FIRE of HEAVEN
TRILOGY

Other Books by Bill Myers

Blood of Heaven

Threshold

Fire of Heaven

Eli

Blood Hounds Inc. (children's mystery series)

Faith Encounter (teen devotional)

The Dark Side of the Supernatural

Novellas

Then Comes Marriage (with Angela Hunt)

When the Last Leaf Falls

FIRE of HEAVEN
TRILOGY

Blood of Heaven

Threshold

Fire of Heaven

BILL MYERS

GRAND RAPIDS, MICHIGAN 49530

ZONDERVAN

Requests for information should be addressed to:

Zondervan, *Grand Rapids, Michigan 49530*

Library of Congress Cataloging-in-Publication Data

Myers, Bill, 1953-
Fire of Heaven trilogy / Bill Myers.
p. cm.
Contents: Blood of heaven—Threshold—Fire of heaven.
ISBN 0-310-24108-1
1. Christian fiction, American I. Title.
PS3563.Y36 F58 2001
813'.54—dc21

2001026335

This edition printed on acid-free paper.

Published in association with the literary agency of Alive Communications, Inc., 7680 Goddard Street, Suite 200, Colorado Springs, CO 80920.

Interior design by Beth Shagene
Printed in the United States of America

01 02 03 04 05 06 07 08 /❖ DC/ 10 9 8 7 6 5 4 3 2 1

CONTENTS

BLOOD OF HEAVEN

To Jim Riordan,
for his love and friendship

ACKNOWLEDGMENTS

Many people have given their time and expertise to help me write this book. I'm sure I've still made a few mistakes, but these folks deserve credit for what I managed to get right. My grateful appreciation to Dr. Dennis Revie and the department of biology at California Lutheran University, Dr. Rick Stead, Dr. Murray Robinson, Dr. Jeff Hutchins, Kristy Woods, Fred Baker, Nebraska State Penitentiary administrative assistant Charles Hohenstein, Hugh and Beth Geisbrecht, my brother, Dale Brown, Marta Fields, Larry and Julie LaFata, Ed Penney, Sue Brower, Lori Walburg, Scott Wanamaker, Frank Peretti, and Angela Hunt. Thanks also to Lissa Halls Johnson, Robin Jones Gunn, Carla Williams, Scott Kennedy, Lynn and Peggy Marzulli, Doug McIntosh, Dorothy Moore, Bill Myers Sr., Bob and Helen West, John Tolle, Bill Burnett, Gary Smith, Tom Kositchek, Cathy Glass, Criz Hibdon, and the rest of my "extended family" for their intercession. Also, to my agent and friend, Greg Johnson, and my editor, Dave Lambert, another friend who first heard me weave this yarn nearly a decade ago. Lastly, always, and most importantly, to Brenda, Nicole, and Mackenzie.

For in my inner being I delight in God's law; but I see another law at work in the members of my body, waging war against the law of my mind and making me a prisoner of the law of sin at work within my members. What a wretched man I am! Who will rescue me from this body of death?

THE APOSTLE PAUL

PART ONE

CHAPTER 1

"You dis me."

There was no response.

"You hear what I say? You disrespect me."

Michael Coleman didn't have to look up from his Thanksgiving meal of turkey loaf and yams to know who was talking. It was Sweeney. Big, brooding, tattoos across the back of his bald head. As a member of the Aryan Brotherhood, he had been convicted for stabbing a Jew to death during last year's Nazi rally in Omaha. He'd come onto the Row a week ago, and this was his move.

"You hear me, Cole?"

Imperceptibly, Coleman tightened the grip on his spoon. He cursed himself for not slipping a homemade shank into his waistband before coming to mess. He'd known a power play was coming; he just hadn't expected it so soon. Still, if a spoon was all he had, then a spoon would have to do. Already his senses were tightening, sharpening. The contrast between the orange yams and the green fiberglass meal tray grew vivid. The eight other men stopped eating and looked in Coleman's direction. In the sudden silence, the hum from the overhead heating duct grew to a consuming roar.

"Sit down." Coleman's command came strong. He was grateful he didn't have to clear his throat. That would have betrayed weakness, and weakness could spell death.

Sweeney shifted slightly.

Good.

Coleman finally raised his eyes. But not to Sweeney. It was to the inmate sitting across from him. A young black man, almost a boy, who'd made the mistake of hitting a white man one too many times in a bar fight. He wouldn't even have been here if he could have afforded a real lawyer. The kid quickly rose and moved out of the way so Sweeney could take his seat.

This was Coleman's gauntlet. If Sweeney obeyed, if he sat, that meant he honored Coleman's position and really did want to talk. If he didn't, then this was clearly a challenge of Coleman's authority.

Sweeney didn't move.

Coleman wasn't surprised. His heart pounded—but not in fear. This was exhilaration. An exhilaration he would carefully hold in check until the perfect moment.

Again Sweeney shifted, but this time to brace himself for what was coming. "You disrespect Garcia and me."

Hector Garcia was the weakest on the Row, which made him the most vulnerable. A bomb freak, he had inadvertently killed an elderly couple who were in the wrong place at the wrong time. Thanks to Oklahoma City, that put him near the bottom of the prison food chain, barely above a child molester.

Sweeney had come onto the Row and immediately made Garcia his punk. No one seemed to mind, not even when he forced Garcia to shave his legs and start wearing jockey shorts dyed pink from cherry Kool-Aid. But after the boy's third or fourth beating, Coleman finally drew the line. He knew Sweeney had clout: major outside heroin connections. In fact, he'd even heard that Sweeney was supplying one or more of the baton-wielding hacks inside, which would explain why they looked the other way during Garcia's beatings.

Still, enough was enough. Maybe it was the memories of his own childhood, his own father. Coleman wasn't sure. But he had passed word down the chain of command that there would be no more beatings. And now Sweeney stood there, not only challenging his decree, but his position as well.

Coleman had several options. Talk it out, which would be read as weakness, or—well, there was really only one other choice. And by the electricity shooting through his body and the razor-sharp focusing of his senses, he knew there was no time like the present.

Sweeney didn't know what hit him. Coleman's five-foot-eleven frame was off the bench and going at him before the man could move. Deliriously out of control, adrenaline surging, Coleman was a wild man, punching and stabbing and tearing and kicking in a euphoric, overwhelming rush.

He barely noticed the hacks descending on him, pulling him off, doing their own brand of kicking and beating. Nor did he really care—although he couldn't help noticing that at least one of them was Sweeney's client. He saw Sweeney stagger back to his feet, flashing a newly acquired, toothless grin and brandishing a pair of aluminum knuckles. Coleman tried to move, but the hacks held him in place as Sweeney came at him. Apparently the man had more connections than Coleman had thought.

There was some solace that it took two guards to hold him as Sweeney did his work. But even as the punches fell and consciousness slipped away, a plan was forming in Coleman's mind. It would take more than this to oust him from power. This was child's play. An excuse for revenge. And revenge would come swiftly. It always did. For Michael Coleman, revenge was not a dish best served cold, but rather piping hot, full of rage, and in a manner they would never forget. That was Coleman's style. That was what made him great. That's why they feared him.

Dr. Philip O'Brien had a problem. His briefcase was packed with so many papers and files that it left no room for the framed picture of Beth and the kids. Now what? Here he was, CEO of the fastest growing biotech firm in the Pacific Northwest, and his brain was gridlocked over what to take and what to leave behind on a forty-eight-hour business trip. In anger and contempt over his indecision, he pulled the core group's "Toxicity of Epidermal Growth Factor" out of his briefcase, tossed it on his desk, and scooped up the photo.

He turned and headed out of his office toward the elevators. Tall, on the downhill side of his forties (though the gray hair made him appear closer to mid-fifties) he still had a boyish, Jimmy Stewart charm. Except for the quiet padding of his Nikes on the carpet and the occasional brush of blue jeans against his briefcase, the hallway was absolutely silent. Just as it should be. No one worked holidays at Genodyne. Except for Security, and the die-hard kids down in Research, the six-story complex would remain closed until Monday. So would the manufacturing plant a quarter mile away. That was O'Brien's style, his vision from the beginning. Happy employees make relaxed employees make imaginative employees make significant breakthroughs in genetic engineering—a theory spawned in the brain of a Berkeley biochem student back in the early eighties. But after dozens of patents and one, soon to be two, products out on the market, it was a theory that had led to a hundred seventy-five million dollars' worth of business last year alone.

Biotech companies come and go. Of the fifteen hundred or so that had started, only fourteen had actually placed a product on the market. And for good reason. With the public paranoia over genetic engineering, as well as impossible FDA guidelines and innumerable testings, it cost between one hundred and three hundred million dollars to develop a single drug. But, as Genodyne had proven, once a drug hits the market, it can become a blockbuster overnight.

O'Brien passed on the elevator and took the stairs. So why was he here? Why had he, head of this flourishing, feel-good company, rushed through Thanksgiving dinner, leaving his wife and two kids alone for the remainder of the weekend? O'Brien arrived at the next floor landing, pushed open the door, and beheld his answer.

"Glad you could make it." It was a twenty-four-year-old kid, well built, with black hair that always hung in his face, and, according to Sarah, O'Brien's twelve-year-old daughter, a major babe. "The freezer and lab equipment have already been loaded. The jet's been on the runway half an hour. Where have you been?" It was Kenneth Murkoski. Murkoski the Terrible. Murkoski the Ambitious. Murkoski the Boy Genius.

"I had some pumpkin pie to finish."

The man-child didn't smile. "Got a call from Lincoln. There was an incident on the Row."

"An *incident?*"

"That's what they called it."

"Was our guy involved?"

"Big time. They said we should hold off a few days."

"And?"

"I said, 'No way.'"

"Kenny . . ." He saw Murkoski wince. He knew the kid hated the name, so he used it only when necessary. He'd handpicked Murkoski right out of M.I.T. almost eighteen months ago. He was the country's brightest, best, and most ambitious. He was also a showboat and publicity hound—a volatile combination, but O'Brien had decided to take the risk. Actually, he hadn't had much choice. Having to continually oversee Research and Development, Manufacturing, Administration, Sales, Marketing, and Logistics had sapped all of O'Brien's creativity. If the company was to survive, O'Brien needed a blue-skyer, some fresh blood (not to mention fresh brain cells) to run the Gene Therapy Division. In short, he needed someone who would think like O'Brien used to think back when he'd had time to think. Of course, that meant more than the usual amount of fires to put out and ruffled feathers to smooth. (Murkoski's social skills were as underdeveloped as his humility.) It also meant losing control of more and more of the details—details that O'Brien occasionally felt Murkoski deliberately hid from him. Still, despite the risks and frustrations, the kid was worth it. Even now.

"You sure we're not pushing too hard?" O'Brien asked. "What did they say?"

"What *could* they say? They're not playing around with some 'B' league biotech firm anymore. We've got the whole Mom-and-apple-pie U.S. government on our side."

"But if they suggest we wait, what's the hurry?"

Murkoski scowled but was interrupted by the ringing of a phone. He reached into his Italian linen sports coat and pulled out the cellular as he answered O'Brien's question. "By the time we get there, things will settle down. The truth is, it will probably make him more willing to play ball with us." He turned and spoke into the phone with a demanding, "Yeah?" The expression on his face shifted, and he turned to walk away. "So what are you saying?" he asked, lowering his voice. It was obvious the kid wanted some privacy, and O'Brien was happy to oblige. Besides, he wanted to check in on Freddy before they left. So as Murkoski continued his conversation, O'Brien headed down the hall.

A biotech company landing a government contract in gene therapy research was unheard of. So was the amount of money they were throwing around. But this was big. Very big. And, in less than a year, the results had proven staggering. No wonder Murkoski kept pushing. It wasn't because of competition—who was there to compete with? It was simply impatience. What they had uncovered, when it was finally developed and ready for the public, would quite literally change the world.

O'Brien arrived at B–11. He held his wallet containing the mag ID against the little black box. He then entered his six-digit PIN. An electronic bolt snapped back, and he pushed open the door.

The room was twenty by forty. The right end looked like an outdoor playground with swing set, monkey bars, slide, and half a dozen boulders of different sizes scattered about. The walls were painted in cartoon-style trees and hills, and the ground was covered in real grass sod that had to be replaced every six weeks. In the far corner a dead tree with three gnarled limbs was held in place by inch-thick cable. The other side of the room resembled a kitchen: cupboards, counters, stools, several toys, and a child-sized table with four chairs. Everything was painted in bright pinks, blues, purples, and greens.

O'Brien allowed the door to shut behind him, then crossed to a park bench near the center of the room. "Freddy," he called. "Freddy, where are you?"

A three-and-a-half-foot baboon scurried up over the rocks and loped toward him. He weighed sixty-five pounds and had a long snout, dark brown, gray-tipped fur, and eyes so close together they almost looked crossed. The animal kept his tail arched high over his back and put on an affected swagger that was almost comical. This was intentional, a baboon's way of saying, "Hi there, look how goofy I am, I can't possibly be a threat." And for good reason. Even though Freddy weighed less than seventy pounds, baboons can be fierce fighters, with the strength of half a dozen other creatures their size.

O'Brien placed the briefcase on the bench and sat down. "How you doing, boy?"

Freddy hopped up beside him and immediately began exploring the briefcase. His long, black hands, almost human, ran over the textured surface, fingering the brass latches, flipping the handle back and forth, looking for some way inside.

O'Brien chuckled. "Sorry. There's nothing of interest in there. Believe me."

But Freddy would not be put off. Now he was lifting the case, looking under it, checking its sides, searching for some means of entrance.

O'Brien watched in silent amusement. The animal had joined the experiment fifteen weeks ago. He was not the first. There had been two other primates before him. Neither had survived. Too many complications. But Freddy had pulled through. And, like the mice in the earlier experiments, his behavior had dramatically changed.

O'Brien reached over and probed the animal's chest. The fur was coarse and bristly. Freddy stretched out for what he obviously hoped would be a good scratch and rubdown.

"Let's see how that sternum is coming, shall we?" O'Brien adjusted his glasses and carefully studied the shaved section encircling what had been a small needle puncture where they had extracted the bone marrow. There had been a minor infection several weeks ago, but now it was completely healed.

"Looking good, dude."

Freddy's response to O'Brien's kindness was instant; he released the briefcase and wrapped both of his arms around O'Brien's arm. It was an embrace. Common among females in the wild, and even between males and babies. But never between male and male. And never with another species; there was too much fear. Yet here he was—a full-grown male embracing and nuzzling O'Brien as if they were father and son.

This wasn't the first time. Freddy had been embracing for almost a month now. But every time it happened, O'Brien felt his heart swell just a little. This was why they were doing what they were doing. This was why he endured Murkoski, why he left his wife and children during a holiday weekend. They were disappointed about his frequent absences now because they didn't understand. But in a matter of a few years, before his children were grown, they *would* understand, and they would rejoice with him just as he was rejoicing now.

O'Brien began parting Freddy's fur and gently kneading the skin. This was grooming. In the wild he would be searching for fleas or lice or flakes of salt, another sign of affection among baboons. And the more O'Brien kneaded the animal's fur, the more Freddy nuzzled in and hugged his arm.

How odd, O'Brien mused. As a scientist he had been taught that baboons occupied a necessary step in the process of human evolution as they made the transition from swinging in trees to walking the open savannas. And now, once again, these same animals were necessary to make what O'Brien hoped would be an equally astounding leap in evolution. A leap just as important, and perhaps even more necessary for the survival of the human race.

O'Brien thought again of Beth and the children. He would call them. In the car on the way to the plane, he would call and say how much he loved them. But first he needed to sit just a moment longer. To sit, to dream, and to savor Freddy's affection.

Katherine Lyon hated Thanksgiving. For that matter, she wasn't too fond of Christmas, Easter, or the Fourth of July. It wasn't so much the holidays as the memories they brought—along with the blitz of TV and magazine ads: All those perfect little families gathered around their perfect little turkeys, or Christmas trees, or whatever.

Katherine sighed wearily as she ran her hand through her cropped, auburn hair. It wasn't the most flattering cut for her, but she didn't care. She hadn't cared for a long, long time. She crossed to the front of the store, set the alarm, and peered back into the darkened interior. Over on the side wall, past the latest-model boom boxes, stereos, and color TVs, she could see the telltale glow from one of a dozen displayed computer monitors.

"Let's go, Eric, I'm not telling you again."

The blue-green light was instantly extinguished, and the head of a blonde, bespectacled eight-year-old floated above the center display of telephone answering machines. How fiercely she loved this boy. Of course the resemblance to his father brought back other memories and emotions. But whenever she looked at him, those feelings of bitterness and loss mellowed into a dull, longing ache.

The rest of his body emerged from behind the display. Slight, skinny, elbows and knees mostly. He was already the object of ridicule from some of the tougher third graders. She couldn't help thinking how he must have looked like Gary when Gary was that age. Until Gary had grown up and filled out into his impressive six-foot-two frame.

"Come on, let's go." Her hoarseness carried a weary impatience. But what else could she expect at the end of another ten-hour day of complaining customers, salesmen on the make, IRS letters, and threatening landlords.

"Got your homework?" She tried to sound pleasant, but it fell flat.

The boy nodded silently and slipped past her to the outside. She followed, pulled the door shut, and inserted the key into the dead bolt. As usual, it was a fight to get the thing to click into place. And, as usual, she cursed softly and promised to complain to the owners. The way they hassled her over the slightest delay in rent, she was entitled to expect a few things in the building to work.

"Lyon Computer and Electronics" was wedged into a tiny strip mall on old Highway 99. The shops surrounding her included the obligatory video rental store, hair salon, music hangout, and Szechwan restaurant. All were closed for the holiday except the Albertson's supermarket at the far end, its dull blue-and-white glow spilling out into the unlit parking lot.

Katherine glanced to the sky. It was dark gray and hung just above her head like wet cement. Another typical evening in Everett, Washington. How she hated this place. But the city, located on Puget Sound, was the furthest she could get away from Iowa. And "getting away" was something both she and Eric had desperately needed.

As the lock finally clicked in, Katherine grew aware of a presence three doors down. He sat on the sidewalk, back against the building. She didn't look. She didn't have to. She knew he was one of the homeless men who haunted the area at night. It's not that she resented these guys. In fact, more than once, when she and Gary had found the rare opportunity to grab a lunch together, she had begged him to buy an extra Big Mac to share. But that was back when life was kinder, back when she was a devoted wife and the loving mother of a newborn, back when she was naive and weak and didn't know how hard and cold the world could be.

She turned toward the parking lot. Her Datsun, a gray beater with a crease running along its back fender, was parked thirty feet away. "Come on," she said, giving her son a nudge.

Eric slouched forward and obeyed. As they stepped off the curb, Katherine discreetly reached into her purse. Somewhere amid the clutter was her leather-cased pepper spray. A gift to herself last Mother's Day. No bigger than a tube of lipstick, it was supposed to be attached to her key ring, but she'd never found the time to do it.

Then she heard it. The scrape of shoes and the rustle of clothes. He was getting up. She kept her stride even and continued digging into her purse.

"Ma'am?"

She fought the panic. She was halfway to the car. Even if she broke into a run, there was no way she could unlock the door and get both her and the boy inside.

Eric turned to look.

"Don't turn around," she whispered.

"But, Mom—"

"Keep walking."

Eric obeyed.

"Ma'am, excuse me . . ." The sound grew louder. Worn tennis shoes scuffing gravel. They were heading toward her. Katherine picked up her pace. So did he.

She continued digging. *Where is that stupid spray? What's this? Lipstick? No! Mascara? No! Where is it?*

"Excuse me?"

The car was ten feet away, but the footsteps were nearly on top of her. He was so close she could hear his breathing.

There! She found it.

Hand still in the purse, she felt for the little red safety tab and clicked it over to the right. Now it was armed. Let him try what he would—she was ready.

Fingers closed around her arm from behind. This was it. If there was one thing Gary had stressed, it was to never be forced into a defensive position. Always play offense. In one quick move, she spun around, pulled out the spray, and fired the thin orange line directly into the assailant's face.

The young man let out a scream and covered his eyes. "What are you doing?" he yelled, dropping to his knees.

Katherine moved in, continuing to unload the spray on his face. *It'll be a long time before he tries this again,* she thought.

"Are you crazy? What are you doing?" Blindly he pushed at the stream, trying to shove it back with his hands. It was then that she noticed the checkbook he was holding. Her checkbook.

"Are you crazy?" he kept shouting. "Are you crazy?"

"What—"

He coughed and gagged. "You dropped this—back there, you dropped this!"

Katherine released the spray. The man threw the checkbook at her as he remained on the asphalt, coughing and choking.

She stepped back and took a deep, ragged breath. As her fear drained away, so did her strength. She wanted to cry, but she wouldn't. Katherine Lyon had not cried in years.

Coleman's hospital bed was located in the north end of the Nebraska State Penitentiary Administration Building. The long, two-and-a-half-story brick building stood at the front of the prison, overlooking the parking lot. Besides the hospital and medical facilities, it housed all the administration offices, attorney/client conference rooms, and a large general visiting area that seated three hundred people. It also contained the execution chamber with the electric chair and adjacent witness room.

As Coleman lay in the evening's silence, he couldn't help thinking that, should his appeals fail, this would be the same room in which they'd prepare him for execution. In less than seven weeks, should the Supreme Court refuse to hear his case, should the three-person pardons board refuse to offer a stay of execution, this room in which he now lay was the exact room in which they would spruce him up so that he could take the fifty-two steps necessary to reach the execution chamber for his ride on Ol' Sparky.

Coleman turned, trying to push the thought out of his head, and pain shot through his body. He had two cracked ribs, a broken nose, and a mild concussion. Yet when they'd brought him into the hospital tonight, he had refused all painkillers. In fact, even before the X rays and stitches, he had insisted on making a phone call. That was nearly four hours ago. Now Coleman forced himself to remain awake, and to wait.

Forty-five minutes later, his vigilance was rewarded. The wall across from the window began reflecting red-yellow-orange, red-yellow-orange. Coleman didn't have to rise and look out to know that it was an ambulance. Someone else in the prison had been injured, but far worse than he. So badly, in fact, that the assistance of an outside hospital with its bigger and better-equipped ER facility would be needed.

Coleman smiled. His phone call had paid off.

He heard a tray rattling down the hall. They were bringing him food. Here, in the hospital, in the middle of the night. A moment later the overhead fluorescents flickered on. He winced at the light. "What's going on?" he demanded.

"Cook said you'd want this." A trustee in a gold shirt and khaki pants pushed the cart toward Coleman. He removed the lid to reveal an enormous portion of tomorrow morning's sausage and eggs.

Coleman sat up, fought the pain in his head, and reached for the cart. He was starved. "What's the action with the ambulance?"

"Your buddy Sweeney. Guess he dealt some bad dope to one of the hacks. The guy OD'd at home couple hours ago."

"Dead?"

"Coma."

Coleman's appetite quickly increased. He dug into the eggs. "And Sweeney?"

"The other hacks weren't too thrilled about it."

"Too bad," Coleman said, cramming his mouth full of food. "Guess these things happen."

"Guess so. Anything else?"

"Tell the cook thanks."

The trustee nodded.

"Oh, have the guys on the Row take up a collection for Garcia."

"A collection?"

"Yeah. Tell him to burn those jockey shorts and get some real underwear."

The trustee smiled and headed out of the room. Coleman inhaled his food ravenously. Once the rage and aggression were spent, they gave way to an incredible hunger. It had always been that way with Coleman. Ever since he was a little boy.

"Hey, Hon, McKenney's got me doing paperwork again. Sorry. I'll get home soon as I can. Maybe pick us up a video. Kiss Eric good night for me. Love you guys."

Beep.

Katherine sat on the kitchen floor listening to the answering machine. These were not new messages. They were from an older tape she had saved from seven years ago. A few of the voices belonged to her, or her friends and family, but most were Gary's:

"If you get this before noon call me, and let's grab some Chinese."

Beep.

The linoleum floor was hard and cold. She leaned against the fridge and felt its vibration against her back. Staring vacantly into her glass, she slowly swirled the Cabernet, watching as the vanishing patina slipped back into the liquid. It had been thirty months since she'd had a drink. The three and a half years before that, the ones immediately following Gary's death, were pretty much a blur. Unfair to Eric and definitely unfair to herself. But with the help of a few friends, she'd gotten back on her feet, changed locale, opened a store, and joined the masses of single parents fighting to keep their heads above the emotional and financial waters.

She usually succeeded. But tonight, with the work hassles, the holiday loneliness, the attack in the parking lot—well, the glow from Albertson's and their acclaimed wine department had been more than she could handle.

"Don't be mad, Hon, but I just got us this puppy. I know, I know, but a kid needs a dog, right? He's a Black Lab. Eric will go ballistic. Trust me on this. See you soon."

Beep.

Katherine had never seen the dog. Somewhere in the confusion of that evening, then the weeklong vigil at the hospital and the funeral arrangements, the dog was neither seen nor heard of again.

Katherine held the glass closer and stared into the crimson liquid. Finally she raised it to her lips and began to drink.

CHAPTER 2

Harold Steiner loved the Law. There was something pure about it, almost holy. In a world of disorder and impending chaos, it was the only mortar holding civilization together. A stronghold, separating man from the animals.

So, nearly forty years ago, at the tender age of nine, Harold Steiner had pushed up his wire-rimmed glasses, cleared his tiny throat, and announced to the world that he would be a lawyer. By twenty-five he had become the youngest assistant D.A. in the history of Nebraska.

But that was a long time ago. Before his life fell apart. Before Melissa's murder. Oh, he still loved the Law, but now he knew it to be a double-edged sword, one just as easily wielded by the barbarians, by those who could twist and distort the Law to destroy the Law. Savages like Michael Coleman.

Steiner reached into the glove compartment, pulled out a faded bottle of Tylenol, popped the lid, and tossed his head back to swallow another handful. The headaches usually came three or four days before Melissa's birthday and lasted until a day or two after. Today his daughter would have been twenty-six.

No one was sure how many people Coleman had killed, or in how many states. There were the convenience store clerk and cop in Council Bluffs, the hooker in Omaha, and the half dozen or so unsolved murders that he'd never really copped to. But it had been Melissa's murder that finally nailed him.

Of course they hadn't let Steiner anywhere near the case, not only because of his emotional involvement but also because it had been outside his jurisdiction. He had lived and worked in North Platte, near the southwest corner of the state. Missy had been killed at Creighton College in Omaha. But that hadn't stopped Steiner from investing his own time, unofficially observing the collection and evaluation of evidence, talking daily with the assistant district attorney, helping behind the scenes, at the trial, the appeals, testifying at clemency hearings. In short, every time Coleman tried to exploit the law to his advantage, Steiner was there to help block him.

It was exhausting work. Friends warned that he had crossed the line. Coworkers said he'd become obsessed. But the Law was the Law. Coleman had broken it. He had defied civilization, endangering it. And in the process, he had destroyed everything precious in Steiner's life. For that, Coleman would pay. Regardless of the price, he would pay.

Unfortunately, the cost to Steiner had also been high. Two years after the murder, Theresa had left him. Fourteen months after that, he had lost his job. Not really lost—"indefinite leave of absence" was the term they had used. And still Coleman's lawyers found loopholes, and still they made their appeals, pleaded for stays, begged for mercy.

Steiner turned off Blondo Street and headed north on 60th. Not one of Omaha's classier neighborhoods, but it was something Theresa could afford. She hadn't returned his last dozen phone calls, and this morning's had been no different. But it should be different. This was Melissa's birthday.

He turned into the driveway of a worn, two-story rental and brought his Volvo to a stop. Checking what was left of his thinning hair (after all, he and Theresa still weren't officially divorced), he stepped out of the car, switched on the alarm, and headed up her walk. Junipers sprawled over the cracked concrete, and some unknown vine encroached upon the steps. Melissa's death had affected Theresa as much as it had him, but in a different way. She had simply quit caring.

He pressed the buzzer, but it didn't work. He opened the sagging screen and knocked.

"Go away," a muffled voice called from inside.

"Theresa?"

"Go away, I said."

"Come on, Therese. It's me. Open up. Come on, Sweetheart."

There was no response.

"Theresa?"

Finally the lock clicked open and a woman appeared in a blue terry-cloth bathrobe. She squinted up at him in the brutal morning light. She'd been an attractive woman once. More handsome than beautiful. She could be still, despite the extra twenty-some pounds she'd put on, and the drawn and weary face from too many late nights at too many bars.

"Theresa?" He frowned. "It's ten-thirty."

"So?"

A smell wafted from the apartment. "Are you smoking again?"

"What do you want, Harry?"

"It's the 26th."

She raised her hand to block the sun. "What?"

"The 26th. Missy's birthday. Don't tell me you forgot."

"Of course I didn't forget."

He could tell she was lying. "So, are you coming?

"Harry . . ."

Steiner stood in silence.

Theresa swore. "Harry, it's been eight years."

"What's that supposed to mean?"

"Harry—"

"Listen." He could hear his voice growing thin and tried his best to stay calm. "It could be eight hundred years. The point is, it's her birthday. We'll never forget her birthday. Right? Come on, Theresa, for crying out loud. After all, it's . . ." The phrase was already dissipating, falling apart before he could finish. ". . . her birthday."

Theresa stood a long moment. "Okay," she finally sighed, "I'll be there. But not right now."

"When?"

"Later, all right? Later."

"Therese—"

"I promise."

"But—"

"Good-bye, Harry." She closed the door.

"I'll wait," he called. "If you want, I can wait."

There was no response.

"Theresa?" Steiner stood a full minute before turning and heading back to his car. He would go to his daughter's graveside by himself. He would wait for Theresa there. Melissa at least deserved that: both of her parents, side by side, together at her grave. On her birthday, Missy at least deserved that.

"This is a joke, right?"

"I assure you, Mr. Coleman," Murkoski said, trying to regain control of the conversation, "this is no joke."

"You come in here with some story about the blood of Christ, and you—"

"No one said we had the blood of—"

"—expect me to be your guinea pig?"

"Please, Mr. Coleman . . ." Murkoski swallowed. He appeared to be regrouping, trying to start again. He threw a nervous look at O'Brien, who sat beside him in one of the three fiberglass-molded chairs. They had been in the attorney/client room with Coleman for only thirty minutes, and the killer already had Murkoski on the ropes, looking like a fool.

And not just Murkoski. O'Brien had underestimated the man as well. They had carefully researched him, studied his psychological profile, medical workup, X rays, blood chemistry; they had even run covert EKGs, EEGs, PETs, and a CAT scan on him last summer. Clinically, they knew everything they could know about the man.

But, like most people, they had erred in assuming that multiple killers were ignorant animals with underdeveloped mental skills. After all, here he sat—ribs taped, nose broken, one eye still swollen shut. How could somebody like this possibly be an intellectual equal? Unfortunately, neither of them had taken into account an inmate's worst enemy: time. Next to sleeping, the best killers of time were reading, writing, and learning the skills of fellow prisoners. Whether it was the careful, step-by-step procedure for making a bomb, courtesy of Hector Garcia, or the intricate nuances of the Nebraska legal system, garnered from the books in the prison library, years of reading and listening had sharpened Michael Coleman's intellect to a razor's edge. Then, of course, there was the psychological gamesmanship he'd acquired in running the Row. All this to say, that in less than half an hour, he had reduced Murkoski, the boy genius, into an agitated knot of frustration.

The kid was flailing; O'Brien decided to step in. "Mr. Coleman. Regarding the identity of the blood. We can only say that it is extremely old, and that—"

"'A couple thousand years,' you said."

"Yes, but—"

"So how were you able to keep it from disintegrating? And don't tell me you found it inside some mosquito embalmed in tree sap. I saw that movie, too."

O'Brien took a long breath, but before he could answer, Murkoski jumped back into the fray. The kid never gave up. "The blood was sealed in candle wax. A small section of vine with fragments of bloodstained thorns was encased in the substance. We suspect it was revered as some sort of religious artifact for centuries. Kept on an altar where dripping candles inadvertently covered and sealed a portion of it."

"And what altar would that be?"

"Pardon me?"

"Where?"

"The southern deserts of Egypt. A monastery. The same one that claims to house St. Mark's bones."

"How convenient."

"No, it wasn't convenient. Not at all, Mr. Coleman." Murkoski's voice rose, trembling. "A lot of people risked their lives to bring it to us, and if you're not interested in helping, then we'll find somebody who is. In case you don't know, there are three thousand other inmates on death row."

Coleman opened his hands and closed them quietly. "Three thousand twenty-six. Perhaps you should contact one of them."

Murkoski blinked. Coleman had just called his bluff. Of all the nerve. Murkoski appeared livid, but O'Brien was more impressed than angry. Coleman had no idea how many months they'd researched him, nor the time constraints they were now working under. And yet he'd uncovered Murkoski's vulnerable underside, pressed all his buttons, and taken control of the conversation—in record time. The man was far more clever than they had imagined.

O'Brien cleared his throat and tried again. "Mr. Coleman—whoever's blood it is, and we can't say for certain, we do know that this individual had a genetic makeup slightly different from the rest of us." He could feel Coleman's eyes searching him, looking for a crevice, for a weakness to take hold of. But he held Coleman's stare and kept his voice even as he went into the details. "Human DNA molecules consist of over six billion base pairs. If strung out in a line, that's enough to stretch to the moon and back 16,000 times. In the ancient blood sample we have, most of those have not survived. But what portions we do have, those that have remained intact, have proven quite interesting."

"How?"

This was the hard part. The part O'Brien rarely shared. But it was Coleman's body they were asking to experiment on, and it was certainly his right to know. "As far as we've been able to tell, the blood contains all the usual maternal genes, but there are some fairly unusual genes we've discovered on the male side."

Coleman raised an eyebrow, waiting for more.

Murkoski moved in. "Certainly a man of your intelligence knows about X and Y chromosomes?" It was a patronizing question, and it was met only by Coleman's silence. Murkoski continued. "Two X's together make a female, while an X and Y chromosome determines a male?"

More silence.

"The X chromosome carries up to five thousand genes, while the lowly Y chromosome, that which makes us men, contains only a little over a dozen. So far science has only determined the function of one of those dozen-plus genes, the one that tells the embryo to develop testes instead of ovaries. The remaining male genes appear totally useless."

"Until now," O'Brien corrected. "We don't know how or why, but for some reason the portion of those Y genes that we were able to recover from the blood have a totally different makeup than any other male gene."

"Meaning?"

Murkoski leapt to the punch line. "Whoever's blood this was could not have had a human father."

Silence settled over the room. O'Brien watched Coleman. Not a muscle moved. Murkoski, on the other hand, leaned back in his chair, obviously assured that the playing field had once again been tilted to his advantage.

The silence continued. O'Brien coughed slightly then resumed. "Most of these new genes still appear useless, but one in particular has stood out. When it is introduced into other organisms—when we replicate it in the blood of say, mice, the creatures' behavioral patterns shift dramatically."

Coleman's voice grew strangely quiet. "You've done this with other animals?"

"Yes. Mice first, then more recently primates."

"And?"

"The mortality rate has been higher than we'd like, but for those who have survived, the results have been staggering."

Murkoski continued. "They are no longer concerned with what's best for themselves. Instead of focusing on their own needs, they act in a manner that's best for their community."

Coleman sat motionless. Although he didn't take his eyes off the men, it was obvious that wheels were silently turning.

Unable to endure any silence for too long, Murkoski continued. "And now we're ready to take the next step. To introduce this blood into a human being."

A flicker of a scowl crossed Coleman's face.

Murkoski didn't appear to notice. "There are no promises," he said. "The process could kill you. Or it could turn you into a lunatic or some type of mental vegetable. But if the experiment succeeds, think of the ramifications." His voice rose slightly as his excitement grew. "We would be able to rid our society, our entire race, of its violence and aggression. Our tendency toward evil would be totally eliminated. We would create world peace. Nirvana. Heaven on earth."

Coleman's voice remained quiet. "You're playing God. You're changing how we're made."

Murkoski shook his head. "No. We're merely accelerating the evolutionary process within our species. Some insects are already doing this, bees for instance. Several varieties commit suicide by stinging an intruder to save the community in their hive. Some birds risk their lives by warning if a hawk or other predator is in the area. There's little doubt that our own species has already begun that evolutionary step—elevating the community over the individual. We're merely picking up the pace a little, that's all. Doing in a few months what would take evolution thousands of years to accomplish."

Another pause. "Why me?"

"You're scheduled for execution in six weeks. The Eighth Circuit has already denied your appeal. That just leaves the U.S. Supreme Court and the Appeals Board."

Coleman gave no reply.

Murkoski was once again taking charge. "If you agree to participate, and *if* you survive, you have our guarantee that the governor of the state of Nebraska will commute your sentence to life."

For the first time, Coleman showed expression.

"Mr. Coleman," Murkoski continued, "we have contacts in very high places."

Coleman held Murkoski's gaze. He'd been in the penal system long enough to know that, with enough clout, anything was possible. He sat for nearly a minute. Finally, he rose to his feet. The meeting was over. The decision made.

"No," was all he said.

Murkoski sat stunned. "What do you mean, *no?* We're offering you your only hope."

"Walking the yard as some do-gooder holy man is not hope. I wouldn't last a week. No, if you want my cooperation, the deal is you get me a pardon."

There was no hiding the incredulity in Murkoski's voice. "How do you expect us to do that?"

"You're the hotshot player here. If you've got the power to pull the governor's strings for clemency, you've got the clout to pull a little harder and get me out."

Murkoski rose to his feet. "Listen, pal, we're offering you your life. Who do you think you are, trying to negotiate with us?"

"I'm a nobody, son. But apparently a nobody you need." He turned, rapped on the eight-inch square of bulletproof glass in the door, and a guard instantly appeared. "Thanks for stopping by."

A moment later, Murkoski and O'Brien stood alone in the room, Murkoski in shock, O'Brien in quiet amazement. Coleman wasn't only smart, he was also a high roller. He'd just taken control of the game, upped the ante, and escalated the stakes to double or nothing. The man was either very foolish or very, very fearless. O'Brien suspected the latter. And if they intended on using him, he knew at that moment that they'd better be careful. Very careful.

Katherine had put off the meeting with Eric's teacher for nearly a month. It wasn't due to lack of concern for Eric. He was the most important thing in her life. It didn't even have to do with having to close the store for ninety minutes as she schlepped down to the school and met with the man. No, Katherine didn't like meeting with Eric's teacher, because she didn't like Eric's teacher.

The last meeting with Mr. Paris had not gone well. The first few minutes, discussing Eric's mathematics and computer skills, had gone okay. Eric was impressive on both accounts. It was even okay when Eric's teacher had discussed Eric's need to work on his reading comprehension, physical fitness, and social skills (it seemed lately Eric had become the all-school punching bag). What was not okay was when the man hinted at Eric's need for a good male role model, Katherine's need for a good man, and Mr. Paris's need for a good roll in the hay.

Katherine was quick to spot his moves and draw the line, making it clear that she wasn't interested, which led to Paris's observation that he liked spirited women, which led to his hand gently taking her arm, which led to the outside edge of her shoe scraping down his shin from his knee all the way to his foot, which she stomped good and hard just in case he had missed her point. More training from Gary.

But that incident had taken place over two months ago. And, ever since that little trip to Albertson's, Katherine's attitude had been changing about a lot of things. Maybe she had been overreacting. Maybe it was time to loosen up a bit. At least that's what she was thinking as she sat at a student's desk in the front of Mr. Paris's empty third-grade classroom, burping back the taste of the Cabernet she'd just had for lunch.

Paris, on the other hand, sat behind his oak desk, working hard at sounding professional while reviewing Eric's scores.

As the man droned on, Katherine couldn't help noticing that he was not quite as repulsive as she had remembered. Oh, he was still going for the twentysomething cropped hair look. His pants and neckties may have both been a couple or three inches too short. And somebody should tell him that goatees were better suited for the Brad Pitts of the world. But there was something almost . . . well, not unattractive about him. Something she couldn't put her finger on. The thought surprised her, and she immediately tried to forget it.

". . . even though he's in the ninety-eighth percentile for mathematics, and his computer skills are exceptional—"

"He got that from me."

"Pardon?"

Katherine felt foolish for blurting it out, but she had committed herself, so she explained. "The computer skills. I used to work in computers for the government. He got that from me."

"I see. Actually, that's about the only way Eric and I have been able to connect. I'm a bit of a computer nut myself." He redirected his attention to the printed results in his hand. "In any case, your son is still very far behind in reading comprehension, language arts, social studies—in fact, in nearly *all* the other areas."

Katherine nodded.

Mr. Paris continued staring at the printout. "I don't think it's intellectual. He's proven he can think. I'm afraid much of it has to do with lack of incentive and self-esteem—along, of course, with his lack of social interaction."

"Social interaction?"

"Does Eric have any brothers or sisters?"

Katherine shook her head. "It's just the two of us."

"What about neighborhood kids to play with? He keeps entirely to himself here at school."

Again Katherine shook her head. "He stays with me at the store 'til I close. When we finally get home and eat, it's time for bed."

Mr. Paris frowned. Was it her imagination, or did this man seem legitimately concerned about her son? Whatever the case, this was a much different individual from the one she had seen in action last September. Again she caught herself beginning not to dislike him.

"What about Little League—any kind of sports?"

Katherine almost laughed. "I'm afraid not. Coordination is not one of my kid's specialties. Besides, like I said, we don't have the time." She sensed what she thought to be an expression of disapproval. "Look, I know it's not fair to Eric, but—"

"No, I understand. Believe me. My own mother was a single parent. She was our sole breadwinner. I know how difficult it can be."

Their eyes seemed to connect just a fraction longer than necessary. There was no mistaking it, the man was sincere. Either that or it was the wine. Maybe both.

He glanced away and frowned again, this time tapping at the paper in his hands. "Listen, I coach a soccer team on weekends. Do you think he'd be interested in trying out?"

"He doesn't know the first thing about the game."

"I could give him a few pointers. Besides, as coach," he almost smiled, "I bet I could pull a few strings to get him on the team."

Katherine fought back a rising suspicion. "You'd do that for him?"

"Only if you think it's appropriate."

Again their eyes locked, again perhaps just a little too long.

"Appropriate," she repeated. "Well, I suppose—sure. I mean, let me talk to him first. But if it's okay with him, I guess it would be okay with me."

Mr. Paris finally broke into a smile. It wasn't a bad smile. Not bad at all. "Good," he said. "Good." With that he scooped up the test scores, apparently bringing the conference to a close. "I think we're done for now. Unless you have any further questions."

Katherine shook her head.

"Well, if you do," he said, rising to his feet, "don't hesitate to give me a call. He's a bright, sensitive boy, and I'll do whatever I can to help."

Katherine took the cue and rose from her chair.

They crossed toward the door. "Oh, here," he said, handing her the test scores. "You may want to look these over when you get a chance."

"I wouldn't know where to start," she said as he opened the door for her and they stepped into the hall. At this proximity, she was certain he could smell the wine on her breath, and for some reason that made her feel a little embarrassed.

"It's really not that difficult," he said. "If you'd like, I'd be happy to explain them to you sometime?"

She gave him a look.

He grimaced. "I'm sorry." Already she could see the color rising to his face. "That wasn't supposed to be a come-on."

She held his look, knowing better.

"Well, okay." He shrugged. "Maybe it was, but just a little. The point is—I know we got off to a pretty rocky start last fall, but—I really do find you attractive and, well . . ." He cleared his throat. "What I'm trying to say is, you have every reason not to trust me, but, if you wouldn't mind, maybe we could, you know, have dinner sometime?"

Katherine tried not to smile. It wasn't over his request, but over the delivery. Like a tongue-tied teenager on his first date, he was blushing and fumbling for words. She liked the vulnerability, of course, but it was also nice to know she could still have that type of effect on somebody. In fact, it was so nice that, before she knew it, she heard herself saying, "Sure, why not?" For a second she was as surprised as he was.

"Well, thanks," he said, looking a little startled. "I'll, uh, I'll give you a call, then."

She nodded. Then, without a word, she turned and headed down the hall. She could feel his eyes on her, but she was too busy berating herself to care. What did she think she was doing? The man was a pig. He'd proven that the last time.

Still, people can change, can't they? Doesn't everybody deserve a second chance? He's got a steady job, he's looked up to in the community, and he made it clear that he knows he behaved like an idiot. He says he's interested. Who knows, maybe it's time to get back into the field again. Maybe not all men are dogs. Maybe Gary wasn't the only exception to that rule. She had her doubts. But what would it hurt to step out again, just to see?

It had been seventy-two hours since Harold Steiner had watched the sun set over his daughter's grave. His wife had never shown. He had driven home that evening confused, outraged, and more determined than ever.

Seventy-two hours had passed, and still he couldn't sleep. Oh, there was the occasional hour or so of dozing, filled in by the nonstop drone of CNN, books he couldn't concentrate on, calls to his law office about having the flu, and visits to the Golden Arches at irregular hours. But he had no rest. How could he when the Law was being ignored, when justice was slowly being forgotten, first by the state, and now by his very wife?

It was 1:30 Monday morning when he stepped into the shower. He cranked up the temperature and let the water pound against the back of his neck. The headache had not gone away this time.

Did they think, did they honestly think that seven years of maneuvering, appealing, squirming for a way out—in their wildest imaginings did they think that Michael Coleman's crimes would be *forgotten?* By some, maybe. By those who watched news as entertainment. Those who, after the third or fourth appeal, felt they were watching a rerun and switched over to more current amusement. But for Harold Steiner, this was no amusement. He would not forget. Everyone else could—even his wife, or what was left of her. But he would not. He could not. The Law was the Law. Michael Coleman had broken it, he had been sentenced, and now he must pay. No amount of stalling or exploiting the legal system would cancel that debt. Justice would be served. Steiner owed it to society; he owed it to Missy.

When the shower ran out of hot water, he toweled himself off and slipped into a pair of boxers. A thought had come to mind, and he padded down the hall to the bedroom. The room was neat as a pin. It always was.

He crossed to his desk, snapped on the computer, and logged on to the Internet. With a few clicks of the mouse, he brought up the photograph of Coleman he had previously scanned from a mug shot. It was perfect. Unrepentant, unfeeling, an animal at the peak of savagery. To make sure that the viewer felt no sympathy,

Steiner had erased the convict's serial number at the bottom. Today, in its place, he typed two words. Bold, centered, and in caps:

NEVER FORGET

A few more clicks of the mouse brought up his e-mail address book—people he'd communicated with over the years. Carefully, one by one, he went down the list, highlighting those who had been involved with the Coleman case: family members, friends, cops, attorneys, judges, relatives of past victims, members of the media, politicians, and the list went on. One hundred fifteen in all.

Once he'd selected them, he brought up the photo of Coleman, dragged the mouse down to the "SEND" box, and clicked it. He sat back and closed his eyes. In a matter of hours, all one hundred fifteen parties would receive a special marker on their computer indicating they had received an e-mail message. They would punch it up and watch as their entire screen filled with the photograph of Michael Coleman and Steiner's admonition: "Never Forget."

Steiner snapped off his computer. Sending that message had helped to ease a little of the pain, but not enough.

CHAPTER 3

Death Row at Nebraska State Penitentiary in Lincoln is one of the finest in the country. No sweltering, rat-infested cells. No shotgun-toting guards busting heads, no insane droolers clinging to the bars and screaming hysterically through the night. In fact, as far as accommodations go, this Death Row gets four stars. Built in 1981, the cells are air-conditioned and single occupancy, with steel doors to assure a certain amount of privacy and aesthetic value—though no one can figure out why the outside of those doors are painted a ghastly lime green. Each eight-by-twelve-foot, beige, cinder-block cubicle contains a tile floor, bed, toilet without seat (toilet seats can be used as weapons), wash basin, and long (52" by 24") bullet-proof window with two one-and-a-half-inch-thick horizontal bars running through it to prevent any unscheduled leaves of absence.

A centrally located dayroom, a cafeteria, access to showers three times a week, two fifteen-minute phone calls a week—not to mention opportunities to visit the law library, to purchase personal goods from the canteen, and to spend up to forty-five minutes a day in the exercise yard—add to the home-away-from-home ambiance for the convicted killer. The only way Coleman could have made out better was if he had been captured and convicted next door in Iowa. There is no death penalty in Iowa.

There are seven two-story housing units at the penitentiary. Each is shaped like an X, with four wings. Death Row takes up the top wing in the unit furthest to the northeast. The ten men (actually nine—Sweeney, thanks to Coleman, was still visiting Lincoln General Hospital) have an entire floor to themselves. They are cut off from the general prison population, forming their own community—eating, socializing, reveling in one another's accomplishments, and walking the exercise yard—all as an elite, fraternal order sentenced to the same fate.

The guards are few. Most of the interaction with inmates is handled by trained case managers and caseworkers with degrees in psychology, sociology, or criminal justice. The bywords for all staff involved with Death Row inmates are *discretion* and *compassion.*

In short, there is no torture on Lincoln's Death Row, except perhaps the torture of time . . . and the mind.

For the next five days, Coleman sat in his cell and thought about what he was rejecting. He'd never considered himself a lucky man. In fact, he figured his luck ran out the day he came home from the hospital with his mother, when she was beaten by his father for insinuating that their newborn son, the man's own flesh and blood, may not actually *be* his own flesh and blood.

As time passed, the beatings transferred from Coleman's mother to Coleman himself. He really didn't mind; he figured they helped make him strong. If he could survive his father's explosive outbursts and relentless poundings, while learning to read the man's erratic mood swings and compensate for them, he figured he could survive anything. And for thirty-five years, he had been right.

But this . . .

Five days he sat in his cell, holding to his bluff. He received no phone calls from Murkoski or O'Brien, no more requests for meetings. If they could meet his terms, fine. If not, with less than six weeks to live, his remaining hours were far too valuable to waste on crackpot scientists, no matter how much clout they claimed to wield. Of course, they had insisted that he keep their proposal a secret; they had even threatened to call the whole thing off if he went public. No problem there. Who would believe it? He certainly didn't. At least most of the time.

But there were those other times, the ones that stole up on him when he was the most vulnerable, when he thought that maybe, just maybe, it might be true, that maybe science could pull off something like this, that maybe he could have a second chance.

Like most men on the Row, Coleman seldom thought of the chair. Oh, it was always there—but for the other guy. The chump. Coleman had gotten himself out of too many jams too many times to be worried. And what was Ol' Sparky but just a little bigger jam, requiring just a little more ingenuity. True, every con talked about how they'd go—some bragging that they'd go down fighting to the end, others vowing to take the chair like a man, still others planning to make a long filibuster speech for the media about the injustice of the justice system. But deep inside, no one ever thought they'd die. The same was true with Coleman. He was a hero in his own movie, and heroes never die.

But this . . .

What kind of mind game were they playing? It was an impossible hope, it was crazy—so crazy that he couldn't quite shake it. To appeal was one thing; that was a game everybody played. But this teasing of the imagination, this absurd flaunting of impossible hopes that were just crazy enough to be possible—this was inhumane.

The news came with the dawn of the sixth day. O'Brien and Murkoski would meet his demands. It would entail unprecedented maneuvers with the Witness Protection Program, not to mention some clandestine cooperation with the highest state officials and a tiny handful of prison personnel. But, *if* he survived the treatments, and *if* there was the expected shift in his personality, then Coleman had their word that somehow they would remove him from the Row and relocate him in society, a free man.

His head pounded. His suspicions rose. He had offered them impossible terms, and they had accepted. What made them so anxious? What was their angle? They were the ones holding all the cards; why did they fold? Maybe they already knew the experiment would fail, that it would kill him, make him crazy. Still, dying this way might be better than electrocution. And if he went crazy—wasn't being a little crazy for forty more years better than being dead in a few weeks?

Coleman wrestled with these thoughts all morning, then did what he always did when faced with fear and indecision. He acted on instinct. He met these fears like he met every other fear. Head-on and from the gut. If they wanted this deal badly enough to meet his terms, then he would make the deal. He would play the odds, take his chances.

For the second time in a week they shuffled him out of Death Row, his hands and feet fettered with nylon bracelets called flex cuffs. Except for their length and strength, the cuffs were almost identical to the ties used to seal household garbage bags. The symbolism was never lost on Coleman.

The late afternoon air was crisp and clear. The sapphire sky already revealed traces of pink on the horizon, giving promise of a spectacular sunset. But Coleman barely noticed. He seldom did. Beauty was a luxury he had no time for, not even as a child. Beauty was for poets and women, not for a man fighting to survive. In his world, such weakness could spell death. As the hack escorted him across the yard to the administration building, the only thing Coleman noticed was the conflicting thoughts warring inside his head.

When Coleman reentered the upstairs hospital room, he was surprised to see Murkoski alone.

"Dr. O'Brien had to get back," the kid explained. "This is a straightforward procedure; his presence wasn't necessary."

Coleman didn't mind. He didn't like Murkoski, but he knew how to play him. In some ways, he sensed that they were cut from the same cloth. The only difference was that Murkoski loved to talk, to pontificate. Coleman preferred to listen and learn. Knowledge was power. And power was something Coleman could always use.

"Will you sit on this table, please?" Coleman crossed to the metal examining table they had wheeled in. Murkoski nodded to the guard, who removed the flex cuffs and stepped outside. "Take off your sweatshirt."

Coleman obliged, pulling off the hooded sweatshirt they'd loaned him for the walk outside.

"Listen," Murkoski said, "we're going to be spending a lot of time together, and I want you to know right off the bat that, despite my education and position in life, I do not consider myself your superior."

Coleman thought of dropping the punk right there. Instead, he pushed back the impulse and remained silent.

Murkoski opened the Igloo ice chest on the floor near the drug cupboard; a circular biohazard decal was plastered to it. "Also, I do not hold you in contempt for your past."

"Neither do I."

Murkoski looked up. "Seriously?" he asked. "You never feel guilty?"

"Why should I?"

Murkoski looked at him a moment, then nodded and knelt beside the ice chest. "In any case, the only difference I see between you and me is the cards we were dealt."

Coleman sighed and rattled off the rest of the bromide. "And since I'm just the unwitting product of my environment—"

"No, actually, just the opposite." Murkoski lifted a small plastic container from the chest. It was gray, the size of a small cigar case. It had no markings. "We are products of chemistry, Mr. Coleman. No more, no less. Chemistry determines who we are. Everything we say, think, or do is a chemical reaction—electricity firing across neurons, which in turn release chemicals to fire more neurons, racing down our nerves at four hundred feet per second until they reach our brain, which kicks in its own chemical agents. Simply put, you and I are nothing but chemical laboratories."

Coleman frowned. He didn't like being controlled by anything, much less something he didn't understand. "You're saying I'm who I am by how a bunch of chemicals got thrown together?"

Murkoski had opened the plastic case to produce a small vial wrapped in foam. "No, I'm saying you're a product of your mother's and father's chemical factories."

Coleman liked this idea even less. "So why isn't my brother like me?"

"Please, Mr. Coleman. That's like asking why every child of blue-eyed parents doesn't have blue eyes."

Coleman hated the condescending tone. As the kid flashed a syringe from the case, he thought how little effort it would take to change that tone forever. But, of course, there was the guard outside, and the experiment . . .

Murkoski continued his lecture. "You're right, though. Studies of identical twins raised apart, in entirely different environments, usually show they have similar characteristics. Not only in IQ, but in personality traits like boldness, aggressiveness, inhibition. In fact, the Center for Twin and Adoption Research at the University of Minnesota has data on twin brothers separated from birth who actually preferred the same cologne, the same hair cream, even the same imported toothpaste. Then there were the separated twin sisters who counted themselves to sleep in exactly the same manner."

Murkoski produced a milky white pair of latex gloves and snapped them on. "Or the results from the National Institute on Alcohol Abuse and the National Institute for Child Health and Human Development. Through selective breeding, they've managed to create different families of rhesus monkeys with entirely different personalities: some shy, others outgoing, and others aggressive."

Coleman watched with a slight uneasiness as Murkoski inserted the needle into the vial and extracted a small amount of clear liquid. He was supposed to be receiving blood. Why the injection?

"There are dozens of other studies. But the one you'll find most interesting is the Danish family with an abnormal history of violence. One of the brothers raped his sister, then stabbed the warden at his psychiatric prison. Another tried to run over his employer. Another forced his sisters to undress at knifepoint, and two more were arsonists."

"Not exactly the Brady Bunch."

"And the cause?" Murkoski didn't wait for an answer. "An abnormally low level of serotonin."

"Serotonin?"

"Yes." He tapped the bubbles out and carefully inspected the syringe. "It's a chemical, Mr. Coleman. A neurotransmitter that reduces aggression. One, I might point out, that is present in thirty percent lower quantities in men than women—which may explain why nine out of every ten violent crimes are committed by males. It also takes a dip during adolescence, which no doubt accounts for their erratic behavior. Pull up your shirtsleeve, please."

Coleman obliged, pulling up his government-issued goldenrod shirt while watching Murkoski's every move. "And all of this has been proven?"

"Absolutely. Unusually low amounts of serotonin have been linked to violent criminals, suicides, even arsonists. In fact, one researcher now at Columbia University was able to create a strain of mice lacking fourteen serotonin receptors."

"And?"

Murkoski crossed to the glass-enclosed cupboard of drugs, laid the syringe down on a metal shelf, and reached for a cotton swab and a bottle of rubbing alcohol. "They became wildly impulsive. Incredibly violent. In fact, and you will appreciate this as well, they are often referred to as 'Killer Mice.'" He smiled at his joke.

Coleman didn't bother. "This Danish family, they all have low levels of serotonin?"

"Genetically, all the men lacked monoamine oxidase, MAO, an enzyme directly linked to the production of serotonin. And keep in mind that serotonin is just one of dozens of classical neurotransmitters that we inherit. And who knows how many undiscovered neuro*receptors* we may have." Murkoski stepped back toward him and began swabbing his arm with the alcohol. "We've discovered an 'Obese Gene' that tells us when to stop eating. We've even altered the genes in male fruit flies to make them behave like females."

"Why isn't all this publicized?"

"Oh, it is. But right now genetic behavior, the study of how we act because of our heredity, is a political hot potato. Everyone's afraid to touch it because of the race and bigotry connotations. In fact, the National Institute of Mental Health has yanked funding from at least one study because they're afraid of the repercussions."

"That people will judge others because of their genes instead of who they are."

Murkoski stepped back to the counter, dropped the alcohol swab in the trash can, and picked up the syringe. "You still don't get it, do you? People *are* their genes, Mr. Coleman. You have no choice. You are the result of chemicals received from your parents, who received similar chemicals from their parents, and so on and so forth, all the way back to our primordial ancestors."

"And you're going to change all that?"

Murkoski shrugged and approached with the needle. "We'll soon find out. It's certainly been the case with our mice and with Freddy."

"Freddy?"

"Our baboon. His behavior has dramatically shifted to something much less aggressive. But as far as what he or the mice or any other lab animals actually feel, we have no idea. We can measure their heart rate and blood pressure, but we don't know what they're thinking."

"Enter Michael Coleman."

"Precisely." He took Coleman's arm with his left hand and prepared to insert the needle with his right.

"What's in there?"

"A retrovirus."

"A what?"

"A retrovirus. Like HIV."

"Hold it." Coleman pulled away.

"Relax. All of the harmful elements have been genetically removed."

"You're injecting me with the AIDS virus."

Murkoski laughed. "No, I'm injecting you with a virus that works in a way similar to the AIDS virus. But it has been genetically altered. There's no way it can reproduce itself inside you."

"I thought you were giving me blood. What happened to the blood of Christ?" Coleman looked and sounded like a little boy making excuses not to get his shot, but at the moment he didn't much care.

"For starters there's no guarantee whose blood we've discovered. But for argument's sake let's say it is Christ's. This virus holds the code for one of the genes of his blood. We inserted that code into this virus, so that when the virus attacks your own blood, your T cells, it will infect them with his DNA. And that's the crux of it. For reasons we don't fully understand, this new blood alters the function of certain neurotransmitters and receptors. As a result, we wind up with a brand-new Michael Coleman. Now will you hold still, please."

Coleman hesitated a moment longer before finally submitting. The tiny prick of the needle was barely noticeable. And the burn of five ccs being pumped into his vein was over before it began.

"So you're not giving me his blood, you're changing my blood into his."

Murkoski nodded. "You're receiving part of his genetic code."

"But not all of it."

Again Murkoski nodded. "That's correct. You'll receive one gene in particular, along with the usual junk DNA."

"Junk DNA?"

"Portions of DNA we don't understand. Probably mistakes in nature left over from when we were swinging in the trees as apes."

"When will it start?"

"Start, Mr. Coleman?"

"When will his DNA start infecting me?"

"Why, Mr. Coleman, it's already begun."

CHAPTER 4

A five-year-old face looks through the rectangular holes of a wire fence. He shivers violently; tears stream down smudged cheeks, leaving tracks through the dirt. He looks like a younger Michael Coleman, but he isn't. He is wearing only his underwear.

"Please," he cries, "please don't leave me here!"

He's outside, and it's winter. There are no colors. Everything is black and gray and white. The rolling hills are covered with hundreds of acres of cornstalks sheered off at their base. It is near Coleman's home.

"Please, Mikey, don't leave me here. Please!"

Coleman is there. He's sitting on a thick tree branch fifteen feet above the boy. It's his little brother, Eddie, trapped inside an empty corncrib. The floor is concrete, about twelve feet in diameter, with a wire fence rising high above him and topped by a cone-shaped aluminum roof. Someone has shoved a large log up against the gate. They are the only ones there. The nearest farmhouse is over a mile away. The winter wind howls and bites.

"Please, Mikey . . ."

But Coleman doesn't notice the wind as much as he notices the smell. Raw chicken. The disgusting smell of uncooked chicken fat and flesh, an odor Mom can never completely wash from her hands. Some adults have vivid childhood memories of smells: their father's aftershave, the mixture of cut grass and gasoline from mowing the lawn, Grandma's musty basement. Coleman's only memory is the smell of his mother's hands after she has put in eight grueling hours at the Campbell's Soup factory. Like many of the poorer women in Tecumseh, Nebraska, her job is to debone and eviscerate the birds, removing their skeletons and scooping out their guts.

"Please . . ."

Coleman looks back down. His brother is small and frail, shivering in the crib. In fact, he looks so helpless that Coleman has to laugh. He can't help himself. It serves Eddie right. If Dad always beats Coleman and lets Eddie go, then this is only fair. Eddie's perfect little world must be shattered from time to time. Of course this isn't Eddie's first wake-up call, nor will it be the last. It is Coleman's self-appointed task to even the score and prepare his sibling for the hardships of the real world, a task in which Coleman revels.

But as he sits in the tree laughing, a cold shiver runs through him—a shiver that has nothing to do with the wind. He isn't sure whether he hears it or senses it. But somebody is there.

"Mikey, my feet don't got no feeling."

He squints into the wind, searching the field. He and Eddie are the only ones there. And yet—there it is again. A cracking sound, below him and behind. He twists around until he can see behind the tree. Nothing. Just a rusting, '58 Ford pickup with one door sprung, the other missing.

"Please, Mikey. I won't tell, I promise."

There it is again. Twigs snapping. Right below him. He looks underneath.

Nothing.

Now he hears grunting. Grunting and the sound of heavy boots scraping against bark.

"Please, Mikey . . ."

It's coming after him. Whoever is there is climbing the tree and coming after him. The grunting grows louder. But Coleman sees no one. He can only hear the scraping bark and the grunting. He panics, scrambling to his feet.

"Mikey . . ."

He nearly loses his balance and throws himself against the trunk for support. The noise approaches. He frantically searches for a getaway. There is none.

Now, all at once, he feels a different cold. Harsher. It's no longer the cold of his fear, but the cold of the wind. Eddie's cold. He shivers violently. The sound is closer. He thinks he hears breathing. His father's breathing. He is certain of it.

"Mikey . . ."

His teeth chatter. He shivers so hard that he must cling to the tree for balance. He hears clothes flapping in the wind. But not Coleman's clothes. They belong to the father he can neither see nor hear. The cold is intense. Before he knows it, he is also crying.

He looks back down at Eddie. Amazing. Their sobs are in perfect synchronization. As his little brother gasps, he gasps. As Eddie sobs, Coleman sobs. He is sharing his brother's fear, his loneliness, and feeling the icy wind—the awful, icy wind that will not stop until—

Coleman awoke. It took a moment for him to catch his breath and realize that he'd been dreaming. He tried to move, but the blanket had wrapped around him in a knot. Angrily, he untangled it and flung it aside. Throwing his feet over the edge of the bed, he took another deep breath, forcing reality to return.

The incident was real, though he hadn't thought of it in years. Nor had he ever had a dream quite so vivid. Yet what really unnerved him was the empathy, the remorse. Michael Coleman had never felt anything for any of his victims. But now, he had experienced his brother's emotions—the cold, the terror, the unbearable ache of being alone and abandoned.

Coleman ran his hands over his face and noticed something even more startling. His cheeks were wet. But not from sweat. Moisture had filled his eyes and spilled onto his face. And when he swallowed, his throat was tight and constricted.

He rose and stepped across to the window. The moon hung over the horizon. It was full and flooded the yard with a serene stillness. Its stark light glinted off the rolls of razor wire atop the fence and bathed the distant highway in silence. Nearly two miles across the road, grain elevators he had never noticed before glowed in the moonlight. It was the most beautiful thing Coleman had ever seen. The ache in his throat grew stronger.

"Don't tell me you're going like that."

"Why not?" Katherine shifted uncomfortably under the scrutiny of Lisa. The downstairs neighbor was a disgustingly slender twenty-five-year-old, with rich, ebony skin. She stood in the bathroom doorway carefully checking Katherine out. Lisa had agreed to watch Eric while Katherine had her evening on the town with Mr. Paris.

"It's a new world out there, girl. If you want his interest, you've got to advertise."

Katherine turned to check her profile in the bathroom mirror. The moderately cut dress of burgundy crepe hung well, accenting her figure and covering the slightest trace of a pooch she'd been fighting. "It's the best thing I own. Besides, I think it's flattering."

"Flattering?"

"Yeah."

"*Flattering?* Nobody wants flattering. When's the last time you were on the dating scene?"

"I, uh—" Katherine resumed fluffing her cropped hair, trying her best to give it some body. "I grew up pretty sheltered, being a preacher's kid and all."

"Your daddy was a minister?"

Katherine ignored Lisa's surprised tone. "That was long ago and far away."

"I should say so, girl. What about your old man?"

"Gary and I, we met as freshmen in Bible college, so—"

"So you don't know nothing, do you?"

Katherine continued working her hair, pretending not to hear.

Lisa glanced at her watch. "What time are you meeting him?"

"He'll be here at 8:00 to pick me up."

"Here?"

"Well, yeah."

"You invited him *here?"*

"It's not like I'm not going to ask him inside."

"Girl, have you ever heard of stalkers, rapists—"

"Sure, but—"

"Muggers, perverts? You think he's going to wait for an invitation if he wants to assault you?"

Katherine reached for the half-empty glass of wine on the counter. Lisa was immediately at her side, removing it from her hands and setting it beside the sink. "And this you save for later. Till you make the decision. Otherwise, you need all your wits about you."

"Lisa—"

"It's a jungle out there, survival of the fittest. And you never let some man know where you live. Not till you check him out. Even then you don't invite him back here. Always go to his place."

"He lives on a boat in the marina."

"I don't care if he lives in a pup tent. You never, never invite a guy to your place. At least not till the second or third date."

"It's a little late now," Katherine said as she reached for her glass. "He's going to be here in fifteen minutes."

Lisa shook her head. "All right, all right." She raised her hands as if making a magnanimous offer. "I'll stay till the two of you leave. That way he'll think I'm baby-sitting here."

"Thanks."

"But that dress . . ."

"The dress is perfect."

"Have it your way. What about that makeup?"

Katherine gave her a look.

Lisa folded her arms and waited for an answer.

"I always use this mascara, and I bought the lipstick special to highlight the dress."

"That's it? Lipstick and mascara?"

"And blush."

"Don't go away, I'll be right back."

Ten minutes later, Lisa finished applying a hasty combination of concealer, foundation cream, powder, blush, eyeliner, lipstick liner, lipstick, and peach, emerald, and almond-roast eye shadows. "Now put your finger in your mouth, wrap your lips around it, and pop it out."

Katherine followed her order, making a little popping sound. "Like this?"

"Perfect."

"What does that do?"

"Keeps the lipstick off your teeth." Finally Lisa stepped back to carefully inspect her work.

"So what do you think?" Katherine asked skeptically.

"See for yourself."

Katherine rose from the edge of the bathtub, crossed to the mirror, and gasped. "I look like a hooker!"

Lisa grinned. "Exactly."

The doorbell rang. Instant panic. "Oh, my gosh, he's here." For the briefest second the two women were fourteen years old again.

"I'll get it," Eric called from the bedroom where he was working on his computer.

"No, sweetheart, let me get that." Dashing into her bedroom, she grabbed her white shawl, threw it on, and spun around to Lisa, who had followed her in. "What do you think?"

Lisa tried to smile while reaching out to adjust the bottom of the shawl. "Well, at least he won't try anything."

"Lisa—"

The doorbell rang again.

Lisa pushed her toward the door. "Go go go."

One last adjustment of the hair, and Katherine headed down the hallway of the apartment, into the living room, and to the front door. "Who is it?"

"Thaddeus Paris."

Katherine threw a forlorn look back at Lisa, mouthing, "Thaddeus?"

Lisa shrugged, and Katherine motioned for her to step back out of sight. Reluctantly, Lisa agreed.

"Hello?" came the voice.

Katherine reached for the dead bolt and slid it back. She could hear her heart pounding in her ears. Then, with a breath to steady herself, she opened the door.

Mr. Paris stood in the hall wearing white Reeboks, designer jeans a couple sizes too small, and a burgundy sweatshirt with *Just Do It* printed across the front. To complete the ensemble, a laptop computer hung from his shoulder.

"Hi." He grinned.

Katherine swallowed back her surprise. "Hi."

"You're all dressed up."

"Uh, yeah."

Suddenly the lights came on. "Oh, I'm sorry. I thought Eric told you."

"Told me what?"

"My new software."

"Software." She sounded like a parrot repeating every phrase, but she was still trying to get her bearings.

"Yeah." He motioned to his computer. "I'm having a dickens of a time with some new software. I thought maybe we could work on it for a while." He flashed what was supposed to be a sexy grin while raising a six-pack of Budweiser in one hand and a bottle of wine in the other. "Then maybe work on some of our own moves."

"Moves?"

"Well, yeah."

Katherine stood a moment, then she reached for the door—

"Hey, wait a min—"

—and shut it, clicking the dead bolt back into place.

"Daddy, Freddy won't share his apple with me."

O'Brien looked up from his picnic lunch—a dripping peanut-butter-and-jelly sandwich, partially baked Tollhouse cookies, chocolate milk, and Snickers bars. The lunch had been packed by Julie, his seven-year-old. Julie was partial to sweets.

Both Julie and Sarah, her twelve-year-old sister, had been playing on the gym set with Freddy while O'Brien and his wife sat on a blanket spread across the newly laid sod. Granted, no one would catch a tan in the artificial environment, but it sure cut down on the flies and ants.

"Daddy." Julie stood with her little hands on her little hips. It was a pose she had learned early from her mother. "Make him share with me."

"Sweetheart." Beth threw a concerned look to O'Brien while addressing her daughter. "I don't think you and Freddy should be sharing food. There's no telling what type of germs he may be carrying."

"Mom—"

"I'm sorry." She reached into the Tupperware and pulled out a carrot stick. "Here, chew on this for a while."

Julie took the carrot with an overly dramatic sigh, then trudged back to her sister and the baboon. The three were playing a game of tag. Of course Freddy didn't completely understand the rules, but it was obvious that he loved chasing and being chased. He also loved the hugs and cuddles that followed each capture.

O'Brien turned to his wife. "Actually, it's the other way around," he explained. "In this environment, Freddy's the one with the fewer germs."

Beth said nothing as she watched their raven-haired beauties play. O'Brien knew she still had some trepidation about Freddy, but that was small potatoes compared to the resentment she harbored. Through the years, their marriage had often hit rocky ground. You don't raise a multimillion-dollar company from nothing without a little stress and a few thousand hours of overtime. Then, just as things were beginning to settle down and the marital stress was starting to mend, along came this new project and, of course, Freddy. Suddenly everything went into hyper speed, with every problem needing to be solved yesterday, and O'Brien's family having to take the farthest seat in the back. The recent eat-and-dash routine at Thanksgiving was the perfect example—an example O'Brien still found himself paying for.

"They'll be okay," he said, rubbing the back of his hand against her arm.

She nodded and tossed her black, shoulder-length hair to the side. It was obvious where the girls inherited their beauty. She had classical Italian features, a strong profile, dark eyes, full lips, and a figure to match. She was also a great mom and wife. Despite their fights over his time spent away, O'Brien knew he needed her as much as the girls did. In fact, if he hadn't had her there, reminding him of home and family, his work would literally and quite completely consume him. She was his tent peg, a reminder of what was really important. That was the purpose of the picnic. If Mohammed wouldn't come to the mountain this Saturday afternoon, then Beth would bring the mountain to him.

For as long as O'Brien could remember, science had been his passion. As a kid, he'd wanted to know how everything worked. Now, as a genetic engineer, he wanted to make everything work better. So far, he and his peers were doing just that. Slowly, of course, but step-by-step, discovery after discovery, they were making progress.

Gene therapy had already been used in treating over three hundred people, beating cystic fibrosis, ADA deficiency, hypercholesterolemia, as well as certain forms of anemia. Meanwhile, everyone was hot on the trail of ways to use it to cure breast cancer, sickle-cell anemia, melanoma, attention deficit disorder, schizophrenia, alcoholism, and the list went on. The opportunities were mind-boggling. By current estimates, there are four thousand human diseases caused by malfunctioning genes. That's four thousand opportunities to make the world a better place. Four thousand ways of not only increasing the quality of life, but in many cases actually saving life.

Granted, social problems resulting from improved genetic science were rising almost as quickly as the cures—like employers refusing to hire individuals if they didn't like what showed up on their genetic screening, or health insurance companies dropping clients because genetic tests indicated a high risk. O'Brien still shuddered at the HMO group who'd told an expectant mother of a cystic fibrosis child that they would pay for an abortion—but not for treatments if she chose to give birth.

Still, these were problems to be worked out in the courts, not the laboratory. O'Brien had neither the time nor the interest to deal with people's greed or prejudice—unless, of course, he could find a gene for that, too.

"So what do you think?"

O'Brien turned back to Beth, who waited patiently for an answer. She'd obviously been having another of their conversations without him. His mind raced. What had they been talking about? He was clueless, and she knew it.

"About getting away this winter," she repeated. "Maybe Mazatlán."

"Yeah," he said. "I think that would be good."

"If I could clear it with the schools, maybe we could stay a few weeks."

"Well," he stalled, somehow suspecting that this was a test. "I mean, we don't have to decide that just yet, do we?"

Beth sighed and looked away. It *had* been a test, and he'd just flunked.

Trying to regain lost ground, he continued, "Actually, you're right. A few weeks might do us all some good."

"Fine," she said flatly, without looking back at him. "I'll get the information."

"Great," he said, sounding a little too enthusiastic. "And we can look it over and decide as a family."

Nice try, but still no response.

He gave it another shot. "But you're right, a few weeks would be really good for us." He stared at the back of her head, unable to tell if he'd made any progress. "Real good."

Before she could respond, his beeper went off. He had been careful to switch it to vibrate instead of beep, knowing how Beth hated the sound. He stole a peek at his belt: 3798. That was Wolff, one of Murkoski's assistants. The man never called unless it was important. And since Murkoski was still in Lincoln . . .

"Listen, I, uh—"

"You need to answer that," Beth said, without turning.

He looked at her, surprised. How did she do that? "I shouldn't be long," he said, rising to his feet.

"It's okay, I understand."

"No, really, I won't—"

"I said I understand. And I appreciate your letting us have this time."

He wasn't sure whether she was serious or sarcastic. After fourteen years of marriage, she still had her mysteries. In any case, he bent down and kissed the top of her head. "Thanks." Then, turning to the kids, he shouted, "What does a guy have to do to get a good-bye kiss around here?"

The children ran toward him, shouting "Daddy! Daddy!" and began protesting his leaving. Even Freddy showed some disappointment as he loped up to him, wrapped his arms around one leg, and indicated that he'd be happy to pick off a few lice if O'Brien stayed.

"Sorry, fella," O'Brien chuckled, "duty calls." After another round of hugs and kisses, he left the room. His heart was heavy, but only for a moment. Back in the hall, the thousand-and-one migraine makers of running Genodyne Inc. quickly returned.

How he envied people like Wolff. People completely immersed in research. No worries about funding, no P and L statements, no keeping an antagonistic board of directors satisfied, or disgruntled employees happy, or impossible FDA compliances met—all this while trying to remember why he had started the company in the first place. It was more than one man could handle, and too many things were slipping through the cracks. That's why he'd brought Murkoski on board for the new project. And that's also why he was always having to play catch-up with the kid. He didn't like it much—particularly when it appeared that Murkoski was keeping him out of the loop.

That seemed to be happening more and more lately. Despite O'Brien's efforts to stay informed, Murkoski seemed to be gradually building a wall around the project, slowly turning it into a company within a company. More than once O'Brien had wanted to slow things down, but the pressure they were receiving from the government, coupled with the potential for incredible financial reward, and Murkoski's own brazen ego, made it difficult to find the brakes.

He'd thought they'd hit a barrier when Coleman had made his impossible demand to be removed from Death Row. And yet, in just a few short days, Murkoski had secured permission. "If that's what it takes to do it," Murkoski had said of his government contacts, "then that's what they'll do. This project is too important to balk at details."

O'Brien shook his head as he moved down the hall. Was there nothing the kid couldn't pull off? He was amazing. But just as amazing was how the project had become so complicated. When you get right down to it, gene therapy is anything but complicated. In fact, in its basic form, it's so simple a child can grasp it. Both Sarah and Julie thoroughly understood the concept.

Every living cell contains DNA, that spiral ladder magazines are so fond of drawing. Inside this DNA are genes that we inherit from our parents. These genes tell us whether we're going to be turtles or people, short or tall, die from breast cancer, or live to be a hundred. You'd think such important messengers would be impossibly complex. They're not.

In fact, it all comes down to just four building blocks, four basic chemicals: guanine, adenine, thymine, and cytosine, better known as G, A, T, and C. These are the rungs that hold the strands of the famous spiraling DNA ladder together. That's it, just four chemicals. But it is the way these four chemicals are combined that creates the fifty to one hundred thousand different genes found in the DNA in every human cell.

Genodyne's job is relatively simple. Discover the gene or combinations of genes that creates a specific characteristic (one gene can contain a group of hundreds or even thousands of these chemical rungs), find which rung it begins at and which rung it ends at, snip out that characteristic at the appropriate rungs with chemical scissors called *restriction enzymes*, and replace the old section with the new one. Don't like brown hair? Find those genes, snip them out, and replace them with the genes for blonde hair.

But having one cell in your body that says "I'm a blonde-haired person" when millions of other hair-producing cells are saying, "No way, we're brown," is a losing battle. The trick is to find some way to tell all the cells that influence hair color to change from manufacturing brown hair to blonde. That's where a virus like the one injected into Freddy and Coleman comes in. Since viruses love to multiply by infecting other cells, why not inject the new genes into a virus, and turn the virus loose in the bloodstream to infect the appropriate cells, changing their brown-haired genes into blonde-haired ones.

That's gene therapy in a nutshell. Of course, there are thousands of minor problems, which explains Genodyne's staff of four hundred fifty and counting. Just to find the right gene is a near-impossible task. That's why there are programs like the Human Genome Project discovering new genes every week in the hope of having all 100,000 mapped and labeled by the year 2005.

Once the genes have been discovered, snipped out, and replaced, there's still the problem of making sure they'll really do what they promise they'll do. That's where Wolff's mice come in. Since the DNA rungs in all animals are made up of the same four chemicals, G, A, T, and C, the mouse doesn't know from where it's receiving these snippets of DNA—it could come from anything from humans to insects. (One of O'Brien's favorite stories was the grad student who isolated the genes for making fireflies glow and inserted them into a mouse to see if the mouse would glow. It did. Well, sort of.)

Once the genes from the precious ancient blood sample had been identified and reproduced, they were inserted into the eggs of Wolff's mice. They could have been inserted into the blood of adult mice, but since the gestation period for mice is only twenty days, it's simpler and cleaner to change the creatures before they're even conceived. These genetically altered eggs were then replanted back inside the mouse, where they were fertilized and eventually birthed.

Still, the new generation of mice infected with genes from the ancient blood didn't necessarily show any change of appearance or behavior. Much of genetic research is guesswork, hit and miss, looking for the right combination of genes. So they had repeated the process, again and again, generation after generation, until they were finally able to isolate and identify the "GOD gene." Murkoski had come up with the name—a hangover, he said, from his Catholic school days. By gene standards, it wasn't terribly long, only 1,058 ladder rungs. But when inserted into the mice, the results were astounding. They no longer scrambled for food, but shared it. In fact, the purest strain (the DNA Freddy and Coleman shared) seemed to actually make the mice more concerned about the welfare of their fellow mice than about themselves.

Incredible. But to O'Brien, no more amazing than the fact that the key to the difference in every animal—from flies to mice to baboons to man—is controlled by the combination of those same four chemicals, G, A, T, C. The concept never ceased to amaze him. And, more and more often, as he made entries into his personal lab notebook, he found himself referring to the "Genius" behind it all—spelled not with a small *g,* but with a capital.

O'Brien entered the research wing by shoving his billfold against the five-by-five-inch black box. The magnetic ID card in the wallet buzzed the door. He then entered his six-digit PIN. The door unlocked and he stepped inside to the bottom floor of an impressive, six-story arboretum. Balconies of each of the other floors looked down on him from all sides. Thirty-foot palm trees and assorted flora and fauna stretched toward the frosted skylights. Of course, his board of directors had told him that this was a waste of square footage, but O'Brien, who had spent more than his fair share of time cooped up in a lab, had insisted. Any scientist working in the dozens of labs along the halls that opened up onto the balconies would relish the fresh air and glimpse of nature that the arboretum provided.

He walked past a small trickling waterfall and shoved his billfold against another box, reentering his PIN. The door to the Transgenetic Mice Area clicked open. He moved down the hall and entered a small room where paper gowns and booties were folded neatly on stainless-steel shelves. He unfolded the gown, slipped it over his shirt and jeans, and buttoned it. Next came the paper booties. These were a little trickier. There was a line painted across the floor, dividing the room into two sections. The first half was for street shoes, the second half was for paper booties. One had to balance on one foot on the street-shoe side while slipping the paper bootie over the other foot. When the paper bootie was in place, the papered foot would come down on the bootie side of the floor, and the whole process could begin again with the other foot.

Once O'Brien had suited up, he stepped onto a sticky floor mat to pick up any dirt or organism that may have contaminated his paper booties while he was putting them on. He then opened the other door and entered a hallway.

He crossed to one of the four metal doors with square, viewing portholes in their center and rapped on the glass.

Wolff, an athletic, red-haired surfer type in his late twenties, looked up from dozens of racks. These held the clear Lucite boxes that housed the individual mice. But these were no ordinary mice. They were pampered beyond belief. Not only was the whole gown-and-bootie process for their benefit, but so were the special temperature and humidity controls, the filtered air, the low-fat food, and the vast array of other amenities you would only provide mice that, after months and months of genetic alteration and breeding, cost thousands, sometimes hundreds of thousands of dollars to produce.

Wolff crossed to the door and opened it. O'Brien felt the gentle breeze against his face as the positively pressured room blew any contaminants he may have brought in back outside into the hallway.

"What's up?" O'Brien asked.

Wolff looked grave as he silently escorted O'Brien over to the racks near the far wall. Unlike the other racks, these held larger Lucite boxes containing groups of four to eight mice, housed together to see how they would behave in a community environment.

"This is our last generation," Wolff said, "the same strain we have in your guy back at Lincoln."

"And . . ."

Wolff stooped down to the third shelf. "They were fine this morning, but when I checked them after lunch—well, see for yourself." He pulled out the Lucite container, and O'Brien bent down for a better look.

Five mice were huddled together at one end, some eating, others cleaning and sleeping. They looked and behaved perfectly normal. It was the sixth mouse, at the other end of the box, that made O'Brien catch his breath. The mouse that lay all by itself, perfectly motionless. The mouse whose body had been shredded apart and partially devoured.

At times Coleman thought he was losing his mind. One moment he'd be holding his own, maintaining the mental and emotional steel necessary to run the Row. The next he'd be suddenly distracted by the beauty of the low winter sun striking a brick wall, or the crisp, cold air in the exercise yard, or the soft rustling of pine needles in the tree just outside the fence. These experiences unnerved him. Not only because they were new, but because he wasn't sure when they would come. Lack of control angered him, and when he wasn't marveling over the beauty, he was cursing its intrusion. Frequently he tried to push the thoughts and feelings out of his mind. Sometimes he succeeded. More and more often he did not.

But there was one feeling he could never push away: the terrible loneliness from the dream. It never left. As the days progressed, the ache grew deeper. It was more than his brother's pain. It was his own. A feeling of abandonment. Of emptiness.

More than once, it was all he could do to fight back the tears. And when the sense of wonder and beauty surrounding him struck at the same time as the loneliness, it was impossible to hold back the tears.

But it wasn't just *his* loneliness. He started seeing it in others, too. The way their shoulders sagged as they sat. The way they slowly walked the yard when they thought no one was watching.

But mostly he saw it in their eyes.

"Something wrong, Cole?"

Coleman blinked and came to. He was in the showers. Skinner, a big black man who had been on the Row a couple of years longer than he had, stood under an adjacent nozzle. Just as he had learned the details of bomb making from Garcia, Coleman had learned the intricate nuances of lock picking from Skinner. They weren't friends, but after seven years of living together they were definitely comrades.

"You're staring again, man."

Coleman blinked again, then resumed lathering with his bar of soap.

Skinner leaned closer. "What's wrong with you?"

Coleman dropped his head and let the water pelt his forehead and scalp. It was a pleasant sensation: the way the water pounded against his skin, the way it gently massaged the roots of his hair. It's a wonder he'd never noticed it before. He tried not to smile at the pleasure, but didn't quite succeed.

When he came out from under the water, he opened his eyes to see Skinner standing with a quizzical look on his face. "I don't know what's going on with you, man, but you better be careful."

"What do you mean?" Coleman asked.

Skinner lowered his voice, making sure they weren't overheard. "Word has it you're getting soft."

Coleman shook his head and swore.

"No, I'm serious, man. Losing your grip, that's what they're saying. And with Sweeney coming back from the hospital next week . . . all I'm saying is you better be smart, man. Just be smart."

Coleman held Skinner's look. He was finding it easier and easier to tell when people were lying, and as far as he could make out, Skinner was shooting straight. He gave a faint nod of acknowledgment. Skinner turned off the shower and walked away. A moment later Coleman followed suit, furious. How could he have been so stupid? It was one thing to feel what he was feeling, but to let others see it? That was insanity. Any weakness on the Row meant trouble, and apparently he had shown that weakness more than once. What was happening?

He crossed the white tile to a metal bench, where he scooped up his towel and began drying off with the other men. No one said a word to him. They knew. Something was coming down. Coleman was losing his touch, and with Sweeney returning, any allegiance to Coleman now could be dangerous. The thought infuriated him.

"All right, men, let's head back." It was McCoy, one of the 9:00 A.M. to 6:00 P.M. hacks. He'd been with them almost four years. A good man, though impossible to con. They obeyed and shuffled into the hall, their thongs flip-flopping as they headed back to their cells.

It was then that Hector Garcia pulled up alongside him. "Listen, Cole, I never got to, you know, say thanks."

Coleman stared straight ahead.

"And if I can ever, you know, show my appreciation . . ." He gently let his arm brush against him.

The punk was putting a move on him! Gratitude or not, you never broke protocol by talking to someone of Coleman's status without being spoken to first. And you never, *never* disrespected him by making an offer like this.

The fury over Skinner's comments, the silent betrayal of the men, his own stupidity—it was more than Coleman could contain. His vision grew sharp and narrow. The sound of the men's thongs exploded in his ears. The colors of the beige walls and the lime-green doors burst in vivid contrast. It was time to reestablish his authority.

It took a single blow to double Garcia over, and one double-fisted uppercut to throw the boy's head back and reeling into the wall. Garcia was unconscious before he hit the floor.

McCoy's baton came down hard, but Coleman felt nothing. He never did in this state. He spun around, grabbed the stick from the startled McCoy, and was about to smash his skull when he came up short.

It was the fear in McCoy's eyes that stopped him. The fear that said he had a wife, kids, a mortgage. Fear that said he was only trying to do his job and please, please, don't hurt me. I'm lonely and scared and faking it just like everybody else. Please . . .

The rage began to dissolve. There he was, in front of all the men, standing with the baton in his hand, staring at McCoy and doing nothing. But how could he strike when there was such fear and loneliness in McCoy's eyes? He threw the baton down in disgust and turned back to Garcia. The kid lay on the ground with a trickle of blood running from his nose.

Overwhelmed with empathy, he stooped down to check on the boy. He could feel the other men's eyes, but he no longer cared. He knew he'd already lost their respect by refusing to go after McCoy. And by kneeling to check on Garcia, it was doubtful that he could ever regain it. But that didn't matter. Right now, all that mattered was Garcia's injuries, and the tightness of emotion constricting Coleman's throat.

He was barely aware of the rattling sounds behind him as McCoy retrieved his baton from the floor. There was a sudden, powerful blow to the back of his head. Pain exploded in his brain for a split second before he lost consciousness.

CHAPTER 5

"What do you mean, he's withdrawn his appeal?" Steiner sat up rod-straight in his legal clinic work cubicle. "He can't do that!"

"He can do anything he wants," came the voice at the other end of the line. "It's his life."

"But—" Steiner fumbled for words. "What's his angle?"

"No one knows. Could be he's grown tired of the fight; we've seen that before."

"No. Coleman doesn't get tired. He's a machine, an unfeeling machine."

The silence on the other end did not disagree. "Of course there is the other theory . . ." The voice hesitated. It belonged to Robert Butterfield, assistant D.A. for Douglas County. The two had worked together on the case since its beginning. Unofficially, of course. Steiner knew Butterfield had caught heat from the press over their alliance and on more than one occasion he had received some questioning memos from his boss. But Steiner also knew Butterfield's respect for professional courtesy. More importantly, he knew the man had a daughter. And whenever Steiner's relentless naggings put an edge to Butterfield's voice, Steiner only had to ask, "What if it had been your daughter, Bob? What if she were the one who was stabbed to death and found with her throat slit?"

"What other theory?" Steiner demanded.

"Rumor has it something's happened on the Row. Coleman's supposedly gone through some sort of change. Moping around his cell, feeling remorseful, that sort of thing."

Steiner scowled. He knew Coleman inside and out. Men like that didn't have remorse. An accidental killer might. Or someone who kills out of passion, sure. But not multiple killers. They never have feelings for their victims; it's simply not in their nature. So what was he up to?

Steiner cleared his throat. "What does his counsel say?"

"They're as puzzled as the rest of us."

"They're playing straight?"

"Whatever scam he's trying to pull, he's pulling alone."

"Maybe he's going for insanity—proving he's not mentally fit for execution because he agrees he should be executed? Others have tried it."

"I don't know, Harold. I'm only telling you what his lawyers say and what I hear from the Row."

Steiner's mind raced. Coleman was clever, crafty. And he was absolutely amoral. What *was* he doing?

"Harold?"

A thought was forming.

"Harold, you still there?"

"Yeah. Listen, Bob. If this is legit, and we know it's not, but if it was—wouldn't the best way for him to prove it to everybody, wouldn't the best way be for him to finally let me visit him?"

"We've been through that a hundred—"

"I know, I know, but think about it. The man claims he's repentant. The father of his victim wants to meet him. What's he going to do, say no? Who would believe him then? Don't you see, he's played right into our hands. If he says yes, I get my meeting. If he says no, I prove he's a fake."

There was a pause on the other end. "It could backfire. He could play the media and turn public opinion around. 'Repentant Killer Begs Forgiveness.'"

"Like Walking Wily in '94?"

"That's right."

"But we still fried him, didn't we?"

"True."

"And with the public so pro-death these days, and this being an election year . . ."

Butterfield finished the thought. "It would be political suicide for the board to pardon him."

"Exactly. Let me take my chances, Bob. Ask Coleman's lawyers to run it past him again. See if you can get me in. Tell them it's a good litmus test to see if he's legit."

"And if they refuse?"

"Then I'll be the one to go to the press. If Coleman wants to play a new game, that's fine with me. He's still not getting away. I won't let him. The Law won't let him."

There was a long pause on the other end. Finally: "I'll get back to you later this afternoon."

The stench of raw chicken fat is replaced by disinfectant, an overwhelming odor of pine and ammonia that makes Coleman's nose twitch. It's a new smell for the fourteen-year-old, but it's a smell he will grow accustomed to over the years.

A Ping-Pong ball clacks back and forth. Kids talk, swear, laugh. Boys and girls. A billiard ball cracks. Coleman reaches into his pocket and pulls out a white sweat sock, the same type they issue every day in this juvenile center located behind Douglas County Hospital. White socks, white T-shirts, and blue jeans.

He is waiting for Father Kennedy. He steps back—black, high-top Keds squeaking on yellowing floor tile. He feels the pool table behind him and turns. Discreetly he reaches into the leather-thonged side pocket.

"Get your paws outta there."

He flashes the boy with the cue stick a leer and pulls out a single billiard ball.

Cue Stick Boy momentarily considers making an issue out of it but appears to remember Coleman's reputation and decides otherwise.

"Oh, here you are." It's an older voice with a trace of an Irish accent. Coleman stiffens but does not turn to face Father Kennedy.

"Thanks for meeting me here, son. May I buy you a Coca-Cola?"

Coleman shakes his head.

"Listen," the man says, "I'm sorry if I embarrassed you at chapel."

Coleman slowly opens the sock. His back is still toward the Father.

"I really am quite open to hearing opinions and answering questions."

Cue Stick Boy pretends to line up another shot, but it is obvious he is watching everything.

"Still, there's a time to speak and a time to listen."

Coleman drops the billiard ball into the sock. It stretches the material three or four inches. He raises it so it does not clunk the table.

"And by challenging my authority in front of the group, well, I'm afraid your comments were a little too disruptive. That's why I had to ask you to leave."

Coleman discreetly wraps the long neck of the sock around his right hand one time.

"I hope you understand. No hard feelings?"

He hesitates.

"Now, if you have any questions, I'd be more than happy to discuss them with you."

Coleman spins. His arm flies into the air, whipping the ball, whirling it toward the man's face. It is only then that he recognizes the eyes. They are not Kennedy's eyes. They are his own eyes. He can tell by the emptiness, their aching loneliness.

But it is too late. The ball smashes into Kennedy's left cheekbone. Yet it is Coleman who cries out in pain. The impact is jarring, searing. He feels his own face give way, sees his own eyes staring back at him in pain and confusion and betrayal.

But he cannot stop. He swings the ball again, then again—each time feeling the blow himself. As victor and victim he screams. And still, he continues.

Somebody runs toward him. Construction boots against tile. His father's boots.

He continues swinging. The eyes in the battered face no longer register any expression. Coleman hits his face again, shrieking in pain, weeping at the cruelty.

His father is there. Coleman's eyes are too battered to make out the blurry form of the man, but he can smell the whisky on his breath. He will kill Coleman. The boy begins flailing his arms, but he hits only air. His eyes no longer work. The pain is unbearable, resonating from his skull through his body and into his gut. He doubles over, convulsing. Once, twice, until finally . . .

Coleman woke up vomiting. He rolled onto his side and managed to spew most of it onto the floor. When the convulsions ceased, he sat up and threw his feet over the edge of the bed. He ran his hand over his face. It was covered in sweat and tears.

They were coming every night now. The dreams. Acts of violence he had completely forgotten. Brutality where he becomes his own victims, feeling their pain, screaming their anguish. Each dream ending the same way, with uncontrollable tears of remorse.

As he sat on the edge of the bed, catching his breath, he heard a train's distant and mournful whistle. He paused to savor the sound. Over the years he'd been vaguely aware of it, but never really heard it. It was painful and beautiful. A distant, sorrowful wail that cut through the stillness of the night.

Over the past weeks Coleman had grown accustomed to the beauty surrounding him. It was still just as breathtaking, but it was no longer quite as unnerving. But the other thing—the ache in his chest, the tightening in his throat, the gnawing loneliness—once that pain came, it never left. No matter what he did, no matter how he tried to ignore it, it was always there.

The only thing worse than the loneliness was the look in other people's eyes. The inmates', the guards', the caseworkers'. They seemed so haunted, so full of their own emptiness. They were Coleman's brother's eyes, forsaken and abandoned. They were Kennedy's eyes, full of searching anguish. That was the reason Coleman spent more and more time in his cell, away from the rest of the population. It was their eyes. He simply could not bear to see the loneliness.

Shadows crossed the window of his door, and he stiffened. Somebody was out in the hall. A key slipped into the lock and the door swung open. Glaring light poured in from the hallway, and Coleman squinted as two, three, maybe four forms shuffled inside.

"Who's there?" he demanded.

No answer. The door shut. It was dark again.

"What do you want?"

"Hello, Cole."

A chill swept through his body. He recognized the voice. It had a different diction, thanks to the missing tooth, but there was no mistaking its owner. Sweeney was back. Other silhouettes became distinguishable. Three men from the Row. No hacks. Just inmates. Apparently Sweeney had been busy all afternoon recruiting and convincing them to change their alliance. Coleman wasn't sure, but for a second he even thought he saw Garcia.

"You wouldn't come to my welcome-home party," the voice sneered, "so I thought I'd bring it here."

"That's ridiculous," Murkoski protested. "How can you say I'm pushing too hard?"

O'Brien held the phone against his left shoulder, bending and unbending a paper clip in his hands, trying his best to remain calm. "Kenny, a mouse from the

GOD gene colony has been killed by one of its own kind. We've got to slow down. We've got to retrace our steps to see what went wrong."

"I'll tell you what's wrong," Murkoski's voice scoffed over the phone. "Wolff's an incompetent buffoon, that's what's wrong. I've said that from the first day we brought him on board. Did you run a biopsy on other animals in the colony? Run some gels? See if one of them's mutated?"

"No, he suggested we wait until you—"

"See what I mean? Incompetent! The man won't even run a gel without me there. Totally incompetent!"

O'Brien paused a moment to let the conversation cool. "It's not going to hurt us to put off the transplant a few more weeks."

"He's scheduled for execution in thirty days."

"So have your federal guys talk the governor into a stay."

"It's not that simple."

"Kenny, I just don't understand the rush. What would it hurt—"

"Look, if you want to run this thing, then you come back here and run it!"

"Kenn—"

"The guy is off the prison grounds and in a local hospital. His behavior is exactly as we hypothesized. And this latest beating is the perfect alibi to keep him out of circulation for the next several weeks. I'm telling you, the timing couldn't be better."

"Have you checked with him?"

"What do you mean?"

"I remember you conveniently forgetting to mention anything to him about a bone-marrow transplant when I was there."

"He'll go along with us. What other choice does he have? Besides, I've already pulled his stem cells and infected them."

"You've already pulled his marrow?"

"He was unconscious when they brought him in, what better time? The departments here are top rate. X ray has the sophistication to kill the cells, and their isolation ward is good enough to keep out infection until he can regenerate new ones. I'm telling you, it can all be done right here and now."

O'Brien's head spun. He knew that a bone-marrow transplant was necessary, just as it had been with Freddy. It was one thing to give Coleman the virus injection every few days to infect his new blood cells as the old ones died off. But those effects were only temporary. To make them permanent, one had to actually change the way the blood cells were made. And since blood cells are manufactured inside bone marrow, it's necessary to change the marrow.

"It's like a car factory," he had explained to little Julie. "They make red and blue and green cars. But if you want a bunch of polka-dot ones, you can either stand outside the car plant and individually paint each car as it rolls out, or you can install new machinery inside the plant that automatically makes them polka dot."

That was the case with Coleman. They could either change the blood cells one at a time, or change the bone marrow—the blood factory—itself.

A bone-marrow transplant was simple enough. Insert a needle deep into the big bones, such as the pelvic bone. Do this fifteen to twenty times to withdraw an adequate portion of the gooey red bone marrow. This is where the stem cells are located, those tricky, hard-to-find cells that actually produce the white and red blood cells. Once outside the body, the marrow is infected with a virus that instructs the stem cells on how to create the new kind of blood. When these stem cells have been reprogrammed, they are reinjected back into the body. In theory, this would allow Coleman to create the new blood all on his own, permanently.

In theory.

"I'm telling you," Murkoski said, "we're all set here. Just say the word, and we're on our way."

O'Brien was losing control of the situation. It was time to test the waters. "And if I don't give the go-ahead?"

He was not surprised by the pause on the other end. Nor was he particularly shocked at the answer when it finally came. "We're talking about a lot of money here, Phil—not to mention power. A lot of rich, influential people who will be very disappointed in us. In you. For crying out loud," he blurted, "we're about to change the entire course of human history!"

O'Brien said nothing. He suspected there was more. He was right.

"To be honest, I don't think McGovern or Riordan or *any* of your board would be too happy to let this type of money and prestige slip out of our hands . . ."

O'Brien closed his eyes and waited. Here it came.

" . . . slip out of our hands and go someplace else. No, they would not be happy with that at all."

O'Brien took a long, deep breath. Just as he had feared. If he pulled the plug now, Murkoski would go to the board. No question about it. He had the audacity and the ego to do that sort of thing. But that was the best-case scenario. The worst case would be that Murkoski would simply quit and go to another company. The kid would pick up all of his toys (along with all that government funding) and go find a company that was willing to let him continue at his own accelerated pace. It was blackmail, pure and simple. Of course, there would be lawsuits and court battles, but by then it would be too late.

O'Brien stalled, trying to change tack. "What about the execution?"

"We'll be running the GSR as soon as his risk of infection stabilizes and we get back to the penitentiary."

"Will you tell him? About the GSR test?"

"I don't think we can. If he knew what was going on, it would ruin the results."

"That seems rather cruel."

"Of course it does, but can you think of any other way to get an accurate reading?"

O'Brien couldn't.

"I'm also nailing down the other details," Murkoski continued. "The Witness Protection guys are making contact with somebody in our area. Looks like we may have ourselves a little bonus in that department. Also, I'm flying out Hendricks, one of our own electricians, to rewire the chair."

"Everyone back there is sitting tight on this?" O'Brien asked. "Only a few people will know the execution is a fake?"

"Not even the coroner. She's going to get sick that day and will be replaced by an assistant she doesn't even know about."

O'Brien was weakening. "But what about the mice?"

"Have Wolff run the gels and get back to me. I'm sure it was just mishandling, maybe some mislabeling. Typical techie incompetence."

"And Coleman? If something should go wrong with the execution? If he should accidentally . . ." O'Brien searched for the right word. "Expire?"

"Then we'll find someone else."

"Kenny . . ."

"Listen, Phil, it's time you realize that this program is more important than one man's life. Or, for that matter, several."

A dull cold tightened around O'Brien's stomach as his worst fears resurfaced. Did this kid know any boundaries?

"We're talking about changing the human race here. With stakes like that, a few sacrifices, especially like a Michael Coleman, are of little consequence. Not when you look at the big picture. Besides, he's scheduled to die anyway, what's the difference?"

O'Brien's head began to ache. Again, he changed the subject. "If you're successful, if we get him out of there alive and free, how will we convince him to keep working with us?"

"I'm adding a viral leash to the marrow. If he doesn't come to us every five to six days, his body will create such massive quantities of cytokines he's going to feel like he's having the flu five times over."

O'Brien's intercom buzzed. He tried to ignore it, but it continued. He pressed the button and snapped, "I thought I said no interruptions."

"I'm sorry, Dr. O'Brien, it's Mr. Riordan, line two. He insists on talking to you about the epidermal drug."

"Can't he wait?"

"He's pretty insistent."

"I'll be with him in a minute."

"He wants to speak to you *now.*"

O'Brien rubbed the back of his neck and spoke into the phone. "Kenny?"

"Yeah, I heard."

"Okay, look, it's your call, but give it another day, all right? Phone me tomorrow and let me know your final decision."

"Phil—"

"Twenty-four hours won't hurt anything. And it will give you an extra day to catch your breath and think through any options. All right?"

Another pause. Then, "All right."

"And please be careful."

"No prob, Phil. Talk to you tomorrow."

Before O'Brien could respond, Murkoski hung up. The CEO of Genodyne Inc. took a long, deep breath. He had done the right thing, he was certain of it. Even though he felt spent and used, at least for now he had done the right thing.

That thought provided little consolation as he reached for line two, preparing for another confrontation with his most demanding board member. Dr. Philip O'Brien did not much care for his job today. And he was caring for it less and less as the day dragged on.

Kenneth Murkoski smiled as he hung up the phone inside the pre-op room. He'd pulled it off without a hitch.

A nurse already in scrubs poked her head into the room. "Dr. Murkoski?"

"Yes?"

"The patient's prepped. We're ready to begin when you are."

"Excellent." He stuffed the cellular into his pants. "I'll be right there."

"Don't you mock me!"

"I wasn't—"

"I'm still your mother."

Katherine's mind replayed the scene again and again. It was a continuous loop. No matter what she did, she couldn't stop the memory of Eric's voice or hers.

" 'Scuse me . . . 'scuse me," she called to the passing bartender. He was a cutey, in his early twenties. "Give me another one of these . . . these, what are they called?"

The bartender grinned. "Surfer on Acid."

"Right." Katherine nodded. "I'll have another . . ." The name had already escaped her. "Another one."

"Don't you mock me!"

"I wasn't—"

"I'm still your mother."

"I wasn't—"

"I demand your respect, do you hear me?"

Though her brain was fogging, the scene wasn't. It remained as clear as when it had unfolded nearly two hours earlier.

It had been another long and trying week. The IRS was closing in fast, demanding she pay for some honest miscalculations made over three years ago.

"How can I pay what I don't have?" she had pleaded for the umpteenth time over the phone.

"We can work out a payment plan, Mrs. Lyon, but this is the United States government—and you *will* pay."

She'd had a similar conversation with her store's landlord that same afternoon. Same basic threat, same bottom line. Bills were piling up faster than she could keep track. Now she was dumping her mail on the floor at the end of the sofa, refusing even to open it. Not that she had time. With work and shopping and creditors and chauffeuring Eric, she had time for nothing.

Except the booze. And the guilt.

The only daughter of a Baptist minister, Katherine had grown up in a strict, religious home. No one drank in her family. In fact, she had not even tasted beer until she was a senior in high school. Even as an adult, drinking had never been a part of her life. Oh, she and Gary would have an occasional glass of wine during one of those rare and infrequent dinners they couldn't afford, but that had been merely an attempt by the young newlyweds to be sophisticated.

Then Gary had been murdered, and everything went wrong. Her trust in a loving God. Her belief that good people were protected from evil. Her fights with her father. And on one particularly rough evening, the visit by a well-meaning friend with a four-pack of wine coolers to help her get through.

What relief they had brought. What blessed, numbing relief. For seven weeks she had been trying to shut down her mind, to stop the pain. Nothing had worked. But there, in those four little coolers, she had found the switch. Those few hours were the only peace she had known in nearly two months of visiting the hospital, enduring the death and the funeral, pretending to be the strong police officer's widow, the faithful preacher's kid. Those four bottles had given her more comfort than any of the hundreds of well-meaning clichés and spiritual bromides shoved at her by friends and relatives.

It was a comfort she had pursued more and more often until she had slowly lost herself to it. That's when she had taken a stand, sworn it off, allowed her dad to enroll her in AA. He was no longer welcome to speak about his God, but he was welcome to help her kick the booze.

And he had. He'd been there every minute she'd needed him. Until eleven months later, when he'd died of a massive coronary, and whatever vestiges of faith Katherine had were snuffed out. It was then she had moved halfway across the country to get away from the suffocating do-gooding of friends and family, to make a go of it in a world with little compassion and no mercy.

She *could* make a go of it, she was certain. She just had to lessen the pain.

"I demand respect, do you hear me?"

The boy mumbled something she couldn't hear.

"What?"

"Nothing."

"What did you say?"

"I said what am I supposed to respect?"

That's when she had hit him. Tears had immediately sprung to his eyes. Not tears of pain, but of betrayal. He'd tried to fight them back, but couldn't.

It was then, seeing the expression in her son's eyes, realizing what she had done, that she'd called Lisa and asked her to baby-sit. She had to get away, she had to stop the pain.

"Here you go, Ma'am."

She looked up surprised as the bartender placed another drink in front of her. She thanked him and asked, "How much do I owe you?"

"No charge. The gentleman over there sent it."

Katherine followed the boy's gesture and squinted at an oily-looking fellow in a worn suit sitting at a nearby table. He raised his glass to her and smiled.

Katherine turned back to her drink. Her last binge, three years ago, had proven to her that men were pigs, animals waiting to take advantage of another's weakness. She would not fall into that trap again.

"Tell him no thanks," she said, fumbling for her wallet. She may be a drunk, but she wasn't for sale.

CHAPTER 6

"What's going on! What are you doing?"

The two men said nothing as they finished strapping Coleman's left arm and leg to the gurney. They had entered the room while he slept and pinned him down before he had a chance to awaken. Now Coleman fought, but with little success, as they forced down his other side and strapped him in.

"What is this? What are you—"

His shouts were cut short by a roll of gauze shoved into his mouth, then quickly sealed in place with surgical tape. Coleman breathed hard, nostrils flaring, eyes wild. He raised his head,trying to see faces, but was quickly shoved back down onto the gurney.

Three weeks had passed since the bone-marrow transplant. His recovery was on schedule, and just that afternoon he had been transferred back to the prison hospital. He had complained about having to sleep on a hospital gurney for the night, and they'd given him some excuse about a lack of beds. Now Coleman realized—too late—that there had been another reason.

Again he raised his head, this time searching for Murkoski. Lights flickered on, and he squinted into the brightness. Again his head was forced down, and this time it was held in a rigid hammerlock by two muscular arms. He tried to bite the arms, to shred them with his teeth, but the man was a pro. Coleman couldn't move an inch.

Suddenly there was electrical buzzing and a harsh scraping atop his head. They were shaving his hair! Why? The only time they shaved a Death Row inmate's head was . . .

Adrenaline surged through Coleman's body. He twisted and strained, but accomplished nothing. The straps and armlock held him firm. Suddenly he heard the distinctive squirting sound of an aerosol can spewing foam and felt cold lather smeared onto his head. Then came more scraping, slower this time, burning and stinging—a razor nicking and cutting his skin.

Shaving the head was the first step in executing a condemned prisoner. It assured the cleanest contact between the skin and the electrodes implanted in the chair's headband. But not now. Not tonight. They were eleven days too early!

Hadn't Murkoski carefully explained it? To keep everyone happy, they would have to stage a mock execution with all of the frills. It would be the only way to convince the public that he was actually dead. And it would have to include everything, the whole nine yards: staged before witnesses, verified by the prison physician, confirmed by the county coroner, extensive coverage by the media, everything to satisfy the folks who wanted to see him fry. But not now. The date had already been set by the courts. He was scheduled for execution January 14. This was January 3!

Now they shaved his left calf, where the second electrode would be placed. The circuitry of the chair was simple. There was a three-and-a-half-foot gap between the chair's head electrode and calf electrode—a three-and-a-half-foot gap that needed one condemned prisoner to slip in and make the circuit complete. That circuit contained 2,450 volts. It would shoot through him, immediately knocking him unconscious and disrupting his heart's electrical pattern.

But not for Coleman. His was to be different. And it was scheduled to be in eleven days, not now.

Unless they were pulling a double-cross.

With their attention on his calf, he was able to raise his head again and look around. Still no Murkoski. Just the two burly men. Coleman might have been able to take them out, if he could move. But he couldn't.

A moment later they smeared a clear, oily gel over the top of his head and then his calf. This was standard procedure to insure maximum contact between the metal electrodes and human flesh.

They pushed open the hospital door and wheeled him out of the room. Coleman's mind raced as they headed down the hall. Seventy-five feet later they arrived at the elevator. Beside it was a blue door and a narrow flight of stairs, the stairs he would have taken if he'd been allowed to walk to his execution. They keyed the elevator, and it opened. They wheeled him in, and the doors closed. As they rode down to the first floor, he tried to read the two men's faces, to make human contact with them. But neither would look at him.

The elevator came to a stop, and the doors rattled opened. He raised his head. He was sweating now, and the tiny rivulets carried the gel down his forehead and into his eyes. It stung fiercely, but he forced himself to keep them open. Directly across from the elevator was the closed door of the execution chamber. To his immediate right was the control room that would hide the humming transformer and the man who would rotate the single dial. The man would be paid around three hundred dollars to stand behind that door and twist the dial on and off four times.

But tonight the door was open. Two men stood inside. One was a stranger, the other Murkoski. Hearing the elevator open, Murkoski turned toward him. Coleman tried to make out his expression, but the sweat and gel blurred his vision.

"I'm sorry to have to do this to you, Mr. Coleman, but there is no other way."

Coleman tried to talk, to plead, to threaten. He shook his head, hoping to signal with his eyes for Murkoski to remove the gauze so he could speak. But Murkoski turned from him and nodded to another large man, who pulled open the door to the execution chamber and went in before them.

It was a nine-by-nine, off-white, cinder-block room. What looked like an old oak throne sat majestically in the center. The chair had been built sometime between 1913 and 1920; it looked like a crude antique. The seat and back were covered with black rubber mats—insulation. Near the top, a small block of wood, which served as a headrest, was also covered with the grooved rubber matting. The four legs, made of four-by-fours, rested on two parallel skids, also made of four-by-fours. They were anchored to the floor by heavy wires threaded through attached ceramic insulators. There wasn't much room to move as the three men unstrapped Coleman from the gurney, carried him across the rubber floor mats, and dumped him into the chair.

Of course Coleman fought, but it served little purpose. These men knew exactly what they were doing.

They began buckling him down with brand-new leather straps, bought expressly for the execution. First the lap strap, then the chest strap, then one for each biceps, one to hold each of his forearms to the armrests, two more to strap his thighs down, and two more around his calves. The purpose of all these straps was not to prevent him from running, but to prevent his body from convulsing and flying out of the chair when they turned on the electricity.

As they attached the electrode to his left calf, Coleman looked ahead at the large rectangular window, not three feet in front of him, covered by a heavy, gold drape. On the other side was the twelve-by-fifteen-foot witness room where the ten chosen witnesses should be watching. But Coleman knew they wouldn't be there. Not tonight. Tonight was eleven days too early.

He turned his head to the left and saw Murkoski standing in the doorway, watching with scientific detachment but avoiding eye contact with Coleman.

The first two men filed out as the last one attached the metal electrodes to Coleman's head, making sure the strap fit snugly. Then he turned and left. Only Murkoski remained, standing in the open doorway between the control room and the execution chamber.

Sweat streamed into Coleman's eyes, continuing to sting them with jelly. But he kept them open. If he'd known how to pray, this would have been the time. He didn't. Instead, he braced himself, preparing for the worst, trying to forget the stories he'd heard. Most of the inmates had speculated that he would feel nothing—

"Knock you out before you know what hits you." But Coleman had read an entirely different account from former U.S. Supreme Court Justice Michael Brennan:

> The prisoner's eyeballs sometimes pop out and rest on the cheeks. The prisoner often defecates, urinates, and vomits blood and drool. The body turns bright red as its temperature rises, and the prisoner's flesh swells and his skin stretches to the point of breaking. Sometimes the prisoner catches on fire, particularly if he perspires excessively. Witnesses hear a loud and sustained sound like bacon frying, and the sickly sweet smell of burning flesh permeates the chamber.

Coleman glanced down. Under his left wrist was what looked like a round coffee mug stain. There were plenty of rumors about that stain. Historians believed that it wasn't a coffee stain at all, but the stain from an ink bottle. In the old prison, the execution chamber had also served as the clothing storeroom. The inmates who had run the store used to sit in the chair to write letters.

Coleman was breathing hard now, trying to catch his breath. Again he looked at Murkoski, who turned to the control room and nodded.

And then it hit.

But it was nothing like Coleman had expected. No jolt. No spastic convulsing. No burning. In fact, he barely felt anything, just the slightest tingle across his skin for several seconds, and then it was over.

Had the chair short-circuited? Had they made a mistake?

He turned back to Murkoski, who was still looking into the control room. "Did you get a reading?" Murkoski asked.

"Yes," came the reply.

"Let's do it again, just to make sure."

Again Coleman prepared himself. The first attempt had failed. This time he closed his eyes, preparing for the worst, and felt—

Nothing. Again.

"Got it?" Murkoski asked.

"Yes. Two good responses."

Coleman opened his eyes just in time to see Murkoski turn to him and smile. "Good," he was saying, "very good." He looked over his shoulder and called, "All right, gentlemen, go ahead and release him."

Two of the three men reentered the cubicle, looking far more relaxed. The first thing to go was the surgical-tape-and-gauze gag. But Coleman, who had earlier wanted to shout and swear and scream, said nothing. He could only pant, trying to catch his breath, as he stared at the smiling Murkoski.

"We had to measure your galvanic skin response," Murkoski said.

Coleman still didn't speak. He wasn't sure he could.

Murkoski continued. "If we're going to stage a mock execution, we have to know what type of jolt your body can withstand. By running this test, Hendricks here"—he motioned into the control room—"will be able to install the correct ballast resistor as well as determine the proper voltage, enabling us to stop your heart without frying your brain."

The men finished unstrapping him, and Coleman continued staring, still trying to comprehend.

"Galvanic skin response, or GSR, is a measurement of the electricity your skin conducts. It changes depending upon the amount of stress you are under. That's why it works so well in lie detectors."

Coleman's hands were free, and he wiped the sweat and gel out of his eyes.

Murkoski continued. "If we had told you this was just a test, you'd have been far more relaxed, and we would never have received an accurate reading. To obtain the proper measurements, you had to think it was real. I trust there are no hard feelings."

"Hi, Kate."

Katherine Lyon looked up from the hard disk drive she had been installing in the store's back room, removed her glasses—and saw a face from the past.

"Jimmy!"

James Preston was thirty-seven years old and built like a tank. He barely had time to enter the room before Katherine raced around the worktable and threw her arms around him.

"Jimmy, it's so good to see you! How are you?"

"I'm fine, Kate, just fine."

He seemed a little stiff, a little uneasy. It may have been the years since they'd seen each other, or the presence of his companion, a tall somber man in a dark suit. Either way, it was a reminder that times change and so do people. She couldn't suddenly return to being the person she had been. Nor could he. She pulled away, a bit more reserved. "Come on in," she offered, then called into the store, "Eric! Eric, come here a minute." Turning back to Preston, she said, "He'll flip when he sees you."

Preston smiled.

"So what brings you all the way out here? Don't tell me you've moved."

"No, Kate, I came to see you."

Eric appeared in the doorway.

"Eric, this is your uncle Jimmy."

"Who?"

"Your dad's partner. You remember Uncle Jimmy."

Preston crossed to the boy. He had a pronounced limp. It came with the artificial leg. "Hi, Eric."

"Hi."

Preston spoke gently. "You don't remember me, do you?"

"Yeah, a little." Eric pushed up his glasses.

"I was with your dad on the police force. We were partners."

"Were you with him when he got shot?"

"Yes I was, Eric. It was my life your father saved."

Eric said nothing.

"He was a brave man, Eric."

The boy nodded. "Uh-huh." Then turning to Katherine he asked, "Can I go now? I got somebody on the Internet."

A shade of disappointment crossed Katherine's face. "Sure." She nodded. "Go ahead."

The boy quickly turned and headed back into the store.

"I'm sorry," Katherine said. She ran her hands through her cropped hair. "You two used to be such buddies."

"That was a long time ago, Kate."

"I'll say." She moved behind her table, then motioned to the broken-down sofa across from her. "Please, have a seat."

The men made their way through the cluttered room to the sofa, where they rearranged a few catalogs and electronic odds and ends to find a place to sit.

"Can I interest you fellows in a drink?" she asked as she sat.

She caught Preston's disapproving look at the glass and bottle on her table. "I thought you quit."

She resented the reprimand and purposely reached for the bottle to pour herself a refill. "It's one of the few pleasures I've got left, Jimmy. That and Eric." She recapped the bottle and set it back on the table. "So, who's your friend?"

The suit was immediately on his feet, extending his hand over the table. "I'm Agent Kevles, Ms. Lyon. Witness Protection Agency."

Katherine shook his hand with less enthusiasm. She took a drink and turned back to Preston. "How's Denise? The kids?"

Preston glanced down. "We've been divorced three years now. She moved back to Vermont eighteen months ago." He continued more quietly. "The shooting took a lot out of us, too."

Katherine said nothing. She was already beginning to dislike the meeting. "So why are you here, Jimmy?"

"Agent Kevles asked me to come with him. The Witness Protection Program has done a lot of research for a special project, and they think you're a prime candidate for the job."

She turned to Kevles. "Job?"

"We have a client we need to place. I can't tell you his name. But I can tell you that he is very, very special. Perhaps the most important placement we have had in years."

"By placement you mean somebody who's informed on somebody else, right? Is he a con?"

Kevles started to respond affirmatively, but Katherine cut him off. "I don't know if Jimmy has filled you in on all the details, but my husband was killed by an ex-convict."

"We are well aware of your history, Ms. Lyon."

"Then you're also aware that I'm not too keen on helping any of the creeps."

"This man is different. I guarantee it."

Katherine said nothing but slowly finished her drink.

Kevles leaned forward more intensely. "I should clarify something. This man is *not* an informer. He's part of an experiment."

"Experiment?"

"Up in Arlington. With a firm called Genodyne."

She waited for more.

"It's a biogenetic company. The project is classified, so I can't give you the details, but I can tell you that we are prepared to pay generously if you would consider hiring this man as your employee."

Katherine held his gaze. "Why me?"

"Well, as I said, you fit the profile—"

"Why me?" she repeated.

Kevles adjusted his glasses, obviously uncomfortable revealing any more information than he had to. But it was also obvious Katherine would settle only for the truth. "Much of this experiment is sociological in nature. And because of your past—your bereavement, your psychological profile, even the fact that you have a seven-year-old son—"

"Eight. My boy's eight."

"Even the fact that you have an eight-year-old son—all of this has strongly influenced our consideration."

"So what does that mean? He's not some kind of pervert, is he? I'm not going to have my kid exposed to—"

"I guarantee you that he is one of the most sensitive, loving people you will ever meet."

"Right. He's still a man, isn't he?"

Kevles appeared unsure how to respond.

"How much?" she asked.

"Pardon me?"

"You said pay was involved. How much?"

She could see the relief cross his face. He was back to familiar territory. "We are prepared to pay eight hundred and fifty dollars a month."

Katherine didn't believe her ears. Eight hundred and fifty dollars a month *plus* free help around the store. But she'd learned much from being on her own, and she knew that the figure had come far too easily for him. She had room to negotiate.

She met his gaze firmly and said, "Twelve fifty."

"Ms. Lyon, twelve hundred and fifty dollars per month seems a bit—"

"Take it or leave it. I have no idea who this creep is. Or what he'll try to pull. You're asking me to spend ten hours a day working beside somebody I don't even know, risk my safety, risk my son's safety, all because you *say* I can trust him. You know, you may have a point: twelve fifty isn't enough. I'd say fifteen hundred is more realistic, wouldn't you, Jimmy?"

Preston stared at her.

Kevles removed his glasses and folded them. "Ms. Lyon, I don't think fifteen hundred dollars is a reasonable—"

"You're right, you're right. I don't know what I was thinking. I'd have to train him, he'd always be underfoot, he'd—

"All right—"

"There's no telling what he could break or—"

"All right, all right, I understand." Kevles put his glasses back on. "I suppose fifteen hundred dollars isn't all that unreasonable."

Katherine almost smiled. "Good. Of course, I'll have to run it past Eric, but we'll see what we can do."

Please, take anything you want. Please, but don't—

"Augh!" Coleman cried, as if he'd been slugged in the gut. But no one had touched him. Not Harold Steiner who stood four feet away in the attorney/client room, not the guard who remained glued to his side. Neither had moved.

It was the picture of Melissa Steiner someone had set on the table that had doubled him over. A pretty girl. Auburn, shoulder-length hair, a smile bordering on mischievous. Coleman leaned on the table with both hands, trying to steady himself.

I've got a stereo upstairs, take it. Please—

Cold sweat broke out on his face. He continued breathing deeply, refusing to give in to the nausea and dizziness trying to overtake him. He didn't recognize Melissa's face. Except in his dreams, he never remembered his victims' faces. But there were those eyes. Different in color and shape, yet somehow similar to his brother's and Father Kennedy's.

And her voice. *You're scaring me, please don't—*

As clear and real as if she were standing in the room with him. He hoped this was another dream. But he knew it was something new, something stronger.

"What's wrong?" It was Steiner's voice, far away in another world. "What's happening?"

Coleman watched the beads of sweat falling from his face and splattering on the table beside the photograph. He had agreed to meet Steiner, not because he wanted to, but because he had to. He had to tell the man how sorry he was, that he now understood the unfathomable pain he had inflicted.

"Mr. Coleman."

Of course the press would have a field day with it, but this wasn't for the press. It was for Steiner. And, somehow, for himself.

"Mr. Coleman, what is wrong?"

Coleman nodded, but he wasn't okay, not at all. Once again his senses were tightening, focusing. But not tightening and focusing on the present.

Please, I'll do whatever you want, but please—

Coleman watched the sweat drip and splatter, drip and splatter. But he could no longer look at the photograph. He no longer had to. Now he could see the eyes without looking at them. Lonely eyes. Begging for mercy.

He felt something in his right hand. It was still the edge of the table, but it wasn't. It was a knife. Her knife. From the kitchen. And that sound. That irritating laughter of a TV sitcom. Mocking him, taunting him.

"Mr. Coleman . . ."

Please—if you want money—

He feels his left arm wrapping around her neck. He is standing behind her. His right hand suddenly jerks inward, toward her, hard, again and again. Now the gasping cries. Hysterical. Pleading, like the eyes. And the rage, the uncontrollable rage as his hand continues thrusting inward. But not rage at the girl. Rage at himself.

He continues stabbing, again and again, only now the girl is gone. Now he is stabbing himself. Now he feels each burning penetration of the knife, each slice and tear of his own flesh. Now he is crying out in her pain. He is in the attorney/client room, gripping the table, and he is back at her apartment in Omaha, jabbing the knife, but not into her. Now it is into his own chest, his own abdomen, again and again and again. Gasping in her anguish. Weeping.

Then the footsteps. His father's, he is sure of it. Louder and louder. They thunder in his head. Just before he arrives they dissolve into another sound. Someone rapping on glass—the guard, signaling for assistance. He hears the door unlock, he hears voices, but the gasping cries in his head are too loud, his own weeping too overpowering.

Arms take his shoulders, leading him away. Other voices ask what is wrong. He cannot answer. It takes all of his effort just to breathe, to walk. He is in the hallway, tears blinding his eyes, making it impossible to see. Sobs of unbearable pain and remorse escape from his throat. Someone is swearing. It is Steiner. He can't make out the words, but the man is not happy.

The meeting has been canceled.

"A little to the left. No, left. There you go."

Theodore Wolff, better known as "Teddy" to the handful of women vying for his interest, was grateful for the gym Genodyne had installed. If there was one thing he hated about genetic research, it was the long hours cooped up in the lab. Of course he loved working his mind, but he also loved working his body. In fact, his greatest inspiration often came in the midst of a grueling racquetball session, or tussles with the Universal Gym. And nothing finished off a good workout like a great rubdown.

"Attaboy. A little more. Good. Now to the right just a bit. The right."

Wearing only a sweatshirt and gym shorts, Wolff lay facedown on the sod of B–11 as Freddy walked up and down his back, gleefully kneading the muscles with his handlike feet, while occasionally giving a little jump, just to liven things up.

"Oaff! Come on, Freddy, that's not funny."

But of course it was funny, so Freddy frequently added the little surprise.

"Up a little . . . there you go."

Besides his athletic build and thick, red hair, Wolff was also known for his perfectly trimmed and manicured nails. He wasn't a neat freak; he just preferred things tidy. Even his workstation, that five-foot area of personal lab counter each researcher staked out as his or her own, was uncustomarily clean.

He also liked to shower. A couple times a day. "If you knew the mites and microbes crawling around on your skin," he joked, "you'd be showering, too."

Wolff was as fastidious with his research as he was with his personal hygiene. That's why he worked so well with Murkoski. Where Murkoski would race through a study, impatient over the details, Wolff would remain behind, cleaning up, verifying, and triple-checking everything. If there was ever a scientific Odd Couple, it was Wolff's Felix to Murkoski's Oscar.

"Thanks, Freddy." He patted the grass beside him, signaling for Freddy to step down. The animal obeyed, but not before giving one more playful hop.

"All right, you!" Wolff rolled over and tried to catch him, but the animal was too fast. Freddy ran off screaming in mock panic, his mouth opened wide while keeping his teeth covered with his lips. This was the "play expression" for baboons. It made no difference what noise or gesture they made—just as long as those needle-like canines were covered, it was all in play. And Freddy loved to play. The swings, the gym set, the tree, the slide, they were all fine. But baboons are social creatures, and no amount of toys compare to a good game of tag or roll-and-tumble with another animal.

Before Wolff could sit up, Freddy raced in from behind and gave him a good slap in the ribs. Wolff shouted in surprise and lunged for him but missed again. Freddy ran off screaming in delight, obviously hoping Wolff would follow.

"I can't right now," Wolff said, rising to his feet and brushing off the grass. "I've fooled around enough for one day. Maybe I'll stop by for dinner."

Freddy responded by racing at him full tilt, screaming all the way. But instead of ducking or running, Wolff turned back toward him—just in time to catch the animal leaping directly at him. The impact sent Wolff staggering backwards until man and baboon both crashed onto the grass, Freddy hooting in delight, Wolff laughing in spite of himself. "Come on, boy. I'm serious! I've got to go."

But Freddy continued the wrestling and tumbling as long as possible, chortling the whole time.

"Freddy! Come on now, Freddy." At last Wolff was able to untangle himself from the animal and rise to his feet. Once again Freddy raced off, turned, and prepared for another assault until Wolff held out his finger and gave a stern command. "No, Freddy. No."

The animal's countenance sagged as he slowed to a stop. Then, raising his tail over his head, he loped toward Wolff in his favorite goofball fashion.

"I'm sorry, boy, but I really have to go."

Freddy leaned hard against Wolff as the man reached down to give him one last series of pats. "Tonight, before I go home. I promise."

As Wolff turned and headed toward the door, Freddy stayed glued to his side, then raised his arm for the mandatory last hug. Wolff stooped down and held the animal for a moment. "See you in a few," he said. Freddy chortled and seemed almost to sigh as Wolff withdrew and headed out the door.

Wolff's specialty was mice. Transgenetic mice. Once the specific DNA was recognized and isolated, it was his job to oversee the placement of that DNA into the eggs of the mice, creating and raising up each new generation of the animals.

The actual insertion of the DNA into the egg was fairly simple: Remove the egg from the mouse and stick that egg under a stereoscopic microscope. With the left hand, turn the micromanipulator knob that holds a tiny pipette—a microscopic glass rod that uses small amounts of suction to position the egg and hold it in place. Once the egg is in place, move the right micromanipulator knob and insert a hollow needle directly into the egg. Once the membrane of the egg has been penetrated, inject the DNA. It's as simple as that. In fact, a good technician can insert DNA into one egg every twenty seconds.

Once the egg's DNA has been altered, it is surgically reimplanted into the mouse, and just twenty days later, there is a new brand of mice that the world has never seen.

Of course, the obvious question is: Why not do this with human eggs? A good question, and one that provides a field day for dozens of sci-fi writers. But there are drawbacks. First, it is highly illegal. Second, to obtain the desired results, one would have to wait for the fetus to develop, be born, and in some cases grow to adulthood. For humans, that period is at the very minimum nine months, and depending on the characteristic being developed, possibly twenty years or more. For mice, twenty days. And with the competition and breakneck speed of genetic research, every day is like a year.

Wolff suited up in the paper gown and booties, headed down the hall, and entered the pressured room of his mice colonies. It had been nearly three weeks since the malicious slaughter of one of the mice. Quite a shock at the time. And, despite the tests, no one was entirely sure what had happened. Some abnormality, yes. A mutation in one of the mice, of course. But the jury was still out as to how and why.

Wolff reached for the Plexiglas clipboard and double-checked the day's charts. It wasn't until he strolled toward the back of the room that he noticed it. One of the upper Lucite cages had no movement inside. Colony 233. He reached for the container, slid it out, and gasped.

The cage was covered in blood. All six mice were dead.

CHAPTER 7

Coleman stood silently in the snow, awed by the absolute stillness. He'd seen snow every year of his life, but not like this. Not with this tranquility, this soothing, calming peace. It had fallen steadily all night and had just let up now, a little before sunrise. He scanned the exercise yard. Every harsh edge, every sharp corner was smoothed and rounded by the soft whiteness. The administration building, the picnic tables, the fences with their rolls of razor wire, everything was covered in gentle serenity. The grime and dirt and mud were completely gone. Erased. Even the sounds from the distant highway were cleansed and absorbed by the smooth, chaste blanket. It was as if the snow had removed all evil from the world—softening its hardness, covering its filth, replacing its vulgarity with silent, pristine purity.

The intensity of Coleman's emotions had been leveling off for the past several days. He still marveled at the beauty surrounding him and grieved over the painful loneliness he saw in individuals, but as the days came and went he was able to gain more and more control over his reactions to those feelings.

He took a deep breath of the cold, fresh air. He felt a tingling all the way to his fingers. He was alive. For the first time that he could remember, really alive. By comparison, his past had been a faded, black-and-white photograph. For thirty-five years he had been sleepwalking, barely aware of his surroundings. Now he was awake. Seeing and hearing and feeling everything as if for the very first time.

But with the exhilaration came the other feeling. His own loneliness. It never left. It was a gnawing hunger he could not shake, an ache that the beauty and wonder around him only heightened. It was as if that beauty were part of something greater and grander than he could ever be. It made him feel cut off, like a perpetual outsider—a fleeting shadow dancing over the surface of creation without ever really being able to connect with it. Though he never ceased to marvel at the world's beauty, whether it was the reflection within a drop of water or the intricate designs in the palm of his hand, he knew that something much grander and deeper was calling to him. But calling him to what?

He took another breath. The air bit his nostrils and stung his throat. Today was the day. Actually, tomorrow at one minute after midnight. That's when one of four electrical jolts would shoot through his body. That's when Michael Coleman would finally die.

"Why can't I just fake it?" he had asked.

"Fake electrocution?" Murkoski had scorned. "I don't think so. We'll greatly reduce the other three shocks, but the first will knock you unconscious and stop your heart, so you won't have to worry about faking anything."

"And if you don't revive me in time?"

"We'll revive you. The assistant coroner will actually be one of our people. He'll roll you to the waiting ambulance and restart your heart in there. We have roughly six-and-a-half minutes. It will be close, but we can do it."

Coleman had not been reassured.

"Relax," Murkoski had grinned, "we've been practicing for days. You're too valuable to us to watch you go up in smoke."

Coleman didn't grin back. "No more surprises?" he had asked, looking into Murkoski's eyes, searching for the truth.

"No more surprises," Murkoski had answered solemnly. "We'll run you straight from the prison to Saint John's, where one of the top plastic surgeons in the country will make alterations."

"How much of my face will they change?"

"Enough that you won't be recognized. Might even fix that nose you're so proud of."

Coleman lightly touched his nose. It had been broken two, maybe three times in fights, and had not always been set with the greatest of care. "How long will all this take?"

"You'll be at the hospital a week to ten days. Then we fly you out to Washington State where you're set up with a nice job and an apartment."

They had discussed a thousand and one other details about the continuation of the experiment and what would be required of Coleman. But, in his usual insensitivity, Murkoski brought it down to the bottom line: "You're our guinea pig. We're giving you a second chance, and you owe us big. We won't ask much. Come into the lab once or twice a week for tests. But we're the boss, and whatever we say—"

"What if I get tired of it?" Coleman interrupted. "What if I decide to walk?"

Again Murkoski smiled, a smile Coleman was growing less and less fond of. "First of all, I doubt that a man of your integrity would double-cross us like that, and second . . ." Murkoski seemed to hesitate, unsure whether to continue.

Coleman pressed him. "And second?"

"And second, I've included a little chemical leash to insure that we'll always stay in touch."

"Leash?"

"Have you ever had the flu, Mr. Coleman?"

"Of course."

"Remember all those aches and pains? Well, those aches and pains don't really come from the flu virus. They come from your own immune system, from chemicals that your body releases called cytokines."

"What's that got to do—"

"During the bone-marrow transplant I took the liberty of altering your DNA in another area."

Coleman felt his anger rising. "You did *what?*"

"It was the only way to insure that you wouldn't, as you say, 'walk.'"

With effort, Coleman held his anger in check. "What did you do?"

"Actually, it's pretty basic. If you don't come in every five to six days for an injection, your own body will release so many cytokines that it'll make your worst flu experience seem like a picnic."

That conversation had taken place four days ago. And, although Coleman's anger had quickly subsided, his lack of trust for Murkoski had not. The youngster was ruthlessly ambitious.

Back in the yard, the sun was just rising. The bank of clouds resting on the horizon diffused it like a light behind fine china. Snow started falling again. Coleman tilted his head back and felt the cool flakes softly touch his face. Then Michael Coleman did something he had never done in his life. He closed his eyes, opened his mouth, and caught a snowflake on his tongue. It was incredible. Absolutely amazing. Joy spread through his chest, and he had to chuckle. If the boys back on the Row could only see him now.

"Cole?" The voice was quiet and considerate. "Coleman?"

Coleman lowered his head and opened his eyes. It was one of the guards standing in the open doorway to the administration building. "Hour's up. Sorry."

Coleman nodded. He turned and started crunching back through the snow toward the door. "Where to now?" he asked.

"Back to the hospital wing. That's where they'll keep you under observation until . . . well, until tonight."

Coleman nodded again, appreciating the man's sensitivity. He lifted up his face one last time and felt the cool flakes gently brush his cheeks. Then, lowering his head, he stepped back into the building for the very last time.

Sixteen hours later, Harold Steiner stuck his hands deep into his overcoat pockets to fight off the freezing night. It was 11:00 P.M., and despite the cold, he and three hundred other people stood in the prison parking lot, some of them in favor of capital punishment, others opposed. The two factions were separated by a simple snow fence and about a dozen state troopers, heavily armed and wearing riot gear. Michael Coleman had made quite an impression.

Steiner's side was the loudest—and drunkest. Chants went up every few minutes, ending in applause or slowly dying out. Some spectators waved signs and placards with such incredibly witty sayings as "HEY, COLE, IT'S *FRY*-DAY" or "LIGHT UP THEM COLES FOR A BBQ." The atmosphere outraged Steiner. Instead of an equitable and impartial execution of justice, these people were treating it like a sporting event.

The folks on the other side were no better. They cradled their candles and held their flashlights while praying and crying and singing. A mixed lot. Shallow thinkers, mostly. Religious do-gooders and knee-jerk emotionalists, more concerned about saving a diseased killer than preserving society. He knew that at least a dozen had been imported by Amnesty International, and probably that many more by the ACLU.

His side was just as diverse, including anticrime groups, good ol' boys looking for a good ol' time, and women's rights advocates. Yes, indeed. Capital punishment could make for some very strange bedfellows.

Steiner was disappointed that he was not being permitted to actually watch Coleman die. He blamed himself for that. After all, the man had played him like a fool. Coleman's performance at their meeting had quickly leaked out, and the media had had a grand old time. "Incensed Victim Confronts Broken Murderer," "Convicted Killer Has Change of Heart," "Cole Begs Forgiveness." The headlines and articles had all been variations on the same theme. Michael Coleman had finally seen the error of his ways, and now his victims, like Harold Steiner, were suddenly being cast as the guilty aggressors. The gall! Harold Steiner guilty? Of what? Of upholding the Law? Of honoring the only thing holding civilization together? If that was the charge, fine. Consider him guilty. He could think of no higher honor than being accused of maintaining the majesty of the Law.

Of course he'd heard all the arguments . . .

"What about mercy?" some demanded.

Mercy had its place. But no one seemed to remember Missy's own screaming for mercy as she was stabbed to death in her apartment.

"People change," opponents insisted. "The Michael Coleman you are executing today is not the same Michael Coleman who killed seven years ago."

Maybe so. Then again, who knew what type of person Missy would be if she had been allowed to live.

"Public execution does not deter murder."

A nonissue. For Steiner, capital punishment was more principle than practical. A line drawn in the sand that says you may go only so far in your attempts to unravel society, and no further.

Then there were the fringe arguments. The liberal Christians who insisted that the only time Jesus Christ commented on the death penalty was when he released the woman caught in adultery. Or the Jews, with their provisions in the Torah for forgiveness of the repentant. All valid arguments, he was sure. But it was one thing to live in the pristine world of theological theory, quite another to survive in an imperfect world that contained monsters who wanted to destroy it.

TV lights glared suddenly in the parking lot. Steiner craned his neck and caught a glimpse of someone trying to raise a swastika. It was quickly torn down.

The media. It was because of the media that he was out here in the cold instead of inside where he belonged. He'd expected Coleman to pull some sort of theatrics at their meeting; he just hadn't expected anything so extensive. Unfortunately, Coleman's dramatics had thrown Steiner back on the front page of the *World-Herald*—and straight to the bottom of the waiting list of those wanting to see Coleman die.

That was the bad news. The good news was that, no matter what spin the press put on it, or on him, the people of Nebraska were no different from the rest of the seventy-five percent of the nation who endorsed the death penalty. Since its reinstatement by the Supreme Court in 1976, nearly three hundred people had been executed—and that figure was rising quickly. By some estimates, the U.S. would soon be executing one hundred convicted killers a year. Not a lot when, last year alone, twenty-two thousand Americans were murdered (nearly thirteen times the death rate of England). But, again, it was a line in the sand. Some justice was better than no justice.

There was another stir in the crowd. "Look, it's Cole!"

"Isn't that Coleman? Right up there?"

Steiner looked toward the administration building, a hundred yards away. The second-story window to the far right had been lit all night. Rumor had it that this was hospital room 7, Coleman's holding room for the last twenty-four hours. And now, just on the other side of the horizontally barred window, there was the silhouette of a man—the outline of his head round and clean, as if it had been shaved.

Jeers and chants immediately rose from Steiner's side of the parking lot.

Waving candles and prayers from the other.

Steiner glanced at his watch. In fifty minutes, the circus would be over. Unless the three-person Board of Pardons granted last-minute clemency, the craziness of this evening, not to mention Steiner's seven-and-a-half years of suffering, would finally come to an end.

The process had been long and arduous. Nebraska law provides that any death sentence be automatically reviewed by the state supreme court. From there, Coleman had gone to the U.S. Supreme Court—but the justices had had the good sense to refuse to hear him, and the case had been returned to the original court for review. When that appeal failed, Coleman's lawyers once again brought him to the state supreme court, then the U.S. district court, and finally to the Eighth U.S. Circuit Court of Appeals in St. Louis. From there, they had again appealed to the U.S. Supreme Court.

Around and around they went, playing the justice system for every delay they could. Then one day, for whatever the reason, Coleman had suddenly had enough. He had fired his lawyers and refused any more appeals or hearings. Some thought he was trying for an insanity plea. (If you're crazy enough to want to die, you're obviously too crazy to die.) Others, like Steiner, thought he was up to something else. But whatever his plan, it had backfired. Now, unless the governor were suddenly to have a change of heart, unlikely in today's political climate, Coleman would soon be killed by electrocution.

Many states still executed with gas; a few even used firing squads and hanging. But more and more were turning to what was considered the most humane process: lethal injection. No pain. Just sleep. Too bad Missy couldn't have gone that way. Fortunately for her, Nebraska was one of eleven states still using the archaic, sometimes painfully inefficient electric chair.

Another song rose from the other side of the parking lot: "We Shall Overcome." The old Negro spiritual they had used during the civil-rights days. The comparison of civil liberties with the liberties of a convicted murderer filled Steiner with rage. But as the hymn softly rose from the parking lot, Steiner almost caught himself smiling. Let them sing. Let them cry. Let them pray. Michael Coleman would soon be dead. Justice may not be swift, but at least in this case, it would be inevitable.

"We've got a problem."

Murkoski turned from the door of hospital room 7 and looked into the hallway. It was Hendricks, the electrician he'd flown in from Genodyne. "What are you doing up here?" Murkoski asked. "You should be downstairs with the chair."

"We've got ourselves a major problem."

Murkoski frowned. They'd run through every possibility, every permutation, a dozen times. Not only had they recorded Coleman's response earlier that week, but they had continued the fine-tuning by using a fifty-five-gallon drum of water (somewhat similar in resistance to a 180-pound male). The chair had been recalibrated and retested, leaving nothing, absolutely nothing, to chance.

"What do you mean, *problem?"* Murkoski asked.

"See for yourself." Hendricks motioned toward Coleman, who was still standing at the window above the parking lot. "The man is as cool as a cucumber."

"Why shouldn't he be? After what we put him through last week, this is old news."

"It may be old news, but if he's this relaxed, it's going to completely invalidate our GSR measurements."

Murkoski's frown deepened.

Hendricks continued. "In this relaxed state, his body's resistance will be much higher than what we've calibrated the chair for."

"But you can change it, right?"

"If you don't mind guesswork. Here's the problem: If we keep the current as is, with his higher resistance, we may not be able to knock him out, let alone stop his heart."

"And if you increase the current?"

"We could go too far, and you'd have a real execution."

Murkoski nodded and felt a faint trace of coolness on his forehead. He'd just broken into a sweat. He forced himself to relax. The past few weeks had been hard but exhilarating. For the first time in his life, he felt as if he'd actually been able to use all of his mental capabilities. It was like playing several games of chess at once: securing state permissions, running security checks, producing bogus reports, monitoring Coleman's physical and mental state, running the electrical tests—all this under intense secrecy and the mounting pressure from his investors.

His decision was swift. "Increase it thirty percent."

"Thirty percent?" Hendricks whispered. "No, you're overcompensating. That's too much, you'll kill him."

"Thirty percent," Murkoski firmly repeated, then turned and headed for Coleman. Even though Hendricks was sure that the increase in voltage would be too much, Murkoski still wasn't satisfied. He was used to winning at any cost, even if it meant stacking the deck. And he was about to add a few more aces to the game.

He scowled. He hated working with people. Give him cold data, lab findings, clinical results, computer hypotheses. But introduce a human being into the mix, and suddenly the variables skyrocketed. Still, as with everything else in Murkoski's life, he was sure that he could improvise and overcome any surprise.

The most recent improvisation had been just last night. Everyone involved had agreed that, like the electrician, Ms. Irene Lacy, the county coroner, must also be replaced by someone from Genodyne. That replacement would be the one to hustle Coleman's body into the ambulance, revive him, sign the false autopsy report, and supply a John Doe body from the morgue for cremation and burial. Everyone had agreed, that is, except Ms. Irene Lacy. She was in no mood for an unplanned, three-day weekend. And when pressed on the issue, she had become hostile.

To smooth things over, Murkoski had invited her to dinner. Just the two of them. How could she refuse? After all, she was a single female, and he was the young and ever-so-good-looking Dr. Kenneth Murkoski. That she had agreed mostly out of curiosity had barely registered with him.

Over the French onion soup, he had explained how sorry he was that he couldn't divulge the details of this "matter of national security." Lacy had been unimpressed, and over the baked salmon she had questioned the legality of his plan.

He had been planning to wait until dessert to raise the monetary issue—ten thousand dollars tops—but decided early that there would be no point. He already knew her answer. Bullheaded, pragmatic, false sense of morality—people like that often said no and even feigned offense when someone tried to buy them. She might even try to file charges against him for bribery.

Murkoski had no choice. When she rose and excused herself to the lady's room, he reached into his finely tailored suit coat and removed a Visine bottle. Earlier that day, he had rinsed it and replaced its contents. Discreetly, he leaned over and measured out four drops of the new contents into her coffee. It would be undetectable, but the genetically altered botulism would multiply in her digestive tract until she was so sick she would be unable to go to work the following day.

That had been his fallback plan. But, now that he had spent an hour with her in conversation, Murkoski held the Visine bottle in his hand and reconsidered. She was a strong woman. Determined. Four drops would be enough to make her sick, but a die-hard like Lacy might insist on showing up for work anyway.

Murkoski reached over and poured another three drops, hesitated, and then added two more drops into her coffee. The cramps and nausea would be severe. Maybe lethal. Of course, the latter possibility wasn't his preference, but he had to be certain. There was too much riding on this. Regardless of the outcome, the tests would show that she had simply contracted an extreme case of food poisioning.

Murkoski felt little remorse as he watched her drink the coffee. It wasn't his fault that she'd been so uncooperative.

And now to the current problem of Coleman being too relaxed.

The convicted killer stood near the window saying final good-byes to three of his friends who would also serve as witnesses. He had no living relatives, at least no one who cared. And it had been agreed upon that none of these friends would be told the truth. For in reality, they really *were* saying good-bye. The Michael Coleman they knew would soon be dead. Regardless of whether the chair worked as expected or not, in a matter of minutes, this Michael Coleman would no longer exist.

On the other side of the room stood one of the prison physicians, a short, rotund man. Beside him, the remaining witnesses—four from the media and three from legal and law enforcement offices.

Before Murkoski could reach Coleman, he was interrupted by John Hulls, one of the associate wardens. The actual warden had been "called away" on out-of-state business. Hulls had known that something was up for weeks, but he had been instructed to carry out the execution to the letter, no questions asked. Despite the recent changes in personnel and Murkoski's free-reining presence at all the proceedings, Hulls, the prison physician, and the guards had been instructed to run the execution by the book. "Excuse me, ladies and gentlemen," he called. "May I have your attention? Excuse me, please."

The room settled down as Hulls unfolded a single piece of paper. "I have here the death warrant. I'm supposed to read it now."

The room grew even more quiet, and he began:

"To: the Warden of the Nebraska State Penitentiary, Lincoln, Nebraska, from the Supreme Court of Nebraska.

"Whereas, the Nebraska Supreme Court has released its opinion in this matter on January 2, directing the Clerk of the Supreme Court to issue her warrant, under the seal of this Court, to the Warden of the Nebraska State Penitentiary.

"Now, therefore, you are hereby commanded to proceed on Friday, January 14, between the hours of 12:01 A.M. and 11:59 P.M. to carry said sentence of death by elec-

trocution into execution by causing the passage of an electric current through the body of Michael Hutton Coleman, until dead, as provided by law.

"You shall make return hereof of the manner of your execution to this warrant and of your doings thereon to the Clerk of the District Court of Douglas County, Nebraska.

"Signed, Brenda J. Elliott, Clerk of the Supreme Court."

Associate Warden Hulls folded the piece of paper and in a much less official tone added, "It's time to start wrapping up, folks. We'll be needing you witnesses to follow your escort to the observation room while we make final preparations up here."

Murkoski waited as Coleman said his last good-byes to his friends. He was impressed by the tears filling the man's eyes. Amazing. In just six weeks he, Kenneth Murkoski, had turned this killing machine into a compassionate, caring human being. And that was only the beginning. Regardless of whether the chair worked as planned or not, Pandora's box had been opened, and the world would never be the same again.

As Coleman finished his final set of hugs, Murkoski approached. "Excuse me, Mr. Coleman?"

Coleman wiped the tears from his eyes and looked at him. Murkoski was careful not to meet his gaze. Lately, the way the man searched and probed people's eyes, it was almost as if he knew what they were thinking. At this point, that would definitely be a disadvantage. He cleared his throat and continued. "I'm afraid we have a problem."

"A problem?"

"It's the power supply. There's a major glitch." He saw the rhythm of Coleman's breathing change. A good sign.

"What type of glitch?"

"I don't understand it all. It's something to do with switching to another power company. As you know, the local carrier feels it's bad publicity to be killing you with their juice, the same juice that goes on down the line and lights up somebody's home. We had to transfer to another company. But when we did, well, somehow the resistance has changed. I don't know the details, but now our readings are off."

He could feel Coleman's eyes searching him, and he was certain the man knew that he was lying. But that was okay. The details didn't matter, just as long as he thought he was being double-crossed, just as long as he thought he might actually die.

"You gave me your word." There was a faint trembling in Coleman's voice. Mostly anger. Hopefully a little fear. Things were getting better by the minute.

"Cole?" Associate Warden Hulls approached. "I'm afraid it's time."

Coleman's eyes darted to the associate warden, then to Murkoski, then back to the warden again. He was beginning to panic. "You gave me your word!" he repeated.

Murkoski shrugged. "These things happen." Then, turning, he headed for the door.

"You gave me your *word!*"

Murkoski said nothing. The past weeks of observing prison dynamics had taught him something about playing people.

"Murkoski!"

"Please, Mr. Coleman," the associate warden said, trying to calm him.

"Murkoski!"

"Cole—"

"You gave me your word!"

Murkoski stepped outside and let the blue metal door slam behind him. He headed down the hall and descended the stairs to the basement. In the control room, he joined Hendricks and William Pederson, the other Genodyne employee, a good-natured Norwegian from their medical staff who would serve as the substitute assistant county coroner.

The ancient transformer that filled most of the room looked like something from an old Frankenstein movie. It had been turned on at 11:15 and now hummed in ominous anticipation. Hendricks brooded over the machine as Pederson stood at the one-way glass, staring past the chair and into the witness room where the ten witnesses were nervously taking their seats. A guard at the door was discreetly offering them small paper bags, a precaution in case anyone got sick.

"Everything on schedule?" Murkoski asked.

Pederson nodded.

Hendricks didn't look up from his tinkering with the transformer. "I think you're making a mistake," was all he said.

"If necessary, can you cut it from a thirty percent increase down to a fifteen?" Murkoski asked.

"What's the point of doing all these tests and rehearsals if we're just going to keep guessing and shooting from the—"

"Can you cut it down to fifteen percent?"

Hendricks returned the curtness. "I can cut it any way you want it."

"Then do it." Without waiting for a reply, Murkoski turned toward Pederson. "Where's your stopwatch?"

Pederson pointed to the sports watch on his wrist.

"You've got six-and-a-half minutes."

Pederson nodded. "The ambulance is running. The defib is inside and charged. A backup is on standby."

"Good."

The elevator doors rattled open. Coleman, two guards, and the rotund prison doctor emerged. Once again Coleman's head was jelled and he was perspiring. Not like last week, but far more than before Murkoski's little lie. Murkoski refused to meet the convict's eyes as they silently escorted Coleman past him and into the execution chamber.

Murkoski and Hendricks joined Pederson at the one-way glass. The guards had closed the gold curtains between the death chamber and the witness room in case there was a struggle from Coleman. But he gave no resistance as they silently and efficiently strapped him in and buckled each of the nine buckles.

Murkoski tried to swallow, but his mouth was bone-dry. "What do you think?"

"What did you say to him?" Hendricks marveled. "He looks a lot worse."

"You think he's nervous enough, then?"

"I think even the fifteen percent could kill him now. Let me cut it back to—"

"No," Murkoski ordered. "Keep it as is."

"But—"

"Keep it as is," Murkoski repeated as he looked back out the window.

When the final strap was buckled, they reopened the curtains. The first row of witnesses sat ten feet from the glass, the second just behind them. Each could clearly see that it was Michael Hutton Coleman who was about to be executed.

Murkoski watched as Coleman looked each of the witnesses in the eye. The man seemed to be trying to comfort and encourage them. Murkoski was stunned. Coleman actually appeared more concerned over what *they* were about to experience than what *he* was about to face. Murkoski swore softly and gave an angry swipe at the sweat trickling down his own temples.

"I strongly recommend we cut it back to what we had," Hendricks said.

Murkoski gave no answer but took a deep breath to steady himself. Through the glass he could hear the associate warden asking whether Coleman had any last words.

"We might fry him," Hendricks warned.

Murkoski took another breath.

"I'm serious. I know what I'm talking about."

Murkoski gave no answer.

Pederson reached for his watch, preparing to start it.

Coleman was saying something to the assistant warden, but Murkoski couldn't hear.

"Come on," Hendricks insisted.

The guards closed the curtains and quickly and efficiently attached the electrodes to Coleman's head and his left calf. When these were secure, they finally placed the leather mask over his face—a crude affair with a V cut out for the nose. But it didn't quite fit, and it flattened the cartilage against Coleman's face. Most thought the mask served as a courtesy for the condemned, allowing them to face their final moment in privacy. Prison officials understood that it was to spare the witnesses from the condemned's expression as 2,450 volts surged through his body.

Hendricks crossed toward the rotary switch at the far end of the transformer. Murkoski felt the man's eyes still on him. "He deserves a break," Hendricks insisted. "After all he's done for us, he deserves a break."

Murkoski continued wrestling with the pros and cons. If the current was too weak, the doctor, the guards, the associate warden, the media, the witnesses—somebody would suspect something was wrong. There would be questions that would have to be answered, questions that might expose either the experiment or Murkoski's superiors.

Too much current, and Coleman would be killed. They would have to start over from scratch.

The curtains reopened and the associate warden stepped out of the execution chamber, closing the door behind him.

"Come on," Hendricks whispered harshly.

Murkoski stared at the masked form, sitting on the other side of the glass, three feet away.

The assistant warden appeared in the doorway and nodded to Hendricks. Hendricks saw him but did nothing as he stared at Murkoski's back, waiting.

Finally Murkoski made his decision. Ever so slowly he shook his head. The answer was no.

Hendricks stared in disbelief.

"Gentlemen?" the associate warden called softly from the doorway.

Hendricks did not move.

"Gentlemen?" the associate warden repeated.

Murkoski turned to Hendricks. Clearly and firmly he whispered, "Keep it as is."

Hendricks scowled, reached for the black rheostat knob, then hesitated.

"Do we have a problem?" the associate warden asked.

"Keep it as is," Murkoski repeated.

Hendricks's grip on the rheostat tightened as he held Murkoski's gaze. Both men were perspiring.

"Come on, boys," Pederson warned, "let's do something here."

At last Hendricks obeyed. Refusing to take his eyes from Murkoski, he turned the knob.

The machine made a dull thud as the electricity surged.

Coleman's body jerked violently, but the straps held him in place. His hands clenched into fists, and his feet pulled back out of his slippers.

Murkoski heard the tiny beep as Pederson set his stop watch. He glanced at his own. It read 12:18.

The first jolt of electricity ended and Coleman's body slumped. There was no movement except for a few drops of sweat falling from his face.

He had stopped breathing.

Thirty seconds later, Hendricks fired a tiny fraction of the first voltage through the body. Another thirty-second pause, followed by another weak charge. And one final pause followed by one last charge.

Murkoski glanced at his watch. 12:20. The process had taken just under two minutes. They had four and a half left.

According to the schedule, the prison doctor was now supposed to move into the chamber, take Coleman's pulse, and declare him dead. Murkoski looked out into the hallway. The doctor stood by the chamber door but was not opening it. "What's the holdup?" Murkoski called.

"I'm not going in yet," the doctor said, waving his hand in front of his nose, indicating that he expected to find the acrid smell of burning flesh inside.

Murkoski threw Pederson a look, and the phony assistant moved to action. "If you're not, I am," he said heading out of the control room and toward the chamber.

"What do you think you're doing?" the doctor complained. "That's *my* job."

"Then do it."

"What's the hurry? He's not going anywhere."

"I am," Pederson said. He had arrived at the chamber door and was reaching for the handle. "I've got work to do, and I don't plan to be up all night."

"All right, all right," the doctor grumbled. He reached for the stethoscope in his pocket. "You're new, aren't you? With that attitude you won't be making many points around here, I can tell you that." Pederson gave no answer as the doctor pushed past him and opened the door.

Murkoski glanced at his watch: 12:21.

Three-and-a-half minutes left. Time was running out, and they hadn't even unstrapped Coleman. He looked back out through the glass. The doctor had entered the chamber and hovered over the body, taking his own sweet time. Putting on a show, no doubt, for the reporters in the witness room. After listening to the chest, he pulled the stethoscope from his ears and nodded to the witnesses. Michael Hutton Coleman was dead.

Murkoski looked to his watch. Another minute and a half had slipped by. That left two.

The doctor stepped out of the room and the two guards moved in, closing the curtain and unstrapping Coleman's dead body. Pederson was right behind, urging them to hurry as they lifted the body, hustled it out of the room, and laid it on the gurney in the hallway.

Fifty-five seconds.

"This is unprecedented!"

Murkoski glanced up. It was the doctor again.

"There's no need for this reckless haste. This is how mistakes are made." He had stopped the gurney, blocking its path with his body. "I don't understand what's going on. What is the hurry? The man is *dead.*"

Murkoski was grateful to see Pederson move into action. The man knew how to take advantage of his considerable Norwegian bulk. He shoved the doctor against the wall. "You did your job," he growled, "now let me do mine." Then, taking the gurney himself, he shoved it onto the elevator, pressed the button, and stood glowering as the doors lumbered shut.

Murkoski glanced at his watch. Twenty seconds.

"Did you see that?" The doctor turned to the others. "Did you see what he did? That was completely unprofessional. There is no excuse for that type of behavior.

What is his name? It'll be in my report, I guarantee you that. This sort of thing cannot go unreported. What is his name?"

Murkoski watched and listened—realizing that he would have to invite the good doctor out to a special dinner as well.

Harold Steiner walked the dirt road alongside the prison as he headed toward the Sutherland Lumber parking lot where he and most of the demonstrators had left their cars.

It was over. Finally. All of it. But, unlike the others, he didn't cheer, light firecrackers, or pray. Instead, he was struck by a peculiar emptiness that he didn't understand. Everything he had worked and sweated over for so many years had finally come to pass. He had won. Justice had been served. And yet he felt so hollow, so empty. Probably just exhaustion. Yet, somehow, he suspected that it was more.

An ambulance bounced out of a side gate, spitting gravel as it turned, then raced past him. He watched, puzzled. No doubt, this was the ambulance taking Coleman's body to the mortuary. But what was the hurry? Steiner slowed to a stop and watched as the vehicle slid around another corner and sped out of sight.

Something wasn't right. In a few days, after he'd rested, he'd have to ask. In the meantime, he stuffed his hands back into his overcoat and continued down the road.

PART TWO

CHAPTER 8

"Do you need a hand with that?"

Katherine's response was swift and accurate. Before she had even finished her startled scream, she swung around the garbage can she'd been emptying into the dumpster and struck her assailant hard in the face. His sunglasses flew off, and he staggered backward until he hit the wall of the building. His head struck the bricks with a melonlike thud, and he crumpled unconscious to the alley.

Eric raced out the back entrance of the computer store. "Mom! Mom, are you okay?"

Katherine nodded to reassure him as she tried to catch her breath. The unconscious man wore a crisp white shirt and a designer tie. At the moment, he didn't look much like the mugger she had taken him for.

Eric kept his distance from the motionless form. "Do you . . ." He swallowed hard. "Do you think you killed him?"

Katherine cautiously walked toward the body. "Go to the bathroom and get me some wet paper towels."

Eric didn't move.

"Now."

He backed through the door, unwilling to take his eyes off the man.

Cautiously, she knelt down to investigate. He was a handsome man. Rugged, closely cut dark hair, late thirties. And the way he filled out his shirt and slacks indicated that he definitely knew how to take care of himself. In fact, except for the faint trickle of blood escaping out of the corner of his mouth, he was an excellent specimen of manhood. Another reason for Katherine to mistrust him.

He stirred slightly. She waited and watched. His face was weathered, with a trace of acne scars across the cheekbones. But it was the bruises around both of his eyes that confirmed her suspicions. Either this man was a prizefighter, or he had just undergone plastic surgery.

She suspected the latter, and with that suspicion came the dull realization that she had just decked her new employee. The Witness Protection Agency had said that he would arrive around 4:00 that afternoon. She glanced at her watch. It was 3:59.

She swore to herself and shouted back into the store. "What's the holdup? Where are the towels?"

"We're all out."

"Try under the sink."

She had been told his name was William Michaels—an alias, of course—and that she would have no other obligation to him than providing work. Other than that, he was on his own. She hoped so. The less involvement with somebody like this, the better.

Eric raced out the door and handed her several dry paper towels. "Here."

"You didn't soak them?"

"I forgot."

Katherine sighed and took them. She began dabbing the blood off the man's face.

Eric scooted in closer and watched with awe. "You really clobbered him, didn't you?"

"People shouldn't sneak up on other people," she answered. "It's not polite."

At last the man's eyes began to move under his lids. Finally they opened. They were good eyes, so brown they almost looked black. And even in their state of confusion, Katherine could see a gentle sensitivity in them.

"Are you okay?" she asked.

He winced, trying to move. "Yeah." Raising his hand to explore his cheek, he asked, "Was that aluminum or plastic?"

"What?"

"The garbage can. Felt like aluminum."

Katherine almost smiled but was quick to cover with an admonition: "You shouldn't go sneaking up on people like that."

He nodded and rose to one elbow, again wincing in pain. "I think you made that pretty clear." He struggled to sit. Katherine started to help, but caught herself. He glanced around the alley, still trying to get his bearings.

"Are you William Michaels?" she asked.

He frowned, then smiled, remembering. "Right, right, William Michaels. I'm not crazy about the name. And I hate Bill. But Will's okay." With some effort he extended his hand. "Call me Will."

She shook his hand. It was warm and strong. "I'm Katherine Lyon, Mr. Michaels."

"And I'm Eric."

The man looked to his right and managed to smile. "Hi, Eric."

The boy stared at him.

"Giving your mom a hand at the store today?"

"I'm here every day. You know anything about computers?"

"No. I've, uh, I've been out of circulation for a while, but I'm willing to learn."

The boy sounded disappointed. "Oh."

"Maybe you can teach me."

"Sure." Eric shrugged, then rose and quietly headed for the door.

Katherine watched the man watching her son. Again she noticed the eyes. Not only were they sensitive, they were also vulnerable. Just a little too open, just a little too wide. Poor guy. Obviously he hadn't yet experienced the uglier sides of life, the struggling, the taking, the abusing. But he would. No one could escape it forever. The knowledge seemed to sadden her just a little.

"Listen, do you want a glass of water or something?" she asked.

"No, I'll be fine."

"Well," she said, rising to her feet, "if you're sure you're okay."

He took his cue and started to rise.

"It was good of you to stop by. But you're not scheduled to start work till Monday, so go get yourself settled in, and we'll see you then."

He nodded, locking his eyes firmly onto hers. It was an unnerving sensation, almost like he was trying to read her thoughts. She accepted the look as a challenge and rose to the occasion. "I'm your employer, you're my employee. That's it. If you've got personal problems, I don't want to hear about them. As you've probably been told, I'm not crazy about this setup, but the money's good, so there you have it."

"I understand."

She shifted uneasily. What was he looking at? What did he see? "All right, then. You're welcome to come in and clean up, but if you'll excuse me, I've got work to do." She turned and headed toward the door.

"Do you need a hand?"

She turned and faced him.

"I mean for the rest of the day—do you need some help with anything?"

"No, Mr. Michaels, I don't need any help. We have everything under control." With that she headed back into the store. She wasn't sure what about him flustered and irritated her. It didn't matter. She had established the boundaries. And if he had any doubts about the consequences of crossing them, the newly acquired cut on his mouth should serve as a reminder.

"Julie, how come your knapsack is moving?" O'Brien stood in the open doorway of their two-story colonial home, blinking at the knapsack that lay on the entry hall tile. Something was inside it, and by the looks of things it wanted to be outside in the worst possible way. "Julie?"

But Julie didn't hear. She was upstairs with her mother and sister, making frantic, last-minute preparations for the trip. The family's flight to Mazatlán was scheduled to leave Sea-Tac at seven that evening, and at the moment it would be nip and tuck whether they could make the seventy-minute drive to the airport in time.

"Who took my Barbie car?" Julie's voice cried from upstairs. "Where's my Barbie car?"

"You're not taking your Barbie car," Beth called. "There's no room. Sarah, did you brush your teeth? Sarah?"

"They're just going to get dirty again."

"But Sarah's taking her ant farm," Julie whined.

"She's what?"

"You little snitch!"

"You're taking *what?*"

O'Brien looked back at the knapsack. It was growing more frisky. "Uh, guys," he called. "Guys, what's in this backpack?"

By now Julie had broken into tears and Sarah was in her best preteen, nobody's-taking-me-seriously form. "Why *can't* I take my ant farm? It's science. I need to see if ants act differently in different countries."

O'Brien thought of calling again but knew it would be futile. As with most of these family outings, he was pretty much along just for the ride. Beth was the one in charge. And that was fine with him. Both of them knew that he would never give the family one hundred percent of his attention. Oh, he tried—but his absent-mindedness made it clear that part of him was always back at the lab somewhere. It was another sacrifice Beth had made in their marriage; another crack in the widening rift of their relationship.

The knapsack gave a desperate lunge. That was enough. O'Brien reached down and carefully unlaced the string tie. The neighbor's kitten, the one Julie had been adoring for the past week, hopped out of the bag and made a mad dash past him and out the door. O'Brien watched, realizing that it would probably be good to have another talk with his youngest about honesty.

The phone rang. He hesitated. The car was nearly loaded and already warming up in the driveway. In just a few minutes they'd be gone. Three weeks of rest and relaxation and some much-needed time with his family. Better to let the service pick up.

It rang a second time. Julie continued crying, Sarah continued demanding, and Beth was doing her best to deal with both. "Philip, will you answer that?"

"Let it go," he called.

"Mother, are you listening to me?"

A third ring.

"It might be the Wilson boy," Beth shouted. "He's taking care of the animals while we're gone. He was supposed to call back."

It rang a fourth time. Against his better judgment, O'Brien walked to the end table and picked up the receiver.

The answering machine had already kicked in with Beth's cheery and concise message: *"Sorry. We're out, but you're on."* The machine beeped, and O'Brien heard a voice cough slightly on the other end.

"Dr. O'Brien." It was Wolff. O'Brien listened silently. "I'm sorry to call you at home like this, but I wanted to flag you before you left."

"Hi, Wolff."

"Dr. O'Brien, thank God you're still there."

"We're just heading out the door. What's up?"

"I think we've got a problem."

O'Brien closed his eyes. "More dead mice?"

"No. Worse."

"Wolff, I'm on vacation. Murkoski is back. His man Coleman is in the area now. If you have a problem, talk to Murkoski."

There was a pause.

"Wolff?"

"Yeah, uh, I did. About forty-eight hours ago."

"And?"

"I think that's part of our problem. Look, can you come to the lab?"

"Wolff—"

Beth and the kids had clambered down the stairs and were dragging the last of their suitcases past him toward the door when she asked, "Who is it?"

O'Brien rolled his eyes, indicating that he was trying to get rid of the caller.

"I've run some new gels," Wolff was saying. "I've run them several times."

"Who?" she whispered.

"Work," he mouthed.

She sighed heavily, then turned to children. "All right, you two, get in the car, I'll be right there."

Wolff continued. "And I'm getting some bizarre results."

O'Brien covered his free ear to hear over the commotion. "What do you mean, *bizarre?*"

"I'm not certain, but things aren't as they appear."

"And you can't tell Murkoski, because . . ."

"Because I think he's the reason."

O'Brien said nothing. He saw Beth watching, anticipating the worst. Wolff's silence was articulate, insisting there was a crisis that only O'Brien could solve. The back of his neck started to ache. He turned slightly, cutting Beth from his sight.

"Dr. O'Brien? Are you there?"

He could feel Beth's presence, silent, critical.

He closed his eyes.

"Dr. O'Brien?"

"All right." He sighed. "Listen, I'm going to run my family down to the airport and get them on the plane. Then I'm going to come back up. But so help me, Wolff, if this is something Murkoski or someone else could have handled—"

"I don't think it is, Dr. O'Brien. Not this time."

O'Brien rubbed his neck. "All right. I'll see you later this evening. Oh, and call my office, have Debra book me on the next available flight to Mazatlán."

"Right."

"Have her do that immediately." The urgency was for Beth's sake, but he knew it wouldn't help.

"Will do. Thanks, Dr. O'Brien."

"Yeah." O'Brien slowly hung up the phone. Then, even more slowly, he turned to face his wife.

Steiner eased his Volvo into the parking lot of St. John's Hospital. The winter sky was a vivid blue, and the sun hung just low enough to stab into his eyes, heightening his headache and making him wince. He had some serious doubts about this meeting. Gabriel Perez was just an orderly, and he could barely speak English. Still, experience had taught him that occasionally it's the little guy, the one everybody ignores, who becomes the unseen eyes and the forgotten ears. That's what Steiner was banking on now. Maybe lightning would strike here, as it had two days before in the cemetery.

Steiner still wasn't entirely sure why he had visited Coleman's grave. It was partly to assure himself that it was over, that the ordeal could finally be put to rest. But there was something more. He couldn't put his finger on it, but he was searching for a type of peace. Because, as much as he tried to will it, peace would not come. True, some of his pain had been excised on that early January morning, in that nine-by-nine, cinder-block execution chamber. But the death of pain, the absence of hurt, is a far cry from the presence of peace.

It was different with Theresa, his wife. Somehow she had been able to let go, to let the healing begin. Not Steiner.

Of course he had tried. But there was a problem: The harder he tried to push the anger and resentment out of his mind, the more the images of Missy began to slip away. And that was unacceptable. If the two had become that intertwined, if he couldn't forget the one without forgetting the other, then so be it. If anger and resentment had become the only way he could remember his daughter, then he would hang on to that anger and resentment regardless of the cost.

Those had been his thoughts as he stood in the county burial section of Holben Cemetery—as he stood gazing down at the ten-inch-by-ten-inch plot that held Coleman's ashes. In fact, he had been so preoccupied that he had barely noticed the caretaker's approach.

"Friend o' yours?" the man had asked.

Steiner had looked up, startled. The old-timer was gray and grizzled and immediately began coughing up a large wad of phlegm. When he spit it out, it was nearly the size of a silver dollar. "Sure caused a stir, didn't he?" the man said as he wiped his chin.

Steiner watched with mild disgust but said nothing. He turned back toward the tiny plot, hoping that the old fellow would leave. He didn't. Apparently he was a talker and didn't get much opportunity to do so out in this older section, especially in the middle of winter.

"Even when we put him down. Never seen such commotion over a pile o' ashes. Like they thought he was gonna rise from the dead."

Steiner looked at him. "What do you mean?"

"Some big fella from the coroner's office, he was a-hoverin' and a-stewin' over everything."

"Some people like to be thorough."

"S'pose. 'Cept once a fella's dead, he's s'posed to be dead. The coroner folks, they usually just turn the body over to the mortuary, and they take it from there. But not this time. No, sir, this guy hangs around from start to finish, like he can't be sure enough we'll get him in the ground."

That's what had started the wheels turning. That and the rushing ambulance Steiner had seen the night of the execution.

The following day he had visited the prison, but found nothing—though he did hear of the prison doctor's fatal bout with food poisoning, and about the presence of a couple of scientist types who were said to have had a morbid fascination with the execution process. Other than that, nothing unusual.

It was only after Steiner made a call to the coroner's office that his suspicions really began to take on substance.

"I'm sorry," the clerk had said, "we're still a little disorganized after Ms. Lacy's death."

Steiner had read of the death in the *World-Herald* but had given it little thought. "There must be some record," he had insisted. "Whose signature is on the autopsy report?"

"That's just it. I mean the report is all filled out and everything, but . . ."

"But what?"

"Well, none of us recognize the signature."

Images of that racing ambulance came to mind.

After a handful of calls to Lincoln hospitals, Steiner had information on all the emergency admittances during the early morning hours of January 14. It had been a light night. There had been only three. A gunshot and a passing kidney stone at Lincoln General. And a burn victim here at St. John's.

Steiner pulled his car into an open stall, stepped out, and crossed the hospital's parking lot. The sun continued to glare, and his head continued to pound.

Fifteen minutes later he was sitting in the cafeteria of St. John's, staring hard at the steam rising from his Styrofoam cup. He never drank coffee, he hated it. But it was important for the orderly across the table to feel relaxed, and "Let's grab some coffee" had sounded as informal as anything Steiner could think of.

"What about special treatment?" Steiner asked. "Do you recall anyone who may have been, say, treated differently from other patients?"

Gabriel Perez, a young Nicaraguan, scrunched his thick eyebrows into a furrow of thought.

"No hurry," Steiner encouraged. "We've got plenty of time."

At last Perez cleared his throat. "I, uh—there was one, in the burn wing. They treat him like he was very special."

Steiner looked on, trying to hide his interest.

"No one was allowed in or out. Not even to clean and bring meals."

Steiner leaned forward. "How long was he here?"

"A week, maybe two. I don't remember."

"What about a name? Do you remember a name?"

He shook his head. "No."

"Did you ever see him? Can you describe what he looked like?"

"No, he was a burn victim. His face, it was all bandaged."

"What about visitors? Do you remember anybody?"

"No."

Steiner fought back his frustration. There had to be something. "How'd he get home? Who picked him up?"

"I do not . . ." Perez hesitated, scowling at the table, trying to remember. "Some young man. Expensive suit, dark hair."

"Ever hear a name?"

"No."

"What type of car did he drive?"

Another frown. "I am sorry." He looked back up at Steiner. "That is all I remember."

"Are you sure?"

He thought another moment and shrugged. "I am sorry."

Another dead end. Steiner nodded and rose to his feet. "Well, thank you for your time, Mr. Perez. And if anything else should come to mind"—he pulled a card from his jacket—"please, give me a call."

Perez rose, nodded, then turned to leave.

Steiner was disappointed. Of course he would go downstairs and check the hospital records, but he knew he would find nothing there. Either there was nothing to find, or else those obvious tracks would already be covered. He reached for his briefcase. Somewhere, there'd have to be another lead. It couldn't be over yet, not until—

"Excuse me?"

Steiner looked up. Perez stood three tables away.

"The reason I could not remember his car?"

"Yes?"

"It was because he did not have one."

"I'm sorry?"

"He and the man in the expensive suit, they took a taxi."

Steiner's eyes sparked to life. "A taxi? Are you sure?"

"Yes. I wheeled him out, and they got into a taxi. That is why I could not remember the car. They took a taxi."

"Which one? Did it have a name—do you remember the name of the company?"

"No, but we have only two taxi companies in this town."

"Thank you, Mr. Perez."

"That is helpful?"

"Yes, more helpful than you can imagine."

Coleman enjoyed Katherine's company. And, though she was careful not to show it, he sensed that she was growing more comfortable with his. He was glad that Genodyne had persuaded him to give in and let her drive him the twenty or so miles from south Everett up I-5 to Arlington. He'd been resistant and defensive when they'd first questioned his driving skills. It was true that he hadn't been behind the wheel of a car for several years, but they were also skeptical of his driving record—a record showing definite signs of irresponsibility and recklessness. "You're just too expensive an investment to end up as roadkill," Murkoski had said. By itself, that argument had carried little weight with Coleman, who hated to rely on anyone and would have preferred to drive himself. But once he'd experienced the dizziness and vertigo that accompanied the treatments, and had considered the prospect of driving home in that condition, Coleman had given in to their demands.

So, with Eric in school, and after some lively negotiating on a price, Katherine had agreed to make the weekly run up to Genodyne for Coleman's checkup and injection to control the viral leash.

Arlington was a picturesque town of five thousand people with a main street seven blocks long and a single stoplight. Nestled at the foot of the Cascades, its east side was surrounded by the mountains, while its west was flanked by dairy farms—creating an interesting population of farmers, lumberjacks, and service industries to support them both. But, like so many small Pacific Northwest towns, the farms were giving way to housing developments, and the loggers were having a harder and harder time finding trees that didn't house spotted owls.

Amidst the sawmills, dairy cows, and newly constructed homes lay the Arlington Municipal Airport. Surrounding the airport was the usual industrial complex with dozens of manufacturers who had fled big-city hassles and big-city bureaucracies for a calmer, more bucolic life. One of these industries was Genodyne, housed in a two-building, six-story complex.

"Why two buildings?" Katherine asked, after Coleman had finished his first checkup and they were receiving a somewhat grandiose tour of the facilities by Murkoski. "Why not put all of this into one?"

"More FDA red tape," Murkoski explained. "They insist that our manufacturing plant, which is a quarter mile away, be completely separate from this, our administration and research division. Guess they're afraid our multimillion-dollar creations from research are going to sneak out and hop into one of our manufacturing vats. Not that you can blame them. When it comes to what the more gifted of us are able to do in biotechnology these days, I suppose just about anything's possible."

Coleman had the distinct impression that the kid was trying to impress Katherine. Of course, that only made her less receptive, which made Murkoski try all the harder, and the cycle continued until the bottom line became apparent to all: The great Murkoski was going down in flames.

Coleman smiled quietly. It was true, he liked Katherine a lot. But it was far more than just her beauty or her in-your-face honesty. Underneath the abrasive, tough facade, he saw a tender, sensitive heart. He wasn't sure what all had happened to her—she was careful to maintain a wall between them—but during his few opportunities to look past the barricade, he was able to see it. There was something rare and precious inside. Something pure. And something terribly, terribly frightened.

This ability to sense a person's thoughts and innermost feelings had rapidly increased since his first treatment back in December. At times it almost made him feel psychic, as he picked up on things no one else seemed to notice. Then again, maybe there was nothing mystical about it at all. Maybe he was simply so alive that he was able to see the details he had previously overlooked—a quiver in the voice, a nervous shift in the eyes, little mannerisms that he had been either too self-absorbed or too frightened to notice before. He didn't understand how it was happening. All he knew was that the ache and loneliness he saw inside other people removed any fear he might have had of them. And without that fear, he felt something he had never felt before the experiment began: compassion.

Coleman, Katherine, and Murkoski walked across the first-floor atrium with its palm trees and waterfall. They took the elevator to the third floor. When the doors opened, they stepped into the hallway and Murkoski motioned somewhat grandly. "These are my labs," he said. "Eight teams of the finest researchers on the West Coast."

He reached for the nearest door and threw it open with a flourish. A handful of researchers, youngsters barely out of grad school, hovered over their cluttered, black Formica workstations. Above their heads were cupboards with glass doors holding a variety of clean, orange-capped tubes and bottles. Beside them were Lucite electrophoresis boxes and power supplies, racks of Eppendorf pipettes, and centrifuges.

"This is where it all happens," Murkoski said. "This is where we rearrange the building blocks of life—changing and fixing creation's blunders." He crossed toward a common household refrigerator and opened the door. Inside were rows and rows of tiny Eppendorf tubes. He took one from the top shelf and held it up to the light for them.

"See that milky white substance? That's what it's all about. That's DNA."

"That's human DNA?" Coleman asked in quiet awe.

Murkoski scoffed. "DNA is DNA. It doesn't matter whether it comes from humans or monkeys or slugs or bacteria. It's always the same four building blocks, regardless of the animal. It's simply a matter of how they are arranged." He replaced the tube and shut the refrigerator door. "And here, in these labs, is where we cut the DNA apart, splice in different sequences, and put it back together again."

"What are these other rooms for?" Katherine asked, pointing to a closed doorway nearby.

Murkoski smiled. Finally she was paying some attention. "Let me show you."

At first Coleman had been surprised at how candid Murkoski had been with Katherine regarding the project. The only secret he had felt necessary to maintain was Coleman's past identity. He had no qualms about her knowing the rest. "After all," he had said, "she's a part of the team now." And then, with a flirtatious smile, he had added, "And a very attractive member at that."

They stepped into a smaller room. There were no people, only the quiet hum of the air-conditioning and a few electronic apparatuses at work. Some were the size of dishwashers, others the size of coffins.

"Once we redesign the DNA, we have to grow it," Murkoski explained. "That's what these little babies are about." He rested his hand on what could almost pass as a large copy machine.

"Bacteria divide, splitting into two every twenty minutes. That's why we use it as our primary workhorse. First we insert the new DNA into the bacteria. Then we put the bacteria into these incubators, where we provide it with the perfect nutrients, temperature, and climate to make it multiply as quickly as possible." He turned to Coleman. "Hard to believe, isn't it? Everything you've become, you owe to microscopic bacteria inside these machines."

Before Coleman could respond, Murkoski turned and escorted them into the next room. "Once we've grown enough of the DNA, we inject it into various organisms to see how they will react. Sometimes we inject it into cells themselves, which we store in these –70-degree freezers here, or into mice, or"—he threw what could be a contemptuous smile in Coleman's direction—"human guinea pigs."

Instead of growing angry, Coleman felt a strange pity for the kid. Was he really that insecure? Was he really that lonely and afraid and—what else? There was something else going on inside Murkoski that Coleman couldn't quite put his finger on. In any case, when their eyes connected, Murkoski's grin faded, and he glanced away.

He turned and escorted them into the next room.

"What are these?" Katherine asked. She pointed to a number of shallow trays with clear Plexiglas covers and red-and-black electrical terminals at either end.

"Those are the gel boxes. This is where we perform what we call electrophoresis." Katherine seemed interested, and Murkoski rushed to offer more. "Each gene is a different size. When a current of electricity is passed through them, they move through a special gel at different rates according to their size—the gel is more resistant to bigger genes, making them move slower, and less resistant to smaller genes, allowing them to move faster. When electrical current is run through them, they move across the gel at different rates, forming very specific and definitive patterns of bands."

"Those bands, they're what the police use to identify people?" Katherine asked.

"Precisely. Genes have their own distinct banding patterns. You can never mistake one for another. Never."

There was something about the way Murkoski emphasized *never* that caught Coleman's attention. Again, he didn't really understand it, but there was something here, something that upset Murkoski, something that made him uneasy.

"Now, if you don't mind," he said, herding them into the next room, "let me show you something that I think you, especially, Ms. Lyon, will find interesting. You said you worked with computers?"

"Yeah, I worked computers for the defense department. Back in the NORAD days."

"Well, take a look at this." Murkoski motioned to a piece of beige equipment on the counter. It stood three-and-a-half-feet high by two-and-a-half-feet wide. Beside it, a computer screen glowed with row after row of multiple-colored bands. "This is our ABI PRISM 373 DNA Sequencer. In many ways, these are our brains. We have lots of these beauties scattered throughout the complex."

Katherine stepped in for a closer look. "A DNA sequencer?"

"Yes."

"What does it do?"

"Remember those gels in the last room?"

"Yes."

"These automatically read them. They record the bands, label the gene, hold it in memory, then fire it off to our main computer."

Coleman watched as Katherine examined the computer and equipment. For the first time that he could remember, she appeared totally absorbed, at peace—almost happy. She seemed to lose herself as she poked, prodded, and explored the fascinating new machine. And as he watched her face fill with awe, he began to experience her wonder himself. He knew nothing about the equipment she was examining, but it didn't matter. Not only was he able to feel people's pain, he was also able to experience their joy.

Unfortunately, the moment was short-lived.

"Dr. Murkoski!" A young technician burst into the room, a look of urgency on his face.

Murkoski turned, angry at the interruption. "What is it?"

"B–11, we have an emergency."

Murkoski's attitude instantly changed. "It's not Freddy, is it?"

"I tried to beep you, but you didn't—"

Murkoski pulled up his beeper, looked at it, then threw it to the floor in disgust. Without a word, he raced out the door, the technician on his heels.

Coleman and Katherine looked at each other. Neither was sure what to do, but since neither wanted to be abandoned in this labyrinth of labs, they hurried after the other two.

Murkoski moved briskly down the hall. He took the stairs two at a time, then crossed the atrium. Coleman and Katherine managed to keep him in sight down another long hallway until they finally arrived at the open doorway to B–11.

Two paramedics hovered over a body lying on grassy sod. One checked for a pulse while the other squirted goop over the paddles of a heart defibrillator. A handful of Genodyne staff gathered around, watching. In the far corner, clinging to a dead tree and shaking it, a baboon screamed hysterically.

"Who is it?" Murkoski shouted as he raced toward the group. "What happened?"

"It's Wolff," one of the staff called back.

Coleman and Katherine moved closer as the paramedic placed the paddles on the chest and yelled, "Clear!"

There was a faint thud as the body convulsed. The baboon barked and screamed louder. Murkoski scowled at the animal and demanded, "Was Freddy part of this?"

"They were just playing," someone said, "roughhousing, and suddenly Wolff keeled over."

"Cardiac arrest," the first paramedic explained.

Murkoski scoffed, "A heart attack? He's young, he's in great shape—look at him!"

A chill swept over Coleman. There was something about Murkoski's tone. Even over the animal's shrieking and screaming, Coleman could hear a falseness in Murkoski's voice. Something was wrong. Terribly wrong.

"He's back!" the second paramedic shouted.

All heads turned toward Wolff as he began coughing up a clear pink fluid. His eyes fluttered, then opened. He was searching, desperately looking for something. But it lasted only a moment before the eyes quit moving. Now they simply stared. And it was that expression that brought the cold sweat onto Coleman's face, making his mouth fill with salty brine.

"Hey, are you all right?" He looked up and saw Katherine. Though she tried to hide it, there was no missing the concern in her face. "You don't look so hot."

He nodded. "Yeah, I just have to sit down a—" But he was unable to finish the phrase before he doubled over and threw up. He wretched once, twice, three times, spewing vomit onto the freshly lain sod.

"Get him out of here!" the paramedic shouted. "Someone get him out of here!"

He felt Katherine take his arm and direct him toward the door. They had to stop one more time as his stomach contracted with another set of heaves. At last he was able to rise and make it out into the hallway, as the shrieks and screams of the baboon continued to echo inside the room.

CHAPTER 9

First time you've seen somebody die?" Katherine asked as they headed back down the freeway toward Everett.

Coleman looked out the passenger window. "I've seen a lot of death," he answered quietly. "It wasn't his dying that hit me. It was the expression on his face."

Katherine nodded, thinking she understood. "That *how-could-this-be-happening-to-me* look?"

"No, it wasn't that." Coleman continued to stare out the window. "That wasn't his question."

Katherine glanced at him. "What do you mean—what was it then?"

Coleman slowly turned to face her. "The man was not asking why he was dying. He was asking why he had ever lived."

The statement stunned Katherine. She wanted to respond but couldn't find the words. Instead, she studied the road in silence.

It had been a week since their first run-in, and this was not the first time he had left her speechless. In fact, it was happening more and more often. But it wasn't just his insight into people that silenced her. It was also his lack of self-consciousness. Whether he was waiting on a customer at the store, horsing around with Eric, or trying unsuccessfully to scale the barriers she kept erecting between them, she had never met a person so completely empty of self.

At first she had mistaken this lack of ego as some major self-image problem. But instead of making him weak, it seemed to make him strong. And the more she saw him in action, the more she found herself envying him. By taking himself out of the picture, by having no focus on self, he was completely *free* of himself. That freedom allowed him to be perfectly honest and to focus intently on others. He saw things in people. Deep things. Like with that dying man back at the lab.

Once again, she felt him looking at her. Searching, exploring. She shifted uncomfortably. "You're doing it again," she warned.

"Oh. Sorry." She could almost hear amusement in his voice as he turned and looked ahead.

The man enjoyed her company, she could tell. And, if she were being honest with herself, she'd have to admit she was beginning to accept his.

No, actually, it was more than that. She found his freedom exciting, his concern for others moving. And these emotions set off a quiet trembling somewhere deep inside her. She was starting to feel things again, things she hadn't felt in a long, long time. But she was through with those types of feelings—she'd sworn them off long ago, and she wasn't about to give in to them now.

"So," she said, trying to change the subject. "Do you think this blood stuff is for real?"

"What do you mean?"

"I mean, what does it feel like to have what could be the blood of Jesus Christ running through your veins?"

"I don't know." He shrugged. "To be honest, I really don't know that much about the man."

"You've never read the Bible?"

Coleman smiled sadly. "Guess I was too busy with other things."

"Come on," she insisted, "everybody's read the Bible—at least some of it."

He shook his head. "Sorry." Turning back toward her, he asked, "What about you?" She could feel him probing again.

"Sure," she said. "When I was a kid I used to read it every night." She couldn't resist glancing over to see how that bit of information was received.

But instead of surprise, his face was filled with questioning concern. "I'd like to hear more."

She knew he wasn't talking just about the Bible. He was also talking about her, about what she'd been through. His sensitivity sent a faint quiver through her body. Effortlessly, without even trying, he had reached in and touched her. She suspected that, in time, if she let herself, she would be able to open up to this man. If she wanted, she would eventually be able to talk with him about the Bible, about God's betrayal, about the brutal loss of the only man she'd ever loved. She could speak of the injustice of losing her father, the only man who'd tried to help, who'd loved her even when she was ugly and unlovable. But Katherine would not—could not—give in to that temptation. Instead, she swallowed back the emotion and remained silent.

"I'm sorry," he said, "I didn't mean to pry. I won't do that again."

She wanted to say something clever, something wry and sarcastic. But she wasn't sure she could pull it off. Fortunately, the Mukilteo Interchange was coming up, so she was able to busy herself checking the mirror, changing lanes, and jockeying for position as they left one freeway and entered another that headed west toward Puget Sound.

By the time she had finished the maneuvers, she had managed to partially reerect the wall holding him out. And to ensure that there would be no further assault, she went on the offense. "What about you?" she asked.

"I'm sorry, what?"

"What Murkoski said, doesn't that concern you? That everything you are, that it's all a bunch of chemicals? Doesn't it bother you that you're nothing but some big kid's chemistry experiment?" She saw Coleman wince and immediately hated herself. Why had she said that, just when they were getting so close? But of course, that was her answer. They were getting too close.

He shook his head. "No. That doesn't bother me."

"What does?" she asked. "I mean, there must be something that gets under your skin, something that sets you off. Or did they take that away, too?" It was another poke, and she hated herself even more.

Coleman remained silent a long moment before answering. "I guess . . . I guess what really bothers me . . . is the pain."

She glanced to him. He was deep in thought. "Pain?" she asked.

"I never knew that people were in such anguish. I never knew there was so much loneliness. Sometimes when I see it in them, I actually *feel* it, right along with them." He hesitated, then continued, almost sadly. "Sometimes I think it would be better to feel nothing at all than to feel that."

"It's true, then." The edge to her voice was softening. "You do sense what other people are feeling."

He nodded. "On the one hand I experience this incredible beauty all around me, things I've seen every day of my life but have never seen—drops of dew on a spiderweb, steam rising from a wooden fence in the early morning sun. On the other hand, I see our inability to connect with that beauty, to be a part of it. I see in every pair of eyes this frustration, this fear that we're nothing but vapor or shadows, that we're skimming across the surface of reality without ever touching it, without connecting to that—that intangible something, that *deepness* that makes all the other beauty possible."

Katherine realized that she was holding her breath and forced herself to exhale.

He continued. "That's what I saw in his eyes this afternoon. It wasn't his fear of death, it was his searching. The realization that he was nothing but a shadow without substance—dancing across creation's surface with no purpose, no reason for being."

Coleman looked back out the window. "I guess that's what bothers me the most. Sensing all that pain. Feeling all their . . . hollowness."

Katherine nodded, then quietly quoted, "'A man of sorrows acquainted with grief.'"

"Pardon me?"

"That's one of the descriptions of Jesus in the Scriptures." Coleman turned toward her as she nodded. "Yes, sir, I think we definitely need to get you a Bible."

Steiner's body cried out for sleep, but he wouldn't listen. He stared at the computer screen while throwing another handful of Tylenol into his mouth and washing them down with a Diet Coke. He'd lost track of time. It could be day, it could be night—he didn't care. He only knew that he was close. Very, very close. He clicked the mouse and brought up the names and addresses of the airplane owners he'd requested from the FAA.

The past few days had not been easy. After interviewing the orderly at St. John's, he had tracked down the cabby who had picked up the "burn victim." The driver was a punk, less than cooperative. All he'd remembered was taking two men to the airport on the morning of January 30.

"There's nothing else you recall?" Steiner had asked.

"Nope."

"Any conversation?"

"Nope."

"Can you describe the bandaged man's voice?"

"Uh-uh."

"Did they say where they were flying?"

"Nope."

The conversation was going nowhere fast. "You don't remember anything?"

"Nope. Just that the guy stiffed me on the tip."

"That, you remember?"

"If a man's got his own plane and he's too cheap to tip you, that you remember."

"They had their own plane? How do you know?"

"I didn't drop them off at the commercial terminal. I dropped them off at the general aviation area."

"Why didn't you tell me?"

"You didn't ask."

Next had come the slow and laborious process of elimination. Steiner knew this was always the most tedious part in any investigation. But he also knew that if you had the time and tenacity, it was the most profitable. Steiner had both.

First he had contacted the Air Route Traffic Control Center in Omaha and asked for all noncommercial flight plans filed on January 30 out of Lincoln Municipal Airport. These records were confidential and it hadn't been easy to get them, but a few well-placed lies about working for the Johnson County D.A.'s office did the trick.

He had thirty-five choices, thirty-five noncommercial flights that had flown out of Lincoln on the thirtieth. But he quickly cut that number in half by eliminating all flights that had a destination of five hundred miles or less. If Steiner's suspicions were correct, the stakes and the need for secrecy were high; he doubted they would risk being seen in any airport if they could make the journey by land within a day.

Now the number of choices had been reduced to eighteen.

Next Steiner listed the tail ID numbers of each of the eighteen aircraft and pulled strings at the FAA to get the names and addresses of each of the registered owners.

This was the list he now stared at on the screen. Since Lincoln is the state capital, slightly less than half of the aircraft were government owned, leased, or affiliated. This could, of course, be a government operation, but he had his doubts.

That brought the number down to eleven. Six private, seven corporate. It had to be someone on this list. But who? Steiner rubbed his forehead. His headache was relentless, but so was his determination. There was something here, there had to be. And he wouldn't stop until he found it.

Once again he scanned the column of private owners:

N9745B David Buchanan	Lincoln, Nebraska
N340E Richard Kaufman	Salt Lake City, Utah
N698O Willa Nixon	Rockford, Illinois
N889DG Thomas Piffer	Lincoln, Nebraska
N7724B Susan Smoke	Kalispell, Montana

He ran a cross-check with Coleman's friends, with witnesses of the execution, antideath groups, defense leagues . . .

Nothing.

He popped another Diet Coke, chugged several gulps, and scrutinized the next list; the corporate planes:

N395AG American Containers	Lincoln, Nebraska
N737BA Genodyne Inc.	Arlington, Washington
N349E Johnson Agricultural	Chicago, Illinois
N7497B Kellermen Dye Casting	Omaha, Nebraska
N983C Moore Hardwoods and Lumber	Hershey, Pennsylvania
N5487G Van Owen Seed Company	Des Moines, Iowa

He stared at the list, hoping to force a pattern, to see something, anything. He saw nothing. Well, almost nothing. That second name, Genodyne, sounded familiar. He'd read something about that company not long ago. *Time* or *Newsweek,* he couldn't remember. Wasn't it some sort of genetics firm?

He studied the address. Arlington, Washington. What were they doing all the way out there? Cattle breeding? Hybrid corn?

He clicked the mouse a few times and popped up his phone directory. Scrolling down, he found the home number for Leonard Patterson, head of security at the penitentiary in Lincoln and one of the few men at the facility Steiner had not completely alienated. He clicked the mouse, let it dial, then reached over to pick up his phone.

It rang five times before someone fumbled with the receiver and a groggy voice mumbled, "Hello?"

"Hi, Leonard. Steiner."

"Harry? What time is it?"

"I don't know. Listen, do you remember those scientists you said were hanging around before Coleman's execution?"

"Harry, it's 4:30 in the morning."

"Yeah. Did you ever hear what area of science they were into?"

"Harry—"

"Just—did you hear a company name or location or anything?"

"No, Harry."

"Why were they so interested? I mean, what were they studying?"

"They took some blood samples and stuff, I don't know . . ."

Steiner waited, letting Leonard think.

"They said they wanted to test his genes or something, yeah, they were a couple guys interested in what a murderer's genes were like."

Steiner's eyes shot to the screen:

> Genodyne Inc., Arlington, Washington.

Bingo. His head still pounded, but he no longer noticed.

"And Sarah and Julie, how are they? Can you put them on?"

"They're down at the pool right now," Beth answered. Another wave of static washed over the phone, drowning out the sentence but clearing in time for the words: ". . . and Sarah's turning into this bronze goddess. Oh, Philip, we're having such a good time, I wish you could join us."

"Soon, Hon. I hope, very soon."

"Something happened, didn't it?

"What makes you think—"

"Don't lie to me, Phil. I can tell by your voice. It's something big, isn't it?"

"Beth—"

"You won't tell me when you can come down, you're vague about the reasons. You won't even talk to me over the office phone. Is it Murkoski again? Is it the project?"

O'Brien gave no answer.

"I thought so." There was another barrage of static that ended just in time to hear the words: ". . . more important, our relationship, or working with some scientist you don't even trust."

O'Brien gave a heavy sigh. "Beth, this is more than just—"

"I'm not angry, Philip. But maybe we should start to seriously—"

"Beth—"

"—reevaluate our priorities. Maybe we should ask ourselves what we really expect out of this rela—"

"Wolff's dead."

"What?"

"Wolff died. Congestive heart failure." There was silence on the other end and another wave of static. "Beth, are you there?"

"How?" came the shaken reply. "He was barely thirty. He was so young, athletic." There was a brief pause. "Do you think . . . he wasn't doing drugs, was he?"

Another pause, this time at Philip's end.

"Philip?"

"He's diabetic. The insulin he kept in the refrigerator at work—someone tampered with the vials."

Beth gasped. "Are you sure?"

"One of his colleagues thought they looked suspicious. We ran some tests. Without knowing it, Wolff had been shooting up with a new version of Interleukin."

"Of what?"

"It's an experimental gene used for cancer treatment."

"And it causes heart failure?"

"This type seems to eat into blood vessels, causing them to start leaking."

"Leaking?"

"Like a sieve. The autopsy showed his heart was weak and mushy, like a sixty-year-old who'd had multiple heart attacks. And his lungs were filled with liquid, indicating that the vessels in them had also opened up, filling the lungs with blood."

"Did Wolff have cancer? Could he have been experimenting on himself?"

"No."

"Have you gone to the police?"

"Not yet."

"Phil, what's going—" The rest of her phrase was lost in static.

"Hold it," Murkoski interrupted. "Rewind that last section." He leaned forward toward his desk, ear glued to his receiver, as he heard the whir and whine of voices running backwards. There was a click on the other end and a repeat of the conversation.

" . . . lungs were filled with liquid, indicating that the vessels in them had also opened up, filling the lungs with blood."

"Did Wolff have cancer? Could he have been experimenting on himself?"

"No."

"Have you gone to the police?"

"Not yet."

"All right," Murkoski ordered. The taped conversation stopped. It was 4:50 in the morning. The young man turned to his office window and instinctively checked out the lines of his suit. They were good lines, ones he usually appreciated. But this morning they gave him little pleasure. "What time did she phone him?"

"Shortly after seven last evening." The voice was heavily accented. Murkoski had never been able to tell what nationality, although he knew it was Asian. "Mr. Murkoski, I am certain you can appreciate our concern, can you not?"

Murkoski ran his hand through his hair. "Yeah—no—I mean, sure, I understand."

"If Mr. O'Brien were to connect your technician's untimely death with our project, I am afraid it could seriously jeopardize our date of delivery."

"I agree."

"The situation is not getting out of hand, is it, Dr. Murkoski? You will be able to meet your deadline, will you not?"

"Of course," Murkoski said, turning back to his desk, trying to hide his irritation.

"Good. Word is spreading. Competition is asking very sensitive questions. You can appreciate our need for haste."

"I'll get on the problem right away."

"We were certain you would. Good morning, Dr. Murkoski."

Before he could respond, the phone disconnected. Murkoski slowly leaned forward and replaced the receiver. Then, even more slowly, he turned to look out his window and into the darkness.

The crack stings his throat and burns his lungs. He holds it until he must exhale and gasp for breath. The rush is immediate, exhilarating, running through his chest, his arms, into his fingertips.

He is it.

Unstoppable.

He grabs the shotgun from the front seat and steps out of the car. He sees everything. The ice machine out front. The barbecue charcoal display. The neon Budweiser sign in its final stages of flickering out.

He kicks open the door, a grand entrance that has the desired effect. The clerk, a boy with long hair and earring, is speechless. He won't try anything. He knows Coleman means business.

Coleman heads toward the counter, pumping his gun. The kid's boom box blasts out an oldie, "Hotel California." The guitar licks are intoxicating, making Coleman sail. The crack screams through his body. He is all-powerful.

Omnipotent.

The clerk falters, throws a look at the security camera. With one hand, Coleman lifts the shotgun and blows the intruding eye to smithereens. There is no sound. Only a flash of light and flying glass and plastic. One chamber is still full. He knows it. The clerk knows it.

"Come on! Let's go, let's go!"

The kid hits the cash register. It flies open. Bills are grabbed, stuffed into a Quickie Mart bag. Coleman grabs a Snickers bar, then several more. He knows he'll be hungry.

"Now the safe!"

The kid makes an excuse. A lie.

Coleman points to the floor. He knows where the safe is hidden.

The kid protests.

Coleman levels his gun.

The punk is shouting at him as if volume will prove his sincerity. Coleman's finger wraps around the trigger. He is grinning.

The boy yells at him. Wide-eyed. Terror-stricken.

Coleman's grin broadens.

The boy turns. Coleman thinks it's towards the safe. But it isn't. He's turning back. There's something in his hand. It's a pistol, a .22. The kid is an idiot, one too many Rambo movies. There's nothing Coleman can do now. He squeezes the trigger.

Another silent explosion of light.

A bell rings, keeps ringing. Somehow the kid has tripped the alarm. Coleman reaches for the bag on the counter, then hears breathing. It's coming from behind. Wheezing, coughing. He spins around, but no one is there. The aisles are empty.

It grows louder, bearing down.

Coleman breaks open the gun. With trembling hands he yanks out the spent casings.

The breathing is louder, roaring in his head.

Coleman backs up, shoving his hands into his sweatshirt, fumbling for two more shells.

He smells the breath now. Alcohol. His father's. It's all around. Coming from all sides.

He turns, stumbling toward the door, but it is locked. He bangs on it, desperate to get out.

"Michael!" It's his father's voice shouting, swearing. "Michael!"

Coleman doesn't look back. He pounds on the glass, trying to break it, but it won't give.

"Michael!"

He continues to bang, but it is no longer glass, it is wood. And it is no longer his father's voice. It is a child's. "Mr. Michaels? Mr. Michaels, are you okay?" The banging continues.

Coleman awoke with a start, cowering, preparing for the blows. But none came. His father wasn't there. The breathing had disappeared. The dream was gone. Only the knocking remained—and Eric's voice. "Mr. Michaels? Mr. Michaels!"

The picnic had been Katherine's idea. Another week had passed, and it was time to make the trek back up to Arlington. Since they were paying her good money to take the day off, and since Eric had never really been up into the mountains, she figured—why not take advantage of the situation and go on a little outing.

She glanced at Coleman as she drove. He was in the passenger seat, poring over the Bible she'd given him. In the days since their last trip, he'd been true to his word. He hadn't pried. He hadn't said another word about her past. For that she was both pleased and disappointed. A week ago, it had taken so little effort for him to reach through her barriers and touch her. And now, as the days passed, as she saw his goodness, and as her trust built, she knew it would take even less effort for him to reach in and move her even more deeply. But he respected her; he would not abuse his power. And it was this combination of restrained power and tenderness that made her start finding excuses to spend time with him.

Her walls were crumbling. She could tell by the way she stood at the closet trying to decide what to wear, by the stirring inside when she heard him arrive at the store. She could tell by the way her body began to take on a softness when they talked, becoming curves instead of rigid lines.

Then there was the drinking. She hadn't quit, but when sobriety came, it didn't carry the piercing sharpness it once had. She was beginning to experience a different high.

She glanced into the rearview mirror. Eric was reading. Another miracle. No Game Boy in his hand, no laptop computer. Just a book, a real book.

"You'll like it," Coleman had said when he had tossed it at him. "I got it at the bookstore down the street. It's called *The Last of the Mohicans,* and it's all about Indians and survival in the wilderness and stuff."

Eric hadn't stopped reading it since he'd first opened it.

They'd been on the road forty-five minutes, heading up the Getchel Highway and into the Cascades. Once again she glanced at Coleman. But this time his face was wet with tears. "What's wrong?" she asked, concerned. "Are you okay?"

He glanced up, a little embarrassed. When he spoke, his voice was thick with feeling. "I never knew what ..." He searched for the word. "Wisdom ..."

Katherine smiled. One of the other things she enjoyed about this man was his childlike wonder, his sense of awe, sometimes over the simplest things. She didn't always understand why it happened, but this time she did.

"This ache I have," he was saying, "this emptiness. It's like he understands—like somehow, he's able to meet that hunger and, and ..."

"Help ease it?" she asked.

He nodded and looked up at her in quiet amazement.

"I guess that's why he called himself the 'Bread of Life.'"

"He called himself that?"

"Oh, yeah."

Coleman was dumbstruck. "And people—people know this?"

She couldn't help laughing at his astonishment. "A few."

Coleman looked back down to the page, then up again. "And you?"

The question caught her off guard. "Me?"

"Do you believe it?"

Katherine took a long, slow breath. "I don't know. When I was a kid, that was all I heard about. Then, as an adult, I had a long stint with AA. When everything else failed, my faith was the only thing that kept me sober, that pulled me through. But now—" She took another deep breath and let it out. "I don't know. I guess I just don't see it anymore."

"And seeing is believing."

"It is for me." She sighed wearily.

She could feel him looking at her a long moment before returning to his Bible. She was grateful to be off the hook. Grateful and disturbed. This man was stirring other things inside her as well; deeper things, long-forgotten.

A half-hour later they were at Granite Falls, a huge rocky formation deep in the foothills with towering cliffs and an angry Stillaguamish River that dropped nearly a hundred feet, thundering and crashing into gigantic boulders before slamming, swirling, and crashing into a dozen more.

"Wow!" Eric cried over the roar. "This is so cool!"

"Don't get too close," Katherine shouted, doing her best not to sound like a mother and failing miserably. But neither boy nor man seemed to notice. She watched as, instinctively, Coleman rested his hands on her son's shoulder. The unconscious act of kindness brought a tightness to her throat. She turned, fighting back the moisture welling up in her eyes, pretending to notice something downriver. Eric had missed so many things in his little life. At the store, day in and day out, with only the computers and people on the Internet as his playmates. What type of existence was that? No interaction with others. No men to model after. How could she have been so insensitive, so selfish, not to see this?

They hiked downstream a quarter of a mile for lunch. Banter and teasing came easy between Coleman and Eric, and Katherine was grateful to feel like the third wheel as she watched their friendship grow. She'd seen it at the store, this male camaraderie thing, but it had always been on Eric's turf. Now Coleman was able to take charge, showing her son how to skip rocks, how to sneak through dense undergrowth so quietly that even crows could not hear and sound the alarm.

Later, she watched as the two studied an animal's track in the mud beside the river.

"Looks like a deer."

"How can you tell?"

"See here, this V."

"Oh, yeah. Cool."

"Look at the size. It's a buck. Probably a big one."

Then there were Coleman's Indian stories. How they survived, what they ate in the wild, how they fought. Some of the details were a little too gruesome for Katherine's taste, but the facts seemed to thrill her son.

"How come you know so much about Indians?" Eric asked.

"You don't grow up in Tecumseh without knowing your Indians."

"Tecumseh? Where's that?"

"Little town in Nebraska. Named after Tecumseh, a Shawnee. His name meant 'Panther in the Sky.' He was the greatest Indian ever."

"Oh, yeah? What about Chief Seattle?"

"He was okay for a Northwesterner. But the real Indians, like the Shawnee, they were back in the Midwest."

"Says who?"

"It's common knowledge."

"Oh, yeah?"

"Yeah."

"Yeah?"

"Yeah."

And so the sparring continued, along with the macho challenges, races, and leaps from rock to rock (with more than one slip and crash into the water). But wet clothes and bruised bodies were only a preliminary to the end of their little outing. As they headed back up to the car, they spotted an overgrown path, a shortcut that was clearly only for the strong-hearted.

Immediately they began goading each other to take it. And, of course, they both rose to the challenge. Just before entering the tangled pathway, Eric turned back to his mom. "Aren't you coming?"

Katherine peered into the dense undergrowth. "No, I think I'll stick to the path here."

"Come on, Mom."

"No—too much testosterone in this one for me. You boys go ahead."

She watched as they began plowing through the brush, sometimes racing, shouting, always inciting the other to continue. But in less than a minute their outlook had changed.

"Ow!"

"Ouch!"

"Yeow!"

"What's wrong?" she shouted.

"Blackberry bushes," Coleman called.

"They must be twenty feet high," Eric yelled.

"Maybe you better turn around and come out," Katherine suggested.

"No way!" Eric shouted. "I'm not afraid of a few blackberry bushes. Are you?" he called to Coleman.

"Not me," Coleman shouted back.

"Me, neither. Ouch! We'll be fine, Mom. Don't worry 'bout us."

"I wouldn't dream of it," she shouted back.

Twenty minutes later she arrived at the car, but they weren't there. It took an additional half hour for them to finally emerge from the bushes, their arms, hands, even their faces scratched and bleeding.

"You guys look awful!" she cried. "What happened?"

"A few more blackberries than we anticipated," Coleman said.

"It's not that bad," Eric insisted. "Just a few scratches."

"A few," Coleman had to laugh. He held up Eric's bleeding arm. "You've got scratches on top of scratches."

"Oh yeah," Eric retorted, grabbing Coleman's other hand and raising it up. "What about you? You got scratches on top of scratches on top of scratches."

"Guys," Katherine protested, "look at you, you're getting blood all over each other."

They looked at their hands. It was true. Both had smeared their own blood onto the other.

"Cool," Eric said staring at his palm.

"You know," Coleman said, "some Indians believed that the soul of man resided in his blood. That's why they mixed their blood together to become blood brothers."

"That may be true," Katherine said, pulling her son toward her and trying to wipe some of the blood from his face with a tissue.

"Mom—"

"But in this day of AIDS and every other blood disease imaginable, I think that's one ritual we can live without."

"Too late," Eric said, reexamining his palm.

Katherine glanced at Coleman, who was looking at his own hand.

"I'm afraid he's right, Katherine. Looks like we've become official, honest-to-goodness blood brothers."

Eric looked up and beamed. But Katherine barely noticed. It was the sound of her name that had caught her off guard, that had made her legs a little weak, her hands a little less sure of themselves. This was the first time he had spoken her name out loud, and she quite literally had to catch her breath. The walls were crumbling again. If Coleman had looked into her eyes at that moment, he would have known everything she was, understood all that she was feeling.

But something else had caught his attention. "Look at that!"

Katherine turned to see that he was pointing toward a giant cedar.

"What?" Eric demanded.

"That."

"It's just a tree."

"No, past that. Look."

A huge, pale moon was rising behind it.

"It's just the moon."

"You're not seeing it. Look at it."

"What?" Eric repeated.

"Look!"

Katherine continued to stare with them. And, as she looked she began to see something else. The way the cedar stretched out toward the sky, its limbs graceful and drooping, with the full, glowing orb rising behind it. There was a silent splendor here. A quiet strength.

"Don't be stupid," Eric said. He pulled open the back door of the car and climbed in. "It's just the moon. You see it lots of times in the day."

Katherine turned slowly to watch Coleman, who was still staring, transfixed. Then she looked back to the tree. She couldn't find the words, but she was beginning to understand. There was something about this moment, this tiny detail of life, that seemed bigger and more powerful than all of the grandiose plans and accomplishments of her own noisy, scampering little life. For the briefest second she too felt like a shadow dancing across the surface of something far deeper, far more eternal than she could ever be. She tried to swallow and found a lump in her throat. It had nothing to do with pain and everything to do with joy. Katherine Lyon was happy. Happier than she'd been in a long, long time.

The ride down the mountain was full of more Indian tales, bantering, and laughter. It took nearly an hour to reach Genodyne, but it seemed like minutes. The trembling inside Katherine ebbed and flowed, but it never disappeared. It wasn't until they entered Genodyne's lobby that the joy started to fade. First there was the problem of taking Eric onto the grounds.

"I'm sorry," the receptionist explained. "No children allowed in the laboratory area."

"But he's my friend," Coleman insisted.

"I'm sorry, the rules are specific. He may visit the offices or our cafeteria, but he won't be admitted to the labs. No children are."

"Call Dr. Murkoski, let me talk to him."

"Dr. Murkoski is unavailable, but if you'll have a seat, I'm sure—"

Suddenly Katherine saw Coleman's expression change. It was more than concern. It was fear. She followed his gaze to the front door, where a man was just entering the lobby and approaching the desk. He was short, in his fifties, with wire-rim glasses and thinning, brown hair.

When he glanced up, the man seemed equally surprised by Coleman's expression. "I'm sorry," he said, "have we met?"

Coleman did his best to recover. "No. I don't think so."

But the man's interest had been piqued. "Are you certain?"

Coleman shook his head.

The man extended his hand. "My name is Steiner. Harold Steiner."

Coleman took it. "William Michaels."

Noticing the scratches on Coleman's arms and then Eric's, Steiner said, "Looks like you two had quite a tussle."

"Yeah." Eric grinned. "And the blackberries won."

The smiles lasted a fraction longer than necessary before Steiner again asked, "Are you sure we've not met?"

Coleman shook his head. "I'm sure." Then, resting his hand on Eric's shoulder, he quickly brought the meeting to an end. "Well, if you'll excuse us."

"Certainly."

Coleman nodded and turned Eric toward the door.

"Wait a minute," Eric protested, "I thought we were—"

"Plans have changed."

"But—"

"Let's go."

"But—"

"Plans have changed." The sternness in Coleman's voice surprised Eric, and he allowed himself to be moved toward the exit.

"Excuse me, Mr. Michaels?" It was the receptionist. "Don't you want to wait and see—"

"We'll be back later," Coleman said over his shoulder. "Tell him something has come up, we'll be back a little later."

Katherine hadn't missed a thing, and she had the good sense to play along. After a parting nod to Steiner, she turned and accompanied Coleman and Eric out the door. But as she walked out, she knew that Steiner was still watching.

CHAPTER 10

O'Brien hadn't run an electrophoresis gel since grad school. Although there had been some changes in chemicals and hardware, the process remained essentially the same. It was also the same process Wolff had undertaken seventy-two hours earlier. The one he had called O'Brien about. The one that O'Brien now suspected led to his death.

It was a little after ten in the evening when he quietly slipped into the lab on the third floor. If Wolff had found a problem while running a gel, that must have meant he was getting different identification bands on the DNA. There were only three possible explanations for that. The first was that Wolff had made a mistake, an unlikely option given his meticulous attention to detail. This left only two other possibilities. Either the GOD gene had mutated on its own—or someone had deliberately altered it.

There was only one way to tell. Double-check the gene's fingerprint. Run another gel.

The procedure was fairly simple. First O'Brien pulled out a sample of the GOD gene from the freezer. From this sample he would need to cut out the specific section they'd been focusing on. But instead of cutting with mechanical knives or scissors, they used chemical ones called restriction enzymes. There were hundreds of these enzymes to choose from, but in this case they had been using *Eco*RI, a distant cousin to the deadly E. coli bacteria that had endeared itself to the fast-food chains a while back.

By mixing the DNA with the chemical scissors and then incubating it in an Eppendorf tube for an hour in 37 degrees C water, O'Brien was able to cut open the DNA molecule and remove and dissect the precise section of the GOD gene he wanted.

Next he melted a clear, blue, Jello-like substance in the microwave. He poured this hot liquid into the five-inch-by-eleven-inch electrophoresis gel box. Carefully he inserted a serrated piece of Plexiglas, which looked like a thick comb, into the liquid at one end. He waited patiently as the gel hardened, then removed the comb, leaving several small holes, or wells, where the teeth had been.

It was tedious work, but O'Brien loved it. Being back at a lab bench, working the front lines, was a far cry from the paperwork and politics he was daily subjected to. And, though he appreciated the money and prestige, a large part of him missed the good old days when he and Beth were first starting out. When she had thought him a hero. When he was breaking new ground. The work had been hard, but at least it had carried a sense of accomplishment. For the past several months, he hadn't been so sure *what* he was accomplishing.

He glanced at the clock—11:15. So far there had been no interruptions, no late-night insomniacs swinging by to see how his or her particular batch of DNA-laced bacteria was breeding. And more importantly, no head of the gene therapy division showing up, demanding to know what he was up to.

Once again, O'Brien scolded himself for giving Murkoski so much power. Of course he had his excuses—trying to keep a multimillion-dollar biotech company on course creates a few distractions. Besides, everyone told him that a real leader must delegate, delegate, and delegate. Well, he had delegated, all right. And now something was wrong. Not only had Murkoski refused to return his calls or show up at the office, but the government contacts he knew to be involved in the project were also strangely unavailable. Yes, indeed, something was very wrong.

As O'Brien continued to work, allowing his thoughts to drift, the silence of the lab began to play tricks on him. Whenever the air-conditioning kicked on or the refrigerators turned over, he was certain that someone had entered the lab. It's not that he didn't enjoy returning to his laboratory roots. He just would have enjoyed it more if he didn't suspect that his life was in danger.

Was he being paranoid? Probably. But he had grown so out of touch with the project, and Murkoski had such a raging ego—who knew *what* the kid was up to.

His mind drifted to his children and to Beth. How he missed them. But, until this mess was straightened out, it wouldn't hurt for them to stay in Mexico. At least there they would be safe.

He crossed to the small D.C. transformer and attached the wires to the gel box. The black wire to the black terminal on the left, the red wire to the red terminal on the right. Running a gel was a fairly simple procedure. Since every gene is a different size and moves through the gel at its own rate, he would place the DNA in the little wells he had made and run 100 volts of direct current over them from one end of the gel box to the other. Then, after a prescribed period of time, he would be able to see how far each section of gene had traveled along the current as it pushed its way through the gel. Wherever the sections stopped and congregated, a band would be created. And it was the pattern of these bands that gave the precise length and identification of the gene they were testing. If there was the slightest discrepancy between the bands in the batch he was now running and the benchmarks they had established in their earlier identification and testing of the GOD gene, he would know.

He reached for a small beaker of electrophoresis buffer and poured it over the hardened gel. This was to ensure electrical contact between the two terminals at each end of the box. As he poured it, he couldn't help noticing the beaker shaking in his hands.

Next he mixed a fluorescent dye called ethidium bromide into the DNA. This would allow him to clearly see the pattern of the bands when they were viewed under ultraviolet light.

Now came the hard part. He grabbed an electronic pipette, a measuring device about the size of a small turkey baster. He adjusted it to ten microliters and with a trembling hand sucked up some of the DNA and placed it into the little wells he had made. It was embarrassing how his hand shook, but it served as a clear reminder of just how nervous he really was. It took all of his concentration and willpower just to drop the DNA into the tiny wells.

Then he heard it. The whine of the elevator. He was only two doors down from the elevator, and the lab's door was wide open. He froze and listened.

It stopped. Someone had brought it down to the lobby.

A moment later it started up again. He tried to picture it moving up the elevator shaft, guessing the time it would take to pass each floor. It had passed the second and was heading toward the third. With any luck it would continue right on up to the fourth or even the—

It sighed to a stop. It was on the third floor. His floor. He could not hear the doors open, but he knew that someone was stepping out. He watched the lab door, angry at himself for leaving it open. Quickly he scanned the bench area in front of him. It would be impossible to disguise what he was doing. Anyone looking in would know he was running a gel. He strained, listening for footsteps, but the air-conditioning made it impossible to hear.

He stepped to the right, behind the cupboard, just out of sight. With eight other labs on the floor, the odds were unlikely that whoever had come up in the elevator was heading into this one.

Unless, of course, they were coming for him.

He saw the brief flicker of a shadow on the tiled floor as a form passed the door and continued down the hall. He closed his eyes and let out a quiet sigh. Then he heard:

"Hello? Anybody in here?"

Relieved that it was a woman's voice and not Murkoski's, O'Brien stepped into view.

She was beautiful. Mid-twenties, long dark hair, jade-green eyes. She had a lean yet sensual figure and didn't seem shy about showing it off with the help of a snug knit top and a short, tweed skirt. In some ways, she reminded him of Beth in her younger days. Before the children. When they were helplessly in love. When she still admired him.

"Oh, Dr. O'Brien. I saw the door open and was wondering . . ." She stopped as she saw the gel box and beakers in front of him.

He flashed a boyish, self-conscious grin. "Just brushing up on my lab technique," he lied. "I really miss rolling up the old sleeves and getting my hands dirty."

"I see." She smiled. Was it his imagination or was she flirting with him? The thought both excited him and set off tiny little alarms.

He cleared his throat. "I'm sorry. I, uh—I don't know your name. Are you new?"

She moved toward him, extending her hand, not taking her eyes off him. "Yes, I'm Youngren. Tisha Youngren." They shook hands. Hers was warm and firm.

"Philip O'Brien."

"I know."

He smiled. "Yes, I suppose so."

She stood a moment, unmoving. She seemed to sense the effect she was having on him, and she clearly enjoyed it.

"Well, uh . . ." He motioned to the counter, indicating his work.

"Of course," she said, "I've got plenty to do, myself. It was a pleasure to finally meet you, Dr. O'Brien."

"Thanks. Me, too."

There was that smile again. She turned and glided toward the door. O'Brien couldn't help staring. When she arrived at the door she turned one last time. "Oh, Dr. O'Brien. The next time you're running a gel?"

"Yes?"

"You really should wear gloves."

"Why's that?"

"The ethidium bromide you're using there"—she pointed to a beaker on the counter—"it's a carcinogen."

"Oh, right." O'Brien glanced at his hands, hoping he hadn't spilled any. "It's been a while."

She smiled one last time. "I can tell." Then, without a word, she turned and disappeared out the door.

O'Brien relaxed, thinking again of how much the woman had looked like Beth in their younger days. So attractive. So young and alive. With the thought came the guilt. What did he think he was doing? He had no business flirting with anyone, much less an employee, no matter how beautiful.

Still, with Beth gone . . .

He angrily pushed the thought out of his mind and walked to the gel box. It would take another hour for the bands to migrate and establish their patterns.

"You sure I can't talk you into some wine?" Katherine asked as she crossed to the kitchen counter and poured herself another glass.

"Thanks, but no," Coleman said.

"Come on," she teased, "word has it that even your genetic forerunner tipped a few."

Coleman smiled and shook his head.

As she raised her third glass to her lips, she could see the concern in his eyes. Yet at the same time she knew he wasn't judging her. He never judged her.

The day had been too perfect to end, and she had asked whether he wanted to join her and Eric for dinner. Nothing special, just some leftover chicken reheated in the microwave, a little salad, and anything else she could rummage from the cupboard. Cooking had never been her specialty.

Coleman had gratefully accepted, and the dinner had been as enjoyable as the day. It was late now, but Katherine still didn't want it to end. The more time she spent with this man, the more time she wanted—and the stronger the trembling inside her grew. Whether it was about her son, her life, even her forgotten faith—whatever they talked about, this man seemed to make everything inside her come alive again. And now all she wanted was to do the same. To touch some part of him where no one else had been, someplace deep inside, someplace she could call her own.

She had sent Eric to bed (which probably meant lights off, but computer on) and had spent the past hour and a half in deep conversation with Coleman. They had covered their likes, dislikes, pet peeves, fears, vulnerabilities. Maybe it was the wine, maybe it was Coleman, maybe it was everything, but it had been a long time since she'd been able to talk so openly and so deeply.

Still, there were the secrets. Most of them his.

"There's just no way you'll tell me who that man was, will you?" she said as she crossed to the sofa and sat beside him.

Coleman shook his head. "Somebody from another life."

"More like a ghost, by the expression on your face."

Coleman nodded and rubbed the top of his shoulder.

"You okay?"

"Yeah. It's just Murkoski's little reminder that I should have gone in for my checkup."

"That chemical leash thing?"

Coleman tried to smile. "'Having the flu times ten,' I think is how he put it. When he returns my call, I need to set up another place for the checkups."

"Why?"

"That man we saw today. He could prove a real threat to the experiment."

"But you won't tell me why."

"It's the past, Katherine."

There was her name again. And each time she heard it, it took just a little longer to recover. "And there's no way you will talk about your past?"

He shook his head. "That part of me is dead, that man is no longer alive."

Once again, Katherine felt a mixture of warmth, weakness, and buoyancy. "You're a person of many mysteries, William Michaels—or whatever your name is."

He smiled, then gently turned the tables on her. "What about you? It seems to me you have your own share of mysteries."

"But women are supposed to be mysterious. It makes us more alluring." The phrase came out sexier than she had intended, but that was okay.

He looked at the carpet, almost embarrassed, which made him even more attractive. She changed the subject. "What about your childhood?" she asked. "You said you grew up in Nebraska?"

"Tecumseh."

"Named after some Indian chief."

"That's right. Population 1,702. Not much to say, really. We were dirt poor, lived in a little trailer." He shrugged. "But we managed."

"Your family? Brothers, sisters?"

"I had a dad who beat me, a brother who overdosed on heroin, and a mother who killed herself trying to hold us all together."

Katherine's heart swelled in sympathy. "I'm sorry."

He nodded.

"Is that why . . ." She searched for the phrase. "I mean, you did serve some time in prison, right?"

"That man is dead. He was very evil, very violent, and now he is very, very gone."

"And you're a brand, spanking new creature."

Coleman shrugged, then nodded. "I guess so."

For some reason, another Bible verse came to mind. Katherine had heard it dozens of times as a child, but she had long since forgotten it. Until now. What was it about this man that stirred so many things inside of her?

He saw her expression and asked, "What?"

She shook her head.

"No, tell me."

She looked up to him, then took a breath and quoted: "'Therefore if any man be in Christ, he is a new creature: old things are passed away; behold, all things are become new.'"

Coleman looked surprised. "Is that. . . ?" He motioned toward the coffee table where the Bible she'd given him lay.

"Yeah, it's in there. Though I suppose it has more to do with a person's faith than his DNA structure, wouldn't you?"

Coleman nodded, though it was obvious he was still mulling over the concept. They both sat in silence, thinking. Finally he turned to her. "I know I promised not to ask, but . . ."

She looked to him.

"What about you?" He held her gaze, looking so deep into her that she fought back a shiver. "I get the feeling that you've been through a lot."

A weakness spread through her body, but she didn't want to look away. She tried to swallow, but her mouth was dry. She took another sip of wine. He waited silently, his eyes full of compassion.

Finally she began. At first the story came out matter-of-factly. Her sheltered childhood, her preacher daddy, preacher-wife mommy. Bible college. Meeting the man of her dreams. Married right out of college. The perfect couple, who within a year were adoring their perfect newborn.

And then the tragedies. Anguish and sorrows that no twenty-three-year-old should ever be forced to face.

Gary's shooting. Her pretended strength. The days of ceaseless prayers and their obvious futility. The suffocating love and spiritual formulas from family and church. Her discovery of alcohol and its ability to numb the pain. The bingeing. The bad-girl reputation. Her father's persistent love regardless of the tongue waggers.

But Katherine could go no further. Somewhere, deep inside, the shudders began. Deep sobs from inside that made it impossible to speak. She tried to stop, but couldn't. She hadn't cried like this since her father's death. A moment later she felt his arms about her shoulders. A gentle embrace, an attempt to comfort. She turned and buried her face against his chest. And to her amazement, she felt his own body shuddering. He was also crying, sharing her pain. And if he shared such deep things with her, was it possible that he might share other feelings as well?

For days, she'd been searching almost unconsciously for a sign. But he was always so considerate, so tender, it was impossible to tell how he felt about her. She looked up at him through her tears. Moisture streamed down his own cheeks. It was so touching, so moving. Before she knew it, she had raised her head toward his mouth. He lowered his. Their lips found one another. The kiss was delicately tender, the salt of his tears mixed with hers. The passion grew. She could feel him trembling, struggling to restrain himself. And it was at that moment that she knew he could be trusted, that she could give herself fully to him without reservation and without fear of being hurt. He had touched her innermost being, her very soul, and she had touched his.

Their embrace grew. But as the kiss reached its height of passion, she felt him hesitate. She kissed him harder, encouraging him. But instead of complying, he started to pull away.

"It's okay," she murmured, pressing in, "it's okay—"

"No," he whispered.

She opened her eyes. He gently pulled back and looked at her, searching. "I'm sorry," he whispered hoarsely, "it's—it's not right."

She moved in again, closing her eyes, reaching for his mouth. "Of course it is."

"Katherine."

She looked at him again. The depth of his gaze was unnerving. "This isn't right. Not now. Not for you."

She frowned. Who was he to tell her what was right and wrong?

"I'm sorry." He shook his head.

She pulled back, trying to understand. Hurt and rejection flooded in. "Sure," she said, trying to regain her dignity, "of course." But the anger and humiliation continued to pour into her. Already she could feel herself shutting down, closing off. "I don't know what I was thinking." She pulled back and sat on the couch, straightening her clothes.

"Katherine . . ."

"After all, you're part God now, right? I mean, what would happen if—"

"That's not it." He searched for words.

She took her glass from the coffee table and rose unsteadily to her feet. "No, you're right. Besides, it's late, and we've both got work in the morning."

"Katherine." He rose toward her.

She held up her hand, bringing him to a stop. "I said you're right, this isn't what I want. I don't know what I was thinking."

"I didn't mean to—"

"Listen, maybe you should go. All right?"

He looked at her a long moment. She held his gaze, refusing to back down. She didn't care what he saw inside now. If it was her anger, fine. Her humiliation, so what?

Finally he nodded. He turned and crossed the room to retrieve his coat. "I didn't want—"

"It's not your fault," she said. "I don't know what came over me." She wanted to say more, but the anger and embarrassment kept her from continuing.

"Thank you for dinner, Katherine. I had a terrific day."

"Right, terrific."

"Will you tell Eric—"

"Tell him yourself," she interrupted. "He's still up, working on his computer."

"That would be okay?"

"I just said so, didn't I?" She turned on him. "He deserves at least that much, don't you think? For you to at least say good night to him. He at least deserves that." She wasn't sure what she meant, but she suspected that somehow he'd know.

At last he nodded and walked past her into the hallway.

Katherine stood, still smarting. Then, seeing the dinner dishes piled on the counter, she moved toward them, grateful to find something to do.

A weary O'Brien headed out of the research building of Genodyne Inc. and into the parking lot. The night air helped a little to clear his head, but not enough. He was both relieved and puzzled. The bands from the gel had proven to be exactly the same as the GOD gene. It had not mutated, it had not been changed. It was the identical pattern Murkoski, Wolff, and the team had been using for months. So what was the problem? Why had Wolff called him at home? More importantly, why had he died?

There was one other thought: the mice. What had happened to that one mouse, then to the entire community of six? And why only to them and not the others? And what did this have to do with the gels and Wolff's fate?

O'Brien was so deep in thought that he barely noticed arriving at his BMW. He was practically inside the car before he heard the girl's shouts.

"Excuse me! Excuse me, Dr. O'Brien?"

He turned to see Tisha Youngren approach. She looked as good under the glow of mercury vapors as she had in the lab.

"Ms. Youngren. Is . . . everything okay?"

"Yeah," she said, arriving just a little breathless. "I left my keys in the car."

"Ah . . ."

"Boy, do I feel stupid." She gave a helpless little-girl smile.

"It happens to the best of us."

"I suppose."

He reached for his cellular. "Let me give Security a call. They have one of those flat metal things to jimmy it open."

"Oh, don't bother them."

O'Brien looked up.

She stuck her hands in her coat pockets and boldly held his eyes. "I've got an extra set at home. I just live a mile away, over at Smoky Point. Since it's on your way, I thought maybe you could drop me off."

He looked at her. "Uh, actually it would probably be better just to call Security. I mean, they've got the metal thingie and all."

"Better for who?" There was that smile again.

He stared at her, feeling his face flush slightly.

She tilted her head, waiting for his answer.

For the briefest second he forgot the question. She was so young, so lovely, and it was becoming very apparent what she had in mind.

"Listen, Ms.—uh, Youngren—"

"Tisha," she said, her smile growing more coy.

"Yes, uh, Tisha—"

"It would only take a few minutes." She took a tentative step toward him. Now they were less than two feet apart, plumes of white breath rising above their heads. "And if you wanted, I could fix you something to eat or something. I mean, with you being alone and everything, and it being so late."

More color rose to O'Brien's face. An indefinable rush of excitement spread in his chest. It had been a long time since someone so beautiful had shown such interest. Oh, there were the occasional flirtings, but nothing like this. This girl seemed truly impressed by him. Unlike Beth, who grew more critical each year, this girl seemed so accepting. No put-downs, or reminders of clay feet. Just a beautiful girl, half his age, who seemed to really admire him.

He wondered how she knew he was alone, then realized that she was part of another generation, a smart generation who knew how to go after what they wanted. He was both flattered and cautious. But why the caution? Other execs did this all the time, didn't they? Wasn't this one of the perks of power? The stress, the worry, the anxiety—didn't these call for special benefits? Didn't this come with the territory? No one appreciated the pressure men like him were under, certainly not their wives. And this girl seemed so willing. How many times had he been faithful at the hotels, the conventions, the international meetings—with no one there to pat him on the back for his integrity. And he was so stressed, and she was so lovely, and there was no one at home waiting.

He took a step toward her. The plumes of their breath intermixed. She reached out and touched the lapel of his topcoat. "You won't be disappointed."

He was glad to hear that her voice carried a trace of nervousness. This wasn't something she did every day. She was putting herself on the line, taking a risk, and all for him. Once again he was struck by her deep, jade-green eyes. So inviting. And he was so alone. He reached up to his coat and placed his hands over hers. She moved closer. No one would know. And she was so young and beautiful and she admired him and no one was at home waiting.

She rose up on her toes and they kissed. It grew passionate, full of hunger, a foretaste of what the night could hold. He pulled her closer, drawing her into himself. She surrendered, but at the same time pushed against him, as if trying to turn him. He was too caught up in the moment to notice. She pushed harder until he stumbled, shifting his feet, and turned slightly. It was then that he opened his eyes and saw it.

In the distance, directly ahead. A van.

Tisha pulled back his topcoat, pressing herself into him. O'Brien closed his eyes, trying to lose himself again, but the image of the van would not go away. He reopened his eyes. This time he saw movement inside the van, silhouetted by one of the parking lot lights. Someone was behind the wheel, watching.

Sensing his distraction, Tisha's kisses grew more demanding. He tried to pull from her, but she clung to him. At last his insistence prevailed and they separated.

"What's wrong?" she asked, almost breathless.

He motioned behind her, and she turned to look.

Suddenly the van's engine turned over and its lights blared on. Tisha shielded her eyes from the glare. "What—"

The van's wheels spun, throwing gravel as it lurched forward. It was heading directly for them.

With memories of Wolff fresh in his mind, O'Brien suspected the worst. Perhaps Murkoski was thinking of another way to silence his questions.

He looked around. They could run for it, but the building was too far away and the van was picking up speed.

"Get behind the car," he ordered.

"What?"

"The car! Get behind the car!"

She started to back away from him.

"Tisha!"

The van roared closer.

"Get behind the car!"

She turned and started running.

"Tisha!"

The van accelerated. It was less than fifty yards away when it veered to the right, and O'Brien realized the sickening truth: It was not heading toward him, it was heading toward her!

"No, Tisha!" He started for her.

The van closed in. Twenty yards from the girl. Fifteen.

It kept Tisha in the center of its headlights.

O'Brien was running now, pushing his legs for all they were worth. "Tisha!"

She threw a frightened look over her shoulder. The vehicle bore down.

Five yards.

"TISH—"

Adrenaline pumped through his body. He was flying—but he was too late. The van would hit her long before he arrived.

Ten feet. Five.

Then, just as it was about to strike, the van suddenly swerved to the left. The passenger door flew open and the van slowed its speed to match the girl's. Now she was running parallel, directly beside it. To O'Brien's amazement, she turned and leaped inside, tumbling into the darkness of the open vehicle.

The van accelerated and roared for the exit.

O'Brien slowed to a stop and watched as the vehicle smashed through the security gate, fishtailed a turn, and raced down the perimeter road. He bent over and propped his hands against his knees, gasping for breath, plumes of white vapor rising above him.

And there, alone, bent over in the parking lot, Philip O'Brien realized that Murkoski didn't need to resort to murder. He could find other means of securing people's cooperation.

Coleman headed down the hallway toward Eric's room. He felt terrible. He had humiliated and betrayed Katherine. And he had no idea how to make it right. Maybe he couldn't. That thought made his heart even heavier as he knocked on Eric's door.

"Who is it?" Eric asked. "I'm asleep."

"It's me, can I come in?"

"Sure."

Coleman opened the door and saw the eight-year-old sitting at his desk in the dark, his face bathed by the blue-green glow of a computer screen.

"Hey, Eric."

The boy didn't look up but continued working the keyboard and mouse. "You're not going to sleep with her, are you?" he asked.

Coleman joined him. "How does somebody your age know about that stuff?"

The boy shrugged. "We get cable."

"What are you doing?"

"That guy at the laboratory today?"

"Yeah."

"He said his name was Steiner?"

"Something like that."

Eric clicked his computer mouse twice more and a picture slowly started to scan, from the top of the monitor down.

"It's going to take a little bit of time, since my equipment is like from the Dark Ages. But there's this guy on the Internet, a real nutzoid. Mom doesn't like for me to read anything he writes."

"So, of course, you do."

"All the time. I've been downloading his stuff into my general file folder forever."

The scanning lines had already revealed dark, closely cut hair and a forehead. Now they were defining the slightly crooked bridge of a nose.

"His name is Steiner, too. Anyway, he's always writing these weird letters and sending these pictures telling us not to forget about the man who murdered his daughter."

Eric's voice grew fainter as Coleman watched the monitor. A knot twisted in his stomach as he stared at the emerging eyes.

"And Steiner," Coleman heard himself ask. "He sends this stuff out to everybody on the Net?"

The rest of the nose was forming.

"Nah, just to a few of us."

"Why you, Eric?" His voice was faint now, unsteady. "Why does he send this stuff to you?"

The mouth slowly appeared, followed by the chin. Next, two words in block letters began to form at the bottom of the screen.

"That's easy." Eric answered, his voice was coming from another world.

"Why, Eric?"

" 'Cause the man who killed his daughter killed my dad."

The picture of executed killer Michael Coleman was now complete. And directly below it, in large printed letters, were two words:

NEVER FORGET

CHAPTER 11

Coleman closed Eric's door and somehow made it down the hall. The walls blurred as he stared at the threadbare carpet passing under his feet. He was the one responsible. For their struggles, their pain. He was the one.

He passed the kitchen and heard Katherine scraping the dinner plates. She was eight feet away, but he didn't look up, didn't speak. He had to get out.

He reached the front door and opened it. The knob was tarnished, loose, and like everything else in this impoverished apartment, ready to fall apart. And he was the reason they were here.

Everything would have been different. Katherine would be back in Council Bluffs, in a real home. She'd be a different person, full of the tenderness and innocence he had been able to see inside her. She'd be in her kitchen loading her dishwasher, preparing to join her husband on the sofa to watch TV, or maybe talk about their dreams, their kids, how to swing payments on that new minivan.

But thanks to him, she had no future. Thanks to him she had no life.

He closed the door, headed down the hall, and took the elevator to the lobby.

He had stepped out and was headed toward the main door when, not eighteen inches from his head, he heard the distinctive click of a revolver's hammer being cocked. He froze. Had he been more alert, he might have seen the shadow that had approached from behind.

"Good evening, Mr. Coleman."

He didn't have to turn to know it was Steiner holding the gun. The voice quivered, trying to control its fear and rage. For the first time in months, Coleman felt a trace of anger. Didn't this twit know how easily he could remove the gun from his hands, how he could break his fingers, or just as easily break his neck? The thought startled Coleman almost as much as Steiner's presence.

"I don't know what happened or what's going on," the voice was saying, "but I think it's time the two of us had a good long talk."

Coleman nodded, his anger turning to empathy over the man's fear and confusion. "You're right, there's a lot we need to talk about."

He could sense Steiner wavering a moment, unsure what to do. He took the opportunity to slowly turn and face him. Steiner was blinking hard, as the gun, which trembled slightly in his hands, remained leveled in Coleman's face.

Coleman kept his gaze fixed on the man's eyes and spoke quietly and calmly. "It would be better for both of us if you took a couple steps backward and loosened your grip on the gun a little."

Steiner dug in, bracing himself, refusing to budge.

"That way it won't accidentally go off in your hand. But if I tried to jump you, you'd still have time to shoot."

Steiner remained unmoving.

Coleman understood. The man was so frightened and full of emotion that he could barely hear what was being said, let alone act on it.

"Do you want me to go with you somewhere?" Coleman asked. "Is that what you have in mind?"

For a second Steiner appeared lost. Then, summoning up all of his concentration, he answered. "Yes, that is exactly what I want."

Coleman continued looking into him. The man was completely out of his element, functioning on raw fear and hate. That's all that drove him, pushing him to do things he normally wouldn't, or couldn't, do. But that mixture was a dangerous combination, and Coleman had to try to keep him calm. "Where would you like to go?"

"Outside." Steiner shoved the gun closer to his face. Coleman nodded, then turned and moved through the deserted lobby. Steiner followed directly behind and to the right, never letting the gun drift more than a few inches from the back of Coleman's head.

They passed the mailboxes on the wall and arrived at the glass door. Coleman started to push it open when Steiner suddenly ordered, "Stop."

Coleman obeyed.

Steiner motioned across the street, over to two men who sat inside a gray Audi, drinking coffee. He swore. "They've been following me ever since I left Genodyne." He grabbed Coleman by the jacket and pulled him back out of sight before they were spotted. "Looks like we're staying here for a while," he said. "Let's go pay that lady friend of yours a call."

The words sounded tough, but Coleman knew the man was terrified. He turned. "Listen, I don't think—"

Steiner shoved him forward and took several steps back. "Move!"

Now, even if he wanted to, Coleman could not disarm him. He was too far away. The man was a fast learner.

Reluctantly, Coleman obeyed.

"Hello?"

"Hi, Connie, this is Dr. O'Brien."

"Dr. O'Brien?" The voice grew clearer.

"I'm sorry to be calling so late."

"No, it's okay, I, uh . . ." There was a pause. O'Brien could imagine her turning on her light, trying to force the grogginess from her mind. "I really haven't been able to sleep that much anyway."

"I understand. Wolff was a good man. He's going to be missed by all of us." It was O'Brien's turn to pause. He picked at the rubber molding around what had once been Wolff's desk. He stared at the empty corkboard, the vacant shelves. After the incident in the parking lot, he'd known that he wouldn't be able to get any sleep, so he had gone back. Now he was in Wolff's office.

"Listen, uh—" He cleared his throat. "Wolff's personal belongings, his notes and so forth . . ."

"Yeah, they're all here. They couldn't find any next of kin, so they figured I'm like the closest."

O'Brien had guessed as much. Although Wolff had pretended to be a free agent, it had been obvious since last year's company picnic that he and Connie were becoming an item. Company policy scowled at such relationships, but what are you going to do? It was love. Besides, she was all the way over in accounting.

"Did they give you his lab book?" he asked.

"Yeah, it's right over here on the dresser."

"Connie, I know my timing stinks, but I wouldn't be calling if it weren't important."

"Is there something you want from it?"

O'Brien sighed gratefully. She was making it easier for him than he had hoped. "Yes. His last few entries."

He heard her moving, getting up. "Hang on. Here we go." Pages were flipping. "That's weird."

"What's that?"

"The last page. He ripped out the last page."

"Are you certain?"

"Yeah. Looks like he was in a hurry."

"How can you tell?"

"It's not in his usual, neat-freak style. It was just torn out any ol' way. In fact . . . oh, that explains it."

"Explains what?"

"Here it is."

"Here what is? What are you doing, Connie?"

"They found a piece of paper stuffed in his pants pocket."

"And?"

"Well, I've got it right here, and it looks like the piece he ripped out of the notebook. Now, why would he do that?"

O'Brien's heart began to race. "What's it say, Connie—what did he write on it?"

"Nothing. It's completely empty. There's nothing—well, except up here at the top."

"What's it say, Connie?"

"It's just some name with a Roman numeral after it."

"Some name?"

"Yeah. *Hind. Hind*III."

O'Brien stopped breathing. *Hind*III was another restriction enzyme—another chemical used to cut and identify genes. Whatever Wolff had discovered, he had discovered by running the gel with the *Hind*III enzyme instead of the *Eco*RI that they had been using since the GOD gene's discovery.

He glanced at his watch. 2:18 A.M. It looked like it was time to run a few more gels.

"You're not telling me anything new," Katherine growled. She was outraged, and had a right to be. Busting into her apartment and holding a gun on Coleman and herself was not a way to win her cooperation. "I know he's got a past," she continued, "I know he's served time. But people change. Can't you see that? He's not the same man who—"

"Men like him don't change!" Steiner brandished the gun toward Coleman, whom he had ordered to sit on the sofa. Earlier, Eric had stumbled down the hall to check out the commotion and had been immediately sent back to his room with orders not to come out. That had been fifteen minutes ago. Now Katherine and Steiner hovered over Coleman, who remained strangely quiet. She thought it odd that since they had entered her apartment, he had not looked at her. Not once.

"Of *course* they can change," she insisted. "Old things can pass away, all things can become new." It was obvious that Steiner didn't understand the reference, so she continued. "This man, he's the kindest, most sensitive person I've ever—"

"You don't know what he's done!"

"I don't *care* what he's done!" she yelled back. Then, regaining control, she tried again. "Look, I don't know how he hurt you, or how he may have wronged you. But you have to understand, he's changed. He's not the same man. Where's your sense of mercy, your compassion?"

"Mercy?"

"Yeah."

"Compassion? You want compassion? This man is a murderer!"

Katherine blinked. She showed no other emotion, but inside she felt as if someone had smashed a baseball bat into her gut. She took half a step back and found an armchair to lean against. Her eyes darted from Coleman to Steiner, then back to Coleman. "That's not true."

Neither man answered.

She repeated her statement, but this time it was a demand: "That's not true!"

Coleman stared at his hands.

She waited, forever.

Then, ever so slowly, he began to nod. "Yeah." His voice was a raspy whisper. "I, uh," he coughed, then with obvious effort forced out the words, "I killed his daughter."

Katherine closed her eyes. She eased herself down into the armchair.

"And who else?" Steiner's voice quivered with rage and triumph. "Tell her who else you've killed!"

Coleman continued to look down. He took a deep breath then shook his head. "I don't know."

"Oh, really? Let's see if I can help. There was that prostitute in Des Moines . . ."

Coleman kept his head down.

"The convenience store clerk in Council Bluffs."

Katherine stiffened. "Council Bluffs? You killed somebody in Council Bluffs?"

Steiner answered for him. "Of course, none of these can be proven."

Coleman stared at the floor, unmoving.

"Then there was the cop."

"You shot a cop?" Suddenly Katherine's head felt very, very light, as if it were trying to float off her body. "When? When did you shoot a cop?"

Coleman gave no answer.

Now she was on her feet, unthinkable suspicions rising. "Was he a patrolman? Did you shoot a patrolman?"

At last Coleman looked up. His cheeks were wet with tears. "Yes," he croaked. "I . . . think so."

"What's your name?" Blood surged through her body. She was floating high above the scene, somewhere else. "Who are you?"

Coleman held her eyes, confronting her glare. "My name is Coleman. Michael Coleman."

Katherine's head exploded. She barely heard the rest.

"I murdered Mr. Steiner's daughter. I may have murdered your husband, too. I . . ." His eyes faltered. "I don't remember."

"You don't remember?"

He didn't respond.

She moved toward him. "You don't remember!"

He shook his head and looked down. That's when she attacked him. She leaped at him, arms flying, hitting him with everything she had, venting her fury, pounding on his chest, his shoulders, his arms.

"You destroy my life, and you don't even have the decency to *remember?*"

Coleman made no move to protect himself as she flailed and swore, calling him every name she could think of, hitting him so hard her hands were bruising.

It was Steiner who finally pulled her off. "Stop it. That's enough. That's enough, now. Stop it!"

She managed to land several more blows before her anger spent itself into exhaustion and Steiner was able to drag her off and back to the armchair. She was crying now, gut-wrenching sobs. But even then, over the tears, she could hear Steiner's gloating words:

"So much for mercy and compassion."

O'Brien placed the new gel under the UV light so that he could study its bands. He had run it several times, thinking he'd made a mistake. After all, it had been a long time since he'd worked in the lab like this. He'd even cut the gene with enzymes that were different from Wolff's suggested *Hind*III.

But the mistake was not at his end. Something else was wrong. The bands were entirely different. And yet, as he studied them, as he compared their lengths and added them together, he found them to be exactly the same gene.

What he had before him was the GOD gene, and yet, somehow, it wasn't. A cold dread took residence somewhere deep in his chest.

He photographed each gel with the overhead black-and-white Polaroid, then gathered the pictures and headed back to the offices.

The dread grew stronger as he studied the conflicting patterns, and as he remembered the mice . . .

He could understand the effects of the experiment breaking down and wearing off. With all of the unknowns they had to deal with, it was possible—in fact, quite common—for some unforeseen element to arise, causing the tests to fail and allowing the mice to revert back to their old behavior. But these mice had not reverted. They had attacked and murdered each other. That was not old behavior. That was totally new. Lab mice wouldn't attack and destroy each other, not like that.

Not only was it new behavior, but—and this is what terrified him the most—it was exactly the opposite behavior of what the GOD gene produced. Instead of a compassionate community working together, those animals had completely obliterated themselves.

An unspeakable suspicion had now risen to the surface of O'Brien's mind. He had been trying to push it aside, but now he knew he must pursue it.

He arrived outside Murkoski's office. The locked door was made of quality oak. Fortunately, the quality of the vertical window running along the side of the door wasn't nearly as high. Still, it took three attempts with the receptionist's chair before he managed to break out the glass. Then there was the matter of reaching through the gaping hole and around to the door handle. He succeeded, but not without sustaining a sizable gash in his left forearm from one of the remaining shards of glass.

He decided not to turn on the lights; instead, he used the glow from the large saltwater aquarium against the wall to help him find the computer. He slipped behind the screen, turned it on, and breathed a silent prayer that Murkoski's arrogance and impatience had led him to forego using a password.

His prayer was answered.

Now came the painstaking process of going through file after file after file. It was the only way. If Murkoski was working a different pattern, he would have it recorded somewhere.

But O'Brien got lucky. The files were listed alphabetically, and he only had to go as far as the "D's" to find it. It was under "Diable.gne."

When he brought the file to the screen and studied the patterns, he could only close his eyes and sink into the chair. Now there was no doubt. O'Brien's worst fears had become reality.

"This is too strange," Steiner said. He was pacing in front of the sofa where Coleman sat. Katherine remained in the armchair. Several minutes had passed since she had attacked Coleman, but neither had completely recovered.

Steiner continued to think out loud. "Of all the people to put together, why you two? Why team up a convicted killer with his victim's own wife? It doesn't make sense. Surely they knew you two would eventually find out."

"Unless ..." Katherine spoke slowly, her voice dull and lifeless. "Unless that's what they wanted."

"For you to find out?"

She nodded.

"But why?"

No one had an answer.

"And this Dr. Murkoski." He turned to Coleman. "You said he was bragging about all of his big-time government connections?"

Coleman nodded. "Wore them like a badge."

Steiner shook his head. "If this was the federal government, they wouldn't mess with a state prison like Nebraska. They'd go directly to a federal pen. Someplace like Leavenworth. Fewer people, fewer chances of leaks. I'm not saying officials weren't involved, but there's more power being wielded here than the government's. Two people have been killed, maybe more."

Coleman looked up. "More people have been killed?"

Steiner glanced to him, then almost seemed to revel in providing the information. "The county coroner and a doctor from the prison were killed. Both to protect you."

A numbness crawled through Coleman.

"There's no short-circuiting justice. Someone always has to pay. In this case, it was two lives for one."

The numbness spread into Coleman's mind. How much more pain was he responsible for? How much more destruction?

"You said there's more power here than the government's?" Katherine asked.

Steiner nodded.

"What could be more powerful than the federal government?"

Steiner looked at her. "Greed, of course. There's money involved here, Mrs. Lyon. Lots of it."

"But whose? And what type of sadist would throw the two of us together?"

The sudden knock at the front door startled them.

Katherine was the first to speak. "Is that the guys out front?" she whispered.

Neither man answered.

More knocking. Harder.

Steiner motioned her to her feet with the gun. She obeyed. Coleman also started to rise, but Steiner ordered, "You stay put."

Reluctantly, Coleman obliged and watched as they crossed to the door.

"Find out who it is," Steiner whispered. "Tell them to go away."

More knocking.

"All right, all right," Katherine called. "It's four in the morning, who is it?"

"Sorry to disturb you, Ma'am." The voice from the other side sounded young. "FBI. We have an urgent matter we need to discuss with you."

All three exchanged glances. Steiner whispered, "Ask to see their ID."

Katherine nodded, shoving her face toward the peep hole. "You guys got badges?"

Despite Steiner's orders, Coleman rose to his feet and cautiously approached. Steiner was getting nervous with the gun again, and Coleman didn't want him doing anything stupid with Katherine so close.

"What do you see?" Steiner whispered.

"They look real to me," Katherine answered.

He turned, anxiously searching the room. "Do you have a back door, another exit?"

"Just the bedroom windows."

Steiner looked down the hall nervously, then pointed the gun at Coleman. "You come with me."

Coleman shook his head. "We're on the third story."

Beads of perspiration appeared on Steiner's forehead.

Coleman stood quietly, watching. He was beginning to experience the familiar sharpening of his senses, the focusing of vision.

More knocking. "Mrs. Lyon?"

Steiner was in a panic. "What do we do? What do we—"

"Open it," Coleman ordered as he stepped forward.

"What?"

Katherine looked up at him.

"It's okay," he said. "There's no place we can go. Open it."

Katherine turned to Steiner, who was wiping the sweat from his forehead. He glanced at them both, then took a step behind the door. He cocked his pistol and nodded. With Coleman at her side, Katherine unbolted the lock and swung the door open.

Two men stood before them. A pretty twentysomething on the left, a pudgier man in his forties on the right.

"Mrs. Lyon?" Twentysomething asked.

"Yes."

"I'm Special Agent Briner, this is Agent Irving." Without giving her time to answer, he looked to Coleman. "And you must be William Michaels or"—he almost smiled—"should I say, Michael Coleman."

Coleman gave no answer. He was too busy looking into the boy's eyes, evaluating his clothes, the posturing of his body—and all the time, his senses continued to focus and tighten.

"May we come in?"

"What's this about?" Katherine asked.

"I think it would be better if we came inside."

"What's this about?" she repeated, holding her ground.

Finally, Pudgy Man spoke. "We have reason to believe that a Mr. Harold Steiner is in the area and that he may be planning to jeopardize the—"

Coleman lunged at the youngest first, throwing the bulk of his left shoulder into the boy's chest, while sweeping out his right hand and breaking Pudgy Man's nose with his fist. The boy staggered and fell under Coleman's weight, and his partner was too busy grabbing his nose to be of much assistance.

Coleman had taken Twentysomething's head into his hands, and it was only Katherine's scream that prevented him from breaking the kid's neck. He settled for hitting him squarely in the face and knocking him unconscious.

By now Pudgy Man was fumbling for his gun. Coleman sprang up and delivered a single punch to the man's stomach and one to the jaw, dropping him to the floor to join his partner.

The flurry had ended as quickly at it had begun. Except for Coleman's heavy breathing, silence filled the hallway. He stood over his handiwork just outside the apartment door, stunned, trying to understand what had happened. The old exhilaration, the thrill, had momentarily surfaced. It had come and gone in seconds, but it left Coleman deeply shaken.

"What did you do that for?" Katherine demanded.

Coleman looked up, trying to get his bearings.

Steiner stepped out from behind the door and gasped. "What did you do?"

"They're not FBI," Coleman said.

"How can you be sure?" Katherine asked.

"Look at their suits. Feds can't afford quality like that."

Katherine and Steiner continued to stare.

Coleman knelt next to the older man and pulled aside the suit coat to reveal a holstered, shiny new .40 caliber Smith and Wesson. He removed the gun, pocketed the clip, and tossed the piece into the apartment.

"Why . . ." Steiner asked, his voice unsteady. "What were they after?"

Katherine shook her head. "I don't think *what* is the right question."

Steiner began to tremble more noticeably. "But—why? What did I do?"

Coleman pulled back Twentysomething's coat. Same holster, but a Colt Mustang .380. "You said they already killed two people?"

Steiner nodded as Coleman removed the gun and popped out the magazine. He checked the other pocket and pulled out a small, round silencer.

"Looks like they wanted to make it three."

Steiner leaned against the door frame to steady himself.

"You going to be okay?" Katherine asked.

He nodded, but it was obviously a lie.

Coleman remained standing over the bodies, still haunted by his actions. Finally he turned to Katherine. "Do you have any antiseptic? Some cloths and cold water?"

She looked up at him, not entirely hearing.

"Katherine?"

Coming to, she nodded. "Yeah, sure." She headed back into the apartment.

Coleman knelt to inspect Pudgy Man while addressing Steiner. "Give me a hand with these two. Let's get them into the apartment where we can—"

He heard the click of the revolver and looked up to see Steiner raising his gun at him.

"What are you doing?" Coleman asked, more irritated than concerned.

"I think we'll let the police handle it from here."

"You're not serious."

"Mrs. Lyon," Steiner called to Katherine, who was inside the apartment at the kitchen sink. "Please call 911. Tell them we have two injured men here and an escaped convict."

"What?"

"You heard me."

As Coleman rose, Steiner backed up several steps to keep a safe distance.

"The man just saved your life," Katherine said.

"And for that I am grateful. But he's still a convicted killer, and I think it's about time we—"

"Steiner, be reasonable," Coleman said.

"Oh, I'm very reasonable, Mr. Coleman."

"Do you honestly think that the police are going to stop guys like this? These guys make a living by—"

"If you'll toss that gun in here with the other and step inside, please. And Mrs. Lyon, will you please make that call?"

"Come on, Steiner," she protested.

Coleman looked at the clip in his hand. He felt its weight, its smooth, hard corners. He ran his thumb over the top cartridge, the next one to be thrust into the firing chamber. Its nickel casing was cool to the touch, the copper coating over the bullet smooth and sleek. Only the nose had texture. It was a hollow point, its tip serrated into a six-pointed star designed to flatten upon impact, destroying as much flesh and bone as possible. So much power here. So much potential. In its own way, its ability to destroy was as awesomely beautiful as any morning mist, or setting sun.

Coleman knew it would be risky, but he could shove the clip into the gun and fire a round or two into Steiner. Of course, he might take a couple of hits himself, but considering Steiner's fear and his inexperience with guns, the odds were in Coleman's favor.

"Drop the gun, Mr. Coleman." The voice was high and quivering.

Coleman looked up and was surprised to see something he had never seen before. In the man's eyes was more than the usual fear and questioning. There was something harder, colder. Something was consuming him, controlling him. Here was a man lost and empty, yet at the same time utterly consumed. The helplessness touched Coleman. He wanted to reach out, to somehow comfort the man. He glanced back at his gun. A hastily fired round into Steiner's body would neither kill what consumed him, nor fill his emptiness.

"I'm not telling you again. Drop the gun."

Coleman slowly lowered the gun and tossed it into the living room.

"Now step inside. And Mrs. Lyon, if you don't make that phone call, I will."

Coleman stepped into the apartment as Katherine began to dial. "I can't believe you're doing this," she said angrily.

"Believe it, Mrs. Lyon. The Law is the Law. And in the end, justice will prevail."

"And justice, that's all that matters?" Coleman asked.

"Justice is all that we have."

"Uh-oh."

The men turned to see Katherine, receiver in hand, looking out the living-room window.

"What's the problem?" Steiner demanded.

Katherine motioned toward the street. "Looks like we've got more company."

CHAPTER 12

It was Lisa, the downstairs neighbor, who helped Coleman and Steiner escape. After some hasty explanations from Katherine—plus the additional motivation of Steiner's waving gun—she escorted the two men to her back bedroom window, where they climbed out and dropped the ten feet to the pavement.

There was no need for Katherine to come too. No one was after her. But to be safe, she grabbed Eric, had him throw on his all-purpose, purple-and-gold University of Washington sweatshirt, left some cold cloths for the men in her hallway, and asked Lisa if she and her son could hang out at her place for the rest of the evening. There was no telling what those men would do once they regained consciousness—or what the new arrivals Katherine had seen waiting outside had in mind.

"No problem," a wide-eyed Lisa had answered. "But if this is how you've adjusted to the dating scene, we've got some serious talking to do."

It was 4:15 in the morning. Outside, a heavy drizzle fell as Coleman and Steiner quickly crossed the street behind the building, Coleman in front, Steiner behind him with the gun.

When they reached Steiner's rental, a white Taurus, Steiner tossed Coleman the keys. "You drive."

"I don't think that's such a good idea. It's been a while."

Steiner referred to his gun. "I can't drive and hold this, too."

"Then let me take it. You drive and I'll hold the gun."

Steiner gave him a look. "Get in."

Coleman had barely turned over the ignition when the first shot shattered the right rear window. Both men ducked. When they rose and turned they saw a tall man just rounding the building and racing toward them. His hair was long and blonde. He wore a gray topcoat and was re-aiming his .357.

"Get us out of here!" Steiner shouted.

Coleman tromped on the gas. Unfortunately, he'd dropped it into the wrong gear. They shot backwards into a jarring, glass-shattering crash, devastating the front end of someone's new Blazer.

Another shot. The gunman was good; he hit Steiner's window, missing his head by mere inches.

"Let's go! Let's go!"

Coleman shifted, punched the accelerator, and they spun out as a third round hit somewhere to the rear of Steiner's door.

Coleman glanced into the mirror. Headlights zipped around the corner, momentarily slowing for the blonde man to climb in. "Where to?" Coleman shouted.

"The police."

Coleman threw him a look. "You never give up, do you?" The lights in the mirror picked up speed, and Coleman accelerated. "The police can't offer the protection you need—not from these guys."

"What do you care?" Steiner said, looking out the back. "They want me, not you."

Suddenly the rear window shattered into a million fragments.

"I don't think they're too concerned about making that distinction right now," Coleman yelled. He turned to Steiner, whose eyes suddenly widened in fear.

"Look out!"

Coleman looked back just in time to see a street sweeper filling his vision. He cranked the wheel hard to the left, then straightened it out. But the inertia and the slick street threw them into a skid.

"What are you doing!" Steiner shouted.

"I told you—I'm a little rusty!"

He managed to pull it out of the skid as another bullet sparked off the left fender. Coleman checked the mirror. Through the shattered glass he could see the headlights closing in.

"There!" Steiner pointed.

"What?"

"The freeway entrance. Right there!"

By the time Coleman saw the ramp they were almost past it. He pulled the wheel to the right. Again the car slid into a skid, this time taking out a road sign before bouncing up the landscaped incline and finally making it onto the ramp. Steiner was still shouting as Coleman accelerated and headed for the freeway.

Katherine had collapsed onto Lisa's sofa. She was past exhaustion. So many emotions raged inside her: hate, love, betrayal, worry, fear. She wanted to scream, to shout, to beat the wall, but she was too numb to even cry.

She feared for Coleman's life, yet she hated him with such fury and such a sense of betrayal that her head pounded in anger. This was the man who had killed her Gary, who had destroyed everything. There was no forgiving such a monster.

But that monster had died months ago. *Old things are passed away.* The monster was gone, and in its place was a man who had reached in and touched her heart, who was so kind and sweet and caring that he had refused to have sex with her because it was not the right thing—for her. She trembled with both weakness and rage. She had never seen such sensitivity, such innocence—

NO!

He is not innocent. He is a murderer! The murderer of my husband.

All things are become new.

NO! He is a killer. The killer of everything I had, of everything I was!

The thoughts warred inside her head, back and forth, until finally, with what little strength she had left, she took hold of the door he had opened inside of her and with the greatest effort forced it closed. It slammed with such power that she could feel the reverberation deep into her soul. She had made a mistake. She had started to feel. She had let someone inside. She would not allow that again. Never. Now everything would return to its place, just as it had been, just as it should be. Everything but the tears, which had finally started and which she could not stop.

"Mom?"

She looked up to see Eric's worried face hovering over her. Lisa had tried putting him to bed, but he was up and kneeling over her. "It's okay, Mom." She felt his arms around her shoulders, clumsily patting her, trying to comfort. "We'll find a way to help him."

The tears came faster. Not only had the monster opened her up and touched her heart, he had touched her son as well. "It's okay," he repeated. "Honest. We'll get him back, I promise."

She reached out and drew him to her. But instead of protesting as he usually did, Eric allowed himself to be pulled into the embrace.

Suddenly, the door exploded.

Katherine screamed and leaped up just as Twentysomething and Pudgy Man raced into the room.

They had turned off the Mukilteo Freeway and were heading north on Interstate 5.

"How fast are we going?"

Coleman glanced at the speedometer. "A little over ninety."

Steiner scanned the roadway. "Where's a good cop when you need one?"

Coleman glanced into the mirror. Their pursuers had initially missed the on-ramp. That had put them about thirty seconds behind. But in the distance he could see their lights slowly gaining. Coleman had the accelerator pegged to the floor, but minute by minute the other car was closing the gap.

"Maybe there's some other way to beat these guys," he suggested.

"You'd like that, wouldn't you?" Steiner said. "Take the Law into your own hands. Maybe kill a few extra people along the way."

Coleman fought back the irritation. "People change."

"The Law doesn't."

"You keep saying that, but what about mercy? What about forgiveness?"

"Aberrations. A human invention."

Coleman nearly laughed. "You're not serious?"

"I'm not? Ask yourself, what holds the universe together?"

"You tell me."

"Laws. The laws of physics, the law of gravity, of thermodynamics—all these laws are what hold the stars, the planets, even the atoms in place. Without these laws, everything would fly apart and turn to chaos."

"But we're not planets, we're human beings."

"And that makes us exempt?"

Coleman had no answer.

"Civilization must have rules. If you break a law anywhere else in the universe, you pay the consequences. You jump off a building, you fall. You split an atom, you vaporize."

"You kill a man, you die."

"Exactly. Cause and effect. Since the beginning of time, the equation has been the same. If you break that equation, and do not seek justice, a part of our civilization unravels, exactly as the universe would."

"But *people change.* There has to be forgiveness. There has to be some compassion."

"The Law is the Law."

Coleman glanced in the mirror. The car was two hundred yards away. "I don't want to be petty here, but didn't I just save your rear back at the apartment? Doesn't that count for something in your 'cosmic equation'?"

"Not my decision to make. That's why we have authorities."

"Listen—we have to do something. They'll be here any second."

Steiner looked over his shoulder, then turned forward to search the freeway. An approaching sign read: BROADWAY 1/2 MILE. "There." He pointed. "Take that."

But Coleman had other plans. About a hundred yards ahead he spotted an old plumbing van ambling down the third lane from the median. Instead of pulling to the right and heading for the exit, Coleman crossed to the far left lane.

"What are you doing?"

Coleman gave no answer but began to decelerate.

"What are you doing?" Steiner demanded.

A second later the car was on their tail.

"Coleman!" Steiner shouted. "Turn to the right! Take the exit. Take the exit!"

Before Coleman could respond, the other car swerved to their right and pulled up beside them. He glanced at the speedometer. They were doing seventy-five. He looked over to the car. The driver was motioning for them to slow down and pull over. On the passenger side, the blonde was emphasizing the point with his leveled gun.

The plumbing van was twenty-five yards ahead and two lanes over.

"Get us out of here!" Steiner demanded. "Now!"

"Hang on," Coleman warned.

Steiner barely had time to brace himself before Coleman swung the car hard to the right and slammed into the other vehicle.

The startled driver swerved into the next lane.

"What are you doing?" Steiner shouted.

There was no time to answer as Coleman hit the brakes and they lurched forward. In the other car, the driver and the blonde snapped their heads back, watching Coleman's car in bewilderment as they raced past. But that was only their first surprise. The second came an instant later when they slammed into the back of the plumbing van.

Coleman swerved sharply, making a beeline for the exit. He had gained some time, but not a lot. They sped down the Broadway off-ramp, made a hard left, scooted up a few streets, then made another right. It was a major thoroughfare but completely deserted this time of morning. Malls and stores sped past, slightly obscured by a fog that increased as they approached the river.

Cresting a small hill, Coleman and Steiner saw the flashing lights at the same time.

"What is it?"

"A drawbridge."

Steiner swore, then spotted a side street, off to the left. "There, take that!"

Coleman turned the wheel, but this time his luck did not prevail. They skidded through the slick intersection until their wheels broadsided the traffic island on the other end and the car flipped. Coleman flew hard into Steiner and the passenger door, then slammed up into the roof. The sound of twisting, screeching metal filled his ears as glass exploded, pelting him from all sides. The car's roll flung Coleman down into the steering wheel and dash, then back onto the roof again. There was no pain, the pain would come later, only crazy, out-of-control tumbling amid flying glass and crushing steel.

And then it stopped, as suddenly as it had begun.

Everything was deathly silent. Only the ringing of the drawbridge bell sixty feet away cut through the stillness.

Coleman opened his eyes. He lay on the roof. The car rested upside down. No fire, no explosions. Just the bridge's ringing bell and its flashing red lights.

He tried to move. Pain shot through his left arm. He heard a groan from the other side of the car and twisted to look. In the flashing light he could see Steiner, his face bloodied and his leg crushed by a large piece of metal.

"Steiner? Steiner!"

The man's eyes opened.

"We've got to get out of here."

Steiner tried to answer, but it came out a gurgle. He coughed, then spat a mouthful of blood.

Coleman pushed at his driver-side door. With a little coaxing, it creaked open. He reached across the car to Steiner and grabbed him around the chest. As he began to pull, Steiner cried out in pain. The crumpled metal kept his leg pinned. Coleman tried again, harder, but Steiner could not be budged.

Steiner coughed, spattering blood. "It's no use."

Coleman raised his feet toward Steiner's door and began kicking the metal.

"Leave," Steiner gurgled. "It's what you—" He coughed violently. "It's what you want." He managed to glare in Coleman's direction. "Go ahead, leave me."

The accusation angered Coleman, and he used the emotion to kick the door harder—five, six, seven times—until the metal finally started to bend. After another half-dozen kicks, there was enough room to pull Steiner free. Coleman grabbed him around the ribs again and pulled him across the inside of the roof until they reached his open door. Then, with one final heave, they both tumbled out and onto the pavement.

Coleman lay a second, catching his breath. The bell continued to ring. The light continued to flash. He rose to a sitting position and looked behind them for the pursuing car.

Nothing yet.

He heard a scraping of gravel and turned to see Steiner trying to reach back into the car. For a moment he was confused, then he saw the reason. The gun. It lay just inside, on the roof.

Coleman staggered to his feet and easily cut Steiner off. He reached into the car and scooped up the weapon. He was surprised at how pleasant its weight felt in his hands. It was good to experience that type of power again. And with that power came the anger. It bubbled up from somewhere deep inside. How dare this twisted little man threaten him. How dare he come back and ruin his new life.

Coleman turned toward him. The look of fear he saw in Steiner's eyes said the man knew exactly what Coleman was thinking. The expression made Coleman grin. "What's the matter?" he asked. "Afraid of a little justice?"

Steiner tried to answer but couldn't find his voice. That was fine with Coleman. He'd heard enough of Steiner's lectures, endured enough of his abuse. Now it was payback time. His heart pounded; exhilaration spread through his body. It was just like old times, and it felt good. Very, very good. He raised the revolver until it pointed directly at Steiner's forehead.

But instead of horror, Steiner's expression shifted to contempt. "Go ahead," he coughed. "We both know it's—" More coughing. ". . . this is who you are. Go ahead. Go ahead!"

Happy to oblige, Coleman pulled back the hammer. His senses sharpened. He could no longer hear the ringing of the drawbridge bell nor see its flashing light. Now there was only Steiner and his ragged breathing.

The man went into another coughing fit and Coleman waited patiently. He wanted to make sure he had the man's undivided attention before blowing him away.

Steiner finished, then glared back up at him. "Go ahead," he coughed. "What are you waiting for?"

Coleman wasn't sure. The rage inside him was beginning to waver. It was losing its strength, no longer supplying him with its power. And the longer he looked into Steiner's eyes, the weaker it became.

"Go ahead," Steiner taunted. "It's what you want! Go ahead!"

Coleman's hand began to tremble—not with fear, but with indecision. It was as if compassion was somehow fighting for control, struggling to resurface.

"Shoot me!" Steiner demanded. "Shoot me!"

Now, once again, Coleman was seeing into the man's heart. Understanding the terrible, searching loneliness. The consuming, controlling rage. But there was something else. Like the moon rising in the cedars, the snow glistening in the prison yard, or the distant wail of the freight train, there was something of beauty in this man, something of value. Despite his ugliness, he, too, bore the fingerprint of creation. Something of eternity dwelt in him, something of eternity searching for the eternal.

"Kill me! Kill me!"

Coleman slowly lowered the gun.

Steiner swore. "You're a coward. A coward!"

Coleman released the hammer, uncocking the pistol. He gave an involuntary shudder at what had nearly taken place, then threw the weapon as far into the bushes as he could. He reached down and pulled the shocked Steiner to his feet. "Come on," he ordered. "Let's go."

"Where is he?" Twentysomething shouted.

"I don't—"

"MOM!"

Katherine lunged for Eric, but Pudgy Man was already pulling him away.

"Let him go!" She was on her feet, leaping at him. "Let him—"

Pudgy Man caught her and threw her back onto the sofa with such force that it knocked the wind out of her.

Lisa stormed out of her bedroom, looking as angry as she was frightened. "Who are—what—"

Twentysomething dropped her with a brutal slam of his fist into her temple.

"Lisa!"

"Where are they?" Pudgy Man demanded.

"I don't know!"

"Mom!"

He threw Eric over to Twentysomething and turned on Katherine. "Where did they go!"

"I don't know! They didn't say!"

He grabbed a handful of hair on both sides of her head and pulled her to her feet. She wanted to claw out his eyes, to snap his knee with her foot. But he knew the moves before she could make them.

"Mom!"

"Shut up!" Twentysomething shouted.

Now Pudgy Man held her face directly in front of his, spittle flying. "I'm asking you one last time!"

"I don't know!" she screamed, "I don't know, I don't—"

Again she was flying across the room. This time into the wall. Her head hit hard. She slumped to the floor, trying to hang on to consciousness.

"Mom ..." Eric's voice grew faint. "Mom ..." She thought he might come to her, but he didn't. She hoped he would understand why she couldn't come to him.

The men were talking, but far away, from another planet.

"... Mom ..."

She tried to move, but her body wouldn't obey.

Now a face was talking at her. Pudgy Man. "... if you cooperate. Keep your mouth shut, and he'll be returned in twenty-four hours. Got that? Twenty-four hours. No cops and you'll see your kid again. You got that?"

She tried to nod and must have succeeded because the face disappeared.

"Mom ... *Mom!*" Eric's voice faded. With concentrated effort, Katherine managed to raise her head. But the men and boy were already gone.

The bridge remained deserted as Coleman helped Steiner under the wooden traffic barrier, then supported the hobbling man as they headed out toward the center. Unlike your typical storybook drawbridges, this bridge did not operate by tilting up. Instead the entire midsection, about sixty feet of asphalt and steel, was on a counterweight system that raised it straight into the air like an elevator.

Now it was dropping back into place, slowly, silently.

Forty feet below, amid the swirling fog, a red-and-white barge piled high with cedar chips was being towed down the Snohomish River toward Puget Sound.

Coleman again looked for the pursuing car. Nothing. He hoped they'd lost them. In any case, the sooner they crossed this bridge out of the city and disappeared into the miles of foggy marshland on the other side, the better.

Unfortunately, Steiner was not making it a team effort.

"Why are you fighting me?" Coleman shouted as he half-carried, half-dragged the man along.

"I didn't ask for your help."

"So maybe I should just leave you here for them."

Steiner tried to answer but broke into another fit of coughing. They reached the end of the roadway, and Coleman leaned him against the pedestrian handrail. He looked up at the towering piece of iron and pavement, the center of the bridge. It was twenty-five feet above them, continuing its approach as it lowered into place. Soon the steel tongue-and-groove end of the bridge would lock perfectly into the tongue-and-groove of the roadway.

Power and precision.

Coleman walked to the edge, a few feet from where Steiner stood, and looked down through the fog at the river below. The wake of the passing tug and barge lapped silently against the pylons.

Steiner coughed again, only this time he doubled over, gagging and spitting blood.

Coleman walked back to him. "Here, sit down." Steiner tried to push him away, but Coleman didn't give up. "Take my arm here and sit—"

"No!" The cry was part wounded animal, part human rage. And with it came the strength to shove Coleman so hard that he staggered backwards, nearly losing his balance over the edge.

Steiner half rose and shouted, spraying more blood and spittle. "You—" But he broke into more coughing.

Again Coleman approached to help.

But Steiner would have none of it. Angrily, he lunged at Coleman. The impact knocked Coleman off balance, but he was able to recover. Steiner wasn't so lucky. His momentum carried him to the edge. For a brief second he teetered, eyes wide in realization.

Then he fell.

Coleman dove forward, managing to catch one arm. But the force of Steiner's falling body pulled him down, slamming him hard onto the roadway. Now Steiner was dangling over the bridge, clinging to Coleman, his weight pulling Coleman's arm into the roadway's steel teeth.

"Hang on!" Coleman cried. "Hang on!"

He looked up at the descending section of bridge. It was fifteen feet above him and closing fast.

Steiner screamed, trying to pull himself back up, but each tug and jerk dug the steel teeth more deeply into Coleman's arm. He couldn't hold Steiner, not with one hand. He inched himself closer to the edge and reached out his other arm. "Take my hand!"

Steiner looked up, terrified. He coughed again, and the force weakened their grip.

"Take my hand!" Coleman shouted. "Take it!"

At last Steiner began reaching. Coleman strained downward against the harsh steel teeth. They made several lunges for each other, and each time the movement lessened their grip. But finally they touched—first their fingers, then their palms, until they were able to grab each other's wrists.

Steiner looked past Coleman to the approaching bridge.

Coleman craned his head to see.

It was ten feet away.

He turned back. The steel teeth continued gouging into his chest and arms. "Pull," he shouted. "Pull!"

But Steiner did not pull. He had stopped.

"What are you doing?"

Steiner gave no response, made no movement.

"You've got to help me!" Coleman turned to look up.

The bridge was six feet away.

He turned back to Steiner. Suddenly he understood. "No!" he shouted, "I'm not letting go! Do you hear me? I'm not letting go! Pull! *Pull!*"

But Steiner simply hung, a dead weight. The bridge was nearly on top of them. Coleman could sense it closing in, hear the difference in the sound, feel the air pressure. "I won't let go," Coleman cried. "You hear me? I won't let go!"

He looked into Steiner's eyes—and saw the spite, the contempt. Steiner would not let Coleman win. He had lived a lifetime proving the perfection of Law. Coleman was wrong. His ways must not prevail. There was no room for mercy. The Law was supreme. Absolute. Not Coleman's mercy. Not his compassion. The Law!

An eerie smile flickered across Steiner's face.

"No!" Coleman cried.

It broadened. He would not allow Coleman to win.

"No . . . no!"

And then, with determination, Steiner released his grip. Their hands slipped apart. And he fell silently, victoriously, into the fog and water.

Coleman rolled out of the way, feeling the steel brush his cheek as the bridge came together, the tongue-and-groove teeth interlocking in silent precision.

It was dawn when O'Brien entered B–11 to visit Freddy. The baboon showed mild curiosity at his entrance, but little else—no enthusiastic welcome, no leaning hard against him to be patted or groomed. He simply loped over to see whether O'Brien had any food; when he saw that he didn't, he headed back to the gym set to play.

Freddy's behavior saddened O'Brien as he slowly sat on the park bench to watch. Something had happened. The baboon's personality had changed. He was no longer the loving and affectionate Freddy he had become since the transplant.

O'Brien sat there numb, barely thinking, until he heard the door to B–11 buzz and click open.

"Well, lookie here."

He was not surprised to hear Murkoski's voice. He had been expecting it.

"Rumor has it you've been burning the midnight oil," Murkoski said as he crossed toward O'Brien.

O'Brien gave his answer without looking. "How much money are they paying you, Kenny?"

"They say you've been brushing up on your lab technique."

"How much?" O'Brien repeated.

"More than you or I have ever seen."

O'Brien nodded. The answer was fair. So was O'Brien's next question. "Is it the Defense Department?"

"Not ours."

For the first time he turned to look at Murkoski.

The kid tossed down the satchel he'd been carrying and smiled. "Some Asian cartel. You've never heard of them."

O'Brien frowned, not understanding.

Murkoski scoffed at the man's ignorance and stretched out on the grass before him. "Empires are no longer defined by geographical borders, Phil. You know that." He picked a blade of grass and began chewing on it. "These days, corporations are the kingdoms. Big multinational corporations." Then, growing more serious, he asked. "How much do you know?"

"I know you're a liar, a cheat, and probably a murderer."

Murkoski shrugged. "Perhaps. But I'm talking about the project, Phil. How much do you know?"

"I know we thought we were working on one side of the DNA molecule, the sense side, when in reality you turned it around and had us working on the antisense."

"That's the beauty of the double helix, isn't it? While one side of the ladder is designed to code for one gene, the other side is designed exactly the opposite, completely neutralizing that gene's effects while coding for another."

"And since both sides are the same length, the gels could not detect the new gene until Wolff started cutting with another enzyme outside the coding region."

"Very good."

"So while you had us thinking we were designing a compassionate, non-aggression gene—"

"I had created the opposite. A gene that removes all inhibition towards aggression."

O'Brien closed his eyes. He had known the answer for the past hour, but hearing it verbalized carried an impact he still wasn't prepared for. Finally he asked the inevitable. "Why?"

Murkoski spat out the grass he was chewing. "Can you imagine what the arms market would pay for something like that?"

"What are you talking about?"

"Come on, Phil, think. In today's world of techno-wars, we have the capability to kill thousands, millions if we wanted, right?"

O'Brien didn't answer.

"So what's the one thing we're missing? What are we lacking?" He didn't wait for an answer. "The will, Phil. We're lacking the men and women with will. We have the buttons, but we don't have people willing to press them. Our technology is capable, but *we're* not. Until now."

O'Brien began to understand. "So instead of compassionate, caring individuals, you're creating killing machines with no conscience."

Murkoski grinned. "Armies select specific personnel. They inject the gene, let them wreak whatever havoc is necessary, and when their time is up, they remove it.

Unless, of course there are a few die-hard generals or weapon designers who choose to live with it."

"God help us."

"Too late for that, Phil. He's already been replaced."

"But the mice. I don't understand. There were only six or seven that turned into killers."

"I couldn't very well go around turning everybody into killing machines, now could I? Not unless I wanted to raise a lot of unwanted questions and risk having the project shut down. And why bother? It's the same gene, just reversed. The biological effects will be the same, so why not study them in passive, easy-to-control individuals, instead of killers?"

O'Brien gestured toward the baboon swinging from the gym set. "What about Freddy? His behavior is changing."

"Best I can figure, he's gone into some sort of regression."

O'Brien looked at him.

Murkoski shrugged. "I suspect it has something to do with the junk DNA we introduced. He's gradually reverting to his original state."

O'Brien sadly turned back to the baboon. "And Coleman?"

"He's regressing, too. Of course, it won't be stopping there."

"What do you mean?"

"Wolff noticed it first. There's something about emotional trauma that stops the process. Once they've been exposed to extreme emotional stress, degeneration rapidly sets in. As it progresses, it neutralizes any normal antiaggression chemistry they may have."

"Meaning . . ."

"Freddy and Coleman are both on their way to becoming far more aggressive than they've ever been."

O'Brien could only stare. *"Emotional stress?"*

"Probably some sort of defense mechanism of the body's. I guess if you have your teeth busted in enough, it's time to stop hugging and to start fighting. I saw it coming, though. In fact that's why I set up Coleman with one of his victim's wives. See how far we could push him."

"You did *what?"*

"Sure. It was a bonus to find her, but you know me, always the opportunist. Once that little bombshell explodes, it should be enough to push him over the edge. Truth is, my sources say he's already started regression."

"So we've released a multiple murderer back into society who will become worse than he was?"

"Relax, Phil. He's being taken care of. Even as we speak."

O'Brien eyed the kid, afraid to ask exactly what he meant. "And Freddy? What caused him to revert? What was his trauma?"

"Wolff's death, of course. I'm sure it wasn't easy for this poor creature to see his best friend die before his very eyes."

O'Brien had heard enough. He reached into his pocket for his cellular.

Murkoski made no move to prevent him. "And now you're going to put a stop to it all by calling the authorities, right?"

"That's right."

"I don't think so, Phil." Murkoski unbuckled his satchel. "I mean, seeing as you're such a family man and all."

O'Brien's eyes narrowed, his voice suddenly steel hard. "If you've done something to my family, if you've so much as touched—"

"Oh, not me, Phil, not me." He pulled a pile of 8 x 10 black-and-whites from the satchel and tossed them at O'Brien's feet. "I haven't harmed your little family unit. But if you're not careful, you could."

O'Brien stared at the photos. They were of Tisha and himself out in the parking lot, beside his open car, talking, passionately embracing, hungrily kissing. Suddenly he felt very weak. Rage and helplessness poured in, mixing and swirling together. He barely noticed Murkoski reaching back into his satchel.

"I've been talking to the Board. Riordan, McGovern, all the others."

O'Brien finally looked up.

The kid held a single piece of paper in his hand. "Seems they feel your resignation is in order."

"You—you can't do that."

"I'm afraid it's already done." He shoved the paper toward him. "Not to worry though. Besides a generous severance package, they assure me that you'll be able to keep all of your stock options. Not a bad deal when you consider how our value will skyrocket when this new drug hits the open market. All that plus—and here's the kicker—the Cartel is offering you a cool fifty million. Sort of a thank-you gift, not to mention an assurance of your discretion."

O'Brien's head swam. "And if I don't sign this?"

"Oh, there's no *if*, Phil. You can either resign now or wait until later. In which case, I imagine the offer will be far less generous."

O'Brien stared at him numbly.

Murkoski forced a smile and pulled a pen from his sports coat. "It's a no-brainer, Phil. A win/win."

The kid held the pen out to him, but O'Brien could not yet take it.

"You know, Phil, from what I hear, Beth's not that thrilled with your marriage these days. Something like this could either destroy it, or be the perfect opportunity to bring it together again. All that money. All that time with the family."

O'Brien felt himself weakening.

"Then three, five years from now, who knows—maybe you could start up another company."

O'Brien looked back down at the letter.

"I don't have all day, Phil. We've got sort of a deadline coming up here."

"What type of deadline?"

"Let's just say that, even if you wanted to stop things, it's too late."

O'Brien held his gaze a moment, then looked back at the pictures on the ground.

"You're all set. A lifetime of wealth. Familial bliss. And for what? For just turning your head and doing absolutely nothing." Murkoski shoved the pen closer to him.

O'Brien glanced up from the photos and stared at the pen. It was an expensive Japanese brand. Ceramic. Not all that different from the one Beth had given him for their last anniversary.

PART THREE

CHAPTER 13

The glare of the high beams irritates him. He adjusts the mirror. He doesn't know who's behind him; he doesn't care. No one can touch him. The crack has made him invincible.

Flashers behind him; a siren squawking. Cops. He glances at his speedometer: 65. He smiles. A bit fast for downtown Council Bluffs. He thinks of outrunning them. Omaha is just across the river. But he's been careful, he has nothing to hide. He chalks up the paranoia to the coke.

He forces himself to relax. He pulls the Nova over to the side of the road. Gravel crunches and pops under the tires as he comes to a stop.

He rolls down his window, waits forever, tapping his fingers on the wheel. Anxious. Wanting to get on with it.

In the mirror he sees the approaching officers. They split, one to each side. A flashlight blinds his eyes. Cop One's pleasantries are false and insincere. "Sir" this, "Mr." that. "May I see your license, please."

On the other side Cop Two shines his light through the passenger window, searching. Coleman smiles. He is a professional. They will find nothing.

He hands Cop One his license. It's fake, but too good to tell.

"May I also see your registration, please?"

Coleman reaches for the glove compartment as Cop Two directs his light to the backseat. He hears words spoken over the roof but cannot make them out. Cop One's flashlight darts to the back. It's the shotgun. Peeking out from under the blanket. Coleman meant to throw it in the trunk, but the Quickie Mart alarm made him nervous, sloppy.

"Will you step out of the vehicle, Sir?"

Coleman's senses focus razor sharp. He hears his door handle being opened, the hinges groaning, the whoosh of a passing car.

"Sir?"

His hand is still in the glove compartment. On the surface are crumpled French fry bags with their printed rows of orange, gold, and brown arches. Below that, dozens of lotto tickets, red letters on gray, and of course the candy wrappers. His heart pounds in his ears. He reaches under the trash and pulls out a 9mm Browning High Power, semiautomatic.

Cop One goes for his gun. Coleman is too fast. The Browning recoils. Pants and knee cap explode four feet from his face. Coleman squeezes off a second round, but he is distracted by the shattering of the passenger window. Cop Two is trying to be a hero.

Cop One is down. Yelling. One more round would silence him, but Cop Two is coming in from the other side.

Coleman turns. He sees the fear in the eyes. He fires point-blank, feels the bullet as it smashes into Cop Two's chest. He screams. He fires again. He feels the second impact, ripping, searing. Cop Two opens his mouth, but it is Coleman who screams. He fires a third round, again feeling its explosion. But he will not stop, he fires a fourth, a fifth, shrieking in agony, as he tries to kill his own pain.

Now someone is on the roof. Pounding. "Michael . . . Michael!" It's his father's voice. Drunk. Angry. He will kill Coleman.

Coleman rolls onto his back. He fires into the roof again and again, like a madman. There is a pathetic groan as a shape tumbles past the window and to the ground. Coleman hears him crawling and knows he's still alive. He leaps out of the car to finish him off. He races around to the other side, raising his gun. But it is not his father who is crawling on the ground.

It is himself.

The wounded Coleman reaches out to him. "Michael." It is his father's voice, but it is Coleman's body. It has always been his body. Since the beginning it has been Coleman pursuing Coleman.

He fires into the bleeding Coleman, feeling each bullet as it bursts into his chest, his belly. But the wounded Coleman will not give up. He reaches out and clutches Coleman's ankle. Coleman fires at point-blank range. The riddled body jolts with each impact, but the grip will not release.

The wounded Coleman grabs Coleman's knees, pulling himself up. "Michael!"

Coleman staggers under his weight.

"You're mine . . ."

"No!" Coleman tries to break free, but the hold is too strong. "Let me go!"

"You are me . . ."

"No!" He is losing his balance.

"You are mine . . ."

He is falling. "Nooo . . ."

Coleman sat up with a start. As reality forced its way back and his vision cleared, he saw that he was surrounded by marsh grass. Acres and acres of it. He rose stiffly to his knees. The drawbridge lay three hundred yards away. The first signs of rush hour were already beginning to appear on it.

His clothes were soaked from the mist. There was the taste of salt on his lips. But he barely noticed. He was still thinking of his dream. He understood it now, and it terrified him.

He was losing ground.

He had felt it in the hallway with Steiner, with the two thugs at the door, and later in the overturned car. The old man was returning. The rage, the uncontrollable fury, it was all fighting to return, to take over.

You are mine.

And with each assault, it grew harder to resist.

You are me.

The monster would not stop until it had regained complete control.

Coleman's mind raced. Thoughts spun, whirled. Memories of murders, laughter with Katherine, unspeakable violence in prison, gentle sparrings with Eric, they all tumbled and thundered and cried in his head—along with Katherine's haunting words, "Old things are passed away, behold all things are become new."

He rose to his feet. The mountains were glowing pink and orange as dawn began to spread across their peaks. He recalled the pristine beauty of the snow in the exercise yard, the lonesome wail of the freight train. The exhilaration of breaking bones, smashing cartilage.

Old things are passed away.

He saw Katherine's eyes, the vulnerability, the love.

Behold all things are become new.

He recalled the Bible, their talks about it.

"This ache inside me—it's like he understands."

"I guess that's why he called himself the 'Bread of Life.' "

He is a new creature.

"My faith was the only thing that kept me sober."

Old things are passed away.

"Like he somehow is able to meet my hunger . . ."

Behold all things are become new.

You are mine.

"I suspect it has more to do with a person's faith . . ."

If any man is in Christ, he is a new creature . . .

You are mine . . .

Old things are passed away . . .

You are me.

A new creature . . .

You are me.

Old things are passed . . .

You are . . .

All things are . . .

You . . .

"Noooo!"

Coleman's cry startled a lone crane, causing it to rise up from the marsh and take flight. Its wings beat the air as it rose noisily into the sky.

He took a step. "Please . . ." Then another. He raised his head toward heaven and shouted, "Do you hear me? *Do you hear me!*"

There was only silence.

He started to run, but the ground was soft and uneven. He fell. He staggered back up, but only for a few more steps before falling again. He rose and stumbled forward, still trying to run. Where, he wasn't sure. For how long, he didn't know.

"Help me," he gasped, then fell again. And rose again. His vision blurring with hot tears. Three, four, a half-dozen more steps before he fell again. He rose one last time, but his energy was spent, the fight gone. Slowly he sank back down to his knees.

"I can't . . ." He fought to breathe. "I need . . ." Tears streamed down his cheeks. "Please, I don't want this. Please . . . help me . . . Whoever you are, whatever you want, I'm yours—take me . . . make me yours . . ."

Katherine snapped on Eric's computer. She hit a few keys and waited for the modem to connect. She noticed her hands trembling. When she was done, she'd have to have another glass of wine. Across the room the radio alarm glowed 6:39 A.M.

The phone on the other end rang twice before the modem connected with three irritating tones followed by a coffee grinder buzz. It had been a while since her cyber-hacking days. Installing a hard disk or listening to complaints about the configuration of the latest software wasn't quite the same as when she and the guys at NORAD had spent their time fooling around on the Internet. That had been years ago, before the civilians had come in and taken it over. She just hoped they hadn't messed it up too badly. She needed to get in there and do some serious skulking.

The menu popped up, followed by a little red box in the corner of the screen, a sign that Eric had received some electronic mail. Katherine started to skip past it. The last thing she wanted was to read some yick-yack from one of Eric's electronic pen pals. But it was up there, it would only take a moment, and who knows.

She brought it up and gasped.

>MOM
>DONT WORRY. IM OK. THEY TOOK PHONE FROM ROOM BUT LEFT COMPUTER. STUPID HUH? IM READING FILES. LOTS OF SKAREY JUNK. MEET ME IN COMPUTER FORUM LOBY 9:00. ILL HAVE MORE STUFF THEN. DONT WORRY.
> :-) ERIC

Katherine took a long, deep breath. He was alive. Her eyes darted up to the message's time of transmission: 6:14 A.M. He was alive and wherever they were keeping him had taken less than an hour to get to.

She reread the message two more times. Eric had access to a computer and was reading someone's files. She was to meet him on the Internet in an area called the

Computer Forum at 9:00. Immediately she hit the reply command and started typing an answer.

>ERIC
>WHERE ARE YOU? CAN YOU SEE OUT A WINDOW? ARE THERE ANY LANDMARKS THAT YOU CAN IDENTI

But the modem suddenly clicked and she was disconnected from the Internet. A phone call was coming in. Eric had complained for months about the disadvantages of having only one phone line, and how call waiting always disconnected him. Now she understood. She hit Alt X to escape and picked up the receiver. "Hello?"

"Katherine?" It was Coleman. His voice filled her with a mixture of rage, concern, excitement, guilt.

"Where are you?" she demanded.

"Just north of Everett."

"They took Eric."

No response.

"Did you hear what I said? They kidnapped Eric."

"Yes." Pause. "We've got to . . . we've got to get together. We've got to figure things out."

The last thing she wanted was to get together with the monster who'd killed her husband, who'd destroyed her life. And yet—

"Katherine?"

"They said if I stayed quiet for twenty-four hours nothing would happen. They said they'd return him if I just—"

"And you believe that?"

"I–I don't know. No, of course not. I don't know."

Another pause. "It's wearing off, Katherine."

"What?"

"The experiment. It's . . ."

She could hear him swallow back the panic.

"Katherine, I'm slipping back to what I used to be."

A cold fear gripped her.

"Katherine?"

At last she found her voice. "But you can fight it, right?"

"I don't know."

Katherine wanted her son back. And, like it or not, she needed Coleman's help. "You *can* fight it," she ordered. "You've *got* to fight it."

The voice responded. Weak and hoarse. "I'm trying. I–I've even been praying. But . . ."

Katherine's head spun. She closed her eyes, trying to get her bearings. "Okay, listen—"

"I don't think I can—"

"Listen to me!" He grew quiet and she continued. "You're right—we've got to get together. But not here." She tapped the desk, thinking. It couldn't be public. It had to be somewhere with a computer and access to the Internet, someone who would let her—

And then she saw it. Eric's report card. And on the top line, the name of his teacher: Mr. Thaddeus Paris.

Mr. Paris's cramped twenty-nine-foot Avanti cruiser looked and felt like any other bachelor apartment, including but not limited to the distinct aroma of old socks, old grease, and Old Spice. Katherine knew he'd been picking up the place since she first called, and she kept a cautious eye on the bulging closets lest they fly open and bury her in dirty clothes or empty pizza boxes.

She had arrived with a knapsack of books about the Internet. After enduring the pleasantries and sidestepping the curious questions, she was finally able to scoot behind the computer that sat on his kitchen table and go to work. Several times he offered his assistance, and several times she made it clear that his help was neither needed nor appreciated. Finally, he took the hint and packed up his briefcase for work.

"You sure you don't need anything?" he asked one final time before stepping off the boat.

The keyboard clicked under Katherine's fingers, and she answered without looking up. "I'll be fine."

He stood at the exit, fidgeting. She could tell that this entire scenario was foreign to him. A beautiful woman all alone in his houseboat while he left her behind to go off to work. What was wrong with this picture?

"Well," he cleared his throat, "if you need anything, or just want to talk, my number is next to the phone."

She nodded.

"Oh, and when you leave, make sure you lock the front gate on the dock. Sometimes it sticks open."

"Got it."

Another pause.

"Okay, then."

No response.

"I hope everything works out."

More of the same.

With a shrug, he turned and started to leave.

Then, almost by reflex, Katherine called out, "Thanks again."

He turned back, obviously grateful for the contact.

Realizing she'd have to say more, she continued. "I promise I'll explain all this to you sometime soon. Honest."

"Oh," he said, smiling an idiotic smile, "no need."

She smiled back.

"Well, bye."

"Bye."

He remained standing.

Katherine forced one last smile before returning to the screen. He took the cue and left.

It was 7:30. She had ninety minutes before reconnecting with Eric. Ninety minutes to scour the Internet, to search databases, and maybe squeeze some priority information from old friends.

The first ten minutes were spent finding the street address assigned to the owner of the e-mail account Eric was writing from. It belonged to a Ms. Tisha Youngren of Baltimore, Maryland. A few more clicks of the mouse revealed that Youngren was a biochem grad student who'd recently moved west. Katherine couldn't find the forwarding address.

She tried another route. Any and all information on Genodyne. She'd been at it quite awhile when the boat rocked and she looked up to see Coleman standing on board.

There was the briefest flutter deep inside that she immediately suppressed and berated herself for feeling. Some ridiculous part of her still wanted to race to him, to throw her arms around him. But there was the other part, the part that wanted to tear out his eyes, to beat him, to rip him limb from limb.

"Hi." He tried to smile.

She knew better than to trust her voice and remained silent.

"You find anything?" he asked.

She shook her head. "Nothing. Dead ends. Whoever's running the show is being very, very careful."

He nodded, then with some effort he moved to sit across the table from her. She could tell that he was in pain, probably from the viral leash, but she forced herself to remain matter-of-fact. "I've got all the nonessentials. Everything you'd ever want to know about Genodyne: start-up investments, P and L figures, FDA applications, the works. Even the board members' birth dates and home addresses, but—"

"You got an O'Brien there?" he interrupted.

She glanced up, a little surprised at his abruptness. She looked back at the screen and nodded. "Dr. Philip O'Brien, the CEO?"

"Yeah." Coleman was rubbing his neck. "I met him in November. Pretty decent guy. Maybe we can go straight to the top and call—"

She cut him off. "I hardly think calling their CEO is going to—"

"If you've got another plan, I'm open. But I'm in no mood to sit around here and do nothing."

"*You're* in no mood?" Her voice grew louder. "My son has just been kidnapped, and *you're* in no mood?"

"All right, all right," he said, bringing the conversation back down. "You're right." He closed his eyes, then opened them. "They told you they'd bring him back in twenty-four hours, is that right?"

"That's right."

"Why? Why'd they say that?"

"I don't know—they said if I stayed quiet for twenty-four hours, if I didn't go to the police, he'd be safe and they'd bring him—"

"You can't possibly believe that."

"I don't know! But twenty-four hours isn't that long—"

"I don't *have* twenty-four hours!"

She looked at him.

He rose and began pacing. "Don't you get it? If they have an antidote or something, I need it now. Now! Not in twenty-four hours. *Now!*"

"What about Eric?"

"I'm not talking about Eric, I'm talking about me!"

"But they said he'd be—"

"I need it now!" He hit the paneled wall with his fist. The entire boat shuddered. Katherine stared. Coleman looked at his hand as if it were a foreign object. He turned, not daring to look back at her.

When she finally spoke, it was without anger. "It really is happening, isn't it?"

Without turning, he answered softly, "Yeah." After a moment he crossed back to the table and sat, still careful not to look her in the eyes. He noticed her half-spilled knapsack and poked at it. "What's this?"

"What?"

He reached in and pulled out the Bible she had given him. He gave her a dubious look.

She shrugged. "You're the one who said you were praying. Not that it will do you any good."

Coleman looked at her.

"If it really is wearing off," she said, "I doubt there's anything you can do to stop it. Like Murkoski said, it's all in the genes."

"I'm more than just some kid's chemistry set, Katherine. I've got to be."

"That's right, you're also the murderer of my husband."

It was meant to hurt him, and it did. But he held her gaze. And when he spoke, his voice was quiet and deliberate. "Maybe. Or maybe old things really have passed away."

It took a moment for the phrase to register. When it did, Katherine felt a surge of revulsion. "Please." She rose and crossed to the sink for some water.

He persisted. "You said it yourself, 'If any man is in Christ he is a new creature.' You're the one who taught me that."

"I'm a preacher's kid, what did you expect?"

"Maybe people *can* change, maybe I really can—"

"Save it. I know the routine." She filled a glass and drank the water. It was bitter and brackish.

But Coleman wouldn't let up. "You said it worked for you. Back when you were in AA, you said it was your faith that stopped you from drinking. Isn't that what you said?"

"That was a long time ago."

"But it worked, didn't it?"

"I suppose. When I let it."

"It changed you." His voice was growing urgent. "Didn't you say it changed you?"

She nodded. "It was no cakewalk. But yeah, it broke my dependency."

"So why can't it do the same for me? I've asked for his help. I've given him my life. If I can't get an antidote, why can't that same faith help me?"

She turned and looked at him. His face was full of anything but faith. Desperation, yes. Fear, definitely. But she did not see faith.

"I'm not just chemicals, Katherine. There's got to be a way to beat this."

It was 9:57. For nearly an hour, Katherine had been parked in the lobby of the Computer Forum, staring at the screen, waiting for her son to log on. But so far Eric hadn't shown.

Coleman sat across from her at the table, wearing one of Paris's jackets to fight off a chill, the obvious beginnings of a fever—courtesy of the viral leash. Yet, despite his pain, Katherine sensed a peace settling over him, a peace that grew as he continued staring at the Bible and silently turning its pages.

Peace was the furthest thing from her mind as she sat across from this beast who had destroyed her life—and the saint who had started to revive it. Maybe he was right; maybe they really were two separate creatures. Maybe that old man, the man who'd pulled the trigger that took Gary, really was dead. And maybe he was right on another count. Maybe, with enough faith, that old man would never return.

Katherine glanced back at the screen. Faith. It had been a long time since she'd even thought about the word. But right now, with her baby's life on the line, she would be willing to try just about anything. She had her doubts, but she was no fool. To cover all the bases, Katherine found herself saying a quiet prayer, just in case there was a God out there, just in case he really did care.

Slowly a tiny spark of something began to glow in her. Maybe it was faith, maybe hope, maybe just wishful thinking. Whatever it was, it gave her the strength to leave the lobby and quickly click over to e-mail just in case Eric had written another message.

Nothing.

She reentered the lobby and continued to wait. For the next ninety minutes she waited, refusing the sandwich Coleman had made, the Diet Pepsi he had found, refusing even to speculate on another plan. It wasn't until 11:36 that Katherine Lyon reached up and, with any flicker of faith that might have returned now extinguished, turned off the computer.

She could feel Coleman staring at her. It was obvious that he sensed her hopelessness and wanted to help. But, when he rose to his feet and started to walk around the table to her, she put up her hand. "No," was all she said. As much as she wanted him—needed him—she knew now, more than ever, that some things can never be changed.

CHAPTER 14

Dr. Philip O'Brien was in the middle of another packing dilemma. This time it had to do with socks. He had none. Well, none that were clean. Ever since Beth had left for Mazatlán, his housekeeping skills, including but not limited to laundry, had steadily gone downhill.

He glanced at the VCR clock in the bedroom. In just a few hours he'd be on the flight to Mazatlán. He doubted that there would be enough time to wash and dry any socks. Of course, he could dig through the dirty clothes hamper and pull out a few of the freshest pairs, but he had been performing that ritual for the last several days and somehow suspected that the socks in there wouldn't survive a third or fourth go-round.

Everything else was ready. The pets were in the kennel, the newspaper had been stopped, the home security folks had been alerted. If he wanted, he could stay down there with his family for months. Or they could head to Asia, or do a photo safari in Africa, or buy a villa in Europe. When it came to time and money, the possibilities were almost limitless.

The phone rang, and he absentmindedly scooped it up. "Hello?"

"Is this Dr. Philip O'Brien?"

The voice seemed strangely familiar, but he couldn't put his finger on it. "Yes."

"Head of Genodyne?"

"Who's calling, please?"

"A friend from Nebraska."

O'Brien went cold. "Where are you? Why are you calling me?"

"Do you know where the boy is?"

"What boy?"

"We need your help."

O'Brien's mind raced. Between the preparations for the trip and disengaging from Genodyne, he'd almost been able to put Coleman out of his mind. Almost. "You must understand, I no longer work for Genodyne. I've—retired."

The pause on the other end seemed interminable. Finally the voice answered. "We need to talk to you."

O'Brien shifted his weight. "There's nothing I can do. If you have a problem, you'll have to take it up with Dr. Murkoski. He's in charge of the program, and I'm sure he's more than willing—"

"Murkoski is killing people. I might be next."

O'Brien felt his face grow warm. "Look, I'm no longer a part of any of this. If you have a problem, I suggest you take it up with—"

"I need to talk to you. I need some answers."

The desperation in the man's voice tugged at O'Brien, but he refused to give in. He had a plane to catch. A new life to begin. "I'm sorry."

"Is there a way to stop this thing? Can I get back to the way I used to be?"

"Even if I knew, there's nothing I can do about it. Genodyne is the only place you can go for help. I recommend that you head up there at once." His palms were damp; he wiped them on his pants. "And if you're worried about safety, you need to know that there's a good chance this call is being monitored."

"I need your help!" The voice suddenly exploded. "Don't you understand? You got me into this, you've got to—"

"Good afternoon, Mr. Coleman."

"Listen to me! Listen, you little—"

O'Brien pressed the off button and slowly placed the phone back into its cradle. He stood for a long moment before turning to the suitcases on the bed. He knew this wouldn't be the last time he'd have to turn a deaf ear. The next months, maybe years, wouldn't be easy. But this was the path he had chosen, and he would hold to it.

Looking again at the clothes hamper, he realized that socks were no longer a problem. He didn't have to wash them. He'd throw them away and buy new ones. Come to think of it, he and Beth could now dispose of their wardrobes and buy new clothes every day of the year if they wanted. He smiled grimly at the prospect and returned to his packing.

Coleman lowered the receiver. The combination of rage and helplessness left him shaking. He could feel Katherine staring at him, and he fought to regain control before turning to her.

"So what's next?" she asked. "Genodyne?"

Coleman thought a moment, then shook his head.

"What other choice is there?"

"Do you have O'Brien's home address on that computer?"

"Right here. But it didn't exactly sound like he was anxious to—"

"There was something in his voice."

"There was what?"

"In his voice," Coleman looked up, trying to explain. "I heard something ... in his voice."

"What's with that dog?" Murkoski complained as he threw open his office door and stormed into the hallway.

Tisha Youngren looked up from her work. "He's been barking like that all morning."

Murkoski saw Eric sitting frozen on a nearby chair and motioned toward him. "You feed him lunch?"

"I tried. He wouldn't eat."

Murkoski pivoted and crossed the room to Eric. He stuck his face directly into the boy's. "Listen, brat. You hear that dog?"

Eric nodded, wide-eyed.

"Well, he's the size of a bear and he's barking because he's hungry. Unlike you, he doesn't have anything to eat. But if you don't finish that sandwich, we can change all that. I know for a fact that he just loves tender little boys. You catch my meaning, son?"

Eric nodded.

"Good." Murkoski broke into a smile. "By this time tomorrow, we'll have everything shipped and you'll be back home safe and sound with Mommy." Without waiting for a response, he rose and headed down the hall.

Tisha called after him, "You done with the computer?"

He turned. "For now, why?"

"He likes playing the games."

Murkoski looked at the boy a moment, then shrugged. "If it keeps him occupied." He turned and disappeared down the hall.

"You hear that?" Tisha asked, trying too hard to sound cheery. "Just as soon as you finish your sandwich, you can go back in and play some more games. Won't that be fun?"

Eric could tell that this woman was underestimating his age and his intelligence. That was fine with him; maybe he could use it to his advantage. He pretended to nod eagerly, then tore into his cellophane-wrapped turkey sandwich.

"What do you think you're doing? You just can't break into someone's—"

"Sit down."

O'Brien hesitated.

"Sit down!" Coleman headed toward O'Brien, making it clear he meant business. O'Brien understood and immediately sank into the nearest chair—leather, like all the others in this expensive, high-tech family room at the back of his house.

Coleman began to pace, a conflict of compassion, anger, and terror. The battle inside his head raged relentlessly. Still, he had been able to keep most of the anger in check, holding it back like an attack dog straining on a leash. He still had control, he still held the leash, but with each lurch and tug, his grip grew weaker. In a matter of time, the beast would break free—and Coleman knew when that happened it would never allow itself to be chained again.

Katherine was settling down in front of the computer that sat on a large oak desk near the French doors overlooking the pool. "This thing have a modem?" she asked.

O'Brien nodded.

"What's with the bags?" Coleman asked, nodding toward the three suitcases at the bottom of the stairs. "You going somewhere?"

"Yes," O'Brien said. His voice was husky with fear, and he coughed. "As I told you over the phone, I've retired. I'm going down to Mexico to join my family on vacation."

Coleman continued to pace, rubbing his shoulders, the back of his neck. The pain was worse, and he was damp with perspiration from the fever. "What do you know about the kidnapping? Where are they keeping him?"

"Kidnapping?" O'Brien sounded legitimately confused.

"My son," Katherine said as she pulled off the computer's dustcover and turned it on. "Your pals kidnapped my boy."

"They what? What pals?"

The incredulity in O'Brien's voice seemed real, but Coleman wasn't sure. He pressed in. "They said they're only keeping him twenty-four hours—for what, we don't know. But they've already killed two, three other times, so you can see why we might have a little doubt about their credibility."

O'Brien grew pale. "What? Who's killed—how many times?"

Coleman's instincts had been right. The man was honestly concerned. And, for the most part, O'Brien was decent. Frightened, but decent. It was obvious that he knew nothing about Eric, so Coleman moved to the next subject. "What about an antidote?"

O'Brien looked up. There was no mistaking the sorrow filling his face.

Again Coleman had his answer, but he wouldn't accept it. "I'm slipping back. What can I do, how can I stop it?"

"I'm sorry." O'Brien shook his head, then continued. "According to Murkoski, once the process starts to reverse, there's no stopping it."

The sentence hit Coleman hard.

But O'Brien wasn't finished. "I'm afraid . . ." Again he cleared his throat. "I'm afraid it will continue to reverse until it leaves you in worse shape than when you first started the treatment."

Katherine slowly stopped her typing.

Coleman swallowed, barely finding his voice. "What?"

O'Brien could no longer look at him. "The chances are high that it will remove any inhibitions you might have previously had toward violence."

"You mean—I'll be worse?"

O'Brien didn't answer. The verdict hung heavy in the room. Coleman had no idea how long the silence lasted before the man continued. "Perhaps in a few months, maybe in a year, they can find—"

Coleman exploded: "I don't have a year! I need it now!"

There was another moment of silence as Coleman took a deep breath and fought for control.

O'Brien waited, then softly repeated, "I'm sorry."

Coleman stood lost, unsure what to do. Finally he moved across the room to the sofa near O'Brien and sank into the cushions.

O'Brien shifted uncomfortably. He glanced at Coleman, then quietly ventured, "Still, I wouldn't give up. Not yet."

Coleman looked at him.

"I mean, you still have a will."

Coleman continued to stare, waiting for more.

"It's true, we all have a proclivity toward certain behaviors, we all inherit programming from our parents. But we're not computers. We still have a will. And in many areas that will has proved stronger than any of our genetic hard wiring."

Coleman frowned. "What about Murkoski's research? What about all those studies he rattles off?"

"There's plenty of evidence to back him up, certainly. But there is other research indicating that how we're raised may carry as much of an influence as our genetic heritage."

"How we're raised?"

O'Brien nodded. "We're not shaped only by the nature of our chemistry, but also by the nurturing of our parents."

Coleman deflated slightly and muttered, "Strike two."

"But there's a third element." Coleman looked at him. O'Brien continued, "Our personal philosophy, what we believe, internally."

"That makes a difference?"

O'Brien nodded. "Absolutely. Take male primates. By nature, they tend to be sexually promiscuous. But through the course of history, we humans have learned the value of fidelity—the emotional values, the social values—so our belief has modified our natural behavior."

Coleman nodded, slowly understanding.

O'Brien continued. "The same can be said about crime, or violence, or addictive behavior. We have learned that the long-term consequences outweigh the momentary gain, so we modify our behavior."

"What about the druggie who can't stop doing drugs, the alcoholic who can't stop drinking—the killer who can't stop killing?" Coleman held O'Brien's eyes, waiting for an answer, but O'Brien faltered. It seemed a simple enough question—if there *was* an answer.

Coleman tried another route. "You said 'belief.' What about faith?"

"Faith?"

"If we can't do it on our own, what about turning to someone we believe can help us?"

O'Brien paused to consider the thought. "It's certainly a consideration. We all know people who have been changed through a religious experience." He looked to Coleman. "You think that's a possibility?"

"I don't know."

O'Brien frowned, thinking it through. "I'm certainly not a theologian, but it would seem—"

"I've got him!" Katherine called from across the room.

Coleman was immediately on his feet, crossing to the desk. O'Brien was right behind, asking, "Who? Who do you have?"

"Her boy."

By the time they arrived, Katherine's hands were flying over the keyboard.

>HONEY ARE YOU OKAY? DID THEY DO ANYTHING TO HURT YOU?

The answer came back tortuously slow.

>IM FINE. CANT TALK LONG. INTERESTING FILES.

Katherine immediately responded:

>WHERE ARE YOU? DO YOU SEE ANY LANDMARKS? HEAR ANY SOUNDS?
>DONT WORY. I'M COMMING HOME TOMROW MORNING. THEY PROMISE. RIGHT AFTER THE SHIPMENT.
>WHAT SHIPMENT?
>THERE COMING GOTTA GO.
>ERIC, DON'T GO. ERIC?

But there was no answer. She tried again:

>ERIC!

Nothing. All three stared at the screen.

Coleman was the first to speak. "What shipment is he talking about?"

O'Brien didn't answer, but slowly turned and started back to the sofa and chairs. Coleman and Katherine exchanged looks, then followed.

"That explains why they're holding your boy," O'Brien said, almost to himself. "They can't afford any more delays before shipping the drug, so they're holding your son to prevent you from going to the police."

"What drug?" Coleman asked. "What are you talking about?"

O'Brien slowly sat, then looked at his hands a long moment. Finally he began. "Originally we thought—we thought we were doing so much good. We were going to change the world, change the human race."

Carefully, in painful detail, he told of the death of the mice, the regression of Freddy, the murder of Wolff. He explained how instead of creating a compassionate race, Murkoski had taken over and developed the antisense gene to create conscienceless killing machines. A gene that, according to Eric's newest information, was scheduled for shipment tomorrow morning.

As the minutes dragged on and O'Brien's explanation became increasingly bleak, Coleman found it more and more difficult to contain himself. When he could stand no more, he waved O'Brien into silence. "So, what are you doing to stop it?" he demanded.

O'Brien looked at him sadly, then shook his head. "There's nothing I can do. There's nothing anybody can do."

Coleman was on his feet again, pacing in rage. "What are you saying? There's nothing we can do? I don't believe that. I don't believe it!"

"Coleman...," Katherine warned.

"How can you say that, after all you've done?"

"I'm sorry," O'Brien said.

"You're sorry!" Coleman repeated incredulously. "You're *sorry?*"

Katherine rose and moved closer. "Coleman, if he says there's nothing we can do, then—"

"The man creates a drug that can turn us into killers, and he says there's nothing he can do?"

"I—"

"What are you going to do when it falls into the wrong hands? How is 'I'm sorry' going to cut it when some terrorist gets it? Or some crazed third-world dictator?"

"You don't think I've thought of that?" O'Brien answered. "You don't think an hour hasn't gone by without that crossing my mind?"

"And you're doing nothing?"

O'Brien hesitated, then glanced over at his suitcases.

"Of course you're doing something," Coleman said. "You're running away."

O'Brien rose unsteadily to his feet, trying to defend himself. "He shut me out of the company. He's planned this for months. There's nothing I can—"

"What about the truck or whatever they're shipping it in? Couldn't we blow it up?"

"That would just cause a delay. He'd only cultivate and harvest more."

"From what?" Katherine asked.

"The genetic material in the lab."

"And if that was destroyed?" Coleman asked.

"He's got hundreds, thousands of samples; plus, the genetic code is in all of the lab computers."

"What about outside laboratories?"

O'Brien shook his head. "No, we'd never do that. There's too great a potential for a security breach. That's why he's in such a hurry to get it out now, before any leaks occur." He turned to Katherine. "That's why he's holding your son. By preventing you from going to the authorities, he's ensuring that the shipment won't be delayed by some sort of investigation."

"I don't understand," Katherine said. "Why the big rush?"

"Every day he holds this drug, the chances of it being stolen or leaked to others multiply. Today it's worth billions. But as soon as it's duplicated and pirated, it's worth nothing. So you see the risk—if Murkoski is forced to sit on this for a few months, it may become worthless."

"What about patents?" Katherine asked.

O'Brien shook his head. "Nobody will honor patents when it comes to this. Genodyne has a window of months, perhaps a year, to make their fortune before individuals and governments start pirating it."

"You're saying that any Tom, Dick, or Harry will be able to duplicate this stuff?" Coleman demanded.

O'Brien nodded.

Coleman pressed his aching head with both hands. "And you don't think that's worth stopping?"

"I didn't say that. I said there's no way to stop it. Outside of destroying every sample—"

"How would we do that?" Coleman interrupted.

"What?"

"Destroy the samples. How do you kill DNA?"

"Heat, I suppose. It's like any living organism. But you can't just go in and torch a few test tubes."

"Why not?"

"As I said, there are thousands. The entire third floor is dedicated to this study. That's eight separate labs. You'd have to literally go into each laboratory, pull out all the samples, and destroy them."

"That's it?" Coleman asked.

"And the lab animals. The mice, the baboon, you'd have to destroy them all."

"And that would take care of it?"

O'Brien turned to Katherine. "He can't be serious!"

Katherine kept her eyes fixed on Coleman. "Is it possible? Is that something you could do?"

"You can't just burn the place down," O'Brien argued. "You'd have to be sure every single sample is destroyed, nothing overlooked. You'd have to generate a lot of fire in a contained area. You couldn't miss a single sample."

"No problem," Coleman said.

O'Brien stared in disbelief.

"There's plenty you can learn in prison, Doctor—if you take the time to ask the right people the right questions."

Katherine turned back to O'Brien. "What about the computers? You said the map of the gene is in the computers?"

"Yes."

"But nothing outside Genodyne?"

"That's right, that would be far too risky."

Coleman turned to Katherine. "Is that something you could take out, the computers?"

"Maybe." She sounded less sure than Coleman. "If I introduced the right virus I might be able to wipe out the entire system."

"We've got backup disks in the vault," O'Brien said.

"You've got the combination?"

"An old one. Murkoski changes it occasionally."

"It's a steel vault?" Katherine asked.

"Yes."

"Do you have a 220 outlet nearby?"

"A 220 outlet?"

"Like for a stove or something."

"There's a lunchroom just down the hall."

"That would help you get into the safe?" Coleman asked.

Katherine shrugged. "In a manner of speaking."

O'Brien shook his head. "I can't believe what you two are saying."

Coleman turned to him. "Tell us everything we would need to know."

"It's impossible."

"If you've got any other suggestions, I'm open."

O'Brien glanced at his watch. "You've got eighteen hours before dawn, before he loads up his shipment. You don't know the layout of the building, you don't know the security—breaking into a place like Genodyne isn't exactly like breaking into the local gas station. This is crazy talk."

Suddenly Coleman sprang at O'Brien, grabbing him by the throat and shoving him against the wall. Katherine cried out, but he barely heard. He was in O'Brien's face, spitting out the words. "I'm crazy? *I'm* crazy? You're talking about turning people into killing machines, and *I'm* crazy!" His grip tightened as he raised O'Brien off the floor a good six inches.

O'Brien coughed and gagged, but Coleman ignored him, his senses tightening, aware only of his own breathing and the pounding of his heart in his ears.

"Coleman!" Katherine screamed, but he heard nothing.

O'Brien kicked and fought to get free, but Coleman's grip was iron.

Then from somewhere far away, he began to hear Katherine's voice. "Coleman! Coleman, you're killing him!"

He felt someone pounding on his back, beating his shoulders. "You're killing him! Stop it!"

Angered at the distraction, he looked back—without letting go of O'Brien—and fixed his rage on her.

It was then he saw the terror in Katherine's eyes. Terror of him. The look hit him hard, shocking his system. Sounds returned. He could hear O'Brien coughing. Turning back again, he saw the deep crimson of the man's face.

Katherine's voice grew louder: "You're killing him, you're killing him!"

Coleman released his grip and O'Brien slid down the wall, coughing and gasping for breath. Coleman looked down, frightened and breathing hard himself. Things were getting worse, no doubt about it. Yet somehow, he suspected that he might have made his point.

At 5:34 that afternoon, O'Brien finally looked up from the blueprints of Genodyne that were spread out across the dining-room table. "That's it," he sighed, taking off his glasses and rubbing his eyes. "That's everything I can think of."

Coleman stared first at the diagram and then at the legal pad of detailed procedures he had carefully written out. Everything was there: security policy and routine, the lab locations, all the storage areas, the location of the vault, the overhead fire extinguisher system, the location of the lab animals—plus any possible areas where Eric might be held, if he was being held there at all. It had been an exhausting afternoon, but Coleman felt confident that they had covered every angle. There was still plenty that could go wrong, but at least they had a plan.

"What time is your flight?" Coleman asked.

O'Brien glanced at his watch. "I can still make it, if I hurry."

Coleman nodded. "Go ahead."

O'Brien hesitated, then scanned the legal pad one last time. "That's everything, I'm sure of it." He glanced up. "But if you need me to stick around . . ."

Coleman shook his head. "No, it's better that you go."

O'Brien nodded, then rose and headed up the stairs.

Coleman closed his eyes, trying by sheer will to force out the relentless pain in his joints and the pounding in his head. The viral leash was definitely doing its job. When he reopened his eyes, Katherine was staring at him from across the table.

"Why are you going through all of this?" she asked.

"What do you mean?"

"If I were you, I'd cut my losses and hightail it into the mountains and disappear forever."

Coleman shrugged, trying to understand it himself. "I guess . . . I don't know. All of my life, it's like I've only taken. And now, for once, I just want to . . ." His voice trailed away as he realized how inadequate this explanation was. He shook his head. "I'm not sure . . ."

Katherine almost smiled. "Sounds like part of that gene is still working."

"What about you? You don't have to do this. Just show me how to knock out those computers and the disks—"

"I would if I could trust you." That slight trace of a smile had disappeared. "But they've got my baby, and I'm not trusting you or anybody else anymore. If he's in that building, I'm going to get him myself."

Coleman nodded, feeling the returning sense of sadness. Things would never again be as they had been. The wall between them would never again come down.

O'Brien headed down the stairs, slipping on a jacket. He tossed a small magnetic card onto the table. "This is my I.D.," he said. "I've got another if you need it."

Coleman shook his head, and O'Brien continued. "With that and the PIN you have written down, you'll be able to enter any room in the building."

"If Murkoski hasn't changed the code," Katherine said.

"I doubt he's had time. Besides, he knows I'm leaving." He turned to Coleman and asked one last time, "You're sure there's nothing else you need from me? We've covered everything?"

"As far as I can tell."

"I could stay behind an extra day, if you think I can help."

Coleman shook his head. "No, go to your family. Do everything just like you planned. There's always the possibility that Murkoski is still watching you."

"If he's watching me, he knows you're here."

"Our car's four blocks away."

O'Brien nodded, then turned and headed for his suitcases. He picked up the three bags and started for the door. Coleman followed.

"So honestly," he asked, as he followed O'Brien into the tiled entry hall. "What do you think our chances are?"

"Honestly?" O'Brien asked. He paused a moment to weigh the question. "Honestly, I hope you're right about this faith thing. Because it looks to me like you're going to need all the help you can get."

CHAPTER 15

Coleman and Katherine began their shopping spree in the early evening. Most of the stores in the Arlington area were closed, but Coleman was used to shopping at all hours, with or without anyone's permission.

Katherine, on the other hand, insisted on keeping track of each broken window and smashed lock, along with the estimated retail value of every stolen item. Maybe it was the fact that she was a struggling retailer herself, or that she had been married to a cop. For whatever reason, she had promised herself that when it was all over they would eventually pay for whatever they smashed or stole.

The first break-in was at Dr. Tolle's Family Dental Practice. Nothing of real value would be missing. No dental equipment, no computer, no petty cash—nothing but one size E nitrous oxide tank and some surgical tubing.

Then there was the two-hundred-foot roll of ten-gauge Romex electrical house wiring, the five-gallon gas can, the ax, the roll of duct tape, the 220-volt extension cord, the timer, and the hank of #6 white braided cotton clothesline—all courtesy of Burnett's Hardware and Lumber. That left only the large box of Ivory soap flakes and the five gallons of gasoline, both of which Katherine felt obligated to purchase in a more orthodox fashion.

It was 9:42 when their headlights glinted off the perimeter fence that surrounded the Genodyne complex. The six-story building was lit, but blurred by a heavy fog that lay in the parking lot. They turned onto the wet asphalt that followed the fence and drove until they passed the main gate and adjacent security building—a small one-story affair.

Katherine continued down the road until they passed a large stand of firs that momentarily blocked the building's view of them. She pulled into the wet grass, as close to the ditch as she dared.

Coleman climbed out of the car and walked back to the trunk. He was shivering again. The fever was up full. He opened the trunk, which gave a rusty creak. He cringed, hoping the sound would be absorbed by the fog. He reached inside and removed the tank of nitrous oxide as well as the duct tape and clothesline.

O'Brien had explained that Genodyne was not a high-security area. No sweeping video cameras, no state-of-the-art gadgetry. Just a perimeter fence, guards who patrolled the grounds once an hour, and motion detectors near all the doors and windows of the ground floor. Inside, the magnetic ID cards and the six-digit Personal Identification Numbers were the primary source of security. "It's not like we're a nuclear testing facility," he had joked.

Maybe not, Coleman thought, but what was now being housed inside there could be even more dangerous.

As he approached the security building he heard the dull blare of a TV. Some cop show with shouting and shooting. He pressed close to the damp, concrete wall and crept to the nearest window.

He paused there to listen for conversation. He could only make out the voices of two men. There were supposed to be three. The third must still be out on rounds.

Coleman glanced at his watch. 9:52. O'Brien had said the guards began their rounds, which took anywhere from thirty-five to forty-five minutes, on the hour. By arriving this late, Coleman had hoped to catch all three together. No such luck. Guard Three was taking his merry time. If Coleman waited, another guard might leave. If he began, Guard Three might arrive and discover him.

Then again, Guard Three could be dozing or reading the latest *Sports Illustrated* in the john.

Frustration began to boil up inside Coleman. Wasn't it always that way—the greatest plans thwarted by the tiniest detail? For a moment he thought how much easier it would be to just bust in, take the first two out, then pop the third when he arrived.

Of course he knew the source of that thought and immediately pushed it aside. But it resisted more than he had expected, and that fact unnerved him. He wasn't unnerved that such thoughts were present; he knew they were there and growing stronger every hour. He was unnerved because he now realized that he would have to double-guess his every action. A plan like this was hard enough when all of his faculties were at a hundred percent. But if he couldn't trust his own instincts, if he had to double-think his every move, there could very well be trouble.

The security fence surrounding the complex was butted up to the security building. A neat design that saved money and looked sleek, but it had obviously been created by an architect and not a breaking-and-entering expert. In a manner of seconds, Coleman had used the fence to climb onto the roof. A moment later, he had fed the surgical tubing down a sink's air pipe, sealed the pipe with duct tape, and turned on the nitrous oxide.

Within five minutes, both guards were sound asleep.

Coleman dropped to the ground and entered the building through the door, holding his breath as he threw open the windows for ventilation.

He had two minutes before the effects of the gas would start wearing off. He moved quickly and expertly. When the guards woke, they would find themselves locked in the bathroom, bound together, with their mouths securely taped.

>ERIC: WE ARE GOING INTO GENODYNE. IF YOU ARE THERE, LET US KNOW WHERE. DON'T LET THEM CATCH YOU READING THEIR FILES. YOU ARE IN DANGER. TRUST NO ONE. I LOVE YOU, MOM.

Eric read the e-mail twice before clicking the REPLY box. He was about to type in his answer when he heard the door behind him rattle faintly. Someone had just stepped out of the front door of the large cabin, and the difference in air pressure had shaken his own door.

Eric stood and stepped quietly toward his second-story window. Below him Tisha was racing across the driveway toward the idling Mercedes that Murkoski had started up. Eric had heard her answer the other phone line a moment or two earlier. And now, judging by her urgency as she relayed the message to Murkoski and by his angry response, Eric guessed that the news wasn't so good.

He had no idea where he was. Some fancy cabin up in the mountains. Just Murkoski, Tisha, himself, and the two men who had brought him. The older kidnapper was sprawled out on a bed down the hall, nursing his broken nose. The younger guy was downstairs watching TV.

It had been Tisha's job to keep an eye on Eric. But now she was outside.

He looked back at the screen:

YOU ARE IN DANGER. TRUST NO ONE.

He had a choice. Wait until tomorrow and hope that they would release him like they had promised. Or take Mom at her word and get out while the getting was good.

He crossed to the door and carefully pulled it open. No one in sight. He stepped into the hall, moved past the bathroom, and past the closed door where the older man was snoring up a storm. He reached the top of the stairs. Below, he could see the younger guy on the sofa, his back to Eric, engrossed in some karate flick.

It would be tricky, but there was a chance that Eric could make it down the stairs and to the outside door without being spotted. After that—well. Still, between Mom's warning and his own uneasiness, he figured it was better to do something than nothing.

He eased down the steps, one at a time. There was no chance he could be heard. The whirring fan up in the cathedral ceiling and the blaring TV made certain of that. But he had to make sure that his reflection would not be caught on the TV screen.

He had two steps to go when the front door opened. For a millisecond he froze, then leaped the last two steps and ducked behind the sofa just as Tisha entered followed by the ranting Murkoski.

"Incompetent! Why is everybody we hire incompetent?"

As Murkoski stormed toward the kitchen, Eric edged around the far end of the couch. Now the stairs were to his back, the TV straight ahead, and the kitchen on the other side of the sofa.

He heard Murkoski yank up the kitchen phone and demand. "Yeah, what is it?" There was a pause. "What time?"

Tisha headed for the stairs. Eric scrunched low, knowing that, if she looked in his direction, she would spot him.

"What's wrong?" the man on the sofa asked, his voice less than four feet from Eric's head.

"There was a break-in at the lab," she answered.

Eric tensed, expecting to hear his name called, his escape ruined. But there was nothing. Just the simple padding of feet up the stairs. She had never looked toward the sofa.

"No, don't report it!" Murkoski ordered into the phone. "Not yet."

The man on the sofa clicked off the TV remote and rose to his feet. He gave a slight yawn and stretch. He was so close that Eric could have reached around and touched his leg. But he stayed low, afraid even to breathe.

"No, *you* investigate it!" Murkoski yelled. "You're security, that's what we pay you for! Get in there and—"

"Kenneth!" Tisha called from upstairs. "Kenneth, he's gone!"

"What?" Murkoski shouted.

The man at the sofa cursed, headed for the stairs, and took them two at a time to investigate. Murkoski slammed down the receiver and followed. "What do you mean, gone?"

A moment later, the room was empty. It was now or never.

Eric sprang to his feet and raced for the door. He threw it open and bolted into the fog and darkness. The gravel driveway popped and scuffed under his feet, sending the dog in the run beside the house into frenzied barking.

The woods lay thirty feet away. He made it into the first group of trees just as the light from the front door spilled out onto the driveway.

"Kid! Hey, kid!" It was Murkoski. "You out here?"

Eric froze. He could see the man, but there were enough shadows to keep him hidden, as long as he didn't make any sudden moves.

"Hey, kid! I'm talking to you!"

Tisha appeared in the doorway, followed by the younger man, a flashlight in hand.

"He couldn't have gone far," Tisha said. The light came on and swept across the trees, its beam clearly outlined by the night fog. For a moment it caught the edge of Eric's sweatshirt. But it didn't stop.

"Eric?" Tisha called. "Eric, where are you?"

Eric slowly edged toward the nearest tree, a large cedar, to better hide himself. There was no gravel here, only a floor of soft needles and underbrush. There were, however, plenty of sticks, and one of them snapped when he stepped on it.

The beam darted back in his direction, and he ducked from sight.

"Eric?" Tisha called. Apparently she had the flashlight now. He heard the crunching of gravel as she moved across the driveway in his direction.

The dog continued to bark.

"Eric? Eric, you don't want to be out here all alone. Come on now." Her voice sounded gentle and kind, but there was something wrong. She was lying. Under all that kindness he felt a ruthlessness, an ambition ready and willing to do whatever was necessary to have her way.

It was odd. He'd been experiencing these feelings most of the day—knowing from people's tone of voice what they were really saying, seeing in their eyes what they were really thinking. He hadn't thought much about it—until now. Now he needed all the help he could get.

"Come on, kid," Murkoski called. "Just come on back and everything will be okay."

The beam danced on the branches and bushes around him. In a matter of seconds, he would be spotted. He had no choice. He had to move.

Remembering what he'd learned from Coleman's Indian stories, he slowly, and this time soundlessly, worked his way through the undergrowth, watching every step, taking one at a time, keeping at least one tree between himself and the searching beam.

"Eric?" Tisha had entered the undergrowth now too. She was making enough noise to mask any he might make, so he picked up his pace, slowly veering to the left, ducking or freezing whenever the beam came in his direction.

"Come on, now," Tisha called. "It's too scary to be out here all by yourself."

She had that right. But it would be even scarier to trust her. It wasn't just what Mom had said over the Internet. It was also what he now knew, what he somehow sensed in the weird way he'd been sensing things all day.

There was a clanking noise, iron chain against steel fence. The dog barked louder, more frantically.

"What are you doing?" Tisha called back to the house.

Murkoski's voice answered. "We'll let the dog find him."

Chunks of drywall flew in all directions as Coleman chopped into the forest-green wall of the executive office. With each jarring slam of the ax, his head and body exploded in pain. And still he continued. He had tried opening the two-and-a-half-foot-wide Testron safe with the combination O'Brien had given him, but it hadn't responded. Given the short amount of time they had, it would be impossible to drill, torch, or blow the 1,800 pounds of high-tempered stainless steel. There was only one way to destroy the computer backup disks inside, and Katherine was the only one who knew how.

They had dumped all of their stolen items into an old gym bag Katherine had found in her trunk—a remnant of the days when she actually cared how she looked.

Knowing that the third guard was still at large, they had carefully made their way through the security gate on foot, then dashed across the parking lot to the entrance of the building. O'Brien's mag card and PIN had opened the door. They had skipped the elevator and taken the stairs. The guard, if he was alert, could have easily keyed off the elevator and trapped them between floors. They had arrived at the executive suites and found the office with the safe exactly as O'Brien had described.

Now, as Coleman swung his ax, chopping out the drywall around the safe, Katherine sat at the executive's desk, exploring the computer system.

"All I need is about eighteen inches around it," Katherine called. "Soon as you get that cleared out, let me know."

Coleman nodded and continued swinging, stopping only to pull out the debris and pieces of wall that fell around the safe.

Katherine couldn't resist the temptation to check her e-mail one last time to see whether Eric had left any messages. She switched to the modem, dialed in the phone number, entered her password, and waited. A moment later she had her answer:

NO NEW MAIL

Katherine's heart sank. Where was her son? Why wasn't he answering her mail? She switched over to the Computer Forum lobby that they had originally met in, just in case.

Not there.

Katherine fought a growing depression and returned to her task. Not only would the backup disks in the safe have to be destroyed, but so would the information stored in the computer system itself.

She reaccessed the mainframe. In just over twenty minutes, she had introduced a virus that she hoped would be destructive enough to eat up any info inside the system—as well as any computer that would log onto that system. Of course, Genodyne's computers were well equipped with virus sniffers and blockers, but her government experience still provided a few tricks that the civilians weren't yet aware of.

At one time, Katherine had been good—the best in her field. Maybe she still was. After all, in the twenty minutes she had just spent, a less-experienced hacker might have been able to introduce a virus equivalent to a bad cold, or maybe even the flu. Katherine had just infected the system with something she hoped to be closer to Ebola.

She paused to double-check her work. Then, holding her breath, she hit ENTER.

She stared at the screen, watching. Slowly, a smile spread across her face as the virus began its work. Within five minutes, there would be no stopping it. The virus would continue to infect and destroy all vital information within the mainframe, up to and including all maps and info on the GOD gene.

"Now what?" Coleman called.

Katherine looked up and saw a two-foot hole cut completely around the safe and running all the way to its back.

Coleman was breathing heavily. "What's next?" he repeated impatiently.

Katherine rose and walked to the gym bag, where she pulled out a roll of heavy Romex wire, the same heavy-duty wiring used inside the walls of most homes. She found one end of the wire and began to twist the three conductive strands together.

Coleman approached, sweating from the fever and obviously fighting through the pain. "So are you going to tell me what's next," he demanded, "or do we turn this into a guessing game?"

She saw such hostility in his eyes that a chill ran through her body. She turned back to the Romex and forced her voice to stay calm and even. "Start wrapping this Romex around the safe. Twenty-five turns."

He lugged the heavy wire over to the hole in the wall. That put him less than a dozen feet away from her, but she was grateful for every foot of that distance. Katherine had been through plenty, and it took a lot to unnerve her, but that last look had done it. She knew that he was struggling with more than just the pain. Coleman was changing. Clearly and irrefutably.

"What's all this supposed to do?" he demanded as he fought the stiff wire, forcing it to bend around the safe.

"I've calculated the inductive reactance that comes from a two-and-a-half-foot-diameter coil wrapped around an 1800-pound steel core."

"Meaning?"

She began stripping one end of the 220 extension cord to connect it to the Romex. "Meaning I'm turning the entire safe into a giant electromagnet."

Coleman nodded. "We can't get to the disks on the inside of the safe, so we're turning the entire safe into a giant magnet and erasing them that way."

"Exactly."

Coleman said nothing. She could feel his eyes on her. Maybe it was approval, maybe it was something else. Whatever it was, it made her uneasy and self-conscious. This was not the man she had known just a few hours earlier.

Once she had connected the extension cord to the Romex, she rose and began stringing the cord into the hall and toward the executive lunchroom, where O'Brien had said a 220 stove outlet would be.

But she had barely entered the hallway when she heard: "Okay, Ma'am. I think you better lay that down and turn around to face me."

Katherine's heart pounded; she dropped the extension cord to the floor and turned around.

It was the third guard, a college kid looking very clean-cut and dapper in his crisp white shirt and blue security uniform. He reminded her of Gary, back when they were first married, back when he had first worn his uniform. The boy was twenty feet away, but even from that distance she could see him sweating as he held the gun on her.

"So, where are your friends?" He motioned toward the office between them. "In there?"

Katherine said nothing as he approached. But with each step he took, she grew more and more apprehensive.

He arrived at the doorway. Keeping his attention divided between Katherine and the room, he called inside. "Okay, it's all over now."

There was no answer.

He was obviously afraid to step inside. "This is Security! I have a gun and I am authorized to use it, so come out now before anybody gets hurt."

There was no movement, no sound.

He looked again at Katherine. Then tentatively, reluctantly, he stepped into the doorway. "Hello? Wherever you are, you'd better—"

Coleman plowed into him like a semi, knocking him back into the hallway. The boy was down on the ground with Coleman on top of him before he knew what hit him. Coleman struck the boy's face once, twice, without mercy. By the time Katherine reached them, his nose was already broken.

"That's enough!" she shouted.

But Coleman continued to hit him. Blood covered the boy's face and stained Coleman's shirt.

"Coleman!"

And still he hit him. Rage had erupted inside him like a volcano, directing all of his fury at this boy.

"Stop it!" Katherine tried to pull him off. "Stop!"

Sounds came from Coleman's throat, grunts maybe, or whimperings, she couldn't tell. She dropped to her knees, pushing against him with all of her weight, crying "Stop it! Stop hitting him!" until she finally got his attention.

His eyes locked onto hers. For a moment, his rage was redirected at her.

Color drained from her face. She felt herself growing numb. She had never experienced such anger, never seen such raw hatred. And the eyes—almost satanic, full of malevolence and fury. But then she saw something else, deeper. Underneath. A flicker. Just a glimmer, way down, deep inside. The Coleman she knew was still there, fighting to resurface and take charge.

His glare softened, then faltered. He blinked once, then again. He looked back down at the boy, at the blood, the pulverized muscle, the broken bone.

"That's enough," she repeated firmly.

His eyes darted back to her.

"That's enough."

Coleman wiped the sweat from his face and rose unsteadily. He looked lost, staring first at the boy, then at Katherine, then back at the boy.

She leaned over and checked the guard. He was still breathing. He had probably lost an eye, and he would definitely need reconstructive surgery.

Coleman coughed. "We've . . ."

She looked up. He was steadying himself against the wall, still staring, still looking confused and frightened. "We've got to get him some help."

She nodded. "How long will it take to destroy all the test tubes?"

"No," he said, shaking his head. "It's over."

"What are you talking about?"

Coleman looked at the blood on his hands. "I can't—"

She slowly rose to her feet. "Yes, you can."

"I almost killed him."

"I know, but—"

"I *was* killing him."

"But you didn't. You were able to stop."

He closed his eyes. She knew that the war inside his head was excruciating.

"You can control this thing," she insisted. "I know you can."

"No."

"Yes, you can. I saw it, just now."

"No, I was—"

"You *have* to control it!" she demanded. "This isn't just about you. This is about all of us. You, me, Eric, everybody! You have to control it!"

Her outburst seemed to confuse him. Maybe she was getting through. She couldn't tell.

"Now stay here with this boy. All I have to do is plug in that extension cord, and those disks are history. That only leaves the lab samples and the animals. Then we're out of here. All right?"

Coleman just looked at her. He was starting to shiver again, his face wet with perspiration.

"All right?" she repeated.

He still gave no answer. But no answer was better than a negative one. She picked up the extension cord and headed for the stove outlet in the lunchroom.

The dog raced into the woods, streaks of black and gold in the night. It headed toward Tisha, but Eric knew that it would change course as soon as it spotted him.

He looked at the nearest tree, a huge fir with branches low enough for climbing. But then what? Be treed like some animal? There had to be another way.

He looked back at the driveway. He'd been circling around, moving parallel with it as Tisha had gone deeper into the woods. Three cars were parked there: a van, the car he had been kidnapped in, and the idling Mercedes.

There was no time to think. The dog was already at Tisha's side.

Eric sprang forward. He crashed through the undergrowth, snapping sticks, twigs, and anything else in his path. He no longer cared about the noise. He had only one objective—to reach that idling Mercedes before the dog reached him.

The animal heard him and immediately spun and lunged in pursuit.

Voices shouted.

The car lay twenty feet ahead.

Branches slapped into the boy's face, stinging his eyes, making them blur with tears, but he kept running. He looked over his shoulder. The dog shot through the brush after him—a flash of gold, then shadows, then black and gold, then more shadows. It was huge, bigger than Eric.

The car was fifteen feet away.

He could hear the dog breathing now. Quick grunting gasps with each powerful stride.

Eric flew out of the woods and onto the driveway.

Ten feet to go.

He heard the dog's claws digging into the driveway's gravel.

Six feet.

He reached toward the door handle—just as his left foot caught a chuckhole, buckling his leg and sending him sprawling into the loose gravel. He put out his hands, sliding on them and on his elbows and knees.

He looked over his shoulder. The dog was two strides behind, fangs bared, eyes white and crazed. There was no time to reach up and open the door. Before the slide slowed Eric flattened out and kicked himself forward, continuing the momentum, until he was slipping under the car.

He would have made it if the dog hadn't caught his left leg, sinking its teeth hard into the ankle. Eric screamed and jerked his foot away. He felt the tendons and muscles rip as he heard the thud of the animal's head striking the side of the car.

The impact made the dog release its grip, and Eric scrambled on his belly toward the other side. The animal tried to follow underneath, but could only reach in as far as its chest. Its barks thundered and roared under the car. It gnashed and snapped, fangs just feet from the boy. But the dog was too big to reach him. It pulled out and raced to the other side.

Seeing the move, Eric reversed direction and slid back across the gravel toward the passenger side. He crawled out, scrambled to his knees, and opened the door.

The dog spun around and came back at him.

Eric leaped into the car. But as he reached for the handle to slam the door, the dog lunged for his arm. Eric pulled the door with all of his might. He felt the animal's hot breath against his wrist—just as the car door smashed its head against the car's body. The animal yelped, and Eric opened the door just far enough for it to escape, then slammed it shut. He spun around and hit the locks, gasping for breath, frantically checking for bites. Suddenly there was a pounding on the driver's window.

"Eric!" It was Tisha pounding and shouting. "Eric, open up! Nobody's going to hurt you. Come on now, open up."

It was a lie. Not only could he tell by her voice, but he could see it in her eyes as well. She could not be trusted.

He looked to the ignition. Yes, the keys were there. He was safe. No one could get him. At least for now.

Murkoski had remained just outside the front door of the cabin, watching. The other young man, the kidnapper, joined Tisha at the passenger side of the Mercedes, pounding and pleading. But Eric wouldn't give in. Murkoski knew he was too frightened. The boy would simply stay there in the car until they busted out a window and dragged him out.

Murkoski scowled. The thought of a busted window in his Mercedes SL 600 gave him little pleasure. But what choice did he have? After all, the kid had the keys, so—

Slowly, Murkoski smiled. Well, the kid had one set of keys, anyway.

He turned back toward the cabin, colliding with the older kidnapper, who had just ambled outside. "What's going on?" the man mumbled through his swollen nose.

"Stay here," Murkoski ordered.

Murkoski headed into the house and up the stairs to his office. He pulled open the top desk drawer, and there they were—the spare set of keys.

He scooped them up and started out of the room, then hesitated. Someone had left the computer on. He turned back and looked at the glowing screen. There was a message on it. From the Internet. He slowly approached the monitor and read:

>ERIC: WE ARE GOING INTO GENODYNE. IF YOU ARE THERE, LET US KNOW WHERE. DON'T LET THEM CATCH YOU READING THEIR FILES. YOU ARE IN DANGER. TRUST NO ONE. I LOVE YOU, MOM.

So the kid had been doing more than playing computer games. Grudgingly, Murkoski nodded in admiration, then reread the message. Suddenly he understood the break-in call from Security. It hadn't been a prank or some unknown intruder. It had been the boy's mom, and probably Coleman as well.

Murkoski paused, running through the possible courses of action. If he wasn't careful, things could quickly get out of hand. Gradually, a plan took shape. He would have to beat them to the punch. He would be the one to call the police, to play the victim. After all, Coleman and Katherine were the ones breaking and entering. As for the kid, children wander off all the time. It was their word against his. A broken-down alcoholic and a convicted killer against a world-famous Ph.D.? Not much competition there.

Of course, the boy would have to be disposed of. But Kenneth Murkoski was getting better at that sort of thing all the time.

CHAPTER 16

More window pounding. This time from the passenger side. Eric spun around to see the younger kidnapper beating on the glass so hard that he thought it would break. Meanwhile, Tisha continued pleading and pounding on the driver's side.

Eric's eyes darted back to the keys in the ignition. He knew that the engine was running, that the car was ready to go. But he also knew he'd never driven before. Still, there was TV and all those movies, and hadn't he seen his mother drive a million times before?

He scooted behind the wheel, which didn't seem to make Tisha and the kidnapper any happier. The shouting and pounding grew louder. Eric reached his foot down as far as he could and pressed the pedal.

Nothing happened.

Maybe it was the wrong pedal. He stretched until he was able to touch the other pedal with his toe.

The engine revved loudly, but the car still didn't move. He stretched and pushed harder. The car roared even louder, but it didn't budge.

Suddenly the pounding on the passenger window turned to loud, sharp crackings. The man was beating on the glass with the butt of his gun.

In a panic, Eric searched the dash board, then looked to the gearshift. It was on "P." He wasn't sure what that meant but remembered that his mother always fiddled with her gearshift before taking off. Still pushing the accelerator with his toe, making the engine roar, Eric strained to see over the dash. The older kidnapper was walking toward him, shaking his head, saying something that Eric couldn't make out over the revving engine, the barking dog, and all the pounding and yelling.

The passenger window exploded. Eric screamed as fragments of glass showered over him. The younger man reached inside, fumbling for the lock. Eric pushed the accelerator as far as he could reach. Still nothing. In desperation, he grabbed the gearshift and shoved it hard.

The car lunged forward. The man reaching inside had to run to keep up. "Stop the car!" he yelled. "Stop it!"

Eric watched him, terrified.

"Stop the car!" The man began swearing. "Stop the car, stop the—" Suddenly his eyes went wide. "Look out!"

Eric turned forward just in time to see a giant evergreen coming at them. He jerked the wheel hard to the left and the car swerved, barely missing the tree. The man wasn't so lucky. Inertia broke his grip on the car and threw him forward directly into the tree. He gave a loud *OOF!* then dropped from sight.

Eric thought he'd killed him. He let up on the accelerator and craned his neck over the backseat to look out the window. He saw Tisha running over and helping the man to his feet.

He wasn't dead. Good.

Then, before Eric could turn around, headlights of the second car blazed on, blinding him as they glared through the back window.

He spun forward and pushed hard on the accelerator. The car threw gravel and slid as he fought to keep it on the road.

The security guard had regained consciousness. Coleman and Katherine carefully helped him to his feet. They eased him down the hall and into the elevator. They had been able to stop the bleeding, but it was likely that he'd sustained a concussion—perhaps a bad one.

"We'll get you some help," Coleman assured him. "Real soon. Just hang in there."

Katherine could see the kid watching Coleman suspiciously. It may have been their recent history together, or the fact that Coleman was now in possession of his gun. In either case, she understood why the boy might be a bit skeptical of Coleman's goodwill.

The elevator came to a stop on the main floor. They stepped off and headed down the hallway toward the lab division.

"Listen," Katherine asked, as she helped the guard along, "did you happen to see a little boy?"

"Sorry?" The guard's speech was thick from his swollen tongue and broken teeth.

"A little boy. Eight, blondish hair, U of W sweatshirt? Did you see anybody bring a little boy in here?"

The guard shook his head. He talked, but it was obvious that his pain was severe. "FDA forbids children entering a lab."

"What about the offices, could he be in—"

He shook his head. "Every visit recorded."

"And there's nothing on the record in the past twenty-four hours?"

Again he shook his head.

Katherine's disappointment was heavy. Where was her boy? Was he hurt? Was he even alive?

They reached a set of doors. Coleman shoved O'Brien's mag card against the black box and entered his PIN. Katherine noticed his hands were wet and trembling as he hit the numbers. The door buzzed and he pushed it open. They moved through the atrium, walking beside the trickling stream and under the large palm trees until they reached the other elevator. They entered, and Coleman pressed the button to the third floor.

O'Brien had said that the experiment was confined to the third floor. They would have to go through each of the eight laboratories on that floor and clear out all samples of the DNA. It would be an arduous task. She glanced at Coleman, wondering what he was thinking. Did he plan on taking the guard wherever they went? They would be able to move faster without him, but she knew it would be impossible to convince Coleman to leave this kid behind in his battered condition.

It was frustrating—which Coleman was she dealing with, killer or saint? And, as the battle raged inside his head, he seemed to change from minute to minute. Only one thing remained constant: his deterioration. With every passing minute, he seemed to be losing ground.

The elevator doors opened, and to her surprise she saw half a dozen technicians crossing back and forth between labs. Coleman leaned toward her and said, "Must be the shipment. Murkoski has them working overtime to make the morning shipment."

Katherine nodded as technicians noticed the open elevator and slowly ground to a halt. She figured that their shocked expressions had something to do with the guard's bloody face or the way Coleman held the gun or both. She stood watching them, unsure of the next step.

Not Coleman. He quickly moved into action. Brandishing the gun with one hand and motioning to the gym bag with the other, he shouted, "All right everyone, listen up!" He locked the elevator door open and stepped out, pushing the battered guard ahead of him.

He definitely had their attention.

"You've got exactly three-and-a-half minutes to clear the building!"

No one moved.

"I've planted a bomb. It's going off in exactly—" He looked at his watch. "In exactly three minutes and twenty-four seconds."

People stood, stunned. Mouths dropped. Most of all Katherine's.

"If I were you," he continued, voice rising, "I'd quit standing around and get out of here! Do you hear me?" He waved the gun some more. "Get out of here! Now! Move it! Move it!"

Panic swept through the hall. Some of the technicians raced into the labs to warn colleagues, others started for the stairs.

"Three minutes and ten seconds! Move! Let's go, let's go! Three minutes and five!"

Katherine stepped off the elevator, amazed at his performance. Coleman was doing a very convincing imitation of a madman—though she was no longer sure how much of it was imitation.

"Three minutes!"

Coleman motioned the gun toward a couple heading for the stairs. "You," he shouted. "And you!"

They froze.

"Go to the other floors. If there's any other workers, clear them out. Check everywhere, the offices, the johns, everywhere."

They hesitated.

He pointed the gun. "Go!"

They didn't wait to be told again.

"Here!" He shoved the guard at another passing technician. "Take him and get him out of here."

The technician obeyed. "What about the woman?" he asked.

Coleman reached out and grabbed Katherine's arm. He pulled her to him hard. "She's my hostage."

"But—"

"Get out of here before I decide to take more!"

He scurried off, rushing the guard ahead of him.

"Hostage?" Katherine said, angrily ripping her arm free of his grasp.

But with lightning speed he grabbed it again, this time twisting it behind her back. She started to fight, but he yanked it up so hard she cried out. He hissed into her ear, "You want to share the blame for this?"

Again she struggled, and he pulled so hard tears came to her eyes.

"This way they'll only come after me."

"Hey, man, come on—"

Katherine looked up to see a freckle-faced kid protesting.

"Can't you see you're hurting her?"

Katherine heard a pistol cocking and turned to see Coleman leveling it directly at the kid. Suddenly she feared that Coleman was no longer acting.

"All right, all right," the kid said as he backed away. "Just take it easy, take it easy."

In a little over a minute, the hallway was clear, and Coleman released Katherine with a shove. She grabbed her arm and rubbed it, wanting to shout at him, to curse him. But when she saw the hate that had returned to his eyes, she forced herself to remain silent. Now that there was just the two of them, she had no idea what he would do.

"You go too," he ordered, wiping the sweat out of his eyes. "Your kid's not here. Get out while you can."

She searched his face for signs of the Coleman she'd once known, once admired. "What about you?" she countered. "You have no stake in this. Why not look out for yourself and get out of here, too?"

He hesitated, and for a split second she saw it. He was still there. Somewhere inside, the Coleman she knew was still there, still struggling, still trying to do right, regardless of the cost.

Holding his gaze, she shook her head. "No, this is too important to let you screw it up on your own. I'm staying as long as you do."

Murkoski stepped back outside the cabin just in time to see his Mercedes disappear down the drive. The older man had climbed into the other car, the Audi, to go after it.

"No!" Murkoski shouted. "Take the van!"

The man rolled down his window. "What?"

"I'm driving this one to the lab."

"Why can't you take the—"

"The van's got a plastic tarp in the back. That way you won't get blood on the carpet. And take a couple shovels so you can put the body somewhere it won't be found." The order had been given, and Murkoski held the man's gaze to make sure there was no misunderstanding.

Coleman and Katherine scoured the labs, emptying every refrigerator of every Eppendorf tube, checking all the centrifuges, the incubators, the sequencers, everything O'Brien had said could contain samples of the GOD gene. They had to be certain. Every sample on the third floor had to be torched.

Katherine wasn't sure why Coleman had chosen to dump all of the tubes into the open elevator. It was getting to be quite a pile, nearly five feet high, and they still had two more labs to go. She wanted to question him on it, but she knew that it was time to keep the arguments to a minimum. He was unstable, a primed bomb ready to explode, and there was no telling what would set it off.

No, she wouldn't question his methods. If there were to be any confrontations, she'd save them for the most critical issues.

She dumped another wastebasket full of tubes into the elevator.

"Hey . . ."

She turned. He stood at the entrance to the last lab, worn and drawn and soaked with perspiration. As threatening and unnerving as it was for her to work with him, she couldn't even imagine what it must be like for him—what type of pain the viral leash was inflicting upon his body, and more importantly, what type of monster he was battling within his mind.

"There's something . . ." He swallowed. "I think you should see this."

She followed him into the laboratory.

It sat on a lab bench across the room. He had just removed it from a freezer. It was a clear, round container, looking very much like a high-tech, Plexiglas humidor. It stood twelve inches high with a base five inches in diameter.

Inside was what looked like a translucent rock. Yellow-brown. But as she moved closer, Katherine realized that it wasn't a rock at all.

It was wax. A small piece of ancient, yellowed wax.

She stooped for a closer look. One end of the wax had been sheered off. And from that end protruded a tiny twig. But she knew it was no twig. She stopped breathing. It was not a twig, but the remains of a vine. And although it was hard to make out through the opaqueness of the wax, there appeared to be the remnant of one, maybe two, long, spindly thorns.

She stared in silent, reverent awe. Of course, she could see no blood through the wax, but she knew it was there. Traces of blood two thousand years old.

As she stared, she couldn't help thinking how those traces of blood on this frail vine were responsible for the unimaginable terror about to be released upon humankind.

No, that wasn't true. The blood wasn't the cause. The blood was holy, pure, good. It wasn't the blood, it was how man had twisted and contorted this goodness, how he had once again found a way to turn holiness into horror.

Coleman cleared his throat. "Better, uh—throw it into the elevator with the rest," he said.

Katherine nodded. But neither moved to touch it. Not yet. They would, of course. But for now they wanted to look upon it just a moment longer. And to quietly wonder.

As soon as Eric's car slid out of the gravel driveway and onto the main road, he knew he'd turned the wrong direction. He was going up the mountain; he wanted to be going down.

Then there was the problem of the accelerator. No matter how hard he pressed, the engine only whined louder—the car never moved faster.

Fortunately, his slower progress made it easier to stay on the road—at least what road he could see. It would have helped if he could have found the switch for the lights, but Eric didn't dare take his hands off the wheel to start exploring.

A pair of high beams bounced onto the road behind him. They quickly closed in, blazing through the back window and into the car. Their approach terrified Eric, and it was all he could do to hold the car on the road. Now the vehicle behind him began honking, long and loud, over and over again.

Eric's anxiety skyrocketed and his driving grew worse, until he was swerving back and forth across the road.

The lights backed off.

It took forever to bring his car back under control. When he did, Eric noticed how hot and damp his hands had become. He wiped them off on his jeans, one at a time.

Once again the headlights approached, flashing from high beams to low and back again, the car horn blaring.

"Stop it!" Eric cried. "Stop it!"

The vehicle pulled directly behind him, so close that he could see it was the van that had been in the driveway, and he could see the faces of both kidnappers.

"Stop it!" Eric screamed.

They eased to his left. Their lights no longer flooded the inside of his car; now they illuminated the road beside him. He knew that they were pulling up. He looked over to see, but lost his bearings and began swerving again.

Once again the lights dropped back.

It was then that Eric noticed a red warning light glowing on the instrument panel. He figured that whatever he was doing wrong, whatever was making the car's engine race without moving, was making the light burn.

He checked the speedometer. Thirty miles an hour. He pressed down on the accelerator as hard as he could. The engine whined louder.

Suddenly the car lurched forward with a loud CRASH.

Eric screamed.

Another crash, another lurch.

The bad guys were ramming him. He had to do something. He looked down at the gearshift. It was on "1." When he had pushed on it the first time, it got him going; maybe it was worth another try. He shoved it into another position. Something labeled "N."

What power he had suddenly vanished, and the engine roared wildly, as if it were going to explode.

They rammed him again.

Eric screamed.

Then again.

But this time they didn't back off. Instead, they kept their bumper pressed hard against his. Suddenly he had more power than he knew what to do with. They were pushing him. They picked up speed. Thirty miles an hour, thirty-five, forty . . .

"Knock it off!" Eric shouted, as he fiercely gripped the steering wheel. "Stop it, *Stop it!*"

But they didn't stop.

Forty-five.

Eric was losing control. He began to swerve.

To his right rose a steep cliff. To his left, the ground fell away in an equally steep drop-off. He played it safe and oversteered to the right. The car scraped, then banged against the cliff, glancing off the protruding boulders. It was a bone-jarring ride. He cringed at the smashing and screeching of sheet metal against granite. He knew that he was making plenty of scratches and dents and figured it would probably get him into lots of trouble. But he also figured that being grounded for life was better than not having a life.

And still the van continued to push.

The road swerved to the right. The rocks and boulders he'd been banging against disappeared, and Eric found himself shooting across the road into the left lane.

"Stop it!" he cried. "Stop it!"

He cranked the wheel to the right, but he was too late. The car crashed through the guardrail and suddenly became airborne.

Eric screamed, taking his hands off the wheel to cover his face. The car glanced off a large tree, then everything went topsy-turvy, like a carnival ride gone berserk. He flew into the roof, then into the doors, then the roof again. It was happening too fast to feel any pain. He figured the pain would come later.

The windshield exploded, spraying glass over his face, his arms, his hands. And then he felt nothing.

When Murkoski arrived at Genodyne, he slowed the car and eased past the dozen or so employees milling outside the security gate in the fog. When he turned and tried to enter the gate, a man with a Greater City of Arlington Police Department uniform stepped from the security building and waved him to a stop.

Murkoski rolled down his window. "It's okay, officer, I'm Dr. Murkoski, head of the—"

"I'm sorry, Sir, no one is allowed inside the parking lot."

"You don't understand. I'm in charge of—"

"I'm sorry, Sir. No one is allowed within a three-hundred-yard perimeter of the building."

"A three-hundred-yard perimeter?"

"Those are my orders, Sir. Now if you'll please back up and—"

"But—"

"I'm sorry, Sir."

Murkoski hated the man's politeness. Underneath all of that courtesy was just some hick who loved to flaunt his authority. Without a word, he threw the car into reverse, spitting just enough dirt and gravel to show his contempt.

He found a level place on the opposite side of the road and parked just as a local TV cable van approached. "Great," he sighed, "a media event." Then he shrugged. It wouldn't be that bad. After all, he was getting quite good at spinning stories and manipulating truth.

He threw open the door, nodded to some of the huddled staff, and strode through the fog toward the gate. The first cop, apparently expecting a confrontation, had already signaled his partner, who was a few years his senior.

Murkoski wasn't concerned. There were only two of them, and from his lofty perspective they were nothing but hayseeds.

"Mr. Murkoski?" the older cop asked.

"*Dr.* Murkoski, that's right."

"I'm Officer Sealy of the Arlington—"

"Did you find them?"

"I'm afraid it's not that simple. Apparently we have a bomb threat here."

"A bomb threat? Why do you say that?"

"Several of your employees were threatened by a man with a gasoline can and other paraphernalia. He claimed to have set a bomb."

"A gasoline can?" There was no hiding the condescending tone in Murkoski's voice. "You don't make a bomb with a can of gasoline."

"It could be a hoax, that's true. His first deadline has already come and gone, but we have to be certain. Fortunately, except for a hostage, everyone else has been cleared from the building."

"A hostage?"

"Yes, a woman."

Murkoski's mind raced. He knew it was Coleman up there. And with him, the boy's mother. But what were they up to? From the e-mail he'd seen on the computer screen, it sounded as if they'd been looking for the boy. But if they'd cleared the building, then they already knew he wasn't there. So why were they still in there? Unless . . .

Sensing a significant danger, Murkoski's thoughts snapped into sharper focus. The e-mail message had also said something about the kid reading computer files. If the kid could open Murkoski's files and navigate the Internet, then he could also transmit those files. And if he had transmitted the wrong file to Coleman and the woman, and if they had read it . . .

Murkoski turned to the cop. "You said he had other paraphernalia?"

"Yes, a gasoline can and a gym bag full of unspecified items. Now we're no experts in this field, but . . ."

The officer continued rattling, but Murkoski didn't listen. Why would Coleman take a can of gasoline into the plant? That's not enough to make a bomb. Enough to start a fire, certainly, but . . .

Destroy all the samples? No, there was far too much material for him to try and destroy on his own. Besides, the new Coleman he'd invented wouldn't be that brazen. Then again, if the old Coleman had returned, the one who'd run Death Row, there was no telling what he was capable of.

". . . a bit out of our league," the officer was saying. "So we'll just sit tight and wait for the Snohomish County Sheriff's Bomb Division to come up from Everett."

"Officer?"

"Yes, sir."

"I know who the man is."

"You do? Are you certain?"

"He is one of my volunteers, a patient."

"Well, then, maybe you could talk to him. If we can establish communication—"

The cable crew had arrived, and a light suddenly blasted into their eyes, momentarily distracting the officer.

"Maybe you could talk to him by phone, I mean, if we set it up."

"It would be better if I talked to him in person." Murkoski flipped the hair out of his eyes and spoke just a little louder for the camera.

The officer looked surprised. "Dr. Murkoski, I don't think that's such a good idea."

"He won't hurt me. He trusts me."

The officer fidgeted. This was obviously not a decision he felt qualified to make, and making it under the glaring light of the camera was even worse.

"Trust me on this, Officer . . . Officer. . . ?"

"Sealy."

"Officer Sealy of the Arlington Police Department?"

"Yes."

"Officer Sealy, if you go in there, you'll frighten him, and he may indeed kill his hostage and blow up the entire facility. I'm sure you don't want that."

"Well, no, of course not."

"And if we wait, he may kill her and blow it up anyway. You did say one deadline has already passed."

"That's true, but—"

"If you allow me in there, if you let me reason with him, I'm sure he'll listen."

"But, risking your own life—"

"That's a risk I'm willing to take, Officer." Murkoski knew he sounded a bit melodramatic, but, after all, this was TV. "For his life, for the hostage's life, for the sake of the company, I'll take that risk."

The officer frowned, still undecided. Murkoski knew that he needed a last push. He patted the man's arm and smiled in gratitude as if he had just received permission. Then, without a word, he turned and started across the parking lot for the building.

"Dr. Murkoski. Dr. Murkoski?"

Murkoski pretended not to hear. He was sure the camera was still rolling, and that was good. The cop was out of his league. No way would the hick want to make a public scene now—especially with somebody of Murkoski's position.

Murkoski smiled quietly. Once he got through all of this, he would have to call up the station and ask for a copy of the tape. He always enjoyed seeing himself on TV.

O'Brien sat in the Pizza Hut snack shop at Sea-Tac. He stared out at his Mexicana Flight #142 to Mazatlán. As they had for the past several hours, a half-dozen ground crew members meandered around the 757, trying to look busy.

O'Brien sighed heavily and tore open another pack of Equal. If someone would just take the initiative and cancel the flight, he could go home or grab a hotel room for the night. Instead, every half hour or so, they would announce that the problem was nearly corrected and that they should be boarding shortly.

O'Brien slowly poured a stream of tiny Equal granules into his third cup of decaf. The late news droned on an overhead monitor, but he took little notice—until he heard the name Genodyne. Suddenly his ears perked up:

"... a bomb threat by a man with a hostage. We have a crew en route to this late-breaking story, and we hope to have a full report before the end of the broadcast."

O'Brien stared at the screen in disbelief. He felt numb and guilty and nauseous all at the same time. Coleman had been found out. The plan had failed before it had even begun.

Eric awoke to the sound of voices—thick and blurry and far, far away. His head ached and he wanted to keep his eyes shut, but there was a light flickering against his lids and he knew he should see what it was.

The voices grew clearer.

He pried open his eyes, but his glasses were gone. Without them it was hard to make out the details, but he definitely saw the flames. He sat up. The pounding in his head grew worse. Fifty yards below him, at the bottom of the hill, a car was on fire. There were no explosions, just roaring, lapping flames.

"Eric! Eric, where are you, son?" The men from the van were down below, looking for him. "Eric!"

Across the ravine, maybe a quarter of a mile away, he saw a light. Maybe a farmhouse, maybe a cabin, he couldn't tell. But he knew there were people there. Good people. He wasn't sure how he knew, he just knew.

"Eric!"

Mustering what strength he had, Eric rose to a squatting position. The throbbing in his head grew worse and he wanted to cry, but he couldn't. Instead, he slowly stood up and quietly made his way through the woods toward the light.

CHAPTER 17

Katherine poured the last of the tubes onto the pile in the elevator. A handful tumbled off, rattling and clinking as they rolled into the hall. She bent over, scooped them up, and tossed them back onto the pile. When she rose, she caught Coleman staring at her. But it was more than a stare. She'd seen that look a thousand times from a thousand different men. It made her feel self-conscious, belittled, and angry. Normally she would have called him on it. But since she no longer knew whom she was dealing with and since they were in such a hurry, she did her best to ignore it. They had one more job after this. Destroying the lab animals. She didn't want to jeopardize their mission with a confrontation now.

As a reward for her restraint, he flashed her a lascivious grin. "Nice. Very nice."

Knowing he wasn't referring to the pile of Eppendorf tubes, she shot him a glare. His grin only broadened. She turned away.

He changed the subject. "All right," he said, kneeling by the gym bag and pulling out the large box of soap flakes, "move that cute little rear of yours down the hall and start closing the lab doors."

His tone was demanding, condescending, and enough to push Katherine past the point of better judgment. "Why?" she challenged.

There was that smile again. He tore open the box of soap flakes and began sprinkling it over the pile of tubes, pushing and kicking the top layers aside so the flakes would filter down. "The labs here are equipped with automatic Halon fire extinguishers."

"What?"

"Fluorocarbon. They use it instead of water. It puts out the fire by replacing the oxygen. Regular water would short out and destroy all the expensive lab equipment. If you close those doors, we'll have enough oxygen for our weenie roast out here. If you don't, who knows."

"What about these?" She pointed to the overhead sprinklers above them in the hall.

"Just water. That's why everything's going in the elevator. No sprinklers in there."

"And the soap?" Her anger was giving way to curiosity.

"Poor man's napalm. Turns the fire into liquid jelly so it sticks to the tubes and doesn't run off."

She watched as he reached for the can of gasoline and began pouring it over the pile. "Get going," he ordered, "we got lots to do."

Still not fond of taking orders, but knowing it was for the best, Katherine turned and headed down the hall. Even then she could feel his eyes watching her. Angrily, she shut each of the eight doors. When she returned, he had finished pouring most but not all of the five gallons of gas onto the pile. He screwed the lid back onto the gas can.

"What about the rest of it?" she asked.

He grinned. "We save the rest to toast the lab animals downstairs."

She shuddered at the thought—and could tell that he enjoyed it.

He reached into the gym bag, pulled out a packet of matches, and lit one. Without hesitation, he tossed it onto the tubes. The pile ignited with a *whoosh.* Hot air slapped against Katherine's face, and she took a half-step back.

Coleman turned and started for the stairs. "Come on." But Katherine remained, watching the flames melt the soap into a thick, burning goo that stuck to the tubes and dripped further into the pile, cooking all that they touched. What a waste. What an incredible waste. Things could have been so different. So much good could have been accomplished if this had landed in the right hands.

Then again, with the type of money they were talking about, what type of hands *would* be right—or could remain so?

The overhead sprinklers kicked on. Water rained down, soaking her shirt, running down her neck. The cold made her shiver, but she continued standing, watching.

She gave a start when Coleman grabbed her arm. "Come on!" he yelled over the hiss of the sprinklers. "Let's go!"

She pulled away angrily. But instead of releasing her, he grabbed her other shoulder, turning her around. She opened her mouth to shout at him, but stopped. There was that grin again. Only now it had twisted into an obvious leer.

"Let me go," she demanded.

His grip tightened, and his gaze dropped from her eyes to her wet, clinging blouse.

She tried to pull away, but he held tight, looking into her eyes again. Water streamed down his face as his leer broadened, growing more frightening.

She forced herself to sound calm and cold. "I said, let me—"

He pulled her toward him.

"What are you—"

She felt his hand on the back of her head, shoving her mouth toward his. Her resistance was no match for his strength. His mouth covered hers. She tried to turn away, but his grip tightened, preventing it. He pushed harder, his mouth demanding and animal-like.

With a sharp twist, she pulled her head back for a moment and glared at him with venom. But his eyes were mocking, spiteful. The Coleman she had known, the one she had been so deeply drawn to, was not behind those eyes. This was someone else—the old Coleman.

She felt his hand reaching, pulling at her soaked blouse. She tried to raise her own hands to stop him, but she couldn't. They were pinned. "Come on, babe," he said, "you know you want—"

She spat at him.

He stopped and blinked, stunned. For a moment she thought the other Coleman, her Coleman, was returning—until he swung his arm back, clearly intending to smash his hand across her face.

It was the wet floor that saved her. He slipped as he swung, spoiling his aim. She turned and nearly broke away, but not quite. He grabbed her shoulder from behind.

This time she remembered her training. She clenched her left hand over her right fist and sent her elbow flying backwards as hard as she could. It met its mark, catching him in the stomach. He gasped and let go.

She started to run, slipped, and then he had her again. She tried to break free, but suddenly she felt herself lifted off the ground and shoved face-first against the unyielding wall. Her instincts protected her nose—she turned her head as she saw the wall coming—but her cheekbone hit hard. She fought to retain consciousness as Coleman held her upright, her toes barely touching the ground.

"I like a woman with spirit," he growled, moving closer until his breath was hot in her face.

Tears streamed down her face. She hated herself for them, but couldn't stop. "Coleman, please—"

Suddenly she heard another voice shouting over the sprinklers: "Well, well, well. What do we have here?"

Coleman spun around. Katherine turned, her vision just clear enough to make out the form of a man. Murkoski emerged from the stairwell.

"A little domestic spat?"

Taking advantage of Coleman's distraction and using the wall as support, Katherine slid several feet away from him. She reached up and touched the wetness on her cheek. At first she thought it was water, but water wouldn't be that warm. Then she looked at her fingers and saw the blood.

Murkoski stepped toward her, the sprinklers soaking his sports coat, his hair, making him look like a drowned rat. With a mocking flourish, he handed her a handkerchief. She batted it away. Murkoski chuckled, shrugged, and stuffed it back into his pocket. "You should have that looked at. I'm afraid you'll wind up with a rather unpleasant scar."

"What do you want?" Coleman seethed.

Murkoski flipped his wet hair out of his eyes. "The question is, what do you want?"

As an answer Coleman broke into a wry grin and stepped aside so Murkoski could have a full view of the fire burning in the elevator. "We had a long talk with Dr. O'Brien."

"I see. And you think that's all of it?"

Coleman said nothing.

Murkoski shook his head. "You *are* ignorant, aren't you?"

Katherine glanced nervously at Coleman. She could tell he was straining not to attack.

"You don't think we have that genetic information recorded?" Murkoski asked.

Coleman's voice was low and quiet. "We've destroyed all the computer files, erased all the backups in the safe."

Murkoski registered a trace of surprise, but held his ground. "What about the gene sequencers?"

Coleman hesitated, then looked at Katherine.

"We emptied them," she said, barely hearing herself over the spray of the sprinklers.

"And their memory?" Murkoski asked, unable to contain his mockery.

She stood a moment. A dull, sick feeling began to spread through her body. She'd completely overlooked the independent computers, the ones reading the genes and temporarily storing their data.

"Don't tell me you've already forgotten the features of our expensive gene sequencers," he pretended to scold.

Coleman turned to Katherine. "Which labs are they in?"

Before she could answer, Murkoski motioned grandly to the building. "Why, throughout the entire wing, of course."

"You're lying!" Katherine shouted over the sound of the sprinklers. "O'Brien said everything was limited to the third floor!"

"Yes, well, Dr. O'Brien has been a bit out of the loop lately."

Coleman turned to Katherine. "Can you knock them out?"

She looked at him helplessly.

"If they're computers, can you knock them out?" he repeated impatiently.

She opened her mouth to answer, but Murkoski cut her off. "Don't be stupid. She doesn't have the know-how. Even if she did, you don't have the time. I told the police if we didn't come out in five minutes to come in shooting."

Coleman stared at him. It was obvious he was trying to determine whether Murkoski was bluffing. But whatever discerning ability Coleman had possessed appeared to be gone by now.

"And if you ask me," Murkoski continued, "I think those rednecks out in the parking lot would enjoy a little action, don't you?"

Without missing a beat Coleman turned to Katherine. "Check out the sequencers. I'll go down and start killing the lab animals."

Katherine nodded, and they both started for the stairs.

"Killing—that's what you do best, isn't it?" Murkoski called.

Coleman stopped.

Murkoski seemed to revel in the moment. Standing there with water pouring over him, taunting and baiting like a school-yard bully. "Just like old times, isn't it, Mr. Coleman? That emotional rush of taking another life. All that control. It's the ultimate power trip, isn't it?"

Coleman's breathing slowed as he focused on Murkoski. Katherine had seen this before. She knew what was coming.

"But then, what can we expect? After all, you're just a product of your chemicals, aren't you? This is how you're programmed. You have no other choice. Once a monster, always a monster."

Coleman's body tensed. Katherine reached out and touched his arm. He didn't respond.

"But you see, there's one lab animal you won't be able to kill. One you can't."

Coleman's voice was barely audible over the sprinklers. "Which one is that?"

"You."

Katherine caught her breath.

Murkoski grinned at his little surprise. "You don't think there are remnants of that gene in your blood? You don't think there will always be a remnant that somebody can pull from you to start all of this all over again?"

Doubt and confusion crossed Coleman's face.

"He's lying," Katherine ventured.

"Am I? Everything's been thought out, Mr. Coleman, down to the most minute detail. You see, that's the difference between you and me. I'm at the top of the evolutionary chain. I'm a thinker. In fact, I come from a long line of thinkers. You, on the other hand ..." His lips curled into a cold smile. "Well, as I've said, we're all products of our genes, no matter how primitive our parentage may be."

Coleman lunged. Katherine screamed as he threw Murkoski into a choke hold, his eyes wild, his face filled with exhilaration.

"Coleman, don't!" She yanked at his arm, but his grip was immovable. "Coleman!"

Murkoski gasped for breath. "That's right," he coughed, water streaming down his face. "Go ahead, prove my point. You're only—" Coleman tightened his grip, choking off the words.

"Coleman!" Katherine cried. "You're killing him! Coleman!" She leaned into his face and shouted. "You're better than this! Stop it!"

"You heard what he said," Coleman sneered. "I'm no more than—"

"You don't have to do this!"

Murkoski kicked and struggled, his eyes bulging grotesquely, as Coleman tightened his grip.

"Listen to me!" she shouted. "Listen to me! He's wrong! You're more than a bunch of genes!"

Coleman shook his head. "It's too late."

"You're a man, not a chemistry set—you've got a will, you've got faith."

The last phrase touched something—in his eyes she saw a fleeting spark. It disappeared as quickly as it had appeared, but she had seen it, and she knew she had found the key. She pressed in.

"'If anyone is in Christ, he is a new person.' Remember? 'Old things have passed away.' Remember that? Do you remember?"

He looked at her. The spark behind his eyes remained a fraction longer this time. There was understanding, a common ground. She had him.

"Let him go. Coleman, let him go."

He shook his head. "I can't."

"Of course you can! You don't have to do this. 'Old things have passed away.'"

"I've tried. All night I've been trying."

"Then maybe you should stop."

Surprise and confusion filled his eyes.

"Stop trying. Stop trying to do it on your own."

He scowled.

"Those are your own words—don't you remember? Stop putting your trust in you. 'If any man is in *Christ* he is a new person.'"

Coleman was listening now. Carefully.

"'Old things have passed away, all things are new.' That's what you said, remember? Stop trusting in you. Put your trust in him, Coleman. Not you. Him, him, Coleman!"

Coleman closed his eyes. Was he praying? Searching for faith? It didn't matter. She didn't care. She didn't even know if she believed it. She just hoped it would work.

"You can't do it on your own. You've tried. Turn it over!"

Coleman hesitated.

"It doesn't have to be forever. Just now. Just one moment at a time. Turn it over to him. Now, Coleman. Turn it over!"

Ever so slowly, Coleman released Murkoski. The kid slumped to the floor, coughing and choking, gasping for breath.

Coleman turned and stepped away; Katherine was right at his side. "You did it," she encouraged. "You did it!"

He shook his head. "Not me," he whispered. "I would have killed him." Looking into her eyes, he repeated in quiet amazement, "It wasn't . . . me."

Katherine searched his face, daring to hope that somehow he was right.

"That's it?" Murkoski said, coughing and struggling to stand in the deepening water. "You beat it one time and you think you've got it conquered? You think you've changed? You'll never change, Coleman. You're chemicals. Chemicals!"

Coleman refused to turn around. Katherine remained at his side, watching him.

"You'll always be this way! You can't keep fighting it, not forever. You'll always be—"

An unearthly shriek echoed through the room. All three spun to see a baboon flying through the rain directly at Murkoski. It hit him in the chest, sending him splashing onto the floor. The animal went straight for the man's throat, tearing, clawing, screeching. Murkoski screamed as he fought and kicked, but his cries bubbled and choked in his own blood.

Quickly, Coleman pulled the guard's gun from his pants and tried to take aim. But they were rolling and thrashing too wildly. As soon as he had a bead on the animal, they'd roll or twist and suddenly Murkoski was in the way. Coleman moved in, searching for a clear shot. But there was only a blur of wet fur and clothes and blood and flesh. He dropped the gun into the water and fell to his knees, trying to grab the animal, to pull him off, to save whatever was left of Murkoski.

"Let him alone!"

O'Brien entered from the stairway.

"Stay back!" he shouted at Coleman. "It's too late—he'll only kill you too."

Coleman looked from O'Brien to Murkoski. The kid was no longer fighting. His body lay in the water, still moving and jerking but only from the animal's ripping and tearing.

"Stay out of his way!" O'Brien warned. "He's a killer now; he'll want to keep killing."

Still on his knees, Coleman reached toward the baboon, one last try. Freddy turned on him, ferocious, shrieking, baring his needlelike fangs, his face covered in blood.

O'Brien slowly knelt in the doorway to the stairs and began to call: "Freddy? Freddy, come here, fellow."

The shrieks gently subsided as the animal looked first one way, then the other, until his eyes focused on O'Brien.

"Hey, boy."

Freddy cocked his head. He seemed to recognize the voice. It looked as if he were trying to remember something else, something from long ago.

"Freddy, it's me. How are you, boy?"

Freddy whimpered faintly.

"It's me, fellow, remember?" O'Brien stretched his hands out through the rain.

But whatever memory the animal had quickly disappeared. He shrieked again, baring his fangs. Suddenly he jumped on Murkoski's lifeless body, striking him with both fists one, two, three times. Then he leaped to the ground, raced past O'Brien, and disappeared down the stairs, barking and screaming as he ran.

CHAPTER 18

"Stop it," Coleman growled as he paced back and forth in the hallway. "Stop saying that."

"But it's the truth," O'Brien insisted. "It's over. We've got an entire bomb division waiting outside, a hundred lab animals not yet killed, and—" He glanced at Katherine. "Who knows if we can knock out those gene sequencers."

"I could probably get into their memory," Katherine speculated, "but if they're scattered throughout the building, it'll take time to make sure I get them all."

"And time is the one thing we don't have," O'Brien said.

Coleman nodded as he continued to pace and think. He was slightly stooped now—from the debilitating pain in his body and in his head.

The three of them stood at the other end of the hall, near the window. O'Brien had managed to shut off the main valve to the overhead sprinklers. There was still the sound of water dripping and trickling, but the deafening hiss had finally been stopped.

Katherine looked out the window, down into the parking lot. It was buzzing with the Snohomish County bomb squad and Arlington police. Behind her, at the other end of the hall, sat the elevator with its charred pile in the final stages of smoldering. Directly in front of that, Murkoski's body lay in half an inch of water, covered by O'Brien's jacket.

"I can talk to the authorities," O'Brien offered, "explain what has happened."

"And that will stop it?" Coleman asked. "That will stop the gene from being manufactured, from being sold?" He motioned down the hall toward Murkoski's body. "That will stop something like that from spreading throughout the world?"

Katherine watched as O'Brien said nothing. All three of them knew the answer. Whatever political, military, and financial powers that had enabled Murkoski to go this far would not be stopped until they had their way.

Coleman resumed pacing, then changed the subject. "Everything is contained in this building? The animals, the sequencers?"

O'Brien nodded. "Everything. Why?"

Before Coleman could respond, a light glared through the window. The sound of the approaching helicopter had been registering somewhere in the back of Katherine's mind, but she'd paid little attention, until now. The thumping grew intolerable as the aircraft slowly dropped into view. All three ducked out of its sight, under the window.

"This is the Snohomish County Bomb Division. You have three minutes to vacate the building or we will come in after you."

O'Brien turned toward Coleman, who was kneeling beside him. "It's over," he said again. "Let me go out and—"

"No," Coleman said.

It was Katherine's turn to try and reason. "Coleman—"

"No!" he insisted. "It's not over. Not yet."

Katherine and O'Brien exchanged looks.

"Your Shipping and Receiving," he asked. "It's in this building, too, right?"

"That's right," O'Brien said. "First floor, the entire back section."

"What about solvents?"

"I'm sorry, what—"

"For the labs, you guys use solvents, don't you?"

"Of course."

"What type do you have?"

"We use several."

"Toluene?"

"It's one of the more common, certainly."

"You have lots of it?"

"I imagine. But what—"

A second light blazed through the window, striking the ceiling. This one came from ground level. Those outside had obviously located their position. Instinctively, the three pressed closer to the wall under the window.

"Okay," Coleman said, "this is what we'll do. First, you two need to get out of here."

Katherine protested. "Cole—"

He cut her off. "You need to stand up. Let them see you stand up. Then walk down the hall, take the stairs, and head out of the building."

"What about you?" O'Brien asked.

"They want a bomb, I'll give them a bomb."

"Coleman, you can't—"

He threw Katherine a harsh look and she stopped. Then, seeing her fear, he continued more softly. "I don't see any other way. The sequencers have to go, the animals have to be destroyed—"

"Let me stay with you, I can help."

He hesitated—then shook his head. "No."

"But—"

"You've still got to find Eric. If something goes wrong, I don't want to be responsible for killing both of his parents."

She held his look a moment, then asked quietly, "What about you?"

"I'll be okay."

She knew he was lying. He tried to smile, but with little success. He was frightened, and he couldn't hide it. Not from her.

"You have two minutes and thirty seconds."

O'Brien shook his head. "It won't work. As soon as we're out of here, as soon as your hostages are gone, they'll come in after you."

"Not if you tell them I have a bomb. Not if you say I've jury-rigged it to go off when they enter."

"Why would they believe me?"

"It used to be your company."

"Two minutes, fifteen seconds."

Another pause. "Are you sure you can do it?" O'Brien asked.

"Just don't let them cut the power."

O'Brien nodded.

"Coleman . . ." Katherine's voice was thick with emotion.

He looked at her. He was seeing inside of her again, she knew it. Just as he had so many times before. He was seeing—and understanding—her worry, her heartfelt concern. And when he spoke, it was with the same quiet sensitivity of before. "We talked about faith."

"Yes, but—"

"I don't know if I can pull this off—I don't know if I have the strength, the faith. But if I don't try, who will?"

"You don't have—"

"Katherine, listen to me."

"You don't have to be the one—"

"Listen."

His gentle intensity silenced her.

"There's a lot I don't understand. You're the expert in this field, not me."

"But—"

"And if you don't think it will work, if you don't think I have what it takes, you need to let me know."

"And if you don't?"

He searched her face, looking for the words. "Then . . . I truly am lost."

As she stared into his eyes, realization slowly set in. He wasn't doing this just to destroy the gene. That was important, of course. If the gene, if all record of it, weren't completely destroyed, the powers behind Murkoski would simply retrieve it and continue again. But Coleman wasn't doing this just to stop them. He was also doing it for himself. If he could overcome his old nature, if he could hold it at bay and destroy the project—then he would be winning a much deeper, more important battle.

Moisture welled up in her eyes.

He waited, seeking her assurance, needing to know if she thought his proposal possible.

Finally, slowly, she began to nod.

He smiled. "Go then," he whispered. "Let them see you at the window and go."

Before she knew it, she was reaching out and touching his face. She wanted to say something, to encourage him, to tell him how good he was. She also wanted to tell of her overwhelming fears and doubts. But no words came.

He understood and moved her hand from his cheek to his lips. He gently kissed it. He was trembling again, and her heart swelled so full that she thought it would break.

"Go," he urged.

She closed her eyes and swallowed hard.

"One minute."

"Go!"

She nodded. She took a breath to steady herself, then slowly rose to her feet. O'Brien joined her. They stood in front of the window, their bodies glowing eerily white from the intense beam of the helicopter that hovered some thirty feet in front of them.

"Put your hands on top of your heads and come out of the building."

They nodded, raised their hands above their heads, and turned to head down the hall.

The dripping of the sprinklers had almost stopped. Now, there was only the sloshing of their feet in the water. The journey took forever. Katherine was crying hard now, but that was okay—Coleman couldn't see.

They passed Murkoski's body. It lay motionless. Beyond that the charred pile of Eppendorf tubes continued to smolder. At the door to the stairway, Katherine hesitated for just a moment and looked back.

Coleman appeared tiny and helpless as he crouched under the window in the shadows of the blinding light. But even through her tears, even in the glare and shadow, she could see him smiling. The new Coleman was still in charge. The thought gave her comfort, at least enough to help her through the doorway, to start her down the stairs.

Toluene, also known as methylbenzene, C_7H_8, is one of the Ts in TNT. According to Hector Garcia, the bomber punk Coleman had defended on Nebraska's Death Row, in its liquid form it is highly flammable. In its vapor form, its explosive power is incredible. Forget the fertilizer and diesel fuel. According to Garcia, this stuff, if properly mixed with air, could really do some damage.

On the Row, Coleman had listened to Garcia's stories. Knowing that knowledge is power, and having nothing but time on his hands, he had asked the right questions, challenged the hyperbole, and filed the information away for future reference. If prison is anything, it's a classroom for the hungry to learn. And Coleman had always been hungry. Now it was time to put what he had learned to work.

The anger inside continued to boil and writhe and seethe, looking for the slightest frustration, the slightest crack to rise through and overtake him. But instead of fighting it, Coleman began to use it. Instead of trying to destroy the anger, he focused it toward accomplishing his purposes, using it to push through the sweat and pain and mind-dulling exhaustion that were clouding his thinking.

Still, he was at the edge, and he knew it. He nearly exploded with impatience while cooped up inside the freight elevator, pacing in frustration as it slowly lumbered its way down to Shipping and Receiving.

Then there was the anxiety of trying to locate the toluene. Why hadn't he asked for more specifics? Shipping and Receiving went on forever. It could be anywhere down here. Yet, somehow, through his own tough mental discipline and with whatever understanding he had of faith, he was able to focus and refocus until his efforts paid off.

He found six fifty-five-gallon drums of the solvent. He only needed two.

Getting those drums onto the freight elevator was another matter. He opted for the mini electric forklift sitting outside on the loading dock. But it was too big to bring in through the doorway. He'd have to roll up one of the large loading doors. No problem, except it would rattle and draw the attention of any sheriff's sniper who might be hanging out on that side of the building.

Something about that last thought outraged him. Here he was risking his life to help the very people who were trying to kill him. Why? If they wanted him so badly, maybe he should just run out there and let them fire away. And in six months, a year, maybe two, they could start warring against terrorists without conscience, gunmen without feeling. That would show them.

The thought grew more and more appealing until it was all Coleman could do to fight off the urge to throw open the doors, yell his vengeance at the world, and go out in a blaze of glory.

Instead, barely holding his anger in check, he stole out onto the loading dock. This part of the building was L shaped. What exposed area remained was concealed by a ten-foot-high fence. Still, he moved quickly and quietly to the forklift and disconnected it from its charging bay. He climbed on board the machine, backed it up as close to the edge of the dock as possible—and then, finally, he released his rage. He stomped on the accelerator with all of his might. The forklift raced toward the metal door and crashed into it. The impact sent such jarring pain through his body that he let out a stifled cry. But when he looked, he found that he'd ripped out only part of the door's bottom seam; he hadn't broken through.

He dropped the forklift into reverse. He expected any minute to feel bullets explode into his back, but he didn't care. In fact, it might be a relief compared to the pain he was already enduring. He ground the gears, found forward, and raced at the door again. This time he broke through, tearing metal and sending brads flying in all directions.

The rush was exhilarating, filling Coleman with such a sense of power that he momentarily lost control. For several seconds he wasn't sure if he wanted to regain it.

But the next task called for concentration and focus, and he fought back to the surface to take charge. Carefully, he maneuvered the forklift, sliding the steel teeth under the first fifty-five-gallon drum. Then he turned, approached the freight elevator, and gently loaded the barrel inside. He repeated the process with the second. When they were in place, he maneuvered the lift inside between the drums and jumped down. He grabbed the nylon strap and pulled down the heavy steel door. It slammed shut, and he hit the button for the top floor.

Once again, the elevator's slow, lumbering speed irritated him, and once again his anger started to rise. But this time there was nowhere to direct it. He didn't even have room to pace. He pounded his fist into his palm. Again and again. "Help me," he muttered, "help me, help me, help me . . ."

All ten officers and two reserves of the Greater Arlington Police Department had arrived on the scene. They had set up a perimeter around the Sheriff's Bomb Division to hold back the growing crowd. They were successful with the crowd. They weren't so successful with the experienced TV crews arriving from Seattle.

"Excuse me, excuse me!" The camera lights pushed and jockeyed toward Katherine, who was kneeling behind the open door of a sheriff's car. "Were you frightened—where did you meet him—did he threaten you—can you give us any idea of his motives—did he display obvious signs of mental instability—did he tell you . . ."

Katherine stayed low and mostly out of the lights, ignoring the news crews as she gave a detailed description of her son to the deputy. From time to time she looked toward the building. So far, no one was going in. O'Brien was doing his job. For how long she wasn't certain.

"Ms. Lyon, Ms. Lyon?" a policewoman was working her way through the crowd. "Ms. Lyon?"

Katherine looked up, shielding her eyes from the lights. The officer was motioning for her to look across the parking lot toward the crowd at the gate.

Katherine rose, but the reporters blocked her view. She stepped up into the doorway of the car and scanned the crowd. In the distance, toward the back, there was a disturbance. People were parting under the orders of an officer, who slowly made his way through the crowd. An older couple walked with him. And by the way they kept looking down and speaking, it was obvious that there must be somebody much smaller by their side.

Katherine held her breath, straining for a better view. She thought she saw a flash of blonde hair through the crowd.

She hopped down and bolted around the car, sending more than one reporter staggering. She ran across the parking lot and started to wade through the crowd. "Eric, Eric!"

There was no response.

"Eric?"

She caught a glimpse of a purple shirt—maybe his U of W sweatshirt, she couldn't tell.

The crowd was parting faster now.

"Eric?"

There was the hair again, then the sweatshirt, then hair—

And then she saw the face.

"Mom!"

Her heart leaped. She shoved through the crowd, running now, giving no thought to anybody or anything but her son.

"Eric!"

At last she dropped down, and he threw himself at her so hard that she nearly fell.

"Mom!"

They hugged fiercely, burying their faces into one another, neither wanting to let go.

"I'm sorry, Mom, I'm sorry."

She pulled back to look at him. His face had a few small cuts, but other than that he was fine. "Sorry for what?" she asked.

"My glasses. I lost my glasses."

She laughed and pulled him into another embrace. "It's okay, honey. We can get new glasses." She closed her eyes tightly and allowed the waves of love to wash over her.

"He came to our house," the older gentleman was saying, "clothes torn, all cut up like that. And he come right up to the door, knocked as polite as you please."

Katherine looked up at the weathered old man, but before she could respond, somebody in the crowd shouted. "He's on the roof! Look, he's on the roof!"

Heads spun. Hands pointed. Katherine slowly rose to her feet and turned to watch.

With a grunt, Coleman swung his ax into the base of the large intake duct that rose half a dozen feet from the roof. It was part of the building's high-volume air-conditioning unit. The blade easily ripped into the galvanized metal. He swung three more times. When he was certain the hole was large enough, he turned to the toluene drums behind him and began to pry them open.

It had been a little tricky getting the barrels up onto the roof, since the elevator only went as far as the top floor. He'd had to drive the forklift out of the elevator, scoop up a drum, then position it just below one of the frosted skylights. Then he had raised the fork high into the air, busting the barrel through the skylight. When the shards of glass had stopped raining, he had placed the barrel on the roof, then repeated the same procedure with the second one.

Next, he had switched on the giant double fans of the air-conditioning unit. They had begun to beat the air with low, ominous thumps. But as the blades picked up speed, the pounding had quickly blurred to a deafening roar.

Finally, using the forklift as a ladder, he had climbed through the skylight out onto the roof and taken an ax to the duct.

When he had both of the fifty-five-gallon barrels open, he pushed and eased the first onto its side. It fell hard, and the liquid began to chug out. With some minor adjusting, he was able to channel the toluene directly into the gaping hole he had chopped out at the duct's base.

The giant fans below immediately began pumping the explosive fumes through the building. They were strong fumes, reminding him of his younger, glue-sniffing days. Knowing he'd have to keep his wits about him, he turned his head to the side to breathe in as much fresh air as possible.

The first drum finished draining and he kicked it aside, sending it rolling and clattering across the roof. He opened the second barrel just as the helicopter crested the building and blinded him with its spotlight.

"This is the Snohomish County Sheriff's Department. Exit the building at once."

He scrambled behind the vent. The glaring light, the beating rotors, and the interruption of his work all helped rekindle his anger. But once again, he was able to channel it. Even though his position behind the duct was awkward, giving him little leverage, he reached out to the open drum and pulled it toward him. He rocked it once, twice, three times before it fell, washing its contents over him, his legs, his waist, before spilling across the roof. It burned and felt cold against his skin, and the fumes made his eyes water, but he fought with the emptying drum until he was able to direct the remaining toluene down into the duct.

By now the helicopter had crabbed to the right, bringing him into full view, once again blinding him with its light.

"This is the Snohomish County Sheriff. Cease your activity and exit the building at once. This is your final warning."

He gave no indication that he'd heard the commands, much less intended to obey them, as the drum continued to empty. Now the fumes were burning his nose. Try as he might, he couldn't avoid inhaling them. Already he could feel his head growing light.

Then he saw it. A little red dot, smaller than a dime, first reflecting off the ductwork to his left, then quickly darting toward him. A sniper in the helicopter was taking aim.

Frantically, he looked over to the broken skylight just fifteen feet away. It was how he'd gotten onto the roof, and now it was his only way off. But a wide pool of toluene lay between him and the skylight. He knew that the fumes hadn't had time to work their way deep into the building. He also knew that, if he ran across that pool and the sniper missed him, hitting a piece of ductwork, there was a good chance a spark would end the show before it even began.

His only hope was to circumvent the toluene—to go around it to the skylight. That would be far more dangerous, and meant an extra thirty or so feet of exposure, but it would have to do.

The drum finally emptied, and he gave it a push across the roof to join the other. His clothes were saturated with toluene, making it impossible to avoid breathing the fumes. Their effects grew stronger. He crouched low, prepared himself, then sprang forward, putting every bit of his concentration, every ounce of strength, into speed.

The first shot missed and thumped into the thick tar.

The helicopter adjusted.

Coleman was nearly there—ten feet, eight, five—when the second shot found its mark. His left leg exploded with pain, sending him crashing onto the roof and sliding across the shattered glass.

But he was there. The skylight was within reach. He grabbed the busted-out frame and dragged himself toward it—the jagged, wire-reinforced glass dug into his arms, then his chest, but he continued to pull. Suddenly the entire frame gave way and he tumbled the twelve feet down to the next floor, missing the steel frame of the forklift by mere inches.

The fumes inside the building and from his own soaked clothes were nearly overwhelming. He ripped off his shirt, found a dry section, and tore it in two, using half as a tourniquet to tie off his bleeding leg, the other half as a filter to breathe through. It did little good. Already his head was spinning, his vision blurring.

It was too early; the fumes hadn't completely spread through the building. But he had no choice. He had to do it now, while he could still think. He reached into his pocket for the matches. When he felt them he went cold. He pulled them out. They were soaked, completely saturated with liquid toluene.

His mind groped. He knew there was another book downstairs in the gym bag. He'd been smart enough to throw in two. But the chances of making it downstairs through these fumes were slim. No way could he stay conscious, let alone remain coherent long enough to make it back to the third floor.

Still, what choice did he have?

With stubborn resolve—and a prayer—he steeled himself and half-limped, half-dragged his body past the roaring air-conditioning fans toward the freight elevator.

The fumes took their toll. His mind was drifting now, starting to float. He entered the elevator and pressed three. The doors rattled shut and the elevator descended.

Mikey, please . . . It's so cold . . . please don't leave me here.

Coleman spun around. It was his brother's voice. Was he hallucinating? Yes, of course. No, it sounded too real.

Mikey . . .

He clenched his eyes, forcing the voice out of his head.

It took forever for the elevator doors to finally open.

When he stepped out, his vision was worse, colors twisted and blurred into one another. Still, he was able to make out the form of Murkoski's body lying on the floor in front of the burned out passenger elevator. Not far away sat the gym bag.

He staggered forward. Time was distorting, telescoping, moving in painfully slow motion.

He floated down to his knees beside the bag and his unfeeling hands began searching for the matches. He was drifting, high and far away, on automatic pilot. Yet his hands kept working.

They found the second book—just as the footsteps began; construction boots against tile. His father's boots.

Michael . . . Michael . . .

He could smell the stench of whisky.

"Help me," he whispered. "Dear God . . . help me . . ."

He pulled out the matchbook. It felt damp. The overhead sprinklers had done their job too well. An alarm bell began ringing. It sounded like the one in the Quickie Mart where he'd shot the clerk. He couldn't tell; it was too far away. The guitar licks from "Hotel California" wafted through his head. So real, so clear, so lovely.

Michael . . .

He felt his fingers opening the matchbook cover, more from impulse than from will. He saw them pulling off the first match and dragging it across the striker.

Nothing.

His fingers were wet. They'd soaked the head of the match. He saw his hands wiping themselves on the dry part of his shirt he'd used as a tourniquet. They tried again, this time ripping out a wad of four matches.

Michael . . .

You are mine.

It was time to quit, to give in. To let that lovely music carry him off.

You are me.

The euphoria lulled him, lifted him . . .

"No! NO!"

His shout cleared his head long enough for him to struggle to his feet. He looked down at his hands. He was still holding the wad of matches. Four of them. He tried striking them all at once.

Too wet. He threw them away.

You are me.

Michael . . .

He tugs at the remaining matches, hands shaking now so badly that he can barely rip them out. He is drifting again, floating, floating . . .

The matches tear away.

Michael . . .

We are one.

He drifts back for a moment, long enough to try one.

Nothing.

Another.

Nothing.

There is only justice. The sound of Steiner's voice startles him.

"NO!" Coleman cries. His shout brings him back long enough to see that he is holding a match—the last one. He forces his hand to drag it across the striker.

Michael . . .

Nothing.

He is gone, in another world, no cares, no pain.

Michael . . .

"Please," he hears himself mumble.

Michael . . .

His hand starts to strike it again, but it cannot. He is on his knees, his throat knot-tight in emotion.

You are mine.

Justice . . .

Michael . . .

"Please." The words barely spoken. "Dear God, help me."

Again he feels the match. It is still between his fingers. But it no longer matters, it is time to—

Michael . . .

Something deep inside him stirs.

Michael . . .

Again he feels the match between his thumb and forefinger. He tries one last time. He is dragging the sulfur head across the striker. It is sparking, flaming to life . . .

A spherical shock wave, consisting of supercompressed air, CO_2, and water vapor, forms at the match head. It rapidly expands until it reaches the walls of the hallway; at that point it is traveling at a detonation rate of 4000 feet per second and has a density equal to that of very hard wood. It slams into the walls, demolishing them and continuing to move outward.

But that is only the beginning.

The trail of exploding solvent vapor roars up the air-conditioning ducts at almost four times the speed of sound, rupturing them as it moves through them to involve every room in the building. The shock wave of expanding gas crushes tile and splinters wood. Most importantly, it creates what is referred to by Hector Garcia as "overpressure." In this case, several hundreds of pounds of overpressure per square inch. It disintegrates the concrete walls and twists the steel support girders until they are unrecognizable—until even areas of the building that have not been touched by the blast collapse and tumble under their own weight.

The research building of Genodyne Inc. no longer exists.

Michael . . . Michael . . .

Coleman looks up. At first it is his father's voice, but then it isn't. Unlike the other times, this voice resonates with kindness and compassion. Coleman is awestruck.

He's unsure where he is. But there is light, everywhere light. Standing above him is a figure. It is his father, but it isn't. It is inexplicably tender, carved from a light brighter than the other light. It is the source of the light, of all light. But the figure is more than light; it is love, a consuming, all-encompassing love. It reaches down to Coleman, taking his hands, gently helping him to his feet.

Unable and unwilling to stop himself, Coleman falls into the light, feeling its arms wrapping about him, its love permeating his body.

He hears three words. Spoken yet unspoken. Powerful, roaring like thunder, tender as breath. They thrill him, but he is afraid to believe. They say he will never again be alone. He will never again be a shadow, dancing, searching, aching to belong. He does belong. Completely. Intimately. Eternally. They are only three words, but they tell him all of this and much, much more. They simply say: "Welcome home, son."

CHAPTER 19

Katherine rested on the tailgate of the sheriff's van, wrapped in a blanket and sipping some very bad coffee. Eric sat up front, checking out the cool radio equipment. A hundred yards away, on the other side of the police barricade, the media lights glared as reporters filed their stories with the hollowed-out shell of Genodyne Inc. as their backdrop.

Katherine knew that her name had been leaked to the press and that it was just a matter of time before she would have to face them. But for now, it felt awfully good to simply sit and close her eyes.

"You doing okay?"

She looked up to see O'Brien standing beside her, trying to drink the same coffee.

"Yeah," she said, scooting over to let him sit. The movement caused the cut in her right cheek to throb slightly, and she reached up to explore the two-inch gash with her fingers.

"You should have them look at that," he said. "You'll probably need stitches."

She said nothing. There was a lot she should do.

"They'll want to talk to you, you know."

She nodded. "What did you tell them?"

"Not much. I don't work here anymore, remember?"

She gave him a look. He shrugged. "I didn't give them a name. I just said he was some friend of Murkoski's. Very angry, very confused, and with a history of mental instability."

Katherine turned away, deeply saddened by the thought. Coleman had given everything he had, everything he was, and he wouldn't even be allowed to have a name. Worse than that, he would be labeled now and forever as some lunatic.

"What about the kidnapping?" she asked.

"That one's up to you. I did suggest he might somehow be responsible for that, as well."

"And they bought that?"

"For now. Keeps everything nice and tidy. 'Course I'll be in Mazatlán by the time they realize the pieces don't quite fit."

Katherine nodded, wondering where she would be, how her life would ever come back together.

Silence stole over the two as they sat in the damp air, with the bad coffee, staring vacantly at the remains of the building. A handful of investigators were already beginning to scramble over the rubble and sift through the debris. On the horizon, the sky was beginning to glow with the promise of another dawn.

O'Brien took a long, deep breath and slowly let it out. "Poor soul," he muttered. "Poor, poor soul."

Katherine looked to him. "Why do you say that?"

"He came so close to winning."

"You don't think he did? You don't think he won?"

O'Brien glanced at her. "He destroyed the project, sure. In that sense, I suppose. But, dying—" He shook his head. "Not much victory for him in that."

"How can you say that?" Katherine felt herself growing defensive. "All he wanted was to be kind and loving and giving. All he wanted was to defeat the old Coleman with the new, loving one."

"And you think he did that? In the end, do you think he overcame the old Coleman?"

"He gave up his life for us, didn't he?" She motioned to the crowd across the parking lot. "For all of them. You don't get any more loving and giving than that."

O'Brien looked at her.

"'No greater love has a man than he lay down his life for his friends,'" she quoted softly.

O'Brien nodded. "I've heard that."

"Me, too. All of my life. But now . . ." Her voice dropped off.

"But now?" O'Brien repeated.

"Now I think I'm finally starting to understand." She paused a moment to look up to the brightening sky. "Coleman won, Dr. O'Brien. Maybe not by your standards, maybe not by mine. But he won."

O'Brien started to answer, but fell silent. He had much to think about.

"Mom! Hey, Mom."

Katherine turned. Eric was standing just outside the van.

"Mom, check it out."

She rose wearily to her feet and walked to him. He was pointing toward a tall pine tree. "Look at that," he said.

At first she saw nothing. "What?"

"There?"

"I don't—"

"Right there."

She kneeled down to his level. It was only then, when her face was beside his, that she saw it. The moon was rising just above the top set of branches.

"Isn't that cool?"

Katherine stared, her throat tightening.

"Isn't it?" he repeated.

He was right; it was cool, very cool. She wanted to tell him so, but she didn't trust her voice. Instead, she wrapped her arms around her son and held him tight. Once again she felt her eyes beginning to burn with tears.

Eric turned to her. "Are you all right?"

She nodded as the tears spilled onto her cheeks. The wetness stung the cut in her face and she winced slightly, raising a hand toward it.

"It's okay, Mom," he said, reaching out to touch her face. "You'll be okay."

The concern in his little eyes and the tender touch of his hand were almost more than she could bear. She reached up and took his fingers. They felt warm, almost on fire as she kissed them. He was right, she would be okay. She had her son, she had her life. And she had something else. A glimpse, a taste of the eternal had started to return. She looked back up to the moon. At that particular moment, it was the most beautiful thing she had ever seen.

"Cool," her son repeated joyfully.

But when she turned to him, he wasn't looking at the moon. He was looking at her, practically beaming as he stared at her cheek.

It was then she noticed how warm her face felt, almost as hot as his fingers. She reached up to touch the cut, but couldn't find it. She ran her fingers over her face, but she couldn't feel it anywhere. Only the heat.

Eric's grin broadened.

"What?" She rubbed her cheek again, searching for it. "What did you do?"

He giggled. "I'm not sure, but it's gone, Mom. It's not there."

She looked at him in rising astonishment. Then spotting the side-view mirror of the van, she moved to it to see.

But there was nothing. The wound was gone.

"How?" she asked. "That's not possible." She turned to him. "How did . . ."

He shrugged, and smiled. "Got me."

She turned back to the mirror.

"But that's not all," he said thoughtfully. "Something else is kinda weird, too."

She turned back to him.

"Lately, when I look at people—real deep and stuff? Well, it's kinda like I know what they're thinking."

Katherine could only stare.

"Isn't that weird?" he said. "That's how I knew those kidnappers were lying. And those old people who brought me here? I could tell that they were good and that they'd help me just by looking at them."

Katherine knelt by her son and held his shoulders. "When," she swallowed, fighting to stay calm, "when did this start to happen?"

"Back when Mr. Michaels and I got all cut up. Remember, with all those blackberry vines and stuff? Remember when we became blood brothers?"

Katherine did remember. She turned back to the mirror, reexamining her face, hoping to find something. She pushed and stretched the skin, searching. There was nothing. Not even a scar.

"Pretty cool, huh?" Eric said.

She turned back to her son, trying to hide the growing panic she was feeling.

"Katherine?" It was O'Brien calling from the tailgate. "Is everything all right?"

She looked at Eric with rising wonder and fear.

"Hey, you two?"

The van rocked slightly as O'Brien rose and started toward them.

"Yeah," she called back. There was a tremor in her voice, but she was able to cover it. "Everything's fine."

She looked at her son another moment, then pulled him into a fierce embrace.

"Mom," he protested. "Mom, I can't breathe."

But she would not let go; she pulled him even tighter. Then, looking up at the pine tree and the moon rising behind it, she blinked back her tears and whispered a quiet prayer.

THRESHOLD

Another one for Brenda . . .
who has stayed faithful for richer or poorer,
better or worse . . .
and everything in between.
Thanks for hanging in there with me.

PREFACE

If I've learned anything in writing this book it's that truth can indeed be stranger than fiction. As with *Blood of Heaven* I've tried to make all of the science as accurate as possible—which includes the paranormal research being conducted to one degree or another in laboratories around the world. The same can be said regarding the various supernatural experiences. Except for the climax, which is more symbolic and allegorical in nature, most of the mentioned encounters have to one degree or another been experienced, documented, or verified by myself or others. When it comes to these two areas, science and the supernatural, I'm afraid what fiction I've added only pales by comparison.

My research began as early as 1976 when John Smalley, Keith Green, and I were involved in the deliverance of an influential West Coast psychic from intense demonic activity. It was then the story began to take shape. I wanted to show how crafty and deceptive the Adversary can be in comparison to the purity and power of Jesus Christ.

Other elements came from my trips around the world as a film director for various mission groups. The spiritual warfare some of these men and women are waging overseas is worth a book in itself.

Recently, I've spent hours in prison interviewing David Berkowitz, the serial killer once known as the Son of Sam—a man who had been deep into the occult and who was charged with shooting thirteen people, but who is now a dedicated brother in Christ.

There was also an extensive and gracious conversation with Dr. Edwin May, who for twenty years headed up a psychic research program for the CIA and who also provided the information on current Russian progress in this field. Dr. Richard S. Broughton was kind enough to speak with me and allow me to visit the Institute for Parapsychology, one of the top psychic research labs in the world.

There were also numerous conversations with pastors, physicists, medical researchers, and followers of Eastern religions.

Their stories and research were both encouraging and chilling. Encouraging in that their ongoing studies clearly demonstrate the presence of a supernatural world and the power of faith. Chilling in that sometimes many of these well-meaning men and women are entering into areas of the occult without even knowing it.

Grateful appreciation also goes to Dr. Schelbert, the Biochemical Engineering and Nuclear Medicine department at UCLA, Dr. Craig Cameron, David Carini, Angie Hunt, Al Janssen, Scott Kennedy, Jim Bass, Lynn Marzulli, Aggie Villanueva, Julie LaFata, Kenneth and Rebecca McCrocklin, Heinz and Maria Fussle, and to Thomas Gray for his "Elegy Written in a Country Churchyard." Special thanks also to Doug McIntosh, a talented writer who served as my research assistant, as well as to my agent and friend, Greg Johnson.

Writing a novel is one thing. Getting it ready out there for reading is another. And for that I want to thank the Zondervan team from sales, to marketing, to editorial. You folks are amazing.

And for their ongoing intercession I want to thank Greg Dix, Gary Gilmore, Robin Jones Gunn, Rebecca and Scott Janney, Lissa Halls Johnson, Larry LaFata, Lynn and Peggy Marzulli, Dorothy Moore, Bill Myers Sr., James Riordan, Carla Williams, as well as my extended family, John Tolle, Bill Burnett, Gary Smith, Tom Kositchek, Cathy Glass, Criz Hibdon, Mark Brown, and Dave Wray.

Finally and always, thanks to Brenda, Nick, and the Mack.

For our struggle is not against flesh and blood, but against the rulers, against the authorities, against the powers of this dark world and against the spiritual forces of evil in the heavenly realms.

EPHESIANS 6:12

PROLOGUE

The sand is hot. It sears the bottoms of her feet, raising welts wherever it touches, but she feels nothing.

She never does.

The scorching wind makes her eyes water. It whips and tears at her faded housedress, but it carries no heat.

It never does.

Grains of sand bite into her face, chapping her cheeks. Talcum-fine grit works its way deep into her nappy hair, into the creases of her mottled black skin, beneath the elastic band of her dress. But it doesn't matter. None of it matters.

Gerty has stood in this desert, at this riverbank, a hundred times. A hundred times she has waited, and a hundred times she has been disappointed.

Once again she hears faint gurgling. She looks at the river—at a small patch of water. It is starting to boil. It always begins this way. Slowly. First one bubble. Then another. Then another and another and another, and faster and faster the bubbles rise until the small area in the river churns furiously.

Gerty struggles to hold back her excitement. She has come this far many times before.

She steps into the river. There is no sensation of warmth, or cold, or wet. Just the knowledge that once again she is in the river.

She sloshes toward the bubbles. Her dress wraps around her legs, binding her movement. She thinks of hiking it above her waist. But there is always the chance that this will be the time, and she would not dare stand half naked. Not on holy ground.

She arrives at the patch of boiling water. Steam rolls up and blows into her face. She blinks, squinting through it.

And then it happens . . .

A small dark form appears under the water. For a moment it looks like a fish, but as it surfaces it is obvious that this is no fish. It is a piece of metal. Iron. An ax head.

Maybe this will be the time.

The boiling comes to a stop. Now there is absolute silence as the last wisps of steam disappear. The ax head continues floating on the water as effortlessly as a newly fallen leaf.

This is the crucial part. She hopes, she prays that it will not disappear as it has so many times in the past. She takes a breath to steady herself, and finally she reaches for it. The tips of her fingers touch the cool surface.

Yes, cool. It is a sensation. A feeling. For the first time the ax head has substance. She can actually feel it!

Carefully she scoops it from the water, fearing that any minute it will dissolve and slip through her trembling fingers.

But it doesn't.

Tightness grows in her throat. Her eyes burn with tears of gratitude, but she blinks them back as she turns the ax head over and over in her hands.

This is *the time.*

Then she sees it. Senses it, really. The light. It hovers over the bank of the river. Brighter than the sun, so brilliant that it is difficult for her to distinguish any shape or detail, though for the briefest moment, she catches a glimpse of what could be wheels . . . and eyes. The rest is light. Everywhere light. And sound, like a roaring waterfall. But there is no waterfall in this river. The sound comes from the light.

Fear and awe grip Gerty; tears spill onto her cheeks. She hears the voice. It has been there all along—in the roar. It is *the roar. It thunders all around her, yet resonates gently through her body. It is all-powerful and infinitely tender:*

"HIS TIME HAS COME."

Gerty nods, the tears now flowing freely. Through her blurry vision she sees movement in front of her. A young man with long, dark hair is kneeling in the water. He wears a coarse, burlap robe. He is kneeling exactly where the water had been boiling. He looks up to her with gray, penetrating eyes. They are filled with fear and confusion. But, even more alarming, they are filled with a lack of hope. Gerty's heart swells with compassion. She has known of him since he was a child, has prayed and interceded for him these many years. She wants to comfort him, to encourage him, but he bows his head before she has a chance to speak.

She looks back up into the light, puzzled. But the light gives no answer. There is only the tender, thundering, consuming roar.

She feels the ax head move in her hands. She watches in alarm as it grows soft, starting to melt.

No. Please, dear God!

Has she come this far only to fail again?

And still it melts, becoming nothing but a puddle in her hands.

But only for a moment.

Immediately it reshapes itself. She watches in amazement as it grows, as its texture shifts from cool metal to rough, porous clay. Seconds later she is holding a squatty cylinder—a flask. The ax head has become an ancient clay flask.

Joy floods through her. It radiates into her arms, her hands, even her fingertips. This is what she has been waiting for. This is what she has been hoping and praying for.

Instinctively, she removes the flask's stopper. Her hands tremble in excitement. Without a word, she tilts the flask and a thick, clear oil spills over its lip, falling in uneven spurts onto the boy's head.

Her tears turn to quiet sobs. "Thank you . . . Thank you, thank you . . ."

As the last of the oil drains, the light before her begins to dim. The roar also fades. The boy, the river, everything around her wavers like a mirage until, in a matter of moments, they have all disappeared.

Gerty Morrison opened her eyes. She was back home, still kneeling before her bed. She kept her head bowed, resting it on the thin, worn mattress that had become soaked with her tears as she continued to pray, "Thank you, dear Lord. Thank you, thank you . . ."

PART ONE

CHAPTER 1

Brandon hated it. How many years had they been pulling these stupid pranks? Three? Four? Ever since they were seniors in high school. Sure, it was fun back then, back when they were kids. But now it was getting old. Real old.

But not for Frank. Frank thrived on it.

Brandon stood alone, inside the giant trophy case. With a roll of gray duct tape in hand he carefully worked his way past the cups, plaques, signed bats, tournament balls, pennants, group photos, silver plates, silver bowls, and other awards on display. Bethel Lake Country Club prided itself on its members' athletic prowess. And if you couldn't tell it by their arrogance, you could see it in the new trophy room they were about to dedicate—a room complete with this enormous, dust-proof trophy case that covered nearly the entire front wall.

Frank was right about one thing. Pride and pretension like this couldn't go unrewarded. They owed it to their people. They owed it to the Townies.

Brandon tossed back his long, dark hair and knelt. He yanked off a sizable strip of duct tape and ran it along the seam, right where the clear Plexiglas wall of the trophy case met the floor. He carefully sealed it so no water would leak through.

Meanwhile, behind the back wall of the case, Del gave the Black and Decker drill the workout of its life as it moaned and groaned in his incapable hands.

"You're pushing too hard," Frank's voice whispered from behind the wall.

"No way," Del's voice answered.

Brandon glanced over his shoulder at the back of the case; the thick cherry wood bulged under Del's pressure. There was more moaning and groaning from the drill until the head of the bit popped through the wood, followed by the rest of the shank.

Then the drill stopped. Then started again. Then stopped. It was jammed. Another start. Another stop.

Hoping to loosen it, Del began to wiggle the drill back and forth.

"Stop!" Frank's voice whispered. "You're going to break it, you're going to break the—"

SNAP!

Too late. The bit had broken off in the wall.

In the adjacent room, Tom Henderson, a twenty-one-year-old Aryan dream, complete with blonde hair and blue eyes, listened to a pompous master of ceremonies delivering another pompous speech. Tom stood with the forty or fifty other firm-bodied club members as the emcee continued his jibes at the locals:

". . . can well remember when we first entered these events seven, eight years back. Why, no one ever gave a thought to Bethel Lake—unless, of course, they found themselves downwind of the hog farms."

Henderson and the crowd chuckled condescendingly. They always chuckled condescendingly when it came to Bethel Lake—at least the Bethel Lake that existed before they had moved in and started taking over. The old Bethel Lake of corn farmers and hog raisers, along with the usual variety of hicks and poor-as-dirt mobile-home owners who prided themselves on being called *Townies.*

But now things were changing. Henderson could see it every time he came back home from college. Cornfields were giving way to golf courses; three-quarter-ton pickups with gun racks were being replaced by four-wheeler yuppie mobiles. There was even talk of remodeling the bowling alley and turning it into a mega-bookstore with espresso bar.

In the past five years, the sleepy, Indiana farm community located just off Highway 30 between Fort Wayne and South Bend had come to life. And now it was growing faster than they could slap up townhouses and condos. Part of this was due to Orion Computech, a new computer manufacturer with a workforce of over eleven hundred and counting. Already the Chamber of Commerce was flirting with aspirations of becoming the Midwest's Silicon Valley. Besides Orion, there was the Diamond Cellular Corporation, Lasher Electronics—and, of course, Moran Research Institute.

Part think tank, part psychic research lab, the only thing more imaginative than the Institute's research were the rumors about that research. The latest had them housing extraterrestrials and breeding them with humans so we'd sweep the next Olympics. Henderson shook his head in amusement. The Townies may be ignorant, but you couldn't fault them for their lack of imagination. The truth was, no one really knew exactly what went on behind the Institute's low-lying, modernistic architecture, but the Townie rumor mills never lacked for grist.

The emcee continued to drone on as Henderson glanced at his watch. His father, a vice president at Orion, had moved here against Tom's wishes when the boy was a senior in high school. Now, home for the summer from Ball State, Henderson had to admit that the town was changing almost enough to make living in it bearable.

In the trophy case, Brandon heard Del asking from behind the wall, "What do I do now?"

"Tap it out," Frank's voice sighed. "Tap it out and get that hose in. We don't got much time."

Brandon heard the sound of something heavy, probably the drill itself, hitting the bit three, four, five times. Finally, it popped out of the hole and fell with a dull thud. He turned to see the bit rolling to a stop just a few feet from his knees.

"Bran," Frank called quietly, "aren't you finished yet?"

Brandon didn't bother answering. He smoothed the last of the tape against the Plexiglas and rose to his feet. As he crossed to the back of the case, he saw a garden hose being shoved through the newly drilled hole.

Things were right on schedule.

He stooped, opened the small door, and stepped out of the rear of the trophy case to join his partners. Frank, the leader of the three-man hit squad, was good-looking, volatile, and athletic enough to be a club member—if it hadn't been for his genealogy. He was a third-generation Townie. Del, on the other hand, wore Coke-bottle glasses and on a good day could almost stretch himself to a height of five-three.

Brandon turned to the trophy case door and ripped off one last strip of tape to seal it as Frank and Del quickly followed the hose down the hall toward the kitchen faucet.

Twenty more minutes passed before the emcee finally started winding down. Henderson sighed in relief. Earlier, he'd spotted a couple of beauties at the far end of the room, and he was hoping to introduce himself. But if the old duffer rambled on much longer, they might slip away without the pleasure of making his company.

"In short," the emcee concluded, "I can't think of a more fitting way to open the new trophy room than with the addition of the Beckman Memorial Tennis Cup."

He turned to the paneled doors behind him and, with a modest flair, slid them open.

The lights came up, and before the members stood their new trophy room. Dark cherry paneling, rich emerald carpet, paisley print chairs scattered around end tables that supported brass lamps with green china shades. And at the far wall stood the focal piece of the room: a massive Plexiglas trophy case—six feet high and eighteen feet long. Inside, near the top and center of the case, was a vacant space waiting to receive the most recent addition—a large silver trophy bowl that sat on the lectern in front of the case.

The emcee approached the lectern as the crowd moved in and settled down. "Peter? Reggie?" he called. "I think it's only proper that you two do the honors."

The group broke into polite applause as a couple of jocks, the winners of the trophy, broke from their dates and came forward. Henderson knew the guys. Even liked them. In fact, they'd spent more than one summer night cruising in his Firebird, putting down the brews. The applause increased as they arrived and held the bowl over their heads.

Meanwhile, the emcee turned to open the trophy case doors. At first they seemed stuck. Either his key wasn't working, or the doors were jammed, or . . .

Henderson was the first to spot it: the trail of tiny air bubbles rising to the surface of the case. For a moment he was confused. What on earth were air bubbles doing . . . ? Then the horror registered. He started to call out, to push his way through the crowd. But he was too late.

With one last tug, the emcee opened the doors.

Water roared out of the case, knocking him to the ground. Club members screamed and scrambled back as the water poured into the room. Some lost their balance, slipping and falling.

Across the room, through the oval window of the kitchen door, Frank and Del watched in delight. They were laughing so hard they could barely catch their breath—until Reggie, one of the fallen, rose to his feet, looked around, sputtering and coughing, and caught a glimpse of them. Frank and Del saw his eyes widen. They saw his trembling finger point. And they saw his mouth open as he cried out a single word:

"Townies!"

Frank and Del ducked from the window, but they were too late. The announcement had been made, their location spotted. Now club members slipped and sloshed toward them with a vengeance.

Brandon was standing farther back in the kitchen, checking out the contents of the stainless-steel freezers, when Frank and Del raced past and grabbed him, yelling, "Come on, come on!"

They flung open a hallway door and started down the corridor. When they rounded the first corner, they discovered most of the club members heading directly for them.

They doubled back.

Even now, running as fast as his little legs could carry him, Del couldn't resist firing off a few jabs. "'I know this place,' Frank says. 'Like the back of my hand,' he says."

"Hey," Frank shot back. "How'd I know they were going to remodel?"

They rounded another corner, then another. At last they spotted an unlikely looking door. "In here!" Frank shouted as he threw it open.

Brandon and Del followed. The door slammed behind them with a foreboding boom. Suddenly they found themselves in total darkness.

"Oh, Frank?" Del's voice echoed.

"Hold on . . ."

"Yo, Frank!"

"Relax, there's gotta be a light here somewh—"

Suddenly the overheads came on and the boys winced at the four brilliant white walls surrounding them.

Del squinted. "A racquetball court? You led us into a racquetball court!"

Before Frank could answer, the door opened and an attractive woman with amber, shoulder-length hair stood in the opening. She was a few years older than they were. But Frank, who made it a policy to recognize any and all of the local beauties, stepped forward. "Hi," he ventured. "Uh, Sarah, isn't it?"

She simply looked at him.

He tried to smile.

So did Del.

It was a joint failure.

"Anybody in there?" a man's voice shouted from down the hall.

The woman stood silent. Still looking. Still deciding.

They fidgeted.

"Sarah?" the voice repeated.

Finally she turned and called back. "Nobody worth mentioning."

"Be careful," another voice warned as the group headed down the other hall.

Sarah didn't answer and waited for the footsteps to fade. Then, without a word, she opened the door wider and stepped back for them to exit.

Frank and Del exchanged glances, then quickly scurried past.

"Thanks, Sarah," Frank offered. Then, to further express his gratitude, he continued, "You're lookin' real good."

She ignored him and turned to Brandon.

For the briefest second their eyes locked. And for the briefest second Brandon couldn't look away. He sensed that she couldn't, either. There was a moment, a connection. He knew he should say something. Something cool, something witty. But he wasn't much good at talking to pretty women. Lately, he wasn't much good at talking to anybody. Instead, he gave a slight nod of thanks, moved past her, and headed down the hall.

The parking lot of Bethel Country Club was cut out of the side of a large hill. There was only one exit: along the bottom of the hill and down the private, tree-lined drive. Already several of the men, including Henderson and his buddies, along with a handful of women, had gathered along that drive. They stood just a few yards past the parking lot, forming a roadblock. Waiting. Watching.

"Just a matter of time," one of the men said.

"You phone the police?" a lithe blonde asked.

"Yeah, right," another scoffed. Others in the group voiced similar scorn. They knew the police didn't encourage these pranks. But they also knew they didn't *dis*courage them either. Like the kids, most of the police were Townies. Their attitude was simple: If these outsiders wanted to come barging into Bethel Lake uninvited, that was their business. But there were certain customs to be followed, certain dues to be paid—and if that included this type of occasional, low-grade harassment, then so be it. It was just normal social interaction.

A pair of headlights suddenly appeared as a half-ton pickup slid around the corner of the parking lot.

"There they are!"

It accelerated toward them.

"Hold your ground," the first man shouted. "They wouldn't dare try to—*look out!*"

Some leaped to the side of the road, others scrambled up the dirt embankment as the truck roared past.

Inside the cab of the pickup Frank yelled, "Eee-haaa!" as the last of the human roadblocks hit the bushes. "We did it, boys!" he shouted. "We did it!"

Del's voice was a little less sure as he glanced back for casualties. "This is insane!"

Brandon, who was driving, gave no response.

Meanwhile, Henderson, Peter, and Reggie scrambled to their feet and raced toward Henderson's '97 Firebird. Unfortunately, in his haste, Henderson had forgotten to turn off the alarm, and it began honking incessantly.

"Let's go, let's go!" Reggie shouted over the noise.

Henderson fumbled with the remote on his keys until he managed to shut off the alarm. They piled into his car, and he brought the 5.7-liter V–8 roaring to life. He dropped it into gear and hit the accelerator. Gravel spit in all directions as the car spun out and began pursuit.

In the pickup, Frank was exultant. "You see the look on their faces?" he cried as he popped a brew. It foamed, but he quickly slurped it up, careful not to let any get away. "I tell you, boys, I can die a happy man."

Looking over his shoulder, Del muttered, "You might get your chance."

Brandon glanced up at the mirror and saw the headlights appear behind them. But he was unconcerned. They reached the end of the private drive, and the pickup bounced out onto the main highway.

"Who's the girl?" Brandon asked, shifting down and quickly accelerating.

"Sarah Weintraub," Frank answered through a loud belch. "Used to work at some fancy college out West."

Del watched through the back window as the pursuing lights bounced onto the road and continued after them. "Uh, guys?" But, as usual, the guys weren't paying him any attention.

"She started at the Institute a few months ago," Frank continued.

"She's a Techie, then?"

"Yeah."

"Too bad."

"Uh—Frank? Bran?" Del tried to keep his voice even as the approaching lights grew closer and began flashing their high beams at them.

Brandon glanced at the mirror. Then suddenly, without warning, he threw his truck into a hard left and hit the brakes.

"Brandon!" Del cried.

The truck slid sideways, its tires screaming. Del and Frank flew across the cab, but Brandon remained fixed at the wheel.

In the Firebird, Reggie shouted, "What's he doing?"

Henderson had no answer as he watched the pickup continue its spin and then bounce to a stop. It had done a complete 180 and was now facing them, headlights glaring.

Back in the cab, Frank shouted. "What's goin' on? What're you doing?"

Brandon gave no answer. He simply downshifted and stomped on the accelerator, leaving behind smoke and flying gravel as he sped toward the Firebird.

"Brandon!" Del repeated.

Brandon swerved the pickup into the Firebird's lane.

"Brandon!"

Inside the Firebird, Henderson's mouth dropped open. The pickup was in his lane and heading directly for them.

"What's he doing?" Reggie cried.

In the pickup, Frank had the same question. "Bran—yo, Brandon?"

But Brandon didn't hear. He gripped the wheel tightly and concentrated on the lights of the Firebird.

A confused Henderson edged his car closer to the right shoulder, trying to get past.

Brandon countered by bringing his pickup just as close to the shoulder.

They were a hundred yards apart, speeding toward each other.

Reggie swore and shouted, "He's crazy! He's crazy!"

Henderson agreed. He swerved hard to the left, to the other side of the road.

Brandon followed suit. Concentrating, barely blinking.

"Brandon?" Del's voice cracked.

Brandon gave no answer.

Henderson squinted against the approaching lights of the pickup. He saw no shape, no detail, only lights—two bright beams below, and four orange running lights on top. Well, actually, three. The light over the driver's side of the cab was busted and glowed white. Desperately, Henderson whipped the Firebird back over to the far right.

The pickup duplicated his move exactly, once again heading toward him.

The vehicles were fifty yards apart now.

Back in the cab Frank began to laugh—it was the only way to hide his fear. "You're crazy, Brandon—crazy!"

Brandon's silence seemed to confirm it.

Panicking, Henderson searched for some way out, *any* way.

Thirty yards . . . twenty-five . . .

Henderson looked at the side of the road, hoping to veer off, but they were in a thick tunnel of trees.

Twenty yards.

With no other option, Henderson slammed on the brakes. Not that it would do any good. If the crazy in the pickup wanted to hit them, there was nothing Henderson could do to stop him. With tires squealing, he threw the Firebird into another left. It skidded and started to spin . . .

. . . just as Brandon swerved to *his* left, missing the Firebird by mere feet.

"Wooooo!" Frank screamed, enjoying the rush of his life.

Del would have shouted, too, but he was too busy trying to keep his pants dry.

The Firebird spun once, then half around again, before bouncing and sliding to a stop on the opposite side of the road, kicking up a huge cloud of dust that hovered above the car.

Brandon relaxed his grip on the wheel. He slowed the pickup, then made a careful U-turn to investigate the damage.

The Firebird's lights were on and its engine running, but there was no one at the wheel. Henderson had thrown open the driver's door and was racing to the back fender.

"You're certifiable, ol' buddy!" Frank laughed as they approached the Firebird. "Certifiable!"

"How'd you know?" Del mumbled, checking his pants for dampness.

Brandon pulled up to the Firebird and rolled down his window. Inside the Firebird, Reggie and his buddy were at various shades of white, coughing from the dirt and dust. Outside, Henderson was leaning over the rear fender, heaving his guts out.

Despite his feigned indifference, there was no missing a trace of concern in Brandon's voice. "Everybody all right?"

They gave no answer. Just more coughing, until, at last, Henderson raised his head. He managed a faint nod before being hit by another wave of nausea.

But for Frank the temptation was too great. He leaned past Brandon and, beer in hand, yelled, "How many times do I have to tell you Techies—'If you don't drink, don't drive!'" He let out a cackling laugh.

But no one in the Firebird responded. They'd had enough. They simply shook their heads, coughed, and waved Brandon on.

But Henderson would remember Brandon's face. More important, he would remember the broken running light on top of Brandon's cab. They would meet again; he'd see to it.

Brandon dropped the pickup into gear and pulled away as Frank let out another whoop—his infectious laughter lingering on the remote road.

"How'd you know?" Del asked again. "How'd you know—"

"How'd he know what?" Frank burped.

"That the guy was going to turn left."

Frank broke into more laughter. "He always knows that stuff." He reached past Del and gave Brandon a slap on the back. "Ain't that right, Bran? You always know."

Once again Brandon did not answer.

Dr. Helmut Reichner cursed softly as the 757 bounced and bucked on its final approach to Tribhuvan International Airport just outside of Katmandu. It wasn't the turbulence that bothered him, nor the fact that the Himalayas, which friends had predicted he would find so breathtaking, were completely shrouded in monsoon clouds. It was that every bump and jar reminded him of his last-minute inoculations for tetanus/diphtheria, hepatitis, typhoid, Japanese encephalitis, and of course, the ever-popular gamma globulin—three ccs in each buttock. And it was those buttocks that were suffering the greatest abuse during the bouncings and buckings.

True, he could have spread out the injections over a few days, resulting in less discomfort. But that would have meant delaying his flight—and the mysterious donor down there in the mountains of Nepal had wanted to see him immediately. If there was one thing Reichner knew about securing financial gifts, it was to make the people with the money think you were jumping whenever they said jump.

As executive director of the Moran Research Institute, Reichner was a pro at playing people to get what he wanted. Those from other parapsychology labs around the world described him in less generous terms: huckster, manipulator, shameless con artist. Let his peers say what they would. While they were busy scrapping and fighting for the few funds available for paranormal research, he was enjoying a free ride from a single donor. It had been that way since the construction of the 2.8-million-dollar complex at Bethel Lake nearly three years ago. He had never understood why the donor had insisted that he build it in the backwoods community of northern Indiana, but that was a small price to pay for total and complete funding. Funding that would later include the purchase of expensive PET scan and MRI equipment. And funding that, if Reichner played his cards correctly, he would continue to enjoy for many years to come.

He didn't know who the guru down there was, where he got his money, or why he hid in the remote mountains of Nepal. Reichner had never actually met him; all their interaction had, until this point, been handled through the guru's intermediaries. There were rumors that he was a young man, perhaps even a boy, the result of a genetic experiment in the States that had gone awry. An experiment that had supposedly left him with incredible psychic powers—powers currently being groomed and guarded by some sort of international cartel. For what purposes, Reichner hadn't the foggiest. But the boy and the cartel had been sponsoring the Institute for three years now. And if Reichner handled this hastily called face-to-face correctly, it should not only answer some of his questions about his donor but ensure uninterrupted financial support for several years to come.

After all, using people and situations was what Reichner did best.

The plane lurched again. Reichner readjusted his meticulously kept six-foot frame, searching for some portion of his anatomy to take the final abuses. He was grateful to hear the dull whine of the landing gears as they opened and locked into place.

He glanced up; the flight attendant he'd been flirting with since New Delhi approached the bulkhead in front of him and folded down the flight seat. Her name was Gita. This was her first month on the job and she was still a little nervous. But the details didn't concern Dr. Reichner. The point was that she was slender, attractive, and very, very young—nearly thirty years his junior.

Just the way he liked them.

He'd been playing the powerful yet understanding father figure during the trip, and it had been working perfectly. Of course he'd made his occupation clear, and of course she found it incredibly intriguing. The younger ones always did. But now they were about to land and he'd have to work fast.

The plane gave another jolt and he winced.

"Are you okay?" she asked as she buckled in. "You look a little pale."

Reichner smiled. Adding a trace of vulnerability would only work to his advantage. "Just a little air sickness. I'm okay." He grinned, wincing just enough to make it clear that he was lying.

"We'll be on the ground in a few seconds," she said sympathetically. "Hang in there."

He smiled and nodded. She smiled back.

Good.

There was another jar as the wheels touched down and they began to taxi toward the terminal.

"So," he cleared his throat, "you've never met anyone involved in psychic research before?"

"No, never. It is most intriguing."

"Yes, well, we are a rare breed." He straightened his tropical wool slacks and folded his hands. "There are only fifty to sixty full-time parapsychologists in the entire world."

"Really?"

"Yes. With less than a dozen labs."

"That is all?"

He nodded. "Two in England and Russia, one in Beijing, Edinburgh, Bombay, the Netherlands, Brazil of course, and a small handful in the States. But that's all. As the leader in this field, I try to visit them often. But you can imagine how having no family and being on the road can make one lonely from time to time." He threw her a look.

She didn't get it. The kid was obviously too naive to appreciate his subtlety. They were approaching the terminal. He'd have to be more obvious.

"But the amazing thing is, I believe everybody on our planet has psychic abilities."

"Really?"

"Absolutely. In fact, right here, right now, I bet you could telepathically communicate to me what you're thinking."

She laughed. "You are not serious."

Reichner glanced out the window. The terminal was three hundred yards away. He'd have to work fast. "Of course I'm serious." He reached out to her. "Here, give me your hand, and I will tell you what you are thinking."

She hesitated.

"I'm serious. Simply focus your thoughts upon me and I will be able to tell."

She threw a nervous glance at the rest of the cabin, then leaned discreetly forward and held out her hand. Reichner took it. It was cool and smooth. So young, so firm.

He fixed his eyes onto hers and looked deeply into them. She faltered, glancing away, then looked back.

Good.

He dropped his voice into a soothing, controlled tone—the one he used on his subjects during their sessions at the Institute. "Just relax and concentrate . . . Concentrate." He noticed the terminal out of the corner of his eye. They were nearly there.

"Oh my, I am getting lots of thoughts." He smiled.

She fidgeted.

"First of all, you are feeling a bit lonely, too, are you not? In fact—hmm, you are wondering what you will be doing this evening." He could feel a slight dampness break out in her palm. Excellent. He tightened his grip so she couldn't easily pull away. Still staring at her, he continued. "You do not want to be cooped up in that hotel room . . ." His eyes widened, pretending surprise. "Well, now."

"What?" she smiled self-consciously.

"No, I—"

"Please, tell me."

"Well, somewhere in the back of your mind you are wondering . . . you are wondering if I will invite you to dinner."

Her smile wavered.

He'd gone too far. Immediately he went in for damage control. "It might be deep in your subconscious, of course, but—"

She pulled back her hand.

"I am sorry," he feigned embarrassment. "Sometimes our subconscious thinks things that we are not even aware—"

"Excuse me." She fumbled with her safety harness and unbuckled it. Without another word, she rose and entered the other cabin.

Reichner leaned back in his seat as the plane shuddered to a stop. He'd been clumsy, hadn't taken enough time. Too bad. In the proper environment he could talk anybody into anything. It was a gift he'd developed over the years. That's how he'd survived his childhood poverty in Austria. That's how he'd risen to his current level of success in his field.

He just hadn't taken enough time, that was all. But there were others. There were always others.

After retrieving his carry-on from the overhead and donning his Hickey-Freeman suit coat, he moved down the aisle. A moment later he passed the girl at the front exit. "It was very nice meeting you," he said, smiling.

She returned the smile and reached out to shake his hand. He was surprised, but he took her hand, once again enjoying the soft firmness of her touch. When he withdrew, he discovered a folded piece of paper in his palm. He waited until he'd stepped out of the plane to read it. Outside, the rain-soaked air was hot and humid, hitting him like a sauna. As he moved down the portable stairway toward the tarmac he unfolded the paper. It read:

Hotel Ganesh
312 Sukrapath Rd.

He smiled. Yes, he was good. He was very, very good.

"Mr. Reichner."

He glanced up to see two Westerners approaching the foot of the stairs. One was short and stocky, about five-five. The other was nearly Reichner's height and had a steel prosthesis for a left hand. Both wore suits almost as expensive as his.

They met him at the bottom of the steps and moved off to the side, out of the flow of traffic. "Are you Mr. Reichner?" the tall one asked.

"*Dr.* Reichner," Reichner corrected. "Who are you?"

"The Teacher has sent us."

Reichner frowned. They were obviously disciples of the boy guru. "We aren't scheduled to meet until tomorrow."

"The situation's gettin' a lot worse." Tall Suit's accent was lower British class. Reichner guessed Liverpool.

"Yes," Reichner cleared his throat. "Well, I have another appointment this evening, so I am afraid—"

He felt a hand lightly press against his back. "I'm sorry, but this can't wait." Not fond of being manhandled, Reichner held his ground. The taller man repeated, "The Teacher, he needs to see you. *Now.*"

Reichner considered his options. He could resist, but since these goons were connected to the money man it would be better to let them play their hand, at least for now. Later, he could complain, maybe even use their inhospitality to his advantage.

As if reading his mind, Tall Suit cranked up a feeble excuse for a smile. Reichner turned to the shorter man who was struggling to look equally as pleasant. The two seemed intent upon having their way, and judging by how they both filled out their suits, Reichner guessed that they were used to getting it. Well—best to play by the house rules. At least until he learned how to manipulate those rules to his advantage. And he would. That was his style. The secret to his success.

SLAUGHTER! KILL! DESTROY! MUTILATE!

The voices inside Lewis's head had been screaming for nearly three days. In calmer times they spoke in complete sentences. But when Lewis refused to obey, their demands grew louder, shriller. The rantings stirred other voices in him. Voices he didn't often hear but that he suspected were always there. Voices that joined in the screaming.

KILL! DECIMATE! ANNIHILATE!

He didn't always understand the words, but he knew what they wanted. They demanded destruction. They hungered for the hot, rusty smell of blood. They demanded the rush of power that came only from taking another life. Of course, Lewis wanted it, too. In fact, at times like this, he couldn't tell where their desires ended and his began. Not that he cared. At least not now. Now his appetite and their screamings had to be silenced—the throbbing, all-consuming hunger had to be fed.

"Which one?" a young teen with an acne-ravaged face whispered.

Lewis stood silently under the cover of trees near the pen. He stroked his red, ragged goatee and carefully surveyed the eight pigs. The moon made their lovely pale skins luminescent. They were beautiful animals. Any one would do.

"Let's go. Let's do it, let's do it." It was the other teen, a little older—the one with the long greasy hair and double-pierced eyebrow.

Lewis said nothing but watched in silence. The urgency of his companions caused him little concern. They were slackers. Hangers-on who were nominally attracted to his power. They were far more interested in witchcraft, Satanism, and the other childish games misfits like them needed to try to gain control of their lives. Neither boy fully appreciated Lewis's real powers—or what he would soon become.

The animals, aware of the strangers' presence, were growing uneasy.

"Come on," Pierced Eyebrow urged, casting a worried glance at the farmhouse. "Let's do it."

Lewis ran his hand over the red stubble atop his head. Yes, it was definitely time. He reached for his belt to check on the Buck hunting knife—one of the few things his daddy had given him before he'd killed himself.

KILL! DESTROY! RAVAGE!

Lewis's heart pounded as he surveyed the animals. Finally he focused on one to the far right. It seemed to be the youngest, the fairest, the most pure.

MUTILATE! DESECRATE!

This was always the best part. Just before the kill. The teasing. The building up of desire until it practically exploded inside him.

"Let's do it!" Acne Face whispered.

Lewis's breath came shorter now, in ragged pants of excitement. He had never killed an animal this large. Hamsters, yes. Stray cats, several. Even a neighbor's puppy. But never this.

Suddenly, he broke from cover and ran toward the fence. Five steps, up, over, and he was inside the pen. A moment later his partners joined him. The pigs squealed in panic, running in every direction. A chained dog began barking over at the house. But that was okay; they'd be done before the porch light came on.

"That one!" Lewis shouted. "That one, right there!"

They closed in on the young animal. It cut to the left, then to the right, then left again. In seconds they had it cornered. Pierced Eyebrow lunged; the others followed until they were all holding it. The thing kicked and jerked and squealed, but it was outnumbered.

"Hold him!" Acne Face yelled. He'd made the mistake of grabbing the haunches and was now suffering considerable abuse because of it. "Hold him!"

Pierced Eyebrow yanked up the animal's head, exposing its neck. Lewis reached for his knife, and then everything turned to slow motion. Ecstasy exploded in his chest, rushing through his veins, firing every nerve.

It was over in seconds. Lewis's legs buckled in euphoria, dropping him to his knees. Already the voices were subsiding. Of course, they would return. They always did. And each time their hunger and desire was greater than the time before. But that was okay. Lewis knew the reason. He was being prepared. There was a stirring in him. He'd felt it, known it, been told about it by the voices. He was about to enter his season. After years of patiently waiting, being ignored and humiliated, Lewis Thompson would shortly—very, very shortly—begin fulfilling the destiny for which he'd been born.

CHAPTER 2

Something was wrong at Moran Research Institute. Terribly wrong.

An exhausted Sarah Weintraub entered one of the two narrow labs and dimmed the lights. It had been a frustrating evening, and these rooms, with their subdued lighting and gray, ribbed panels of sound-absorbing material, always comforted her. She dropped into one of the two swivel chairs in front of a black console that contained a handful of controls, a couple of joysticks, some unwashed coffee mugs, a half-used legal pad, and a computer keyboard. Above this were two or three computers, some video monitors, a pair of speakers, and four red floodlights directed toward a plush leather recliner to the right. Behind her, almost within reaching distance, were waist-high racks of DATs, more computers, and other monitoring equipment. And finally, above that was the three-foot-high by seven-foot-long, one-way glass of the observation room, which housed even more state-of-the-art electronics and dirty coffee mugs.

Earlier that evening, she had made an obligatory public relations appearance at the country club—on the arm of some Neanderthal who had tried more moves on her than he had words in his vocabulary. That had been a mistake, but she had paid her penance by spending the rest of the evening and early morning hours here, at the Institute. Other twenty-eight-year-olds had their boyfriends, their husbands, their kids, but Sarah Weintraub had her work. And over the years it had become a demanding lover, one she seldom refused.

It hadn't always been that way. Granted, she was ambitious and even aggressive, more than most. As the only girl in a family with four brothers, she'd had to be. But at the appropriate time, she'd always been able to fit in and unwind with the best of them. Until her second year at grad school. That's when she'd gotten pregnant, and that's when the fights with Samuel had started. "Come on, Babe," he had insisted, "I want a kid as much as you. But not now. We've both got school to finish and careers to launch. After that, sure. The more the merrier. But not now."

Sarah hadn't wanted the abortion, but Samuel's persistence had worn her down. He understood her ambition perfectly, and he'd used it to get his way. At the end of her ninth week, she'd found herself on the table, legs in the stirrups, staring at a poster of a smiling Garfield up on the ceiling.

She knew the fetus was a boy, had sensed it from the beginning. She'd begged him to please understand, to please forgive her. But apparently he hadn't. There had been an accidental perforation of the uterus wall, followed by severe bleeding. By the end of the day, Sarah Weintraub had found herself the recipient of an emergency hysterectomy. Eight months later, she and Samuel had broken up. He'd never admitted it, but she suspected "damaged goods" to be a contributing factor on his part. And for her, there had been the guilt and overbearing depression that she just couldn't seem to shake.

Fortunately, there had been her studies and later, her work. Not only had they kept her mind occupied and held back the depression, but they had also earned her the reputation as a diligent researcher and a go-getter—proving that she really was a good girl. Proving that her work really did count for something. Proving that maybe, after enough accomplishments in her field, that maybe, just maybe, the sacrifice of her son could someday be justified. Until then, all Sarah Weintraub needed were two to three dozen hours of overtime each week to keep the guilt and self-loathing at bay.

She leaned over the console and punched on the power. The board lit up, and one of the computers started to whir. She had spent the past several hours alone at the Institute, checking and rechecking last week's data. But no matter how carefully she scrutinized the procedural notes and reworked the probabilities, the results remained the same.

Something was wrong.

The red light on the board glowed, indicating that the random number generator, or RNG, was up and running. The original RNG had been developed nearly thirty years ago by a brilliant but bored Boeing employee out in Seattle. Today, its offspring are found in nearly every parapsychology lab in the world. Although it has many uses, it's particularly effective in measuring a person's psychokinesis, or PK—the ability to move physical objects through mental concentration.

In the old days, this meant trying to manipulate the outcome of tumbling dice or flipping coins. The process was slow and cumbersome, sometimes taking hundreds, even thousands of trials. But now, thanks to modern science, this and nearly every other area of paranormal research had turned high-tech.

Sarah never completely understood the electronics behind the RNG, but she knew it was designed to fire a random set of pluses or minuses over a given period of time. All the human subject had to do was hold down a button on the joystick and concentrate, trying to force the computer to fire more pluses or more minuses than would be normal for random chance.

Sarah had been working with a dozen volunteer subjects who came in weekly. Some demonstrated very strong PK. Others showed no giftedness in the area whatsoever.

But in the past seventy-two hours, all of that had changed.

Everything had gone haywire. Subjects with consistently high PK readings were flat lining. Those with no past history were going off the chart. Incredible. It was as if somebody was playing an elaborate hoax. That's why Sarah was here in these early morning hours. That's why she had reexamined every result, every figure, every procedural report.

But the outcome was exactly the same: Other than impossible PK scores, there was absolutely nothing unusual.

Sarah leaned back and sighed. Almost absentmindedly she reached to the console and snapped on a monitor. With the same lack of thought, she scooped up the joystick and started fiddling with the button in the handle. The speaker in front of her began to ping—high pings meant *plus* firings, low pings meant *minus* firings. On the monitor, a graph with a line appeared. It showed visually what she was hearing audibly. The more plus firings, the higher the line rose on the graph, the more minus firings, the lower it dropped.

Earlier that day a technician had run careful calibrations on all six of the Institute's RNGs. He'd found no problems. Not a one.

Having no energy to concentrate, Sarah lowered the volume. This wasn't an experiment, just something to do as she tried to relax. But she couldn't let her mind drift too far. After all, this was the first week of August—the week of bad dreams and deepest depression. The week of drinking just a little too much wine and working doubly hard to keep her mind occupied. The little whirlpools of memory were always present, but this week, the anniversary of her abortion, was always the worst. If she was careless, she could accidentally step into one of those memories and be pulled under—dragged into a spinning vortex that would take days, sometimes weeks, to pull out of. Over the past three years she'd grown to accept this period of time. She figured it was the price of admission. And, truth be told, she considered it mild punishment for her offense.

It had been about this time last year that Dr. Reichner had begun pursuing her. Having her Ph.D. in neuroscience and doing research for UCLA, Sarah initially had been repulsed at the thought of joining a parapsychology lab. There are few branches of science given less credit than parapsychology. But, like Samuel, Reichner knew how to get what he wanted. His offer had been nearly double what she had been making at the school and, gradually, his phone calls and persistent e-mail accomplished their purpose. She had agreed to move to this backwoods Indiana town and take a position as senior researcher for Moran Research Institute. New job, new part of the country, longer hours—maybe this would be what she needed to finally bury her grief and self-hatred.

She'd found research into the paranormal more credible than she had anticipated. In fact, she was surprised to observe the painstaking care and scientific objectivity with which studies in the paranormal were being undertaken throughout the world.

She was also surprised at some of the results.

Such as the PK research in Russia. A group of so-called psychics were brought in to focus disruptive thoughts upon preselected laboratory rats from a larger colony. They attempted to make the selected rats act more aggressively. Professional animal behaviorists observed the colony to determine which rats appeared to be most disruptive. Without knowing it, the behaviorists chose the identical rats that the psychics had been concentrating upon. To further verify the results, biologists were brought in to dissect all of the rats' brains, particularly studying the chemicals and regions that indicate aggression. Once again, this group selected the identical rats that both the psychics and animal behaviorists had chosen.

Of course, this was just one of dozens of PK experiments being conducted around the world. Others measured the human mind's effect on plants, atomic particles, even the human nervous system—often with impressive results. In fact, just recently the U.S. Department of Defense had admitted to pouring over twenty million dollars into their own special parapsychology studies. A waste of taxpayers' money? Perhaps. But if the human mind could maneuver the electrons necessary for firing the RNG, couldn't it do the same on an enemy's computer? If they could disturb a mouse's mind, couldn't they do the same with the thoughts of a military general?

Sarah's own thoughts were jarred by a faint, electronic whine. Earlier, she had turned down the RNG's volume, but now the soft shrillness caught her attention. She looked up at the monitor. The line on the graph was gone. It had completely shot up and off the screen.

Immediately, she released the button on the joystick. But the high-pitched whine continued.

That was impossible. She wasn't influencing the machine now. It should drop back down to the flat line of random chance.

But it didn't.

Instead the whine's pitch actually increased. Sarah rose to her feet, staring at the screen, wincing at the shrillness. It was a malfunction. Had to be. There was no other explanation.

She had to record this. Get the results on tape. She turned to the DAT machine behind her and punched up RECORD.

But just as the recorder came to life, the whine stopped.

Sarah looked back at the monitor. The line on the graph had gone flat. It had dropped back down to the acceptable level of probability.

And then she felt something. A chill. A damp, freezing sensation swept across the lab. From right to left. She gave an involuntary shiver as it brushed against her skin, then moved on toward the open door to the hallway.

Word of last night's Townie exploits rapidly spread through the plant of Bollenger's Printing and Lithograph. The fact that Brandon and Frank both worked there certainly helped. The fact that Frank loved retelling the story and thrived on all the attention didn't hurt, either. And since most of the employees were Townies like himself, they hung on his every word, vicariously reliving last night's escapade and sharing the victory. Even now, as Brandon drove his electric forklift past the giant printing press, he could see Frank recounting the story to Warner, the ponytailed operator.

Warner listened and laughed as he manipulated the reverse button of the press, inching the mammoth rollers backward with his left hand as the right deftly darted in between them with a cleaning rag.

Looking up and spotting Brandon, Frank shouted to him over the plant's noise. "Hey, there he is now. Hey, Mario—Mario Andretti!"

Both guys laughed and Brandon threw them a half-smile before turning his attention back to the forklift.

That's when he saw her . . .

His eight-year-old sister. She was wearing a white nightgown and looking even more lovely than he remembered. In her hand she held a pot, and in that pot was a small, ornamental tree.

Brandon slammed on the brakes.

The girl said nothing.

Quickly, he dropped the forklift into neutral and hopped off.

"Jenny?"

His heart began to pound. He felt a joy he hadn't experienced in months as he started toward her, anxious to hug her, to scoop her into his arms, to say how much he had missed her.

But she held out her hand, motioning for him to stop.

He slowed, confused. What did she mean?

She extended her finger and pointed. Brandon followed it to Frank and Warner. He looked back at her. He started to speak, to ask what she meant, but before the words came he was interrupted.

"Hey, Martus."

He turned to see Roger Putnam, the foreman of their shift, a lumbering mass of muscle and fat who was busy reading his clipboard as he rounded the forklift. He glanced up and spotted Jenny.

"How'd she get in?" he asked. "No one under eighteen on the floor, you know that."

Brandon looked at him in surprise. Was that all he had to say?

Tapping his clipboard, Putnam continued. "Listen, you're screwing up on the orders again. You know I can't keep covering for you."

As he spoke, Jenny again raised her hand and pointed.

"I mean, I've got my rear end to protect too, y'know."

Again, Brandon followed Jenny's gesture to Frank and Warner. What was she trying to say? They were just shooting the breeze. Just standing and talking—

Except for Warner's right hand, the one darting in and out of the rollers. He glanced at Jenny. Her face was filling with urgency. That was it.

He looked back at Warner, who was still laughing, paying little attention to his work.

"Now, you got another delivery over at the Institute today," Putnam was saying, "so try not to ..."

But Brandon barely heard. He stared at Warner's hands as the man carelessly pushed the reverse button with his left, while darting the cleaning rag in and out of the rollers with his right. Suddenly, his left hand hit the reverse button too recklessly and slipped off, pressing the forward button instead.

Before Brandon could shout a warning, the rollers reversed. They grabbed the cleaning rag, yanking Warner's hand with it. The massive rollers crushed his fingers, then his hand. Warner opened his mouth, trying to scream, but no sound came—only Brandon's own anguished cry as he bolted up in bed, his face covered in sweat.

He glanced at the crimson glow of the radio alarm on his nightstand. It read 4:22 A.M.

"How long a drive do we have?" Dr. Reichner called from the backseat of the Peugeot. "Where exactly does your Teacher live?"

It had been twenty minutes since they'd met at the airport outside Katmandu. Now they had doubled back into the city and were making their way through the crowded, stone-paved streets. Both of his escorts sat up front—the shorter one on the passenger side, the taller one gripping a knob on the steering wheel with his steel prosthesis. The sunlight had started to fade, making the city look surreal—white plaster walls now orange from the sun, umber tiled roofs, holy shrines, strange statues covered in multicolored candle wax and flowers. And the people, everywhere people. Street vendors, barefoot children, emaciated holy men with painted faces and white, flowing hair.

"So," Reichner tried again. "How long before we get there?"

For the first time since they'd met, the shorter one spoke. Unlike his British partner, this man sounded Danish. "You have your degree in physics?"

Reichner didn't appreciate having the subject changed, but he decided to answer. "That is one of my doctorates. My first is in theology at Princeton Seminary. But when I couldn't find God in religion, I turned to physics." It was an old joke, but one that carried more truth for him than humor.

"So tell me," Short Suit continued, "don't you find the similarity between quantum physics and Eastern philosophy amazingly similar?"

Wonderful, Reichner thought, *a pseudo-intellectual. This guy will want to talk forever.* He glanced out the window and again wondered how long the ride to guru-land would take. "Yes," he answered almost mechanically. "There are interesting parallels."

Short Suit nodded. "I am reading about Schrödinger's cat. What an intriguing concept."

Reichner said nothing. It always surprised him how excited laypeople became when they first grasped quantum mechanics, as if it were something entirely new. The truth is, it had been around for three-quarters of a century. And in that time it had done some major damage. In fact, many would say that it had overthrown much of Isaac Newton's and Albert Einstein's thinking, causing Einstein himself to complain, "God does not play dice with the universe."

Well, guess again, Al.

Until the 1920s everything was clear-cut. Everyone knew that the movement and position of any object could be predicted. Just find its speed and direction, then do a little math. Of course this is still true with larger objects like cars or planes or planets, but when it comes down to particles the size of atoms or smaller, look out. At that level everything can turn topsy-turvy. The fact is, there's no telling where one of those particles could suddenly pop up, or in what direction they'll be heading—until we observe them.

Observation, that's the key that baffles everyone. Because somehow, someway, it's that very act of observation that determines where those objects will be. Until the observation is made, the particle is merely a ghost located in several places at the same time. It's only when we observe it that it materializes at the location in which it is observed.

At first the concept sounds absurd, unbelievable. So for beginners, Reichner usually explained it as if a subatomic particle were a magical car, one that is in St. Louis, New York, Seattle, Los Angeles, Dallas, and a hundred other locations all at the same time. It is only when we, the observers, go to St. Louis and see it there, that its ghostly appearances in all of the other locations disappear and it materializes in St. Louis. The same would have been true if we had first seen it in New York or Dallas. The car would have appeared in those cities instead. It was a crude comparison that left out more than a few details, but it helped Reichner make his point: Our act of observing has a profound impact upon subatomic objects. In truth, it actually determines where those objects will be or what direction they will be heading.

Astonishing? Yes.

True? Absolutely.

As a teen, Reichner used to think such theoretical double-talk belonged more to philosophers than to scientists—following such hypothetical questions as: "If a tree falls in the forest and nobody hears it, does it make a sound?" But quantum mechanics is far more than theory. It has been proven mathematically and through hundreds of lab experiments such as Thomas Young's two-slit system, or Alaine Aspect's work at the University of Paris as early as the 1970s.

Then, of course, there was Reichner's own work with Sarah Weintraub and their PK experiments back at the Moran Research Institute. The chain of logic was clear. If we can determine the location of a subatomic particle by observing it with our minds, can't we also *influence* that particle's behavior with those same minds? Isn't that really what PK is all about? When the Institute's subjects direct the firing of the random number generators to either pluses or minuses, are they not simply practicing everyday, run-of-the-mill, quantum mechanics?

But quantum mechanics is more than just some scientific laboratory's novelty. It is also responsible for such practical inventions as the transistor, electron microscope, superconductor, laser, and even nuclear power.

Unfortunately, Short Suit wasn't done talking. Not yet. "I am sure you and the Teacher will have many fascinating hours of conversation, particularly regarding the Buddhist and Hindu beliefs of the nonlocal mind."

Reichner rolled his eyes and looked back out the window. Once quantum mechanics had become accessible to the public, the Eastern religions had quickly jumped on the cosmic bandwagon. If subatomic particles don't really exist until we view them, couldn't the same thing be said about larger items, like the earth, the stars, the universe? And if the universe didn't really exist until we observed it, doesn't that make us its creators? And if we've created the universe, doesn't that make us all God, all part of a great single cosmic consciousness that has created itself?

It was an interesting theory, and one that had left the Western religions and philosophers in the dust.

Until now.

Now there were some new and powerful scientific theories on the block involving *superstrings* and the *eleven-dimension universe.* Theories that indicate higher dimensions, suggesting a reality beyond our perceived three-dimensional world—a reality that the less sophisticated could misconstrue as belonging to "God" or the "supernatural." Such theories didn't completely nullify quantum mechanics, but they thoroughly and quite effectively put Judeo-Christianity back into the system. Not that Reichner cared one way or the other. He just hoped he wouldn't have to be the one to break the bad news to his Eastern mystic sponsor. News like that might have a serious impact on his guru's check-writing ability.

"Here we go," Tall Suit said as he eased the car to the side of the road.

Reichner glanced around. They had reached the outskirts of the city. For the first time since they'd left the airport, they weren't surrounded by people. In fact, the place was nearly deserted. The nearest building was almost thirty yards away. "This is it?" he asked.

Without a word, both men opened their doors and stepped out. Reichner started to open his own door, then noticed that Short Suit was doing it for him. But instead of allowing Reichner to exit, Short Suit scooted in beside him.

"What is going on?" Reichner demanded.

"May I see your arm, please?"

"What?"

Short Suit produced a syringe and needle.

"What are you doing?"

Now the other door opened and Tall Suit moved in and sat next to Reichner on the other side. "The Teacher, he's very particular about revealing his location."

"I don't really see what—"

Short Suit took Reichner's right arm and shoved up his shirtsleeve as Tall Suit grabbed the other arm.

Reichner resisted, trying to push them away. "What are you doing? I don't want—what is that stuff?"

"Ativan," Short Suit explained as he wiped an alcohol-soaked swab across the arm. "It is a sedative."

Reichner continued struggling. "I know what Ativan is."

Tall Suit pushed him farther back into the seat as Short Suit continued. "It is four milligrams. You will be asleep before you know it."

Reichner struggled. "I will not be sedated!"

The two men were strong. Reichner twisted his body, kicking against the front seat, but they held his arms firm while keeping him pinned down.

Reichner felt a tiny burn in his right arm. He looked down. Short Suit had found the vein and was pumping the liquid into it.

"Just sit back," Tall Suit encouraged. "You'll be there before you know it, Mr. Reichner."

He could feel the drug rushing through his body. "It's *Dr.* Reichner." The chemical swept into his brain. "*Dr.* Reichner. I have a Ph.D. I have *two* Ph.D.'s."

"You certainly do, Dr. Reichner." The voice grew fainter, more distant.

Reichner fought the fogginess. He had to continue talking. "I have a degree from Princeton Seminary. I also . . . I'm . . ." He felt an irresistible urge to close his eyes, fought it, then obeyed, but only for a moment, just to gather his wits. "I also . . . in physics . . . I have two degrees. Princeton . . . and in, one in . . ."

That was the last Dr. Reichner remembered of Katmandu.

Brandon shuffled into Momma's kitchen wearing nothing but jeans and an old T-shirt. He'd have worn less than that if he thought he could get away with it. But Momma was from the South, and though she had been up here in Indiana for over twenty years, there were still certain customs, certain civilities she insisted upon from her family. And wearing a shirt to the breakfast table was one of them.

"Morning, darlin'," she called from the stove.

"Mornin'," he mumbled as he pulled out a chair and took his seat.

It wasn't seven in the morning and the kitchen was already sweltering. The weather had been hot like this most of the summer. But Momma didn't complain. It wasn't her way.

Sunlight blasted through the screen door, forcing Brandon to squint and turn his head. But the back door would remain open. That was where his father sat—every day, unmoving in his wheelchair, staring out at the world through the screen. The expensive, silver-and-turquoise wristwatch Brandon had given him six Father's Days ago glinted in the sun. Back then it had cost Brandon most of his savings, but it had seemed a small price to pay. Even now Momma made sure the man wore it every day. Not that it mattered. As a stroke victim, he couldn't look at it. Probably didn't even know he had it on. Even if he did, he could never show any appreciation. He was incapable of showing any emotion.

Brandon glanced down at the table. After all he'd put his father through, it was probably just as well.

"He sure loves that mornin' sun on his face, doesn't he?" Momma asked.

Brandon said nothing.

Momma continued, uncomfortable in any silence. "Looks like we're gonna have ourselves another blisterin' day." She scooped the pancakes from the griddle. "Weatherman says we're settin' ourselves some kinda record. Comin' up to thirty days without a speck o' rain. And none in sight."

She crossed to the table and set the plate of eggs and hotcakes before him. Brandon saw the sweat glistening off the hairs of her forearm, knew a thin dark stain was already working its way down the back of her housedress. He hated to see her working like this. He'd made it clear a hundred times that he didn't need breakfast. But she insisted. There were certain civilities expected from a family.

He picked up his fork and began to eat. She moved to the fridge. He could feel her standing there, pretending to busy herself by pouring a glass of milk but scrutinizing his every move.

"'Course, the farmers are complainin' to beat the band." She forced a chuckle. "Guess they need somethin' to complain about, though. If it's not too dry then it's too wet, or too cold, or too somethin'." She crossed to him and set the glass on the table, then nervously brushed the damp strands of hair behind her ear. "Still, I bet they could use a little help."

Brandon continued to eat in silence. He could feel her eyes still on him.

She turned back to the stove. Nearly half a minute passed before she finally turned and said what was on her mind, what he had suspected she wanted to say since he'd entered the room. "You had another dream, didn't you?"

He gave a half shrug.

"Jenny?" she asked.

There was no need to reply. She already knew the answer. She crossed back to the fridge and opened it, striving to be matter-of-fact. "You know, if you took that medicine like the doctor says, you wouldn't have to be puttin' up with those things. You slept real well when you took it before. Remember?"

He gave no answer.

"Oh, sugar." She had turned back to him and was now speaking from her heart. "Your sister's gone." She took a tentative step toward him. "She's gone and there's nothin' we can do about it."

More silence. Brandon continued to eat. She moved closer. "And you gotta stop blaming yourself. It was . . . her time. And the good Lord knew it. You just happened to be the one there, that's all."

"A tool in his hand—is that right, Momma?" The sarcasm came before he could stop it. "I just have to believe it was his will." They were hard words, stinging words, and he regretted saying them as he watched her retreat back to the stove.

Another minute passed before she spoke again, her cheeriness a little forced. "I'm dropping by the Wilson's this afternoon. Thought I'd pick us up some more of that cider your daddy likes so well."

Brandon looked toward the door. His father sat motionless, just as he always did.

"Remember—remember that jug we forgot and left in the cellar all winter?" She chuckled. "My, oh my, now that had some bite to it, remember? Wasn't too long 'fore we all got a little tipsy? Remember?" Her voice grew softer, drifting into memories. "What people would've said . . . the pastor's family gettin'—"

But Brandon had had enough. His chair scraped against the yellowed linoleum as he rose.

"Where you goin'?"

"The shop's got another deadline," he said as he turned and started for the door. "Putnam wants everybody there by 7:20."

"But you've barely touched your—"

"I'll grab something later."

"But—"

He squeezed past his father, careful not to look at him. He never looked at him, not if there was a chance of their eyes meeting. He headed out the door and down the porch steps. When he reached the bottom, Drool came lumbering after him. Normally, Brandon would have stooped to give the big old dog a scratch and rub, but he had to get away. He knew Momma was trying to help, but he also knew her suffocating ways and that he could literally drown in her chatter. He gave the dog a quick pat on the side and moved for his pickup.

He climbed inside and started up the engine. He dropped it into gear and started down the dusty, potholed lane that ran a hundred fifty yards to the highway. He knew she was standing at the screen, watching, and it took every ounce of willpower just to raise his hand and give her a wave.

He didn't know if she waved back. He didn't care.

He just had to get away.

Sarah stood in front of her bedroom closet, more asleep than awake. She'd spent less than four hours in bed. But four hours would have to do. Now it was time to put down the coffee and stumble out the door to work. But first, what to wear. Not that it mattered. Most of her wardrobe was the same: dark colors—grays, browns, greens, nearly all loose-fitting. Not that she'd planned it that way. It had just happened.

Friends scoffed at her. "You got a body most would die for. You can't keep hiding it. You've got to get back out there and ad-ver-tise."

But Sarah wasn't interested in advertising. Not anymore. In her high school and college days, oh yeah. Big time. It had been great fun, and she'd been good at it. But that was long ago and far away. Another life. Now there was her work and the lab and her research. Oh sure, she could still force the smiles, be charming, flirt and play the game. But that's all it was: a game.

And the truth was, she was no longer interested in playing the game, much less winning it.

She reached into the closet, pulled out a nondescript sack of a dress, and quickly slipped it on. It was important to hurry, today more so than ever. Because, although she was careful not to let the thought completely form, in the back of her mind she knew: This was the date, this was the third anniversary of her abortion.

Brandon slipped the hand dolly under a four-foot stack of pamphlets. He tilted them back, then turned and wheeled the pile across the floor of Bollenger's Printing and Lithograph. He'd started working for the plant part-time back in high school. After graduation, some friends headed off to college, but Brandon remained behind. What good would college do anyway? Just postpone the inevitable: searching for a halfway decent job. Besides, there were no guarantees, not for his generation. Skeptical, figuring America's best years lay behind, Brandon did what many of his so-called "Generation X" did. He found a safe place, then quietly and silently began giving up his dreams.

It hadn't always been that way. As a boy, he'd been everybody's favorite. Especially his father's. He had adored the man, and the man had adored him. They'd done everything together, and there wasn't the slightest doubt that he was destined to follow in his father's footsteps. It was believed by all who knew him that Brandon Martus would be a bright and shining light for his generation. Some thought he'd become a pastor like his father; others said a famous teacher or evangelist. Whatever the details, everyone knew that he was destined for greatness. Everyone told him so.

And Brandon had believed them. He had believed everything—until his father's stroke six years ago. After that, no amount of believing did any good. Not that he didn't try. At first he had tried everything, even insisting that Momma drive all the way to Chicago and later to Indianapolis to attend faith-healing crusades. But no matter how hard Brandon prayed, no matter how hard he believed, his father remained paralyzed.

That's when the doubts crept in. If God couldn't be trusted with a little thing like healing his father, how could he be trusted with bigger things? And if he couldn't be trusted with bigger things, then how could Brandon trust God with anything—including this supposed "call" that everyone said God had placed on his life?

The answer became crystal clear: He couldn't.

And that's when the downward spiral began—a spiral of doubt, anger, guilt, but most of all, self-hatred. A spiral that made it difficult to talk to his mother and impossible to look at his father. A spiral that had finally reached bottom just seven months ago when Brandon had sealed his fate by killing the only other thing that mattered in his life. That was the night he had accidentally killed Jenny, his little sister.

With the stack of pamphlets balanced on his hand dolly, Brandon crossed the plant, heading for the loading dock. As he approached the giant printing press, he could hear Frank laughing, no doubt reveling in last night's exploits at the country club. Word of their antics had spread quickly, due in no small measure to Frank's gift for gab.

Brandon rounded the corner of the press and saw Warner, the ponytailed operator, listening and laughing as he inched the press's big rollers forward, cleaning them with a rag. He spotted Brandon and shouted, "Hey, Martus—sounds like you boys done all right against them Techies!"

Brandon gave a nod as he moved past.

"I tell you, it was beautiful," Frank laughed. "And this guy"—he motioned toward Brandon—"this guy was insane, man. Thought he was Mario Andretti."

The familiarity of the phrase caught Brandon off guard. He glanced over his shoulder as Frank rattled on and Warner listened with admiration. Brandon's gaze shot to Warner's right hand.

It held the same rag as in the dream. It darted in and out of the same rollers.

He looked at the other hand.

It carelessly pressed the reverse button on and off, on and off, also as in the dream.

But before Brandon could react, he ran his dolly into Roger Putnam, the plant foreman. The stack of pamphlets tumbled to the floor, and Putnam grabbed his shin, swearing. "Come on, Martus!"

Brandon muttered an apology and quickly moved to restack the load—at the same time, keeping an eye on Frank and Warner.

With a groan, Putnam lowered his massive bulk to help him. "When you gonna start putting some mind into your work?"

Brandon gave no answer. Frank and Warner were still laughing.

"Listen," Putnam continued, "you're screwing up on the orders again."

The phrase chilled Brandon. Hadn't that also been in the dream? He shot another look at the press.

"I can't always be covering for you, man. I mean, I've got my rear end to protect too, y'know."

Incredulous, Brandon rose, staring first at Putnam, then at the press and at Warner's left hand pushing the reverse button.

"Now—you got another delivery over at the Institute this . . ."

Warner's right hand darted dangerously close to the rollers.

". . . so try not to—"

That was all Brandon could stand. He leaped to his feet, shouting: "Your hand!" He started toward them. "Look out, your hand, it's going to—"

Just as Warner hit the off button to shut down the press.

Brandon slowed and stopped as the big machine wound down. Frank and Warner turned to look at him. He could feel Putnam and other workers doing the same.

What had happened? He'd been so certain. It had been exactly like his dream.

Frank was the first to speak. "What's up, buddy?"

Brandon stared at the rollers of the machine, then over at Frank, then Warner.

"You okay?" Frank asked.

Slowly, Brandon nodded. "Yeah. I, uh—I'm fine." For another moment he stood, unsure what to do. Finally, he turned back to the dolly and finished restacking the pamphlets. He rose and quickly wheeled them off, more than a little grateful to be away from everyone's curious gaze.

CHAPTER 3

"If he is in such a hurry to see me, why is he not here?" Reichner paced back and forth on the bare, earthen floor. The building was a single room, ten by twelve feet, constructed of stone and plaster. At one end sat a combination fireplace and open-hearth oven. At the other, a roughly hewn wooden door and a single window that looked out into the night rain. The furnishings consisted of a spartan bed complete with microthin mattress, a wooden chair and table, a chipped porcelain washbasin, and a small thatched mat, probably used for meditation.

A tiny barefoot woman was replacing fruit in a bowl at the table while a man in a yellow, long-sleeved robe smiled politely. He was small and brown, like any of the peasants Reichner had seen swarming the streets of Katmandu earlier that evening. But when he spoke, there was no mistaking his university training. "Patience is a great virtue, Dr. Reichner."

"I have been waiting nearly four hours!"

"I assure you, Teacher will arrive at the perfect time."

The woman completed her work and stood silently, waiting to be dismissed. The man nodded and she opened the door, exiting into the night.

"So you are holding me prisoner?" Reichner demanded. "Is that it?"

"You may leave at any time you wish. Although I suspect it is as advantageous for you to see Teacher as it is for him to see you."

Reichner hesitated. For the second time that day, he'd heard that the guru wanted badly to see him. This was good. Valuable information to store for later use. "What about my laptop and my suitcases?"

"They will be returned to you in time."

Reichner ran his hand through his brown crewcut. He was getting nowhere fast. "Why won't you tell me where I am?"

"You are one-half kilometer from the main compound."

"And where exactly is that?"

"Now, Dr. Reichner, if Teacher had wanted you to know such things, we would not have given you the sedative."

"Yes, well, in the future it would not hurt to ask your guests' permission before you start pumping drugs into them."

"I hope the experience was not unpleasant."

"It was rude and frightening and entirely unwarranted."

"I am sorry. I suppose we could have thrown a gunnysack over your head and knocked you unconscious."

It was meant as a joke but Reichner didn't smile. The man nodded in understanding. He reached into his long, flowing sleeve, pulled out a small piece of paper, and handed it to Reichner.

"What's this?" Reichner asked.

"Teacher wishes you to have it."

Reichner looked down at the paper. One very long word was written upon it. The penmanship was sloppy, like a child's, and it was in language he didn't recognize.

"That is Sanskrit," the man explained. "An ancient Indic language."

"What does it say?"

"It is a special mantra the Teacher wishes for you to meditate upon."

"Mantra?"

"It is the God-name of Teacher. Just as our Hindu brothers recite 'om' to more fully connect with the universe, if you meditate upon this name, it will help cleanse your mind and allow you to more fully communicate with Teacher's spirit."

Reichner eyed the man, then glanced back at the words. He knew all about meditating. Back in his college days he'd practiced it. Even now at the Institute he used similar techniques to help relax his subjects before beginning their sessions. But he seldom practiced it himself, and never by chanting Eastern mantras.

"Please." The robed man motioned to the small woven mat on the floor. "You will find that meditating upon his name will facilitate both his arrival and your upcoming discussion."

Reichner's frustration rose. "What will facilitate his arrival is your telling him that I do not intend to stay here much longer." It was a bluff and they both knew it. "I have a busy schedule. I have many pressing engagements."

The robed man nodded and turned toward the door. "As you wish." He reached for the wooden handle and pulled it open. Rain and wind blew inside, whipping his clothes. He turned and motioned to the mat one final time. "I assure you, Dr. Reichner, Teacher will arrive much sooner if you simply prepare yourself for his visit."

Reichner stared at him coolly. The man forced a polite smile, then turned and stepped out into the rain. Reichner stood at the door watching as the deluge soaked the man's clothing, causing his robe to droop and cling to his body. But he barely noticed as he calmly plodded up the muddy road toward the compound.

Reichner slammed the door with an oath. It swung back open and he had to push it closed, then latch it. He wadded up the paper the man had given him and threw it across the room onto the bed. He wasn't about to be drawn into some sort of mystical hocus-pocus. "Prepare himself," indeed. More likely, relax and be lulled into a more susceptible mood so that his sponsor would have the upper hand in their discussion. Well, if anyone was going to have the upper hand, it would be Reichner. That was his specialty. "The Teacher" obviously had his own agenda, but Reichner would manipulate it to fit his.

Fifty minutes passed. Twice Reichner opened the door and thought of heading up the muddy road to the compound where the Peugeot would be, where he would insist on being taken back to Katmandu. But both times the wind, the rain—and most important, the guru's money—had persuaded him to exercise a bit more patience.

Having eaten the fruit from the bowl, and with absolutely nothing else to do, he eased himself onto the bed. The thin mattress and broken springs quickly reminded him of his recent inoculations. He spotted the crumpled piece of paper nearby and reached for it. He smoothed it out, then examined the name.

Other than the length, eight syllables, and the fact that it was in a foreign language, there seemed nothing unusual about it. He read it again, this time out loud. The soft consonants and gentle vowels rolled pleasantly enough off his tongue. He repeated them again. Interesting how gentle and comforting they sounded. But a "God-name"? Hardly.

Reichner sighed. He tilted back his head and stared up at the cracked, plastered ceiling. The things he put himself through to keep the Institute going. He turned toward the window and stared out into the wet blackness. He looked at the door, examining its rough, hand-hewn planks. Then to the table and chair, equally as crude, then to the fireplace, until he eventually found himself looking back down at the paper.

He repeated the syllables again. Slowly. Reichner knew it was no accident that they conveyed such warmth and peace. That was their purpose: to bring the meditator into a more relaxed alpha state, perhaps even increase his theta and delta brain waves as well. Sarah Weintraub was more familiar with these patterns than he was, but he did know that the lower frequencies often created the most peace while also making the mind more receptive to the paranormal.

Again, he repeated the syllables. He mused over how organic they sounded, how naturally they fit into the mouth. Without even trying, he'd already memorized them. He closed his eyes and recited them again. His warmth and sense of well-being increased. He could actually feel the tension in his body easing, the muscles along his shoulders and into his neck beginning to loosen. He'd be sure to keep the paper, perhaps run the syllables past Sarah when he returned home. Maybe even do a few tests.

Knowing the meditation routine, he decided to continue. What would it hurt? He focused on the sounds, gradually allowing his mind to empty, pushing aside extraneous thoughts, concentrating only upon the syllables. He spoke them again, softer. Then again. And again. Everything grew wonderfully still. Tranquil. And again. There were no other sounds, just the syllables, and the wind, and the rhythmic dripping of water from the roof, and . . .

What was that? Music? He strained to listen. Where was it coming from? Through the door? Down the road? No. It wasn't coming from outside the room. It was coming from inside. But from inside himself. Deep within. And soft—softer than the wind, as soft as a breeze brushing a feather. And he could hear harmonies, harmonies too beautiful to describe, too subtle to ever remember. They resonated through his mind, filling him with their beauty.

He listened, spellbound. He'd read of this type of thing in Eastern mysticism but had never experienced it. Then he noticed something else—an energy, a light. A tiny pulse began somewhere in his feet and gently rippled up through his legs, his stomach, into his chest, through his shoulders, and on into his head. When it was gone, another wave began, washing up through his body, a little brighter, a little faster. Then another, brighter, faster. And another. It was as if his entire body was beginning to breathe, to vibrate to this organic, euphoric rhythm of light. The sensation grew until he realized that he must either give himself over to it entirely or put an end to it. He hesitated a moment—then released control.

Immediately, he began to merge, to meld, to blend into all that was around him. He was no longer Dr. Reichner, owner of two Ph.D.s. He was no longer a single individual. He was part of something greater. Vaster. The vastness was him and he was the vastness . . . growing more and more into the vastness . . . growing into everything . . . everything growing into him . . . one with everything . . . one with the universe . . . becoming the universe . . . he was the universe . . . the universe was he and—

Excellent.

The voice didn't surprise him. It came naturally, as naturally as the music. As the light. As himself.

You do that very well, Doctor.

It was the voice of a child, a boy, maybe eleven or twelve years old. He used adult words and tried to sound grown up, but there was no mistaking his youth.

If you want, you may open your eyes.

Dr. Reichner's lids fluttered, then slowly opened. He was still in the room. Still on his bed. But coiled on the floor before him was a python, at least fifteen feet long. Its head was raised, and its pale golden eyes were locked directly onto his. But Reichner felt no fear. He was part of the python and the python was part of him.

Good evening, Dr. Reichner. Although the jaws did not move, it was obvious the voice came from the creature.

Reichner gathered his thoughts, preparing to speak, but he was surprised to hear his thinking broadcast before he opened his mouth. *Is this—a vision?*

You may call it that, the creature thought back. *I find it a more accurate form of communication.*

Are you— Reichner hesitated. *Are you the one they call . . . Teacher?*

I am called by many names. My mother of birth called me Eric.

Reichner was surprised. Eric was a Western name, certainly not Eastern. Then perhaps the rumors were true. Perhaps he did originally come from America. Perhaps there was some truth to the rumor of a genetic experiment gone haywire.

The python swayed its head silently, waiting for Reichner to complete his thought before it continued. *Others refer to me as Teacher. Some call me Shiva.*

Reichner recognized the name. Shiva was a major god in the Hindu pantheon. The god of destruction.

Still others call me Krishna, Buddha, Mohammed, the Christ.

Reichner nodded. The boy certainly had no lack of ego.

My appearance, does it frighten you?

Even now, amidst the experience, Reichner knew he'd have to be cautious. Provided that he was not going crazy, and provided that this was really the guru he was scheduled to meet, he knew he would have to play him very carefully. *You are a Nagas,* he answered. *In Eastern religions, deities often appear in the form of serpents.*

Very good . . . but of course you don't believe I'm a deity.

Reichner hesitated, already caught.

There was gentle amusement in the boy's voice. *Don't worry. What you believe is of little consequence to me.*

What is . . . of consequence?

This age is drawing to a close. And there's a stirring.

A stirring?

The one we've been waiting for has finally arrived.

Reichner scowled.

He's young, but his spirit has already been stunted. His narrow religious training has prevented his growth. We've decided he needs a tutor to help unlock his gifts.

We?

The cartel who first introduced me to my powers and . . . The voice seemed to hesitate.

Reichner pressed in. *And?*

I also have a tutor. The one who guides me in all knowledge of good and evil, but he is not your concern.

Why are you telling me this?

Because we've chosen you to be the youth's instructor.

Reichner's suspicions rose. *Me?*

You understand these things more than most. We sponsored your institute because we knew that this day would come. We told you where to build, because we knew that Bethel Lake is where he would surface.

Reichner's frown deepened. He'd always wondered why they'd been so insistent he locate at Bethel Lake. In the three years he'd been there, he'd encountered only one person in the area who had shown any pronounced psychic ability—a kid, Lewis Thompson. That had been nearly eighteen months ago, and it had been a bust. True, the first few months had been remarkable; he and Lewis had made tremendous strides in developing the boy's paranormal abilities. But then Lewis had lost control, the voices had taken over, and he could no longer control his impulses. As far as Reichner knew, Lewis was still there in the vicinity, but the kid was far too unstable to work with.

You're not talking about the young man I experimented with last year? Reichner thought. *He's psychotic, far too risky to—*

Lewis Thompson was a mistake! the voice angrily interrupted. *Your mistake!*

The outburst surprised Reichner, and he grew quiet. It was time to wait and watch.

The voice regained control. *This one is far more gifted, Doctor. And you will instruct him in how to release and develop those gifts so that he may usher us all into the new paradigm.*

Reichner almost smiled. The boy was obviously trying to sound older than his years. And yet, at least for this meeting, he seemed to be the one calling the shots. Of course Reichner knew that there was a high probability that this was all a delusion, that the sedative probably wasn't the only drug they'd slipped him in the car. But if there was any element of truth to this hallucination, if this guru boy in the guise of a snake was actually communicating with him and making this request, the financial possibilities could be staggering. Who cared whether such a "stirring" actually existed, much less lived near the Institute. If Reichner played his cards right, he could ride this financial bandwagon for another year, maybe two. Who knew how long he could milk money out of—

I am not a fool, Dr. Reichner.

Reichner looked up, startled.

The voice continued. *If you won't find him and work with him, then we will utilize another. We will—*

No, wait. Reichner fumbled, flustered at having his thoughts read. *Who is this kid? Does he have a name? How will I know him?*

There is a dangerous road ahead for him, Doctor. Many enemies surround him. That is why he needs your help. That is why you have been chosen.

Before Reichner could respond, the python dropped its head to the floor. Then it silently slid over its coiled body toward the door.

That's all? Reichner silently called out. *You brought me all the way over here to tell me this?*

There was no answer.

Reichner threw his feet over the side of the bed and rose. *What if I make a mistake? What if the same thing happens to him that happened to Lewis? What if—*

He stopped and watched in amazement as the head passed through the door as effortlessly as if the wooden planks were mist.

You will make no mistakes, the voice spoke as the rest of the python's body vanished through the wood.

How can you be so sure? Reichner called.

The response was distant and faint but still clear enough to hear. *Because I will be with you, Dr. Reichner. Wherever you go, rest assured, I will always be with you.*

A moment later Reichner opened his eyes. He was surprised to see that he was still sitting on the bed. He looked about the room. The door remained closed, the rain still poured, and the python was nowhere to be seen.

Apparently, his meeting with the boy guru had been brought to a close.

Gerty's hand rested on the worn handle of the refrigerator. It had been three days since she'd last eaten. Three days since she'd had her vision of anointing the boy with the long black hair and piercing gray eyes in the river. She was weak and starting to grow light-headed. Common sense told her to eat, or at least to drink some juice. But sometimes common sense carried little weight in spiritual matters.

This kind can come forth by nothing but by prayer and fasting.

She'd read that verse many times during her seventy-eight years. And she'd practiced fasting more times than she could remember. In her younger days, a week-long fast, even two, hadn't been that unusual. But the older she got, the less tolerant her body became of the practice, and the longer it took to recover.

And still the impression stirred and rose within her:

This kind can come forth by nothing but by prayer and fasting.

It really wasn't a voice. Just a knowing. And it certainly wasn't a demand. Instead, it was a quiet request. If she refused, she knew it would go away. There would be no condemnation. After all, she'd been praying and fasting for the boy three days now. Surely, three days was long enough.

She pulled on the refrigerator door. The seal around the edges cracked and popped as it opened. Inside were the usual: bread, bologna, apple juice, tomatoes, a few vegetables. Not well-stocked, but enough, considering the size of her social security check.

For the past several minutes she'd been thinking of toast. A nice, gentle way to break the fast. Warm, soft, crunchy toast—maybe with some of that peanut butter she'd bought the other day. Already her mouth began to water.

She took out the loaf of bread, shut the refrigerator door, and shuffled over to the counter. She undid the plastic fastener, opened the wrapper, and pulled out two slices. But before she dropped them into the toaster, she held them to her nose and breathed in. What a marvelous smell.

This kind can come forth by nothing but by prayer and fasting.

It wasn't incessant, just a tender reminder making sure that this is what she really wanted to do.

She dropped the bread into the toaster and pressed the lever. As she waited, she thought of the words. They were the words of Christ, when he'd spoken to his disciples about casting out demons. But what did demons have to do with the boy? She'd known him when he was a baby, had watched him grow up from afar—had even drawn sketches of him and written letters she'd never mailed, hoping they'd all be of help to him someday. His gifts were pure, she knew that. They were God-given, God-ordained.

This kind can come forth by nothing but by prayer and fasting.

Unless . . .

Maybe those pure gifts were being threatened by something *im*pure, something demonic. Maybe *he* was being threatened. It had happened before, during other times in his childhood. That would explain why the verse kept coming to mind now, why she felt the need to continue interceding.

But it had been three days. *Three days* of not eating. Surely her Lord didn't expect more than that.

She opened the cupboard and pulled down the small jar of peanut butter, yet her mind was still on the boy. He was so young. And when he had looked up at her from the river, he'd seemed so lost, so frightened.

She removed the lid to the peanut butter and pulled off the aluminum foil. The aroma of peanuts filled her senses, almost making her dizzy. If she had been hungry before, she was ravenous now.

Of course, she knew that the boy's emergence would not be easy. She had always known that the forces of hell would do all they could to stop him.

But she was so hungry.

But he looked so frightened.

She opened the drawer and reached for a knife to spread the peanut butter.

This kind can come forth by nothing but by prayer and fasting.

Again, she saw his eyes, felt her own beginning to well up with moisture. She stared at the toaster, watching it blur as tears filled her vision. The boy needed her help. Her continued prayers.

The toast popped up. The combination of warm bread and fresh peanuts was more than she could stand.

But hell was preparing to destroy the boy and God was giving her the opportunity to help protect him—if she wanted.

Another moment passed. And then, ever so slowly, Gerty's veined and wrinkled hand reached for the lid of the peanut butter. She screwed it back on as tears spilled from her eyes. "Thank you," she whispered. "Thank you, dear Lord, thank you."

She turned and headed into the hallway, her slippers shuffling along the threadbare carpet. She entered her tiny room and crossed to the bed. Reaching out both hands, she eased herself down onto her bony knees.

And there, on her knees, Gerty resumed her prayers for the boy. Not because she had to, but because she wanted to. Because she understood the high calling. Because she counted it a privilege.

"Thank you, dear Lord. Thank you, thank you . . ."

CHAPTER 4

It had been several hours since Brandon's little scene at the printing plant. Now he was in the company's delivery van, grinding the gears in an effort to find reverse. Once he'd found it, he eased the vehicle backward into the loading dock of Moran Research Institute. It was a low-lying building, mostly brick and tinted glass. On its roof were multiple rows of solar panels. Frank, who'd been there more times than Brandon, had always made a big deal about the cool futuristic equipment they had inside. Brandon had never taken the time to check it out, but he did know from experience that their employees' lounge had the best junk food in town.

He brought the van to a stop and rolled down both front windows to keep the insides from roasting. The outside air hit him like an oven. It was three o'clock in the afternoon and pushing a hundred and five. And with the Indiana humidity, forget the oven—it was more like a sauna.

From his side mirror he spotted a grizzled Afro-American approaching. It was Billy, the one-man shipping and receiving staff.

"You're late," the old man groused.

"C'mon, Billy," Brandon said as he popped open the door. "What's a week or two between friends?" He stepped out into the pounding sun. "Am I gonna have to unload this, or will your pet gorilla take care of it?"

Billy shouted over his shoulder. "Simpson! Simpson, get your sorry butt out here!"

A gangly teen suddenly appeared from the comforts of the air-conditioned building. He was summer help, an obvious favor somebody in management owed a friend. Unfortunately for the kid, Billy wasn't impressed by anybody in management.

"Let's move it, boy!"

The kid hopped off the loading dock and quickly moved to the back of the van.

"Come on, come on!" Billy hounded him. "Let's see if you can actually break a sweat today."

Brandon shook his head sympathetically and started for the building.

"Hey, Martus?"

He turned back to the old man.

"Heard what you guys pulled off at the Country Club last night."

Brandon nodded. Good news traveled fast. But before he turned toward the building, Billy hobbled closer. "You guys ever decide to pull off something like that again ..." He lowered his voice and glanced over his shoulder to make sure he wasn't overheard. "You just count ol' Billy in, you hear?"

Brandon broke into a smile. "I'll keep that in mind." He turned and headed toward the building, as Billy resumed his favorite pastime of chewing up and spitting out his summer help.

Brandon entered the building. Inside, it was a good thirty degrees cooler. It took a moment for his eyes to adjust to the dim, recessed lighting as he started down the hall. The carpet was maroon with gray rectangular patterns, and the walls were paneled in thick oak. On both sides, running the entire length of the hall, hung modernistic pieces of art composed of torn paper and cardboard. He thought they were pretty stupid—and undoubtedly pretty expensive. Everything about this place was expensive.

It hadn't been a good day. Nor had it been a particularly good night. His dreams of Jenny were coming back again. The past three nights had been worse than ever—so real, so detailed. When they'd originally come, during those first few weeks after her death, they'd left him crying, sobbing her name, until Momma would wake him, until she would hold him and gently rock him as tears streamed down both of their faces.

And now they were returning, more vivid than ever.

The shrinks said it was just his guilt, a way of "achieving closure" and saying good-bye.

His Christian upbringing insisted that the dead never come back and appear to the living—no wandering souls dropping by séances to say hi, or spooky ghosts sticking around to haunt houses. "Absent from the body, present with the Lord," that's what the Bible taught. And those attempting to make contact with the departed, to try to cross the barrier were called sorcerers, practitioners of the occult—a crime so heinous that in the Old Testament those who practiced it were to be put to death.

But Jenny had seemed so real ...

And now his dreams of her had begun incorporating pieces of reality. Not accurately, not completely, but what had happened at the plant a few hours earlier was certainly no coincidence. Or was it? Part of him hoped so. But there was another part, the part that wanted so desperately to reach out to his little sister, to bury his face into her hair, to hold her and never, never let her go.

For a moment Brandon felt his eyes start to burn with moisture. He quickly blinked it back. Those first few months had been an embarrassment, breaking into tears at the most inconvenient of times. It had taken quite a while to get a handle on his emotions, and he wasn't about to let them start sneaking up on him again.

Up ahead was another hallway, but he ignored it because to his immediate right was the employee's lounge. The place was deserted. Just tables, chairs, and the twenty-seven-inch TV mounted up in the corner, currently featuring Oprah with her latest alien-abducted guest. Brandon wiped the sweat off his face with his T-shirt and headed over to check out the vending machines. With any luck there still might be some—ah, yes, there they were: barbecued sunflower seeds. There were still half a dozen packages left, about the same number as the last time he'd visited. Apparently, word of this delicacy had not yet spread. Their loss, his gain. It wasn't much, but drowning his anxiety in a couple bags of these culinary delights wouldn't hurt. He dropped in fifty cents, pushed D–15, and watched the first pack fall into the bin. He repeated the process for another.

After retrieving the bags, he tore one open and poured a few into his mouth. Excellent. Weird, but excellent. He walked back into the hallway. It was the end of the day and the place was deserted. And since he wasn't particularly excited about going back out into the heat, and since he could stand a little diversion, and since Frank had always made such a big deal about the equipment—now would be as good a time as any to do a little exploring.

"I think I can handle her from here, Dr. Weintraub," the stocky orderly said.

"Are you sure?" Sarah asked. She looked dubiously at the sedated patient between them as they walked her down one of the Institute's hallways. "Do you want me to call anybody at the hospital?" The three of them proceeded slowly down the hallway.

"No, I should get her back there and settled in with as little fuss as possible. If you know what I mean."

Sarah knew exactly what he meant. She'd had ethical questions about using patients from Vicksburg State Mental Hospital ever since she came on board. Unfortunately, Dr. Reichner hadn't. He was certain that some of the mentally ill had more highly developed paranormal abilities than others. And, thanks to his manipulative charm, along with the proper financial incentive discreetly slipped to the proper assistant manager, a carefully screened handful of patients participated in the tests. It was a dangerous game to play, but one that Reichner insisted was worth the risk.

Sarah slowed to a stop in front of Observation Room Two, where they'd been viewing this subject since early afternoon. She turned and spoke directly to the woman. "Thank you for your help today, Francine."

The woman turned her head, but the glazed look in her eyes made it unclear whether she'd heard. Her mouth hung open, and she gave no response. Sarah watched sympathetically. Earlier she had tried to convince the orderly that sedation wasn't necessary, that she could verbally talk the hysterical woman back down. But when Francine's agitation turned physical, the orderly insisted that it was better to be safe than sorry.

"Say 'You're welcome,'" the orderly said.

Francine moved her mouth, but no sound came. Just a small trickle of saliva.

Sarah pulled a tissue from her dress pocket and gently wiped the woman's chin. It wasn't exactly professional detachment, but Sarah could never feel detached, at least not with the physically or mentally impaired. She wasn't sure why, though she suspected that much of it had to do with little Carrie, her sweetheart of a niece who suffered from Down's Syndrome. Her brother and sister-in-law had known of Carrie's condition long before her birth, but they had decided to go through with the pregnancy anyway—a choice that pricked Sarah's own conscience. Maybe that's why Carrie held such a powerful place in Sarah's heart. And maybe that's why the Francines of the world, the weakest, the most vulnerable, always brought out the mother and nurturer in her.

Maybe. Then again, maybe it was her simple understanding that they were no different from her. That we are all cripples in some way. If not mentally or physically then, at least for some, as in her case, emotionally.

"Come on, girl," the orderly said as he eased Francine's arm forward and started her down the hall. "Let's get you home."

"Bye-bye," Sarah said.

Francine looked at her, gave what could have passed as a smile, then shuffled off toward the exit. Sarah stood, watching, until they rounded the corner and disappeared. Then, at last, she turned and took the three steps that led up into the observation room.

The back wall of the narrow room was full of racks of electronic equipment—recorders, computers, monitors. At the front was a console equipped with an intercom and a variety of complicated controls. Above the console was the one-way mirror, three feet by seven, that looked down into Lab Two, the very lab she'd worked in the night before—and the one housing the leather recliner where Francine had sat most of the afternoon.

Sarah reached to the console and snapped off the four red floodlights that were directed at the recliner. The lab grew dark, although the recliner was still clearly visible. On its seat lay a set of headphones, a pair of clear safety goggles, and two halves of a Ping-Pong ball. These had been used to help ease Francine into a deeper state of rest. Through the headphones, Dr. Reichner's prerecorded voice had taken Francine through the standard yoga relaxation exercises, tightening and releasing various muscle groups in her body. Meanwhile, the two halves of the Ping-Pong ball, with felt glued to their cut edges, had been placed over her eyes and held in position by the safety goggles. This was far more satisfactory than using a blindfold, which could press against the eyeball, creating distracting images. Meanwhile, the floodlights had filled Francine's vision with lovely, red nothingness.

The first hour had gone according to schedule. As soon as Francine had reached a relaxed state, another subject, in this case a retired Marine Corps officer who sat next to Sarah up in the Observation Room, stared at a randomly selected video image on a monitor. From here he had tried to mentally transmit to Francine what he had seen by sheer concentration. This was a common procedure, one Sarah had performed dozens of times. Everything had gone by the book—until, suddenly, for no explained reason, Francine had started growing agitated. They had tried to calm her, but nothing seemed to work. She had grown worse and worse until the orderly finally had sedated her and insisted that they stop the session.

Sarah plopped into the seat behind the console and sighed wearily. Like it or not, this day had become just as unpredictable as the last three. What *was* going on?

She punched up the DAT controls. Immediately, the speakers began to play back a voice. Francine's voice. The one they'd recorded just minutes before the outburst.

"And it makes my mouth all tingly inside. Everyone has it on their food and when they laugh I can see it on their tongues. It's all yellow and icky. I wonder if I have it on my tongue and I'm afraid to laugh in case they see it. I must be very—"

"Sounds like mustard."

The voice startled Sarah and she spun around to the open door. Silhouetted in it was a young man with long hair and impressive shoulders.

Her nerves already on edge, Sarah demanded, "What are you doing sneaking up on people like that?"

He gave no answer.

"Who are you?"

He entered the room. "I wanted to say thanks for last night."

Now she saw them. The eyes. The same piercing, steel-gray eyes she'd seen the evening before. "You're the boy from the Club."

He gave a half nod, holding her gaze. She sensed the power of his eyes again, the way they locked onto hers without letting go, making her a little unsteady inside. But she saw something else as well, something deeper, something very sensitive.

She forced herself to take a breath, then demanded, "How'd you get in here?"

He stepped toward the EMG monitor against the back wall and looked at it a moment. She could feel her senses sharpening, coming alive, aware of his every move. She tried to cover her uneasiness. "Excuse me?" she repeated. "How did you get in?"

"Deliveries."

Besides the power and sensitivity, there was an earthiness, a lack of pretension. From his worn Levi's to his T-shirt, what you saw was what you got. Still, she wasn't exactly wowed by his social skills. She tried again. Another tack, not quite as abrasive. "That was quite a stunt you boys pulled last night."

"You use all this stuff?"

"Pardon me?"

"All these monitors and stuff, you use them?"

"Yes. Well, most of them." She shifted. Along with his power and sensitivity came an unpredictability that both attracted and challenged her. "Lately, we've—uh, been experimenting with the Ganzfield Technique."

He looked at her.

Good, she had his attention, or at least part of it. "Ganzfield," she repeated.

His gaze was unwavering. She felt her face hike into a self-conscious smile, hoping for some response. There was none. She gave her hair a nervous push behind her ears and continued talking. "You see the lab down there?" She pointed through the one-way mirror to the room below.

He crossed for a better view. As he leaned past her, their bodies were less than a foot apart. She cleared her throat. It was important that she keep talking. "A volunteer is subjected to sensory deprivation—that's what the recliner and Ping-Pong balls are for."

He seemed unimpressed. She felt herself growing more flustered. "Once they're relaxed, they try to visualize an image another volunteer is viewing on this TV monitor here."

"ESP?" the kid asked as he turned and moved past her. The room was so narrow that he accidentally brushed against her hair. At least she thought it was an accident.

"Well, actually, we call it PSI."

Still not looking at her, he was examining more equipment.

"Excuse me." The edge had returned to her voice as she swiveled in her chair to more directly confront him. "Is there something specific you're interested in here, or did you just decide to take a personal tour?"

He didn't look at her. "Not really."

"Then would you mind telling me why you're here?"

Finally he turned to her. There were those eyes again. His lips moved slightly. Was that a flicker of a smile? Was he flirting with her? Or was it something else?

"What?" she asked.

His smile grew—and then he looked down to the ground and shook his head.

"No, please," she demanded, "I would appreciate your telling me what is so amusing."

"You Techies." He glanced up at her. Was that still a smile? "You come in here with all your money, all your fancy equipment." She strained to hear some teasing in his voice, some humor. "And all you're doing is hanging out playing fancy video games."

The phrase hit hard. That was it. Eyes or no eyes, the kid had definitely hit a nerve. Maybe he was kidding, maybe he wasn't. It didn't matter, not now. She swallowed, trying to keep her voice level despite the anger. "These *games,* as you call them—they may very well answer some of humankind's most basic questions."

The kid shook his head in amusement and moved past her toward the door.

The civility in Sarah's voice slipped a couple more notches. "Haven't you ever wondered who you are? Where you've come from, where you're going?"

He reached the door and turned to her. "Haven't lost much sleep over it."

"Maybe you should try it sometime."

It was meant as a slam, but he didn't seem to notice. "I doubt that some flake staring at a family picnic is going to help anybody."

Sarah swallowed again, though now her mouth was bone dry. "I think it's time you leave."

"You got that right." He turned and headed down the three steps into the hallway.

"Hold it—wait just a minute."

He turned back.

"The tape I was playing. How'd you know the subject was describing a picnic?"

"I heard it."

"No, you didn't." Sarah watched him carefully. "We never got that far, she never saw a picnic. The other subject was concentrating on it, but she never saw it."

The kid shrugged. "Guess it's just my PSI." With that he turned and was gone.

Sarah remained sitting, staring at the empty doorway. Frustrated, unnerved. And, although she hated to admit it, very, very intrigued.

"This is too weird. The board's never done anything like this before."

"Shut up," Lewis snapped.

Pierced Eyebrow stared at the plastic, triangular pointer under his and Lewis's fingertips. It continued moving as if under its own power, flying across the Ouija board, stopping at letters, spelling out words almost faster than Acne Face, the third member of the party, could write them down.

Lewis also watched the pointer but with far less interest. He no longer relied on such barbaric forms of communication. So crude, so juvenile. This was nothing but a children's board game that could be purchased at nearly every toy store in the country. "Communicate with the dead," its advertising proclaimed. "Contact spirits."

Yeah, right.

It was a kids' game, plain and simple. He'd even read that it was the most popular kids' board game in America. Hardly a tool for someone with his giftedness.

But the past twenty-four hours had again grown intolerable. The voices had resumed their screaming. One shrieking over another, over another. Too loud and numerous for him to discern any meaning, they were now a continuous cacophony of screaming rages and incessant urgings.

But urgings for what?

SLAUGHTER, BUTCHER, OBLITERATE, KILL!

Yes, but kill what? More animals? Not even the pig had satisfied them for long. He had to find some way to reduce the voices, to filter out the craziest screamings and understand what the others wanted.

They'd started seven years ago. The voices. Back in high school, back when Mr. Johnson, the philosophy teacher, had turned him on to Eastern mysticism, particularly Zen Buddhism. It was no big deal—just a cool way of relaxing and "connecting to the cosmic consciousness within." To heighten the effect, Lewis and a few friends started using pot, then later, hallucinogenics.

And then the whispering began. A gentle presence. Then another, and another. It seemed that the more he emptied his mind, the stronger and more numerous those presences became. Sometimes they whispered things to him, warned him, revealed information that no one could possibly have known. And the more he gave himself to them, the stronger they became.

That was when Dr. Reichner over at Moran Research Institute took him under his wings. He was one of the few who believed that Lewis wasn't crazy, that the voices really did exist. He began running tests on Lewis. And the more tests he ran, the more Reichner reassured Lewis that there truly was something remarkable about him, something "gifted." That was his exact word: *gifted.*

For a while everything had been great. Lewis had been Dr. Reichner's golden boy. But, as the tests went deeper and deeper, as he surrendered more and more of himself to the voices, they began to take more and more control. Eventually Lewis, growing frightened, tried to silence the voices, to demand that they leave.

That's when they became ugly.

That's when they grew terrifying, demanding. That's when they began disrupting the experiments, filling Lewis's head with shrieks and screams, causing him to explode in violence. And that's when Reichner turned traitor, insisting that it was just too dangerous to continue his experiments. Of course Lewis had pleaded with him, had begged him to understand. His giftedness was certainly worth the risk of a few outbursts. But Reichner disagreed and had said no to Lewis.

Unfortunately, it wasn't possible for Lewis to say no to the voices. They kept growing, in power and in number. And they kept increasing their demands. Usually there seemed to be one or two in charge, and Lewis could pick out their voices and understand what they wanted. But not when the others joined in. Not when they all began screaming and shrieking their demands for violence at the same time.

Yet, even now, he knew they didn't just want violence for its own sake. Even now, Lewis sensed a broader purpose. There was some sort of plan behind all of this, some logic. If he could just figure out what it was that they really wanted.

He looked down at the list of words Acne Face was writing from the letters that appeared on the board:

Slay
Execute
Kill
Exterminate

What did he need the board for? These were the same words he heard on his own. There must be some sort of pattern here. If the voices would just stop screaming long enough for him to—

"Is anybody else getting bored?" Acne Face asked as he stopped to rub the cramp out of his hand. "We've been doing this like for a couple hours, now."

Pierced Eyebrow glanced up. "Yeah, maybe we should give it a rest."

"Or start asking it other stuff," Acne Face said.

"Like what?" Pierced Eyebrow asked.

"I don't know. Hey, I got it. Let's ask it if I'm going to be rich."

Pierced Eyebrow frowned. Suddenly his face lit up. "No, I got it. Ask if—ask it if I'm going to get lucky with Julie Nelson."

Acne Face snickered.

"No, better yet, ask it if there's like some kinda spell I can cast on her—you know, words or something that will make her—"

Lewis leaped to his feet. He grabbed the board and threw it across the room. Then he turned his rage on the boys, swearing vehemently at them, using only a fraction of the words filling his head.

"Hey, take it easy," Acne Face protested as he rose to his feet.

Pierced Eyebrow did the same. "What'd we do?"

"Get out!" Lewis screamed. "Get out of my house!" He wasn't sure if it was he yelling or one of the voices. Maybe it was both. Didn't matter. He'd had enough of the two boys, of their childishness, of their need to be entertained. What was happening to Lewis was far more important than entertainment.

"Easy, man," they said. "Just take it easy."

Lewis swept the beer bottles and ashtray off the table. They exploded against the wall.

"Hey, come on," Pierced Eyebrow protested.

Lewis focused on him.

The boy took a half step back. "Take it easy, man, just—take it easy, okay?"

Spotting a half-empty bottle of Jack Daniels on the floor, Lewis scooped it up and smashed it on the table. Booze and glass sprayed in all directions. Before Pierced Eyebrow could move, Lewis lunged at him with the broken bottle. "Get out!"

Pierced Eyebrow stumbled back. "Hey!"

Lewis rounded the table and lunged again, this time catching the boy's arm, slicing through his shirtsleeve.

Pierced Eyebrow grabbed his arm. "You're crazy!"

Acne Face was already pulling his buddy back, trying to get him out of the room. "Let's go. Let's get outa here."

"Get out!" Lewis shrieked. "Get out! Get out!"

The boys turned and broke for the front door.

"Get out!"

"You're crazy, man! You're cra—"

"Get out!"

They threw open the door and raced into the night.

Lewis stood in the tiny living room, all alone, breathing hard, trying to get his bearings. Something was about to happen. Inside, he was about to explode. But he felt something else, too. A focusing. A focusing that would direct the explosion. And God help whoever it was that would receive the brunt of—

Hold it—*whoever?* That was the word he'd thought. "*Who*ever."

Then it *was* a person. The senseless animal slaughters had been only a harbinger, a preparation for the real thing. A real *person.*

But who?

Lewis stumbled back into the kitchen, kicking aside the empty pizza boxes and beer bottles. He yanked out a kitchen drawer, letting it and its contents spill to the floor. He dropped to his knees and in the dim light began searching through the clutter. A moment later he found it, wrapped in a cellophane bag. A joint. But not just any joint. He tore open the bag. This was a joint soaked in PCP, angel dust.

It had been partially smoked. That's how it was with this stuff. So powerful that he only took one or two tokes at a time. That's all he needed to make the connection, to feel the universe swelling up inside him, to open his mind to the infinite.

But not tonight.

He rummaged through the spilled debris on the floor until he spotted a book of matches. With trembling hands he placed the joint between his lips and struck a match. It flared, momentarily lighting the room and his face.

He took the first drag, inhaling deeply, letting it burn the back of his throat, his lungs. He held in the smoke as long as possible, making sure none of it was wasted. Then, a moment later, he felt it. The growing sense of perception, the strength surging through his body and mind. Normally, he would take one more toke and butt it out. But not tonight.

He exhaled and took another long drag. Perspiration popped out on his forehead. But it was only perspiration for a second. Soon it became beads of enlightenment. Rotating like colored prisms, vibrating in perfect synchronization, each connected to the consciousness of the universe, each pumping its power through the pores of his skin and into his brain, filling him with indescribable wisdom, overwhelming strength.

He exhaled and took a third toke. Then a fourth. He would continue until he had finished the joint. Then he would know exactly what he was to do. More important, he would have the unlimited power necessary to do it.

CHAPTER 5

I'm telling you," Frank said, letting out a burp that swelled to a belch, "if we formed ourselves a band, we'd have to fight off the chicks."

Brandon said nothing as he inched the pickup along State Street. It was Friday night and summer. This meant that all four lanes of the main drag through Bethel Lake were packed with teens and young adults enjoying the ageless American tradition of cruising. Several shouted to one another from passing cars; others checked out the newest wheels or the added accessories to those wheels. Then, of course, there was all that guy-and-gal action.

Spotting an interesting prospect, Frank leaned past Del and shouted out Brandon's window. "Hey, Marty! Where'd you find the babe?"

A young man in a four-wheeler beside them flashed Frank a grin as his free arm tightened around the buxom blonde sitting beside him.

"Listen, sweetheart?" Frank shouted.

The girl turned toward him, all smiles.

"You stick with ol' Marty there. You got yourself a real nice boy."

She agreed, snuggling deeper into his arms.

"But when you want a man, you be sure to look me up, hear?"

The girl giggled and Marty pretended to laugh. But as they pulled away, his free hand was firing off a universal gesture of contempt.

Frank's laughter reverberated through the cab. No sooner had it faded than Del pointed at something up ahead and asked, "Say, guys?"

There, two lanes over, in the oncoming traffic, was Henderson in his Firebird. Beside him sat Reggie, the other kid from the Club. And crammed in the back were two passengers who could have passed as linebackers for any Superbowl team.

Frank was the first to speak. "You don't suppose . . . They're not looking for—"

The occupants of the Firebird spotted the pickup and immediately broke into a tirade of oaths and gestures.

"Lucky guess," Del replied.

Henderson began honking, trying to force the cars ahead of him to pull out of the way.

Brandon glanced up the street. The traffic in front of him was queuing up to stop at a traffic light. Luckily, he was in the outside lane, a good two lanes away from the approaching Firebird. But, judging by their anger, two lanes might not be enough.

As if proving his point, the doors to the Firebird flew open and the backseat passengers climbed out, rising to their full Herculean stature.

Frank cleared his throat. "Uh—Brandon?"

The hulks started across the lanes toward the pickup.

Immediately Del reached past Brandon and rolled up the driver's window. "I hope we're talking safety glass, here."

They closed in, less than twenty feet away. Other passengers in other cars turned to watch.

Fifteen feet.

"Yo, Bran."

Ten.

Suddenly Brandon yanked the steering wheel hard to the right and punched the gas. The pickup bounced up the curb and onto the sidewalk. Brandon hit the gas harder, causing the rear end to slide out—and the approaching hulks to leap out of the way.

"Alrighteeeee!" Frank shouted.

Pedestrians scattered as Brandon guided his pickup carefully down the sidewalk. Del turned pale and a wide-eyed Frank gulped his beer.

Brandon threw a look over his shoulder. The linebackers had already clambered back into Henderson's car. Copying Brandon's action, the Firebird bounced up on the opposite sidewalk and quickly backed up after him. Apparently, they had no intention of letting the pickup get away.

Brandon reached the end of the block and headed out into the intersection. Oncoming cars hit their brakes and horns blared as he made a hard right, tromped on the accelerator, and peeled out down the street.

The streams of water pelted Sarah's back, her neck, and the top of her head. But she didn't move. She remained on the floor of the shower, legs drawn in, head down, huddled into a tight ball as the water beat against her body. She was done crying now. At least she hoped so.

She had made a mistake. Maybe it was the lack of sleep, the second glass of wine, or just bad luck. Whatever the reason, she had momentarily lowered her defenses. It had taken only a moment. She'd started off by thinking about her day at work and the strange effect the boy from the Club had had upon her earlier that evening, which had led to memories of Samuel, which had led to memories of the baby . . . which led to . . .

. . . the grinning picture of Garfield up on the ceiling, and the shots of Novocain, and the soothing voice of the doctor, and the pain from the metal rods forcing open her cervix, and the assurance to herself that it was only a thing—a nine-week growth of her body, and then remembering that it had different DNA, which made it different from her body, and the grinning Garfield, and the doctor's soothing voice, and the digging and poking of the nozzle, and the sound of the suction machine with its clear vacuum cleaner canister, and the blood filling the tube, and the screams in her head begging the baby to forgive her, and the hope that he wouldn't feel pain, and the knowing that his pain receptor cells and neuro pathways were already forming, and the doctor's soothing voice, and the grinning cat, and the dizziness, and the doctor's concern over her loss of blood, and her demands to know what was wrong, and the panic, and the fighting for consciousness . . .

And waking up in a hospital room with a major portion of her reproductive system removed, followed by the helplessness, the outrage, the guilt, and the loss.

Back in the shower, Sarah's body convulsed in another sob. And then another. The crying had started again. "No!" she whispered harshly. "Stop it!" She forced herself to her feet. But another sob escaped and then another until she was leaning against the wall, her arms wrapped tight around herself.

For a moment, she thought of crumpling back to the floor. But experience told her she had to stop. *Now*. Not another sob, not another tear. This was nothing but self-pity, and self-pity served no purpose. It could undo no wrong; it could never bring him back. Now all she could do was make sure his sacrifice meant something. Now she had to be the best she could be, to work harder, to prove herself, to prove his death was not entirely in vain.

With a deep breath, Sarah stood upright and reached out to shut off the water. She stepped out of the shower and numbly reached for the towel. She was spent and exhausted, but she had to keep moving, to keep pushing. She was good at that. She could do that. She'd been doing that for years.

Five minutes later, Sarah Weintraub scooped the keys off her kitchen counter, passed the sink buried in two weeks' worth of dishes, and headed out the back door to her car. It was almost 11:00 P.M. Fortunately, she had keys to the Institute, which meant she could go to work anytime she wanted to.

Anytime she had to.

Things were coming to a head faster than Gerty had imagined possible. She was now conscious of the forces gathering, moving into position around the boy. Tonight there would be at least one assault. Maybe more. And others would follow, stronger, more frequent.

The hunger pangs were gone. They usually left during the third day. Now there was only the sense of urgency—and her prayers. There were no visions, no supernatural experiences, just prayer.

Over the years, she'd learned that although they were interesting, the supernatural experiences weren't usually necessary. More often than not, it was simple prayer that was the most effective . . . and the most powerful. Sometimes this merely involved singing, or directing quiet thoughts of adoration toward the Lord. Sometimes it was the slow, thoughtful reading of Scripture. Other times, she found herself confessing her failures, asking him to forgive her. And finally, like tonight, there were times of heartrending supplication and intercession.

"Please, dear God, protect him. Whatever he's goin' through, whatever he's about to meet, save him, protect him, dear Lord."

She had prayed for him frequently over the years. On more than one occasion, forces had tried to rise up and destroy him—but none like those coming at him now. Still, such attacks shouldn't surprise her. If he was to become such a formidable threat to evil, why shouldn't the forces of evil concentrate their attack upon him? It made perfect sense.

However, there was one thing that she had never understood: the boy's own weaknesses—his internal doubts, his external sins.

Why? Why did her Lord always choose to fight the impossible wars? Wasn't battling against the outside evil enough? Did he always have to choose as his champion someone who was wounded and weak on the inside as well? And what of the young man's sins? He was certainly no saint. How could her Lord use someone like him to accomplish such great purposes?

The thought had barely risen before Gerty broke into a quiet smile. Wouldn't she have said the same thing about other great men of God? Jacob the con artist, Moses the murderer, David the adulterer, Paul the persecutor?

Her eyes welled with moisture. It was true, his ways were not hers. And if one of his habits was to choose the weak to confound the wise, then so be it.

But this boy . . .

A picture came to mind. She'd sketched it years ago. It was a picture of the boy as a weak sapling, a tiny olive tree struggling to grow in a desert. At his roots were a thick, impenetrable mass of weeds that choked out the water and nourishment of the soil. Higher up, on the trunk, were dense parasitic vines that sucked out what little life he had managed to acquire. She sighed heavily. There were so many fronts on which to battle. The desert heat, the thick weeds, the attacking vines, his own internal weakness.

Should she pray against the vines, those demonic counterfeits trying to sap all of his strength? But what about the other outside forces—the heat, the weeds? And what of his internal struggles—his deep emotional scars, his obvious lack of faith?

She shook her head. No, a higher level of prayer was needed. Not a prayer of pleading and begging and groveling. But a prayer aligning itself with her Lord's will.

A prayer thanking God in advance for accomplishing his purposes, whatever those purposes would be.

The smile returned to Gerty's lips. Thanking God in the midst of attack and confusion made absolutely no sense at all. Which was another reason she believed she was on the right track, that this was how she was supposed to pray for the boy.

She never understood why God didn't simply accomplish his will on his own—why he insisted upon his children joining him, why he allowed them to become the catalyst for releasing the will that he had already determined. But she always thanked him for the opportunity. What a privilege to work side by side with her Creator. What a privilege for the God of the universe to release his awesome will through her frail prayers . . .

Once again tears of gratitude sprang to Gerty's eyes as she remained on her knees, beginning to quietly and persistently pray in tandem with God's will—not fully knowing what it was but thanking him and worshiping him in advance as he began to accomplish it.

Brandon raced out of the city on old Highway 17. It twisted and turned, following Hudson Creek some thirty feet below.

"Whoooooeee!" Frank shouted, popping another brew. "Mario baby does it again!"

But there was little time to celebrate. Brandon had spotted headlights in his rearview mirror. They had just rounded the last bend and were quickly gaining on him. Suddenly, without warning, he cranked the wheel hard to the left and threw the truck into a screeching 180.

"Oh no," Del moaned, grabbing the dash for support.

"Déjà-vu!" Frank shouted.

Brandon straightened the pickup, hit the gas, and they shot back down the road, heading directly toward the other car.

Inside the Firebird, Henderson squinted as the glaring headlights approached. He steeled himself. He would not back down. Not this time. He'd been humiliated once, and once was more than enough. He just hoped that the driver of the pickup would be smart enough to know this.

Brandon pressed harder on the accelerator, and they picked up speed. Del desperately searched the seat beside him. "Where's my seat belt? I can't find my seat belt!"

The car and truck bore down upon one another.

Inside the Firebird no one said a word. They were somber and silent. Henderson flashed his lights on high. "Come on," he whispered to the driver of the pickup. "Don't be stupid, don't be stupid . . ."

The lights blinded Brandon as the Firebird approached, steady, veering neither to the left nor to the right. Brandon set his jaw.

They were seventy yards apart. Sixty. Fifty.

"Come on," Henderson whispered under his breath, "come on, come on . . ."

Forty. Thirty.

Suddenly, Brandon knew. He sensed, with complete conviction, that the Firebird would not budge—that if they were to survive, *he'd* have to back down.

Twenty yards.

He yanked the wheel hard, swerving to the right just as the Firebird roared past. Brandon fought the steering as they slid down the highway—until they ran out of asphalt, dropped six feet into a steep ditch, and bounced to a jarring stop.

A moment of silence passed before Frank observed, "They learn fast."

But Brandon wasn't finished. Not by a long shot. He threw the pickup into first and stomped on the accelerator. The bank was steep and the gravel was loose. The back tires spun, spitting stone and gravel, but the truck barely moved.

Brandon let up on the gas and wiped his face.

"Oh, well," Del offered hopefully.

Frank remained silent, waiting to see what Brandon would do next.

Again he pressed the accelerator, and again the tires spun. He pushed harder. The engine roared. The tires threw gravel and whined. Ever so slowly, the pickup began to move. They inched their way up the bank. The tires began to smoke, but Brandon would not let up. At last the tires caught the edge of the asphalt and squealed as they dug in and pushed off.

Brandon made another U-turn and they were on their way. But the Firebird was nowhere in sight.

"Where are they?" Del asked.

"Don't worry," Frank assured him, "we'll find 'em."

Del moaned and sank back into the seat.

A quarter mile up the road, Henderson had turned the Firebird around and eased it to a stop in the center of the road, directly behind a sharp, blind curve.

"What are you doing?" one of the hulks in the backseat demanded.

Without answering, Henderson turned off the engine. He left his lights on and climbed out of the car.

"What!" Reggie asked. "Are you crazy?"

"They want to play hardball," Henderson said, "let 'em play hardball."

"Yeah, but—"

"Relax," Henderson said. "He'll see the lights in time. Barely, but he'll see them."

"This is crazy," Reggie protested.

But the driver had already pocketed his keys and was heading for the side of the road.

"Henderson? Henderson!"

Reggie glanced at the other passengers. It was obvious that they didn't approve, but it was also obvious that they weren't going to remain in the car for a debate. They quickly piled out and joined Henderson as he headed up the steep embankment for a better view.

Back in the pickup, Brandon was a study in concentration. Wherever the Firebird had gone, it couldn't be far. Up ahead was another curve. He picked up speed. Neither Frank nor Del said a word; their eyes remained fixed on the road.

Up on the embankment, Henderson and the guys heard the pickup approach. A couple of them fidgeted in concern, but no one spoke.

Brandon hit the curve. He'd barely started into it when his eyes widened in surprise: His headlights caught a white reflection directly in their path.

It was Jenny! She was wearing her white gown and holding a lantern.

He slammed on the brakes and steered hard to avoid her. Unfortunately he was too distracted to see the parked Firebird appear just around the bend.

"Look out!" Frank shouted. "Look out!"

Brandon spotted the car and threw the truck in the other direction. It made a three-quarter spin, barely missing the Firebird, and slid to a stop on the far side of the road, just inches from a steep drop-off overlooking Hudson Creek.

Suddenly everything grew very silent. A dog from a nearby farm began to bark.

At the top of the bank Henderson gloated. It had gone perfectly. Not only had he humiliated the driver, but he'd also impressed his buddies. He began to slide down the embankment, back to the road. "Come on," he called. "Nothing worth sticking around here for."

The others agreed and followed, laughing and scoffing—more as a release of tension than for humor's sake. They threw a few gibes and taunts at the distant pickup before finally arriving at the Firebird and piling in. Once inside, Henderson fired up the engine and, after his buddies shouted a couple more oaths for good measure, he took off. He glanced in the rearview mirror and caught a glimpse of the long-haired driver. The kid was already out of his truck. It would have been nice to stick around, rub his nose in it a bit, but justice had been served. And sticking around to bask in the victory would have definitely been uncool.

Outside, Brandon barely noticed the Firebird pulling away. He was too busy searching the road. "Jenny!" He raced to the bend where she had stood. "Jenny! Jenny!" He was breathing hard, trying to catch his breath. "Jenny!"

But nobody was there. He slowed. "Jenny . . ."

Peering through the darkness, he searched the bank above him. Nothing. He spun around, looking all directions, then dashed to the other side of the road, looking down toward the creek.

"Jenny!"

He blinked back the tears burning his eyes. He held his breath, straining to hear the slightest crack of a twig or rustle of brush. Nothing but crickets and the barking dog.

"Brandon! Yo, Brandon." Frank was approaching from the truck.

But Brandon barely heard as he continued searching the bank, the woods, the creek. *"Jenny!"*

"Hey, Bran." Frank slowed to a stop. "Jenny's not here, man."

Brandon turned to him.

Frank continued, softer. "She's dead, man. You know that. She's not out here. Nobody's out here."

The tears spilled onto Brandon's cheeks.

"You all right?"

Angrily, Brandon swiped at his eyes.

"Hey, don't worry 'bout it. We'll get 'em next time." Frank forced a grin. "I promise you, ol' buddy, it's our turn. We'll get 'em next."

Brandon stood in the road, searching the bank above them, the creek below. Finally, he turned and looked back down the deserted highway. Of course, Frank was right, there was nobody there. Nobody.

At least, not now.

It had taken nearly an hour for Sarah to lose herself in her work. But at last she'd been able to pull out of the relentless whirlpool of memories. The anniversary had nearly gotten her, but finally she had managed to pull out. And she'd do her best not to swim so close to those emotional waters again.

Over the past several minutes, she had begun to feel something else, another emotion. At first she'd thought it was the remains of her little pity party in the shower. But it wasn't. It was a strange, uneasy feeling, like she was being watched. But that was impossible. It was after 1:00 A.M. on a Saturday morning. No one had been in the Institute for hours. Just her. She'd parked her car in the front lot, entered through the lobby, and made sure the door locked behind her.

Still . . .

She took off her glasses and rubbed her eyes. It was probably exhaustion, or the anniversary, or her nerves—maybe all of the above.

She redirected her attention to her work. Sitting before the console in Lab One, she stared up at the figures on the monitor's screen. She sighed and put on her glasses. She was a neurobiologist, not a statistician. But, from the start, Dr. Reichner had made it clear that like all of the other parapsychology labs, they needed to include a "probability value"—the number that indicates the probability of an event happening simply by chance. This creates a standard that all tests can be compared to. For instance, take a test result with a probability value (p) of .05 or less. That simply means that the possibility of it happening by chance is less than five percent, or "$p < .05$." That's the normal cutoff point in PSI research. Anything higher than .05 is not taken seriously, but anything lower, such as "$p < .01$" (the chances of an event occurring as less than 1 in 100) is considered significant.

Sarah stared at her figures. She couldn't be sure, but her best estimate was that the probability value of this week's events in the lab was somewhere around $p < .0000000000001$.

No wonder her nerves were on edge. Maybe she was entitled to be a little paranoid. Something was very weird here.

For the second time in as many minutes Sarah stole a glance over her shoulder. There was nothing but the equipment and the three-by-seven, one-way mirror looking down on her from the observation room. Yet it was the mirror that caused her the uneasiness. Anybody could be up in that room spying down on her and she would never know it.

Or would she?

Like everybody else, hadn't she, at one time or another, known when someone was watching her? And wasn't that exactly the feeling she was experiencing now? Once again she tried to shove the thought out of her mind, only this time it wouldn't budge.

With a heavy sigh, she pushed herself back from the console. Something had to be done. Reluctantly, she rose, passed through the narrow room directly beside the one-way mirror, and out into the hallway.

Everything was perfectly still, perfectly normal, except—

How odd. Hadn't the door to the observation room been closed earlier? Maybe not. She couldn't be sure. But they always kept the doors closed overnight and through the weekend to help protect the equipment from dust.

With more than a little trepidation, she moved toward the observation room door. She thought of calling out, of asking if someone was there. But she was being ridiculous. She stepped up the three stairs leading into the room, then reached around the wall to the light switch and turned it on.

Light flooded the room. No one was there. Nothing but racks of equipment and the faint hum of the overhead fluorescents. Of course, someone could be hiding behind one of those racks or crouched under the console, or maybe behind the—*Stop it,* she chided herself. *Stop it right now.* She turned, hit the lights, and headed back down the steps—but not before firmly closing the door behind her. And locking it.

She shook her head. Definitely paranoia. Still, even paranoia had some scientific validity. She remembered one of the Russian PSI studies where a subject was placed in a room with a TV camera focused upon him. Galvanic skin response sensors attached to his skin to measure any increased anxiety he might feel. In the next room, another subject sat before a TV monitor. Most of the time the second subject was only shown a test pattern. But at randomly chosen times, the first subject appeared on the monitor and the second subject stared at him. When the experiment was complete and the results analyzed, it was discovered that the first subject's skin sensors recorded increased anxiety at exactly the same times the viewer had been looking at him on the TV monitor.

So maybe there was some validity to that uneasy feeling we've all had of being watched. What was the old joke—just because you're paranoid doesn't mean that they're not out to get you?

As she reentered the narrow lab and passed along the one-way glass, she did her best to ignore it. She moved back to the console and took her seat.

And then the room exploded.

She spun around to see a chair sailing through the one-way mirror as pieces of glass flew in all directions. She leaped back, barely dodging the chair as it smashed into the console behind her. She bolted for the door, trying to get past the gaping hole in the mirror, but the room was too narrow—a hand reached through the hole and grabbed her arm. She cried out and twirled around to see a head emerge through the opening. He was a kid—eyes wild, ragged goatee, stubbly red hair.

"Where is he?" he screamed.

Adrenaline surged as Sarah pulled to get away. But the boy hung on—even as she began to drag him through the hole, even as the shards of glass tore into his upper arm.

"Where is he?"

"Let me go! Let me—"

"You are the one!" he screamed. *"You are the one, you are not the one!"*

She pulled with all of her might, dragging more of him through the jagged opening. He was bleeding now, but he didn't notice. *"You are the one, you are not the one!"*

He found a foothold and braced himself. Suddenly Sarah could pull no farther. In a panic, she searched the room for something, anything. There, over on the console. A coffee mug. She reached for it, stretching as far as she could.

"You are the one, you are not the one!"

At last her fingertips touched the handle. She scooted it, rotating it, until she was able to grab it.

"You are the one, you are not— "

She spun around and smashed the mug into his face. It shattered, cutting her hand and slicing into his forehead, but he didn't seem to notice. Blood streamed down his face, running across his brows, into his eyes, but he didn't react.

She stared, astonished.

His grip tightened on her arm. He began dragging himself through the opening—across the shards of glass, and toward her.

"You are the one, you are not the one! You are the one, you are not the one!"

Wild with fear, Sarah fought and pulled, doing anything to get away. She dragged the weight of his body through the opening until he finally tumbled out onto the floor. The fall broke his grip, and she lunged for the door. She nearly made it—until he grabbed her leg. For a terrifying moment he had her. She kicked two, three times until she managed to break free. She staggered out into the hallway, but she could hear him behind her, already struggling to get to his knees.

"You are the one, you are not the one!"

She ran down the hall, stumbling in fear until she entered the lobby. She could hear the distant popping and scraping of glass as he staggered out into the hall after her. She fumbled for the lock on the double doors and was surprised to see one already unlocked. She threw it open and raced toward her car. It was a beater, a ten-year-old Ford Escort, the only car in the parking lot.

She arrived at her door, gasping for breath, her sweaty hands fumbling with the key. She shoved it into the lock—just as the lobby door flew open.

She looked up. He'd spotted her and started toward the car.

She opened the door and threw herself inside.

"You are the one, you are not the one!"

She hit the door lock, then shoved the key into the ignition.

He was nearly there.

For weeks she'd had trouble with the carburetor, planned on getting it fixed, never found the time. She turned the key, hoping desperately that it would cooperate.

It didn't.

She looked up. He was ten feet away. Through the blood streaming down his face she could see the grin, mocking through crooked teeth.

She kept turning the key, pumping the gas. "Come on—please, please, please—"

He arrived and yanked at her door.

"Please!"

He banged the glass with his fist and she gave a start. He continued pounding it, again and again, leaving bloody hand marks.

She kept grinding the starter.

Through her peripheral vision she saw him step back several feet. He was searching the ground, looking for something to break in with.

"Come on, come on . . ."

He reappeared just as the engine kicked over with a roar. She glanced up; he was coming at the car with a giant rock in his hand.

She yanked the transmission out of park and stepped on the gas. It fishtailed, her hands so sweaty she could barely hang on to the wheel. There was a loud thud at the back. He'd thrown the rock. She glanced into the rearview mirror. He stood there, swearing at her. Swearing and shouting. Over and over again, shouting:

"You are the one, you are not the one!

"You are the one, you are not the one!

"You are the one, you are not the one!"

PART TWO

CHAPTER 6

Brandon went to church for the same reason he wore a shirt to the breakfast table: Momma believed that civility required it. Every Sunday morning, the two of them sat in the front pew, just as they had when Dad was the preacher. Only now, Dad sat beside them, in the center aisle, unmoving in his wheelchair.

Brandon had learned, over the years, that it would do no good to protest coming. There were some things Momma would not be swayed from. So he consented to this Sunday routine while at the same time quietly and efficiently perfecting the fine art of zoning out.

"As you know, a week from this evening we will be holding our final service here in this building—a farewell celebration as we prepare to join our Unitarian brothers across town. Now I suppose some would consider the closing of this fine old church a defeat, but I assure you that the Higher Power in his infinite . . ." The Reverend continued droning on through his justification for shutting down the church. But whatever his rationalization, the bottom line was simple: Attendance was so meager that there was no way they could afford to keep the doors open.

Brandon didn't mind. True, he'd spent his entire life going to this church; he'd been dedicated here as a baby, baptized here as a child. And he'd spent years listening to his father deliver sermons from that very pulpit. But maybe the change would do them good. It might even cool Momma's fanatical ardor for constant attendance—although that was doubtful. He guessed that whenever and wherever the Reverend decided to speak, she would always be there to listen. Yes, Momma and the Reverend had grown close—but there was nothing immoral about their friendship. After all, it had been six years since Dad's stroke, and Momma was entitled to a little male companionship.

Brandon stole a look at his father. Did he know what was going on—that they were about to tear down the church he had fought so hard to build? Who knew what was going on behind that slack, impassive face—except, of course, for the contempt Brandon always sensed lurking behind his silence. Contempt for him—for everything Brandon did, for everything he was and was not.

Brandon looked back up at the Reverend and pretended to listen as the man continued rattling off his bromides. It's not that Brandon hated church. He didn't even hate God. You have to care about something to hate it. And Brandon didn't care one way or the other. Not anymore. When he was a kid, sure. He'd followed the party line, wowed everyone with his zeal, even subbed as a Sunday school teacher for the little ones. But that was back when he'd thought life had guarantees, when he'd thought faith counted for something. Now, of course, he knew it didn't. Not after his father's stroke. And not after Jenny's death.

Brandon stared at the brass pipes of the organ mounted on the wall behind the pulpit, then at the white ash cross positioned immediately in front of them. The cross. What a perfect symbol of life's futility. Brandon shook his head at the irony: How Christians cherished and worshiped the very thing that proves that, no matter what you do, no matter how good you are, you die. Everything dies. He remembered hearing some comedian say that if Jesus came today, instead of crosses, Christians would be wearing electric chairs around their necks. What a joke. What a sad, hopeless joke. Yes, Brandon thought, if there was any symbol to capture the futility of life, it was the cross.

For the thousandth time, his mind drifted back to Friday night, to little Jenny standing in the road . . . if it had been Jenny. Of course it had been Jenny. What else could it have been? And yet nobody else had seen her. Frank, Del—they hadn't seen a thing. Had it been a hallucination, something he'd just imagined? Brandon closed his eyes and pressed his fingers against his lids. If so, then he was *really* in bad shape.

It sounded like the Reverend was finally running out of steam. "At this time, we have some special music. Lori Beth, would you like to come forward now and share with us?"

Brandon watched as a fourteen-year-old blonde nervously walked down the aisle and took her position in front of the altar. Over the past year, Lori Beth had gotten quite a figure, and she was still painfully self-conscious about it—a little girl trapped in a woman's body. She took the mike from the Reverend and nodded to the soundman at the back of the church. A music track blared through the speakers until the volume was lowered. A few bars later, the girl started to sing. Her voice wasn't bad, though a little thin and tentative. That's how it always was with the new ones. A little nervous at first but gradually, as the song continued, their confidence increased.

Not so with Lori Beth. In fact it was just the opposite. With each line she sang, she seemed to grow less and less sure of herself, and more and more nervous. But it wasn't the congregation that unnerved her. It was something else, something toward the back. At first Brandon tried to ignore the problem, but by the second verse the girl was practically trembling.

Brandon stole a look over his shoulder. Mr. Gleason, the middle-school English teacher, a large man with thinning blonde hair, had risen from the back and was heading up the aisle toward her. Brandon remembered him as a friendly guy, always making jokes. But instead of his usual good-natured expression, his face was twisted into a leer.

Brandon turned back to Lori Beth. She still sang, but her eyes remained fixed on the approaching man, and her voice was beginning to quiver. Gleason passed Brandon. He was loosening his tie as he approached the girl. Lori Beth's voice grew more and more shaky. Finally the teacher stopped directly in front of her. He raised his big, meaty hands and placed them on her white, delicate shoulders.

And still she sang. Staring at him, terror-stricken, she continued to sing.

Brandon looked at Momma, then at other members of the congregation. Everyone was calm, some even smiling. Wasn't anybody concerned?

Suddenly the man pulled Lori Beth toward him. She gasped and tried to resist, but he was insistent. He grabbed the back of her head and pulled it toward his face—and then he kissed her. Hard. His mouth covered hers in consuming passion.

The Reverend smiled, nodding his head; the congregation sat complacently. Didn't they care?

After the kiss, Lori Beth took a shaky breath . . . and *still* she sang. But Gleason wasn't finished. He began kissing her neck, hungrily, demandingly.

No—no, Brandon had seen enough. Disgusted at Gleason, outraged at the congregation, he rose to his feet. "Stop it!" he shouted. "What do you think you're doing! Leave her alone!"

Gleason ignored him. He began pawing at Lori Beth's blouse, tearing at it, ripping off buttons. That's when Brandon moved to action. He leaped across the few feet separating them, grabbed Gleason's arm, and tried to pull him away. "What are you doing? Leave her alone!"

With little effort, the big man flung him aside. He turned back to the girl, kissing her, pulling at her clothes while, amazingly, she continued to sing!

Brandon lunged at him, grabbing his shoulders, using all of his strength to pull him away.

"Stop it! Let her—"

Then he felt a pair of hands on his own shoulders. He whirled around. It was the Reverend. But he wasn't helping to pull the teacher away. He was pulling *Brandon* away.

"Easy, son, take it easy."

"What are you doing?" Brandon shouted. "Look what he's doing to her!"

"Easy—everything's okay."

Surprised at the calming voice, Brandon looked first at Momma, then at the congregation. Their complacency was finally broken; now, everyone was staring in astonishment. But they weren't staring at Mr. Gleason; they were staring at *him,* at Brandon.

Confused and breathing hard, Brandon turned back to the teacher. He wasn't there. Only Lori Beth stood before the altar—her blouse neatly pressed, her hair and face showing no signs of the struggle. True, her eyes registered fear, but not fear of Mr. Gleason. It was fear of Brandon.

"It's okay, son." He could feel the Reverend's grip tighten as he gradually pulled him away. Brandon looked out over the congregation. There was Mr. Gleason at the back. Like Lori Beth's parents and several other members of the congregation, he had risen to his feet in apparent concern. But his tie was perfectly straight; there was no sign of a skirmish.

The Reverend eased Brandon away, toward Momma who was now standing. "It's okay, son," he kept repeating, "it's okay." Numb and confused, Brandon allowed himself to be guided to his mother, who helped him sit back in their pew. "It's okay. Just have a seat, son. Everything is all right. It's okay, everything is all right . . ."

Three hours later, Brandon was sprawled on the sofa in the living room. It was stifling. The fan drew air in through the front screen door, but that helped little, since the outside air was even hotter than the inside. Sweat trickled down his temples as he stared at the TV, pressing the remote, one channel after another after another, barely watching.

Drool, good old faithful Drool, had sensed Brandon's turmoil. Several minutes earlier, the massive, chocolate-colored mongrel had plopped down at the foot of the sofa with a heavy sigh. Over the months, the years, he had become Brandon's only confidant.

At one time, it had been Brandon and his father—Brandon and his father camping out, Brandon's father coaching Brandon's basketball team, Brandon and his father working on model cars when he was a child, then graduating to the real thing as Brandon grew older. Everyone who knew them envied their friendship. If ever there were two people who found joy and purpose in one another, it was these two.

But that was a long time ago.

Now there was only Drool. Brandon may no longer be able to talk to his father, he may not be able to stay in the same room with his mother, but there was always Drool. Quick to listen, slow to judge, and always faithful. Good old Drool. At the moment, the animal's devotion was being rewarded by Brandon's absentminded scratching behind his ears.

It had been seven months since Brandon had killed his little sister. Seven months of self-torment by day and agonizing dreams by night. Everyone had said that the dreams would go away, that he'd get better.

Well, everyone was wrong.

After the incident on the road last night, the fragments of conversation at the printing plant, and the weird whatever-that-was at church this morning, it was clear that not only were the dreams *not* going away—they were starting to plague him even when he was awake.

What had happened with Lori Beth this morning made no sense at all. But what he'd seen the other night out on the road, that was different. It had been Jenny. And that meant that the Bible was wrong—the dead *do* come back, at least in her case. But what did she want? What was she trying to say?

Brandon shook his head and let out a long, slow sigh as he surfed the channels.

Outside, on the porch, he could hear Momma talking to someone. Probably just another "concerned" neighbor or church member dropping by. Yes, sir, good news traveled fast in little Bethel Lake. He hit the mute button for a better listen.

"I'm sorry," Momma was saying, "but he needs his rest and I—"

"He's entering his season, Meg." It was an older woman's voice—thin and crackly. "You *knew* this day would come."

"It's been a very tiring morning for him—well, for all of us. Perhaps if you stopped by another time."

Bored, Brandon threw his feet over the side of the couch. He stepped over Drool and shuffled toward the screen door.

"If you'd just let me look in on the boy. Maybe offer a few words of encouragement. Let him know that . . ." The woman's voice trailed off as Brandon arrived at the screen. She was a frail old woman. Black skin, graying hair, dressed in her Sunday best, which wasn't much. Besides a print dress of tiny flowers, she wore slightly yellowed gloves and a small white hat. Brandon was sure he hadn't met her before, and by the way Momma stood on the porch, blocking the woman's approach, it was clear that things were going to stay that way.

As the woman stared at him, a look of wonder slowly spread across her face. Momma glanced over her shoulder at him. But before she could make the introductions, the old woman began to quietly quote: "'Behold, I will send you Elijah before the great and dreadful day of the Lord.'"

Brandon glanced quizzically to his mother, but she was already looking away.

The old woman continued: "'And he shall turn the hearts of the fathers to the children and the hearts of the children to their fathers.'" She stopped, then slowly smiled at him.

Momma glanced at him again and cleared her throat. "Uh, Sugar—this here is Gerty, Gerty Morrison. An old and dear friend of the family's. She used to attend your father's congregation. 'Course that was a long time ago, when you were just a baby."

"Eli." The woman's eyes filled with moisture. "Eli, we've been waitin'. Waitin' over twenty years for—"

"Brandon," he interrupted.

"'Scuse me?"

"The name is Brandon."

The woman glanced at Momma, then nodded. "Yes, of course." She continued: "The Lord would say much to you, Brandon."

"Now, Gerty," Momma warned her, "you promised."

"But he must be warned of the counterfeits." She turned back to him. "You do understand the difference? How to discern the spirits, and how to prepare for the battle you're about to—"

"Gerty, please!" Momma's outburst surprised them all, and she immediately struggled to recover her civility. "You promised, now. Remember? You promised."

Brandon continued to watch. He knew that most church circles had one or two well-meaning fruitcakes who insisted that they could hear God speaking. It came with the territory. At best, they were harmless—just folks looking for attention. At worst, they could be deluded, even dangerous. Brandon wasn't sure which category this old woman fell into.

"Yes." Gerty was nodding to Momma. "Yes, you are right, I did give you my word." She broke into another smile. "And I thank you for this opportunity, Megan. I thank you from the bottom of my heart."

Momma nodded, still keeping a wary eye on the woman.

Gerty turned back to Brandon. "It was a pleasure meetin' you, Brandon."

He nodded.

She nodded back. Then, in the silence, she turned and started down the porch steps. But, when she reached the bottom, she turned back to him, a look of concern filling her face. "Your shield," she asked. "You won't be forgettin' your shield of faith?"

"Gerty. . . ," Momma warned.

"No, ma'am," Brandon answered kindly. It was obvious this old-timer fell into the harmless category, so it wouldn't hurt to play along. "Got it right here in the house where it's good and safe."

Gerty nodded, though it was clear she was confused by his answer.

"Yes, ma'am," Brandon offered helpfully. "I never leave home without it."

Still confused, she smiled nonetheless. Then, slowly, she turned and hobbled toward her car.

Brandon watched, quietly amused and a little sad.

But not Momma. Even with her back to him, he could see the nervous tension in her body—a tension that remained even after the old woman was in her car and heading down the lane to the main road.

Dr. Reichner took another long sip of coffee—his third cup since he'd left the Fort Wayne airport ninety minutes ago.

"How long were the police here?" he asked.

Sarah Weintraub knelt beside the console in Lab One, examining a patch of blood-stained carpet. "About an hour."

"They have any idea who it was?"

Sarah shook her head. "If they did, they weren't saying."

Reichner fingered the jagged shards of glass still protruding from the one-way mirror that separated the lab from the Observation Room. He was exhausted, but he could not, would not sleep. It had been seventy-two hours since his encounter with the boy guru, or python, or whatever it was back in Nepal, and he was still a little shaken.

Initially, he had chalked up the experience to some sort of hallucination, an imagined mystical encounter. He had certainly been in the right place for it. That along with the drugs, the exotic location, and a person's normal susceptibility to suggestion—well, it was definitely a plausible explanation. Then there'd been that mantra and the Eastern meditation thing. Some medical studies he'd read hypothesized that the chanting of mantras and meditation was simply a way of depriving the brain of oxygen while increasing carbon dioxide. Since the temporal lobe of the brain is sensitive to the delicate balance of O and CO_2, altering that equilibrium can easily create a sense of well-being, the so-called Eastern mystical experiences, or even that tunnel sensation so many "near-death" participants babble about.

At least that's what the medical books said. But after his experience on the flight back home, he had begun to question the textbook explanation. It had only happened twice. During the New Delhi to O'Hare leg of his flight. But twice was enough. Reichner had closed his eyes, drifting into that in-between state of sleep and wakefulness, when he had suddenly seen the pale yellow eyes of the python floating before him. It had no doubt been some reaction to his dramatic earlier encounter with the guru. At least that's what he told himself. Yet it had seemed so real. Then, of course, there had been those parting words from the Nepal vision: "I will always be with you."

In any case, for the time being at least, he preferred to throw down a few more cups of coffee and stave off sleep just a little bit longer.

"Maybe we should get this typed," Sarah said, indicating the blood on the carpet.

Reichner stooped beside her for a better look. She smelled nice. Her hair was still damp from the shower she'd been taking when he'd called. He could smell the scented soap on her skin. Some sort of berry. Yes, very nice indeed.

Of course, he'd tried talking her into bed when she'd first joined the Institute. But she'd made it clear from the get-go that she was not interested in another relationship, especially with her employer. He knew that he could have manipulated her, worn her down (*nobody* said no to Reichner, unless he wanted her to), but she was already approaching thirty, which meant she really wasn't his type anymore. After all, he did have his standards.

Besides, she was an overachiever, a workaholic—the type who buried themselves in their job, looking to their work for all of their fulfillment and self-esteem. He had run a background check on her that hadn't been conclusive, although he assumed that her workaholism was a reaction to something unpleasant in her not-so-distant past. But the reason made little difference. The point was that someone like this could be exploited in far more profitable ways than for a little roll in the hay. And it was so easy. All he had to do was appear unsatisfied with her work and imply that she could do better. Or toss a brief compliment her way if she had nearly killed herself over a project. "Praise junkies," he called them. Like devoted dogs, they would kill themselves just to hear a kind word from their master. Everybody had an Achilles' heel, and by exploiting hers, Reichner was able to squeeze out twice the amount of work he would have gotten from a healthier employee.

Yes, he was a man who knew what he wanted, and he always knew how to get it.

"You said he had red hair?" he asked.

"And a goatee," Sarah added. "Looked like he was in his mid-twenties."

Dr. Reichner stood back up and took another sip of coffee. "What about his teeth?"

"Pardon me?"

"Were his teeth crooked?"

Sarah hesitated. "Well, yes. I'd forgotten but, yes, they were in terrible shape."

Reichner nodded.

"You know him?"

Reichner said nothing. He was rethinking his conversation back in the mountains of Nepal. At least that portion of it involving Lewis Thompson, the kid who had blown up on him some eighteen months earlier. How odd: They'd just spoken of him and now, suddenly, he was resurfacing. Reichner turned back to her. "Did he say anything else?"

"No," Sarah shook her head. "Just the same phrase over and over again—'You are the one, you're not the one.'"

Reichner nodded and glanced around the room. "Have you been working with any new subjects here? Anybody showing exceptionally high PSI?"

Sarah shook her head. "No. Just the usuals. Though as I told you, some pretty weird stuff's been happening here the past few days."

Again, Reichner said nothing. He continued rearranging the pieces, first one way, then the other, trying to fit them together.

"So are you going to have him arrested?"

Reichner looked at her and frowned. "No. If it's who I think it is, we have some history together. I should probably take care of this myself."

"You don't think he'll come back?"

"No."

Sarah glanced at the smashed mirror. "I don't understand. I mean, what was his purpose?"

Reichner shook his head. "He wants very badly to destroy something or someone."

"Why?"

"I'm not sure. Maybe . . ." A thought began to take shape. "Maybe it's jealousy."

"Jealousy?"

Reichner rifled through his thoughts, testing the theory. It seemed to hold. He nodded slightly.

"Of whom?"

He gave no answer.

After a moment, Sarah repeated, "You're sure he won't come back?"

Barely hearing, Reichner glanced at her. "What?"

"Here? You're sure he won't be coming back?"

He saw that she was worried and shook his head. "No, not here." He picked up a shrapnel of glass from the console and examined it. "Whoever he wanted is close, but he's not here."

"How do you know?"

"'You are the one, but you're not the one.'"

"Then *who?*" Sarah persisted.

Reichner shook his head. He fingered the jagged edge of glass in his hand. "I don't know. But whoever it is, it would be better if we found him first, before our friend does."

Late Monday afternoon, Brandon stood in the delivery bay, tossing one twelve-pound box of flyers after another into the back of the delivery van. Burton's Music and Video up on Lincoln Avenue was having a blow-out sale, and by the amount of print work they ordered, it looked like everyone in the county would know.

"Hey, Martus."

He looked up to see Putnam, the foreman, approaching.

"Think on your way home you could drop some boxes off at the Institute? They're still a couple short, so—"

Brandon cut him off. "Hey, I delivered exactly what you—"

"Easy, Cowboy. My mistake. I take full responsibility." He glanced up at Brandon. "At least this time."

Brandon nodded. He'd overreacted. With all that was happening, he was definitely on edge. But Putnam wasn't finished.

"Listen, uh . . ." He coughed slightly. "I heard what happened yesterday—you know, at the church and everything. Are you gonna be all right?"

Brandon reached for another box and tossed it in. "I'll be fine."

"'Cause if you're not, if you wanted like a little rest or something, you got some sick leave coming."

"I'm fine."

"You sure? 'Cause, I mean I've got my rear end to protect here, too, y'know."

Brandon hesitated. There was that phrase again. The same phrase he had heard in Thursday night's dream, the same one Putnam had used during the false alarm Friday. Brandon shook it off and continued.

"Well, all right then. I mean if you're sure."

Brandon nodded and continued loading.

"So, you'll catch the Institute this afternoon on your way—"

Suddenly a loud scream echoed through the plant. Putnam and Brandon spun around. Fifty feet across the floor, next to the press, Warner, the ponytailed operator, was on his knees, one hand holding another, both covered in blood.

"What the—" Putnam broke into a run. Brandon followed.

Frank was already there, quickly wrapping a rag around the screaming man's hand. Blood was everywhere. Other workers moved in as Putnam arrived. But Brandon slowed to a stop. Already he could feel himself growing cold, a tightness spreading through his chest.

"Call 911!" Putnam shouted. "Get an ambulance over here!"

A worker started for the phones. Both Frank and Putnam remained at Warner's side, trying to hold him down, trying to stop him from writhing.

An icy sweat broke out across Brandon's face. He had known. Down to the tiniest detail—Putnam's phrase, the press, Warner's hand—he had been warned.

"Is somebody calling an ambulance!"

Just as Jenny had saved him from the Firebird, just as she had tried to save Warner's hand, he had been warned. And, like it or not, his dreams, his visions, had started to come true.

CHAPTER 7

Two hours later, Brandon leaned against the vending machine in the employee's lounge of Moran Research Institute and opened another bag of sunflower seeds. As Putnam had requested, he'd swung by to drop off the remaining shipment on his way home. Although Billy and most of the Institute's staff had already gone, there were still a couple of cars left in the parking lot, so Brandon had entered through the loading dock and dropped off the boxes. Now, in the silence of the lounge, he closed his eyes and rested.

It had been another painful and confusing day.

Instead of waiting for the paramedics, Putnam and Frank had driven Warner to the hospital themselves. Word had it that the press operator would probably lose his hand. Brandon took a long, deep breath and slowly let it out. He had known. In the dream, Jenny had told him. Why hadn't he warned them? Why hadn't he been stronger, made a bigger deal about it way back last Friday? He popped a small handful of seeds into his mouth. Things were growing worse.

At the other end of the Institute Sarah Weintraub was fighting her own internal battles by doing what she did best: working hard and late. The one-way mirror had not been replaced between Lab One and the Observation Room, so she was using the other pair of rooms. Except for the carpeting and a different set of coffee stains, they were identical.

Sarah was testing two more patients from Vicksburg State Mental Hospital. The first one, Sheldon, was a wiry man in his mid-fifties. He sat calmly with Sarah in the Observation Room and stared at a video image on the monitor. It was a scene of a dairy farm, complete with barn, cows, and a tractor. Karen, a heavy woman with mousy brown hair, sat in the leather recliner down in the lab, on the other side of the glass. Attached to her body were numerous sensors: GSRs, EMGs, and EEGs. Her face was bathed by the four red floodlights, and she wore the Ganzfield goggles (complete with the Ping-Pong ball halves) over her eyes. The relaxation tape of Dr. Reichner's prerecorded voice played softly through the speakers.

"Tighten, tighten . . . and relax. Tighten, tighten . . . now relax. Good. Very good. Now your calves. Tight, tighter, tighter . . ."

The GSR showed the first anomaly. By measuring the amount of electricity her skin conducted, it indicated how nervous she was. And Karen was nervous. Very nervous. Instead of gradually relaxing during the test, her anxiety was actually increasing. Dramatically.

Sarah checked the EMG. The results were the same: a marked increase in Karen's muscle tension. The EEG followed suit, registering a rapid increase in beta waves, the brain waves present during stress and agitation.

Sarah reached for the intercom button. "Karen, are you all right? Sweetheart, just try to relax, okay?"

She glanced at the monitors. Karen's anxiety levels continued to rise. She looked back through the glass. Karen was scowling, starting to move her head.

"Karen? Karen, try to remain still. Just listen to Dr. Reichner's voice. Just listen to his voice and try to—"

She stopped, trying to locate the strange sound she'd just heard, something like a faint gurgle. She turned to Sheldon. He was still staring at the video picture, completely lost in it. She looked back into the lab. The sound was coming from Karen. Her head had begun to roll from side to side, and the sound grew louder. But it was no longer a gurgle. It was low and continuous, like a growl.

"Karen?"

No response. The growl increased.

"All right, Karen. Listen, sweetheart, we're going to end this session. Okay? You can come back up now, all right? Just open your eyes and join us."

The head rolled more violently.

Sarah pressed another button. She wasn't sure where the stocky orderly was, but she needed him. "William," her voice echoed through the Institute's PA, "William, please come to Lab Two, stat."

She turned back to the monitors. Some readings were beginning to spike, going off the screen. Karen's growls intensified into muffled cries as she began twisting and squirming.

Sarah rose to her feet. Sheldon was still oblivious to anything but the picture on the screen. She turned, raced down the steps into the hall—and was shocked to see the boy from the country club approaching. She started to say something, to demand an explanation for his presence, when suddenly an unearthly shriek came from the lab.

She threw open the lab door. Karen was writhing in the recliner. The big woman screamed again, and Sarah raced to her. "Karen! Karen, listen to me!" Sarah pulled off the woman's goggles.

Karen's eyes darted around the room in wild, animal-like panic.

"Karen—"

Karen's eyes froze on something. Over by the door. Suddenly she was scrambling, fighting to get out of the recliner.

"Karen!"

She struggled to her feet, breathing heavily. Then, pointing with a trembling finger, she growled, low and vehemently, "You."

Sarah followed her gaze to Brandon, who was standing at the door. "Get out!" she cried. "Can't you see you're scaring her? Get out!" She spun back to Karen and tried to calm her. "Karen, listen to me."

"No," the voice hissed.

Sarah grew more firm. "I want to speak to Karen."

"No!"

"Yes, I want to talk to—"

The woman shoved Sarah aside and ripped off more of the sensor wires.

"Karen—"

But Karen lurched toward Brandon.

When the woman headed toward him, Brandon had the good sense to back away. She was slightly smaller than he was—but there was no mistaking the look in her eyes: She meant business. She panted heavily, her eyes glaring into his. *"You!"* she seethed.

He gave an involuntary shudder. It had been a long time since he'd seen such hatred—but this was more than hatred. There was something else: a reverberation, a unison of voices, as if more than one person was speaking.

"What have you to do with us?" The woman glowered in the doorway. *"Have you come to persecute us before our time?"*

"Karen." It was Sarah, approaching the woman from behind. "Karen, listen to me. I want to speak to Karen." She touched the woman's arm, trying to calm her. "I want to speak—"

"NO!" With an anguished shriek, the woman spun around, grabbed Sarah by the shoulders, and threw her into a rack of equipment. Brandon immediately moved to help Sarah, but the woman turned and lunged at him, screaming. She hit him hard, and they staggered to the ground. She landed on top, screaming, punching, scratching, clawing, mostly at his face and eyes. Her strength was incredible. He was able to hold his own, but barely. Off to the side, he spotted Sarah coming at them again.

So did the woman.

She twisted and punched Sarah hard in the stomach, sending her staggering. But Brandon took advantage of the woman's distraction and grabbed both of her wrists. They were sweaty and strong, already twisting, already breaking his hold, when suddenly another man appeared, a much bigger man. He came from behind and wrapped his arms around the woman's arms and shoulders, binding her movement, pulling her off Brandon.

"Come on, Karen," he ordered, holding her in what amounted to a fierce bear hug.

"Our name is not Karen!" she shrieked as she fought.

But the man was a pro. "Right, well, whoever you are, just calm down now. Calm down . . ."

Brandon pushed himself against the wall, wiping the sweat from his face, trying to catch his breath. In the background, he heard a recording of a man's voice with a slight German accent. "Tighter, tighter . . . and relax. Good, very good. And now your shoulders. Tighter, tighter . . . and relax. Excellent . . ."

"And that's legal, using crazies to experiment on? Ow!"

Sarah continued cleaning the young man's wounds, using the cotton balls and rubbing alcohol just a little too briskly. If he wanted to mouth off, that was fine with her, but he'd have to pay the price.

The rest of the staff was already gone. William, the hospital orderly, was on the road chauffeuring his two patients back to Vicksburg. Now it was just Sarah and the kid in the employee's lounge. His shirt was off, and she applied her limited first-aid training to the scratches on his neck and back with a definite lack of bedside manner. "Our work with the mentally ill isn't official. At least not yet. We're still clearing up some red tape." She hoped he wouldn't miss her meaning. "I'm sure you can appreciate the damage it would cause us if word of their involvement leaked prematurely."

He said nothing and she trusted he understood. She moved around to his back, grateful to be out of his line of vision. What was it about him that made her so self-conscious? He was just a kid, half a dozen years her junior, maybe more. And still she heard herself rattling on, sounding like some nervous schoolgirl. "Actually, the tests are harmless. Just some simple relaxation exercises—"

"And since it's for science and they're just loonies, it doesn't make any difference if—ow!"

She'd got him good that time. She continued, doing her best to keep an even tone. "These *loonies,* as you call them, are people just like you and me—except the chemistry of their brain is slightly different." It was time to move around to his front again, but she kept her eyes from his as she talked. "We have over fifty billion neurons in our brains. They fire ten million billion times per second. That's a lot of information. A healthy person's brain filters out much of that input before it reaches conscious level. We're interested in those people whose brains can't."

She waited for a response, some indication that he was listening. There was nothing. What was with him, anyway? And still she heard herself continue: "The theory is that there is paranormal activity all around us but that you and I filter it out. Some of the mentally disturbed may not be able to do that."

He cocked his head up at her and she glanced down. A mistake. Once again those intense gray eyes locked onto hers. And once again she felt herself growing the slightest bit weak inside.

"What about the voices?" he asked.

She looked back at the cuts on his neck and dabbed them with cotton. "What voices?"

"You know—how'd she make her voice sound like it was more than just one person talking?"

Sarah slowed to a stop and looked back down at him. "You heard voices?"

"Didn't you?"

She shook her head, this time holding his gaze. And it was then she saw it. A flicker of vulnerability. He was afraid. He was afraid and now, suddenly, he was the one who looked away.

She hesitated, then resumed dabbing the scratch along the top of his shoulder. When she spoke, she tried to sound casual. "How many voices did you hear?"

He said nothing.

Now his rudeness was beginning to make sense. He wasn't acting out some misguided machismo. He was just afraid. She could tell by his increased breathing rate, the rapid pulse in his neck. She dabbed the cotton along a nasty gouge near his left clavicle and saw him wince. This time his discomfort gave her no pleasure. "I'm just about finished," she offered.

He didn't speak. She tried to do the same. But curiosity, professional and otherwise, got the better of her. "So. You didn't answer my question. How many voices did you think you heard?"

He glanced up at her again—the strength of those eyes was now lost in his fear, and vulnerability. Once again she felt herself being drawn to him. He looked away and shrugged, but this time his feigned indifference was less convincing. "Three," he said, "maybe four."

The comment brought Sarah to a stop.

He looked back up. "Why? What's wrong?"

"Karen suffers from multiple personas."

"What's that?"

"She becomes different and distinct people at different times."

"So?"

Sarah began to treat his cuts again, more slowly this time. "So at last count Karen's number of personalities . . . came to four."

The boy sat motionless. Sarah saw his larynx rise and fall as he swallowed. Without warning, he reached for his shirt. "I gotta go."

"I'm almost done here, why don't you—"

But he was already on his feet, slipping on his shirt, buttoning it.

She quickly sealed up the alcohol and tossed the cotton balls toward the trash. He was heading out of the room. She couldn't let him get away, not yet. She grabbed her bag and moved into the hall after him. "You said you heard voices?" she persisted as she joined his side. "Three, maybe four?"

He didn't answer. Her mind raced. Wasn't this the same person who'd scored a direct hit with the Ganzfield test Friday? Coincidence? Maybe. But what about Karen's reaction? What about his "hearing" her personalities?

"Listen," she fumbled, "I'm sorry, I don't even know your name."

"Brandon."

"Listen, Brandon—what would you think about stopping by here again sometime? After work?"

"For what?"

They continued down the hall.

"I don't know. Maybe run a few tests. Get to know each other a little better."

It was a lame attempt at flirting, and his look told her he'd recognized it for what it was. She flinched and tried a more candid approach. "Remember your perception last Friday—about the hot dog and the picnic?"

No response.

"First that, then Karen's reaction to you—and now you say you heard voices, the same number as her personalities. Doesn't that strike you as all just a little bit odd?"

They'd nearly reached the door to the parking lot. He still refused to look at her, but at least he answered. "You never stop working, do you?"

The response caught her off guard. Was she that obvious? He barely knew her, and yet—well, no matter. She pressed on. "Something happened in that room. You know it and I know it. And it wasn't just with Karen. *You're* the one who heard the voices."

They had reached the door and he slowed, almost stopping. Then suddenly he pushed it open and headed outside. "I think I'll pass."

"Why?" She followed him, making sure the door locked shut before racing to catch up. Although it was early evening, the heat was intolerable. "Aren't you the least bit curious? Wouldn't you like to know if you're somehow . . . gifted? If there's a way you could use those gifts to help others?"

She was at his side again, and again he gave no answer.

"Why not?" she asked. "Why wouldn't you want to know?"

"Doesn't interest me, that's all."

She looked at him and felt her anger rising. So that was it. Vulnerable? Afraid? Hardly. That had been wishful thinking on her part. No, he was just like the others—jaded, self-centered, only looking out for himself—typical of so many men in her generation—younger, older, it made no difference. Her words came a bit sharper. "And if it doesn't interest you, then it's not important, is that it?"

"You got that right."

Sarah came to a stop and watched as he approached his pickup. It was time to take off the gloves. "And what does interest you?" she called.

No answer.

"No, I'm serious. Pulling those sophomoric pranks with your buddies at the country club? Is that what's important, is that what counts?"

He opened his door.

"Is it?" she persisted.

"Makes me smile."

"Well, I don't want this to come as too great a shock to you, but maybe there are more important things in this world than what makes you smile."

Brandon hesitated, giving it a moment's thought, then shrugged. "I doubt it." With that he climbed into the cab and fired up the truck.

Sarah stood steaming. Somehow, once again, he had managed to push all of her buttons. She turned and stormed toward her own car. She had barely arrived and was reaching for her keys when she heard him call, "So—when will I see you again?"

A half-dozen zingers ran through her head, but none of them befitting a lady. No, the best thing was to simply ignore him, to not let him know he'd gotten under her skin.

"How 'bout a pizza?" he called.

She couldn't tell if he was serious or trying to be funny.

"I'll even spring for an extra topping."

Well, at least she had her answer—and Robin Williams he was not. As she opened her car door she could sense him still sitting there in his pickup, watching her every move. This made her more self-conscious and awkward, which made her all the more angry.

Inside, her car reeked, probably the result of a half-eaten Whopper or one too many yogurts left all day in the broiling heat. She closed the door and reached for her seat belt. The smell was enough to gag her, but she wasn't about to roll down her window and risk more conversation.

She inserted the key and turned it. It ground away, but nothing happened. The carburetor. She stopped and tried again. "Come on," she muttered, "not now, not now . . ." But no amount of coaxing helped. She stopped and blew the hair out of her eyes. Then, deciding she would not be intimidated, and having this irrepressible urge to breathe, she finally rolled down her window.

She tried the car again. Still nothing.

She could feel him sitting over there, no doubt smirking away.

She tried again. This time, not letting up. With dogged determination she kept turning the engine over and over again as it ground slower and slower—the battery showing surer signs of giving up the ghost.

She stopped and waited.

He called out. "Need a lift?"

"I wouldn't want to put you out," she answered bitingly.

"No problem," he replied. "It might even make me smile."

Sarah ignored him and tried the car again until it finally ground to a halt. Wiping away the hair sticking to her face, she made one last attempt. But there was nothing left. Only a dull click followed by silence.

She could imagine him grinning, probably yucking it up. But she couldn't sit there forever. They were a half mile outside of town and at least that far from the nearest service station.

Okay, fine, maybe she'd lost this round, but it wasn't over. Keeping her cool, she removed the key, grabbed her bag, and climbed out. Then, summoning whatever dignity she had left, she started for the pickup.

Reichner pulled up behind the white, rust-streaked VW bug just as Lewis Thompson was opening its door to climb in. The young man looked terrible—dirty, barefoot, stained Grateful Dead T-shirt. And the sweat. Even through his windshield Reichner could see the sweat running down the boy's face.

Reichner turned off his Lexus, opened the car door, and stepped out into the intolerable heat. He'd always found this quarter-mile stretch of homes between Bloomfield and Second Avenue disgusting. Even when he had been working with Lewis, he'd made a point of avoiding this neighborhood, with its unpainted houses, sagging porches, and front yards sporting more abandoned cars than lawn. His distaste may have stemmed from memories of his own childhood poverty back in Linz, Austria, or simply from his contempt for people ignorant enough to live in such squalid conditions.

But none of that mattered. Right now he had to find out what Lewis was up to.

He slammed his car door, and the kid spun around, seeing him for the first time. Reichner walked to him, slow and deliberate. This was how he dealt with the kid—in exact contrast to the boy's own agitation and anxiety. It was a means of establishing power and superiority.

"Dr. Reichner." Lewis gave a nervous twitch that almost passed for a smile. He appeared distracted, torn between climbing into his car or staying outside to talk.

Reichner approached, keeping his voice low and stern. "Good evening, Lewis." It was a voice that Lewis had learned to obey during all those months of experiments, a voice he would want to please whenever he could. Reichner had made sure of it. "Where are you off to?"

"I, uh—church." Lewis was disoriented, looking at the horizon, the ground, anything but Reichner's eyes. "I'm going to church."

"We've not seen each other in some time."

"Yeah, uh . . ." Lewis ran his hand over his sweaty face, then over his red stubble of hair.

"Why church, Lewis?"

Lewis winced, still looking everywhere and nowhere. Reichner watched and waited. It was obvious that the kid was hearing the voices again—and equally obvious that he was doing drugs to heighten their intensity. Such a pity. Because the more hallucinogenics he took, the more demanding the voices became, insisting that he take even more drugs, which he would, which only increased their demands—and around and around he would go. A vicious cycle that would eventually destroy his sanity, stripping away any rational will, until he'd lost all control. Reichner had seen it happen before, and he shuddered to think what this pathetic young man would be like in seventy-two, even forty-eight hours from now.

The voices Lewis was hearing were no doubt the same ones he had heard before, the same ones that had been so helpful in the beginning but had later destroyed their experiments. What a waste. He had shown such potential, such promise. During that period they had made astonishing breakthroughs, more rapid than anyone in the field of paranormal research—until the kid blew up. Until he was no longer able to control the voices and they began turning on him, controlling him. Now Lewis was only a shell of what he had been, his powers completely unfocused, and by the looks of things once again losing control.

"Why church?" Reichner repeated.

"Because . . . I'm not—I'm not sure."

"Why church, Lewis?"

"I don't know!" The eruption was sudden. "I don't know, all right?"

Reichner said nothing, allowing his silence to play on the boy, making it clear that penance was due for the outburst. Lewis fumbled with his keys, repeating the words, mumbling them softer now, an obvious apology, "I don't know, I don't know . . ." He turned, then clumsily, haltingly, entered the car.

"You don't want to go, Lewis. Not yet."

Lewis hesitated. Reichner could tell that the kid wanted to shut the door, that something inside him was driving him to shut it. But he couldn't. The doctor smiled. Apparently all those months of hypnosis still gave him some control over the boy. He continued, keeping his voice low and even. "As a matter of fact, you would really prefer to step back out of the car for a moment."

Lewis's face showed the struggle. He had to obey his internal voices, but he just as desperately needed to please Reichner. Reichner watched and waited, curious to see how much power he could still exert over the boy. Finally, Lewis rose unsteadily from the car. He seemed more disoriented than ever.

Reichner was pleased.

"What do you want?" Lewis tried to sound angry, but he still could not look Reichner in the eyes.

"Why the church, Lewis?"

"I don't know, all right?" His breathing was heavy. Reichner guessed that his internal torture was overwhelming—needing to obey his internal voices, needing to obey Reichner's. Suddenly the boy began to pace, repeating the words. "I don't know, I don't know, I don't know."

Reichner knew he was telling the truth. Lewis seldom lied. He decided to change the subject. "I understand you paid us a little visit Saturday morning."

For the first time Lewis's eyes darted to Reichner's, then away. It was an admission of guilt. He resumed pacing.

"Talk to me, Lewis." Reichner waited. "Talk to me."

"He was there!" Lewis blurted. "He was there, but he wasn't!"

"Who was that, Lewis? Who was there?"

Lewis's eyes flashed at him, seething in anger. "You know who."

"Why don't you tell me, Lewis."

"The fake! The impostor!"

Reichner waited.

"The one you're trying to replace me with." Lewis stopped pacing and turned to confront him. "But I'm the one! I'm the one! I'll always be the one!"

"Of course you are, Lewis. You have always been the one."

Lewis's eyes seemed to soften. "And your favorite!" It was part declaration, part plea. "I will always be your favorite! I will always be the one!"

"Of course, Lewis, you will always be the one."

The words had their desired effect. Lewis began to relax, almost to wilt under the affirmation.

"But tell me about this impostor, Lewis. Is he here? Do you know who he is, where he lives?"

Lewis shook his head and resumed pacing, his internal distractions once again rising. "No, I, uh—church. I need to go to the church. I need to go."

"Okay, Lewis," Reichner spoke softly. "You may go to church. You may return to your car and enter it."

Lewis turned, quickly crossed to his VW, and climbed in.

"But Lewis."

He looked up at Reichner, blinking the sweat out of his eyes.

"No more uninvited visits to the Institute, all right?"

Lewis nodded and reached for the ignition. He turned on the engine, put it into gear, and released the brake. But, even now, he seemed to hesitate, unsure whether he had been given complete permission.

Reichner smiled and stepped back so that the boy could close the door. "It's all right, Lewis. You may leave now."

Gratefully, Lewis reached out and pulled the door shut. He inched from the curb and headed off. Reichner remained standing and watching while the car picked up speed, its chain whining, as it disappeared down the street.

The late afternoon attack on Brandon had not caught Gerty off guard. Though her physical condition was weakening from the fast, her spiritual perceptions had increased. She didn't know the details, only that the attack had come from a level low in the demonic hierarchy and that it was somehow associated with a patient from Vicksburg State.

Gerty was well aware of the dangers of associating mental illness with demonic activity. In her earlier, more zealous days she had seen the cruel treatment of such patients by well-meaning believers who insisted that every mental and emotional problem was demonic.

Even now, she wasn't sure where to draw the line. She knew all too well the verses where her Lord had cast out demons from an epileptic, and from another who was deaf and dumb. Did that mean that every epileptic was infested by demons? That every deaf and dumb person was possessed?

Of course not. And what about the patients diagnosed with multiple personalities? Were their symptoms always the result of demons, those rebellious angels who had been cast out of heaven with Satan?

Again, Gerty did not know. The adversary was clever. If he could inflict pain and suffering by having people underestimate his power, then he could do the same by having them overestimate it, by working believers into such a frenzy that they were casting demons out of every dark shadow and unexplained bump in the night.

And yet, demonic activity no longer lurked in the shadows. Not anymore. Scripture clearly warned that the Enemy, himself, could come disguised as "an angel of light." And as this age quickly drew to an end, such deceptions would become increasingly apparent. She was painfully aware of the growing acceptance of the counterfeit spirituality of New Age and Eastern spiritualism. She'd heard that over half of the world now believed in reincarnation. And it was nearly impossible to turn on the TV without hearing something about UFOs, the supernatural, the occult, or someone having some sort of mystical experience.

Yes, these were sobering times. Times, according to her Lord, in which "false christs and false prophets will rise and show great signs and wonders to deceive, if possible, even the elect."

No, Gerty did not have all of the answers. But she did have a gift. Something Scripture described as an ability to "discern spirits." She did not know all of its workings. She didn't have to. All she had to do was trust her Lord. Trust in his operation of the gift. A gift that increased as she devoted her time to prayer and fasting.

But at this particular moment, her concern was not the supernatural counterfeits coming at the boy. They would continue. Throughout the course of his ministry, they would continue, and he would learn to recognize them. No, it was his lack of faith that concerned Gerty now. It was his stubborn refusal to believe.

Because time was running out. A cold shudder had begun somewhere deep inside of her. It was coming. She was sure of it. Tonight. It was coming and he was not ready.

So far, the attacks and counterfeits—they had come only to confuse and wear him down.

But not now. Now, at last, it was here. It was approaching the city.

"Dear God—please, he's not ready, not yet. He doesn't have the faith, he doesn't have the tools." Her once serene prayers of praise and thanksgiving had suddenly given way to panic.

She had been lying on her bed. The lack of food and the earlier demonic assault on the boy had tired her, but she was ready to resume battle. She had to. For his sake.

It was coming and he was not prepared.

"Please, Lord," she murmured. She scooted across her bed and lowered herself back onto her knees. "Be merciful. He's not ready. He doesn't even believe. Without his shield he will be destroyed. Please, give him eyes to see. Protect him. Give him faith. Please, dear Jesus, give him your faith. Please, dear Lord. Holy Lord. Holy God. Holy. . . . Holy. . . . Holy. . . . "

The scratches on Brandon's face and neck burned. But that was nothing compared to the pain inside. The dreams, the plant accident, his little sister, the attack of the patient. In just four days everything had gone insane—and it was getting worse. If that wasn't bad enough, now he had a beautiful woman sitting in his truck, a woman to whom he was attracted. But one that he'd said incredibly stupid things to, and who now obviously hated his guts.

And how could he blame her? He'd been a first-class jerk. He knew how arrogant and uncaring he'd sounded back at the Institute. But what other defense did he have? There were too many things that she didn't know, that she shouldn't know. Add to that his natural inability to talk to any woman he found attractive and, well—there they were.

He glanced over at Sarah. She sat sullenly, as close to the passenger door as possible. Yes sir, he'd really outdone himself this time.

He looked back at the road. Twilight was settling over the fields. Off to the right, between the stands of trees, he noticed glimpses of a dark, billowing cloud. Grateful for a conversation starter, he motioned toward it. "Looks like we're gonna finally get ourselves some rain."

The woman glanced in that direction but said nothing. Brandon shifted his weight. This was going to be harder than he'd thought.

The road took a slow turn to the left. As he followed it, the cloud came more into view. There was a faint glow reflecting off the bottom. At first he thought it came from the setting sun, but the glow had movement. It seemed to shift and flicker.

The road continued to turn, and once again the cloud disappeared behind some trees. Brandon hesitated, then decided to keep it in view by slowing and turning off onto a side road.

"What are you doing?" Sarah asked, her voice still a few degrees below freezing.

"Looks like some sort of fire." He motioned toward the bottom of the cloud. "Check it out."

Sarah craned her head. "Where?"

"Right there, right in front of us."

She looked in the direction he pointed, then turned back to him, a puzzled expression on her face. He wasn't sure what her problem was, but this cloud was definitely weird, and worth investigating. As they approached, he realized that it was the only cloud in the sky. He estimated it to be a hundred feet wide and nearly three times that tall. It could have almost passed for a miniature thunderhead. And there was something else . . . it seemed to be drawing closer to the ground.

The road angled to the left and for several seconds a large stand of poplars completely blocked the cloud from sight. When it came back into view, it was off on Sarah's side. They were much closer now—so close that he could see a tremendous turbulence inside it as the cloud churned and boiled upon itself.

Another turn, this time to the right. And another stand of trees. When the cloud finally came back into view, it was dead ahead, less than two blocks away. And it was hovering directly over the church. *His* church. Brandon stared in unbelief as it slowly descended toward the structure—as if the building, itself, was somehow attracting it. Trees on both sides of the road started to toss and bend from the approaching wind. But there was something else, something even more astonishing.

The glow on the bottom of the cloud was not reflecting a sunset or a fire. It was reflecting light, yes, but a light that blazed through every window and opening of the church below it.

Urgency filled Brandon, and he quickly sped up.

"What's going on?" Sarah demanded.

"It's Monday night—they've got choir practice in there!"

Now they were a block away. Dust and debris flew all around the truck. And still the cloud descended, dropping closer and closer to the building until, finally, to Brandon's alarm, it enveloped the steeple.

He pushed harder on the accelerator.

He could hear the wind now. Like a roaring freight train, it grew louder and louder. And something else. Something inside the roar. A type of . . . groaning. Almost a wail. Voices, human voices. Dozens, perhaps hundreds of them.

The wind kicked up more dirt, making it nearly impossible to see the road. Brandon leaned over the wheel, peering through the windshield.

"What are you doing?" Sarah called, "Brandon, what's going on?" But he could barely hear her over the noise.

They were almost there. The trees writhed and twisted violently. The pickup shuddered, and Brandon had to grip the wheel just to keep it in the road. There was a loud snap, and suddenly the windshield exploded into a spiderweb of cracks as a tree limb smashed into it.

Brandon hit the brakes, and they skidded to a stop across the road from the church. He threw open the door and staggered into the wind. It pushed and pulled at him, throwing dirt and grit into his eyes. He squinted, covering his face with his arms, and continued forward.

"Brandon!" Sarah called from the other side of the pickup. "Brandon!"

He turned to her and shouted. "Get under the truck! Get under the truck!"

"Brandon, what are—"

"There are people in there!" He turned back into the wind. It bit into his face as he fought his way across the road. The howling voices grew to a deafening roar. He looked up at the steeple. It was completely engulfed by the cloud.

He was halfway across the street when he noticed another vehicle—a white VW bug approaching from the north. But no sooner had he seen it than he heard a thundering, rippling clatter. He spun back to the church just as the steeple ripped apart, flinging wood and rubble into the wind, creating a barrage of flying shrapnel. He ducked as pieces struck his legs, his back, his shoulders.

"Brandon!" He could barely hear Sarah's voice over the wind.

Another explosion. He turned to see a side window of the church blowing out. Then another. And another, and another, in rapid succession. But they didn't explode from wind rushing into the church; they exploded as its light rushed out—as shafts of blazing, piercing light burst through the openings.

Just as Brandon reached the sidewalk, he heard a loud crack. He looked up to see a giant cottonwood falling toward him. He leaped aside, but a branch caught him from the back and threw him hard onto the concrete. And then there was silence.

"Brandon . . ." Sarah's voice was far, far away. Another world. "Brandon . . ." He felt her shaking him by the shoulders. "Brandon . . ."

Dazed, regaining consciousness, he rolled onto his back. When his eyes focused, he saw her staring down at him, her face filled with concern, her hair flying in the wind.

And directly behind her—the cloud, much closer now. So close he could make out what appeared to be faces—swirling, contorting faces. Faces that were inside the—no, they weren't *inside* the cloud, they *were* the cloud. They were the source of the roaring winds, the deafening groans. It was these twisting, agonizing, tortured faces that made up the cloud.

"No!" Brandon shouted. "Stay away!"

But the faces continued their approach. As they came closer, they condensed, coming together, forming something new. A head. But not a human head. This was something more grotesque, more ferocious. It looked part leopard, part lion, part he wasn't sure. He could clearly see it, suspended in the air. There were the eyes, the mouth—and there were horns. But not two horns. No, there were several of them. He guessed at least ten.

"Stay away!" he shouted. "Stay back!"

The head drew closer. But it was no longer approaching the church. It was coming after them. Its mouth opened as it closed the distance. Brandon went cold with fear. But he was feeling something else as well. A stirring. Deep inside his chest. A swelling. There was a power he couldn't explain. A burning power that rapidly grew inside of him. It filled his chest then rose into his throat and his mouth. He gulped in air, but nothing would cool the searing heat. His lungs were on fire. The burning power had to escape. The approaching head had to be stopped. He took in another gulp of air; it did no good. The fire within him had to be released. He opened his mouth. A word came to mind; it formed in his throat, his mouth. Somehow it was part of the fire. And before he knew it, he had tilted back his head and shouted. *"GO!"*

The word roared from his mouth. But it was more than a word. It was also flame. Burning, leaping flames that shot high into the air. They struck the vaporous head, momentarily igniting, then completely evaporating one of the horns. The head howled in agony as it veered to the side, avoiding the rest of the fiery blast.

When the flames ceased, Brandon turned to Sarah. She looked back at him, terrified. He saw it again. Beyond her. The monstrous head. Only now where the horn had been destroyed, another had replaced it—a hideous thing, covered in eyes. He pulled Sarah to the ground. "Get down!" he shouted. "Get back under the truck!"

He struggled to his feet. Looking over his shoulder, he saw the thing coming directly at him. He raced to the church and ran up the steps, half staggering, half falling.

"Brandon!"

He yanked at the doors but they were locked. He banged on them, shouting, beating the glossy white wood with his fists. But the people inside were too frightened to help. Either that or they were already—

He shoved the thought out of his mind and looked back over his shoulder. The vaporous head appeared below the awning and quickly approached, once again opening its mouth. Brandon turned and slammed his shoulder into the door. It budged, but not enough. He tried again. Still nothing. The swirling head closed in. He leaned back and tried one last time.

The door broke open with such force that he stumbled, nearly fell, into the foyer. Inside, the room glowed with a brilliant, blinding light. So bright that he didn't see the three-tiered water fountain until he ran into it. He threw out his hands to catch himself and they splashed into the water. He'd never seen the fountain before and looked at it with astonishment. But even more amazing was the water he'd touched—it had suddenly turned blood red.

He pulled back with a gasp. Staggering, head reeling, he finally spotted the sanctuary doors. They were closed. On one side stood a strange olive tree, on the other, a giant lampstand holding lanterns identical to the one Jenny had held in the road. And directly over the doors was something else he had never seen before. A sign. But a sign whose words seemed vaguely familiar:

ENTER NOT WITHOUT THE SHIELD OF FAITH

With rising fear, he headed for the doors. He didn't want to go in, but knew he had to. He grabbed the handles, hesitated a moment to gather his courage, then threw them open. He staggered inside two or three steps before finally coming to a stop.

The sanctuary was absolutely calm. There was no storm. No howling wind. No blinding light. Only the sound of his gasping breath broke the silence.

Up at the front, below the organ pipes and towering cross, he saw the choir. Members he'd known since childhood—his mother, the Reverend, old man McPherson—they were all staring at him, their startled faces filled with concern.

Brandon closed his eyes, then opened them again. He looked back out the door behind him. There was no light. No cloud. Only Sarah. She stood at the foyer doors, looking on with the same worry and concern as the choir. He reached out to the nearest pew for support. Unable to fight back the exhaustion and the flood of emotion pouring in, he slowly lowered himself into the seat. Tears sprang to his eyes. He leaned over and rested his head on the pew in front of him. The tears continued to form until one fell from his face. It splattered onto the worn oak flooring. Another followed. And then another. He tried fighting them back, but it did no good. They continued to fall, one after another, after another, and there was nothing he could do to stop them.

CHAPTER 8

Even at a quarter past nine, the living room was sweltering. Damp with perspiration, Sarah sat on a worn sofa, waiting for the next sweep of the electric fan. The meeting could have taken place out on Mrs. Martus's porch, but at this time of year and in this part of Indiana, unless they had an extra pint or two of blood for the mosquitoes, it was better to stay inside.

At the moment, Mrs. Martus was upstairs helping her son get into bed. Meanwhile, her husband, Brandon's father, sat in a wheelchair, staring out the screen door. He hadn't moved a muscle, hadn't even acknowledged Sarah's or the Reverend's presence since they'd arrived. She guessed that he was the victim of a severe stroke or some other brain injury.

She petted Drool, a huge dog who did not get his name by accident, as she carried on small talk with the Reverend. He was a handsome man in his late fifties—intelligent, well-read. Like everyone else in the community, they'd begun their conversation by discussing the drought—what it was doing to the crops, how it was affecting the farmers, the future impact upon corn and soybean prices. It wasn't long before the Reverend added, somewhat sardonically, "And in one more week we'll finally hit the forty-day mark."

"Is that significant?" Sarah asked.

The Reverend shook his head with a sigh. "Not to you or me. But you would be surprised at how folks, particularly in these more rural areas, still look to the weather as a sign of God's favor or disfavor."

"You're serious?"

"I'm afraid so. And, like it or not, forty days and nights of the heavens being sealed has a distinct biblical ring about it."

Sarah nodded, then look up just in time to see Mrs. Martus make her entrance from upstairs.

"Well, now." The woman was all smiles as she glided down the steps from Brandon's room. "I think he's going to be just fine. 'Course it took a bit of doing, but I finally convinced him to take his medication." She entered the room, full of poise and Southern grace. Still, there was a certain nervousness about her. An uneasy energy. "Gracious me, where are my manners. You've been sittin' here all this time without anything to drink?" She turned toward the kitchen. "Let me get us some iced tea. I'll only be a—"

The Reverend was immediately on his feet. "No, Meg." He smiled. "Please, let me get that for us."

"Nonsense. It's already made. The pitcher's in the—"

"Meg, please." He motioned toward the sofa.

She hesitated, seeming to waver. And for the first time since she'd arrived, Sarah caught a glimpse of the strain she was under.

"Please," the Reverend repeated, "you've had a very trying evening, Meg."

At last Mrs. Martus nodded and the Reverend headed for the kitchen. He'd no sooner left the room than she turned to Sarah with a smile. "Well, now, this is service, isn't it?"

Sarah smiled back as the woman sat beside her.

As if unable to endure any silence for long, Mrs. Martus continued, "So tell me, Dr. Weintraub—"

"Please, 'Sarah.'"

"All right, Sarah." Another smile. "How long have you known Brandon?"

"Actually, not very long."

"I didn't even know he had friends at the Institute." She pushed a damp tendril of hair to the side. "'Course gettin' any information from him these days is like squeezin' blood from a turnip—if you know what I mean." She chuckled quietly.

Sarah nodded. Now, at least, she understood his silence. If he was having such experiences as this, no wonder he was afraid to talk to anybody about them. "Mrs. Martus? How long has he been having these—attacks?"

"Oh, they're not attacks, dear. Sometimes—well, sometimes he just thinks he sees things that aren't there, that's all."

Sarah nodded. "How long?" she gently repeated.

"Dear me." The woman scrunched her eyebrows in thought. "As a boy, he always had himself a real vivid imagination. Tellin' stories that'd take your breath away." Once again she pushed her hair aside. "'Course his daddy, there"—she indicated her husband—"he'd always be encouragin' it. Thick as thieves those two; no separatin' them. But that was a long time ago."

Once again Sarah could sense the woman's weariness. "Mr. Martus—he's suffering from . . . ?"

"A stroke. Been almost six years now."

"And he has no use of his arms or legs?"

"Or speech," Mrs. Martus added. "Least that's what the doctors tell us."

Something about that last line led Sarah to believe there was more. "And you believe them?"

"Me?" Mrs. Martus chuckled. "Well, of course I do, honey. If the good Lord wants to send us a trial or two, then that's his business. Ours is to take what comes in life and make the best of it." She paused a moment, then glanced upstairs. "'Course, not everyone can accept that fact."

Watching her carefully, Sarah ventured a guess. "People like Brandon?"

Mrs. Martus nodded, almost imperceptibly. "Poor soul." She glanced at Sarah with a nervous smile.

Sarah waited, cocking her head inquisitively, making it clear she'd like to hear more.

The woman looked toward the wheelchair, then down at her lap. And then, after another pause, she started to talk. "The first few months he used to stay up, sometimes all night, praying at his daddy's side. He was so positive that if he prayed hard enough, if he just had enough faith, he could make his daddy walk." Her voice trailed off into sad memories.

Sarah looked back toward the wheelchair, touched by the woman's emotions but even more moved by this unseen, sensitive side to Brandon. She was about to ask her to continue when the Reverend entered carrying a tray with a pitcher of iced tea and three glasses. "Here we go."

Suddenly Mrs. Martus was all smiles and good cheer. "I do declare, Reverend, you are a man of many talents." He smiled as he set the tray before them and began filling the glasses. "Sarah was just askin' how long Brandon's been havin' these spells."

The Reverend nodded. "They really didn't get bad until after the accident, wouldn't you say?"

Mrs. Martus agreed. "At least that's when the dreams started."

"Excuse me?" Sarah interrupted. "Accident?"

"Oh, didn't you know?" Mrs. Martus asked. "We lost our little girl about seven months ago. An automobile accident. Brandon was driving."

Sarah's heart moved with compassion.

"'Course as Providence would have it, he barely had a scratch—but you can hurt a person deeper than in the physical, if you know what I mean."

Sarah glanced down. She knew exactly what the woman meant. That's why she had the lab, her work, the long hours. But what did Brandon have? She turned back to Mrs. Martus. "You mentioned dreams?"

The Reverend answered, "The doctors say Brandon is suffering from acute guilt—compounded by his inability to accept his sister's death."

"So he dreams about her?" Sarah asked.

"They say it's a release."

"But weird dreams," Mrs. Martus explained. "Not healthy at all."

The Reverend nodded.

Sarah continued a bit more tentatively. "Were they ever—the dreams—were they ever partially manifested?"

The Reverend frowned. "What do you mean?"

"Have they ever contained facts or bits of information that, later, seemed to come true?"

Mrs. Martus shifted slightly. Sarah couldn't be certain, but it seemed she'd grown more uneasy.

Once again the Reverend answered. "Why do you ask, Dr. Weintraub?"

"Well, the average person spends a total of six years of his life dreaming, and—"

"Usually emotional or psychological in nature," he interjected. "Unless, of course it's just plain fantasy."

"Not always," Sarah corrected. "PSI studies indicate that precognitive skills—the ability to perceive an event before it happens—most often occur when we're in the dream state."

Mrs. Martus and the Reverend exchanged a discreet glance. Sarah noted it, then continued. "What about premonitions? Feelings that he'd been someplace, seen something before the event actually occurred?"

"Dr. Weintraub." The Reverend quietly set down his drink. "We appreciate your interest, particularly given your area of expertise. But let me assure you, Brandon's experiences have nothing to do with what you folks refer to as 'the paranormal.'"

"How can you be so certain?"

"Brandon has suffered a severe emotional loss, and he holds himself responsible. To encourage him, to suggest that these experiences come from anything else, much less the supernatural—well, it would only do him more harm than good."

"But you do believe it is possible?"

He took a breath and folded his hands. "I believe the human mind is a remarkable instrument, capable of far more than we give it credit. But to think of these incidents in the context of the supernatural—well . . ." He gave a little smile. "I'd like to think we've all grown past those days of superstition, wouldn't you?"

Sarah looked at him, unsure whether to be offended. "Still," she insisted, "as a minister, as a man of faith, you're aware of these things. I mean, your own Bible talks about dreams, prophets—"

"The Bible was written a long time ago, Dr. Weintraub. Certainly, it contains great wisdom and insight into the human condition, not to mention its poetic grace and beauty. However, I'm sure you are aware of the problems created when people start taking it too literally, when they begin treating it as if it were infallible, the final word of authority in any type of social, historical, or even scientific issue."

"Certainly, but as a—"

"If that were the case, where would we stop?" he chuckled. "Would you also have us believing in a six-day creation, or handling snakes, or raising people from the dead?"

"All I'm suggesting is that, as a minister, you're certainly aware of—"

"As a minister, I'm aware that it is my responsibility to care for my flock." His voice grew more firm. "And if that means protecting them occasionally from half-baked theories or the latest fads in pseudoscience, then so be it."

Sarah felt her ears growing hot with anger. "Excuse me?"

"What I mean to say is that—"

"Gracious me," Mrs. Martus laughed, as she held out her hands, making it clear that the discussion was at an end. Sarah and the Reverend looked at her. She chuckled. "Yes, sir, there's nothing like a lively debate between friends." She reached over and poured more tea into Sarah's glass. "I guess it's like my momma always said, if you want some spice in the conversation just add a little religion and politics."

The interruption gave Sarah a moment to cool down. She stole a glance at the Reverend. He was doing the same. She'd obviously hit a nerve. But what?

"Brandon will be fine," Mrs. Martus cranked up her smile a little higher. She patted Sarah's hand. "He just needs a little rest, that's all. Just a little rest and he'll be as good as new. Mark my words."

Mrs. Martus and the Reverend reached for their iced tea. The cubes in their glasses clinked, and Sarah watched as they raised the drinks to their mouths in almost perfect unison.

Dr. Reichner started awake. He blinked, once, twice, before finally getting his bearings. He sat up. His face was wet with perspiration and his heart hammered in his chest. He took several breaths, literally forcing himself to calm down and relax. It had been five years since his heart attack and he did not intend to have another.

It was only a dream, that's all. A flashback to his encounter with the python. He reached over and snapped on the light.

See, the room was empty. Only his Siamese cat lay at the foot of his luxurious, satin-sheeted bed. Nothing else. And definitely no python.

Still the words of the boy guru's voice had seemed so real, echoing in Reichner's head as clearly as the first time he'd heard them:

"We've chosen you to help him . . . to unlock his gifts . . ."

There had been no other communication from Nepal. Not by fax, nor e-mail, nor phone. But that's how it had always been. Besides the money that was wired every month into the Institute's account, there was virtually no other communication with the cartel. They definitely liked their privacy, and that was fine with him. The less interference the better.

Of course he was required to keep his financiers up-to-date on his research through semiannual reports and by copying them on all published articles, but that was about it. That's why the summons to Nepal and his conversation (if you could call it that) with the boy guru had been so significant. For three years the money had always been there when he needed it. And, except for their insistence that the Institute be built here in Indiana, they'd pretty much given him free rein.

Until now.

And yet it was a simple request. Find some young man with pronounced PSI abilities and run a few tests on him. No problem—virtually a carbon copy of what he'd done with Lewis. Although it would be fine with Reichner if they could forego the "voices" this time.

No, it wasn't the request that bothered him as much as it was the method in which it had been made.

More and more, he had begun to regard his initial vision in Nepal as legitimate. It was too vivid, too precise, to have been induced by drugs or the exotic environment. And he'd certainly read about such things happening—not only in Eastern mysticism but in the West as well, where shamans supposedly communicate with the spirits of animals. And there was at least one famous psychic in the States who claimed to receive her prophecies through a talking snake. The concept certainly wasn't new. In fact, it was as old as the Garden of Eden myth. But Reichner had never personally experienced anything like that, and it had definitely left him unnerved.

Then there was the other matter: this sudden urgency. The boy guru obviously believed something was going to happen. And judging by the pressure he was exerting, he believed it was going to happen very soon.

But all of that had little to do with tonight's experience. Tonight it had simply been a dream. Reichner had merely dreamed that the python was curled up on his silken sheets repeating the phrases. Phrases Reichner had obviously pulled from his memory. Phrases that his subconscious was using to urge him to begin the search. Of course it would have been easier to believe this if it hadn't been for that other phrase, the new one still ringing in his ears, the one that hadn't been used in his encounter in Nepal—the phrase that had finally awakened him.

"If you do not help," the voice had whispered, *"we will lose him. And if we lose him, you will pay."*

Reichner shook his head. It was only a dream. He glanced at the alarm on his bed stand: 12:11. He reached over to turn off the light, then hesitated. Maybe it wouldn't hurt to sleep with it on, just for tonight. Angry at the thought and at the weakness it betrayed, he snapped off the light and lay back down.

But sleep would not return.

Nor did sleep come for Brandon. It had been nearly three hours since Momma had helped him up to his room. The medication she'd given him hadn't even taken the edge off his torment. How could it? How could two little pills be expected to stop a living nightmare? The storm, the vaporous head with horns, the fountain of blood, the lampstand, the sign—they all seemed vaguely familiar, like pieces from forgotten dreams, or stories he'd heard as a child. But nothing made sense. His mind raced—to where, he wasn't certain. How to stop it, he hadn't a clue. The only things he could be sure of were the tears, his increasing confusion, and his ever-growing anger.

Sometime after midnight, he got up, dressed, headed out to his pickup, and quietly drove into town. Unsure where to go, he eventually found himself back at the church. He didn't expect to find any answers there, but he did expect to vent some rage.

The doors were unlocked. They always were. It was a policy his father had started way back when the church had first opened. And, over the years, it was a policy that potential thieves and vandals usually respected. Brandon stepped into the foyer. Everything was deathly still. This time, the sanctuary doors were open. There were no fountains, no olive trees, no lampstands, and definitely no hanging sign. Everything was real.

He entered the sanctuary and made his way down the slight incline of the aisle toward the altar. He didn't bother turning on the lights. He'd grown up here. The diffused glow from the outside streetlight provided what little illumination he needed.

He stopped just a few feet from the pew he'd sat in every Sunday for over twenty years. He glared up at the cross hanging on the wall, the same absurd symbol he'd seen each of those Sundays. The symbol of death and sacrifice and futility.

When he spoke, his voice quivered with rage. "What do you want from me?"

Silence.

Again he spoke, louder. *"What do you want?"*

But, of course, there was no answer. Just his own echo as it faded into the silence. A tightness grew in his throat. He tried to swallow it, but it wouldn't go away. Tears sprang to his eyes, but he fought them back. Not here. Not now.

He spoke again—a final, harsh whisper. "What do you want?"

"Maybe he just wants you to believe."

The sound spun Brandon around. He peered into the darkness, searching for its source. There. Almost at the back, near the center, a small sitting figure.

"Who's there?" he demanded.

With some difficulty the figure rose from the pew.

"Who are you?" he asked again. "What are you doing here?"

Slowly, the figure made its way toward the center aisle. "I'm here 'cause I knew you'd be here." It was a woman's voice—craggy and old. It sounded familiar.

"Who are you?" he repeated.

"I s'pose I could be askin' you the same question, Brandon Martus."

The figure stepped into the aisle. A faint pool of light spilled across her face. Now he recognized her. "You're the old woman. The one who stopped by the house yesterday."

Gerty started toward him, hobbling painfully down the aisle. "And you're the boy who refuses to believe."

Brandon watched in silence as she approached. She spoke again. "I'm sure gonna miss this place. Hear they're gonna be tearin' it down for a—what'd they say? Some sorta bank building?"

Brandon said nothing.

She continued, "Did you know that right there, right where you're standin' in front of that altar, your momma and poppa dedicated you to the Lord? You musta been only seven, maybe eight days old." She stopped halfway down the aisle to catch her breath.

Brandon said nothing.

"Believe you me, that was one special morning. 'Course we knew before that, before you were even born we knew that the Lord had his hand upon you." She chuckled softly. "Yes, sir, that was one special day. We were all standin' around singin' and believin' somethin' real special was gonna happen, right then and there. 'Course nothin' did. But still ..."

Her voice trailed off and Brandon quietly answered. "A lot of things people believe don't happen."

At last she arrived and looked up at him. "But that don't mean you stop believin'."

Brandon carefully eyed her.

"Your belief, that's what makes it happen, Brandon Martus. All you need to do is the believin'. He'll take care of the rest. But you gotta believe. Do you hear me, son? You got to believe. Faith, that's your only shield."

"Well, then, I'll have to do without."

She looked at him.

He glanced away, then mumbled, "The only thing I know about faith is I don't have any."

The old woman watched him, saying nothing. Finally she looked past him to the cross on the front wall. "There are two types of faith, child. Earthly faith and heavenly. The earthly faith, that don't mean a thing. It's just man-made, just a way to try to make the good Lord do what you want him to." Her eyes fell back on him. "But there's another type. The type that surrenders to his will. Completely. And once it learns what that will is, it speaks it into existence. And that type of faith, anyone can have."

Brandon closed his eyes. He'd heard religious double-talk all his life. "Yeah," he said, preparing to move past her, "well, I'm fresh out of both."

"You're wrong."

Her comment angered him. "What?"

She said nothing, which only irritated him more.

"Look, I don't have any faith, okay? Not anymore." She remained silent. He continued, "Maybe once, when I was a kid, sure. But I've gotten a little older now. And smarter, if you know what I mean. I understand a lot more."

"You understand nothing."

His irritation grew. "I don't have faith, all right?"

The woman shook her head. "You're wrong, Brandon Martus."

He tossed his hair back in frustration. "What's with you, anyway?"

She held his look. "Anyone can believe who wants to believe. You just don't want to."

This was absurd. What was he doing arguing with a nutcase in the middle of the night? "I *can't* believe." His voice grew louder. "You got that? I *cannot believe.*"

"You *will* not believe."

He took a breath, holding back his anger.

"Your will is the key. If you'd turn that key, God would give you his faith. He is the author of faith, Brandon Martus, not you. You need only surrender to him."

Brandon shook his head. There was no reasoning with this type. He'd run into them before. It was best just to let them go on and live out their little delusions. "Look, I should have never stopped by here in the first place." He started to pass her. "Why don't you just—go back to whatever you were doing and—"

She grabbed his arm. Her grip was weak, but he let it stop him.

"Your will is the key, Brandon Martus. You just got to surrender."

He looked at her, then down at the hand on his arm. She released it and he started back up the aisle.

"Brandon Martus."

He kept walking.

"Beware of the seducers. Be keepin' your eyes open for the counterfeits."

He slowed to a stop.

"If you refuse the Lord's way, your adversary will be tryin' to seduce you down other roads." He turned to her and she continued. "There's only one path, Brandon Martus. His path. And it's narrow. Beware of the broader ways. Don't be reachin' for heaven with the arm of the flesh. Such ways lead to the occult, to destruction. All paths but the Lord's lead to destruction."

He held her look another moment before turning and continuing back up the aisle. Maybe it was good they were tearing down the place. Who knew what type of wackos were starting to show up.

He exited through the foyer and walked outside into the sultry night air. The moon was nearly full, but its edges were blurred by a faint haze. He headed down the steps and crossed the grass to his pickup. Then he heard footsteps behind him. Apparently the old gal could move a lot faster if she set her mind to it. He turned, ready to confront her one last time. "Look, I—"

That's when he was hit. Someone jumped him from behind and they both crashed into the side of his truck. Before Brandon could recover, his attacker was already landing punches. Brandon raised his arms to block the blows and staggered back, away from the truck.

He saw a young man with a shaved head, red goatee, and wild eyes. Crazed eyes, like an animal's.

"We knew you'd return!" the assailant screamed, spittle flying. *"We knew!"* But it wasn't a single voice. It was like the patient's at the Institute. Multiple voices. Dozens of voices. Dozens of voices all shouting and directing their anger at him.

"Look," Brandon said, catching his breath, bracing for another assault. "I don't know who you are, but I don't want any trouble, all right? So why don't—"

Once again the attacker leaped at him, and they tumbled to the ground. As they rolled, Brandon swung his fists, striking ribs, kidneys, gut, but nothing mattered.

The assailant seemed oblivious to pain. They rolled one way, then the other, until the attacker wound up on top, and Brandon found himself pinned. He tried to buck him off, but the man seemed to have superhuman strength.

With Brandon's arms pinned by his assailant's knees, the man began landing punches squarely into his face. Blow after blow, sharp and powerful. Brandon did his best to resist, trying to roll, trying to throw him off, but it did little good. Lights began dancing across his vision. A loud ringing filled his head.

With the attacker's blows came the swearing. Vile oaths, all directed at Brandon. But they were sounding farther away, fading . . . as was Brandon's pain. He was passing out. Any second now and he would—

"Get off him." It was the old woman's voice, faint and from another world. "Get off! In the name of Jesus Christ I command you to stop!"

The blows ceased instantly. At first Brandon thought he'd passed out, but no, he still heard her voice.

"By the power and authority of Jesus the Christ I order you to stop!"

Brandon felt the weight of the young man shift on his chest.

"Who are you?" the voices demanded.

"Who I am is of no importance." Her voice was clearer now. Brandon was coming back, regaining consciousness. "In the name of Jesus Christ, I order you to get up."

With a struggle, Brandon finally managed to open his eyes. His vision was blurred, but he saw the man on top of him and, beyond that, the old woman.

"Now," she ordered.

The attacker rose from Brandon and staggered to his feet. Brandon rolled to his side, coughing and spitting what he knew to be blood. When he looked back up, he saw the young man catching his breath and speaking. *"He must wage the war himself,"* the voices screamed.

"In time," the woman replied.

Slowly, unsteadily, Brandon struggled to his hands and knees, keeping his eyes on the confrontation. The woman had taken a step or two closer. She now stood face-to-face with the man, who towered over her by nearly a foot.

"He is ours!" the voices shouted.

The woman held her ground, unflinching. "Liar."

"He has chosen to— "

"You are the author of lies."

"He has turned. He has chosen to follow our— "

"You are the author of lies, and I order you to be silent."

Everything grew quiet. The woman and the young man remained glaring at one another, but the young man no longer spoke.

Brandon knew an attack was imminent. The man was about to grab her. The last thing in the world he wanted was to get back into the mix, but the old lady would definitely be needing his help. With painful effort he rose to his feet. His head throbbed and the ground still moved under his wobbly legs, but at least he was standing.

Yet, instead of attacking her, the man's head swiveled toward him—his eyes still wild and terrifying. *"You will not prevail,"* the voices seethed. *"Victory is ours."* The hatred sent a shudder through Brandon.

The young man turned back to the woman. Brandon prepared himself to leap to her defense.

But she showed no fear. "Go," she commanded.

The man glared at her, but she didn't yield. Her voice was not loud, but it was clear and spoken with unmistakable authority. "In the name of Jesus the Christ, I command you to leave."

Brandon watched. It was amazing. Instead of attacking her, the man's stature, his very countenance, seemed to wilt.

"Now," she ordered. "Go, now."

The young man hesitated, then momentarily looked around as if trying to get his bearings. When he spotted Brandon, he tried to maintain the bravado. "I am the one. It is *my* season. You are the impostor." But it was only one voice now—a hollow imitation of the power and hatred Brandon had felt moments earlier.

"Now," the old woman repeated. "In the name of Jesus Christ I order you to leave, now."

The man turned back to her. He shifted his weight, as if unsure what to do, where to go. Then, spotting a beat-up Volkswagen across the street, he turned and walked toward it. Brandon and the woman watched in silence as he approached the car, climbed in, and started it up. Not a word was spoken as he finally pulled away and headed down the street.

At last Brandon turned to the old woman. She was staring at him. He could feel his face already swelling from the blows, and he knew some of the cuts were still bleeding. But when she took a concerned step toward him, he backed away. Whatever was going on, whatever had happened, he wanted no more of it.

"Brandon ..."

He raised his hands, motioning her to stay away. She ignored it and continued to approach. He turned, stumbled, then headed for his truck.

"Brandon Martus."

Keeping a hand on the truck bed to steady himself, he moved along it to the cab.

"You understand now," she called out. "Do you understand?"

He threw open the door and climbed inside.

"Eli."

He stole a look over his shoulder. She was still shuffling toward him. He reached into his jeans pocket for his keys. His right hand screamed in pain. It was either sprained or broken.

"Eli—you have the same authority, you have seen it work."

Gritting his teeth against the pain, he yanked out the keys and shoved them into the ignition.

"Child—"

He fired up the truck.

"You have the authority."

He dropped it into gear and released the brake.

"You need only surrender to his will. You need only believe."

He revved the engine and quickly pulled from the curb. She was still talking, but he no longer heard. He traveled nearly fifty yards before glancing up at the rearview mirror.

The old lady was still there, standing all alone in the road, watching after him.

Dr. Reichner sat in the passenger seat as Sarah drove. Her car was running, but barely. He'd been the one to suggest they take it—after all, she knew the way. But now he cursed himself for the idea. Besides worn-out shocks and the world's roughest-sounding engine, she had no air-conditioning. A serious oversight in this record-breaking heat.

The car gave a couple of extra shudders as she turned onto Highway 30 and accelerated. "I think it's a bad carburetor," she shouted over the roar of the open windows. "Last night it didn't want to start at all."

"Maybe you should have taken the hint," Reichner said, fingering a piece of window molding that disintegrated under his touch.

"All she needs is a little loving care," Sarah insisted. Then, throwing a gibe back in his direction, "That is, if her owner could ever get some time off to visit the garage."

Reichner smiled quietly. Sarah wouldn't take the time off, even if he gave it to her. And that was fine by him. As long as he could capitalize on her desperate need to achieve, she would always be of use.

This morning was a perfect example. Initially, she had balked when he suggested they drive out to visit the boy. She didn't want to exploit his trauma, to take advantage of his sister's death. Reichner pretended to understand—but all he had to do was remind Sarah that if this kid was for real, the potential breakthroughs in their field would be unparalleled. Minutes later they were in the car, heading out to pay him a little visit. Again Reichner smiled. It took so little to play this woman.

Earlier, when she'd first mentioned the boy, he had shown little interest. Somebody with a bad case of nightmares and hallucinations seemed a likelier candidate for Vicksburg State than for his studies. But when she had mentioned that he had also been at the lab, and that a patient had attacked him, and that he had been at a church the night before, Reichner had begun to wonder.

Hadn't the boy guru insisted that Reichner would find somebody in this area? Hadn't Lewis wanted to attack somebody else at the lab? And last night hadn't Lewis also spoken of visiting a church? Coincidence? Perhaps. But definitely reason enough to drop by and pay this kid a visit. Besides, it gave Reichner an opportunity to be alone with Sarah, and he liked that. He glanced at her legs. She was wearing a skirt today. Yes, he liked that very much.

"This must be the place," Sarah said, nodding toward a pickup parked along the shoulder of the road. They had just come from the boy's house, where his mother had reluctantly told them that he was probably down at the river. "He's taking the day off," she had explained. "That's where he likes to go and work things out."

Reichner had assured her that they wouldn't bother him, that they would only ask a question or two. It was a lie, but it made no difference to Reichner. After all, it was what she wanted to hear.

Sarah pulled the car to a stop behind the pickup, and they stepped out into the pounding sun.

"He may seem aloof at first," she said as they found the path and started down the steep bank into the woods. "But that's just a defense. Underneath, he's really quite sweet and sensitive."

Reichner arched an eyebrow. Was it his imagination, or did she have a thing for the kid? Throughout their drive, she'd spoken about him with concern—and now he was "sweet and sensitive"? He'd keep this in mind.

They were halfway down the path when they found him. Or at least when his dog found them. But instead of barking an alarm, the old animal lumbered to its feet and headed up the bank to greet them, all pants and slobbers. It recognized Sarah immediately, and she bent down to give it the appropriate pats and praises. Then it turned to Reichner, who for appearance's sake had to do likewise, petting and patronizing the beast while it drooled all over his two-hundred-fifty-dollar-a-pair Ballys.

Sarah called out, "Brandon."

The boy was stretched out on some rocks, shirt off, sunning himself. He was a good-looking kid, muscular build, and with long gorgeous hair that some of Reichner's women would have killed for.

"Brandon?"

He looked up, spotted them, then turned away.

They continued down the path, slipping slightly, as unruly blackberry vines snagged Reichner's slacks and sharp rocks assaulted his shoes.

Again Sarah called his name.

He finally turned back to them. "Come to see another show?" he shouted. "Sorry, the next performance isn't until—" He stopped when he saw Reichner. "You brought a friend. Maybe I should start charging admission."

They reached the bottom of the path and Reichner glanced at his shoes. They were scuffed and covered in drool. This kid had better be worth it.

"Your mother said you might be here," Sarah explained as they approached. "This is Dr. Reichner, my boss. He's head of the Institute."

The kid's eyes locked onto Reichner's. They were steel gray and riveting. Immediately Reichner knew that Sarah had been right; there was a depth here, something that belied the boy's pretended indifference.

But Sarah had noticed something else. "Your face," she asked in sudden concern. "What happened to your face?" She was referring to the cuts and bruises around his eyes and on his cheeks.

Brandon looked away.

"Brandon?"

"I was at a late-night church service."

Sarah turned to Reichner with a concerned look. He frowned and motioned for her to continue.

"Listen." She shifted uneasily. "Do you mind if we talk to you for a few minutes?"

The boy turned back to her. Reichner watched and almost smiled. He'd guessed correctly. There was definitely something between them.

"Please," she asked, clearing her throat a little self-consciously. "I think it might be important."

The boy gave no answer. There was only the sound of the river and the groaning of the dog as it collapsed in some nearby shade.

Taking his lack of reply as an affirmative, Reichner searched for a seat. "Well . . ." He found a flat boulder nearby and eased carefully onto it, mindful of his slacks. "Dr. Weintraub tells me you've been having some pretty unusual experiences?"

The boy simply looked at him. But Reichner was unfazed. "So, tell me, Brennan—"

"Brandon," Sarah corrected.

"So tell me, Brandon, how long has this been going on?"

The boy glanced away.

Reichner waited.

Finally the kid responded. "Not long."

"And it started out as dreams, you say, that is before they became—" He chose to bypass the word *hallucinations*. "Visions." The boy made no response. Reichner pressed on. "Tell me, Brandon, I am curious: What do you know about quantum mechanics?"

The kid threw him a look.

Reichner chuckled. "Actually, it is not that complex a concept." He found a stick near his feet and picked it up. "It merely explains how solid objects, say this piece of wood here, can sometimes act more like waves of energy than as an actual physical object. That is, until we observe it. And then, for some reason, it collapses back into a lower state and becomes a solid object again."

Brandon looked at him. "They pay you money to think like that?"

Reichner forced another chuckle. Let the boy have his fun. At least he'd gotten Brandon's attention. Now he'd better move fast to keep it.

"What if I were to tell you that instead of a solid object, like this stick here, collapsing and appearing into our dimension—what if I were to say that I believe your experiences, your dreams and visions, are *you* actually stepping up into *its* dimension or into dimensions that are even higher?"

The boy looked skeptical but intrigued. Good. Now Reichner just had to wait for him to take the bait. He paused, letting the silence build. Finally, the boy spoke.

"You're talking like sci-fi movies—parallel universes and stuff."

Reichner shook his head. "Not exactly. Mathematically I have trouble with *parallel* universes. However, with existing mathematical formulas I can prove *perpendicular* universes."

"Perpendicular?"

Reichner nodded. It was a stretch, but if this preacher's kid still believed in a heaven and a hell—an 'up there' heaven, and a 'down there' hell—then this concept would work nicely. He continued, "Mathematically, thanks to Green, Schwartz, and dozens of other physicists, we have proof that our universe does not consist of three dimensions, as we once thought. Instead, it consists of at least eleven."

"Eleven?"

Reichner nodded. "That is correct. Eleven dimensions. It can be proved mathematically. Beyond question."

The boy shook his head—either in skepticism or wonder, Reichner couldn't be sure. He quickly moved on. "Now, of course, we can construct models like the tesseract to help us understand higher dimensions. But instead of bringing out the charts and diagrams, there is an easier way." Again he paused, making sure the kid was still on the line. He was, and he was waiting for more. Perfect.

With the stick still in his hands, Reichner rose to his feet. "Now, it is difficult for our three-dimensional minds to comprehend an eleven-dimensional world, so let us talk about two and three dimensions, instead." He stepped to a small pool near the edge of the river. It appeared to have once been a large eddy, but thanks to the drought, most of it had evaporated, leaving it only a few inches deep.

"Let us suppose that there were two-dimensional creatures living here on the surface of this water." He crouched and gently set the stick in the pool. "They would understand length—" He stretched his hands the length of the stick. "And they would understand width." He indicated its width. "But they would have no comprehension of height, of up and down, because they are only two-dimensional creatures. A third dimension, up here above the river, would be impossible for them to see or even comprehend, because they only live in their two-dimensional world."

The boy leaned forward. Good.

"But you and I, up here in the three-dimensional world, we could look down upon their entire world with a single glance." He motioned from one end of the stick to the other. "We could see their beginning, just as clearly as their end. And, even though we are all around, they would not see us at all—until, *poof*—" He poked his finger into the water. "We suddenly appeared in their dimension. Or *poof*—" He removed his finger. "We suddenly disappeared."

"We'd be like gods to them," Sarah explained. "We'd be omnipotent. Able to observe everything they do, being in all places at the same time."

"Now." Reichner reached into the water and lifted out the stick. "What if a two-dimensional creature were suddenly lifted up out of his world and into our three-dimensional world?"

"He'd freak," Brandon answered quietly.

Reichner nodded. "Precisely. He would see things that did not exist in his world, three-dimensional objects that his two-dimensional mind could not comprehend. And, as a defense, his mind would reduce those images into forms he *could* understand—most likely symbols from his existing world."

The boy shifted uneasily.

Reichner was obviously making his point. "You come from a religious background, correct?"

Brandon nodded.

"Think of all the great biblical visions and symbols: white horses, multiheaded beasts, slain lambs. These symbols all come from people trying to explain the inexplicable—using lower-dimensional terms to explain a higher-dimensional reality, a *superreality.*"

"And you're telling me all this because . . ."

"I want you to look upon science, at least our science, as just another facet of religion, just another way of trying to understand God."

Brandon repeated his question. "And you're telling me all this because . . ."

Reichner threw a look at Sarah. He'd done all he could. The fish had taken the bait, now it was up to her to bring him in.

She took her cue. "Because we need your help, Brandon."

The boy glanced at her, then looked away.

She gently persisted. "Let us run a few tests."

He shook his head and rose to his feet.

"In a controlled environment."

"No."

"You'd be in no danger. We'd be right beside—"

"No!" He turned back to her, obviously trying but unable to hide his agitation. "I'm not going to be some guinea pig in one of your laboratory experiments."

Sarah quietly rose to her feet. "That's not what—"

"I'm not one of those loony tunes you bring in from Vicksburg and hook up to a bunch of wires."

Reichner fired a glance to Sarah. How much did the kid know about their use of mental patients?

But Brandon wasn't finished. "It's just guilt, all right? The doctors say I'm getting better. It's just a matter of time and I'll be okay."

"But we're talking about more than just you." Sarah took a step toward him. "The implications of this research could affect the entire world, Brandon. We could be helping the human—"

"Well, *me* is all I got, all right?"

"Brandon, if you'd just stop and—"

"Not you, not the world—me!"

"And you is all that counts?" An edge had entered her voice.

The boy glanced away. "You got that right."

They were losing him. Reichner looked hard at Sarah, a signal for her to play the final card. She scowled, obviously reluctant to go into that area.

But Reichner nodded firmly, making it clear that she had no other choice.

And still she hesitated.

All right, then, if she wouldn't, he would. He turned to Brandon and asked a single question. "What about your little sister—what about Jenny?"

Brandon's eyes shot to him, then to Sarah. But Sarah was unable to look at him.

He turned back to Reichner. "She's dead. Or hadn't you heard."

"Perhaps." Reichner shrugged. "At least in this dimension."

He let the phrase hang, making sure the hook was back in the kid's mouth. Then he rose and began to brush off his slacks. "Well, I see that we have made a mistake. I thought perhaps you would want to help us. If not in the name of science, then at least for ..." He pretended to hesitate, then shrugged. "Well, it really doesn't matter now. We are sorry to have wasted your time, Brandon." He turned to Sarah, who was unable to look at either of them. "Shall we go, Doctor?"

She nodded.

Without another word, they turned and started for the path.

"If I do that ..."

The kid's voice stopped them. Reichner almost smiled. So predictable.

"If I go through with it, you're saying I might meet Jenny?"

Reichner said nothing.

Brandon repeated, louder, "If I go through with it, are you saying—"

"It's a possibility," Sarah gently interrupted. "But nothing's for sure."

Brandon persisted. "But there's a chance?"

Sarah paused, then nodded.

"And you'll be there?" he asked, keeping his eyes fixed on her.

"I'll be at your side the entire time."

Brandon stood a long moment. Then he looked toward the dog and gave a low whistle. The animal struggled to its feet and lumbered toward him. Finally he answered, "All right." With that, he turned and headed back toward the river.

Sarah hesitated, then called, "Brandon."

He started working his way upstream along the edge of the water. He didn't turn to her when he spoke. "I said all right, didn't I?"

To fully confirm it, Reichner called out, "Tomorrow afternoon. That will give us time to set up the equipment. Tomorrow afternoon, at two."

Brandon said nothing. Neither did Sarah as she stood watching.

Reichner turned and started back up the path. Several seconds passed before Sarah joined him. Reichner knew she felt guilty. Too bad. But using people, playing this type of hardball, was all part of the game. And she'd better get used to it if she planned to be a winner. Still, he wasn't worried. Because if there was one thing he knew about Sarah Weintraub, it's that she was driven to win.

CHAPTER 9

"Okay, we're getting images." The Institute's biochemical engineer motioned for Sarah and Reichner to join him over at the computer terminal.

Across the room, Brandon lay on a hard, twelve-inch-wide table that had been rolled inside the PET, or positron-emission tomography scanner. It looked like a giant white doughnut with an opening thirty-five inches in diameter that ran forty-two inches deep. It completely surrounded Brandon's head, which was held in place by two leather straps fastened with Velcro strips. He wore no gown, just jeans and his standard-issue T-shirt. His left hand rested in a plexiglass pan of water heated to exactly 43.6 degrees Celsius. From this hand they would remove multiple blood samples in order to monitor the radioactivity they were injecting into his body through a syringe in the other hand—a syringe surrounded by a silver cylinder designed to shield the technician from the very radiation he was injecting.

Outside the scanner, on a table near Brandon's chest, a small cassette recorder played Reichner's relaxation tape.

Sarah knew that PET scans weren't always available to parapsychology labs, partly because of the machine's 1.8-million-dollar price tag. She also knew that the Institute was preparing to order a second. A wonderful indulgence. But PET scans themselves were no luxury. Unlike SCATs or MRIs, which register the same condition of tissue—whether it's dead or alive—PET scans actually view and record the metabolic rate of a living organism.

Thirty minutes earlier, they had injected Brandon with three ccs of the radioactive isotope Fluoro Deoxyglucose, a sugar that enters the cells of the brain just like any other sugar molecule. But since it is radioactive, it gives off energy—which the special crystals inside the PET's plastic doughnut (over eighteen thousand of them) are able to record.

The purpose? To see which areas of Brandon's brain were the most active when he had his visions.

The process was relatively painless, except for the hard table Brandon now lay on. All he had to do was listen to Reichner's prerecorded voice and let it lead him into the lower-frequency brain waves—the brain waves present when the subject is most susceptible to paranormal activity.

Sarah joined Reichner at the computer screen to watch the first of the sixty-three sliced video images of Brandon's brain appear. To see pictures of the human brain actually working never ceased to amaze her. The organ is by far the most complex in the known universe, and to this day prompts more questions than science has been able to answer.

The brain had not always been held in such high esteem. Aristotle figured it to be nothing but an elaborate cooling system that was good for producing mucus (after all, look how close it was to the nose). But eventually, this relatively small, three-pound organ responsible for everything from a Shakespearean sonnet to the horrors of Hiroshima, received the credit it deserved.

The biochemical engineer sitting at the computer, a young man from Taiwan, whistled softly. "Take a look at that."

Sarah directed her attention back to the screen. Not only did the PET scan show what sections of the brain Brandon was using, but it also showed to what degree he was using them. The areas with the least amount of function were shown in the cooler colors of purple, blue, and green. The more moderate working areas appeared as yellow. And finally there was red—the "hot" areas, the areas where the radiation was most highly concentrated, where brain activity was the greatest.

"His entire right temporal lobe," Reichner whispered in awe, "it's on fire."

Sarah looked on with equal wonder. For ease in research, the brain was divided into regions by function. The frontal lobe controlled some motor activity but was also responsible for giving us our sociability. The occipital lobe was for vision. The parietal lobe received sensory information and helped in special orientation. But it was the right temporal section of the brain that held their attention now. When this area was stimulated during brain surgery, some patients experienced the so-called 'out-of-body experience,' or a feeling of déjà vu, or any number of paranormal sensations.

"Have you ever seen anything like it?" Reichner whispered.

"Not like this," Sarah said, shaking her head and staring. Brandon's entire right temporal lobe glowed a bright red.

"Amazing," the engineer whispered.

"Okay," Reichner nodded. "I have seen enough."

Surprised, Sarah turned toward him. "What?" she asked.

"Let's get him out of here and into the Ganzfield."

"But we're not done," the engineer argued.

"We only have him for a day. Get him unplugged and down to Lab Two."

Sarah frowned. "That wasn't the agreement. We asked him to participate in one experiment, and for only a couple of hours."

Reichner looked at her and scoffed. "We are not going to let an opportunity like this slip through our fingers, Doctor. Now, get him unhooked and moved."

"But . . ." Sarah glanced across the room at Brandon and lowered her voice. "What if he doesn't want to stay? Emotionally, we've put him through a lot already. What if he wants to go home?"

"He will stay."

"How can you be so sure?"

"How?" he asked.

She nodded.

"Because you, my dear, know how to convince him."

Gerty stood at the stove, savoring the smell of the chicken-and-rice soup. This was how she always broke her longer fasts. It was the gentlest way she knew of easing her digestive system back into operation.

She had finally finished her time of prayer and petition for the boy. It had not been as long as some of her earlier fasts, but her Lord had said that it was enough. The concentrated period of intercession was over. The boy would still face counterfeits and challenges, and his fiercest battles still lay ahead, but the Lord had made it clear that her time of interceding was over. His perfect will would be accomplished.

Of course she had no idea what that will would be. And, after last night's talk with the young boy, she had some very serious concerns. After all, despite the Lord's power, he always respected an individual's will. It was always up to the individual whether that person would love the Lord, hate him, obey him, or even believe in him.

And it was that final choice, the choice of *un*belief, that she feared most for the boy.

Of course she had asked her Lord. But in this area he had remained silent. She knew that he wasn't being indifferent to her requests. He simply understood the complexities far more than she did. So, at least for now, she too would have to simply believe. Gerty smiled. Of course she would believe. After all their years together, after all those years of his love and tender mercies, how could she do otherwise?

She reached over to the counter and picked up another of the letters she'd been writing. Although the Lord had said her time of intercession had drawn to a close, he had promised that she could continue writing her letters. How many more, she didn't know. Perhaps as many as she had time for. Because he had promised her one other thing: Before the week was over, he would take her home.

Gerty picked up the letter from the counter and read what she'd written.

Dear Eli:

> I know that you are confused and that you find your gifts frightening. At times you may even wonder if they are from God. It is good to be cautious. That is why he instructs us to "test the spirits." But let me assure you, dear child, as you turn to our Heavenly Father, those gifts will always be from above. Yes, there are counterfeits. Yes, if you strive for the gifts independent of his will, you will enter regions of the occult, a dangerous world where clever impostors promise good but seek to destroy.

The soup was steaming now, nearly boiling. Gerty turned off the stove, then reached up to open the cupboard. The door stuck slightly, squeaking when it finally gave way. She took down a small bowl, opened a drawer, and pulled out a ladle. The smell of the soup was intoxicating. With trembling hands, she dipped the ladle into the pan and slowly dished it up. It was Wednesday afternoon, the ninth day of her fast, and the soup smelled so good she could practically taste it.

When she had finished, she looked at the small formica-topped table, piled with sketches she had retrieved from the attic earlier that morning. Sketches she had been drawing for twenty-two years. She would drop them off at his house. Today, maybe tomorrow.

But not the letter. Like the other letters, this one was meant to be read later. After she was gone.

She took a spoon from the drawer and, holding the bowl in both hands, she shuffled past the counter toward the table.

She slowed as she passed the refrigerator. The Lord hadn't told her how she would die, or the exact day. But she had sensed, she had known, where it would be: right there, right between her old refrigerator and the kitchen table. Strangely enough, the insight hadn't frightened her. It simply helped prepare her.

She arrived at the table and pulled out one of the two chairs. Gently, she eased herself down. She pushed aside the letters and sketches to make more room. Then, after a quiet prayer of thanks, she picked up the spoon and dipped it into the soup. Her hand shook as she raised it to her lips.

It was warm and rich and full of flavor. She held the broth in her mouth, savoring it a moment, before finally swallowing. She dipped her spoon back into the bowl and took another sip. It was as good as the first. She wondered if she would miss this sort of thing in heaven. Then she smiled. How could she? Her Lord had promised a feast, a wedding banquet in her honor. How could there be a feast without food?

She took several more spoonfuls, feeling it warm her throat, her insides. She was less than halfway through when she placed the spoon in the bowl and pushed it aside. She would return to it shortly, but right now there were more important matters.

As she reached for her Bible, she felt a trace of sadness in her heart. She knew she would never see the boy again. Still, she would be allowed to minister to him.

Through the sketches, as well as the letters and the verses in her old Bible, she would still be able to help. The thought gave her some comfort as she opened the worn book and began turning its yellowed pages. At last she found the verses she was to give him. She would return to the soup in a moment, but right now it was more important that she clearly underline the verses for him to see.

"Like a leaf, floating upon the surface of a quiet pond . . ." Dr. Reichner sat in the Observation Room, speaking softly into the microphone. He glanced at the clock. They were twelve minutes into the session.

Down below, in Lab Two, Brandon rested comfortably in the leather recliner, bathed by the four red floodlights. His eyes were covered by the Ganzfield goggles.

Reichner continued speaking. "No cares, no worries, no thoughts. Just quiet, gentle floating . . ."

Sarah sat beside Reichner, still filled with guilt. She'd used Brandon, there was no doubt about it. At Reichner's insistence, she'd taken advantage of Brandon's trust in her and had convinced him to stay. It hadn't taken much; he was already so scared, so vulnerable.

And he had no one else but her to trust.

She winced. Once again, someone had manipulated her, someone had used her to exploit another. It was an all-too-familiar scenario, forcing her back to memories of the fights with Samuel, his arguments for the abortion, how having a child would hamper her career. Sarah closed her eyes. Once again, she was feeling cheap and used and very, very dirty. And, once again, to ease the pain, she focused on her work.

In front of her were the monitors registering Brandon's heart rate, respiration, GSR, EMG, and the all-important EEG. During Sarah's childhood, her MD parents had often discussed the EEG craze. Back then, meditation and biofeedback were the talk of the town. Eventually interest died down, but not for the parapsychologist. In parapsychology, interest in the electroencephalograph and brain waves was still very high.

And for good reason. It was still an important gauge for measuring mental activity. The brain produces electrical current all the time, anywhere from .05 waves per second all the way up to forty. The frequencies of these waves indicate what type of consciousness we are experiencing. Generally, they fall into four categories:

The *beta* wave is the brain wave of highest frequency. When this wave dominates our mental activity, our minds are in high gear, concentrating, solving problems, having panic attacks. Next comes the *alpha* wave. It's strongest when we're in that daydreamy, half-awake state. Then comes the *theta* wave. It's strongest when our subconscious is functioning—when we're dreaming, or experiencing that inexpressible "nagging" feeling at the back of our mind, or suddenly solving a problem that we didn't even know we were thinking about. Finally, there is the *delta* wave. This is the slowest and most mysterious. It's been found to be strong in psychics, telepathics, and others who claim to be experiencing supernatural insight.

In her parents' day, when everybody was busy achieving "inner peace," alpha was the fad. But today, everyone from New Agers to Eastern mystics is focusing on theta and delta waves, the waves operating when the mind seems most susceptible to paranormal energy outside of the body.

Sarah stared at the EEG and frowned. Something wasn't right. She reached over and rapped the monitor.

"What's wrong?" Reichner asked.

"We have a malfunction." She motioned toward the screen. "Look how pronounced theta is. Something's overmodulating."

She reached behind the monitor, preparing to push the reset button, but Reichner shook his head. "No."

She looked at him.

"Let it go."

She pulled back, still looking at him. Did he actually think that Brandon could be generating that much theta, and in such a short period of time?

"That's very good," Reichner spoke into the mike with soft, velvety tones, "very, very good . . ."

Sarah glanced back at the screen. The theta started to shift, to decrease. She motioned to Reichner, who saw it and immediately spoke, "No, Brandon, don't listen to my voice, just feel it, make my voice a part of you. Let it guide you, help you keep your mind free, help you keep it nice and empty . . ."

Sarah watched. This part always made her nervous. She knew that a "free and empty mind" was essential in experiencing the paranormal. After all, the more empty your mind was of yourself, the more open it would be to other input from outside forces. Which was okay, she guessed, except—well, what assurance did they have that these outside forces were always good?

"Now, keeping your mind free and clear, I want you to tell me what you see, Brandon. Tell me what you feel."

Brandon's voice came back as a quiet whisper. "Peace."

"Good."

Sarah stared at the EEG. Now, the delta waves were starting to increase. This was remarkable.

"What type of peace, Brandon?"

"Waves . . . washing over me . . ."

"Any colors, sounds?"

"Wind—so quiet . . ."

Sarah leaned past the console to look at Brandon through the one-way mirror as Reichner quietly cooed, "Good . . . very good."

Brandon barely heard Reichner's voice. The waves of peace had completely enveloped him. He was deep inside them, floating, totally weightless. He was remotely aware that the wires and sensors were still attached to his head, arms, and chest, but he no longer felt them. He knew that he was still in the recliner back at the lab, but he was someplace else as well. Someplace beautiful and deep and crimson. The only sensation he felt was a soft breeze brushing against his face and a sound as gentle as wind stirring through pine trees.

At first he had been uneasy. Try as he might, he still couldn't shake the old woman's warning: *There is only one path. All others lead to the occult, to destruction.* Not easy words to forget, even if you didn't necessarily believe them. But in one sense he did. In one sense, he wondered: How different were all of these expensive machines and intellectual scientists from the crystal balls and sorcerers of old? Besides spending a few extra million dollars and investing a few dozen more years of schooling, weren't they in essence attempting to accomplish the same thing: contacting the spiritual world on their own terms?

The thought troubled him. But Sarah had promised that he would be safe. And there was the possibility of meeting Jenny again, of finding out what she was trying to tell him, of once again holding his little sister in his arms.

As Brandon floated, trying to push the fears aside and keep his mind free, he lost track of time. He didn't know whether he'd been there ten minutes or an hour. Then, finally, through the deep crimson, there was a glint of light. It came and went before he realized that he'd seen it.

There it was again. Piercing bright. A great distance away.

The wind picked up, blowing a little harder. With it, the sound also increased. But it wasn't really a sound. It was more like rapid, irregular puffs of air, like gentle whisperings. He had entered some sort of current. He could feel it pulling him—gently, yet persistently. And the more he gave himself over to it, the stronger it grew.

There was another glint of light, brilliant, and a little closer. Then another. And another, closer still. Yes, he was definitely moving. The current was drawing him toward the flashes. Directly in front of the light was a shadow, a silhouette. It looked human. He squinted, trying to protect his eyes from the blinding flashes, yet trying to see the form. He gave more of himself to the current and quickly picked up speed until, finally, he was close enough to make out that form.

It was a child. A girl in a white gown, her golden hair blowing in the wind. Although he was still some distance away, he immediately recognized her.

"Jenny . . ."

He watched as she reached into the folds of her gown and pulled out the lantern, the same one she had held out on the road. The same type that had been suspended by the lampstand in the foyer. This was the source of the light. It wasn't coming from behind her, but from inside her gown. Yet it was so bright that Brandon had to raise his hands to shield his eyes.

The current grew stronger and he moved faster. The sensation of speed began to frighten him. He wasn't sure why. After all, there was his sister, just ahead. He wanted desperately to reach her, to throw his arms around her, to hug her. But there was something holding him back. Maybe it was his fear of speed—or of giving up control.

Whatever the reason, he began to resist the current, turning his head, willing himself to slow. It proved to be harder than he had expected, but with great concentration he was able to retard his progress until he finally slowed to a tenuous stop. He turned toward her. She was a dozen feet away. He wanted so badly to touch her, to hold her—but he was afraid to give up control.

The current tugged and pulled, but he stood his ground. Part of him wanted to give in and be swept to her waiting arms. But he was simply too afraid.

As if understanding his fear, she raised her hand, the one holding the lantern. She held it out to him, offering to let him see it, to examine it.

Brandon looked on painfully. He wanted to trust her, he wanted to let go. But he couldn't.

The light grew brighter, the current stronger. But Brandon's panic only increased. He concentrated even harder to hold his ground. That's when he saw the hurt on her face. The pain of rejection. His eyes started to burn with tears. He wanted to call out, to explain that it wasn't her, that it was him, *his* fear, *his* cowardice. But no words would come.

Slowly, she withdrew the lantern.

Brandon's heart broke. He hoped she understood but feared she didn't. He watched as she lifted the lantern high above her head. Then, with great purpose, she released it. The lantern dropped, but it didn't shatter. Instead, when it hit the ground, it seemed to melt, to become a pool, a molten pool of light that began to churn and bubble upon itself.

Brandon and his sister stared as the light began to grow, horizontally as well as vertically. And the larger it grew, the more power it radiated. Now he understood. The light was the source of the current. As it increased in size and strength, so did the current. It pulled him even harder. He dug in, struggling to stand firm, to keep his balance.

The pool of light boiled, expanded—and the current continued to grow. Brandon fought harder. He looked back at Jenny, pleading for her to help, to make it stop.

She watched in quiet sympathy but did nothing.

The molten light was much bigger now, taking shape, forming a huge, growing rectangle that looked like some sort of doorway. A doorway that now towered high above him.

He turned away, trying to break free, to fight his way out of the current. His feet slipped once, twice. He was losing ground. He was being dragged toward the opening. He twisted and stretched, fighting with all of his will to break free of the current, until finally, with the greatest concentration—

Brandon's eyes exploded open. They darted about the room. He was back in the lab, back in the leather recliner. He was covered in sweat, trying to catch his breath, but he was back.

"If there was so much 'peace,' why did you resist?" Reichner demanded as he paced back and forth in the lunchroom. "Why did you pull away?"

Brandon sat at the table, staring down at his coffee, looking weary and shaken. Sarah stood nearby, feeling no better than Brandon looked.

"You said it was fear," Reichner said, crossing back to him. He leaned over the table. "Fear of what? Fear of the power? Of the intensity? Fear of what?"

Brandon remained silent. Finally he shrugged. "I was losing control. I don't like . . . losing control."

Reichner slammed his hand on the table and turned. Sarah was able to catch his eye and frown.

"He was there!" Reichner argued. "We were at Threshold. He even had his spirit guide."

Sarah nodded and looked down. Of course, the man was right. It was a shame to have gotten so close and not pressed on. But they'd already pushed Brandon so far.

In exasperation, Reichner turned, then stormed out of the room.

Sarah looked up in surprise. This was a first. Reichner never lost control. He always won his arguments and he never, *never* gave up until he got his way. But, at least for now, it appeared that he had failed on both accounts. She glanced at Brandon, impressed. This young man affected people in surprising ways.

Silence hung over the room. She wanted to say something, to let him know it wasn't his fault, that his fear was a natural response. She also wanted to let him know that if anybody was to blame, it was her. She shouldn't have pushed, she shouldn't have manipulated him to stay. She wanted to say all of this and more, but wasn't sure where to begin.

Fortunately, he saved her the trouble. Picking at the Styrofoam cup in his hands, he asked, "Has this sort of thing happened before?"

She nodded. "In other studies, yes. But never with us."

More silence.

She still wanted to apologize, to somehow make things better. "Listen, uh . . ." She cleared her throat. "It's getting late. Do you want to catch a bite to eat or something?"

He shrugged. "It wasn't that big of a deal." Then, pushing the cup aside, he started to rise.

"No," she said, "it was. A big deal, I mean." He looked at her and she held his gaze. "I'm sorry, Brandon. We had no business putting you through that, and I'm—well, I'm just very sorry."

She glanced down. She could feel him still looking at her. She hoped he could sense her sincerity. She swallowed and finally looked back up. "What do you think? How does—uh, do you like pizza?"

He kept looking at her.

She smiled nervously. "I might even spring for an extra topping."

Then, slowly, a trace of a smile began to spread across his face.

CHAPTER 10

So with scholarship in hand, I left for Stanford vowing never to set foot in Portland again, at least until I was rich and famous."

"And you chose science," Brandon said, his eyes never leaving hers.

She laughed self-consciously. "I wasn't sure whether I wanted to find the cure for cancer or the purpose to man's existence. But since I hate little white mice . . ." She threw him a grin. He nodded but didn't smile back. She took another sip of Chianti. It was her third glass of the evening. It had taken that many just to loosen up around him.

"I guess some people—well, some people would say I might be overly ambitious," she heard herself confessing. "I don't know. Just because I plan on winning a couple Nobel prizes before I'm thirty . . ." She gave another self-conscious chuckle. It wasn't the entire picture. She could have talked about the baby, about her need to keep pushing, to keep driving until his death counted for something—but that was a part of her no one was allowed to see. Ever.

She took another sip of wine and avoided Brandon's eyes by glancing around Eddie's Pizzeria. It was dim and smoke-filled—mostly Townies putting down the brews after a hard day at the drill press or wherever they worked. She and Brandon had just finished off a medium Canadian bacon with pineapple (his choice) and, thanks to the Chianti, she was doing most of the talking. Still, she found herself being drawn to him.

She watched as he caught the waitress's attention and motioned for another Pepsi. Even that intrigued her. She'd figured him to be more of a drink-beer-until-you-drop kind of guy. And yet, here he was, ordering a soft drink. Such a paradox, so full of contradictions—like a man caught between two worlds, not completely fitting into either.

He looked back at her. She smiled. Maybe a bit more flirtatiously than she had intended. Still, it was her third glass.

"What about you?" she asked. "Didn't you ever want to be famous, make a name for yourself?"

Brandon shrugged. "I do all right."

"Terrorizing Techies?" She smiled at her barb.

He frowned, then understood and returned the smile. "It's a thankless job, but—"

"—somebody has to do it." They finished the phrase together and chuckled. It was the second time she had gotten him to smile, and she liked it—the way his face lit up, illuminating their corner of the room. They were starting to connect. At least she hoped so. But he still hadn't answered her question. Instead, he had looked away. This time he was the self-conscious one. And she liked that even better.

"Well?" she asked, waiting for a response.

He shrugged. But she didn't intend to give up until she got an answer.

Finally he cleared this throat. "As a kid, way back when I was little, I always wanted to be . . ." Again he looked away. "I always wanted to be kinda like a pastor."

Sarah nearly choked on her drink. Fortunately, the words were coming so hard for him that he barely noticed. "It just seemed like, you know, the right thing to do. I mean, my dad was a pastor, and his dad before him. It just seemed . . . it seemed good."

He looked back at her.

"What happened?" she asked, a little softer.

He took a breath and slowly let it out. Sarah listened intently.

"I'm not sure," he finally said, "but somewhere along the line I started to learn the truth. About Santa Claus, the Easter bunny—and God." He swallowed hard, looking everywhere but at her. "I tried. God knows how I tried. But there was . . . nothing. Nothing I could believe in anymore, nothing I could hang onto, nothing I could see . . ." His voice trailed off.

Sarah watched silently. There was deep water here, far deeper than she had guessed. She wanted to reach out and touch his arm, to tell him it was okay, that she understood. But she didn't trust herself, she didn't trust the wine. Instead she quietly offered, "Maybe—maybe that's what faith is all about. Believing in something, even when you don't see it." He looked at her, and she shrugged. "Not that our generation is terribly fond of believing in anything."

He nodded, musing.

They'd found another point of contact, and she pursued it. "What is it about us? Why are we always so afraid? I mean, half of my friends are still in graduate school because they're afraid to get out into the real world."

Brandon spoke slowly. "Maybe we've just been lied to by too many people."

Sarah nodded. He was right, of course. They were the ones raised by parents with broken vows, politicians with broken promises, and ads with impossible claims.

Another pause settled over their conversation.

Sarah resumed. "You know, you talk about faith. In a lot of ways, science and faith aren't that far apart. I mean, we're both asking the same questions: Why are we here? How did we get here? And most important, who or what is responsible?"

She glanced at him, but he was looking away again.

"I guess, in some ways, that makes me no different from your dad, or the local rabbi, or some Tibetan monk—we're all out there searching for some sort of God, some sort of Absolute."

He looked back at her, that penetrating look, the one that made her weak inside. She forced herself to continue. "Science doesn't have to be religion's enemy. In some ways it can actually be an ally in proving faith. I mean, look at the study they did at San Francisco General Hospital."

He stared.

"You've heard of it, right?"

Apparently he hadn't.

Her words came faster. After all, this was her work, this was where she felt safest and most secure. "The director of the coronary care unit agreed to put nearly four hundred patients on two lists—those who were to be prayed for and those who were not. A quarter of a mile away, a group of evangelical Christians prayed for the patients on the first list without either the patients or their doctors being aware of it. The study lasted ten months. During that time, the patients who were prayed for showed a significant decrease in congestive heart failure, fewer incidents of pneumonia, less need for antibiotics, and fewer cardiac arrests."

"This was an official study?" he asked.

She nodded. "Published back in '88."

He looked away, thinking.

But she wasn't finished. "Then there's the 1995 study at Dartmouth Medical School, where they discovered that the most religious of those who underwent heart surgery were three times more likely to recover than those who were not religious."

He looked skeptical.

"No, I'm serious," she insisted, "these were all legitimate studies. And there are plenty more, each and every one verifying the power of faith and prayer."

She took a sip of wine. She knew she'd become too chatty, but she didn't particularly care to stop.

"I'm not saying you have to believe in God. I mean, look at me. For me it's science. I've given everything I've got to science, poured my whole life into it. And I'm going to make a difference. You know why? Because I'm committed, because I believe. That's the whole point. You've got to believe in something, Brandon, otherwise your life will never have any—" She searched for the word. "I mean, everything will just keep on being so . . ."

"Pointless?" he asked.

"Exactly. Pointless. Otherwise your life will continue to be pointless, a waste with no meaning or purpose to—" She suddenly stopped. Even in her flushed state, she saw the pain cross Brandon's face. What had she said?

"Listen," she stammered, "I didn't mean to imply that your life doesn't have—you know, that it's a waste or anything like that."

But Brandon was already looking off and away. She'd hit a nerve and hit it hard. She reached out and touched his arm. "I didn't mean—"

"No, that's okay," he said, shrugging, pretending it didn't matter. "You probably have a point. I mean, I know you have a point."

She watched as he struggled to find the words. Why had she done that? They had been connecting so well, they had really been—

"Brandon! Hey, Brandon!"

She looked up to see two young men, the ones she had met with Brandon last week at the Club—a shorter kid with thick glasses and a taller, almost good-looking one. It was the taller one who had called out to them. "Well, well, well, what do we have here?" he asked as he sauntered over to the booth.

Brandon nodded. "'s up, Frank?"

"Not much. At least for me." Turning to Sarah, he smiled. "You're lookin' real good tonight, Sarah."

She nodded, trying unsuccessfully to cover her distaste.

"Hey, Bran." The shorter one in the glasses nodded.

"Del."

"Haven't seen you at work," Frank said as he reached for the remainder of Brandon's drink. "Everything okay?"

Brandon nodded. "Couldn't be better."

"Yeah?" Frank raised the glass and chugged down the rest of the soda. Brandon threw an embarrassed glance at Sarah.

"Great," Frank said, finally coming up for air. "'Cause, if you recall, we've got ourselves a little vendetta to settle with the Techies." Turning to Sarah, he added, "No offense, of course."

She didn't respond. He turned back to Brandon. "It's been almost a week now, and people are startin' to talk. I figured since—"

"Not tonight, Frank."

"No, I don't mean tonight. But it oughta be soon. I mean, we got our reputation to keep up, right, ol' buddy?"

Brandon said nothing.

"So you just think up somethin' real good." Then turning to Sarah, he explained, "Brandon here, he's a genius at comin' up with ideas." He held out his index finger to Del, who took it and pulled while Frank released a giant belch.

Brandon lowered his eyes and stared at the table.

"You just let me know when," Frank said, preparing to leave, "and I'll grab us some brew and away we go." Turning to Sarah, he added, "You're welcome to come too, if you want."

"I think I'll pass." Her words carried an intentional chill.

"Suit yourself, but it's gonna be good times."

Neither Brandon nor Sarah responded.

"Well, all right then. You kids take care." Frank turned, gave Del a nudge, and the two of them headed for the door. "Have a good night," he called, "and don't do anything I wouldn't do." He let out a cackle of laughter and disappeared into the crowd.

An embarrassed silence fell over the table. When Sarah finally looked at Brandon, he was scowling hard at his glass.

Lewis stood on the back porch of the farmhouse, pressing himself against the wall. The kitchen window was directly beside him. It was open, and he could hear the woman washing dishes less than six feet away. She was humming to the radio—country gospel. His heart pounded. Hunger and desire throbbed all the way into his hands.

SLAUGHTER . . . KILL . . .

This was the place. The voices had told him. The impostor lived here. And, as soon as he was destroyed, Lewis could enter into his season.

SLAY . . . MUTILATE . . .

He'd parked his bug down at the end of the lane. This sort of thing wasn't new to him; he'd done it lots of times—sneaking up to people's homes and spying. Even climbing up on their roofs and watching when they thought no one could see. Like Mrs. Cavanaugh, the vice principal's wife. Or some of the girls from high school. He smiled to himself. If they had only known.

The lady began to sing. His smile twisted into a contemptuous sneer. So stupid and unsuspecting. Singing as her executioner lurked so near.

He turned and eased closer to the window until he could see through the screen and inside. He caught glimpses of her head as she moved back and forth. If she looked up at the right time, she would see him. What a delightful scare that would be.

He reached down to his belt and silently unsnapped the sheath to his hunting knife. He could break through the screen in a second. He inched closer, until she was in full view. If she would only look up. His fingers danced along the knife handle. If she would only look up, then scream in terror, and he would lunge through the screen and grab her, pulling her out, kicking and screaming and—

"NO!" the voices screamed. *"THE IMPOSTOR, THE IMPOSTOR . . . DECIMATE, MUTILATE, KILL! THE IMPOSTOR . . . THE IMPOSTOR!"*

But where? Where was this impostor? If he couldn't find the impostor, then taking out this lady would be next best. And it would help silence the voices, and it would—

"THE IMPOSTOR . . . THE IMPOSTOR . . . THE IMPOSTOR . . . THE IMPOSTOR . . ."

Reluctantly, Lewis removed his hand from his knife.

The back door was open, just ten feet away. He ducked below the window and silently crossed toward it. He was practically there when he noticed the shadow—

a man's shadow. It was the impostor, he was certain of it. He was sitting just on the other side of the screen door.

ANNIHILATE . . . SHRED . . . TEAR . . .

Lewis's heart pounded harder. Barely able to contain his excitement, he inched along the wall.

SLICE . . . RIP . . . RAVAGE . . .

He was breathing heavily now—the exhilaration growing out of control as he reached the edge of the doorway.

SLAY . . . KILL . . . DESTROY . . .

He remembered, from their encounter at the church, that the impostor was strong. He would have to surprise him. But he could take him. With the help of the voices and the knife and the adrenaline, he could—

The woman spoke, but he couldn't hear her words. His voices were screaming, one on top of the other, writhing, shrieking, swearing. They were pulling him under, demanding complete control of his body. They could have it. In just a moment, they could have it all. Just let him taste the kill first, to experience the thrill, and then he would turn it over to them.

He reached for his knife and pulled it out.

He crouched beside the door, preparing himself, his heart pounding wildly. He took two gulps of air—and then he sprang.

He threw open the screen door and leaped inside. But he was wrong! It wasn't the impostor! It was some old-timer in a wheelchair. Lewis dug his feet in, aborting the attack. The screen door slammed behind him. The woman screamed. A dog upstairs started barking. He could take them out, he could take them all out. But between the shrieking voices, the screaming woman, the dog, the man, Lewis froze. Then the panic struck. He turned. He staggered back into the door, shoving it open, stumbling off the porch, and running into the night.

He ran until he reached his car. Then he was inside, firing it up and racing for home. The voices screamed louder than ever. Degrading, belittling, demanding, all-consuming. He had to stop them. He would stop them. Someone had to die. It was the only way. And it had to be soon. Very, very soon.

Sarah glanced at her watch. It was nearly eleven when Brandon pulled up to her condo. Forty minutes had passed since she'd made the crack about his wasted life. Although he'd done his best to hide it, she could tell that she'd hurt him. And the visit by his two buddies hadn't helped any. He was distant now, aloof. Once again, he'd retreated into himself.

The car came to a stop and she turned to him. "Are you all right?"

He nodded.

She wanted to say something more, but she'd obviously done enough talking for one night. Then, to her surprise, he spoke.

"I was thinking. Maybe we should go ahead and continue that test. You know, see what's on the other side of that Threshold thing."

Sarah shook her head. "No, Brandon. We shouldn't have pushed you. That was my fault, I shouldn't have—"

"No, no. It's not you."

She looked at him.

"It's me. Maybe—maybe there is something I can do."

She watched him carefully, not sure what he meant.

"Maybe I can—you know, give you guys a hand with whatever you're trying to find out. I mean, if you really think it could be helpful to you . . . and to others." He forced a smile. "At least it would be a change from terrorizing Techies."

"Listen, Brandon, what I said back there, I didn't mean—"

"What about tomorrow?" he interrupted. "Is that—would that be too soon?"

"Tomorrow?"

He nodded. She searched his face. "Are you sure?" she asked. "I mean, is this something *you* want to do?"

"Tomorrow's okay, then?"

"We can make whatever arrangements you want, but I don't think—"

"Then I'll see you tomorrow."

She hesitated. "Brandon . . ."

For the first time since they'd stopped, he looked at her. There was that connection again. Deep, resonating. He smiled, a little sadder this time. Her heart swelled. When she wasn't intimidated or offended by him, she was moved by how vulnerable and sensitive he could be. The feelings were strong, stronger than anything she'd felt since Samuel. And since it was getting late, and since they were connecting so well . . .

"Listen," she said, "would you like to, you know, come in for a while?"

He looked at her, and immediately she knew she'd stepped over the line. He was a preacher's kid, for crying out loud. The same one who didn't drink, who went to church, who as far as she could tell didn't even swear. He may have lost his faith, but there was still something there, something innocent, almost naive. She glanced away, feeling a little embarrassed.

But his answer came without judgment. "Thanks, but I better get going."

She nodded. What had she been thinking of? Besides, he was just a kid and a lab subject, to boot. She knew better than to get personally involved with her work. "Of course," she said. "I understand." She reached for her door and opened it. "We'll see you tomorrow, then."

He said nothing as she climbed out. And then, just before she shut the door: "Sarah?"

She turned to him. He struggled for a moment, obviously trying to put his thoughts into words. But apparently they wouldn't come. Instead, he settled for a simple "Thanks."

She nodded, not entirely understanding. "Sure." And then she shut the door.

He dropped the truck into gear and pulled away as she pretended to head for the condo. But she'd gone only a few feet before she turned and watched the pickup head down the road. She stood there silently, not moving, until it disappeared into the night.

Brandon eased the truck into its usual spot between the house and the barn. It was eleven twenty-five when he turned off the ignition and stepped into the hot, night air. The heat wave hadn't let up. Thirty-six days without rain, and by the looks of things it would soon be thirty-seven. He quietly closed the cab door and paused to stare up at the night sky. Sarah had awakened something in him. He could feel it. Actually it was many things. But mostly it was a type of . . . hope. Was it possible? Could his life really have some sort of purpose? Could it really have meaning again?

He walked across the driveway toward the house. The grass and gravel were bathed in the blue-white light of the mercury vapor lamp mounted on the barn. He was emotionally exhausted, but his thoughts spun and tumbled and churned. Not only about Sarah and the hope she offered, but also about tomorrow's experiment—and about Jenny. After all, Jenny had been there, too, coaxing him, urging him forward, encouraging him to cross Threshold.

Then he was back to Sarah. How he envied her clarity, her sense of purpose. Not like Frank or Del. *Terrorizing Techies.* He shook his head. Truth be told, that really had been about his only reason for existence. Until now. Maybe he really could contribute something.

A moment later and he was back to Jenny. She had looked so loving and understanding. Of course, she'd always been sweet, everyone's favorite, but could it be that she'd actually forgiven him?

Other memories tumbled in, fragments he'd never be able to forget. His speeding car, her begging him to slow down, his laughter. The oncoming headlights. Her scream. The car sliding out of control. More screaming. Then the flipping and everything flying and her screaming and the car hitting the tree and the sickening explosion of glass and crunching metal—and the sudden end of her scream. Forever.

Brandon slowed as he moved up the porch steps. He'd had no idea how tired he really was. He was surprised to see the door closed. In this heat, they kept the windows and doors open all night. He opened the screen. A large manila envelope rested against the back door, his name scrawled across it in a large, unsteady script. He bent and picked it up. Studying the writing, he pushed on the door to find that it was locked. That was odd. They never locked the doors. He glanced at the carport. The van was there; they were home. He reached into his pocket and pulled out his keys.

A moment later he was upstairs. After silently checking to make sure his folks were okay in bed, he entered his room, peeled off his T-shirt and waded through the obstacle course of dirty clothes, car magazines, and, of course, Drool. For whatever reason, the old animal loved to sprawl out directly in his line of traffic. Brandon collapsed onto the bed, snapped on a light, and opened the envelope.

Inside there was a large pack of papers. He pulled them out. On top was a letter written in the same handwriting as the envelope. It read:

Dear Eli:

I drew these the week of your birth.
I hope you find them helpful.

Your servant,
Gerty Morrison

He recognized the name and fought back a wave of uneasiness. The memory of the fight outside the church two nights ago was still fresh in his mind. He hesitated, too exhausted to continue, too curious to stop. He pulled aside the letter to look at the first sketch.

The paper was yellowed and the pencil work smudged. Portions were faded and worn away from age. But there was no mistaking the subject. It was Brandon. Exactly as he was today, complete with long hair, T-shirt, and worn blue jeans. He glanced at the initials in the lower right-hand corner. *GM.* Gerty Morrison. And beside them was a date—it looked like 1976.

He hesitated. Was it possible? Had she really seen this image of him, just as he was today, way back in '76? He frowned and slowly pulled the paper away to look at the next. It was equally yellowed and aged. It was a sketch of a younger Brandon, on his sixteenth birthday. He was grinning and standing beside a used Toyota Celica, his first car, a gift from his father. It was also the car he had killed Jenny with. His eyes shot down to the corner to see the same initials and the same date: 1976.

He swallowed and pulled the sketch aside to reveal the next. In it he was thirteen years old and holding his newborn sister.

He closed his eyes. A dull ache spread through the back of his skull. He pulled the sketch away to look at the next. He was seven and holding another birthday gift: little puppy Drool.

Then the next. Age four.

Then age two.

Age one.

Until, finally, he was staring at a sketch of himself as a newborn. He was at the church, being held by his parents. They looked so young, so proud. And hovering over them, dominating the picture, was the cross. The very one that had tormented him for so many years. Brandon took a long breath and slowly let it out. His head pounded mercilessly.

He looked back down to his lap. There was one sketch left. It was different from the others, larger and folded in half. He reached for the edge of the paper and slowly pulled it back.

Near the left side of the drawing was the lantern, identical to the one Jenny had been holding, identical to the one he'd seen outside the sanctuary doors. He continued pulling, slowly revealing the picture bit by bit, until he saw an olive tree, also like the one at the doors. He faltered. For a moment he could go no further. Whatever was there, he didn't want to see. Whatever she had drawn, he didn't want to know.

Yet his hand continued to pull until the entire picture came into view.

It was of an older Brandon. Older than he was today. He stood in an ancient walled city. His head had been shaved, and he was wearing some sort of burlap robe.

Brandon looked at himself, nearly forgetting to breathe. The eyes were wild and intense, staring directly at the viewer. And the mouth—his mouth—it was opened in a primeval scream, so realistic that he could practically hear the sound. And out of it—out of his mouth roared flames of fire, *exactly* as they had in his vision outside the church.

Brandon sat paralyzed, unable to take his eyes from the sketch. The shaved head, the crazed eyes, the mouth, the flames—it was more than he could absorb. His head was ready to explode. He closed his eyes, forcing the moment to pass. But when he reopened them, everything was the same.

He needed help. He needed to talk to someone. With resolution, he threw his legs over the side of the bed. The sketches tumbled to the floor. He bent, scooped them up, and headed for the door.

A minute later, he was back in the pickup driving toward Sarah's. He wasn't sure what he was going to do when he got there, but he needed her, he needed her clarity of vision, he needed her understanding. He needed her presence.

He arrived in town and headed for Sarah's street. He approached the corner to her condo and rounded it. That was when he saw the jogger. A woman right in his path, too close to miss. He slammed on the brakes, swerving hard, but he was going too fast. Just before impact, she spun around and he saw her face.

It was Sarah.

She raised her arm and screamed as his left front bumper caught her leg and threw her up onto the hood. She rolled and slid across the metal, her expression frozen in horror as she hit the windshield—

Brandon bolted up in bed. His face was wet and he was breathing hard. The sketches lay scattered all around him. He wanted to curl into a ball, to make it all go away. But he knew it wouldn't. And he knew, more than ever, that he needed Sarah's help. He threw his feet over the side of the bed and slipped on his shirt.

Downstairs in the kitchen he flipped through the phone book until he found her name. Still shaken, he reached for the wall phone and dialed her number. Was the dream a premonition? Like the factory accident? Was something going to happen to her as well? He had to talk to her, she had to be warned.

The phone rang seven times before he hung up. Where was she? He hesitated, afraid to take the next step. But this was Sarah. If anything were to happen to her . . .

He stormed out of the kitchen and jumped into the pickup. It started noisily. He slipped it into gear and headed down the lane. He didn't understand the dream, didn't know whether it was like the one at the factory or like the others that made no sense. But he had to make sure she was all right.

He sped down the road, mind whirling, driving on autopilot. The roads were deserted and he made good time. When he arrived at the final corner, the one he'd dreamed of, he slowed down, just to be safe. Tense and nervous, he carefully negotiated the turn—and suddenly, out of the blue, a woman appeared. He slammed on his brakes, trying to avoid her, but they were too close. The bumper caught her leg, hurdling her onto the hood. She slid across it, and just before her head smashed into the windshield, she turned, and he saw Sarah's face—

Again Brandon woke up. Sweating, fighting to catch his breath. His eyes darted about the room, fearfully trying to get his bearings.

Unnerved and shaky, Brandon eased himself from the bed. Several of the sketches tumbled to the floor. He made it out to the hallway and used the handrail for support as he moved down the stairs and into the kitchen. He grabbed the phone book off the counter, found her number, and dialed. It rang twice before she answered.

"Hello?" a groggy voice mumbled.

Brandon hesitated. He wanted to say something.

"Hello?"

Then ever so slowly, he reached down and pressed the disconnect button.

He replaced the phone and eased himself into the nearest chair. He would sit there until dawn.

CHAPTER 11

Brandon passed through the kitchen on his way to the truck. The room still smelled of the bacon, pancakes, and warmed maple syrup Momma had served earlier for breakfast. While he was eating, she had spoken of last night's intruder. Brandon had listened with concern, even insisted that she call the sheriff. Initially she had declined, saying that the young man wasn't as threatening as he was confused.

"In fact," she'd said, "when he ran off, he looked more frightened than *I* was!"

But Brandon had insisted, and reluctantly she had agreed.

That had been fifteen minutes ago; the sheriff was on his way. Now, Momma was upstairs making beds and Brandon was heading for the Institute. He didn't tell her where he was going; he knew she'd only be worried and scared. And the way he figured it, he was scared enough for both of them.

His father sat in the wheelchair, staring out the door, the early morning sun striking his face. Brandon started to squeeze past him, then hesitated. He paused a moment to look down. Finally, with great effort, he spoke.

"Pop . . ."

Of course there was no response. Brandon knelt. He glanced at the silver-and-turquoise watch he had given his father so many years earlier, the one Momma still insisted he wear, as if to prove he still loved his son. Once again Brandon hesitated. He knew the words would be difficult, but he also knew they needed to be said.

"It's been a long time, hasn't it?"

The man stared off into space.

Brandon swallowed. "You and me, we haven't done a lot of talking lately."

More silence.

"But you're always in my mind, somewhere—you're always there in the back of my mind. You, Momma, Jenny . . ." Brandon glanced away and swallowed again. This was harder than he'd thought. "I know—I know what a disappointment I am to you, Pop. And I don't blame you."

Before he knew it, emotion began to well up from somewhere deep inside. "Pop ... Oh, Pop ..." He tried to swallow it back, but it kept coming. "I'd give anything to bring her back. Anything."

His eyes burned. He blinked hard, but they continued to fill with moisture. Something had opened up inside of him, and he couldn't seem to close it. "I used to plead with God—when she was in the coma, I used to beg him, 'Take me! I'm the screwup, I'm the failure. Take me, not her.'"

Angrily, he swiped at the tears, but they continued to come. "I'm sorry," he whispered. "I'm so sorry."

And then, all alone in the kitchen with his father, Brandon did something he hadn't done since he was a little boy. He lowered his head and laid his face down upon his father's lap. "I'm sorry," he choked, his throat aching beyond belief, "I'm so sorry."

He lay there, for how long he didn't know. His father's hands were just inches from his face. He would give anything to feel them touch him, stroke his head, offer some sort of comfort.

But, of course, there was none. Not for him.

At last Brandon raised his head. Through blurry eyes he looked up at his father. "I'm not going to let you down," he whispered hoarsely, "not anymore. I'm going to make you proud of me, Pop. You, Jenny, Momma—I'm going to make you all proud."

His father did not reply.

Slowly, he rose to his feet, wiping his face with his sleeve. He started out the screen door. Then, hesitating, he turned back. "You don't have to love me, Pop." He swallowed. "But you won't have to be ashamed of me, either. Not anymore."

Once again there was no answer, and once again Brandon understood the condemning silence. Quietly, he shut the door behind him and headed for the pickup.

"Are you the woman who called?"

Gerty nodded and adjusted the large parcel she carried under her arm. The young man before her wore a dirty army shirt, worn jeans, and he sported a week-old stubble across his face. He opened the door wider; it creaked as Gerty stepped into the apartment.

The place was an electronics graveyard, Radio Shack thrown into a blender. Stacks of chassis lay here, gutted TVs there, pieces of stereos, cannibalized computers, circuit boards, transformers, half-empty spools of wire, monitors—all dumped and stacked throughout the dimly lit room. Gerty didn't recognize any of them, but she knew filth and squalor when she saw it. Empty pizza boxes, fast-food bags, half-crushed aluminum cans ... along with the distinct aroma of spoiled food, body odor, and a cat box that definitely needed to be emptied. At least she hoped it was a cat box.

The man kicked a pile of junk mail out of his path and crossed toward the dining-room table, which was covered in more circuit boards and monitors. He didn't say a word. Nor did Gerty as she followed. She wasn't intimidated by him, nor by his environment. Knowing that she was soon going home to her Lord did a lot to keep things in perspective. She was here for a purpose. And, regardless of its appearance, this was where she had been sent to accomplish that purpose.

The young man sat down before three large computer monitors. Two of them were glowing. There was no chair for Gerty, and he didn't offer one. To his immediate right sat a pile of magazines with naked women on the cover. Gerty glanced away, embarrassed. But she felt neither revulsion nor disgust for the young man. Only pity. And compassion.

He sniffed loudly and wiped his nose with his hand. "Did you bring the data?"

"Data?" she asked.

"The information you wanted me to enter."

"Oh, yes." She pulled the two-inch stack of papers from her arms—the letters she'd been writing, some new, some decades old.

He took them in his thin white hands and plopped them next to the magazines. Again her eyes caught a cover photo, and again she felt embarrassed. For the briefest moment she wondered if she had heard wrong. How could her Lord possibly want her to work with someone like this? He had promised her that her letters would be used for holy purposes. But here? In this place? With this man? She looked at him and was once again filled with compassion. Not her compassion. This was deeper. It was the Lord's. He was not looking at the boy's crippledness. He was looking past the sickness to a heart, a heart that he longed to heal.

Gerty smiled quietly. In all the years she had known him, her Lord had never changed. He was still drawn to the dregs of society, to the outcast, to those who knew they were sick. Yes, sometimes it was difficult for her not to judge, but if he had chosen *her*, with all of her weakness, then he could and would use anybody. Even this boy.

She nodded in silent awe. Yes, her Lord was good.

The young man carelessly flipped through her stack of papers. Each page had a date on top, followed by a few Bible verses, and then some insight or practical observation on how to apply those verses.

"These dates here at the top." The man sniffed and wiped his nose again. "That's when you want him to get them?"

"Yes. He'll soon be havin' a computer and those are the dates I want him to be readin' these letters."

"Kind of a timed-release thing?"

"I'm sorry, I don't understand your—"

"You don't want him to have access to all of this stuff at once. Just on the date you've written here at the top."

Gerty nodded. "Yes. They're lessons from the Bible, each one needs to be buildin' upon the next."

The young man gave her a skeptical look. "The Bible?"

She nodded.

He smirked, then riffled through the pages. "Sure got a lot here."

She sensed his hesitation. "The price you quoted me over the phone, it was—"

"The price I quoted you was to scan this stuff into the computer, then design a program that would release it to your boy through e-mail at the right time. You didn't tell me it was all handwritten."

"Will that cause a problem?"

"Take more time, that's all. I have to manually type in all of this junk with the keyboard."

Now Gerty understood. "How much more do you want?"

She watched as he ran his hand through his greasy hair. "I don't know. We're talking quite a few man-hours here."

"How much?" Gerty persisted.

He looked at her, gauging. "I'd say—probably an extra hundred and fifty, maybe two hundred bucks."

Gerty held his eyes as she reached down and opened her purse. She pulled out a wad of bills. It was the last of her money, but that was okay. She wouldn't need it where she was going. "There's one hundred and eighty-five dollars here. It's all I have."

He reached for the money. "One hundred eighty-five will be just fine."

But she held it firmly in her grip until his eyes again met hers. "You'll be typin' it in yourself?" she asked.

"Yes, ma'am."

"No one else? Just you?"

"Every word."

She nodded and finally released the cash. He took the wad and stuffed it into his shirt pocket. "I'll start on it right away," he said as he turned back to the computer.

Gerty stood in silence, once again feeling a faint smile cross her face. This was why her Lord had chosen him. And this was why, over the years, regardless of how absurd his requests seemed, Gerty had always obeyed. Because, when she obeyed, he always amazed her. Now she understood. As this lost young man typed in the holy Scriptures she had written, he would be exposed to their life-changing truths. Truths that would give him the opportunity to be healed.

Gerty's smile broadened. Yes, her God was good. He was very, very good.

Brandon lay stretched out on the leather recliner. He was wearing the Ganzfield goggles, and his face was bathed in the glow of the red floodlights. Dozens of fine wires ran to the sensors taped to his temples, eyelids, face, arms, fingertips, chest, back, stomach, legs, and feet.

He was in Lab One. The instruments in Lab Two were being recalibrated; they wouldn't be up and running until the end of the day. Reichner had refused to wait, so they were once again using the first lab, the one Sarah had been attacked in. The pieces of shattered one-way mirror had long ago been cleaned up, but its replacement hadn't yet arrived, so clear window glass had been temporarily installed.

Up in the Observation Room, Sarah kept a careful eye on the monitors and readouts. The heart rate, respiration, GSR, EMG, EEG, all were registering as before. Directly behind her, two DAT machines ran, one to record the multiple readings coming in, the other to serve as backup. This was too important to risk losing the records to a malfunction.

Reichner sat immediately to her left, speaking into the console's mike. As before, his voice was calm and soothing: "Like a leaf, Brandon. Like a leaf floating on the surface of a quiet pond."

"Yes." Brandon's answer was barely above a whisper.

"No thoughts . . . just quiet, gentle floating."

"He's reached level," Sarah said, motioning to the EEG. "Theta is up to where it was before."

Reichner looked at the monitor, surprised. They both glanced up at the digital timer. The readout glowed: 2:20.

Sarah blinked in surprise. He'd reached level in under three minutes—nearly four times faster than yesterday.

Reichner turned back to the mike. "Excellent. That's very, very good, Brandon. Now, Brandon, keeping your mind free and empty, I want you to search for that light again. I want you to find Jenny."

There was no response.

"Brandon? Brandon, stay with me."

Still, no answer.

"Brandon." Reichner's voice remained soothing but carried an edge of authority. "Brandon."

Sarah leaned forward to look through the glass. Down below Brandon's face registered the slightest frown.

"Brandon."

Finally he answered. "I don't see anything. I don't—"

"You're trying too hard," Reichner gently interrupted. "Relax. Let her come to you."

Sarah watched as Brandon took a deep breath and slowly exhaled. She knew he was trying to obey, to clear and release his mind. Again the thought made her just a little uneasy. And again she wished she could see and hear what he was experiencing . . .

Brandon floated in the deep, crimson void. There was no sensation, no up, no down, only the faint brushing of wind against his face and its gentle whispering in his ear. But it was more than wind. This time he recognized it to be something else, something tender, something encouraging, something—alive.

Then he saw the flicker. Like a welding spark. Just as bright as before, and just as brief. It happened again, but longer—a blinding shaft of light cutting through the emptiness. And with that light came the tug, the pulling of the current. He knew it was Jenny holding the light, and he knew if he gave himself over to the current, it would carry him toward her.

After a moment's hesitation he slowly began releasing his will. The wind increased; the current began moving him. There was another flash, a little closer. And then another as Brandon released more and more control to the current and began to pick up speed.

Another flash. Now he could see the light silhouetting a distant form. The form of his sister. His heart swelled as he drew closer. Soon he was able to see her features—her blonde hair blowing in the wind, her white gown—and, as he approached, the smile, that sweet, understanding, angelic smile.

As before, she reached into the folds of her garment and pulled out the lantern. Its brightness stabbed his eyes, forcing him to raise a hand and shield them. With the greater intensity of the light came increasing speed, and with the increasing speed his fear returned. Once again he began to resist the current, willing himself to slow. With all of his concentration and with great determination, he was able to decrease his speed until he came to a stop. The current continued to tug and pull, but he refused to go any further.

Jenny was a dozen yards away. Once again she held out the lantern to him. He knew she wanted him to approach and take it. But he couldn't. He hated himself for it, but he was still too afraid—afraid of coming any closer, afraid of giving in, of losing control.

She nodded, her eyes full of understanding. Then, as before, she raised the lantern high over her head and dropped it to the ground. It hit, and the light spilled out like liquid. As it spread into a large, molten pool, Brandon could feel the force of the current increasing, pulling him harder. The light churned and boiled upon itself, growing in width and height, until it formed the glowing rectangle that had towered over him the day before.

The current increased, and Brandon fought even harder to keep his footing. With rising panic, he struggled, exerting all of his will to resist being drawn in. Frightened, he looked up at the rectangle. It was solidifying, its liquid light turning into a doorway, the Threshold. The intense brightness dimmed slightly, as if the structure were cooling. Now he could see detail: intricate carvings on the pillars of the doorway, words and symbols he had never seen before.

And just inside the opening, waiting patiently, was little Jenny.

The gentle whisperings around him grew louder, clearer. They were voices, low and sustained, like singing.

And still the current increased, and still he resisted.

"Let it go, Brandon." He wasn't sure if it was Reichner's voice or the voices of the wind. "Let it go . . ."

He looked back at Jenny. So much love and compassion filled her eyes. This was where he had failed her before, where he had panicked, where he had shown his cowardice and stopped the experiment.

The wind and voices grew even stronger. He wanted to stop it; there was no need for him to cross through the Threshold. Let the Sarah Weintraubs of the world be the heroes, let them change civilization. Just let him continue to live his life of—he tried to block her words, but they came before he could stop them: *pointless.* That's what she had said about his life. *A pointless waste.*

She had been right. And yet . . .

Perspiration broke out across his forehead. He could still stop this, he *should* stop it. But what about Jenny? He looked up. She waited so patiently, so lovingly. And what about his father? And Sarah?

You've got to believe in something . . .

"Let it go, Brandon. Let it go . . ."

. . . a pointless waste, no meaning or purpose . . .

And his father. *"I'm going to make you proud,"* that's what he'd told him. *"I'm going to make you all proud."*

"Beware of the broader paths." Memories of the old woman's voice surprised him and did little to ease his fear. *"All paths but the Lord's lead to destruction."*

He closed his eyes, shaking his head. *"I have no faith,"* that's what he'd told her. *"I have no faith anymore."*

Pointless, a waste . . .

I'm going to make you proud of . . .

No meaning or purpose . . .

I'm going to make you all—

Other paths lead to destruction.

"Let it go, Brandon, let it go."

A waste.

"Let it go, Brandon . . ."

Beware of the broader—

You don't have to be ashamed . . . I'm going to make you—

Such ways lead to the occult. Beware of the—

No! Brandon's mind screamed. *No!* He turned his head, shutting off the old woman's voice, refusing to listen. With great purpose he forced himself to look back toward Jenny. It was time to end the cowardice. It was time to put aside his fears, to end the old way of believing. It was time to finally make something of himself. Slowly, with determination, Brandon raised his arms. There was one last moment of hesitation, of fear, and then Brandon Martus gave up his will.

The current immediately snatched him up, pulling him so quickly through the Threshold that, as he entered, Jenny leaped aside. She shouted as he passed, but he could not hear over the roaring wind.

Then, suddenly, instantly, it stopped—the current, the speed, the wind. Everything.

Now he was simply floating. In complete silence. Peaceful, serene silence. The towering doorway had vanished; so had its light. And as the quiet peace continued, his fear slowly began to ebb. It was then that he noticed the colors. Beautiful. Sparkling. As diverse as the rainbow, but many times more vivid. They were moving about him, gently brushing against his clothes, caressing his skin, his face, exactly as the wind had. In fact, they were the wind. Only now he could see them. And now he could clearly hear them—they were voices. Human. Human voices singing lovely, sustained chords.

He turned, searching for Jenny. At first he couldn't find her, and his panic began to return. Where was she? Had he left her behind? Had he—

And then he heard it. Gentle laughter. A little girl's giggle. Jenny's. He tilted back his head and saw her floating just above him, surrounded by the sparkling, dancing colors of light.

Brandon's heart leaped. He'd forgotten how much he loved the sound of that laughter. He smiled, reveling in it. What had he been so frightened of? Now, at last, after all these months, they were finally together.

As they floated, she motioned toward his stomach. He looked down and noticed a silver cord passing under his shirt. He pulled up the shirt to see that the cord was attached to his navel. How odd. It was like some sort of umbilical cord.

He looked back up at Jenny questioningly. She giggled and motioned for him to look for the other end, to see where it led. He obeyed and looked back down. To his surprise, he discovered that he was floating ten, maybe fifteen feet above the Observation Room at the Institute. Sarah and Reichner seemed completely unaware of his presence as they continued the session. The cord drifted above their heads, snaking this way and that until it dropped to the adjacent lab—the very lab where his body lay in the recliner.

Strangely enough, Brandon wasn't surprised at seeing himself. He'd watched this sort of stuff on TV, heard the stories of people leaving their bodies and hovering over themselves. Some thought it was a hallucination; others insisted it was their spiritual body looking down on their physical. It made little difference to Brandon. Not now. At last he saw the other end of the cord. It was attached to his *other* navel—the one in his physical body that rested on the recliner.

He looked up at Jenny. She had drifted several yards higher and seemed to be moving on, picking up speed. She motioned for him to follow. There was no fear now, and he nodded. By simply willing it, he started to move in her direction. But he had traveled only a few feet when he was suddenly brought up short. He looked back down to the cord. It had reached its limit and was stretched taut. Now it was acting as a tether, holding him back.

Jenny was moving farther away. She motioned for him to hurry. He noticed that the sparkling colors surrounding her were turning more golden in hue. The singing voices were growing louder, more pronounced. He had to do something. He hadn't come this far to be left behind. He reached for the cord, wondering if he could somehow disconnect it. He looked back up at Jenny. It was hard to tell from that distance, but it looked as if she was motioning for him to pull. Obeying, he placed both hands around the cord. Then he gave it a firm tug. There was no pain, no sensation of any kind, as it easily detached from him. He let it slip through his hands and watched as it fluttered back down toward the lab.

Sarah jumped at the sound of the alarm. Her eyes shot to the monitor. "Blood pressure is dropping!"

"What?" Reichner rolled his chair back to see for himself.

"Like a rock." Sarah scanned the other monitors. "So's his respiration, EMG. They're falling. Everything is falling!"

"That's impossible."

Sarah fought back the panic as she read, "Diastolic is 59 . . . 51 . . ."

Reichner spun back to the intercom button and hit it. "Brandon, Brandon, come back up."

"46 . . . 38 . . ."

Again Reichner spoke into the mike, less calm. "Brandon!"

Still no response.

Another alarm sounded. Sarah spun to the EEG. All of the brain waves were flattening.

Reichner leaped from his chair, sending it rolling backward. He headed for the door, took all three steps in one jump, and raced into the lab.

Brandon was free. Freer than he'd ever been in his life. But it wasn't just his body; it was his mind, his emotions, everything about him—clear, unbridled, free. He was picking up speed, moving faster toward his little sister. And, as his speed increased, so did the volume of the singing and the intensity of the lights surrounding him. They sparkled brighter, gently caressing his body as they slowly changed from the beautiful ambers and golds to deeper, more vivid hues of orange and red.

Above him, Jenny slowed slightly, waiting for him to catch up.

Although he could see no trees or clouds or sky, Brandon knew they were now outside of the Lab. They were someplace in the cosmos, someplace vast and deep and wondrous. Jenny hovered less than twenty feet away. As Brandon closed the distance, he willed himself to slow so that they would not collide. Gradually, his speed decreased.

When they were ten feet apart, she stretched out her hands, waiting for him. He did the same. Seven feet. Four. Finally, at last, he arrived. They stared into each other's eyes, drinking in one another's love and affection. It had been so long. But now, at last, they were together. And for the first time since her death, Brandon no longer felt guilt or shame or failure. Here, everything was forgotten. Forgiven. For the first time in his life, he experienced only love and peace.

The voices grew louder. The beautiful oranges and reds dancing about him were darkening to even more dramatic scarlets. But he barely noticed. All he saw was Jenny, her image wavering from the tears in his eyes.

She smiled, blinking back her own tears.

Moved by her affection, he reached out his hand to her cheek, to brush away one of the tears. His finger touched the moisture, the smooth skin—

There was a tremendous searing, like lightning ripping through air, like gristle tearing from flesh. And with that sound came the transformation. Instantly Jenny's nose grew, turning into a long, doglike snout, its jaw open and panting. Her eyes shifted higher onto her face, then narrowed. Her skin erupted, suddenly bristling with gray and black fur as her lips pulled back, stretching, curling into a snarl that exposed large canine fangs.

It was a wolf! Not Jenny, but a wolf. She had become a wolf!

Before Brandon could pull back, the creature snapped at him. Its razor teeth tore into his arm, ripping and pulling away flesh. Brandon screamed. The animal showed no pleasure, no remorse—only hunger, only a ravenous desire to destroy as it shifted its weight, preparing for another attack.

Brandon lurched away. The force threw him backward, tumbling, spinning, head over heels.

"Jenny!"

But there was no answer.

As he spun, out of control, he saw other changes. He was no longer floating in some peaceful sky. He was falling. Falling into a fiery void that grew redder and redder every second. And the sparkling lights escorting and touching him now had shape and form.

They were humanoid and they were on fire. They were burning cadavers, clinging to him, wailing in agony. These were the voices he had heard. Not gentle whisperings, not beautiful sustained chords but burning corpses, screaming in anguished torture. And they were falling. Falling into a bottomless, burning inferno.

Back in the lab, Reichner grabbed Brandon, shaking him hard. "Brandon!"

Sarah watched as other alarms in the Observation Room began to sound.

"Come back up!" Reichner shouted. "Come back!"

There was no response.

She grabbed the phone.

Reichner dragged Brandon out of the recliner, ripping off a dozen sensors in the process. "Brandon!" He slapped him once, twice, but there was no response.

Sarah watched the scene through the glass as she quickly punched in 911.

Reichner spotted her and yelled, "What are you doing?"

"I'm calling 911!"

"Don't be a fool!"

She looked at him, confused.

"They'll close us down!"

She could only stare at him in disbelief. The phone on the other end began to ring.

"Records!" he yelled. "They'll go through everything. They'll find out about Vicksburg. They'll shut us down!"

Sarah understood, but she didn't move.

"Get in here!" he cried. "Give me a hand!"

The phone continued to ring.

"Dr. Weintraub, I need you, *here!"*

The voice on the phone answered, "Emergency, 911."

"Sarah!" Reichner's eyes flared in anger.

"911," the voice repeated. "Are you reporting an emergency?"

Suddenly a loud drone filled the room. Sarah spun around to the heart monitor.

"He's flatlining!" Reichner shouted. "Get down here, now!"

She looked at the phone, hesitating.

"Now!"

Another moment's hesitation.

"Sarah!"

And then slowly, but decisively, she hung up.

"Come on!"

She ran out of the room and into the lab, her hatred and self-loathing already rising to new heights. As she entered the lab, Reichner was ripping off the boy's shirt. Buttons and sensors flew in all directions. She dropped near Brandon's face, preparing to give him CPR as Reichner placed his hands on the boy's chest and began to pump and count.

Brandon was covered in flames. The burning corpses continued to cling, clawing, shrieking for relief. Pieces of their flesh dripped and fell onto his own body, burning whatever they touched, igniting his clothes, his own skin.

"Jenny!" he screamed. *"Jenny!"*

Through his own cries and the tormented wails of the bodies around him he heard laughter, but it wasn't Jenny's. It was deep, guttural, malicious. He craned his neck and spotted the wolf through the flames. It was heading directly for him, laughing, its mouth opened wide, ready for the attack.

"My God!" he screamed. "Help me! Please, somebody—my God, help me!"

The plea snapped the wolf's head around. His laughter faltered. He was only yards away, moving in for the kill, but now he seemed uncertain, tentative. He began to search, looking one way, then the other.

That's when Brandon heard it. Another, entirely different sound. It began to overpower the shrieks and wailings. Mighty, all-consuming. Like the roar of a waterfall, but a thousand times greater. It increased, booming, thundering, roaring. Not only did Brandon hear it, he could feel it. It vibrated through his entire body.

Then he spotted something high above him. It was another light, brighter than anything he had ever seen, many times brighter than the sun. Instinctively he knew that it was the source of the sound. The wolf and the burning cadavers tilted back their heads, looking up at it with fear and awe. As it approached, Brandon could see that its sides were moving, rotating like wheels. But they were more than wheels. They were alive. They were covered in eyes—hundreds, maybe thousands of eyes—all-searching, all-seeing, all-knowing.

Although its appearance was terrifying, Brandon somehow sensed that it was good. More than good—it was pure. But with that purity came a dread. Not the dread he had experienced with the wolf, or the horror of the burning corpses. This was different. Deeper. Yes, it was terrifying. But terrifying in its awesomeness, in its power—and its unwavering, absolute perfection.

He watched as it slowly came to a stop. Everything around Brandon seemed to be waiting, but the light moved no closer. It simply hovered a hundred yards above them. It offered Brandon no help, no promise of rescue. Just its presence. And yet, somehow, that presence was enough. It began to stir something inside of him. An expectation. Somewhere inside of him a quiet hope and assurance began to swell and grow.

Maybe it was this assurance, or maybe it was simply having a point of reference, an idea of up and down. Whatever the case, Brandon once again willed himself to move—only this time upward, toward the light, toward the wheels of eyes. Of course it frightened him, and of course he knew that its power and purity could kill him. But death by goodness seemed far preferable to destruction by evil.

As he rose, Brandon felt the clinging, burning cadavers start to lose their grip. First one, then another, they began slipping away, falling with horrific screams back into the flaming void below. And the more that fell away, the more swiftly he rose.

He looked up. Although he was traveling faster, he never seemed to draw any closer to the rotating light. It seemed that the more quickly he rose, the more quickly it rose. In fact, it had kept the exact same distance from him as when he'd first started his ascent. He wasn't sure why, but he sensed that this distance might be for his own protection—that if he drew too close, its terrifying purity could indeed destroy him. And as far as he could tell, it had not come to destroy.

Off in the distance, he saw the laboratory approaching. But it wasn't below him as before. Now it was above him—thirty or forty yards *above* him. It was as if he were looking up through a glass floor. There was the recliner, the console, Dr. Reichner and Sarah kneeling beside his body trying to revive him.

But there was something else around his body as well.

A group of creatures. Grotesque, hideous things. There were nearly a dozen, and yet Sarah and Reichner seemed oblivious to their presence. Some were small, some big, but all were equally repulsive. They reminded Brandon of gargoyles, of the trolls and monsters from childhood books and nightmares.

They spotted his approach and immediately snarled and screamed at him. Some shouted threats and obscenities. Others waved their claws and talons menacingly.

All but two. These two were several feet taller than the others. They were clothed in brilliant, shimmering light that made it impossible for Brandon to make out any detail of their features. One stood near the head of his body, the other at his feet. They said nothing and made no movement, but there was a presence about them. A strength.

The last of the burning corpses fell away, and Brandon realized that he was no longer fighting to rise. He found himself in another current—but this time, a current pulling him into his body instead of away from it.

The creatures moved to block his path. They continued waving their claws, gnashing their fangs, screaming their obscenities—some in English, others in languages he could not understand. They did everything they could to intimidate him, to scare him away. But, even if he'd wanted to, he could not have stopped his approach now; he was moving too fast.

He raced toward them with increasing speed. He was going to crash into them, and there was nothing he could do to stop it. He raised his arms to protect his face—

Then, just before impact, just before he felt their claws and fangs tear into him, the two taller figures extended their arms. Effortlessly, they knocked the smaller creatures aside, making a clear and direct path for Brandon to reenter his body.

Reichner sat back on his legs and wiped the perspiration from his face. He had finally restarted the boy's heart. Sarah leaned forward and felt for Brandon's breath. He was breathing. A moment later his eyes shifted under closed lids. They rolled once, twice, and then opened.

Time passed. Ten, maybe fifteen minutes later Brandon was on his feet, pacing the lab.

"Be reasonable," Sarah argued. "At least have a doctor examine you and see—"

"No." He cut her off as he continued buttoning his shirt, preparing to leave.

"But it's for your own good," she insisted.

"*My* good?" His voice trembled in rage. "You nearly killed me, and it's for *my* good?"

She had to look away. It was true. Once again she had caved in to her guilt and ambition, once again she had allowed herself to be manipulated—this time at the risk of nearly killing him. What was wrong with her? Why couldn't she stop? Would the past ever let her go?

"Listen, son." It was Reichner's turn. "I know you are upset. But what we are uncovering here may completely redefine paranormal research. And not only that branch of science."

Brandon said nothing.

"Everything may change. Physics, our understanding of the brain, the soul, even our most rudimentary—"

Brandon turned on him. "Shut up! Just—shut up."

Reichner appeared unfazed. "We are in the midst of a major scientific breakthrough. You, Dr. Weintraub, myself—we could advance science by logarithmic leaps, and—"

"Science?" Brandon was livid. "This isn't about science. This is about *you.*" Reichner glanced away. Brandon spun toward Sarah. "It's so *you* can get your awards, your Nobel prizes. It's so *you* can prove whatever it is you think you've got to prove." His words cut deep. "That's it, isn't it? Isn't it?"

He waited, hovering just a few feet from her. She knew that he was waiting for an explanation, for her to defend herself. But when she looked up at him, there were no words. For a brief moment their eyes connected, looking into each other as before ... until Brandon broke it off. He turned and headed for the door.

"I never said my purposes were selfless." Sarah was surprised at how calm her voice sounded.

Brandon came to a stop but did not turn to her.

"I never said they were pure." She took a breath, then continued. "They may have exploited you, even hurt you—and for that I'm truly sorry. But—"

Before she could finish, Reichner interrupted. "But at least she has one. At least she has a purpose."

She threw him an outraged look, but he ignored her. He'd already sniffed out the boy's weakness, and now he was going for the kill. "But tell me, son. If you walk out that door, what exactly do you have? Hmm? What purpose? What reason do you have for living?"

Sarah turned back to Brandon. He was looking down. Somehow he seemed a little smaller, a little more lost. He stood a long moment, his back to them. Then, without a word, he walked out the door, never to return.

PART THREE

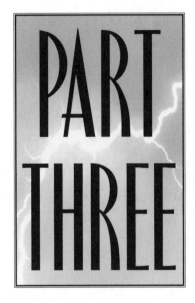

CHAPTER 12

Sarah knew it was only a dream. Nothing weird or paranormal—just churning bits of emotions. It started with another shouting match with Samuel. Of course it was about the abortion. Only now he was no longer Samuel. Suddenly he had become Reichner—using that same smooth logic, the same manipulative reasoning. Only now she was no longer in her apartment but lying helplessly on a table as he stood beside her in a surgical gown, poking and prodding inside her with the vacuum nozzle, trying to calm her with his cool, relaxing voice, assuring her that everything was okay, that it was all in the name of science, only somehow the nozzle was now inside her brain, sucking something from her mind as the vacuum machine grew louder, screaming with sucking air until suddenly she looked up to the clear surgical tubing and saw that it was Brandon being sucked through it, his face distorted in a scream, but instead of his voice it was hers, crying hysterically, trying to move but somehow paralyzed by Reichner's soothing voice until she could stand no more, and then—

Sarah awoke. She was breathing hard, and her cotton nightshirt clung to her damply.

Four minutes later she stood in the shower. It was only 5:30 Sunday morning. But that was late enough. It was time to get to work. She tilted back her head and let the shower rinse the shampoo out of her hair.

She'd felt something with Brandon—something she hadn't felt in years. Something had come back alive, and she had hoped that it would offer a reprieve, an escape from her prison. But she'd only fooled herself. There was no way out for her. It was the same song—the same guilt and driving ambition—only in a different key. It would always be that way. Gradually, week by week, month by month, it would continue to destroy her.

And two days ago it had nearly destroyed Brandon.

The shower took longer than normal. She felt a need to lather up again. She wasn't sure why, but she just didn't feel clean enough.

And somewhere, in the back of her mind, Sarah Weintraub guessed that she never would.

"'What profit hath a man of all his labour which he taketh under the sun? One generation passeth away, and another generation cometh: but the earth abideth for ever.'"

Brandon thought it was odd for the Reverend to read from the Bible this Sunday. He seldom did. But, after urging everyone to attend the farewell service that evening, and reminding them that the top religious leaders of the community would be there to show their respect, he had opened up to Ecclesiastes and was again demonstrating his impressive oratory skills:

"'The sun also ariseth, and the sun goeth down, and hasteth to his place where he arose.'"

But it didn't matter to Brandon. He was already zoning out—back in his pickup, sitting with Sarah, remembering how he had enjoyed her company and how for a brief moment she had given him hope.

"'All the rivers run into the sea; yet the sea is not full; unto the place from whence the rivers come, thither they return again.'"

And what about Jenny? What had happened to her? Why had she become a wolf? Is that what death did to you? Or was that thing Jenny at all? "Beware of seducers." That's what that old lady had said. "Keep your eyes open for counterfeits." Was that what she'd meant? Was that what he'd experienced—not Jenny, but a counterfeit? Was that whole experiment just another way of entering that dangerous region she'd called the occult? And if so, if she'd been right about that, then what about—

A gentle breeze stirred through the church. It caught Brandon's attention and drew him back to the sanctuary. The candles on the altar were flickering.

"'The thing that hath been, it is that which shall be; and that which is done is that which shall be done: and there is no new thing under the sun.'"

Directly above the Reverend, at the apex of the sanctuary ceiling, there was some sort of movement. Brandon looked up and watched as a gray, swirling mist began to form.

Brandon closed his eyes. But when he reopened them, the mist had grown larger and was taking a shape—slowly whirling into faces that twisted and melded into one another. The same swirling faces he had seen in the storm outside the church with Sarah.

"'There is no remembrance of former things; neither shall there be any remembrance of things that are to . . .'"

Again Brandon closed his eyes, this time clenching them tight, concentrating, trying to make the image disappear. When he reopened them he saw that he had at least stopped the thing's growth. Encouraged, he stared at it, trying by sheer concentration to make it go away. He scowled hard until, slowly, stubbornly, the cloud began to recede.

It was exhausting, but he would not stop. This was *his* life, and he didn't have to put up with this. He would deny these illusions, these intrusions. He would make them leave for good. Out of the corner of his eye he saw his mother turn toward him, cautiously watching. She took his hand, but he would not look at her, he could not look at her. Not until he forced the thing away.

"'And I gave my heart to seek and search out by wisdom concerning all things that are done under heaven . . .'"

The cloud continued to recede. So did the faces—until they were only a thinning mist, growing fainter by the second. A moment later, the wind slowed to a stop, and the mist was completely gone.

Brandon closed his eyes. He took a long, deep breath and let it out. He had won. It had taken every ounce of his will, but he had won. He turned to his mother; she gave him a questioning smile. He returned it, then directed his attention back to the Reverend.

"'I have seen all the works that are done under the sun; and, behold, all is vanity and vexation of spirit . . .'"

Reichner settled himself comfortably behind the expensive mahagony desk and turned on his home computer. It had been a good morning. Earlier he'd met a girl at Kroger's supermarket. Some pre-med college student. She looked barely twenty and came with all the accessories—good legs, a pert body, and long, gorgeous hair. Just the way he liked them.

Of course she'd heard of the Institute, and of course she was flattered by his attention—particularly when he commented on her strong ESP potential. She had declined his offer for dinner, but his persistent charm had eventually paid off. By the time they'd reached the parking lot, she'd agreed to stop by the townhouse with a friend, later that evening.

Things were getting back to normal.

Reichner logged on to his Internet server and opened his e-mail box. There was the usual correspondence: a handful of fellow researchers, a film producer who wanted to do a documentary, and some loony tune in Great Britain who needed his CD player exorcised. Reichner saved the letter from Nepal for last. He popped it onto the screen and started to read.

Doctor:

You have failed. He will no longer listen to you.

There was more, but Reichner had to pause. Not only was this a reference to the past encounter he'd had with the boy guru or python or whatever. But now the kid was speaking of events he couldn't possibly have known about. Not yet.

A lucky guess? Perhaps, but Reichner had his doubts. There really had been a young man in this area who really had proven to be exceptionally gifted. And now, just as the e-mail pointed out, Reichner had let him slip through his fingers.

If this was *remote viewing* that the boy guru was practicing, then Reichner had never seen anything quite so accurate. Granted, the U.S. military had trained and used remote viewers for decades. But they had only been able to observe physical sights like military installations, or specific events such as missile launches. They'd seldom if ever observed a situation involving relationships.

The letter continued:

> Perhaps he'll listen to one of his own. She could do more harm than good, but time is running out. Visit Gerty Morrison. Convince her to reason with him. Your window of opportunity is nearly closed, Doctor. If we lose him, you will pay.
>
> Eric

Reichner had no idea who this Gerty Morrison was but figured he could track her down easily enough, especially if she was local. But it was the last phrase that caught his attention. *"If we lose him, you will pay."* It seemed familiar, but he couldn't place it. Obviously, it was a reminder that if he failed, the Institute would suffer financially. But why did it seem so familiar? What about it—

And then he remembered. It was from his dream. The one with the python on his bed. Those were the identical words the thing had used as it had departed, just before Reichner had awakened with his heart beating like a jackhammer.

"But the important thing is, you were able to resist it," the Reverend insisted. "You were able to fight it off. And the next time it will be easier, and the time after that, easier still."

Brandon poked at the green beans on his plate. It was Sunday afternoon and, as happened at least once a month, the Reverend was over for Sunday supper.

Momma sat across from Brandon, lifting another spoonful of potatoes to her husband's mouth. "And with that determination," she said, "along with the help from your medicine, we'll finally be able to close this awful chapter once and for all."

Brandon watched as she slipped the spoon into his father's mouth and encouraged him to chew. Then he turned to the Reverend. "I have a question."

"Certainly."

"Weren't visions and dreams—didn't prophets, like in the Bible and stuff—didn't they have them?" He didn't miss the look between Momma and the Reverend before the Reverend cleared his throat and answered.

"The prophets were a long time ago, Brandon. And even if they did exist, we have no way of verifying whether they actually had such insights or whether their 'future predictions' were simply written *after* the fact."

Brandon glanced at his mother. Was it his imagination or was she doing her best not to look at the Reverend?

The man continued. "To believe in the miraculous or the supernatural today, in this age of scientific reasoning, well, I'm afraid those days of superstition and folklore have long passed. Yes, I know that doesn't agree with the latest trends and TV talk shows, but the supernatural has never been proven, Brandon—whether it's good or evil, it's never been proven."

"So what is there?" Brandon asked. "I mean if you don't believe in—"

"I believe in man. And his choices. What we choose to make of ourselves. Anything more than that is simply wishful thinking, striving after wind." The Reverend reached for a biscuit and broke it apart. "Now it's true there are many people who would take issue with that. Good, sincere people, like your father there."

Brandon looked at his father, who continued to chew and stare off into space.

"He was quite a believer in those early days, wasn't he, Meg?"

Momma nodded and turned to Brandon. "When you were first born, things got a little crazy around the church there for a while."

Brandon frowned, not understanding.

She continued. "Truth be told, we all got a little carried away. Some of us were even sayin' things like the world was gonna come to an end."

Brandon stared at her. "The world coming to an end?"

Obviously embarrassed, she reached for the green beans and began to dish up seconds. "It was all anyone talked about back then—how we were all supposed to be taken up to heaven, how the Antichrist was supposed to be comin', and how some end-time prophets were gonna rise up and fight him."

Drool, who had been asleep near the back door, suddenly lifted his head. The movement attracted Brandon's attention. The poor animal was so deaf he could barely hear, but now he was staring up at the ceiling. Brandon ventured a look and was grateful not to see anything. He turned back to his mother. "You said this all happened when I was born?"

Momma nodded. "Thereabouts. People thought they were havin' all sorts of visions, and prophesyin'. Some even believed there would be a major showdown right there inside our own church." She gave a nervous chuckle. "I'm afraid we definitely got a little carried away."

Brandon scowled. "Why didn't somebody—why didn't you ever mention it?"

Momma shrugged as she brought another spoonful of potatoes to her husband's mouth. "It's not really somethin' we're proud of, Sugar. Fortunately, it only lasted a few months. When nothin' happened, things finally settled down. 'Course your daddy here, he was always hopin' some of it was true."

Brandon looked at his father.

"And that's certainly no reflection on him," the Reverend interjected. "It's not every man who can start a congregation from scratch. But without the proper education, the proper checks and balances—well, something like this can spread through a church like wildfire."

Brandon turned back to the Reverend. "But visions and stuff, I mean, they could happen, couldn't they? I mean, what about all this talk about angels and the Devil—"

"Brandon," the Reverend gently interrupted. His voice was quiet, and he spoke earnestly from his heart. "You must believe me, son, these things just don't happen—not to the educated, not to the rational. And not to the . . ." He hesitated. "Not to the healthy."

Brandon searched his face. The man was sincere, there was no doubt of that. But before Brandon could continue, Drool suddenly broke into a fit of barking. All three gave a start as the animal lumbered to its feet.

"Drool," Momma scolded.

But the animal continued barking as it hobbled out of the kitchen toward the living room.

"Drool, come back here."

They exchanged looks, and Brandon rose to investigate. "Hey, fella," he called as he headed out of the room. He found the dog standing at the foot of the stairs looking up, barking.

"What's wrong, boy?"

More barking.

"What's the problem?" Momma asked, as she and the Reverend entered.

Brandon shook his head, then started up the stairs to see for himself.

"Could be a squirrel," she offered hopefully. "You know how they're always playin' on the roof outside our windows."

The dog continued to bark but remained at the foot of the steps, refusing to follow his master.

Brandon arrived at the top of the stairs and headed down the hall. Before him was the bathroom, his bedroom, his parents' room—and finally Jenny's. For some time now, Momma had been promising to clean out Jenny's room, to save a few mementos, maybe store the bed and furniture up in the barn. There had even been talk of turning it into a guest room. But Brandon knew that would never happen. She didn't have the heart. There were still those times, late at night, when he heard her slip into her little girl's room and have a quiet cry. It had been seven months since her death, and so far the only change had been that they kept her door closed.

Until now. Now it was open. Not by much. Just a few inches. But a few inches was enough. Brandon slowed his pace. He approached, carefully avoiding the floorboards that he knew would creak.

Downstairs, Drool continued his incessant barking.

"Brandon," Momma called. "Brandon."

But he didn't answer. He'd heard something. A tiny tinkling—breezy, far away. And the closer he approached, the louder it grew. It was music. One of Jenny's music boxes had been opened, and it was now playing a song.

He continued down the hall until portions of her room came into view—a canopy bed, her vanity. The afternoon sun struck the pulled window shade and bathed everything in a dim, ivory-yellow glow. As the melody grew louder, he began to recognize it. Something from one of those Disney movies she loved so much.

He caught a glimpse of her bookshelf, then the corner of the dresser. At last he arrived. He nudged the door open a bit further. There on the dresser sat the music box—glass with gold trim and a red rose etched upon the open lid. Other than the music, everything was completely still.

Against his better judgment, Brandon heard himself quietly whisper, "Jenny?"

There was no answer. Only the music.

He pushed the door farther until he saw the entire room—the stuffed animals on her bed, the ballerina poster, the dolphin mobile hanging from the ceiling.

He took a tentative step inside.

"Jenny."

And then another.

"Jen—"

It lunged at him from behind the door. He fell hard, crashing to the floor. Somebody was on top of him. In the dim light he saw the glint of steel—a knife coming toward his chest. He raised both hands and barely caught the wrist in time.

"Impostor!" a chorus of voices screamed.

Adrenaline surged through Brandon as he struggled to push the knife away. Now he saw the face behind it. Short red hair, goatee. The young man who had attacked him at the church.

Brandon squirmed, throwing his body hard to the left, then to the right. The kid toppled off, and for a brief moment the knife disappeared. Brandon struggled until he was on top. But only for a second. He was thrown off, flying through the air until his shoulder slammed hard into the dresser. He heard the popping and shattering of china dolls as they fell to the floor around him.

The attacker lunged again. Brandon rolled to the side, momentarily dodging him. He scrambled to his feet but was broadsided. They fell and rolled—Brandon on top, then underneath. The knife reappeared. Coming down hard, this time toward his face. Brandon jerked his head to the right and heard the blade thud into the wood an inch from his ear.

The voices swore and grunted as the attacker pinned Brandon's arms with his knees and yanked the knife from the floor. Suddenly the blade was high overhead, once again glimmering in the light. Below it Brandon could see the kid's crooked teeth, his leering grin. The knife plunged toward him. With his arms pinned, there was nothing he could do. Nothing but watch the blade and brace himself—until suddenly, the hand and knife were swept aside. Fur and fangs filled his vision as his attacker was knocked off.

Brandon kicked himself backward scooting out of the way as Drool tore into the man's hand, biting it, savagely shaking it.

The multiple voices screamed curses. The knife reappeared in the other hand. Drool continued growling and tearing into the first. He did not see the blade preparing to strike.

"No!" Brandon shouted. "Stop!"

The order startled the attacker, carrying more weight than any punch Brandon had landed. But it lasted only a second before the young man focused back on the dog. He raised the knife high into the air, and this time he brought it down hard.

The dog yelped in pain but continued to fight.

"No!" Brandon shouted again. "Stop it! Stop!"

Again the assailant turned to him, this time with confusion and fear. That's when Brandon understood. That's when he remembered what the old lady had said about his power. His authority.

"I command you—" He took in a gulp of air. "I command you to stop this!"

"You have no authority!" the attacker shouted.

Brandon searched his memory, trying to remember what the old woman had said, the phrase she had used. He had it. "In the name of Jesus—"

"You have no authority!"

"In the name of Jesus Christ I command you—"

"You have no authority! You don't believe! You don't believe!"

The accusation hit hard. Brandon faltered for a second, and a second was all it took. With a mocking grin, the attacker raised his knife high over the animal and drove it down again.

"No!"

Brandon's cry was lost in a thundering roar that filled his left ear; plaster exploded from the wall behind him. He spun around to see his mother standing at the door, holding a smoldering shotgun. Before either could speak the attacker leaped into the window. Glass shattered and the shade ripped away as he hit the roof, rolling and scrambling out of sight.

Glaring sunlight flooded the room. Out in the hall Brandon could hear the Reverend shouting, running down the stairs after the intruder. A moment's silence passed before Momma finally spoke, her voice shaking. "You all right?"

But Brandon barely heard. Drool lay less than a yard away, whimpering and panting.

"Brandon."

He pulled himself through the broken plaster and pieces of glass to the animal. Drool looked up at him, unable to move, eyes begging him to make the pain go away.

"Sweetheart, are you all right?"

But they were deep wounds. One in the chest, the other in the gut.

"Brandon? Sweetheart, are you okay?"

The boy dropped closer to the dog and wrapped his arms around him. There was nothing he could do. He thought his heart would burst as the big animal whimpered again, this time more faintly. With great effort and a slight groan it turned its head toward him. Then, finding Brandon's face, the dog began licking him. It was more than Brandon could stand. He lowered his head and buried his face in the animal's fur. He would not leave. He would stay with him until the end.

CHAPTER 13

Taking a break to walk down the hallway for a cup of coffee, Sarah was surprised to notice that the sun had just set. She'd been in Lab One all afternoon, carefully going over the data and results on Brandon Martus. The whole Martus affair may have been over, but a tremendous amount of ground had been broken, and it was important that someone transcribe and evaluate the information—if not for now, at least for future reference. Then, of course, there was the other matter, the one of her heart.

So far, today's work had revealed nothing new—just a review of the rapid drop of vital signs as Brandon had crossed Threshold, and of the sketchy accounts he had provided after their first session. Earlier she had brought up the PET scans and studied them on the monitor. Again, nothing new—just the pronounced stimulation of the right temporal lobe that they had originally observed.

She reached for her notebook and flipped through its pages. These were sporadic notations she'd taken from their conversations—information on Jenny's death, Brandon's vision outside the church, his dreams, the reaction of the multiple personality patient, and his mention of the old black woman who kept wanting to help him. Sarah paused at her name for just a moment, then reached for the envelope of her sketches that Brandon had brought in.

They were drawings of him in various stages of childhood, nothing unusual—except that the woman had supposedly drawn them all during the first week of his life. Then there was the last sketch, in which he stood in an ancient city wearing burlap and breathing fire from his mouth. Sarah studied the picture. If this woman had legitimate PSI, and if she had accurately seen into the future with this sketch as she had with the earlier ones . . .

Sarah flipped over the envelope to look at the front. It was old and previously used. The name and address of Gerty Morrison had been crossed out but was still legible. She grabbed her notepad and copied it down.

She looked over the other notes, the ones mentioning the factory accident and Brandon's precognitive dream four days before it had happened. Then there was his hallucination involving the young singer at church.

Again she stopped. Brandon's account of the teenage soloist at church had been shaky at best. But it was interesting that this teen and the factory worker were the only two people outside his family to appear in his visions. And if the accident at the factory had come true, then what about this girl?

Sarah hesitated. She didn't particularly want to call up Brandon. She wasn't even sure he would speak to her. But she had to try. Partly to satisfy her scientific curiosity—and partly because, if his vision was accurate, this girl could be in trouble.

Brandon stood in the doorway of his pickup, looking over the top of the cab. He carefully scanned the countryside for signs of danger as Frank and Del continued their shoveling in the back.

"We missed you, ol' buddy," Frank said. He was breathing hard, and for good reason. They'd been shoveling for over ten minutes; the bed of the pickup was nearly full. "Sure glad you're back in the saddle again."

Del, who was breathing even harder, leaned against his shovel a moment to catch his breath. "You've had some pretty classy ideas in the past, Bran, but this is definitely *Guinness Book of World Records* time."

Brandon nodded and continued to search the driving range and the parameter road for any signs of activity. "Just keep shovelin', boys," he said, "just keep shovelin'."

Sarah picked up the phone, dialed, and waited nervously as the phone rang on the other end.

"Hello?"

"Hello, Mrs. Martus? This is Sarah Weintraub. Is Brandon in?"

"No, he's, uh, he's out for the evening."

Sarah hesitated, unsure if she was hearing the truth. "Well, maybe you could help me. Do you remember that girl who sang the solo in your church last Sunday—you know, when Brandon had one of his 'spells'?" There was no response, and Sarah fumbled with her notebook to get the name. "A Lori Beth? Lori Beth Phillips?"

Again, no response.

"Mrs. Martus?"

"Yes."

"Would you happen to have her phone number—maybe an address?"

"Sarah ..." The woman cleared her throat. "Please understand, I appreciate your tryin' to help. But Brandon is much better now, and that's a part of his past I think we'd all do better to forget."

"I can understand that, but if you would just tell me—"

"I'm sorry, dear, but we've got the farewell service at the church tonight, and I'm already runnin' late."

"What about Gerty, the old black woman who—"

"I've got to go now, darlin', but thank you for your concern."

"Mrs. Martus, if you—"

There was a click on the other end, and for a moment, Sarah sat, puzzled at the woman's abruptness. Then she rose and walked to the shelf against the back wall. After some searching, she found the local phone directory and began flipping through the pages.

Hills are few and far between in northern Indiana. Fortunately for Brandon and the boys, Bethel Lake had a couple. Even more fortunately, one of them rose directly behind the Bethel Lake Country Club. It wasn't a huge hill, no more than a hundred, maybe a hundred and twenty feet at best. But in making room for their parking lot, the Club owners had cut away a good third of it, leaving an impressive fifty-foot ridge that dropped sharply toward the lot.

After taking the back way around a gate or two, Brandon had managed to drive the pickup to the top of that ridge. Now he maneuvered it backward until the rear tailgate was aligned over the parking lot below. He remained behind the wheel, keeping the motor idling, as Frank and Del piled outside.

"You sure they're there?" Del asked as he hoisted himself up and climbed onto the load.

"That's his car, ain't it?" Frank asked, climbing up to join him.

Del pushed up his glasses, took another look down into the parking lot, and nodded.

"Then they're there." Without another word, Frank reached down to the tailgate and unbolted his side. Del unbolted the other.

"We're ready!" Frank shouted back to the cab. "Hit it!"

Brandon punched the accelerator. The rear wheels spun out as Frank gave the tailgate a good kick. It flew open, and twenty-three hundred golf balls began to tumble out. Frank and Del tried to help push them, but they were unable to keep their balance as they slipped and fell and flopped around in the back.

"Yee-haaa!" Frank yelled, laughing, having the time of his life—as all twenty-three hundred golf balls bounced down the steep ridge directly toward Bethel Lake Country Club.

The score was 30-Love in the second set. Tom Henderson and Beverly, a new lovely he'd been strutting for all evening, were two games short of winning the match against Reggie and his babe of the month. Henderson delivered a powerful serve that hit the baseline before zipping past Reggie's racket.

That's when they heard the first explosion. It sounded like a small firecracker. It was immediately followed by another, and then another, and more and more in rapid succession.

Reggie called to Henderson. "Is that hail?"

Henderson wasn't sure, and they both crossed the court, heading for the lobby to investigate. By now the entire structure was thundering. Jogging into the lobby, Henderson saw movement through the front glass door. Giant, white somethings were bouncing into the glass and pounding against the aluminum wall.

The girls arrived, and everyone edged closer for a better look. It was then that Henderson recognized the little white somethings.

"Golf balls!" he shouted over the roar. "They're golf balls!"

Golf balls pounded everywhere—against the door, the front wall, ricocheting around the walk, raining down on the parking lot. He approached the door, cupped his hands against the glass, and searched the cars. His beloved Firebird sat directly in the center of the downpour, its carefully waxed finish slowly but quite surely breaking out in a severe case of acne.

Reggie pushed past him, shoving open the door, attempting to brave the onslaught. But the pounding balls forced him back in.

Not Henderson. That was his Firebird out there, his pride and joy. He raced outside and was instantly hit by a stinging ball against his shoulder. Then his thigh. Then his head. They hurt. So did the other dozen that hit. He raised his arms to protect his face as he fought his way forward, staggering toward his car. He'd made it only ten feet from the building when, over the din, he heard a distinct and unforgettable cackle of laughter. He looked up to the ridge and caught a glimpse of a pickup—the one with the broken running light on the cab—just before it bounced and disappeared out of sight. And then he opened his mouth and shouted.

"Townies-s-s . . ."

Sarah's car was acting up again, but she managed to coax it out of the Institute's parking lot and up Brower Avenue to Third. Then it was just a short jaunt over to Lambert, then left to Klaussen. That was the address the phone book had for Herb and Margaret Phillips: 339 Klaussen.

It was an older ranch home, mostly brick. The porch light was off, but Sarah could see lights on inside. As she stepped out of the car and approached the house, she heard the TV blaring. Some mindless sitcom. She headed up the porch steps, pushed the doorbell, and waited.

There was no answer. She tried again. Still nothing. She opened the aluminum screen door and knocked. A moment later the porch light glared on. A worn woman in her late thirties opened the door.

"Mrs. Phillips?" Sarah asked.

The woman squinted. "No, I'm . . ." She glanced past Sarah to make sure no one else was there. "I'm her sister."

"My name is Sarah Weintraub. Is Lori Beth in?"

"Are you a friend?"

"Well, not exactly." Sarah heard a car slowly pull up to the curb behind her. "I tried to call earlier, but—"

"I don't believe it," the woman muttered half under her breath. But she was no longer listening or even looking at Sarah; she was staring past her. Sarah threw a glance over her shoulder to see that a white Taurus had pulled up to the curb. The driver's side opened, and a large man with thinning blonde hair stepped out.

The woman turned and called into the house. "Jim? Jimmy, he's here!"

The front door of the house opened wider, and a burly mountain of flesh appeared. At first his eyes glared at Sarah. They were angry and bloodshot. Then they moved past her to the man on the curb.

The man at the curb came to a stop and called to him. "Hello, Jim."

The burly man answered, low and intense. "You've got a lot of nerve coming here. Go. Now."

"I just, uh . . ." The man at the curb coughed slightly and took half a step closer. "The parents, how are they doing?"

Jim seethed. "What do you care?"

The man at the curb continued his approach. "Listen, I, uh—"

"Get out of here!" The response was so venomous that it brought the man at the curb to a stop. "You take another step, and I'll come out there and kill you myself."

"I need to talk to the parents, Jim. I need to explain. It's not as it appears—"

"Get off their property!"

The man hesitated.

"Get out of here!"

The standoff lasted another moment before the man at the curb lowered his head, turned, then slowly headed back to his car.

But Jim wasn't finished. "Filth! Pervert!" He stepped out onto the porch, pushing past Sarah. "We're going to get you locked up!" he yelled. "They'll lock you up and throw away the key! Do you hear me? Your life is over! It's over!"

The other man said nothing as he approached his car, opened the door, and entered.

Suddenly Jim turned on Sarah. "What do you want?" he glowered.

"She's a friend of Lori Beth's," the woman beside him explained.

"Lori Beth is dead. She killed herself this morning." He watched as the car slowly pulled from the curb. "More like she was murdered."

Sarah stood in stunned silence. She was unsure how to respond. The man gave her little opportunity. He turned and headed back into the house.

Finally Sarah found her voice. "Wait a minute. I don't understand. What happened?"

The woman at the door hesitated, then spoke. "You mustn't hold it against her, honey. The note said that that monster"—she motioned toward the departed car—

"that her teacher there had been . . ." She searched for the word. "You know—'hurting her.' Poor thing, she just didn't know how to tell anyone, how to make him stop."

Sarah's head reeled. It was true then, what Brandon had seen. The teacher had been assaulting the girl. Maybe not right there, right in the church, but behind school doors. Once again Brandon had seen the truth, had seen what really was happening. She was so lost in thought that she barely heard the woman conclude, "I'm sorry." By the time she looked back up, the door had closed in her face.

Gerty sat at the kitchen table, writing another letter. She suspected that it would never get to Brandon. Not that it mattered. All the important notes were already over at the computer hacker's house, being entered for future retrieval. These notes were simply loose thoughts, rambling odds and ends. Still, if she could save Brandon even a little suffering on his treacherous road ahead, it would be worth the effort.

Earlier she had arranged the table so that nothing would be missed. She had carefully laid out the remaining sketches she had not yet given him. She'd also opened her worn Bible to the underlined passages. She hated parting with that Bible; it had been her companion for over thirty years. But now he would need it far more than she.

Her pen had barely begun the second paragraph of the letter when she heard the creaking. It came from the back porch. She stopped writing and held her breath.

There it was again, the groaning of old wood. Somebody was outside, making his way toward the screen door. She tried to remember if she had locked it but couldn't recall. Not that it mattered. If he wanted in, he could easily rip out the little hook and eyelet.

She continued to listen. Another creak, more groans. She forced herself to take a breath. It came out shaky. She had known that this moment was coming, had sensed it for days, but still she was frightened. It's not that she didn't trust her Lord. She trusted him completely. And she was anxious to finally see his face, to fall into his arms.

But still she was frightened.

There was a knock. "Hello?" The voice was young. It attempted to be friendly, but she could hear the pain and torment underneath. "Hello, is anybody home?"

She took another breath to steady herself before answering. "Who is it?"

"I'm Lewis," the voice said, "Lewis Thompson. My car ran out of gas in front of your house, and I was wondering if I could use your telephone."

Gerty paused a moment before slowly rising to her feet. She pushed the chair back, and it squeaked against the worn floor.

"Ma'am?" the voice persisted.

"I'll be right there." She started toward the door. As she approached she felt a peace settling over her. A peace that was beyond any understanding. It was a quiet confidence. A resolve that filled her entire body.

The boy's face came into view through the screen. She immediately recognized the short, nearly shaved hair, the red goatee, and the crooked teeth. This was the child at the church, the one who had attacked Brandon, the one she had sent racing off. She couldn't tell whether he recognized her; he seemed too agitated to recognize anything. He pulled at the door, but the tiny hook and eyelet kept it closed. She could refuse him entrance, but he would only rip the door open and there was really no need to ruin it. She took the remaining steps to the screen door and flipped up the hook.

He pulled it open. He was nervous and sweaty, but he managed to speak. "Yeah, run outa gas right here in front of your house."

His right hand was wrapped in gauze. He saw her staring at it and twitched a nervous grin. "Got attacked by a dog this afternoon," he said, holding up his hand so she could get a better look. The gauze had dark spots where the blood had soaked through.

Gerty nodded, and they stood facing one another in silent confrontation. He was sweating, agitated, ready to explode. She could still stop this. She could still exercise her authority and send him running. But to do that would mean disobedience. It would mean using her powers outside of God's will. The temptation wasn't a surprise. She remembered how the Lord himself had been tempted to turn stone into bread, to oppose his Father's will in the garden, to call down legions of angels as he hung on the cross. She thought of Stephen, or the thousands of other martyrs who had gone before her. God could have delivered any one of them—if it had been his will.

With steely determination, she took her eyes off the boy. She turned and headed toward the refrigerator. "Phone's over on the wall," she said. "Can I get you somethin' to drink?"

He gave no answer. She could hear him waiting, preparing to attack.

"Still mighty hot," she continued. "Never seen nothin' like it in all my days." She arrived at the refrigerator, opened it, and reached for the beige Tupperware pitcher of iced tea. She could hear the brush of his clothing as he moved toward her. Without looking, she closed the refrigerator door and crossed to the cupboard for a glass. She'd washed the dishes earlier that afternoon. No sense having others clean up after her. She pulled down a glass, the one with the little sunflowers on the side. She'd had it for years. Won it at the County Fair dime toss.

The boy moved closer. She could hear him breathing now. Short, labored gasps.

She no longer felt fear. Only compassion and pity. Compassion for the boy and pity over what he would have to live with in the years to come. Unless . . .

Maybe she could still help him. Maybe there was still a way to prevent his pain. She poured the iced tea. "So tell me, you ever go to church?" she asked.

No answer.

"Sunday school?" She turned and was startled to see how close he was. His face was wet and his eyes were wide and wild. She thought she saw him nod but wasn't sure. She held out the glass. He looked down at it, confused. Finally he took it.

She moved past him and headed back to put away the pitcher. "Remember how they was always talkin' 'bout Jesus? How he suffered and died on the cross? How he shed his blood for the forgiveness of our sins—for everything you and I ever done wrong?"

Her back was to him again and she heard movement, a shifting of weight. The topic obviously made him uncomfortable. Either him or the multitude that she knew lived inside of him.

"I just want you to know, son, that there's nothing you can do that's too bad for him to forgive. You just remember that. It's never too late to ask his forgiveness, and to let him come in and be your Lord."

She opened the refrigerator door, placed the pitcher back on the top shelf, and closed it. Now she headed toward the table. " 'Cause he loves you, son. Don't you ever be forgettin' that. No matter what happens, remember he loves you."

She could hear him approaching, his breath faster, heavier.

"All you got to do is ask."

There was a snapping sound, something being unfastened. Then the sound of steel sliding from leather.

"And I forgive you, too. Remember that. I forgive you, too."

He stood behind her, so close she could feel his ragged breath against her neck. She looked at the ground. She was there. Right where it would happen, right between the refrigerator and table. And she was ready. She had told him the truth, the only truth that mattered, and now she was ready.

She heard the rustle of clothing as he raised his arm and then a faint grunt as his hand flew toward her. She cried out, but not in agony. It was in anticipation. The pain would only be a moment. The joy would be eternal.

"Did you hear him shout?" Frank asked as he leaned over the table toward his two buddies. He scrunched up his face and gave a mournful howl. "*Townies-s-s . . .*"

Del chuckled and Frank broke into his infectious laughter, stopping just long enough to finish off another beer. He turned to the locals who were listening. "It was beautiful, man. A work of art. Ol' Brandon here, this time, he really outdid himself."

Del pushed up his Coke-bottle glasses and nodded as Brandon shook his head in modesty. But Frank was right; it had been a great idea, and they had pulled it off beautifully. Only twenty minutes ago the country club had undergone an attack that would go down in the history books.

Unfortunately, the celebration was short-lived.

"Looks like you've got company," Del said.

Brandon glanced up to see him staring out of the window into the parking lot. Sarah had pulled her Escort alongside his pickup and was climbing out. Part of him leaped at seeing her again. But an equal part was cautious.

His eyes followed her as she crossed to the doors of the pizzeria, threw one open, and entered. He made no effort to get her attention. He figured she would find him soon enough. He was right.

She headed toward his table with obvious determination. By the looks of things, she'd been working all evening, and even though she was disheveled, he still found her very, very attractive.

"Hey, Sarah." Frank raised his glass as she approached.

She ignored him and focused directly upon Brandon. "May I speak to you? Alone."

"They're my friends."

She hesitated, then dragged up a chair to join him. "Okay, have it your way. I just came back from Lori Beth's house."

He didn't like the urgency in her voice and braced himself for more. "So?"

"So, she's dead."

"What?"

"Lori Beth Phillips?" Frank asked in equal surprise.

"She committed suicide. Her teacher had been sexually assaulting her—just like you saw. She couldn't find any way out."

Brandon stared, still trying to digest it.

Sarah continued, just as determined but a little softer. "They're coming true. Lori Beth, the guy at your plant."

"No." He began shaking his head. "It's not—look, I'm finally getting better, all right?"

"Better?" She looked around. "You call hanging around these slackers better?"

Frank, who was definitely feeling the beers, allowed his anger to surface. "Listen, sweetheart, I don't know who you think you are, or what your problem is—"

She ignored him, speaking only to Brandon. "What about Jenny?"

The question hit Brandon almost as hard as the news about Lori Beth.

She persisted. "What about Jenny?"

He finally looked back at her. "That thing wasn't Jenny. It never was." He fought to keep his voice even. "I don't know where she is, I'm sure someplace good. But that thing—that thing was evil."

"Out on the road, didn't it try to save you?"

"Or get me killed."

Sarah leaned forward. That dogged persistence that so infuriated him and that he found so attractive focused directly upon him. "What about Lori Beth? What about your friend's hand? You could have saved them both. You could have—"

"I was in hell!" The outburst surprised them both.

The room grew quiet. He tried to pull back his anger but didn't quite succeed. "I saw the fire, all right? I saw the burning bodies. How can you tell me that's not evil?"

His anger only fueled Sarah's intensity. "But if there's a hell, then there's a heaven. Don't you see? 'Perpendicular Universe,' remember? If there's a below then there's got to be an above. An evil, then a good. If there's a counterfeit, then there's got to be the real thing."

"What about the church?" he insisted. "I've seen that—that thing two different times now. It's just as real, and it's scarier than all of the others combined. And nothing, *nothing's* ever happened there."

Her eyes darted up to him. She took a breath, obviously trying to keep her voice even and in control. "Then I'd say it's just about time, wouldn't you?"

They held each other's gaze. A sinking sensation filled his stomach. She was right. Something was going to happen at the church. Something awful and powerful . . .

He noticed a new look coming over her face. A realization. "Your mother." She spoke more urgently. "Your mother said that the last service in the church—it was tonight. Right? Is that what she said?"

Brandon lowered his eyes.

"Is that right?"

He looked away, somewhere, anywhere but at her. He could hear the wheels turning, knew her next thought.

"Brandon—"

"No."

"But—"

"There's nothing I can do." He turned back to her. "Even if it's true, there's nothing I can do."

"What about that black woman? Gerty? The one with the sketches?"

"No."

"I've got her address, maybe we could go—"

"No."

"Maybe she could help, tell you how—"

"No!"

"We're talking innocent people!"

"Leave me alone! Why can't you just . . ." He turned directly to her now, but already he could feel his anger dissipating. "Why can't you just leave it alone?"

She held his gaze until he had to look away, down at the glass in his hand.

"Brandon, I'm not talking about the experiment now. I don't give a rip about the work. I'm talking about—"

Suddenly Frank had her arm. "All right, sweetheart, you heard the man. I think it's time—"

She wrenched herself free, spilling his beer onto the table. The restaurant grew quiet. She rose to her feet, still speaking to Brandon, who was still staring at his glass.

"You may have been to hell, Brandon. But there's another kind of hell." She paused, waiting. When he didn't respond, she continued. "We've both, you and I, we've both lived there."

He looked up at her, knowing exactly what she was talking about. The hell of his purposelessness. The hell of her driving ambition. Both trapped in the never-ending loop of guilt, and self, and pain.

"I just thought . . ." She took a deep breath. "I was just hoping that you might have wanted out."

He tried to think of something cool to say, something flippant. But there was nothing. She waited one more moment before finally turning and heading for the door.

Her words burned in his ears. Frank was saying something, but Brandon didn't hear. He watched as she walked outside, climbed into her car, and tried to start it. But it wouldn't kick over. He could hear it grind and grind but with no success. She grabbed the papers from the front seat and threw open her door.

He lowered his head, preparing for another onslaught. But she didn't come back in. Instead, he suddenly heard his own truck roar to life. He looked up just in time to see the headlights blaze on.

"Hey!" Del shouted. "She's got your truck!"

She found reverse and pulled out.

"She's got your truck!" Del repeated as he leaped to his feet and started for the door. "She's got your truck!"

Brandon rose as Sarah threw his pickup into gear, stomped on the accelerator, and fishtailed onto the main road.

CHAPTER 14

Sarah clung to the pickup's steering wheel with one hand while trying to unfold the map with the other. She knew Gerty Morrison lived on Sycamore. The address suggested that it was a mile or so outside of town, probably past the gravel pit. But she needed to check the map to be sure.

Blinding lights suddenly appeared around the bend, letting her know that she had drifted into the wrong lane. She grabbed the wheel with both hands and swerved back as the passing car blasted its horn in anger.

Sarah blew the hair out of her eyes and again reached for the map. If Brandon's precognitive skills were as accurate as they had been in the past, then something was about to happen at the church. Something dramatic, terrible—and, since this was the final service in the church, it would probably be tonight. There was nothing Sarah could do to stop it, but if this Gerty had had a similar premonition, if she had some sense of what was about to occur . . .

Sarah glanced at the speedometer. She was doing nearly seventy. She let up some, but not much.

The curfew tolls the knell of parting day,
The lowing herd wind slowly o'er the lea,
The plowman homeward plods his weary way,
And leaves the world to darkness and to me.

Momma sat in the front pew, keeping her eyes fixed on the Reverend as he recited another one of his favorite poems. The farewell service was more difficult for her than she had anticipated. But it would be her final act as the church's cofounder, and then it would be over.

Now fades the glimmering landscape on the sight,
And all the air a solemn stillness holds,
Save where the beetle wheels his droning flight,
And drowsy tinklings lull the distant folds.

She turned to steal a glance back at the rest of the church. She was pleased to see so many folks. This was the end of nearly twenty-five years of hard work and tradition, and it brought out some of the dearest and best. Leaders of the religious community, like Reverend Jacobsen over there from the Lutheran church, Father Penney, Pastor Burnett, Pastor Smith, even Rabbi Cohen—none of them to gloat over another church's failure but to bid it a fond farewell.

There were only a handful from this church. That's all that ever attended now. In its heyday, before her husband's stroke, they'd had nearly four hundred members. They'd even had to go to two services. But that had been a long, long time ago.

Save that from yonder ivy-mantled tower
The moping owl does to the moon complain
Of such as, wand'ring near her secret bower,
Molest her ancient solitary reign.

Momma turned back to face the front, but not before glancing at her husband. She was grateful that he couldn't comprehend what was happening, that he didn't understand what had become of all their hard work, of the promises and prayers that had never been fulfilled.

Beneath those rugged elms, that yew tree's shade,
Where heaves the turf in many a mold'ring heap,
Each in his narrow cell forever laid,
The rude forefathers of the hamlet sleep.

Henderson turned the Firebird onto SR 15 and headed north. He and Reggie had started out searching the major roads, but if they had to, they would work their way down to the smaller streets and avenues. The guy had to be out there somewhere. The half ton with the broken running light was out there, and they would find it. If they had to travel every highway and back road in Kosciusko County, they would find it.

It was more cottage than house, and even at night Sarah could tell that it hadn't seen a paintbrush in years. A faint light shone from somewhere deep inside, nearly obscured by the drawn shades, dirty windows, and overgrown shrubs.

Sarah stepped out of the pickup and into the warm night air. She was struck by the sudden silence. She figured much of it was due to the surrounding woods and thick vegetation. Even the perpetual hum of Highway 30 was dulled and absorbed by the jungle of maples, mulberries, and sprawling junipers. At one time it must have all been very picturesque and parklike; now it was a jungle that seemed on the verge of swallowing up the entire house.

She waded through the knee-high grass along what she thought to be a walkway. At the front porch, she carefully made her way up the stairs and knocked loudly on the blistered door.

There was no answer.

She tried again. "Hello," she called. "Gerty? Gerty Morrison?"

Strange. There was a light on inside and two cars parked in the driveway.

She knocked again. "Hello?"

She pushed at the door. It was locked. She moved to the nearest window and tried to peek inside. The pulled shade blocked her view, but she could tell the light was coming from somewhere in the back. She turned, made her way down the porch, and walked around the house. For a second she thought she caught movement inside, the flicker of a shadow. But it was gone before she could be sure.

From the rear of the house, the light was clearly visible. It came from the kitchen. The back door was open, and the light spilled from the kitchen through the screen door and onto the porch.

Not wanting to scare the old lady, Sarah called from the yard. "Hello? Mrs. Morrison?"

She walked up the weathered steps to the screen door. "Hello." Through the screen she could see the kitchen counter. Off to the right was a table cluttered with papers. She reached out and knocked on the door. It bounced and clattered, apparently unlatched. Her instincts told her to stop, that something wasn't right. Still, she had come this far.

She pulled on the door. It opened with a low squeak. "Hello, Mrs. Morrison? Anybody home?"

She took a tentative step inside and let the door close against her back.

The table was stacked with papers, but the rest of the kitchen was as neat as a pin—except for a recent spill on the floor between the refrigerator and the table. It still glistened with moisture and was a little smeared, as if someone had hastily tried to wipe it up. She knelt for a better look. The best she could figure in the poor light, it was some sort of juice, probably grape. She felt no inclination to touch it.

She rose to her feet and looked around. Now that she was nearer to the table, the clutter appeared more organized. She stepped closer. In the very center lay an open Bible. On either side, carefully arranged, were stacks of papers. On the left side were handwritten letters; on the other were sketches like the ones Brandon had given her. She moved closer. The sketches were not of Brandon as a child. They were of the older Brandon—the one in the burlap robe who stood inside some ancient walled city.

Sarah picked up the pile and examined the top one. In many ways it was identical to what she had seen at the Institute. But instead of fire coming from his mouth, this sketch showed Brandon looking toward the heavens with an expression of fear and apprehension.

She pulled it aside to look at the next. It was at the same location, but now Brandon had a companion, dressed in a similar coarse robe. Although the companion's back was to her, Sarah guessed him to be a boy because of his slighter build and shortly cropped hair. He had one arm outstretched as if confronting some unseen force. In the other hand he held a lamp, exactly like the one in the sketch at the Institute—exactly like the one Brandon had described from his dreams and visions.

She turned to the next drawing. Same city, but this time the horizon was filled with a vaporous, monstrous head covered in horns and peering down upon Brandon and his companion. Now Brandon was the one holding the lamp, and now—

Suddenly Sarah went cold.

In this sketch Brandon's companion had turned to look directly at the viewer. The face was drawn in careful detail. Sarah bit her lip and closed her eyes. But when she reopened them, nothing had changed. She felt her head growing light and leaned against the table for support. It wasn't a boy standing beside Brandon. It was a woman. A woman with a jagged scar across her forehead that ran down her cheek. Other than the short cropped hair and the jagged scar, the woman looked exactly like her. Exactly like Sarah Weintraub.

Sarah took a deep breath to steady herself, but it did no good. What type of hoax was this? She looked back at the table, at the pile of letters, then at the Bible. It was opened, and a large portion of one page was underlined. Like the sketches and letters, it seemed to be carefully laid out, on display, as if waiting for someone to find it.

She picked up the book and noticed her hands were trembling. She began to read. Her lips moved inaudibly. Color slowly drained from her face as her mind began to whirl. These words, what they were saying . . . but it was impossible . . . And yet, there they were, clearly written and making perfect sense.

She read them a second time. Her trembling grew worse as unfathomable thoughts rose and surfaced. When she had finished, she slowly lowered the book. That's when she saw him.

He'd been standing in the shadows of the living room. For how long, she didn't know. Realizing that he'd been spotted, he moved into the light. She recognized him immediately. He was the attacker from the lab—same short hair, same ragged goatee, same wild look in his eyes.

She recalled that it was always best to talk to an assailant, to make human contact. They were less likely to attack if they made a personal connection. "Where—" Her voice was shaky. She stopped, took a breath, and tried again. "Where is she?"

He gave no answer.

"Gerty Morrison? Is she here?"

He leaned forward, squinting, as if trying to hear what she was saying.

She spoke louder. "Where is the woman who lives here?"

He looked at her, still not comprehending. His mouth had begun to quiver, then twitch. Finally it exploded with the words she had heard before:

"You're the one, you're not the one!"

She took a half step back, bumping into the table.

"You're the one, you're not the one!"

His eyes darted to the pile of drawings. She followed his gaze. He was staring at the one of Brandon and her as they stood inside the walled city.

"You're the one, you're not the one!"

Her head reeled. "I don't under—do you know what any of this means?"

He frowned, but not at her question; it was at something else, something in his head. His face twisted, contorted. Suddenly he leaned over and gasped in pain.

"Are you all right?"

He groaned, almost mournfully. "You *are* the one."

He ran a shaky hand over his face to wipe off the sweat, and then righted himself. That's when she saw the reflected light in the other hand. It was a large hunting knife.

He saw her eye it and raised the knife into view, grinning, relishing the look of fear it brought to her face.

Still feeling the table against her back, Sarah began to inch her way along its edge. He was going to attack, she was certain. And if she got just a little closer to the back door she might be able to run for it.

He wiped his face again. His eyes darting in all directions, growing wilder.

She had to stall him, to keep him occupied, at least until she got closer to the door. "How did you know?" she asked.

He scowled.

"That I'm the one."

He cocked his head again, as if preoccupied, as if listening to something else.

Then Sarah made a mistake—she glanced at the door. He saw it. Swearing, he lunged for her. She tried to get away, but she didn't have a chance. He was too fast. She saw the knife coming at her, toward her chest. Instinctively, she brought up her hand to defend herself, expecting to feel the burning pain of the blade. But instead to her surprise the knife hit the Bible she'd been holding.

She dropped the book and tried to run, but he grabbed her arm. She swung it hard and tore free, stumbling toward the door, but he threw himself at her, catching her at the waist and bringing them both down to the floor. She was all fists and knees and feet, flailing and kicking, but blindly, barely landing a blow. She finally brought her knee into him, hard enough to make him gasp, allowing her to break free. She scrambled for the door on her hands and knees, but he caught her leg. She screamed and tried to kick free, but he hung on.

"You are the one," he gasped, "you are not the one."

She squirmed and kicked, but he hung on, moving up her legs, fighting to grab her swinging arms.

"You are the one."

She landed a powerful blow to his face, and for a second it looked as if some sanity had returned to him. But only for a second. Instantly it was replaced by the sneering grin. She fought and kicked, but he climbed to her chest now, pinning her shoulders to the ground. That's when the knife reappeared.

Sarah fought and squirmed for all she was worth, but there was no way to move. He was breathing so hard he could barely speak. Sweat fell from his face and splattered onto her neck.

With one hand he grabbed the back of her hair, pulling her head to the ground, exposing more of her throat. With the other, he shoved the blade against her jugular. Sarah looked at him, wide-eyed.

His mouth was open, gasping for air, preparing for another explosion of violence, when suddenly—

"Hello, Lewis."

His head jerked up.

Unable to move, Sarah strained to see Reichner standing at the screen door.

"She's the one," Lewis panted. Sarah felt the blade press harder against her neck. "She's the one, but she's not the one!"

Reichner's voice remained calm and controlled. "I don't think so, Lewis." It was the same voice he used with his subjects during the lab sessions.

"The pictures," Lewis gasped, motioning toward the table.

Reichner opened the door and strolled toward them, slow and deliberate. "She is not the one, Lewis. You know that."

Lewis looked down at her. More sweat fell from his nose and chin. He adjusted his weight but kept the knife firmly against her throat.

"But . . . she's the one, she's—"

"Lewis, Lewis, Lewis." Reichner shook his head. "*You* are the one, you know that. You have always been the one."

She felt the kid catch his breath. Again he adjusted his weight, then looked down at her and frowned in confusion. "But the pictures, the—"

Reichner stood four feet from them now. "It is you, Lewis. Listen to the voices."

Sarah felt the pressure of the knife lessen slightly.

"You are the one, you have always been the one."

Pain crossed the boy's face. "Yes . . . no. Me, I'm the—"

"Where is the old woman, Lewis?"

A scowl crossed the boy's face as if he was trying to remember.

"The one who lives here. Where is she, Lewis?"

"The back. Hall closet. I put her in the—"

"Did you kill her, Lewis?"

The blade left Sarah's throat and he sat up, his weight still heavy on her chest. She wanted to roll him off, to slide away, but Reichner was playing the kid now and it was important that she didn't interfere.

"Did you kill her, Lewis?"

"I . . . I don't—"

"Do not lie to me, Lewis. You know that I know. I always know, don't I?"

Lewis stared at him, transfixed. Reichner's voice was smooth and calm. "You killed someone, didn't you? You killed someone and not the one."

Sarah felt Lewis's body shudder.

"And the one—that is whom you are supposed to kill. That is the one the voices want, isn't it?"

Lewis slowly nodded.

"Not some old woman, not some beautiful girl."

The kid fidgeted—confused, distracted. Part of him seemed to be listening to Reichner, another part hearing something deep in his own head.

"That is what you want, Lewis. To kill the one. That is what your voices really want."

Lewis winced, trying to hear, trying to clear his mind. Reichner took a half-step closer, then quietly knelt down to his level.

"Listen to your voices, Lewis. Listen very carefully."

The anguish on the boy's face increased.

"They want to kill the one."

"But . . ." Lewis's voice was weaker.

"And that is you, Lewis."

Sarah's eyes darted to Reichner. What was he saying?

"You are the one. They want to kill the one, Lewis, and you are the one. Listen to your voices, Lewis. Let them have their way."

The kid continued to stare, mesmerized, almost nodding in agreement, until suddenly he shook his head. "No!"

Reichner's voice continued, softly. "Yes, Lewis, listen to your voices. You are the one. You have known it all along. You are the one. And the one is whom you must kill."

"Doctor," Sarah whispered, but he paid no attention.

"Close your eyes, Lewis."

The kid hesitated. "It's okay, just close your eyes for a moment. They are so heavy, just close your eyes and listen, listen to your voices. Just for a moment . . ."

The boy's lids fluttered, then lowered.

"That is good, Lewis. Very good."

Sarah watched in fear and awe.

Reichner dropped his voice to an intimate whisper. "You are the one, Lewis. You have always been the one. You are the one who must be killed. You are the one the voices must kill."

"Doctor," Sarah protested. But Reichner stared so intently at the boy that she doubted he heard her. "Just have him drop the knife," she whispered.

"You must obey the voices," Reichner continued.

Eyes still shut, Lewis began to nod.

"Dr. Reichner, you can't—"

"Do it, Lewis. Obey the voices."

"Doc—"

"Now, Lewis." His voice became more insistent. "Obey the voices, now."

"Dr. Reichner!" But neither Reichner nor Lewis heard.

"You are the one who must be destroyed. Do it. Do it now, Lewis!"

The boy rose to his knees. Taking advantage of the movement, Sarah immediately slid out from under him and scrambled to her hands and knees. The boy remained transfixed, continuing to nod his head, his entire body beginning to rock under the movement. Silently, he turned the knife around, until the blade was facing himself.

"Dr. Reichner!" Sarah shouted.

"Do it, Lewis, do it now. Obey your voices."

The boy placed it against his chest, directly over his heart.

"Stop it," Sarah protested. "He's going to—"

"That is right, Lewis. Now."

"Stop it! Stop—"

"Now, Lewis!"

Sarah reached out and grabbed Reichner's arm. "Stop it!"

"Now!"

The boy drove the knife hard between his ribs.

Sarah screamed.

Lewis's eyes exploded with pain and realization.

"You're crazy!" Sarah yelled. "Look what you've done, look what you've done!"

But Reichner was too immersed in the victory to hear. "That is good, Lewis. You did well. Very well."

The boy slowly looked at him.

"The voices are proud of you, Lewis. They will be leaving you now, and you will never have to hear them again. Never again."

Sarah moved to try and help the boy, but Reichner's arm shot out and pushed her away. She turned to him, stunned, then to the boy who was looking down at the wound in his chest, the spreading blood on his shirt, his hands. Reichner reached out his hand and set it on top of the boy's head—a blessing, a benediction. "Good, Lewis. You have always been good."

Lewis looked up at him.

"And you will always be the one. Always."

A smile spread across the boy's face. The expression slowly froze, and then he toppled to the floor.

CHAPTER 15

"You . . ." Sarah's voice was hoarse, just above a whisper. "You killed him."

Without looking at her, Reichner rose calmly to his feet. "It was necessary to save your life."

She could only stare at him. "Not like that. He didn't have to kill himself. Not like that."

Reichner said nothing. He turned his back to her and moved toward the kitchen table.

Sarah looked down at the boy. "You killed him. You didn't have to, but you . . ."

Reichner picked up the sketches on the table and casually flipped through them. "He killed once. How did we know he would not do it again?"

Sarah slowly turned to him.

Reichner shrugged. "It was a murder/suicide. That's what it was, and that's what we will tell the police."

Sarah rose unsteadily to her feet. "But it's—it's not true."

"It is true enough for our purposes."

Revulsion stirred deep inside her. "*Our* purposes?"

He ignored her, pointing to the first sketch. "Interesting likeness."

"It's true enough *for our purposes?"* she repeated

"The boy was trying to kill you, Dr. Weintraub. And when he was through with you, he would have gone after your boyfriend here."

Sarah glanced at the sketch in his hand, angry, confused. "What?"

"'You're the one, you're not the one.'"

"Does that makes sense to you?"

He brought the sketch closer to his face for examination. "Not entirely. But if this artist's precognitive skills are anywhere near

Brandon's, it appears that you may very well be assisting him in the years to come." He glanced up at her with half a grin. "That is to say, *we* will be assisting him."

Sarah stared at him.

"He is 'the one,' whatever that means—no doubt somebody of great psychic ability. And you and I, we will be by his side, we will be there observing his every experience, recording his every encounter." He looked back at the sketch, the slightest trace of wonder filling his voice. "Imagine the possibilities, the discoveries waiting to be made."

Sarah's revulsion grew. How could he be so callous? She looked back down at Lewis's body. The corpse of the boy he had killed wasn't even cold, and he was already making plans for the future. What type of creature was this?

"Don't look so shocked, Doctor."

Her eyes shot back to him.

"I was merely protecting our interests. If I did not stop Lewis now, he would have been an obstruction, perhaps even trying to destroy our work."

Sarah stared, trying to grasp all he was saying, sickened at what she understood. She spotted the Bible on the floor and moved to pick it up. There was a deep gash on the front cover where it had saved her from the knife.

Reichner continued examining the sketches. "We are on our way, my friend. What is the saying about the goose who laid the golden egg? We have found that goose, Dr. Weintraub, and now we must be very careful to protect him. At any cost."

She looked back at Reichner, her anger growing.

Reichner smiled at her and tapped the picture. "He is 'the one.' "

"How dare you." Her voice was low and trembling.

Reichner chuckled. "Dr. Weintraub—"

"You killed this poor boy just so—"

"He killed himself."

"—just so you can continue your experiments?"

"*Our* experiments, Doctor. And, as I have pointed out, he would have no doubt tried to destroy your young man."

"How can you be so cold-blooded, so—"

"We are on the verge of a major breakthrough, Doctor. Your boy has crossed Threshold and has returned. He can do it again—anytime he wills, I suspect. You saw the findings, the PET scan, the Ganzfield. And that is only the beginning. With his powers, and our tutelage, there may be no end to the progress we—"

He looked at her and came to a stop. She knew her face showed her disgust, but she no longer cared.

He smiled. "Come, come, Doctor. Don't play pious with me."

She stared at him.

"We are cut from the same cloth, you and I. This we both know."

Instinctively she pulled the Bible into herself, bracing for more.

"We are people of ambition. That is how we are wired. Your ambition is no less than mine. Nor should it be. You are young, with many years ahead of you. And if this sketch is true, if indeed, this boy is 'the one,' there may be no end to our discoveries and advancements."

The words sounded strangely familiar, but she couldn't place them. Her head was starting to hurt. She glanced back down at Lewis. She was numb and sickened. And yet she continued to listen.

"You could be the next Newton, Galileo—think of it. You, a Salk, an Einstein. That is heady company, Sarah Weintraub."

"Please." Her voice was thin. "Stop it."

"A Nobel prize *would* be nice. Not to mention the world acclaim. Think of the—"

"Stop."

"Greatness is nothing to be ashamed of."

Sarah took half a step back. She knew what he was doing. His words both excited and disgusted her. And still he continued. And still she listened.

"Think of the millions, of the billions you will be able to help. Your name will be synonymous with hope and encouragement, with the most important breakthroughs of our generation. You will be—"

"Stop it," she demanded. "Stop it now!"

He took a step toward her.

"Sarah." He smiled again. "It is true. We are cut from the same cloth."

She tried to look away but could not.

"Any mistakes of the past will be forgotten. You have your whole future ahead of you."

Now at last she recognized the words. They were Samuel's. And that boy—she looked down at the body. That could just as well have been her baby, or Brandon, or—

"You're disgusting," she seethed, but she knew her words were spoken more out of desperation than conviction.

Reichner's smile increased. "As are you, my dear. That is the price we must pay for our greatness."

Again he held her eyes, and again she could not look away.

"There is nothing wrong with ambition, Sarah. Not if it means changing the world. Not if it means exonerating us from past mistakes, absolving us from—"

"Leave me alone!" She was slipping, and they both knew it.

"That is the glory of greatness."

Her eyes shot around the room.

"To be remembered only for our good."

She had to make him quit. The door. She had to get away.

"Everything else will be forgotten. Only our—"

She broke for the door, threw it open, and bolted down the porch stairs, running for the pickup. Reichner's heavy footsteps followed. She didn't look back.

"We are cut from the same cloth!" the voice called. "You and I, we are one and the same!"

Sarah flung open the pickup's door, threw the Bible onto the seat, and crawled inside. Quickly, she fired up the engine. She could no longer hear Reichner's words, but their truth, or her fear of their truth, echoed inside her head. She had to get away. She had made it this far, she had to keep going.

"And I still remember those early years when Pastor Martus and I rolled up our sleeves and worked together to create the Kosciusko County Food Co-op."

Rabbi Cohen, a short bald man with a stately presence, stood at the front of the church, near Momma and her husband. Like the clergy before him, he was paying special tribute to both the church and its founders.

"We put some long hours in, my friend." Then with a twinkle, he grinned. "Not always in agreement, mind you. But the fruit of our labors has been well worth it." He smiled at Momma and momentarily rested his hand on her husband's shoulder. "And for that I count it a privilege both to have known you and to have served with you." He gave the man a pat on the shoulder and turned to head back to his seat.

Momma stole another look at her husband. During the past several minutes, as leader after leader shared their memories and spoke their praise, it had taken all of her Southern steel to hold back the tears. Still, as grateful as she was for their kindness, part of her resented how their praise was beginning to sound less and less like a tribute and more and more like a eulogy.

The Firebird slid around a corner and headed up Center Street. Inside, the CD throbbed with another raw and angry group that kept Henderson's adrenaline pumping. It had been ninety minutes since the attack on his car. They'd been down a dozen roads and still hadn't seen a sign of the pickup.

Now they were heading back into town by way of Eddie's Pizzeria. It was a favorite hangout of the Townies. In fact, Reggie was certain that he'd seen the pickup there before. Henderson slowed as they passed the parking strip in front. It held a couple of vans, a beater Mustang, a rusted-out Land Cruiser, and an old blue Escort. No sign of the pickup.

Henderson gunned it and they sped down the road into town. He reached for the CD and cranked it up.

They'd find him. If it took all night, they'd find him.

Inside the pizzeria, Frank called to Brandon. "Come on, ol' buddy, loosen up. This is a celebration, remember?"

Brandon forced a grin and raised his glass. With all the trouble the guys were going to, to cheer him up, the least he could do was pretend to have fun.

But his uneasiness continued. Sarah's words kept haunting him, as did his thoughts about the church. Something wasn't right. And the more time passed, the more un-right it became.

Sarah raced through town, heading back to the pizzeria. She had to tell Brandon what had happened, what was going on. She had to make him see that the stakes were far higher than either of them had thought. She glanced at the Bible on the front seat. It was no longer possible for Brandon Martus to be a passive observer.

The Firebird had just crested a small knoll when Reggie pointed through the windshield. "There he is!"

Henderson peered ahead. Sure enough, above the headlights of the approaching vehicle he could see the telltale broken running light. He pressed down on the accelerator and popped on his high beams.

Back inside the pickup, Sarah squinted at the brightness. It took a moment to find the high beams and give the approaching car a courtesy flash.

Brandon looked up. What was that sound? Where was it coming from? He glanced at the others at his table. Frank, Del—no one seemed to notice. But it was growing louder. Some sort of roar. A car. More than one. And music. Loud and driving. Nothing like the country-western coming from the nearby jukebox.

Sarah flashed her high beams again. But the oncoming car didn't respond. She flashed them a third time.

From the passenger seat of the Firebird, Reggie yelled, "What's he doing?"

"I don't know," Henderson shouted, "but it's not going to work."

Brandon gave a start when Frank slapped him on the back. He turned to see him talking—something about picking up girls, but he couldn't make out the words. Frank's mouth moved and he was speaking, but from another world—his voice was no longer discernible above the roar of engines and the pounding music.

The high beams were blinding, and Sarah had to keep her eyes low and to the right side of the road.

Henderson's grin broadened. Any second now, they would begin the game. Both he and the pickup knew the rules; they'd been clearly established. And he would play them perfectly. Only this time he would not back down. Maybe parking the car in the middle of the road the other night had been a little underhanded. Maybe he had deserved the equally cowardly attack of golf balls. But not this time. This time, he would win fair and square.

Sarah raised her left hand, shielding her eyes from the blinding brightness.

Henderson drummed his thumbs on the wheel to the beat of the music. It was time. He swerved the Firebird into the pickup's lane.

Brandon's eyes shot around the restaurant. Everyone was having a good time. Del was laughing, Frank was flirting with a couple of girls. But Brandon heard only the roar of engines and the swelling, pounding music. He took another gulp of his drink, trying to relax, to force the sounds away.

They only grew louder.

Sarah's heart pounded. The car was in her lane, coming directly at her, high beams blazing. She swerved to the left.

So did the car. *What was he doing?*

Back in the Firebird, Henderson clenched his jaw. It was up to the pickup to make the move, to back down. Not Henderson—the pickup. And he'd better make it now.

Sarah panicked, unsure what to do. Left? Right? Which way would this car turn?

Back in the Firebird, Henderson's eyes suddenly widened in surprise. For a split second his lights lit up the pickup's cab. Those weren't Townies inside but a woman. He swerved back into the other lane . . .

Just as Sarah made a similar move.

Their fenders caught. Red fiberglass collapsed into rusted steel—hoods crumpled, frames twisted. And glass. Everywhere there was flying glass. The air bags in the boys' car exploded open and their seat belts locked into place.

Sarah wasn't so lucky. She flew forward, screaming . . .

Brandon heard the explosion of metal and shattering glass. For the briefest second he saw Sarah's face—exactly as he had seen it in his dream—her terrified expression as she flew into his windshield. Her mouth opened in a scream, but a scream she would never finish.

Brandon leaped to his feet crying, "Sarah!"

Hark! a thrilling voice is sounding:
"Christ is nigh," it seems to say;
"Cast away the works of darkness,
O ye children of the day."

It was an old hymn. Momma knew that the Reverend had chosen it especially for her—because of the memories. It was one they'd sung in the old days, when the church was first starting out, when they were so full of hope and expectation.

So when next he comes with glory,
And the world is wrapped in fear,
May he with his mercy shield us,
And with words of love draw near.

Sarah!

Momma froze at the sound of her son's cry. She turned and scanned the sanctuary, but he wasn't there. All she saw were the townsfolk standing and singing. Some looked back at her, smiling, but no one had heard what she had heard.

Yet that had been her son crying out. She was certain of it.

She looked back up at the Reverend, who smiled down warmly upon her. She hesitated, then closed her hymnal and stepped past her husband into the aisle. Trying to draw as little attention as possible, she quietly headed up the aisle toward the exit.

Brandon threw open the doors to the pizzeria. He heard Frank shouting something, but didn't stop to listen. He sprinted toward town. He had no idea where he was going or what had happened. He knew only that Sarah needed him, and she needed him now.

Momma reached the church steps. Outside, a slight wind had picked up. She felt compelled to turn to the right. She followed the instinct, heading down the steps, and turning onto the sidewalk.

Brandon continued to sprint. He didn't have the endurance to keep up this pace forever, but he'd go as far as he could.

Momma had traveled barely a block when she heard the neighborhood dogs start to howl—and moments later the sound of an approaching siren.

Brandon's lungs began to burn. And still he pushed himself. He had sprinted nearly half a mile, and he was definitely feeling it. His throat was on fire and his legs were growing weak. Up ahead rose a small hill. He started the ascent and was about to slow his pace when he caught a glimpse of red and orange lights flashing against the upper-story windows.

"Sarah!"

He pushed harder, the rushing air cutting a groove into his throat, his legs slowly turning to rubber.

He crested the knoll. At the bottom was an EMS vehicle and a small crowd. Behind them, illuminated by the flashing lights, were two other vehicles, both crushed and twisted. He flew down the hill, barely able to control his legs, trying to convince himself that neither of those vehicles was his pickup.

As he approached the EMS truck he could see Henderson was being eased down onto the curb by a paramedic. He looked shaken, but other than some cuts and an injury to his right arm, he appeared okay.

Brandon arrived, gasping for breath. "Where—where is she?"

Henderson looked up, startled. He tried to rise to face Brandon, but the paramedic forced him to stay down.

"Where is she?" Brandon demanded.

"I didn't know it was her." Henderson's eyes were red, his cheeks still wet from crying. "I swear to God, I thought you were driving. I thought you were—"

Brandon turned from him and headed toward the crowd, toward the center of activity. He pushed his way through the onlookers until he saw another paramedic. The man was huddled over a body on the street. Heart pounding, fearing the worst, Brandon approached. At first the body's face was blocked from his view. Then the paramedic shifted and Brandon saw her. The blood and open wound made it difficult to recognize her, but he knew it was Sarah.

Brandon's throat tightened. He hurried the last steps as the paramedic pressed a blood-soaked gauze against a gash that ran across Sarah's forehead and down her cheek. Brandon knelt. "Sarah." His voice was swollen with emotion. "I didn't . . ." He searched for the words. "I'm sorry . . ."

Through his tears, he could see the lid of her good eye start to move. Finally it opened. It took a moment to focus. When she spotted him, she tried to smile, but with little success. Ever so slowly, her lips parted, then closed, then parted again. She was attempting to speak.

A gurney rattled beside them as the other paramedic arrived and quickly lowered it.

She continued moving her lips. Brandon leaned forward, concentrating until he finally made out the broken, raspy words: "It's . . . you . . ."

He nodded, fighting back the ache in his chest. "Yes, I'm here. I won't leave."

She frowned and tried to shake her head.

"Please," one of the paramedics ordered, "give us some room here."

Brandon pulled back as the first paramedic called to his partner. "On my count. One, two, three." In one swift move they transferred Sarah from the ground to the gurney. They elevated the gurney to waist level and prepared to wheel it toward the EMS vehicle. Brandon saw that Sarah was still trying to speak. Again he leaned forward.

"Revelation eleven," she whispered hoarsely. "It's . . . you."

"Please step back." The warning was severe as the paramedics pushed past Brandon and rolled Sarah toward the ambulance. He stayed as close to her side as possible until they arrived at the back and lifted her in. For the briefest second her eyes found his. Then they slid her inside, closed the door, and she was gone.

Brandon stood motionless in the flashing lights. His mind raced in every direction, but he understood nothing. The wind was much stronger as it whipped at his shirt and blew his hair, but he barely noticed. The vehicle pulled from the curb and started its siren. Brandon watched as it headed down the street and disappeared from sight.

Unsure what to do or where to go, he turned toward his pickup. It lay twenty feet away, a crumpled piece of steel and broken glass. Slowly, numbly, he started toward it. People continued to mill about, but he paid no attention. He arrived and stood silently at what had been the right front fender. It was peeled up and back—much of it shoved into the front seat. It was amazing that Sarah had not been killed instantly.

He walked beside the wreck, slowly running his hand over the twisted metal, hearing the broken glass pop and crunch under his feet. At the passenger's door, he looked inside. More glass, as well as crushed dashboard and torn upholstery. He glanced to the portion of floorboard still visible. There in plain view lay a Bible.

He frowned. He reached inside, careful to avoid the sharp and ragged metal. He took hold of the book and cautiously fished it out. His heart had started to pound again, and he was breathing a little more heavily. "Revelation eleven." That's what she'd said. But it had made no sense. He knew, of course, that there was a Revelation in the Bible, the last book. Could that have been what she meant? No, it was an absurd thought. And yet . . . what was she doing with a Bible in his truck? No, it was too crazy.

So why was he afraid to open it and see?

He held the book in his hands, working up his courage, before finally opening the cover. The wind flipped and snapped at the pages.

"Revelation eleven." He turned to the back of the book and noticed his hands shaking. The wind blew harder against the pages, but he kept them open with his hand as he ran down the verses—two, three, four . . .

He stopped cold. He moved back to the third verse, then began to read out loud, his voice low, barely above a whisper.

"And I will grant authority to my two witnesses, and they will prophesy for 1,260 days clothed in sackcloth."

He gulped air in and continued reading.

"These are the two olive trees and the two lampstands that stand before the Lord of the earth."

His head grew light. *Lampstands? Olive trees?* He was beginning to feel cold. Still he continued.

"If anyone desires to hurt them, fire proceeds out of their mouth and devours their enemies."

He closed his eyes, trying to understand, remembering all too well the fire that had escaped from his mouth during the encounter outside the church. He reopened his eyes.

"These have the power to shut up the sky in order that rain may not fall during the days of their prophesying; and they have power over the waters to turn them into blood . . ."

Images of the drought and the three-tiered water fountain came to mind. He was hyperventilating now, breathing hard but still unable to get enough air. He lowered the book. He could read no further. He now understood what Sarah had meant, and he was very cold and very frightened. Then, from behind, he heard his mother's voice, as she continued to softly quote:

"And when they have finished their testimony, the beast that comes out of the abyss will make war with them and overcome them and kill them."

Brandon spun around. The wind blew her hair as she continued to recite the Scripture from memory.

"And those who dwell on the earth will rejoice over their dead bodies and make merry; and they will send gifts to one another, because these two prophets tormented those who dwell on the earth."

Brandon swallowed. When he finally found his voice, it was afraid and angry. "Why—why didn't you tell me?"

"I wasn't . . ." He could barely hear her over the wind. "I wasn't sure."

He took a step back from her. He had to get out of there. But where? He stepped toward her again, then turned away. He began to pace, struggling, trying to make it make sense.

"Brandon," Momma shouted over the wind. He heard her but would not look at her. "It doesn't have to be you. Someone else will be chosen. You can refuse it."

He spun back to her, staring. What was she saying?

"It doesn't have to be you," she repeated. "You don't have to be the one!"

He opened his mouth but could find no words.

"It's true," she shouted. "You don't have to be the one. You don't have to be anything, if you don't want. We always have a choice. You don't have to be anything at all. Nothing at all."

The phrase struck him to the heart. Had she any idea what she'd just said? Did she know that this was the very issue he'd been battling with? He took another step away from her, and then another. But she continued to plead, driving the stake in deeper.

"We can live like we've always lived. You don't have to be the one, you don't have to be anybody. I can take care of you, it can be just like it's always—"

Brandon grabbed his head, trying to make her stop, trying to make it all stop.

She moved closer. "Sweetheart, you don't have to get involved. We can go somewhere else. We can—"

Suddenly she quit talking. A low rumbling had filled the air. It rattled the windows behind them, shook the ground at their feet. But it wasn't an earthquake. It was an eerie resonance, a deep moaning that rapidly grew in intensity. Brandon turned, searching, making sure it wasn't his imagination. But other people had noticed it, too. Some pointed, others stared. He followed their gaze up the street and to the left. There, eight, maybe nine blocks away, hovering in the sky, a dark, swirling cloud was forming—a cloud exactly like he'd seen in his visions. As it condensed, it slowly approached the earth. And, although he couldn't see the source, he saw that its bottom surface was reflecting light that could only be from—

"The church!" He turned back to his mother and shouted. "It's the church!"

"Brandon!"

He turned and started down the street, first at a trot, then at a run.

"Brandon!" Momma called. "It doesn't have to be you. Brandon! Don't leave. You're all I have left! You're all I have! Brandon, don't leave me. Don't leave me!"

CHAPTER 16

The gurney wheels chattered as the paramedics hustled the unconscious Sarah down the emergency hallway of St. John's Hospital. They were already running an IV of Lactated Ringers into her right arm. Sterile gauze was pressed firmly against the cut on her face.

A nearby elevator rattled open and the on-call surgeon, a Dr. Hibdon, joined them as they continued down the hall. He was an older man, tall and lean, with unruly puffs of gray hair sticking out from both temples. "What do we have?" he asked.

"Compound and depressed skull fractures, fracture of the right clavicle, severe facial laceration." The first paramedic ran down the list. "BP increasing, pulse and respiration depressed."

The doctor pulled a penlight from his shirt pocket and, as they continued moving down the hall, opened her left eye. "Left pupil mid-position and unresponsive." He glanced up at a nurse who had just entered through the swinging doors. "Start eighty milligrams of Manatol. I want a CT scan and then I want her prepped. Stat."

The nurse nodded as the doctor peeled off from the gurney to enter the scrub room.

Explosions pounded the air, one after another. Brandon watched as he ran, but the bottom of the cloud was now obscured by tossing and blowing trees. He bore down harder until he rounded the final corner—just in time to see the last of the church windows blow out. Glass flew in all directions, and piercing light blazed from each of the openings. The wind was gale force, whipping and bending the trees, throwing all manner of dirt and debris into the air. Directly above the church, the black cloud's swirling vortex drew closer and closer to the steeple. By now even the bravest of onlookers was backing away, starting to run. Brandon doubted that they could see all that he saw, but whatever they'd experienced was obviously enough.

"Brandon!" He looked across the street to see old man McPherson yelling, his thin gray hair blowing wildly. "Your father!" he shouted. "When the storm hit—I'm not sure, he still might be in there!"

The steeple exploded. Brandon turned just in time to see the cloud envelop it, spewing pieces of wood in all directions. He held out his hands to protect his face. The exposed skin of his arms and hands stung with flying splinters and rubble. He looked back at McPherson, but the old man was already gone. Lowering his head into the wind, Brandon struggled forward.

From the steeple, the cloud's vortex snaked its way across the roof toward the back of the building, where it tore out another hole and entered the church.

Brandon fought his way across the street as the trees blew wildly. Limbs snapped and cracked. A power line suddenly dropped in front of him, leaping and sparking a crazy dance on the asphalt. He veered to the right, giving it a wide berth. A minute later, he reached the church steps.

By now he had recognized something else in the howling wind. Voices. Human voices. Agonizing voices from his previous visions—crying, screaming, tormented voices—wailing voices.

He started up the steps. The wind was so strong that he had to cling to the railing. A ripping *crack* was followed by a *whoosh-thud* as a giant cottonwood crashed to the porch, missing him by mere feet. He arrived at the double doors and struggled to open them. The right one gave way. As he pulled it open, he was struck by a light so bright that it practically blinded him. Covering his eyes, he inched his way through the door and into the foyer. He could not find the source of the light, but as his eyes adjusted to the brightness he saw the same water fountain he'd seen before. It was in the center of the foyer and already bubbling red liquid. The sanctuary doors lay directly ahead. On each side there stood an olive tree and a lampstand.

Dreading to look up, but knowing he had to, Brandon raised his eyes. Above the entrance, just as he expected, hung the sign:

ENTER NOT WITHOUT THE SHIELD OF FAITH

He hesitated. He knew the warning and the implication. Worse yet, he knew that he did not qualify. But he also knew that his father was in there. Cautiously, Brandon took hold of the doors. He paused one last moment to gather his courage, and then he threw them open—

The wind inside had virtually stopped. The light was nearly normal. But at the front of the sanctuary, spiraling in through the hole in the roof, hovered the swirling cloud of contorted faces. And not six feet above the altar, these misty apparitions had tightened and condensed until they formed a distinct image—the same image Brandon had seen in his earlier vision: a giant, multihorned head.

Brandon gasped.

And there, sitting in his wheelchair, halfway down the aisle, where he had no doubt been left in the panic, sat his father. Brandon knew that if the poor man could see even a fraction of what he, Brandon, saw, he must be terrified.

He started down the aisle toward his father when, off to the right, he noticed movement. Another man. The Reverend. He rose from a place of protection behind the pews and started to approach the altar. He looked up at the hole in the roof but seemed totally oblivious to the cloud swirling through it, and to the monstrous head hovering just above the altar.

"Reverend!" Brandon called. "Reverend, look out!"

The Reverend turned to him, then looked back up at the roof. "I've never witnessed anything like it. The twister came, ripped off the steeple, then tore open this hole, and—"

"That was no twister!" Brandon shouted.

The Reverend shook his head. "And at this time of year, too. A single cloud with no other storm activity. I'm sure there is a natural explanation for the phenomena, but . . ."

As the Reverend talked and approached the altar, the beast's head slowly opened its mouth.

"Reverend." Brandon could barely find his voice. "Look out."

The Reverend followed Brandon's gaze to the altar but saw nothing. He was six feet away now, looking directly at the head, but he seemed totally unaware. "I'm sorry, what did you—"

Suddenly, a dense, pencil-thin mist shot from the beast's mouth. It entered the Reverend's own mouth with such force that he staggered backward, his eyes bulging in surprise. He coughed and choked, trying to catch his breath. When he finally looked at Brandon, it was with bewilderment. His hands began to shake. Then his arms. He looked down at them, confused, staring at them as if they were foreign objects. The shaking grew more violent. He looked back at Brandon, his confusion turning to fear. "What's . . . going on?"

Brandon could only stare as the man's entire body began to bounce, then to shimmy and gyrate. Now the Reverend's fear turned to horror. "Help me!" he cried to Brandon. "Please, help—"

Suddenly his head flew back, and mocking laughter echoed through the room. Brandon spun around, looking everywhere for its source—until he turned back to the Reverend and realized that the laughter was coming from the man's open mouth.

Reichner had eased his tall frame into the calfskin armchair of his living room. With some difficulty, he tucked his stocking feet under until he was sitting cross-legged. He was not pleased with what he was about to do, but he saw no alternative. The e-mail waiting for him when he had returned from Gerty's house was quite explicit:

> We must talk at once. Use my God-name.

It had been forty-five minutes since his encounter with Lewis and the good Dr. Weintraub. He knew Sarah was upset over what had happened, but he also knew it wouldn't last. She was his—if not personally, then at least professionally. She belonged to the Institute; she belonged to her work. In a day or two she'd be fine, and then they would resume their pursuit of Brandon Martus.

He looked up at the computer monitor. The message still glowed:

We must talk at once. Use my God-name.

He could try answering by phone or return e-mail. But the instructions were specific. Very specific. Reluctantly, he reached up to the brushed aluminum lamp that arched over his head and dimmed it to low. He had half an hour before the pre-med from the supermarket was to show up. That should give him enough time.

He stared at the piece of paper, the one from Nepal with the so-called God-name written on it. It had worked before. At least something had happened up there in the Himalayas. But here, in Indiana, the environment was considerably different. And, to be honest, Reichner wasn't particularly thrilled about subjecting himself to the python experience again.

Still, the initial reciting of the mantra had proved relaxing. And with the current level of stress he'd been under, as well as his weak heart, it might not hurt to start practicing a little meditation from time to time. Then, of course, there was the other matter—the fiscal survival of his Institute.

He read the eight syllables of the God-name quietly, barely above a whisper. Then he read them again. They were as smooth and calming as he remembered. He closed his eyes and repeated the sounds two, four, half a dozen times, letting the syllables roll from his tongue. He shifted, trying to relax, to empty his mind of the week's events.

He repeated the syllables over and over again until, ever so softly, he heard the breeze, the delicate wind. As gentle as a baby's breath. The sensation was pleasant and relaxing, allowing him to release even more of himself to it.

As he did, the sound grew louder, melding, merging into those lovely sustained chords, the same wondrous music he had heard back in Nepal. It surrounded him, gently lifting him, welling up inside and washing over his mind, his body, his very being. Once again the light pulsed in his feet, then rippled up through his chest and into his head. Wave after gentle wave followed, until his entire body was again breathing and resonating in this lovely, euphoric rhythm. Until he was again becoming one—one with the music, one with the wind, the light. One with something far greater and vaster than he could ever imagine.

The Reverend danced, legs and arms flying in all directions like some out-of-control marionette. His laughter echoed through the room, tying an icy knot deep in Brandon's stomach.

Brandon ran the remaining steps down the aisle to join his father. Whoever had abandoned him there had at least locked the wheels so that he wouldn't roll down the gentle incline to the front. Brandon faced him, momentarily turning his back on the Reverend and the head. "It's okay, Pop, I'm here now. I'm here. Let's just hurry and get you out—"

Sensing movement, he spun around to see the Reverend's body propelled rapidly up the aisle toward him. He braced himself, preparing for impact, but the Reverend suddenly came to an abrupt halt. The man stood less than six feet away. His eyes were rolled back into his head, and his arms and legs continued their wild dance.

"I HAVE WAITED A LONG TIME FOR THIS."

The voices were multiple—just like the kid who had attacked him, just like the woman at the lab. They came from the Reverend's mouth, which opened and closed as if he were speaking, but they did not belong to him.

Brandon stiffened, recalling his past confrontations with the multiple voices—particularly the one with the kid outside the church, and later in Jenny's bedroom. He remembered the authority with which Gerty had controlled the red-headed kid that night—the same authority she kept insisting he had. The same authority he'd tried back in Jenny's room but with little success.

Unsure what to do, but left with no alternative, Brandon cleared his throat. He would try it again. "Leave him!" he shouted. "I command you to leave him, now!"

The Reverend's head shot back as more laughter filled the sanctuary. Then he spoke. *"HE DOESN'T EVEN BELIEVE I EXIST!"*

Brandon swallowed and tried again. "I command you to leave him!"

"AND YOU BELIEVE IN NOTHING." More laughter.

Brandon steadied himself, remembering all too well how his bluff had been called back in Jenny's room. "I—I do believe." He centered his voice, trying to give it more authority. "I believe and I command you to leave. Do you hear me? I command you to leave. Leave him now!"

This time there was no response. No words. No laughter. Brandon held his breath and waited.

Gradually the macabre dancing slowed, then stopped altogether. Brandon watched, saying nothing.

At last, the Reverend's eyes rolled down. He blinked and looked about, confused and disoriented. When he saw Brandon, he frowned. "What . . ." It was a single voice now. The Reverend's voice. "What happened?"

Brandon stepped toward him. "Are you all right?" The Reverend nodded but wobbled slightly. Brandon reached out to steady him. "It was that head." He motioned back toward the altar. "It—"

Without warning, the Reverend's body twirled. His arms flew out; his right hand smashed into Brandon's face. Brandon staggered backward as more unearthly laughter filled the sanctuary.

Holding his cheek, angered at the deception, Brandon took a step forward and braced himself. "Leave him!" he shouted. "Leave him! Now!"

More laughter.

"I said, leave hi—"

Suddenly, the Reverend's body was picked up, dragged between the pews, and violently hurled against the left wall. Brandon started toward him but stopped when he noticed the beast's head leaving the altar. Its vaporous faces swirled faster as it moved up the aisle toward him. Trembling, Brandon forced himself to step back into the aisle, taking a stand between it and his father.

"Stay away!" he shouted. "Stay back!"

The head slowed to a stop. It hovered at eye level less than a dozen feet away. Brandon could see the horns clearly now. There were ten, counting the new one that had grown back—the hideous-looking one covered in moving eyes. The head did not open its mouth, yet it spoke with the same voices that had spoken through the Reverend.

"YOU HAVE NO AUTHORITY."

Brandon's heart hammered in his chest. He had tried everything he had known, everything he had seen the old woman do. And nothing had worked.

As if reading his thoughts, the head resumed its advance.

"Stay back!" Brandon ordered. "I command you to stay back!"

The voices repeated themselves. *"YOU DO NOT BELIEVE."*

"I do."

"LIAR."

Brandon pulled back a step. Then another. The creature was right.

"YOU DON'T EVEN KNOW WHO YOU ARE," the voices hissed. *"NOT THAT IT MATTERS. LOOK WHERE SUCH BELIEF BROUGHT YOUR FATHER."*

Brandon couldn't resist looking back at his father in the wheelchair. Once again the thing was right. His father had been a strong believer, and look where it got him. But as Brandon stared, something caught his attention. Was it his imagination, or were his father's vacant eyes actually registering emotion? Was it fear? Pain? He couldn't tell, but something was definitely going on inside of him.

"Brandon!"

It was his mother's voice. He spun around to see her entering from the back of the sanctuary. But before he could respond, the beast shot another stream of mist, this time to the wall opposite the Reverend. From it the human wolf of the lab experiment suddenly materialized. It crouched low, baring its teeth and snarling.

Apparently Momma saw it, too. But not the wolf. She saw something entirely different. "Jenny!" Her hand went to her mouth in astonishment; her face filled with joy. "Jenny!" She ran toward the wolf.

"Momma, no!" Brandon cried. "Momma, it's a trick!"

But she gave no sign of hearing as she raised her arms and raced toward what she thought to be her little girl.

Brandon ran along the pew toward the wall to cut her off. "It's not Jenny! Momma!"

He was barely aware of the head. Taking advantage of his distraction, it quickly moved in, rotating to his left. For a moment he couldn't see it.

And then it screamed. An unearthly roar. Agonizing voices. Blaspheming voices. A chorus of cries and shrieks so powerful that they hit Brandon's body with physical force. He fell against the pew as the beast appeared at his left. The voices pushed him, forcing him to stumble, to stagger along the pew until he fell back into the center aisle just a few feet from his father's chair.

The assault had begun.

The head continued rotating until it was behind him. Brandon struggled to his feet but the voices were too loud, their hatred too strong. They blasted him with an even greater barrage of screams and obscenities. The impact threw him off balance, sending him staggering down the aisle. The beast pursued, pushing and driving him toward the front of the church. Brandon turned to confront it, but another blast threw him backward, stumbling, falling, until the back of his head struck the hard ashwood altar with a sickening thud.

This time he did not rise.

When he opened his eyes, he saw through a blurry haze. The beast's head hovered fifteen feet away, in the center of the aisle, staring directly at him. Off to the left stood his mother, apparently torn between running to help him or running toward her daughter . . . until the head rotated, opened its mouth, and shot another stream of vapor toward the wolf. Suddenly a wall of flames ignited and surrounded the animal.

"Momma!" the wolf screamed in Jenny's voice. "Help me, Momma! Help me!"

"Jenny!" Momma ran toward the animal. But the wall of fire was too tall and too thick. Brandon understood. It was merely a decoy—something to keep his mother occupied, to keep her from interfering during the real showdown.

Now the head turned its full attention to Brandon. Slowly, menacingly, it started its approach. Brandon tried to clear his vision, to move his body, but nothing would cooperate.

The thing was ten feet away when something caught Brandon's attention—a glint, a moving reflection, behind the vaporous head. He squinted, trying to clear his vision. Then he saw it. It was his father's silver-and-turquoise wristwatch. The one he'd given him so many years before. But why was it—and then he had his answer. The watch was moving. To be more precise, his father's hand was moving, just enough to catch and reflect the light. Was it possible? Was his father actually moving his hand?

"YOU ARE MINE."

Brandon focused back on the approaching beast. It was eight feet away, its mouth opening wider. And now, for the first time, Brandon could see into its throat. To his astonishment, it was not a throat but a swirling, glowing pit. A spinning whirlpool of fire that stretched as far as the eye could see. A whirlpool that created a tremendous wind, a vacuum so strong that it began sucking in all of the surrounding air. Hissing, howling wind rushed into the creature's mouth. Brandon could feel his hair, his clothes being drawn toward it.

And still the beast approached. The wind pulled harder until Brandon felt his body starting to move. Just as in the experiment at the Institute, the current was attempting to drag him toward it. Toward the mouth. Into the throat.

He struggled to get to his feet, but his unsteadiness coupled with the powerful wind made it impossible. He was sliding toward it faster now. He had to stop himself, he had to grab something. But there was nothing except the altar behind him. Twisting around, he grabbed the nearest corner. It was smooth and slick. His grip wouldn't last long, but it was all he had.

The beast closed in. Brandon tried not to look over his shoulder into its throat, but he couldn't help himself. The swirling fire went on forever. And now he saw faces. Human faces. The same tortured, burning faces that had surrounded him when he was tumbling in the experiment, when he was falling into the fiery void. The same terrifying, burning, screaming faces.

Once again he caught a glimpse of a reflection. Behind the head. The moving reflection of his father's watch. His father's hand was trembling and shaking as it continued to inch its way forward.

The operating lights illuminated Sarah's shaved head in an unearthly glow. Dr. Hibdon could have waited for the neurosurgery team to come in from South Bend, or they could have evacuated her to Fort Wayne. But the CT scan had confirmed his suspicion of an acute subdural hematoma. They'd already run the Glasgow Comma on her. She'd not scored well. It was a judgment call, but Hibdon was a competent surgeon and seconds counted.

He picked up the stainless steel scalpel from the tray. "All right, let's see what we can do for her," he said as he reached down to the marked incision site on her skull.

That was when the EKG went off.

The doctor's eyes shot up.

"She's arrested!" a voice called from the right.

Hibdon leaned past a nurse to see for himself. The green line on the oscilloscope had dropped. There was no tracing. It was smooth and flat.

"Check her leads," he said.

"Leads okay," the voice replied.

"Give her a milligram of Epi," he ordered. "Bring in the paddles."

The team moved into action.

"Give me two hundred joules."

The creature's mouth opened wider. The swirling abyss of fire and faces pulled harder; the tug on Brandon's feet and legs was relentless. He clung to the edge of the altar, but his handhold was too weak. He was already beginning to slip.

And then he saw the wheelchair. It had started down the incline. Somehow, his father had moved his hand far enough to release the brake. Now he was rolling down the aisle directly toward them.

"YOU ARE MINE," the voices in the throat shrieked.

The chair rolled toward them. It was heading straight for the back of the beast's head! So that's what his father was up to. He was trying to stop it!

Brandon's grip on the altar was nearly gone.

"YOU ARE—"

And then the wheelchair struck. But instead of slamming into the head, it passed through the vaporous back and entered it!

The creature roared in surprise. It shrieked and screamed. It pitched its head back and forth, but Brandon's father and the chair remained inside. For an instant Brandon saw the man's eyes. They were wild with fear. But they showed no more fear than the eyes of the beast. It was clear that his father's presence was inflicting pain—but not just his presence. Brandon guessed that it also had something to do with his faith. A faith that had been trapped inside a lifeless body for six years, but a faith that was finally being released—and doing some extensive damage in the process.

As the creature writhed, his father was thrown from side to side. The beast's screams grew to a shrieking resonance that vibrated the entire church. Above, the light fixtures began to crack; some shattered into a rain of glass. On the front wall, behind the cross, the organ pipes began to explode. One after another—fiery, popping explosions. And still the shriek continued. The supports holding the cross vibrated until they shook loose and the entire structure broke from the wall. With a groan, it toppled forward. Spotting it, Brandon rolled out of the way just as it crashed to the floor, missing him by inches.

Thanks to his father's attack, the wind had momentarily lessened, giving Brandon the time he needed to struggle to his feet. But he'd barely risen before he heard:

"YOU ARE MY DEEPEST DISAPPOINTMENT."

He looked up to see his father standing, floating inside the beast's head just a few feet away. The chair had already been flung to the ground, and the man hovered before his son.

"YOU HAVE ALWAYS BEEN A DISAPPOINTMENT."

The words hit Brandon hard. Part of him knew that they were coming from the creature—that his father had put up a gallant fight but had been overcome. Still, the other part of him knew that the man standing before him was his father, that he was finally speaking to him after so many years of condemning silence. And that the words he spoke were the very words Brandon had known he would say, had feared his father had been thinking for all of these years.

Brandon's response was faint and trembling. "Pop—"

"YOU ARE NOT MY SON."

The indictment brought instant tightness to Brandon's throat. It was nearly impossible to speak. "Pop, please. Please don't say—"

"MY SON WAS TO BE A LEADER. TO EMBODY MY FAITH."

"I do. I have faith. I—"

"LIAR!"

The accusation made Brandon's legs weak. He took half a step back, trying to regain his balance as tears sprang to his eyes.

"FAITH DOES NOT DESTROY."

"Poppa, I swear to you. I believe!"

"YOU ARE DESTRUCTION. YOU HAVE DESTROYED JENNY, SARAH—ALL THAT YOU TOUCH!"

The words hit with such force that Brandon gasped. He tried to catch his breath, but couldn't. "Please. I—"

"YOU ARE DESTRUCTION. ALL THAT YOU TOUCH, YOU DESTROY."

The ache in Brandon's throat was agonizing, his breathing impossible. Everything his father said was true. And that truth was relentless, powerful, devastating. Slowly, he dropped to his knees. He was no longer able to stand.

And still the onslaught continued.

"YOU ARE NOT FAITH. YOU ARE DESTRUCTION."

"I . . ." He could no longer look up. "I belie—"

"YOU BELIEVE NOTHING!"

"I do." Brandon's voice was barely a whisper. "I . . ." He felt his body shudder. It was an escaping sob.

"YOU BELIEVE NOTHING. YOU HAVE NO PURPOSE. YOU ARE NOTHING."

Brandon choked, trying to talk. "I . . ." But he could not. There was another sob. Then another. Deep, gut-wrenching. His father was right. He *was* a failure, he *was* nothing. Whatever fraction of faith he might have had before his father's words, was gone. It was all gone.

"I'm . . . sorry."

"YOU BELIEVE NOTHING!"

Brandon lowered his head, silently weeping, nodding in agreement. He was remotely aware of his father's body being tossed to the floor like a rag doll. He knew that it had served its purpose. The beast had used it to break him . . . and it had succeeded.

Brandon remained on his knees. He did not look up. He sensed the beast approaching. He could feel the wind increasing, pulling harder. But he no longer cared. What was the point. This was his fate; this was what he deserved.

The wind grew, pulling with greater and greater force. Brandon was moving now, being drawn toward the open mouth, toward the swirling flames of the throat. But it did not matter. He no longer cared.

CHAPTER 17

Sarah's body lurched under the electrical paddles. The doctor looked at the monitor. The line remained flat.

"All right, give me 370."

The male nurse manning the crash cart nodded and reset the calibrations. He was new—tall and gangly with a steel prosthesis for a left hand. He had spoken only a few words, but Dr. Hibdon recognized them as British. Lower middle class.

An intern placed the paddles back on Sarah's chest, one near the sternum, the other just past the nipple. "Clear," he called.

The body leaped.

The alarm continued to sound.

The open mouth filled Brandon's vision, the swirling abyss of flames and faces were all he could see. Still on his knees, he instinctively leaned back. It was more reflex than resistance and it did little good, except to free his feet and legs. They were the first to be sucked into the mouth. He watched in terror as the howling wind pulled them into the throat. The heat and flames ignited his pants with a pain so excruciating that all he could do was scream . . . and scream. He spun onto his stomach and tried to crawl away, but the wind was too great. He clutched at the carpet in a vain attempt to slow himself, but there was nothing for his fingers to grip; their tips burned raw dragging across the coarse fabric.

To his left he saw a pew, the very one he and his mother had sat in for so many years. He lunged toward it, grabbing the base, and hung on fiercely. The pain in his burning legs hardened his grip to iron. But it made no difference. For the pew itself began to move. He was dragging the pew right along with him into the mouth.

"No!" he screamed, searching for another handhold. Something heavier. Anything. There was only the fallen cross. It had wedged itself against the altar with the crossbeam jutting out toward him. It

was close enough for Brandon to grab, but he had no assurance that it would be any more stable than the pew.

The burning pain exploded around his waist, igniting his shirt, the flames eating into his back and belly. Over half of his body was in the throat now. He grew light-headed; his consciousness started to shut down. Pain was everywhere and nowhere. It would be easier to just—

"Brandon!"

His senses sharpened. It was Sarah's voice. It was softer than the tormented screams surrounding him, softer than the screams coming from his own mouth, but somehow it was closer, clearer.

"Help me," she whispered, *"Brandon . . ."*

"Sarah?" he groaned.

"You must believe."

"Sarah!"

"Believe."

The plea was unmistakable but confusing. Believe what? Believe in himself? He'd already proven the futility of that. Gerty had been wrong. He had no authority. He had no power. He had—

"Believe!"

"What!" he cried. "Believe in what?"

Desperately, he turned his head in every direction. There was nothing he could believe in, nothing to hold on to. Nothing but the flames dancing around the edges of his vision. Nothing but the pew that served no purpose, and the cross wedged behind the—

"Believe!"

No. She couldn't possibly mean the cross. Yes, he could reach out and grab it, he could take hold of the horizontal beam stretching toward him. But there was no promise it would hold.

"Believe."

Was that what she meant? To grab the cross and believe that it would hold? Even now, the irony wasn't lost on him. Once again, that foolish symbol of death was offering help. The very icon that had mocked him since childhood, the perfect representation of all that was hopeless and foolish and futile was again before him—testing him, taunting him, offering its meaningless help.

"Believe."

"I can't!" he shouted—and then screamed as fire enveloped his shoulders, lapping around his neck. He closed his eyes. He wanted to pass out, to put an end to it. But he couldn't. He looked back at the cross one last time—and, despite the pain and the difficulty in breathing, he gasped. For there, on the beam of the cross, was a hand. A human hand lashed to the wood. It hadn't been there a second ago. It had never been there.

And it was alive.

The hand was covered in blood, but its fingers were moving—stretching, reaching out. Stretching toward him!

Of course. What did he expect? This would be his final hallucination. The perfect, mocking end to all of his suffering.

But it looked so real.

No! And even if it was true, even if it was real, even if he did reach out to it, he would have to let go of the pew. And the wind was too strong, the power too intense. He would be sucked away before he ever made contact.

"Believe . . ."

The hand stretched, reaching. Urging. Brandon was no fool. He knew whose hand it was supposed to be. But he also knew how he'd rejected it in the past. How he'd scoffed at it—and worst yet, how he had remained indifferent to it. Even if it was *the* hand, it wouldn't accept him. Not now, after all he'd done. Not after all that he'd become.

And then he saw something else. Through the blood on the hand he saw the open wound. The gaping hole in the center of the palm. It *was* the hand. The hand with the hole. The hand with the perpetual wound. The hand that received its scar because . . .

Sunday school verses rushed in. Songs and sermons and prayers. Memories of why that hand had been wounded. Not because of Brandon's faith or success. It had been wounded because of his doubts and failures. Wounded for his defeats, not his victories. And now it was reaching out to him.

"Believe . . ."

But if he let go of the pew, if he let go of his only security and grabbed the hand, how did he know that *it* would take hold of *him?* It had every reason to ignore him, to reject him, to let him perish. That was, after all, what he deserved.

But there was the open wound—and its promise of forgiveness.

"Believe . . ."

The fire had burned through his skin, igniting flesh and muscle, organs and bones. He had to decide, and he had to decide now.

But he couldn't.

And that, he suddenly realized, was in itself a decision. If he refused to reach out, wasn't that his decision? The skin of his face ignited in the intense heat, searing his mouth, obliterating his vision.

"Believe . . ."

Finally, with a scream from the depths of his doubt and agony, Brandon let go of the pew and lunged for the hand.

But it did no good.

Just as he'd feared, the hand failed him. He was sucked into the throat. He screamed one last time as the fire roared into his mouth, down his own throat, burning his lungs, every inch of his body consumed in flame, everything but his outstretched hand—when suddenly, something gripped that hand. Brandon couldn't grip back—he didn't have the strength. But something was holding on to him firmly, around his wrist.

And it was pulling.

Rapidly. Steadily.

The fire disappeared around his face. He didn't have the courage to open his eyes, but he felt the flames recede from his lungs, his throat, his mouth. He gulped in cooler, soothing air. His head and neck were out, followed by his shoulders and chest, then his stomach. He still didn't have the strength to hang on, but he didn't have to. He knew the hand was holding him. Its grip was firm, and it would not let go.

The cool air hit his waist, then his legs as he continued to emerge. Finally he opened his eyes, looking down just in time to see his feet exiting the mouth. And still the pulling continued. He tilted back his head to look at the cross. It was several feet closer to the front wall than he remembered. But that wasn't the only surprise. Because now it was empty. There was no hand. There was only the cross.

Then the pulling stopped. Brandon lay on the carpet, gasping for breath. The screams and the howling wind behind him slowly subsided. He twisted around to see. The horned beast had closed its mouth and had pulled away several yards.

Brandon looked back at the cross. There was only the wood and his own hand reaching out. And yet, even though he didn't see it and didn't feel it, he knew that it was still there. He knew that the hand was still there, and he knew that it would not let him go. It would never let him go.

Maybe this sense of knowing was faith, maybe it was something else. He wasn't sure. All he was sure of was that the knowing didn't come from him. It wasn't something he'd imagined or worked up.

"*He* is the author of faith," Gerty had told him. "Not you. You need only surrender."

Is that what he'd done? Simply given in, simply stopped trying and given up? Could it really be that easy?

There was no time for reflection. Another sound had replaced the wind. It had started off softly enough, then quickly grew in intensity. Brandon turned, looking back around the church, but he saw nothing except the beast's head—and his mother. She still stood to the left, but there was no longer any sign of her daughter or the wolf or the flames. The illusion had abruptly disappeared, leaving her confused and disoriented. But only for a moment. Suddenly her attention was drawn up toward the ceiling.

On the other side of the church, Brandon saw the Reverend slowly rising to his feet. He was also looking up, staring toward the roof.

Brandon followed their gaze. There, at the apex of the ceiling, a brilliant light was emerging through the rafters. It didn't damage the structure; it simply passed through it. And as it approached, the roar grew louder. But instead of wind, it sounded like water. Like a giant waterfall, pounding, thundering, filling the entire church with its presence.

The beast's head quickly turned inside itself, inverting, until it faced the opposite direction—away from Brandon and toward the blinding brightness. But the brightness really wasn't a light. It was something more. A quality. A purity. A purity so intense that it generated the brightness.

Brandon had seen this same purity before. Back in the lab, during the experiment. This is what had saved him, what had guided him back through the floor of the lab and into his body. He shaded his eyes and squinted into the brilliance. Yes, there were the four spinning wheels he had seen earlier, and the thousands of all-searching, all-knowing eyes. But he saw something else this time. Amidst the brightness he caught glimpses of what looked like faces. Four of them—some human, some animal. Between the four spinning wheels were blinding flashes, a lightning that arced back and forth between the wheels and between the faces. And, at the very center, between these wheels, was a form so excruciatingly bright that it was absolutely impossible to look at.

A voice sounded. It didn't speak; rather, it resonated through every object in the room, as if the molecules themselves vibrated with its power.

"DEPART."

It took several seconds for the sound to fade. When it had, the beast raised its head and spoke to the light—though its mouth never moved. *"HE IS MINE."*

The room responded:

"DEPART. HIS TIME HAS NOT YET COME."

The head did not answer. It could not. The command had been given, and it had no choice but to obey. Slowly, purposefully, the brilliant purity rose back through the roof. It took several seconds for it to disappear, and even after it was gone its presence seemed to linger. The roar took even longer to recede as everyone, including the beast, looked up in awe.

Finally, the head moved. Brandon tensed as he watched it turn and invert upon itself to once again face him.

"OUR BUSINESS IS NOT YET FINISHED."

Brandon swallowed. He was too frightened to speak, and wasn't sure what he'd say if he could. He looked at Momma, then at the Reverend. They had both started toward him. Apparently neither could see the creature, though it was directly in front of them. He began to call out, to warn them, but stopped. Something was happening to the head. It had started to dissipate. The mouth, the horns, everything was growing less distinct. Details faded, dissolved, until the entire creature had become a nebulous cloud.

"Brandon," Momma called. "Sweetheart, are you all right?"

The closer the two approached, the less defined the cloud became until it was nothing but a mist that wisped and swirled, then disappeared altogether as Momma and the Reverend passed through it in their rush to him.

Something wasn't right. Dr. Hibdon had ordered that they increase the wattage from 200 to 370. But the patient's body had convulsed exactly as it had the first time. There was no difference. A less experienced surgeon might not have noticed, but Hibdon did.

"You gave her 370?" he called over the sound of the alarm.

The male nurse checked the cart. "Yes, sir."

A small trickle of sweat started down the doctor's temple. Over the years he'd seen dozens, perhaps hundreds of hearts resuscitated. The reaction of the body varied slightly, but never like this. This was not how a body responded to 370 watt-seconds of electricity surging through it.

"You're sure it's set at 370?" he repeated.

Without looking at him, the nurse shifted slightly. "Yes, sir, 370."

Hibdon frowned and glanced at the intern holding the paddles. He gave him a motion to check. The intern nodded and leaned past the nurse to see for himself. He did not answer immediately.

"Doctor?" Hibdon asked irritably.

"It's set at 150," the intern answered.

Hibdon scowled and the male nurse with the steel prosthesis immediately protested. "That's impossible. I—"

"See for yourself," the intern pointed.

"Set it to 370!" Hibdon barked. "We have a woman in asystole here!"

"It *is* set at 370," the nurse protested. "The calibrations on this machine are wrong. I've made the correct compensation—"

"Nurse! Set it at—"

"But—"

"Set it at 370 and leave the room."

The team froze.

The alarm continued and the nurse blinked. "Excuse me?"

"You heard me," the doctor ordered. "I don't know who you are or what you're pulling, but you're out of here."

The nurse held his gaze a fraction too long. There was no missing his animosity. Hibdon looked at the intern. "Set it at 370 and call security."

There was a shuffle of feet, a commotion as the nurse turned and stormed out of the room. Hibdon wasn't sure what had happened, and he had no time to think about it. Later, he'd find out where the nurse came from and how such incompetence wound up on staff, but not now. He glanced down at his patient.

"370?" the intern called to verify.

"Does everybody have a hearing problem?" Hibdon demanded.

"No, sir—370 joules."

Hibdon watched as the paddles were again placed on the woman's chest.

"Clear."

There was a quiet thud and the body convulsed—this time far more violently, as every muscle contracted, arching the body grotesquely while the electricity surged through it.

The alarm stopped.

"She's back," the intern called. "We've got a rhythm."

Hibdon nodded, then refocused his attention on the brightly lit skull.

CHAPTER 18

The music had swelled, completely enveloping Dr. Reichner. It had lifted him and filled him with indescribable peace. He was floating, now, in a deep, beautiful crimson. For how long, he didn't know. But with each passing moment, he became more of the music, more of the crimson, more of the peace. They had truly become one. Inseparable. Everything had become him and he had become everything.

Finally, from within the center of the music, from within the center of himself, he heard the voice:

Good evening, Dr. Reichner.

He recognized it instantly—the juvenile timbre, the attempt at speaking with a maturity beyond its years.

Slowly, Reichner opened his eyes. To his surprise, he was not in his living room. Nor was he in Nepal. Instead, he was perched on the tallest structure of Bethel Lake, the water tower in the park. He looked around. He was still sitting cross-legged, but at the very top of the tower. Leaning one way or the other would send him toppling down the side of the steel and aluminum sphere. But he felt no anxiety. Peace still permeated him, filling everything—the trees, the distant buildings, the moon, the passing clouds. They were all one, created from the same atoms, the same stardust. He was them and they were him. Everything was one ... including the python curled up at his feet.

You have failed us.

Immediately Reichner's peace began to drain. The boy guru sounded cold, angry.

You have all failed us.

Reichner watched as the python raised its head, beginning to weave and bob. It flicked its tongue in and out, again and again. He thought of ending the encounter, of forcing himself to wake. But there had been so much peace. And he wasn't about to be intimidated, not by some kid—and not when it came to the financial support of his beloved Institute.

It is not over yet, Reichner answered, doing his best to sound in control.

You are wrong.

There was a finality about the statement, a detachment that made Reichner even more uneasy. Maybe he *should* end it—but on his terms, when it was clear he was in charge.

The python drew closer. The boy guru's voice became more agitated. *He has entered his season.*

The python touched Reichner's left stocking-covered foot. Instinctively, the man pulled it back. But not too far—after all, he was balanced high on the pinnacle of the water tower. He felt his heart starting to pound. He resented the rising fear. After all, he could play anybody, especially a child. He swallowed, trying to sound calm and poised. *Then we will try another approach.*

The python's tongue darted in and out even more quickly. It stretched its head out farther until it actually rested on Reichner's foot. It took all of Reichner's willpower to hold back a shudder. But he would not back down; he would not show his fear.

As if reading his resolution, the snake's head moved across his ankle. It drew up the rest of its body as it slithered across his leg and up toward his lap.

His body rigid with fear, Reichner could only watch, swallowing back his revulsion. It was time to end the encounter.

The head arrived in Reichner's lap and began coiling in the rest of its body to join it. Child or no child, money or no money, it was definitely time to end this encounter. Reichner clenched his eyes shut and then, with a jolt, forced them to open.

But he was still on the water tower. And the python was still drawing its body onto his lap. Its tongue darted and flickered even more quickly. Reichner was breathing harder now. His heart pounded faster.

You have failed us, the boy guru repeated. *You have all failed us, and now we must start again.*

Reichner tried to swallow, but his mouth was desert-dry as the python finished pulling its fifteen-foot body onto his lap. The weight was enormous, far more than he had imagined.

Once again he tried to end the vision. Once again he clenched his eyes, tightened his entire body, and forced himself to jerk awake.

Once again he failed.

We have lost him and you will pay.

There it was—the phrase from his dream, from his e-mail. His heart raced. He wondered whether the creature could feel the pulse throbbing through the arteries in his lap. Perhaps its acute hearing could detect the pounding in Reichner's own ears—a pounding that had grown so rapid that it was nearly impossible to distinguish the individual beats.

Again he tried to take the offense. *I'm afraid you are jumping to conclusions.* But his voice was thin, no longer able to mask his fear. His heart pounded so hard and fast that it was growing difficult to breath. He reached his hands to the roof behind him and tried to scoot out from under the creature.

But the snake was far too heavy. He was pinned, unable to move, which only increased his panic.

We have lost him and you will pay.

The thing slowly raised its body. Reichner watched in fear as it rose until its head was level to his chest. It came no farther, staring at the center of his chest as if concentrating. All the time its tongue flicked faster and faster, almost in rhythm to his—wait a minute. Was it possible? Those flickings, those rapid dartings of the tongue, in and out—they were in perfect synchronization to his heart. Of course, they were still one. He was the moon, the trees, the boy, the python, and they were him. And yet ... no. The thing wasn't matching his heart rate. That wasn't it at all. It was *controlling* his heart rate. The faster the tongue flicked, the faster his heart pounded.

Reichner broke into a sweat. He realized the boy would know about his heart condition. There were records, his hospitalization, the weakened muscle. And if he knew all that, and if he could control his pulse—Reichner was finding it more and more difficult to breathe. He was beginning to pant, fighting for air.

At last the creature quit staring at his chest. Now it rose up, passing his throat, his chin, its tongue flicking faster and faster. In a moment they were eye to eye. Face-to-face. Just inches apart. Reichner's panic turned to terror. His chest began to cramp. The pain spread into his shoulder.

But the yellow, black-slit eyes would not move. They remained staring coldly into his own. The tongue, a blur of movement, faster and faster and faster. *We have lost him, and you will pay.*

Reichner's pantings became short, ragged gasps. The pain spread, searing into his neck, cramping his left arm. He was sweating profusely. Gasping and aching and sweating.

Again he tried to force himself awake. Again he failed.

He leaned away, as far back as possible.

The python drew closer until, unbelievably, its whirring tongue began to lightly brush Reichner's lips.

The man stared, wide-eyed, his chest exploding in pain. If he could just get away, pull back. If he could just—

The python lunged. But not toward Reichner. Rather, it lunged away from him, off him, purposefully removing its weight from his lap. The movement startled Reichner, making him pull harder.

And that was his mistake.

With the weight gone, Reichner was off balance. Before he could catch himself, he tumbled backwards onto the steep decline. He tried to turn, to stop himself, but only succeeded in twisting sideways as he began to roll.

His heart thundered in his ears as he rolled three, four, five times before running out of roof.

And then he fell.

If he managed to scream, he didn't hear it. Not over the roar of his heart. And the pain, the unrelenting, excruciating, exploding pain. Now there was only the pain and the roaring and the eternal falling. The falling . . . falling . . . falling . . .

Momma threw her arms around Brandon and began to weep. Even though he was exhausted he held her, feeling her body shudder as she clung to him. He caught sight of the Reverend. The man was kneeling beside his father, who lay on the ground where he'd been tossed. Gently, Brandon freed himself from Momma, took her hand, and crossed with her to join him.

"Poppa?" Brandon called softly as he knelt. "Poppa." He reached out and picked up the man's hand. He pressed it to his face. "Oh, Poppa . . ."

Then, to Brandon's amazement, he felt movement—the hand was beginning to tremble, struggling to move. He looked down into his father's face. The old man's eyes had opened. Now they were staring at his hand, using every ounce of willpower to move it.

"Poppa?"

Brandon loosened his grip and watched as the hand slowly opened. He glanced at his mother, who knelt on the other side. She was looking on with equal astonishment.

The hand opened now, stretching its fingers. To him. Much like the hand on the cross. Brandon pressed it to his lips and kissed it. He closed his eyes against the tears spilling onto his face. When he reopened them, he saw moisture in his father's own eyes. And the lips—his father's lips were starting to quiver.

At first Brandon didn't understand. Then he realized his father was trying to speak. He leaned over and listened. There was nothing but a faint wheezing crackle. Then he heard it. It was dry and raspy, not even a whisper, but it was a word.

"Son."

The tears came faster. It was true, then. He was his father's son. Even when he had failed. Even in the disappointment. He was still his son.

Brandon wiped his face as he sat back up and looked lovingly down at his father, at the faint smile on the man's lips. But there was no longer an expression in his father's eyes. Now they stared off and away. Frozen, vacant.

"Robert!" Momma cried. "Robert, don't go!" She leaned forward, shaking his shoulders. "Robert! Robert, come back!" She began to sob. Brandon looked on sadly as she threw herself onto his chest, crying. He'd had no idea how fiercely she still loved him.

They stayed that way, for how long Brandon didn't know. But when he finally looked up, he saw people—firemen, paramedics, members of the congregation—cautiously entering the building. Another moment passed before he slowly rose to his feet. He looked down one last time at his father, at the faint smile on his lips. Then at his mother, still crying. He exchanged looks with the Reverend, who nodded and gently took Momma's shoulders, helping her to her feet. A moment later she was in his arms, sobbing.

As the paramedics moved in, Brandon turned to survey the church. Everything was a mess. Broken glass, strewn debris. Behind him, the cross lay on the ground exactly where it had fallen. Exactly where it had saved his life. How much of it had actually happened and how much of it had been a vision, he didn't know. But he did know that it was real. All of it. A "superreality," that's what Reichner had called it, and that's what he had experienced.

Dazed and weak, Brandon started up the aisle. More people were entering, many of them heading to the front. Some spoke, most simply stared. He'd nearly reached the back doors when Frank and Del appeared. Not far behind them trailed a silent and very meek Henderson, his right arm in a sling, his wrist bandaged.

Brandon slowed to a stop. Frank was the first to break the silence. "You all right, buddy?"

Brandon looked at him. Even though Frank sounded concerned, Brandon saw something else—sensed it, really. In Frank's eyes, in his voice, he sensed an anger. A hurt and an anger. How odd. They'd been friends all of these years, and Brandon had never seen it before. Not like this. Until that moment, he'd had no idea the kind of rage Frank held inside.

"Bran?"

Brandon blinked, then slowly nodded to the question. The three of them stood another moment. But no other words could be found. Somehow things had changed. Things had changed, and Brandon suspected that this would be their last conversation for a very long while.

He turned and started back up the aisle toward the doors. Henderson stepped aside to let him pass, but Brandon hesitated. Henderson shifted uneasily under his gaze. Brandon sensed his shame, but he sensed something else as well. There was a goodness here. He knew that there was nothing he could do to take away the pain of Henderson's guilt. But, just as he had sensed Frank's rage, he now sensed there was something he could do for Henderson. For the physical pain, for the pain in his arm.

It was an odd impulse, but slowly, tentatively, Brandon stretched out his hand toward the arm. Henderson watched, shifting uncomfortably, throwing a nervous look at Frank and Del.

When Brandon's hand finally touched the arm, Henderson flinched. Not in pain, but in uncertainty. He looked up at Brandon but didn't move. Slowly, Brandon felt a heat spread through his fingers and into his palm. Henderson must have felt it, too, for he watched in amazement. The heat lasted only a few seconds. When it faded, Brandon removed his hand. He looked up at Henderson, who reached over with his good hand to rub his injured arm, then squeeze it. Carefully, he pulled it from the sling, holding it up in amazement, wiggling his fingers, checking for pain. There was none. He looked back at Brandon, speechless.

Brandon gave a reassuring smile. He knew that it had been healed.

And with that knowledge came yet another insight. Somebody else, another person, needed his help. Without a word, Brandon turned and made his way through the crowd and toward the exit.

Melinda Hauser knocked on the townhouse door a second time. She saw lights on inside, but there was no answer.

"You sure you got the right address?" Robin asked.

Melinda glanced down at the business card in her hand. The back read "1223 Ramona Drive." The doctor had written it down earlier that morning while they had stood in line at the grocery store. And that was the address they now stood in front of. As a pre-med student visiting her aunt for the summer, Melinda had heard plenty about Moran Research Institute, and she was more than a little interested. But she knew that this Reichner fellow wasn't only intrigued by her ESP. His wandering eyes had told her that he was also fascinated by other, more obvious attributes. That's why she'd invited her friend Robin. It would be fun to listen to the man, to ask questions, to hear him tell about paranormal studies . . . and Robin's company would ensure that that was all he did.

"Try the door."

Melinda hesitated.

"Go ahead."

Melinda turned the handle. It was unlocked. She pushed it open. The entryway floor was green marble. A chandelier hung above them, and a beveled mirror faced them from the opposite wall.

"Dr. Reichner?"

No answer. They stepped inside. Melinda cleared her throat and tried again. "Doctor?"

Beyond the entryway a dim light glowed.

"Hello? Is anybody home?"

She glanced at Robin, who motioned her forward.

"Hello . . ." They eased through the entry hall and around the corner to see the living room. "Dr. Reich—"

She stopped. By the armchair, a body was sprawled out on the floor.

"Dr. Reichner!" She raced toward it. Even in the dim light, she could see that his eyes were open and frozen. The skin was ashen white. But it was the expression on his face that made her skin crawl. The mouth was open as if caught in mid-scream. And the eyes—she couldn't recall ever seeing such horror in someone's eyes.

She stooped and touched his neck. She could find no pulse, and the body was already cold.

Robin leaned past her. "Should we call 911?"

For a moment Melinda didn't respond. She was still unable to take her eyes off the tortured expression.

"Mel?" Robin repeated.

Melinda glanced up, then shook her head. "No," she said, looking back down. "No need to bother them. Not now."

As soon as Brandon joined the crowd outside, he felt something cold and wet strike his face. Then again. And again.

"It's raining," someone shouted. "Look, it's raining!"

Brandon tilted back his head. More drops splashed onto his face. He could hear excitement sweep through the crowd as the drops came down harder and faster. At last, the long, hot weeks of drought had come to an end.

Brandon lowered his head and surveyed the crowd. They were all looking up at the sky, blinking as the drops splattered on their faces. Old man McPherson had removed his hat. Some of the children started to cheer. The adults were smiling, talking; some were beginning to laugh.

"Brandon?"

He turned to see the Reverend moving down the church steps to join him. "Brandon ..." The rain came harder now. Both were getting soaked, but neither moved to find shelter. "In there—I don't understand. What happened?"

Brandon saw something in the Reverend's eyes he had never noticed before. Fear. A fragile vulnerability. These insights, this seeing into people was growing stronger. Once again, Brandon was moved with compassion. He wished he could do something to ease the man's fear, to remove his pain as he had Henderson's. But healing an arm seemed far easier than healing a man's soul.

"I'm sure it all has a logical explanation," the Reverend continued. "But that voice from the roof. And Henderson's arm. I saw what you did to his arm."

Brandon shook his head. "I don't understand it all—but I've got some ideas."

The Reverend looked at him, waiting for more. Once again, Brandon was struck by the man's eyes, by his searching, his loneliness. Such need.

"Where are you going?" the Reverend asked.

Brandon looked over the crowd, then up the road. "To the hospital."

"The hospital?"

Brandon nodded. "I've got a friend there who needs help."

The Reverend continued to stare. Brandon offered no explanation but turned to leave.

"Brandon?"

He looked back.

"Be careful. God knows what you've gotten yourself into."

Brandon nodded slowly. "Then I guess ... I guess I'll leave it to him to get me out."

They stood silently in the rain. There was much more to be said. Brandon could feel it. But he could also feel a sense of urgency from the hospital. Sarah was in deeper danger than he had thought. Without a word he turned, took a deep breath, and started walking. The battle was over, he knew that. But the war had barely begun. There would be other confrontations on other fronts, far more sinister and far more deadly than what he'd faced in the church. "Our business is not yet finished," that's what the beast had said.

But Brandon would be ready.

Not because he was smarter, or stronger, and not because he'd worked up some sort of synthetic, man-made faith. No, Brandon Martus would be ready simply because he now knew how to trust. It would be just as it had been on the floor in front of the altar. In all of his helplessness and ignorance and failure, he would simply reach out to the pierced hand and put his trust in it.

That was his only hope, the pierced hand. And as he continued walking into the downpour, making his way up the darkened street, Brandon knew that was all he would need.

NOTES REGARDING REVELATION 11

I realize some of the issues in this novel are controversial. That's probably why I chose them. Like Christ's parables, good storytelling should stir up the audience, wake us from our complacency, and get us to think.

One area of disagreement may involve the two witnesses mentioned in Revelation. There are numerous interpretations of this prophecy. Some believe the two are Elijah and Moses, or Enoch and Elijah, or others. Some scholars don't even believe that the witnesses are people at all but that they are symbols of the law and the church, or the Jewish people and the church. No one is certain.

And while we're speaking of uncertainty, I've checked with Greek experts about the gender of the two prophets. According to the original language, if the witnesses are indeed individuals, one of them needs to be male. However, there is nothing in the Greek preventing the other from being female.

All in all, I hope these portions of the story will make for interesting thought and discussion. That's the excitement of finite minds trying to understand an infinite God and his inerrant Word . . . we seldom get the details of prophecy figured out until after they happen. If you disagree with the book's interpretation, that's fine. I'll probably agree with your disagreement. Again, my purpose, while staying within the boundaries of Scripture, was to stir up our thought, not dictate it. I hope it worked.

Blessings,
Bill

FIRE of HEAVEN

For the Bride,
that she may be presented
without spot, blemish, or wrinkle

PREFACE

I wanted to try something different with this book. And I figured I should warn you up front so if you're reading this in a store you can slip it back on the shelf before it's too late, or if you're already at home you can race back and get a refund before the pages get bent.

My point is . . . this book is not for everybody.

First of all, I wanted to try to write Christian fiction. Not just entertainment that you expect to be moral or that has a Christian theme. I wanted to write a piece of Christian fiction for Christians. Something that begins with what we already believe about God and explores him from there. Something for the disciples after the crowds have been entertained and gone home. Something that assumes exploring God's truths (some may call these portions preachy) can be just as engaging as the fastest car chase or steamy romance scene. So if you're looking for some good, old-fashioned, escapist entertainment, go ahead and slip this back on the shelf, no hard feelings. Maybe we'll connect the next time around.

Also, despite what you may have thought, this is not an end-times prophecy book. My purpose is *not* to expound upon end-time events. Lots of other books out there claim to have those answers. This isn't one of them. In fact, I'd be surprised if *any* end-times happenings unfolded the way they're depicted here. That wasn't my purpose. I wanted to explore end-times themes, not events. I wanted to touch upon end-times teaching as Christ might have when talking to his disciples. It seems nearly every time they asked him for the ear-tickling details, he gave a few generalities and then used the opportunity to springboard into a deeper truth. Instead of getting their flesh worked up and excited about the mark of the beast, or the timing of the Rapture, or who the Antichrist will be, he usually went for a deeper, spiritual truth . . . like encouraging them to be ready.

That's what I've tried to do here. The rest is just backdrop, a little scenery that we may or may not see along the way to his Second Coming. As I've said, if you want a clearly marked road map, hundreds of other books claim to know the way. All I want to do with this one is to challenge us to examine our hearts as we make that journey.

As I did in *Threshold* I need to briefly mention the gender of the two end-times witnesses. According to the Greek experts, if these two witnesses are actually people, then one definitely must be male. However, there is nothing in the original language that prevents the other from being female.

And now finally, to the thanks . . .

First of all my deepest appreciation goes to a friend who wishes to remain anonymous. She prayed every day for the book, from its research, through the outlining, and during the actual writing. There were days she fasted, and nearly every day my e-mail had an encouraging word of Scripture from her. No writer could have been more blessed, and in many ways this book is as much the fruit of her labor as it is mine.

There was also that woman from Ohio (I don't think she ever told me her name) who, on the most critical day of the book, tracked my phone number down and called up to say she'd been led to pray and fast for me.

Special thanks also to Dale Brown who made this book much better; as well as to Rolland and Rena Petrello; Dr. Craig Cameron and his wife, Sue; Geog Pflueger for his hospitality in Jerusalem; Oswald Chambers for the "powder of contriteness" quote; Tina Schuman; Scott and Rebecca Janney; my research assistant, Doug McIntosh; James Riordan; John Tolle; Gary Smith; the incredible folks at Zondervan; Susan Richardson and the staff at For Heaven's Sake; Lissa Halls Johnson; Vince Crunk; Erdogan, my guide in Turkey; Carla Williams; Diane Komp, M.D.; Tony Myles; Francine Rivers; Lyn Marzulli; Greg Johnson; and always to Brenda, Nicole, and Mackenzie.

"And I will grant authority to my two witnesses, and they will prophesy for twelve hundred and sixty days, clothed in sackcloth." These are the two olive trees and the two lampstands that stand before the Lord of the earth. And if anyone desires to harm them, fire proceeds out of their mouth and devours their enemies; and if anyone would desire to harm them, in this manner he must be killed. These have the power to shut up the sky, in order that rain may not fall during the days of their prophesying; and they have power over the waters to turn them into blood, and to smite the earth with every plague, as often as they desire. And when they have finished their testimony, the beast that comes up out of the abyss will make war with them, and overcome them and kill them. And their dead bodies will lie in the street of the great city which mystically is called Sodom and Egypt, where also their Lord was crucified. And those from the peoples and tribes and tongues and nations will look at their dead bodies for three and a half days, and will not permit their dead bodies to be laid in a tomb. And those who dwell on earth will rejoice over them and make merry; and they will send gifts to one another, because these two prophets tormented those who dwell on the earth. And after the three and a half days the breath of life from God came into them, and they stood on their feet; and great fear fell upon those who were beholding them. And they heard a loud voice from heaven saying to them, "Come up here." And they went up into heaven in the cloud, and their enemies beheld them. And in that hour there was a great earthquake, and a tenth of the city fell; and seven thousand people were killed in the earthquake, and the rest were terrified and gave glory to the God of heaven.

REVELATION 11:3–13 NASB

PROLOGUE

Katherine Lyon wasn't sure if she'd heard her son scream or if she'd dreamed it. It didn't matter. She flung off the coarse wool blankets and hit the cold stones of the floor running.

There it was again. Faint, distant, but impossible to miss. It *was* her son and he *was* screaming.

Katherine grabbed her robe, raced to the wooden plank door, and threw it open. The first traces of pink reflected off the snow-covered mountaintops and filtered into the courtyard. Dawn was about to break, but she barely noticed. She turned left and ran across the second-story balcony toward the men's quarters. Once again she cursed the fact that they were separated. But Eric was thirteen now. The thickening fuzz on his face and his unsteady voice made it clear he was entering manhood. And segregation in the compound was expected, demanded.

Then there was the other matter . . . the growing number of devotees who insisted upon calling him Master, or in some cases, God. Somehow it didn't seem fitting for God to continue rooming with his mother.

The two of them had been on their own for eleven years now. The first seven after Gary, her husband, was shot in the line of duty. The rest after Michael Coleman, a close friend, had laid down his life for them—but not before accidentally infecting Eric with a special DNA.

A DNA that many believed to come from the blood of Christ.

Katherine passed two young women wearing sandals and loose colorful pants called *punjabis*. As disciples who were privileged to live within the compound, their joy, their pleasure, was to serve Eric and members of the Cartel. And they did so with unwavering devotion. Even now they carried *pujaas*, plates of colored rice and flowers, as an offering that would soon find its way outside Eric's quarters.

Initially, she and Eric had tried to shun the adoration. But their attempts were only mistaken as humility, which only offered more proof of his godhood. This along with his uncanny insight into other people's thoughts continued to deepen his followers' reverence. People talked, rumors spread, and the harder Katherine tried to clear the record, the greater the worship grew.

Breathing heavily, she reached the men's section. She rounded the corner and nearly ran into an armed guard stationed outside Eric's door. He was military but not from Nepal. No surprise there. More and more countries were offering their services in order to court the Cartel's favor. The soldier was simply one of a rotating group of international representatives. Southeast Asian, the best she could tell.

"What do you want?" His accent was thick. He was new and obviously unnerved from the screaming inside.

"I am the boy's mother," Katherine said, trying to catch her breath. Despite the number of months living here in the Himalayas, she had never entirely adjusted to the thinness of the air. She started for the door, but he blocked her path. She looked up, glaring at him. "My son is having a nightmare. If you don't let me in, you may bring his displeasure upon you." She took another gulp of air. "And I'm sure neither of us wants that, do we?"

It was a ploy she used more and more often. And, given Eric's recent outbursts of anger, it usually worked. Changes were happening with her son just as they had with their friend Michael Coleman. Although Eric's supernatural powers continued to grow, the tender mercy and compassion he'd once exhibited had begun to die. The deterioration that Coleman had fought in himself was now happening to her son. It was all Eric could do to control his hostility . . . an unfortunate reversal and not-so-minor side effect of man trying to reproduce the genes of God.

There was another scream. Muffled this time, almost whimpering. Katherine's gaze remained fixed on the guard. She would not back down.

He shifted again, glancing around the courtyard, obviously hoping for someone to rescue him. But there was only Katherine. He took another breath, swallowed, then finally nodded and stepped aside.

Katherine brushed past him and threw open the door.

The room was several times larger than hers—an eclectic mixture of East meets West. Saffron silk drapes here, the latest computers and monitors stacked over there. A giant, blue-skinned Krishna statue leaned against one plastered wall, while posters of the latest rock idols were taped on another. And there, writhing and tossing in the giant four-poster bed, was young Eric.

Katherine raced to him, scooping him into her arms. He was still asleep and whimpered slightly until she began to rock him.

"Shh, now, shhh . . ."

Instinctively, he wrapped his arms around her, clinging to her as he had when he was a baby. Emotion rose deep within Katherine, tightening her throat and making it ache. She'd read once that there was no love more pure than a mother for her child. She agreed. Despite his outbursts, despite the embarrassments he caused, he was her son. He would always be her son.

"It's okay," she whispered hoarsely as they continued to rock. "It's just a dream, it's okay."

He stirred, then opened his eyes.

She kissed the top of his head. "Was it Heylel?" she whispered. "Did he show you something scary again?"

Eric gave no response but turned his head and continued to cling.

Katherine had her answer. Originally, she had been wary of Heylel's appearances to her son. But after listening to half a dozen experts on the subject who insisted Eric was communicating with his guardian angel or a spirit guide, and after reading another dozen books extolling the benefits of such communication, Katherine had begun to relax . . . a little. As an embittered preacher's kid who was toying with returning to the faith, she could find nothing wrong with her son's experiences. Wasn't the Bible chock-full of angels speaking and directing people? Why should Eric, with his heightened sensitivity to the supernatural, experience anything less?

Heylel was careful never to reveal his exact identity. But, because of his piercing insight into political situations and the absolute accuracy of his predictions—which he communicated to the Cartel through Eric—several thought he might be the departed spirit of some military genius, perhaps Napoleon or Alexander the Great. Those with a vivid imagination suggested Eric could be channeling some wise and benevolent alien from another planet, while many with a more scientific bent suggested that Heylel was merely a subconscious extension of Eric's own supernatural giftedness.

It made no difference. The point is, everyone was positive Heylel was good—the books, the counselors, Eric, the specialists Katherine had insisted be flown in to examine him, the Cartel, everyone. Everyone . . . except Katherine. Because, despite the overwhelming evidence, she still found something unsettling about the times Eric would give up control of his voice and become a channel for this entity to speak through.

Still, Heylel was always courteous, never abusive, and he always offered brilliant counsel. A counsel that the Cartel had grown more and more dependent upon. A counsel that this semisecret organization of international bankers, politicians, and world leaders was using for the betterment of all.

And yet . . .

Katherine pushed back her son's damp hair and kissed him on the forehead. He did not pull away. She tried to lift him from the bed, but those days had long passed. He was far too heavy. Instead, she helped him to his feet and gently guided him toward the door.

"Come stay with me," she said softly. "Just for a while."

She was pleased Eric didn't resist as they headed for the door. God or no god, this frightened boy was going to spend the rest of the early morning hours with his mother.

Brandon bolted up in bed. He sat there for several seconds, catching his breath, waiting for the last of the nightmare to fade. It was always the same one. The one where he stood before the altar of his father's church confronting a giant serpent head. As always the vaporous specter had floated above the aisle, just a few feet before him. As always, it had opened its tremendous mouth in preparation to devour him. And, as always, Brandon stood terrified, staring helplessly into its throat, seeing a whirling vortex of human faces, fiery apparitions that twisted and distorted, faces screaming in agony as they swirled around and around, spiraling down into an endless abyss.

The vision was horrifying. It always was.

So was the wind. The fierce, screaming wind that tugged at him, trying to draw him into the mouth. As in the other dreams he had spun around to grab hold of the altar, hoping his grip would somehow prevent him from being sucked into the throat, from joining those thousands of tortured, screaming faces.

The nightmare didn't come often, but when it did, it always left him cold and shaken. The reason was simple. It was identical to the confrontation he had actually had in his father's church over a year ago. Only, in that confrontation, his grip on the altar did not hold. The encounter had been fierce and excruciating. It had taken his father's life, and it had nearly destroyed his own.

But tonight, there had been another difference. As he clung to the altar, he had noticed some sort of crescent moon and five-pointed star carved into the wood. The image seemed vaguely familiar, but he couldn't place it. And, even now, as the last of the nightmare faded, the moon and star continued to linger in his mind.

He turned to the clock radio on his nightstand. It read 2:39. He wouldn't be able to go back to sleep, he was certain of that. He pulled off the damp sheet that still clung to his body, snapped on the light, and sat on the edge of the bed. Scattered on the floor around his feet were the remains of yesterday's newspaper. There were the usual headlines about the recent crash of the Tokyo stock exchange and fears that Wall Street and NASDAQ were following. Another article spoke of the masses of people starving from the drought. There was also something about the rapid spread of a new virus they'd nicknamed "Scorpion." Latest estimates were that 1.3 million of the world's Semite population, mostly Jews and Arabs, were already infected, and it was going to get a lot worse before it got better. Finally, there was another article on the progress Lucas Ponte and the Cartel were making toward world peace.

But yesterday's headlines were of little interest to Brandon now. Now, his eyes were drawn to a pile of sketches on the dresser across the room. Sketches made by Gerty Morrison before she'd died. No one had taken the old woman seriously when she lived, but the prophecies she had given regarding Brandon and Dr. Sarah Weintraub had proven eerily correct, down to the tiniest detail. Still, the past prophecies were nothing compared to the ones she claimed were yet to be fulfilled. The ones insisting that both he and Sarah were the two end-time prophets mentioned in the Bible.

Of course, it took more than one woman's predictions to get them to take such a claim seriously, no matter how accurate those predictions had proven in the past. And God seemed only too happy to oblige with further evidence . . . such as the words of other so-called prophets spoken over his mother when she was pregnant with him . . . and the demoniacs who always screamed whenever he or Sarah entered their presence . . . and the results of the paranormal tests Sarah had run on him when they'd first met . . . and the showdown between heaven and hell that had killed his father and nearly taken his own life.

There was, however, one further piece of evidence, perhaps stronger than all of the others combined: the emergence of Brandon's own prophetic gifts. And, just as importantly, his newfound ability to heal the sick.

If God was trying to make a point, he'd certainly gone out of his way to do so. Yet, at the same time, he was frustratingly silent when it came to any details on the how or the when.

With a heavy sigh, Brandon rose from the bed and shuffled toward the pile of sketches. Many of them were detailed drawings Gerty had made of him at pivotal moments in his childhood. The fact that she had never seen him during this time made them even more compelling. But the last sketch was the one he and Sarah had found the most unsettling. He riffled through the pile until he found it. It was a sketch that featured both of them together. Their hair was cut short and they stood side by side in an ancient walled city. And hovering directly in front of them was the vaporous snake head of his dream. Its mouth was opened wide, and it was poised to devour them. But equally disquieting was that the serpent was held at bay by what looked like flames of fire . . . spewing from Brandon's mouth.

Brandon stared at the sketch a long time before setting it back down on the dresser. Then, taking a deep breath and slowly letting it out, he glanced back at the time.

It was now 2:43.

He headed back to bed. He shut off the light and stared up at the ceiling. It was doubtful he'd be able to sleep, but he needed to try. After all, today was going to be a busy day. Busier than most.

Today, in just eleven hours and seventeen minutes, he and Dr. Sarah Weintraub were to become husband and wife.

PART ONE

CHAPTER 1

"Sarah, your veil, it's all—here, let me straighten it. Sarah, tilt your head this way. Sarah!"

Dr. Sarah Weintraub obeyed and leaned forward.

"A little more. Now please, *please* pay attention."

She stood just outside the sanctuary doors as the wedding coordinator flitted about making last-minute adjustments to her gown, her veil, or anything else that the poor lady could fixate over. But Sarah didn't mind. The elaborate wedding had mostly been for Brandon's mother. Which was okay. It seemed a small price to pay to comfort a woman who had lost her daughter, her husband, and was now about to lose her only son. Of course they would stay in touch with her, try to meet her needs. But as the clinic continued to grow and word of Brandon's healing ministry continued to spread, time for any personal life was becoming less and less of a reality.

Some thought the wedding came too quickly. Others were sure it wouldn't last. It would be hard enough to begin a life amidst the growing famine, the panic sweeping the world over this new virus, and the current financial calamities. But add to that the fact that Brandon was four years her junior, and many were certain that the couple was asking for marital disaster.

Although the other issues were of concern, the age difference was inconsequential. It didn't bother Brandon and it certainly didn't bother her. In fact, Sarah found him less self-absorbed and ego-driven than most men twice his age. Not that he didn't have his moments, but over the past year Brandon Martus had become the most compassionate and sensitive man she had ever met. And, best of all, much of that compassion and sensitivity was directed toward her.

There were other differences, such as their backgrounds and their education. Brandon grew up in this Indiana farm community and was lucky to finish high school. Sarah was West Coast born and bred and held her doctorate in neurobiology. If ever the term "opposites attract" applied, it would have to be to these two.

But there was that prophecy in Revelation . . . and the mound of evidence that indicated they just might be the two end-time prophets who would prepare the world for the return of Jesus Christ much as John the Baptist had prepared it for his first coming. Of course most of that was subject to interpretation, which proved to be a major source of disagreement between the two of them. She never understood why Brandon insisted upon taking every word so literally, while she, although admitting that the two of them might somehow be used, saw the prophecies as more spiritual and symbolic. The truth of the matter was, nobody knew for certain. Not even Gerty. But, at the very least, from what they could tell, the two of them were to work together as a team. And what better way to be a team than to be husband and wife?

Oh, and there was one other detail that carried weight in their decision for matrimony . . .

They loved each other. Fiercely. They were absolutely committed to one another, regardless of the odds.

Sarah peeked through the glass in the sanctuary door. She could see Brandon standing before the altar, incredibly handsome in his tuxedo.

For her, the attraction had been instant, love at first sight. Yes, there was his long black hair and those muscular shoulders. And yes, there were those killer gray eyes which could still make her stomach do little flip-flops. But that was just the wrapping. Because inside, inside was a heart not only full of kindness, but a heart full of her. What had he said the night he'd proposed? "You're the missing piece I've been looking for all of my life . . . you're what fills my hollowness." The words had made her cry then and they almost did now. She knew that whatever the future held, despite graying hair, wrinkled skin, or sagging body, he would always be there for her. Always. And she would be there for him.

Of course there were a few other obstacles to overcome . . . like the forces of hell trying to destroy both of their lives. For Brandon it had been a showdown in this very church, a confrontation with what they believed to be a manifestation of Satan himself. For Sarah it had been a violent collision that sent her flying through a pickup's windshield. If it hadn't been for Brandon's intervention at the hospital, one of the first times he'd put his healing powers to use, she would not be standing here today. And, except for a nasty scar running across her forehead and down to her right jaw, she was as good as new.

Actually, better. Because, in the process of praying to heal her body, Brandon had healed her soul.

"Get ready, Sarah. The prelude is almost done . . ."

Sarah glanced up at the wedding coordinator who was pulling open the doors in preparation for the wedding party processional. She gathered herself together and threw a look at her father. The poor guy appeared more nervous than she was. She leaned over and whispered, "It's okay, Dad—everything will be all right."

He gave what was supposed to be a reassuring smile and patted her arm with his cold, damp hand.

As a little girl she had never seen much of her father. But she did inherit his love for medicine, and even more importantly, she inherited his drive to be the best. If Sarah had learned one thing from her father, it was that success had little to do with brains or beauty and everything to do with ambition and hard work. Although it could be a plus, the ambition had created terrible problems for her in the past, and on more than one occasion it had proven to be her Achilles' heel. Still, as time passed and her love for God increased, she had learned how to deal with it and for the most part kept it under control.

She looked back at her father. He was a good man, full of understanding. Despite their Jewish roots, he made little protest over her conversion to Christianity. "If it's what you want, if it's really what makes you happy, then it's fine by me," he had said. But there was no missing his resigned shrug and quiet afterthought. "Still, I suppose it's best your mother isn't alive to see it."

If he was tolerant about his daughter's change of faith, the good doctor was anything but pleased over his future son-in-law's disposition toward miracles. He did not spend all of that money sending his baby to graduate school to have her marry some backwoods faith healer. That's why he had come a week early. And that's why after several days of carefully examining the clinic's work—both Brandon's healing of the sick, as well as Sarah's medical evaluations of those cases—he grudgingly admitted that there was something going on. Of course Sarah had tried to explain that "something" in terms of her new faith, but the subject fell on impatient and increasingly hostile ears.

The wedding party was in place, and the music began for Sarah's entrance. She stepped up to the doors. Now she was able to look over the entire church. More accurately, as they rose to their feet, the entire church was able to look over her. She felt her face growing warm. Some of it was from excitement, some of it was her self-consciousness over the scar. Funny, Brandon had tried repeatedly to erase the scar, but had never succeeded. Neither of them was sure why. And, oddly enough, it was the only thing that made the normally self-confident Dr. Sarah Weintraub just the slightest bit insecure.

Still, this was their day and she would not be intimidated. As her father escorted her into the sanctuary, Sarah cranked up a smile and made a point to look as many people in the eye as possible. Most were friends and family of Brandon—a definite hometown advantage. Only a few belonged to her. But there were also dozens of patients who had become friends—men, women, children who had entered the clinic doors with severe injury or disease, some diagnosed as terminal, but who now stood perfectly healthy, anxious to share this day with them.

Of course, there were the others. The skeptics, the stone throwers . . . and the media. These were the people on the clinic's "Win Over" list. The list had been Sarah's idea, and she kept it regularly updated. She loved Brandon and respected him more than any person alive. And as his gifts increased, his mercy and compassion followed suit. But it took more than mercy and compassion to run the clinic. With the addition of three full-time staff members and the purchase and leasing of medical equipment, along with Brandon's insistence that they only accept donations—"It's God's work, Sarah, we can't charge them for what God is doing"—it was all they could do to keep their heads above financial water.

Common sense dictated that they had to increase their donor base by increasing their exposure. The more people they won over, especially the skeptical and influential members of the media, the greater their exposure, and the greater their exposure, the greater their chances of avoiding fiscal suicide.

And they were making progress. In fact, just yesterday, Sarah had been contacted by Jimmy Tyler Ministries. They had invited the two of them to fly out to L.A. and sit on the platform during some upcoming, nationally televised event. Because Tyler was one of the leading televangelists in the country, and owner of GBN, the Gospel Broadcasting Network, his endorsement alone could make or break the clinic. Sarah had worked long and hard courting their interest, and now they were finally coming around. But what type of event was it, and how could they best utilize it to fit their—

Stop it, Sarah chided herself. *Stop working. This is your wedding day, for crying out loud.*

But old habits are hard to break. Before she knew it, she was again scanning the crowd, making mental notes of those who had shown up for the event and those who—

"You!" A wizened old man suddenly leaped in front of her, bringing her to an abrupt stop. As he pointed at her, he turned to the crowd and shouted, "Behold . . . the whore of Babylon!"

Murmurs rippled through the congregation as the organ music came to a halting stop.

Sarah stood paralyzed, unsure of what was happening, what to do. She threw a helpless look at Brandon, who stood equally as shocked.

The old man continued. "She who shows her ankles to foreigners."

The murmuring increased. Suddenly, the man's hand shot up to Sarah's veil. Before she could stop him, he'd grabbed the lace and ripped it aside. She gasped along with the rest of the church as he tore it away.

"Behold!" He jabbed his finger at her scar. "The mark of the beast! Proof of her iniquity—"

"That's enough!" Brandon's voice cut through the air with authority. He'd recovered from the initial shock and moved toward them.

The old man spun to him and practically hissed. "What have you to do with us, servant of the Most High?"

A cold chill rippled across Sarah's shoulders. She'd seen this type of confrontation before, at the clinic, and she knew what was about to happen. But before Brandon could respond, her father moved in. He reached for the man's shoulder, trying to grab his arm.

But the old-timer spun around, driving his elbow deep into her father's belly. He gasped and doubled over.

"Daddy!"

"That's enough!" Brandon repeated. His voice brought silence to the commotion. "Leave us."

The old man seemed to hesitate.

"I order you to go."

At last he found his voice. But it was smaller now, a false bravado of what it had been. "You may think you have authority . . . but not forever. Your day will come." He pointed back to Sarah. "The day of destruction will come for you and your harlot. Very soon, victory will be ours."

"Go!"

"Our business is not yet—"

That's when Brandon's two friends, Frank and Tom Henderson, suddenly appeared, each grabbing one of the fellow's arms. And that's when Frank deftly landed two lightning quick blows to a kidney, making sure it would be a while before the old codger interrupted any more weddings.

The man coughed and gasped.

"Guys," Brandon protested, "be careful."

Frank broke into his famous smirk then turned to Tom and nodded. Immediately they half-dragged, half-walked the coughing man up the aisle toward the exit.

Sarah turned back to her father. He was still bent over, clinging to the edge of a pew. "Dad? Daddy, are you all right?"

"I'm okay," he said, coughing slightly and trying to rise.

She wasn't convinced. "Are you sure?"

"I said I'm okay." He righted himself and carefully tested a rib or two. She glanced at Brandon, who nodded to her that he thought the man was all right. "Just tell me where . . ." Her father coughed again. "Just tell me where I'm supposed to sit."

"Over there." Sarah motioned toward the front pew. "But if you're not—"

"I said I'm okay. Let's just get on with this thing, shall we?" He started for the front pew and was immediately joined by the pastor, who had stepped down to assist him.

Meanwhile, Brandon's aunt had risen to help replace Sarah's veil. Another woman began smoothing her dress. For the briefest moment Sarah stood disoriented, unsure of what to do . . . until she saw Brandon reaching out and taking her hand.

She looked up at him. There were those riveting eyes. She felt them looking inside of her again, probing her heart the way they did when he wanted to know what she was really thinking. Sometimes she found the look frustrating, knowing there was nothing she could hide from him. Other times their intensity made her knees the slightest bit weak. This time she knew he was making sure she was okay and that she really wanted to continue.

She swallowed hard and forced a smile.

But Brandon still didn't have his answer. He asked again, this time in a language only she understood—a language they'd first used in the hospital when he'd stayed all those nights at her side, praying for her recovery, when her face was bandaged so completely that she could barely utter a sound. More recently it had been his method to see if she'd fallen asleep as they watched old movies on late-night TV. It was a simple code. Childish, really. But it was theirs.

He gave her hand two gentle squeezes.

Sarah's heart swelled. She swallowed again and then gave one simple squeeze back. That was the signal. It was going to be okay. Things were going to be all right.

They turned and headed for the altar.

Katherine was not fond of these afternoon sessions. Come to think of it, she was growing less and less fond of any of the sessions involving the Cartel. These were the times when Eric was the most vulnerable, when he made himself available for Heylel to speak through him and give them counsel. These were also the times Katherine wandered the adjacent hallway, visited nearly every secretary whose office was in the vicinity of the meeting room, and put down more than her fair share of coffee. Sometimes the meetings would go on for an hour, sometimes several. It all depended upon what international fire had to be put out. The current meeting had just begun its third hour.

She sat in an armchair inside a lobby of one of the offices and idly flipped through another magazine. She didn't mind the Cartel members themselves. In fact she almost liked a couple of them. Even though they were some of the most influential people in the world—international bankers, business moguls, past and present politicians—as human beings, they weren't half bad.

For Katherine and most of the world, the Cartel's history was murky at best. Until they officially acknowledged their presence less than a year ago, many people weren't even sure they existed. And that invisibility, according to the experts, was their greatest strength. Some insisted the group had roots as far back as the Knights of the Temple, or more recently, the Illuminati. Others insisted they were a major force behind the creation of the United Nations, the Trilateral Commission, and the European Union. Whatever rumor you cared to believe, the point was they were heavy hitters who had finally come out of seclusion for one purpose and one purpose only: "To assist global powers in bringing about permanent world peace." That was it. Despite the conspiracy rumors and paranoid hearsay, they insisted they were not interested in "world domination." They didn't want to run the show, merely save it.

And what better man to become their spokesperson than Lucas Ponte? Twice elected president of the United States, he had quickly earned a reputation not only for his compassion, but for his commitment to world peace. In the first term he had become a national hero. By the second, his admirers and followers were international. If anyone had the golden touch for peace, Ponte did. First there was the miracle of bringing fruitful dialogue to the Balkans, a region which except for Soviet domination had not known rest for over a century. Next came his peace brokering amongst the warring republics of central and western Africa. And finally there was his success in easing tensions between India and Pakistan. As his tenure in office drew to a close, many feared the world would become a less kind place with his absence. Fortunately, the Cartel would not let that happen. Instead, they stepped out of seclusion and asked Lucas Ponte to become their chairman—giving him the opportunity to complete the job he had so successfully begun.

Still, even at that, Katherine didn't entirely trust them. Not at first. After all, this was the organization that had bankrolled the research of the GOD gene. They were the ones who tried to have portions of Christ's genetic code reproduced in Michael Coleman and who inadvertently infected her son. In short, they were the ones who had ruined Eric's life.

Of course that hadn't been their intention. They were simply exploring the possibility of gene therapy to curb man's tendency toward violence. And what better DNA to attempt to duplicate than that belonging to the Man of Peace?

It was an intriguing theory. Until it backfired. Until a few greedy individuals tried to reverse the process, attempting to create conscienceless killing machines. Need some general to press the nuke button? Some infantryman to fight without fear or mercy? Just inject the reverse gene, something called *antisense,* into them for a period of time and stand back. Such a drug would prove invaluable to any nation or military with the money to buy it.

Invaluable? Yes.

Unconscionable? Absolutely.

That's why, after Coleman's death, she and Eric did their best to avoid the Cartel . . . until the group's clout and unlimited financial power finally flushed them out. Yes, the Cartel admitted, there had been a handful of "loose and very greedy cannons" in the program. But they had been discovered and promptly disposed of. The Cartel's purpose was the same as it always had been, to promote world peace. And Eric, with his newly acquired powers and, more recently, with his ability for allowing Heylel to speak through him, could become an invaluable player in that process.

But Katherine was not terribly interested in world peace. And, despite all the books she'd been reading and the counsel she'd received, she was becoming less and less excited about her son's channeling abilities. No, it was the other carrot they offered that brought the two of them to the compound and persuaded her to endure these sessions. It was the Cartel's offer to do everything in their power to find a cure for Eric—to stop the degeneration that had begun as a result of their own experimentation. Not a bad promise considering they were major stockholders in some of the largest genetic laboratories of the world . . . considering Eric's condition had taken a turn for the worse . . . considering they were the only hope she had to stop her little boy from turning into some sort of antisocial psychopath.

So, here Katherine sat, flipping through magazines in a plush office amidst the mountains of Nepal while her son met with and offered counsel to some of the most powerful men in the world. Then again, it really wasn't her son. It was somebody or something else. And it was that somebody or something else that was making the Cartel's offer less and less appealing, that was making Katherine think more and more seriously about getting out.

"Only, the Arab Coalition will not call for a cease-fire until Israel agrees to return to the negotiating table . . . and, of course, Israel will not negotiate until there's a cease-fire."

"What about a nuclear threat?"

"Lots of saber rattling. But with the right guarantees, the Jews won't go nuclear if the Arabs don't go biological."

"Guarantees provided by . . . us?"

"Who else."

The group sat quietly around the table as the former NATO secretary general finished his report. He gathered his papers, leaned back, and resumed chewing a cigar almost as big as his ego.

Eric didn't like the man, never had. Even his voice irritated him. In fact, it was all he could do not to shout the pompous old windbag into silence. But Chairman Lucas Ponte hated it when Eric did that sort of thing, especially at these briefings. It not only disrupted them, but it embarrassed Lucas.

And Eric didn't want to do that. After all, Lucas was his friend. In many ways he'd become the father Eric never had. And Eric was becoming the son Lucas had always wanted.

Now, if he could just get his mother to go a little easier on the guy . . .

"Mr. Chairman, once again I must insist that we delay the groundbreaking and that we seriously consider moving your installation into office to another location." It was one of the bankers. The woman from South Africa. Eric hated her almost as much as the secretary general. So did the other nine members of the Cartel gathered around the table. At least that was Eric's impression. "To stage such events at this time in Jerusalem will not only exacerbate the situation, but it will prove dangerously reckless to your own safety."

"I disagree." It was another banker, this one from Germany. "An action like this will only show our resolve. It will underscore our strength and our insistence that world peace will not be held hostage to fragmentary elements."

Some around the table agreed, others did not. But it was the South African's voice that rose above the din. "One can hardly call these Middle East outbreaks fragmentary!"

More comments flew back and forth. But Eric barely noticed. He pushed up his glasses with his little finger and returned to work. At the moment he was secretly carving his initials into the side of the mahogany table with a $750 Mont Blanc pen. Like all the other meetings that were supposed to be so important, this one was going nowhere fast.

A scientist spoke up. Swiss, if Eric guessed right. "One would think Scorpion should make them sit up and take notice. The disease has reached pandemic proportions. Every continent reels under its impact." He turned to Aaron Stoltz, head of media. "A virus of unknown origin striking primarily the Semitic races, the Jews and Arabs . . . I am not convinced we are taking full advantage of this situation."

Aaron Stoltz nodded. "We're continually flooding news services with the latest death toll. We're playing the 'judgment of God' angle to the max, with the hopes that they'll start cooperating with each other, but—"

The secretary general interrupted, "—but everyone is listening except the Jews and Arabs."

Ironic chuckles circled the table. But Eric had had enough. "I say we just nuke 'em!" The words came louder than he had anticipated and the laughter quickly faded. Some glanced around the table; others shifted uncomfortably. Except Lucas. Lucas was cool. Even when Eric had his outbursts, Lucas Ponte always showed him the respect he deserved.

"So tell me, Eric, do you think that would be a solution?"

"It'd sure stop them from wasting all our time at these stupid meetings."

Lucas smiled. "You may have a point. And with all the other issues to cover it's certainly—"

"Eric . . ." It was Heylel. Eric could sense his approach as much as he could hear it.

Lucas continued. "But I'm not sure nuking the entire Middle East will exactly solve the unrest or that it will stop this new disease."

"Eric . . ." Heylel's voice was louder now, so loud that it had started to drown out Lucas's. Eric shifted in his seat, pretending to ignore it.

Lucas turned back to the scientist and asked, "What progress are we making toward a vaccine?"

"Eric . . ."

Not now, Eric thought back.

"I have something very important to share with the group."

Lucas turned back to Eric. He was speaking to him, but Eric could barely hear now. The man's lips moved but he sounded muffled, growing fainter and farther away. Despite Eric's resistance, Heylel was taking over.

"Eric . . ."

It's not that Eric resented Heylel. He'd shown him lots of neat stuff—astral projection, telepathy, bilocation. And the little mind game he'd played with Dr. Reichner, that psychic scientist in the States, was especially exciting. But there was a price: Whenever Heylel wanted to speak, he spoke. Whenever Heylel wanted to use his body, he did. Oh sure, Eric could resist, but lately it was getting harder and harder to say no.

"I have another movie to show you, Eric."

But, things are just getting—

"It's another war."

But I . . . Eric hesitated. *What type of war?*

"Oh, you'll like this one. It's much better than the last. All sorts of soldiers are stabbed and killed. Some even get blown up. And, if you watch carefully, you'll get to see a decapitation."

Eric felt himself weakening. *Really?*

The voice chuckled. *"Child, have I ever lied to you?"*

Of course, he never had. From the moment he'd first appeared to Eric, Heylel had never lied. Granted, only a few of the promises had been fulfilled, but the bigger ones, the ones Heylel had made about worldwide fame and popularity, were definitely on their way. All Eric had to do was keep cooperating.

"Here, just take a little peek . . ."

Before Eric could respond, sound and images flooded his brain. It was like a movie, only a hundred times better. It was as if he was really there. Men in bright blue uniforms running, shouting. Cannons exploding, swords stabbing and skewering. Sometimes a person would explode and fly through the air screaming in agony. It was everything Heylel had promised and more.

And, as Eric gave himself over to the images, he began to sink deeper and deeper—falling from his own mind, falling someplace very, very special. Soon he felt his throat being cleared, his vocal chords vibrating, and his mouth begin to move. But he could not hear what he was saying. It would be hard to come back up and take control. Each time it got a little harder. But that was okay. At least for now. Because right now the gore and killing that surrounded Eric was a thousand times better than sitting in some boring old meeting listening to a bunch of boring old-timers talk about controlling the world.

Brandon sat with his shirt off on the hotel bed, as nervous as a schoolboy. For the second time he clicked on the TV and for the second time he clicked it off. He didn't know much about romance but somehow he figured CNN was not the appropriate background for his wedding night.

He threw another look at the bathroom door. What on earth was taking her so long?

He shook his head, musing at the depth of his feelings. How was it possible? How could one person bring out such tenderness in him, such caring? He once considered himself the most selfish human on the planet . . . and now, in less than a year, he'd become so committed that he would do anything for her, give anything to her, be anything for her.

He rose, crossed over to the twenty-fourth-story window, and pulled back the sheers. It was the same view he'd seen thirty seconds earlier—the Chicago River, the Navy Pier, and beyond that Lake Michigan. It was still just as impressive and still just as intimidating. He'd never been in a hotel, at least not like this. Sure, he'd seen the Hyatt Regency whenever he came up here to Chicago. But he never gave it a second thought. That's where the rich and famous stayed. The hotshots. Not people like him. No way. Well, *no way* had come and gone. Now he was here, with his bride, spending their first night together.

The room was Frank's idea. Brandon had made it clear that neither he nor Sarah had the time or money for a honeymoon. But Frank and the guys at the plant insisted upon pitching in for at least one night. And when Frank made up his mind it was pretty hard to change it.

So here they were.

Brandon gave another look at the bathroom door. He wasn't entirely sure what she was doing, but he had his ideas. Ever since the accident Sarah had spent an inordinate amount of time on her looks—brushing her hair, checking her makeup, that sort of thing. He knew it was because of the scar. Before the accident, her beauty came naturally, something she took for granted. Now it was something she felt a constant need to work on. He sadly remembered her excitement the day she discovered her hair had finally grown out enough to start covering the scar.

Brandon wasn't crazy about the thing, either. But he hated it more for what it did to her on the inside than what he saw on the outside. He hated the way it made the once-confident woman suddenly insecure and self-conscious. And the closer their wedding approached, the more insecure she became, and the more she needed to be reassured of her beauty. Of course he did this gladly, but he also made it clear that there was an even greater beauty inside. Not that he had always been so sensitive. After all, it was her good looks that had originally taken his breath away. But that had been a long, long time ago. A different lifetime, a different Brandon. A Brandon who had been lost, searching for meaning and purpose. A Brandon who—like many of his fellow Generation Xers—had lived aimlessly for the moment and only for himself.

Not that he'd completely changed. He'd be the first to admit that there were still plenty of rough edges to work on. But gradually, day by day, as he and Sarah studied the Scriptures, and as they poured themselves into people at the clinic and into each other, he saw the shift in both of their lives. Why hadn't anyone told him how exhilarating it could be? How liberating? By taking his eyes off of himself and focusing upon others he was becoming a different person. And that was fine with him. It was fine with both of them. The sooner the better. Because from what they'd read in the Bible, it appeared that their role in the end times would be crucial. Very crucial.

But when? And how?

God had spared no effort in making it clear they were to be participants, but when it came to the details, he remained aloof, completely silent. With no course to follow but their own, they put their heads together and came up with the clinic. It seemed the best way of combining their talents . . . his gifts of faith and healing and her background in science and medicine.

Granted, this didn't exactly make them the fire-breathing, turning-water-to-blood prophets spoken of in Revelation. But, as Sarah had always argued, there were other interpretations of this Scripture than just the literal. Those who believed Revelation to be a book covering the entire span of the church age looked upon the witnesses as symbols of devout Christians who, throughout the centuries, had turned the waters red with their martyred blood. Those who believed Revelation applied strictly to the times of Roman persecution immediately following the writing of the book and that the number 666 was a secret code for Nero, believed the two witnesses to be historical individuals such as Peter and James. And those who believed it was completely spiritual and symbolic, believed the two witnesses represented the old and new covenants, or Jews and Christians, or the civil and religious law. There seemed to be endless possibilities in interpreting who they were and what they would be doing. And, although Brandon still leaned toward the literal approach, Sarah's arguments certainly made more and more sense.

Yet they had to do something. The world was unraveling at an alarming pace. Crashing stock markets, worldwide famine, spreading disease—all within the past twelve months. If anyone needed proof we'd entered the end times, all they had to do was read a newspaper. Things were rapidly coming to a head, and the sooner the two of them were ready the better.

But ready to do what? And how? If only God would stop being so mysterious.

There was a gentle rap on the hallway door and a voice calling, "Room service."

Brandon looked up. Room service? They hadn't ordered room service. They couldn't afford it even if they had. Unless . . . maybe this was more of Frank's doing.

"Mr. Martus?"

Brandon rose. Although the voice was muffled, there was something about it. Something nervous. He grabbed his shirt, threw it on, and crossed to the door. When he opened it he saw a young girl, probably high school age. She stood beside a silver cart that was draped in white cloth and held a sweating silver ice bucket. Inside the bucket was a bottle wrapped in more white linen.

"I'm sorry," Brandon said. "We didn't order any, uh . . ."

"Champagne," she said, just a trace too cheerily. "Compliments of the hotel."

"Oh, um . . ." He opened the door for her to enter. She rolled the cart into the room.

"Are you finding everything satisfactory?"

Instantly, he knew. The girl had lied. He wasn't sure how he knew. He was never sure how he knew these things. Some called it clairvoyance, others insisted it was God's gift of discernment. Brandon wasn't sure. All he knew was that as he grew less self-absorbed and freer of himself, he could listen to others more deeply and hear them more clearly. It was the little signs that spoke the loudest . . . a self-conscious glance, a nervous swallow, the slightest increase of pitch in the voice. The signs had always been there, but before, Brandon had been so full of himself that he hadn't noticed.

He leveled his gaze toward the girl and quietly asked, "What would you like from me?"

She glanced up, a little surprised. "I'm sorry, what?"

"Why did you come here? What do you want from me?"

She tried holding his look, but her eyes wavered then glanced away.

Brandon continued, gentle but firm. "Why are you here?"

But she could not answer.

He tried an easier question. "The champagne wasn't the hotel's idea, was it?"

Her eyes dropped to the floor. Her breathing grew more labored. He waited patiently. Finally, she shook her head. As she did, tears fell from her lashes. She reached up to wipe them, and that's when Brandon saw it. Her hand. It was crippled. It twisted inward, turning upon her like a self-accusing claw. It might have been an accident, a birth defect, even polio. Brandon didn't know and it really didn't matter.

The tears came faster. He took her arm and helped her to a chair. "Here." He grabbed a tissue from the counter. Several tissues. By now tiny rivulets streamed down her cheeks. But that was okay. Crying was good. In the beginning, he used to try and stop it, but not anymore. Sometimes the tears cleaned and washed parts of the soul that he could never see.

He handed her the tissues and kneeled down in front of her. "Have you had that all of your life?"

She nodded.

He waited for more.

She gave a loud sniff and continued. "Since I was a baby."

He looked back at the hand and saw two, maybe three, sets of scars running from the knuckles to her wrist. "How many operations?" he asked.

"Three." She sniffed again. "We've been to specialists and surgeons and tons of healing services." She wiped her nose. "But nothin' ever happens. It never gets better."

Brandon nodded. Again, the details really weren't important. They were only a way of helping her relax, of getting her used to her surroundings before he asked the hard question. But she wasn't ready for that. Not yet.

"What's your name?"

"Latisha. Latisha Cooper."

"Hello, Latisha. My name's Brandon."

She nodded at the obvious and didn't look up.

"You go to school around here?"

She shook her head. "Used to. But then I—" She caught herself and started again. "But not anymore."

"Not since you had the baby."

Her eyes shot up to him.

"It's okay," he said softly. "It's all right."

A new wave of tears streamed down her cheeks. And for one brief moment Brandon thought his own heart would break. He understood now. The hand had ruled her entire life. It was the reason behind her pretended indifference to school. It was the reason she hung out with gang members and why she slept around. It was also the reason that she'd finally gotten herself pregnant.

He cleared his throat, trying to hide the emotion in his own voice. "How old is your child now, Latisha?"

"She'll be eighteen months next Thursday."

"Is she as pretty as you?"

She gave a little shrug and pulled her claw in closer. Before she could withdraw it any further he asked, "May I hold your hand?" There was a moment's hesitation. He started reaching for it. "Is that okay? May I hold your hand?"

She watched as he took it. When they first touched he felt the tiniest flinch. But it wasn't fear. It was deeper than that. It was guilt. And shame. And anger. The poor child was consumed by them. They were the real sickness, her real disease. And they were the reason she'd come to him. Of course she didn't know it, probably never would. But he did.

At last, the time had come. He had to ask the question. "Latisha, tell me ... do you really want to be healed?"

Her eyes widened in surprise then narrowed in anger. Was he mocking her?

Brandon held her gaze, waiting for an answer. It was an absurd question, he knew. But on more than one occasion he discovered people really didn't want to be healed. Oh sure, they said they wanted help, but those were merely words. In reality, their crippledness had become their identity, the trademark of who they were. And for those afraid of losing their identity, who in their heart of hearts really didn't want to be changed, the infirmity would not leave. Sometimes, even more tragically, if it left it would return.

Suddenly, he heard the bathroom door open behind him, and he saw Latisha look up.

"What on earth ..." It was Sarah's voice. She no doubt looked more lovely than he'd ever seen her. And probably more surprised.

"Sarah." He cleared his throat. "This is, uh, Latisha. Latisha ... Sarah." He'd been in more awkward situations, but at the moment he couldn't remember when.

The girl started to rise and pull her hand away.

Brandon's grip tightened. "No, please, it's okay."

She looked at him doubtfully.

"No, really." Then, over his shoulder, he called, "She wanted me to take a look at her hand, to see if there was something we can do for her."

He knew Sarah had been caught off guard and was definitely miffed. He also knew she would see the girl's desperation and would understand. After all, they encountered this type of need a dozen times a week at the clinic . . . although, not exactly in these circumstances.

Once again, Latisha started to pull back her hand and rise, but this time Sarah spoke. "No, please, sit. It's okay, please." Brandon heard the strain in her voice, but he also heard the compassion.

Still unable to see her, he called over his shoulder. "Would you like to join us?" He knew she would refuse. She was aware of the procedure and the need to create a bond of trust. If she were to barge in now, they'd have to start over, and that would slow things down.

"No, I've got some work to do over at the desk. You two go ahead."

He nodded and watched Latisha's eyes follow Sarah back into the bathroom. He winced slightly, realizing she'd probably gone back to grab a robe. Yes, sir, things couldn't have been any more awkward. When he heard Sarah reenter he asked again, "Are you sure you don't want to join us?"

"No, that's okay," she said as she crossed to the desk behind him. "You two go ahead." She still didn't sound convincing, but she was trying. A moment later he heard the familiar sound of her laptop opening and the faint whir of a hard disk starting up. He almost smiled. It had been nearly ten hours since she'd checked her e-mail. No doubt some kind of record for his bride, the information junkie.

He turned back to Latisha. It was time to re-ask the question: "Do you really want to be healed?"

This time she was able to hold his look. And this time she nodded.

"Good," he half-whispered. "Good." He wrapped both of his hands around hers. Then, closing his eyes, he started to pray. With lips barely moving, he silently thanked the Lord, expressing his gratitude for Latisha and his gratitude for the opportunity to help her. Then he began seeking God's will, making certain this was the time and place, that the Lord didn't have some greater plan which did not include a healing.

As he continued to pray, he began to feel the heat. It started in his palms, then spread out to his fingertips. Soon, both of his hands were on fire, their warmth encircling hers. He knew it took all of her will not to panic and pull away, but he also knew she was a strong girl.

Nearly a minute passed before he reached for the fingers of the hand. Then, kneading her hand as if it were soft, malleable clay, he began opening the claw. Latisha stifled a gasp, but he kept his eyes closed. From time to time he would release the pressure to feel if the hand would twist back into itself.

It did not.

Another minute passed before it was entirely straight and the healing was complete. At last Brandon opened his eyes and looked up at the girl. Her face was as wet with tears as his own. She held up the hand, astonished. She turned it, staring at it as if it belonged to someone else. Ever so carefully, she closed it. Then opened it.

She repeated the process, faster. She grabbed it with her other hand, squeezing it, testing it. Everything worked perfectly.

Suddenly she threw her arms around Brandon—clinging to him tightly, burying her wet face into his shirt. "Thank you," she whispered fiercely. "Thank you, thank you, thank you." Brandon said nothing, holding her for as long as she needed, silently thanking the Lord.

At last they separated. She struggled to her feet and started talking excitedly. They were the usual promises—she'd live a better life, go back to church, get right with God. Brandon listened and smiled. He knew she meant well. They always did.

Finally, she gathered herself and started toward the door, practically skipping. "Thank you, Mrs. Martus," she called over to the desk. "Thanks so much!"

"You're welcome" was all Sarah said.

Her response surprised Brandon. Normally Sarah would be excited, sharing in the patient's joy and offering plenty of hugs of her own. But this time, though she smiled and was pleasant, she remained in front of the computer, very much preoccupied.

After a few more thank-yous and more promises to live better, Latisha finally stepped out into the hallway. Not, of course, without giving Brandon one more hug. He returned it, wished her the best, and after another set of good-byes, was finally able to close the door. He leaned against it silently. Some healings were harder than others, depending upon the emotional baggage attached. This one had been exhausting.

At last, he turned to Sarah. She was still staring at the computer. Even in the screen's blue-green glow she was beautiful . . . her graceful neck rising from the top of the white cotton robe, that rich auburn hair grazing her delicate shoulders. There were times, like now, that he found her presence absolutely intoxicating. It took a moment before he could find his voice. "Sarah?"

She gave no response.

"Sarah?" Still nothing. "Is everything all right?"

She finally turned to him, her face a mixture of concern and confusion.

He started toward her. "What's wrong?

"We have some very strange e-mail."

He arrived at her side and looked at the screen. "From who? What's it say?"

"It's from . . . Gerty Morrison."

"Gerty Morrison? No way."

She motioned toward the screen. "See for yourself."

He leaned in beside her for a better look. "That's impossible. Gerty's been dead for over a year."

Sarah looked up at him and slowly nodded. "I know."

CHAPTER 2

"Help me! Somebod—" The cry was interrupted by an unearthly scream. Part animal, part little boy. "Help me!"

Katherine exploded into the room. She pushed her way past the Cartel members who hovered over her son. Those who didn't have the foresight to step back were shoved aside. "Excuse me! Excuse me, please!"

She'd been milling around the hallway all afternoon and into the evening, just in case this sort of thing happened. It didn't happen often, but it happened enough—whenever Eric wanted to regain control of his body before Heylel was done using it.

"Help . . . me!"

She pushed aside the last Cartel member and saw her son convulsing on the floor. To the untrained it looked like a seizure, but she could see his eyes were opened, and although they were wild, she could tell he knew exactly what was going on. More importantly, she knew he would continue to fight until he got his way. He always did.

Of course Lucas was already at his side, Lucas was always at his side. He was trying to hold the boy's head, trying to comfort him and convince him to relax. "Take it easy, sport. Take it—"

"Stop it!" Eric shrieked. "Let go of me! Let go!" But he wasn't screaming at Lucas, he was screaming at Heylel. "Let go!"

Katherine arrived at his side. She took his hand and reached over to his sweaty face. "Shh . . ."

"Mom . . ."

"It's okay, sweetheart, I'm here. It'll be over in a minute."

"He won't . . . let . . ."

"It's okay, darling . . ."

"Let go of me! Let—"

"It's okay—"

". . . gooo!" The last word was a wrenching cry from the boy's gut. As it faded the writhing stopped. Eric had resurfaced. Heylel was gone. The room grew quiet, its silence broken only by the boy's heavy panting.

"Sweetheart, are you okay? Sweetheart?"

He didn't answer.

Katherine tried to move closer, but Lucas was in the way.

"Sweetheart, here." She reached in toward him. "Let Mom—"

But Lucas was already helping him sit up. Katherine watched with resentment as the boy clung to him and the man began stroking his hair. "You all right, sport?"

Eric may have given the slightest nod, she wasn't sure. But it was enough. That was her son and she was going to hold him. "Excuse me," she said, reaching past Lucas. "Excuse me . . ."

And then Eric did something that broke her heart. Something that made her all the more resolved to end these sessions. As she reached toward her son, Eric turned to Lucas as if asking for permission.

Her son! Asking for permission? Outrageous!

"It's okay." Lucas nodded encouragingly. "Go ahead."

Incensed, Katherine moved in and pulled him away from the man. Eric didn't resist. "It's okay, baby," she said as she began stroking his damp hair. "It's over. It's okay, it's all over."

"You said the seizures would stop! You gave me your word!"

Katherine and Lucas were alone in his office. A year ago she'd been intimidated by his fame and popularity. Like droves of other women, she was physically drawn to his good looks and emotionally moved by his charm and sensitivity. Add to that the sympathy factor of losing his wife to cancer the last year he was in office, and you pretty much had every woman's dream. But Katherine soon learned that when it came to sex Lucas Ponte's feet were made of the same clay as the next man's. And after he made several smooth but failed attempts to bed her, it was safe to say her first blush of reverence and timidity toward him were gone. Long gone.

Lucas shook his head. "I said *Heylel* promised they would stop."

"Well, Heylel is a liar!"

Lucas remained silent, letting her words reverberate against the rich mahogany walls. He was known for his compassion and for being calm under pressure. Calm and compassionate. She had never seen him otherwise. Another reason she disliked him.

"Katherine . . . I can appreciate your feelings—"

"You know nothing about my feelings!"

He paused then nodded slowly. "You are correct. I'm sorry, I've never had the opportunity of experiencing a parent's heart."

"You've got that right."

"But Heylel has never lied before."

"I don't care what—"

"Once he gives his counsel to the Cartel he leaves. He always has. It's only when Eric insists on interrupting and fighting for control before Heylel finishes that we have these problems."

"It's Eric's body; he's got a right to do what he wants with it."

Lucas nodded, thinking. "It should also be his right to decide on whether or not to continue hosting Heylel. As far as I can tell the dangers are minimal, and Eric's certainly been more than willing."

"He's only a kid."

"He's a young man, Katherine. And he has a will of his own. He's always had the ability to say no. No one is forcing him to cooperate with Heylel."

Katherine's anger rose. Not over what he'd said, but over her inability to refute it. How she loathed this man.

"You know how important Heylel's counsel is to us."

"Not as important as Eric is to me!"

He nodded. "Once again, you are correct. But without his advice, without his insight . . ." Lucas paused, pretending to gather his thoughts, but she knew he already had them. He always did. "Katherine, for the first time in history, we are on the brink of world peace. I know it doesn't look like it now, but deals are being made, bargains are being struck. And much of it, dare I say a greater degree of it, is due to Heylel's counsel . . . and to your son's willingness to facilitate that counsel."

Katherine started to object but wasn't sure how.

He continued. "Nearly every country is supporting us now. In just a few weeks we will hold the groundbreaking in Jerusalem, followed by my installation into office. For the first time in history, the entire world will know peace. Think of it. People from every nation working together for a common good. And your son's participation will be one of the primary factors. In many ways his contribution is greater than mine, greater than any of ours. And perhaps, in the grand design of things, this is a token payment for all of the suffering you two have been forced to endure."

"If it doesn't destroy him first."

Lucas frowned. "He's been in no real danger. I'm not sure exactly what you mean."

Katherine wasn't sure either, which only added to her frustration.

Before she could answer, Lucas continued. "You have paid an incredible price, Katherine. To ask you to do more would be terribly unfair." He took a deep breath and slowly let it out. "But, to deprive Eric of this opportunity, especially if the risks appear to be minimal, would it not be even more unfair?"

She started to answer, but he wasn't finished.

"Especially if it's what he wants? He's not a little boy, Katherine. And if he chooses to be a major historical figure in bringing about the peace of the world, shouldn't he have that right?"

Katherine felt her argument slipping through her fingers and fought to hang on. "*If* he knows the consequences."

"Then explain to him these perceived fears of yours. But be fair, Katherine. Be certain he understands both the risks . . . and the rewards."

"And if he chooses to quit?"

"Then it will be his choice. Of course it may be difficult for me to convince our labs to find incentive to continue searching for a cure to his genetic problem, but at least it will be his choice. You owe him that, Katherine. We all owe him that." He held her gaze, making perfectly sure she understood.

Almost against her wishes, Katherine began to nod. As always Lucas made perfect sense, and as much as she wanted to stay angry at him, she had lost the reason. Still, there was the other issue. "What about this doctor, this neurobiologist that used to be on your payroll?"

Lucas frowned.

"The one who worked for that institute you guys sponsored in the States."

"Oh, yes. Sarah Weintraub?"

"Yeah."

"We've tried contacting her. We've explained both Eric's deteriorating self-control as well as this situation with Heylel. We've asked that she come to observe him and to make an evaluation."

"And?"

"At the moment she's preoccupied with a new clinic she has started . . . and a new husband."

Katherine felt her anger returning. "I want somebody to tell us what's happening to my son. You said she's good—"

"I said she is the best. She's one of the few neurobiologists in the world who also specializes in paranormal research. It's a rare combination."

"Then you get her here."

"Katherine . . ."

"If you want to keep using my boy as your cosmic communication center, then you get her here to tell me what's going on." Katherine was grateful to have found another reason for anger, and she knew it was time to leave before he found another way to diffuse it. She turned and started for the door.

"And if we can't convince her to come?" he asked.

She turned back to him. "I've seen what your resources can accomplish, Lucas. When you boys set off to do something it gets done. If you can't bring one little doctor here to look after my boy, then it only proves to me how unconcerned you are for his welfare. And if that's the case, then you'd better start looking for someone else to help you save the world, because we won't be sticking around."

She turned and stormed out of the office, pleased with her performance and with her terms.

She just hoped he wouldn't call her bluff.

Dearest Brandon and Sarah:

By the time you get to reading this I'll be home with the Lord. I've asked a young man to be sending this note along with a few others at different times to help guide you through your treacherous course.

"Is this for real?" Brandon asked.

Sarah glanced up from the screen. "From what I've read of her other letters, it sounds like the same woman."

"You don't think it's a forgery?"

"There's always that possibility, but how many people knew she even existed?"

Brandon nodded and they turned back to the screen.

I know the following words will be hard. But as his two witnesses he'll be requiring a lot more from you than most.

Like others from Scripture, you will be made an example for folks to see. Trust him. The cost is great, but you must remain faithful. You've read 'bout your deaths in Scripture. Don't let it worry you. Death comes in many forms. Fact, it was the good Lord himself who said, "Unless a kernel of wheat falls to the ground and dies, it remains only a single seed. But if it dies, it produces many seeds."

As you're about to read, the call upon your lives is very real and very great. But he must take you through several steps. Each one requires faith, and they won't always be making sense. But you've already taken his hand. Now for your sakes and the sake of the world, don't be letting go until all is complete.

Your sister in Christ,
GM

"Where's the rest?" Brandon asked.

"In an attached file."

"Have you read it?"

Sarah shook her head and doubled clicked the mouse, bringing a new document up onto the screen. This one was much different in both tone and content:

My Children:

Before I formed you in the womb, I knew you; before you were born I sanctified you; I ordained you as prophets to the nations. Only be strong and courageous. Do not tremble and be afraid.

Sarah took a breath to steady herself.

My heart is heavy, to the point of breaking. For as a harlot looks to many lovers, so my bride has turned her eyes from me.

> As a wife treacherously departs from her husband, so she has dealt with me. With her mouth she says, "Come, my beloved, I eagerly await," but with the fruit of her thoughts she pleads for my absence.
>
> Listen carefully, my children. I have paid a great and terrible price for my bride, and I will not be denied. She is mine and no one may have her. Yet she is neither willing nor ready for my return. And I will not approach her chamber until I am her sole desire.
>
> Warn her, my children. Warn her of her lustful neighings, of the lewdness of her harlotry. This is my decree to you.
>
> This is how she will hear my voice. Though you are wed and your covenant made, your relationship must not be consummated.
>
> You must neither lie together nor become intimate with one another.

"What?" The word escaped before Sarah could catch it. She threw a look to Brandon. He was also scowling. She turned back to the screen and continued:

> For just as my bride and I are legally wed, just as I love and long for her, I will not consummate our relationship until she is cleansed. She must put aside her harlotries and be purified for the arrival of her Bridegroom.

Sarah had reached the end of the screen and scrolled down to read more. But that was all, there was no more. She turned to Brandon. "Did I read what I thought I read?"

The pain and confusion in his eyes made it clear she had.

"But that's . . . that's not possible," she said. "It's a joke, right? Some sick, practical joke."

Brandon said nothing. He reached down and scrolled back to reread the message.

But Sarah had seen enough. She scooted back her chair and rose. "This can't be real." She headed toward the window then back toward the desk. "You're the one who said wait until we were married. You're the one who said sex was so precious it was only to be shared by husband and wife."

He nodded. "That's what the Bible says."

She crossed back to the window, continuing to pace. "And we obeyed. Lord knows it was hard, but we obeyed." She spun back to him, jabbing her finger at the screen. "And this is our reward? Not to 'lie together,' not to 'consummate' our relationship?"

Brandon had no answer.

"No, no, this isn't the God we've been reading about. This isn't the God of love and mercy. No way. This is some sicko God, some sexually repressed—"

"Sarah."

"Brandon . . ." Her voice revealed the hurt. "This is our wedding night."

"I know," he said sadly, "I know."

"And you really think that this could be his will? Weren't you the one who kept telling me how God was the one who created sex, how it was supposed to be the deepest communication between two people? Isn't that what you said?"

"He's not saying sex is dirty—"

"No. He's saying *I'm* dirty!" She felt her throat tightening with emotion. The words on the screen had hurt more than she thought. "Don't you see it? I'm the 'bride.' I'm the dirty one, I'm the filthy one."

Once again the years of guilt and condemnation began welling up inside of her—the ambition, the using of people, the abortion. Of everything Christianity had to offer, this had been the most beautiful and hardest to accept—that Christ had taken the punishment for all of her failures, that her past was completely forgiven, that he saw her as pure and holy . . .

Until now, until this pronouncement that she wasn't even fit to sleep with her own husband.

"Sarah . . ." He held out his arms to her. "That's not what he—"

"Of course it is! It's right there, see for yourself!"

"He's using us as examples," Brandon said, "as symbols. You think this is any easier for me?"

"I don't know why not. After all, you're the good guy. You get to be the bridegroom, you get to play Jesus Christ. While I get the role of some cheap, two-bit prostitute. Fitting, don't you think?"

"Sarah . . ." He reached out to her. She turned away as hot tears spilled onto her cheeks. She gave them an angry swipe, but they kept coming, which only made her more angry.

"Sarah." He wrapped his arms around her from behind. "Sarah . . ."

At first she resisted until finally she turned and pressed her face into his chest. "This isn't the program I signed up for," she said. "It's not fair."

"I know." She couldn't see his face but heard his heart pounding, felt his labored breathing. "You're right," he said. "It's not fair. It's not fair at all." She remained in his arms, feeling his strength, grateful for it. She wished they could stay like that, just like that, forever. He continued. "But . . ."

She closed her eyes, knowing there was more.

"I know you're having a hard time accepting a lot of this end-times stuff—especially when it comes to taking it literally. And, to be honest, so am I. But this . . . I mean, you can't get much clearer than this, can you?"

She gave no answer.

"If we're agreed that Gerty's never been wrong . . . along with all of the other Scriptures and prophecies and things that have been happening to us . . . if we can agree on that much, that she's never been wrong . . ." He took a deep breath and let it out with heavy resignation. "Then what other choice do we have? What else can we do but obey?"

She said nothing. It wasn't the answer she wanted, but it was the one she'd expected—at least from Brandon.

"Sarah?"

She still would not speak. If that's what he wanted, if that's what God wanted, okay, she'd comply. But that didn't mean she had to approve it, it didn't mean she had to gleefully accept it.

"Sarah, please . . . say something."

Still, Brandon shouldn't have to bear the entire burden of making the decision. After all, this was the man she loved. And they were a team.

"Sarah?"

At last, she gave a grudging nod. She could feel relief spread through his body. Although the decision was far more his than hers, they'd made it together. At least that's what he'd think. He tenderly kissed the top of her head. She pressed deeper into him, feeling his warmth and strength and love.

"Hold me," she whispered. "Please . . . just hold me."

CHAPTER 3

"Eric! Eric, lunch is ready!" Katherine rose and shaded her eyes from the blinding snow above. Behind her, terrace after terrace of young grainfields descended like emerald steps until they reached the small village below. A handful of peasants were hunched over, working the fields, as a distant water buffalo pulled a wooden plow through one of the plots.

"Eric?" She scanned an outcropping of rock. That's where she'd last seen him playing with Deepak, his bodyguard. "Eric?"

The picnic had been her idea. To get him away from the compound and its influences. To get him back into the Nepal countryside with its violet blue sky and dazzling white mountains. Later, when the time was right, she'd ask him what he thought about moving on. There were some powerful pros and cons, and she wanted to know his opinion.

"Eric!" With a heavy sigh, she started up the steep slope after him.

Of course the biggest reason for staying was for the help the Cartel continued to offer. Their genetic scientists had already come up with some drugs that had drastically slowed down his progression toward violence. It had been entirely different for Michael Coleman, their original guinea pig. His moral disintegration had taken only a few weeks. For Eric they'd slowed it down to many, many months.

Still, slowing it down was not the same as stopping it. And, as Eric's interest in the supernatural increased, his moral conscience and concern for others seemed to decrease. Not that he didn't try to be good. There were many times Katherine saw his face scrunched into a frown as he struggled to make the right decision. But as the impulses toward evil increased, it became more and more difficult for him to resist. And nothing pierced Katherine's heart deeper than to discover her son off by himself, full of remorse over some recent outburst of violence.

Another plus was his attachment to Lucas. Of course she was jealous, she knew that. Truth be told, she should be honored that such a man had taken an interest in her son. And it wasn't just because he was powerful. Except for his womanizing, you couldn't ask for a better male role model. Everybody loved Lucas Ponte—an acclaimed international leader, respected by men, adored by women. And, although the wheels of power had positioned him as the figurehead to bring the nations together, he always maintained a certain humility, a grace, and compassion.

Against those two strong pluses for staying was the only minus . . . Heylel. No one knew what the name meant, though from time to time he also referred to himself as Light Bearer. Whatever he was, he continued to make Katherine more and more uneasy.

The initial contact with him had come simply enough. One of the compound's Tibetan monks had suggested they turn to meditation as a cure for Eric's violence. If he could successfully empty his mind and enter that quiet place deep inside of himself he would find his guardian angel or perhaps a spirit guide who could help. It didn't take Eric long to master the process, and he said there were lots of guides wanting to assist . . . until Heylel came along. Then everyone stepped aside and allowed him to come forward.

"He's like the head honcho," Eric had explained. "Everyone's afraid of him."

Heylel had never spoken directly to Katherine, but he had been providing invaluable counsel to the Cartel. Lucas was right. Heylel's knowledge and insight into other leaders' thinking, as well as upcoming world affairs, was as helpful in bringing them toward world peace as all of the other Cartel resources combined. Normally, Katherine might even consider this a plus, if it weren't for the power struggles that were starting to end the sessions.

Katherine was breathing hard by the time she rounded the cleft of rocks. "Eric? Eric, where are—" She came to a stop. He sat high atop another group of rocks, some thirty feet away. His legs were crossed and his hands rested on his knees in the lotus position. Several feet below, Deepak lay stretched out, sound asleep in the afternoon sun. But it wasn't the bodyguard's fault. Eric liked his privacy, and entering weaker minds and coaxing them to sleep had become child's play for him.

Now, however, Eric was playing another game . . .

Two large, gray-back shrikes sat perched on the stones in front of him. They had the typical black masks around their eyes and beautiful yellow-gold breasts. Katherine was surprised to see two such perfect specimens side by side, much less so close to Eric. Normally they were cautious of each other and of humans. But not today. Today they were all friends. Today they sat on the rocks staring at Eric, calmly tilting their heads as if listening. Maybe they were. From time to time, one or the other would preen himself then hop a little closer.

It was a touching moment, and Katherine was grateful to see her son enjoying the peace—something that, because of the genetic deterioration, was coming less and less frequently. Figuring lunch could wait, she dropped back behind the rocks to watch, unnoticed. A birch prayer pole rose from the outcropping above her, its hundreds of Buddhist prayer flags snapping and fluttering in the wind.

As Eric continued focusing upon the birds, they began to preen themselves more vigorously. At least Katherine thought they were preening . . . until they began pulling out feathers. At first it was just one or two. But as seconds passed they began tearing out clumps of white down, then some of the larger, blue-gray feathers.

Eric shifted, pushing up his glasses and concentrating more intently.

The more he concentrated, the more violent their actions became. Beakfuls of down and feathers flew as the birds pecked at themselves more and more furiously. Then came the first sign of blood. Bright red against their golden breasts. And still they tore into themselves. Brutally. Insanely. Self-inflicted wounds that grew deeper and more bloody.

Katherine's hand rose to her mouth.

The poor creatures began to stagger under their own blows. But even that wasn't enough. Not for Eric. He focused more intensely until, suddenly, the helpless birds turned against each other with a vengeance. The fight lasted several more moments as beaks and talons ripped and tore, as blood and feathers flew. It was all Katherine could do not to cry out.

And then, at last, the battle came to an end. Both birds lay on their sides, heaving bodies gasping for final breaths. Eric's private cockfight was over.

Katherine turned away as a half-cry, half-groan escaped from her throat. She looked back, hoping he hadn't heard. But she was wrong. The boy's head swiveled in her direction. She pulled further into the rocks. And there, hidden by the boulders, with the flapping prayer flags above her, Katherine began to cry. She'd suspected this behavior before, had done her best to deny it.

But now . . .

She closed her eyes and swallowed back a sob. This monster was not her son. Not her baby boy. Where was the child whose heart broke the time a sparrow hit their picture window? Where was the little boy who wanted to raise ladybugs for a living? What of the toddler who padded into her bedroom at night just to cuddle? Where was he now?

And . . . what would he be tomorrow?

They were trapped, she knew that now. Despite her fears, despite her rantings at Ponte and her objections to Heylel, there was no alternative. They had to stay. The Cartel and their genetic research to reverse the deterioration of her little boy . . . it was his only hope.

It was her only hope.

Brandon had just finished his last session for the day. It had been a grueling one with a mentally disabled girl and her mother. The children always took the most out of him. Their sessions were the most rewarding when the time was right and the healings were successful, but they could also be the most painful when God, for whatever his reasons, said no.

And this time, he'd said no.

Brandon escorted them out of the examination room and into the dimly lit hallway. Of course there were plenty of tears and he did his best to console them, encouraging them to return in a few months to try again. They'd nodded, and after the good-byes and obligatory hugs, he turned wearily into the room to begin filling out the girl's chart.

The paperwork had been Sarah's idea. And she was right. There was no reason why they couldn't run the clinic like any other medical facility—recording each patient's malady, carefully documenting the healing, or the lack of it, as well as the number of sessions necessary before it was finally complete. In short, they were simply removing the superstitious elements from God's work and evaluating it rationally and scientifically.

"Science and religion don't have to be enemies," Sarah had said. "Not if we look upon science as just another means of studying God and his work."

Of course the clinic wasn't the first of its kind. There had been others . . . like the one founded in the early part of the twentieth century in Spokane, Washington, by John G. Lake. Records indicate that up to two hundred people a day were treated at this facility, often with some sort of medical follow-up or scientific verification. Now, Brandon and Sarah were doing much the same, though with their slower style of care and compassion they were lucky to squeeze in ten people a day. And since their success rate hovered between seventy and eighty percent, word was quickly spreading and appointments were having to be made weeks in advance.

All of this was good. Now if they could just reach an agreement on the finances. If he could just get Sarah to see that you don't charge money for God's free gift. The subject was coming up more and more frequently, as were other major and minor disagreements in their marriage. But didn't newlyweds always have problems and rough edges to smooth out? At least that's what he'd heard.

Brandon finally finished the chart and gathered his papers. He crossed to the door and snapped off the lights. But he'd barely stepped into the hallway before Salman Kilyos grabbed his arm.

"Mr. Brandon . . . please!" He was a young man, no older than Brandon. His grip was weak, but desperate. "Help me, you must." His wrists were so skinny that the fake Rolex slid up and down his left arm like an oversized bracelet. The translucent skin on his arms showed three purplish bruises—sickly looking things, Kaposi's sarcoma, a frequent symptom of those in the final stages of AIDS. Brandon's first instinct was to pull back and break the hold. But then he looked into the man's hollow face and pleading eyes.

"I beg you, Mr. Brandon . . ." He began to cough and quickly pulled out a soggy handkerchief, shoving it to his mouth. Brandon's revulsion did not lessen.

Salman continued coughing, each spasm wracking his frail body. "Please . . . for the love of God!"

Brandon watched with compassion. On the man's left forearm he saw the tattoo of a crescent moon with a star hovering over it. They'd talked about it during an earlier visit. It was the symbol of Salman Kilyos's homeland, Turkey. But it was more than that. Because as Brandon stared at it, he realized it was the same symbol he'd seen in his last dream, carved into the altar. What did it mean? A coincidence? He doubted it. If there was one thing he'd learned in the past year it was that coincidences like these were never a coincidence—especially when connected to the dream.

Then what was it?

Salman had originally come to America looking for a remedy to his disease. "God's curse for liking the ladies too much," he had joked, making sure the emphasis was on *ladies*. Although many clinics were experimenting with possible breakthrough drugs and procedures, none was either willing or able to help him. And, now, in his final days, nearly all hope had run out.

All hope but in Brandon . . . and his God.

As the coughing subsided, Brandon gently admonished him. "Salman, what are you doing here? You should be in bed."

"In bed? In bed? What am I going to do in—?" The anger sent his body into another coughing fit, and he had to lean against Brandon for support.

"Here." Brandon gently took his arm and eased him into the chair next to an old metal desk. He glanced up and down the hall for one of the staff members. But they were either up front in the reception area or down the hall helping Sarah. That's when he saw the open window to the fire escape. "Did you break in again, Salman?"

The young man fought back the coughing long enough to gasp, "It is the only way I can get in to see you."

Brandon sighed. This had been typical of his entire day. Better make that the last couple weeks—ever since he and Sarah had received their little edict from the Lord. Although they'd moved into their new apartment, and although it had two bedrooms, they'd decided it was best for him to continue sleeping at his mother's. They may be end-time prophets, but they weren't fools. Of course they still had a thousand and one questions to ask, but there had been no further word and no further answers. Nothing. Now, all they could do was obey and wait. As frustrating and, at times, as angry as it made them, there was no other alternative but to obey and wait.

Tensions were no better at work. Brandon had learned to smile and laugh at the newlywed jokes, but each one felt like a blow driving in deeper the unreasonable demand God had made and—although he constantly pushed the word out of his mind—the *cruelty*.

Finally, there was Sarah. As painful as it was for him, there was no telling what it was doing to her. Being told she represented a harlot, an adulterous bride, that she wasn't even worthy enough to sleep with her husband? When she'd first become a Christian, it had been all she could do to grasp the concept of God's unconditional love. And now . . . who knew how all of this was tearing her up inside?

He directed his attention back to Salman, kneeling down before him as the man continued to shudder with each wracking cough. The poor fellow didn't have enough strength to be out of bed, let alone out in public. He'd been to the clinic a dozen times. And each time Brandon had turned him away. Not because he wanted to, but because he had to. Because every time that he prayed, seeking the Lord's will, he had the clear and unmistakable impression: *Healing is not yet permitted for him, not at this time.*

The response always troubled Brandon. He'd healed several AIDS patients in the past, so why not Salman? Every time he'd turned him away his heart grew heavier. And every time the man walked out the doors of the clinic he looked like he'd received his death sentence. Perhaps he had.

The coughing became more violent.

"Salman . . . Salman, are you all right?"

Salman tried to respond, but it was impossible for him to answer.

"Salman?"

His grip tightened on Brandon's arm.

"Salman!"

The man gestured frantically but could not speak. He wasn't getting enough air. With his free hand, Brandon reached toward the phone on the desk. He grabbed the receiver and pressed 306, Sarah's extension. The line began to ring.

Salman's coughing grew more frightening, his wheezing and gasping more desperate.

The phone continued to ring, but no one answered. Brandon turned and shouted down the hall, "Sarah!"

No response.

"Somebody! We need some help here!"

The door to the reception area flew open and Ruth Dressler, a young part-timer, ran in.

"Where's Sarah?" Brandon yelled.

"She's picking up supplies. Is that Salman Kilyos?"

Brandon nodded.

"Mr. Bran . . ." That was all Salman could wheeze. It was barely a whisper. But his eyes had connected with Brandon, and they cried volumes. *Why? Why won't you do something? Why would God allow this?*

Of course, Brandon had asked the same question. Hundreds of times. Not only about Salman, but about the others. About the thousands of drought victims he saw dying of hunger every day on TV, about those bodies ravaged and destroyed by the Scorpion virus, about the innocent war casualties, about the mentally tormented like that little girl he'd just refused, about the endless stream of humanity whose emotional and physical misery would never come to an end.

But Salman's could . . .

The thought surprised him, yet it made sense. Salman was right there, right in front of him. And it's not like he'd be disobeying God. After all, God had never said, "Never." He'd simply said, "Not yet, not at this time." Well, "not at this time" meant there had to be *some* time. And, by the looks of things, this was about the only time Salman had left. If it didn't happen now, it was doubtful it would ever happen. And since there was so much pain and fear, and since God was a God of love and mercy, and since Brandon had the power to at least end this person's suffering . . .

He reached back up to Salman and placed both of his hands on the man's chest. Silently, he began to pray. Without waiting for confirmation from the Lord, he quietly but firmly began speaking healing into the man's body. It wasn't disobedience. How could it be? After all, God was doing the healing. And if he didn't want to heal, he didn't have to heal. It was as simple as that.

Luckily for Salman Kilyos, it appeared, God did.

Brandon felt the heat begin in his palms, then spread out to his fingertips.

Salman felt it too. His gasps grew more panicked.

"Just relax," Brandon said. "Just relax."

Salman nodded. Soon his breathing started to come easier. In a matter of seconds, the wheezing had all but vanished. But the healing wasn't complete, and Brandon continued to pray. The heat in his hands gradually spread to his arms and then up into his shoulders. He began breaking out into a sweat. But this had happened before. With the more severe cases it happened.

"It is so warm," Salman whispered.

Brandon nodded and glanced up at him. For the first time that he could remember, he saw Salman smiling. Brandon smiled back. "How do you feel?"

"The pain . . ." Salman sat up in the chair. "I can feel no pain."

Brandon shifted his weight, but kept his hands on the man.

"Praise God." It was Ruth behind him. He'd almost forgotten she was there. "After all this time, praise God."

"Yes." Salman nodded. "Praise God." He reached up and took Brandon's arms. His grip was much stronger. "Praise God. Praise the Lord!"

Brandon smiled again and continued to pray.

A moment later Salman rose unsteadily from the chair.

"Easy. . . ," Brandon warned.

"Praise God!" he shouted. "Praise the Lord!" Although he was still weak, Salman was now on his feet.

"Be careful . . ."

The man barely heard. He began dancing a little jig. "Praise God!" He reached down, urging Brandon to his feet. Brandon cooperated, but for some reason, the sudden rise made him a little light-headed. For a moment it was Salman's turn to steady him.

"Thank you, Lord!" Salman shouted. "Thank you, God!"

Brandon looked on, smiling. He, too, was thankful. But instead of feeling the warm afterglow that so often accompanied the healings, he felt nothing. Heaven had grown strangely quiet. He frowned slightly, wondering. But only for a moment, because Salman had suddenly discovered something else about his healing.

"Look!" He'd pulled up his sleeves, showing his arms. Then he reached for his shirt and unbuttoned the top three buttons until he could look down at his chest. "They're gone! My spots. They are all gone!" He pulled out his shirt to check his stomach. "All of them. They are gone!"

He reached out and took Brandon's hands, pulling him into the dance. "Praise God! Thank you, my friend. Thank you from my heart's bottom. Thank you!"

Brandon had to grin. Salman's joy was contagious. But only to a point. Because there was something else. Something that felt no joy or excitement. Something that felt the slightest bit uneasy.

Katherine finished her e-mail to Dr. Sarah Weintraub and hit the spell checker. It had been her second mailing to the neurobiologist in almost as many weeks. Once again she had urged the woman to come see her son, and once again she had promised "very substantial" compensation ... including the power and prestige involved in working with the Cartel. During the upcoming months that sort of connection should prove very valuable. These were the same points she had used in her first mailing, but in this one Katherine had included a slightly different approach.

Instead of facts and figures, with which she always felt the most comfortable, she took a chance and tried speaking from her heart. She tried reasoning with Sarah, woman to woman, pointing out how Eric was her only child, how she loved him more than her own life, and if Sarah had or ever would have children of her own, she would know exactly how she felt. The tone made Katherine uneasy. She hated sounding needy to anyone. But this was her little boy she was battling for, and she'd do whatever it took.

After catching a few typos, Katherine hit SEND, and the mail was on its way.

She never knew if Sarah had read the other e-mail or not. It had been answered, but by a staff member who explained how incredibly swamped Sarah was, and how, at least for now, she had to stay near the clinic. However, the answer had included an invitation for Katherine and her son to come to the clinic for an examination and consultation anytime they wanted.

The naïveté of the offer angered Katherine. They couldn't fly back to the States. Not now. Didn't these people read the news? The Cartel was in the final stages of negotiation. Eric's input was needed now more than ever. Katherine had included this in her latest mailing, but again wondered if Sarah would ever see it. Still, between her mailings and the promised communiqué coming from Lucas's office, something should shake loose.

Katherine keyed back into the main menu. Computers had been a part of her life ever since her Omaha days, way back when she'd worked for the Department of

Defense. But after the murder of her police officer husband, and the next eighteen months of blur lost in the bottom of a bottle, she had decided it was time to make a new start. That was when she packed up little Eric, headed west, and tried to forget everything about her past. Well, everything but her expertise in computers.

She'd opened a small computer store in Everett, Washington. Unfortunately, it had set a record for the most amount of money lost by any company in its first year of business. And that was her good year. From then on things got worse. She may have been a whiz at computers, but she was clueless about business.

When the Cartel had first approached them about staying at the compound, Katherine had insisted she have access to a computer and the Internet. She'd also insisted upon being able to read all files on any DNA research their main lab in Belgium was conducting. After all, it was the Cartel's genetic engineers that had gotten Eric into this mess in the first place. It was only fair she be allowed to check on their progress as they tried to get him out.

She scrolled down to the genetic file named "Antisense." This was the area of most importance to Eric. By inverting specific segments of any genetic code, molecular biologists are able to create characteristics 180 degrees opposite of the original piece of DNA. As best as anyone could figure, that's what had happened to Eric with the genetic code they had replicated from what they believed to be Christ's blood. At first, Eric had exhibited strong, Christlike characteristics—mercy, compassion, a knowing beyond what his five senses could detect, even the performing of some miracles. But the process had eventually reversed itself. And instead of creating a loving, self-sacrificing savior of the world, the Cartel's scientists had created a—

Katherine refused to think the thought. Whatever Eric's problem, it was only temporary. They'd find a way to reverse the process. They'd find a cure. She just hoped it would be soon.

Up on the screen she noticed there had been only one new report filed since the last time she checked—a minor breakthrough in cancer research utilizing antisense to replace deactivated tumor suppressor genes. Not exactly what she was looking for.

Katherine sighed and prepared to shut down the computer. She glanced down at the screen's clock. Dinner was in less than an hour. She turned to look outside. The late spring blizzard continued to rage. And, over there, across the room in his bed, Eric was enjoying a peaceful afternoon nap. She decided to stay.

Turning back to the computer, she scrolled through some of the other genetic research files. Earlier, when she and Eric had first arrived, she'd tried reading everything she could find on the subject. But it was overwhelming; the Cartel was involved in far too many aspects of research on the topic. Eventually she had learned to focus only on the areas that applied to Eric.

As she continued to scroll, the file labeled "Scorpion" caught her eye. That was the street name for the virus that had been attacking the world's Semite population. For the most part other races were immune to it, but there was something about the DNA makeup of Jews and Arabs that made them vulnerable to the virus's fury. A fury that attacked internal organs, eating them up and turning them to jelly. A fury that, like its cousin Ebola and other Class 5 viruses, seemed to come from the very pit of hell.

The disease got its name from its scorpion-like tail that could be seen under an electron microscope. No one was sure where it came from or how to stop its spread, and every continent was reeling under its impact. Latest death tolls were pushing two million. Of course all of the top labs and humanitarian organizations in the world were focused upon the problem, and the Cartel was no different, utilizing a sizable portion of its influence and funding. But, so far, success had been elusive.

With nothing else to do, Katherine opened the Scorpion file and scanned down its subfiles. She'd been here once or twice before but had never gone all the way through. She doubted she would this time. She did, however, come upon the names of the four cities. Cairo, Mecca, New York, and Tel Aviv. These were the first four cities to report the outbreak of the plague.

She scrolled to the Cairo file and double clicked it. Immediately the screen read: "Access denied."

Thinking it odd, she tried again. Again the screen read: "Access denied."

She went over to Mecca and double clicked it.

"Access denied."

The same was true with New York and Tel Aviv.

"Access denied."

"Access denied."

The fact that she'd been closed out didn't bother her. Except for the genetic information, that was the case with most all of the Cartel's files. And who could blame them? With all of their high-powered meetings and maneuverings, they didn't need her browsing through any ultrasensitive information. Of course that made little difference to Katherine. She seldom if ever found a program she couldn't hack her way into.

No, it didn't bother her that she was blocked out. But it did intrigue her. After all, the agreement was that she could have access to *all* files on genetic research. So what was up? Of course there would be some secrecy in the search for Scorpion's cure. Whoever found it would definitely have the world's undying gratitude, a position particularly helpful to the Cartel in their efforts to court world favor.

But why did each of these cities have its own file? And why were they the only ones to which she was denied access?

Katherine glanced at the time. She still had forty minutes to kill before dinner. So, with a shrug, she started to type. Nothing helped pass the time like a good old-fashioned hacking.

"It will be the ecumenical event of the century." Tanya Chase, the anchor for GBN News, was already on her feet. "Think of it . . . Protestants, Catholics, Jews,

Moslems, Hindus, people of every faith coming together before God. And it won't be just at the L.A. Forum. With the satellite feed and local downlinks, we could be reaching every home in the United States and Canada! Not to mention a handful of stations in England, Australia, and New Zealand."

Sarah couldn't help nodding. It was difficult not to get caught up in this petite woman's excitement as she paced back and forth in the clinic's cramped office. She was a lot smaller in person than on TV, but her face was just as tan, her features just as chiseled, and her honey blonde hair (probably not natural) was just as striking. She was dressed to be taken seriously and had a perfect knockout figure (which probably wasn't natural, either). On TV her energy reminded Sarah of someone who'd had a few too many cups of Starbucks, and in person it was no different. Her presence filled the room.

"Let's face it . . ." She finally came to a stop across the table from Brandon. Leaning toward him, she utilized her scooped neck sweater to its fullest advantage. "Something's going on here. The wars, the famine, this new disease. I mean, people are claiming it's the end of the world, and maybe they're right."

"Maybe they are." Brandon kept his eyes leveled at hers, refusing to let them lower. A fact quietly appreciated by Sarah.

"Maybe they are," Tanya repeated. She rose and resumed her pacing. "And if that's the case, then it's time somebody helped us put aside our petty differences. It's time somebody brought us all together with one voice and one accord into the presence of God."

"And you think Jimmy Tyler's the man."

Again she stopped and locked eyes with Brandon. "I know he is."

Sarah watched for Brandon's reaction. Ever since their wedding night, tension had been growing between them. Gerty's e-mail had driven an indefinable wedge between them. They still loved each other, she was sure of that. Probably now more than ever. And the self-control they exhibited did nothing but increase their respect for one another. But every day, Sarah found herself growing more and more resentful. At whom, she wasn't sure. Most likely at God, which did little to help with her feelings of guilt and unworthiness. But she was also resentful toward Brandon. More specifically, she was resentful at his response toward God.

Yes, he was frustrated, she saw that daily. And there were times he could not hide his anger. But, for the most part, he seemed to be taking their command for abstinence as a type of challenge, rising to the occasion and using it to focus more intently upon his work. It was probably just a defense mechanism—she couldn't be sure. The only thing she could be sure of was that as she grew more and more resentful and guilt-ridden, he seemed to grow more and more dedicated . . . which made her even more resentful and guilt-ridden . . . and on and on the cycle went, like a whirlpool, pulling their relationship down lower and lower.

Sarah turned her attention back to the meeting and addressed Tanya. "Why does Reverend Tyler want Brandon and me to share the platform?"

"Actually, just one of you. Probably Brandon, here, since he's the miracle boy."

Sarah nodded.

"There will be dozens of other ministries represented, so room doesn't permit—"

"No, I understand," Sarah said, barely aware she was tugging her hair over her scar.

"You really think our presence is going to be helpful?" Brandon asked.

"What, are you joking? You guys are getting yourself quite the little following."

"You wouldn't know it by looking at our books." Sarah meant it as a joke, but it came off more weary than clever.

Tanya turned to her. "That's because you don't know how to market yourselves."

Sarah's eyes shot to Brandon. It sounded like someone had overheard their arguments.

He cleared his throat and answered, "Listen, when it comes to finances, I know we're not being all that conventional, but—"

"I know, I know." Tanya held up her hands. "I've heard it all before. You're doing the Lord's work, right?"

"As best as we understand it to—"

"And Jesus never charged for healings, and Jesus never held telethons, and Jesus never took an offering."

Now it was Brandon's turn to look at Sarah. The reporter *was* listening to their arguments.

"But let me tell you something." Tanya was back at the table. "Jesus never had to spend $90,000 renting an arena. He never had to pay for TV equipment or deal with unions. And he sure never had to buy satellite time."

Sarah felt a twinge of justification. It was good to hear someone else use her reasonings for a change.

"And what exactly would Jimmy Tyler get out of the deal?" Brandon asked.

Sarah winced. Didn't he know how good this could be for them? Couldn't he let up just a little?

Fortunately, Tanya was unfazed. "Reverend Tyler will be getting no more than you . . . national exposure and the opportunity to bring hope and comfort to a world torn at the seams, to a world that desperately needs to be brought together in a spirit of unity."

"Careful," he half-teased, "you almost sound like the Cartel."

"In many ways we're not that different. Only what they're striving to do on a political level, we are attempting to do spiritually."

Brandon turned to Sarah. He was obviously interested in her input.

She responded, doing her best not to sound too enthused. "I don't know what it would hurt. And, as Ms. Chase has said, we could certainly use the exposure. I mean, think what that type of publicity could do for the clinic."

Brandon nodded, but he still wasn't convinced.

Tanya leaned back over the table toward him, a little further than the last time. "So what will it be?" she asked.

He kept his eyes on hers, refusing to be distracted. Sarah almost smiled. The woman had no idea who she was up against. How deeply she respected this man. She respected his strength, yes. And, although it could be exasperating at times, she also respected his commitment.

Finally he answered, "I think Sarah and I need more time to discuss it."

"Of course, of course." Tanya pulled back and began gathering her papers. "Take all the time you want. And don't forget to pray about it. Praying is important, too."

Brandon nodded.

Tanya dumped her stuff into a leather satchel and closed it before looking up. "But don't take forever. There are plenty of other ministries that would love to be up on that stage with Jimmy."

Sarah rose to her feet and extended a hand across the table. "I know that, and please tell him how much we appreciate this opportunity."

"I certainly will." Tanya turned back to Brandon, who had also risen to his feet. "And it is just that," she said, reaching out to shake his hand. "An opportunity." She held his gaze, making sure he understood. "A very big opportunity . . . for both of you. And for your ministry. An opportunity that you would do well not to miss."

"Brandon, why are you being so unreasonable?"

"I'm not unreasonable."

"It's a terrific offer and you're just throwing it away. If that's not unreasonable, then maybe I need someone to explain to me—"

"I don't like the man, Sarah. It's as simple as that."

"No one says you have to like him."

"He's a huckster. You've seen him on TV. He's a manipulator. Besides, he's got a lousy toupee."

A week ago the humor would have lightened the mood, broken the tension. But not this evening. This evening, as they prepared dinner in the apartment, before he headed to his mother's for the night, they were having another argument. Something Sarah knew was happening more and more often. And if Tyler's invitation created such a stir, just wait until she brought up the e-mail she'd received from Nepal, the one asking her to help some kid involved with the Cartel.

"The man's a crook, Sarah."

"How can you say that? Look how God has used him."

"God also used Baalam's jackass."

Sarah sighed wearily. "Why are you so closed to this? If we work with him, we'd be reaching a good part of the world. Isn't that what the Scriptures say the two end-time prophets are supposed to do? Reach the world? Well, here's a flash for you, partner. It sure ain't happening for us here in Bethel Lake . . . and it sure ain't happening with our little podunk clinic."

She waited at the refrigerator for a comeback, but there was only silence. She turned and saw him staring down at the table. She'd struck a nerve. He'd obviously been struggling with the same thoughts. But he wasn't about to concede. Oh, no, why should tonight be any different from the others?

"So you're saying we'll accomplish all these great things by endorsing the beliefs of the Jews, Moslems, Hindus . . . or whatever New Age fruitcake has a following big enough for Tyler to pander to?"

"We don't have to endorse anybody."

"Being on the stage with them endorses them."

"We don't have to endorse their beliefs, Brandon. But we can at least endorse them as people. We can at least acknowledge them as fellow seekers of God."

"Please . . ."

"What's that supposed to mean?" He gave no answer and she pursued. "Do you think we're the only ones that God listens to? Are we so arrogant that we think he's only paying attention to us?" Again no answer. "We're talking about a God of love here, Brandon, a God of mercy. Half the world is dying—disease, war, starvation—while the other half is so scared they don't know what to think. There's a whole lot of pain and confusion out there. And no merciful God is going to turn his back on that. We're all on equal ground before him, and he's not going to let a little tweaked-out theology get in the way."

He looked up at her. "What did you say?"

She did not answer, realizing she might have stepped over the line.

"Sarah, the Bible says no one comes to the Father but through his Son."

"I know what the Bible says."

"Then how can we—"

"And I don't need you to quote it to me."

"But if you believe it, if you believe Jesus Christ and if you really love him, how—"

She spun on him angrily. "Nobody loves Jesus Christ more than I do, Brandon!" Her throat grew tight. Didn't he know how grateful she was to have her past forgiven? She swallowed. "Nobody . . . not even you." Tears sprang to her eyes. She turned and crossed to the sink, hoping he hadn't noticed. She'd win this argument and she'd win it through logic, not emotion.

When he finally spoke his voice was softer, even a little sad. "I know. I didn't mean that . . ." He hesitated, then tried again. "I didn't . . ." Another failure. This time accompanied by a heavy sigh.

She remained with her back to him. She heard his approach, caught his reflection in the window. A moment later his arms were wrapping around her. The tears came faster, and it was all she could do not to yield to him.

When she trusted her voice, she continued. "Everything's unraveling . . . Instead of becoming clearer, each day is more confusing than the last. There are times I'm not sure what I believe anymore." She took a ragged breath, then continued. "But

I know this. That TV show is the first indication that we're on the road to somewhere, that people are actually starting to pay attention to us. And to turn it down now would be one giant step backward."

There was a pause before he answered. "I know what you're saying. And believe me, I have plenty of my own doubts. But ... it's just ..." He took a breath, then quietly let it go. He tightened his embrace and rested his head on her shoulder. How deeply she loved this man, how he still made her weak and trembly inside. She knew the discussion wasn't over, but at least for the moment a truce had been declared. She reached down to take his arm, to let him know she was still upset but that it was okay.

And that's when she saw it. "Brandon?"

"Hmm?"

"What's this?"

"What?"

"Here, on the inside of your arm. It looks like ..." She turned toward him. "Is that a tattoo?"

Brandon looked at it with her. Although the outline was faint, there was no missing a crescent moon and a five-pointed star hovering beside it.

She glanced up at him but he was still staring at it, obviously as surprised as she was. Then she noticed something else. Higher up on his arm. A faint bruise. And another, off to the side.

"Where did you get those?"

She looked back up to him. His eyes were wide with astonishment. He quickly checked the other arm. There was another bruise, a little larger, a little more sickly.

"Brandon?"

He stepped back then quickly peeled off his shirt.

"Bran?"

Now he was examining his chest. There were two more bruises there. And another one, lower on his belly.

"What are they?" she asked.

"Salman ..." He half-whispered the name.

"Who?"

"Salman Kilyos."

"The guy from Turkey, the one with AIDS?"

He looked up, eyes still wide. "I prayed for him ... This afternoon I prayed for his healing."

"The Lord finally gave permission?"

"I don't know, not exactly ... but he was healed."

"Brandon."

He rubbed the back of his neck. "I thought maybe I was just coming down with the flu—you know, kind of achy and stuff, but ..." He looked back at his arms, examining the bruises. "These were his. I saw them on his arms ..."

"Brandon, you're scaring me."

After another moment, he looked up at her, his eyes filled with wonder and fear. "I've got . . . Sarah, I've got AIDS."

"What?" She took a half step back.

He looked down at the bruises, exploring them with his fingers. "I prayed for him, he got healed, and I—"

"Brandon . . ."

"And now I've got his sickness."

He examined the tattoo again, rubbing it. "This was his, too."

Sarah was finding it hard to breathe. "That's not possible."

Brandon continued examining his body. "Everything is fainter, and I'm sure the pain is nothing compared to what he felt, but—"

"Brandon!" The cry stuck in her throat.

He looked back up.

"What is God doing? What does he want from us now?"

Brandon could only stare, then shake his head.

"What does he want? What type of monstrous thing is he demanding from us this—"

"Sarah . . ." His voice warned caution.

"And you would defend him? After this! This is the reward for our obedience? This is how he loves his children?"

"Sarah . . ."

"No!" She began to pace, incredulous.

"There really isn't that much pain, honest." He started toward her, but she would have none of it.

"This is not what God would do. No merciful God would do this!"

He continued toward her, but she backed away. "No."

"Sarah . . ."

"No! This is not a God of love!" She had to get away, to get some space to think.

"But, the pain, it's barely—"

"Stay away from me."

He came to a stop, then reasoned, "Maybe this is some sort of sign. Maybe he's trying to—"

"And still you defend him?" She was shouting, trying to hear herself over the insanity.

He started toward her again. "Sarah."

Her mind reeled. She had to get away, she had to make some sense out of what was—

"Maybe if—"

She turned and headed for the bedroom, then changed direction and went for the closet.

"Sarah . . ."

She threw open the door and grabbed her coat.

"Where are you going?"

She wasn't sure. But she was no longer willing, she was no longer able to listen.

"Sarah." He was reaching out to her again.

"No."

"But—"

"Leave me alone!"

She turned and headed down the hall, stumbling slightly, vision blurry from tears.

"Sarah . . ."

She opened the door and stepped outside. The cool air hit her face but she needed more, she needed to breathe. She started down the steps.

"Sarah . . ."

He was calling, but she barely heard. She had to breathe, she had to get away.

He was on the porch. "Sarah . . ."

Her feet moved as fast as they could down the sidewalk before she broke into a run. She had to get away. She had to breathe. She had to clear her head.

"Sarah . . . !"

CHAPTER 4

"And the situation with the Jews?" Lucas asked.

"For the most part they're with us." It was the secretary general again. Same smelly cigar, same overfed ego. "You dangle the rebuilding of the temple in front of them, and they're bound to become cooperative."

"Except for the Hasidim and a few other ultraorthodox sects," another member of the Cartel corrected. Eric looked up from his doodling to see a short round man with a heavy Middle Eastern accent. "It is not giving up Israeli land in exchange for a temple that concerns them. Rather it is that the groundbreaking coincides with the day of your installment as chairman. They are afraid that it puts too much focus upon one man."

The secretary general turned to Lucas. "Unless, of course, you can convince them that you're their long-awaited Messiah."

Quiet chuckles filled the room.

"Maybe we can." Lucas grinned. "Maybe we can." He turned more serious. "What about the Palestinians?"

"They are ecstatic. Finally, a homeland that's more than a token West Bank patchwork."

"And the Arab Coalition?"

The secretary general rolled the cigar in his mouth, then pulled it out. "They assure us that, for the most part, they can hold the extremists in check. But it will be no cakewalk. It's not going to be easy convincing the fringe elements to share their beloved Temple Mount."

"Even though the Dome of the Rock and the temple will be two hundred meters apart?" Lucas asked.

The secretary general nodded. "Even if they're two hundred miles apart. You can create a state for the Palestinians, you can give the Jews their temple, but you still can't control the crazies."

Lucas nodded. "Have we made it clear to the Coalition that we'll soon have another means of control at our disposal?"

"Eric . . ."

"They know that's what we're saying. But, of course, they want to know what that means of control is."

Lucas smiled. "Assure them they'll not be disappointed."

"Eric . . ."

Eric returned to his sketching. *What do you want? I'm busy.*

"I've got something very, very special for you."

If it's another movie, I'm not interested.

"Oh no, my young friend, this is not a movie. This is something entirely different."

Eric pretended to sulk. The last two times it had been very difficult to regain control of his body. Heylel had been too stubborn. Now Eric was going to make him pay. He continued his sketch of the secretary general—complete with cigar, donkey ears, and daggers sticking out of his neck. He waited for Heylel to say more, but there was only silence.

A half minute passed. He pushed up his glasses and focused back on the Cartel. They were yacking about Scorpion again and about finding a cure. He continued to wait. Still no Heylel. Eric was sure he was there; he could feel him. But he remained absolutely silent, and silence was something Eric could never stand much of.

So. . ., he finally thought.

More silence.

Are you there? Hello?

"Yes, I am here."

So what do you want?

"I think you are ready for the next level."

Eric felt a rush of excitement but tried to hide it. *Next level?*

"There is much more power that awaits you, my friend."

Like what? You keep promising me more power, but where is it?

"I have promised you great things, have I not?"

Yeah, but so far—

"So far you have merely undergone the preparation. And you have done well. You have allowed yourself to be opened and enlarged. Now you are ready to taste and experience powers you never believed possible."

Really? Eric could no longer hide his interest.

"And not just in this dimension. My young friend, you are now ready to travel and experience the powers of all dimensions."

How? When?

"If you wish, we may start at this very moment."

You'll be going with me?

"I'm afraid I must stay behind and talk to these people. But my other friends will be happy to take you. Many of them know the regions far better than I."

Eric briefly focused back on the meeting. The representative of the European Union was talking. "... complete cooperation, as long as we have assurance that the London market will regain its stability and—"

Eric turned inward, back to his conversation. *Where are these ... friends?*

"We're right here." The voice was so close it startled him.

"Hello, Eric." There was another.

"Hi, there." And another. *"Ready to go on our adventure?"*

I'm not sure. How long will we be gone?

"Time has no meaning where we are going," the first voice explained.

"They need my help now, Eric," Heylel said. *"Let my friends take you with them. When you are done you may return."*

And you'll let me be back in control?

"If I have completed my task, certainly."

Eric immediately saw the fine print. It was the single word *if.* So he replied with a single word of his own. *No.*

"Eric?"

Not unless you let me come back when I want to come back.

"My young friend, be reasonable."

I won't leave unless you let me come back when I want to come back.

Eric waited a breathless moment. He was dying to see what they wanted to show him. He'd never been disappointed with any of Heylel's surprises, and he knew this would be no different. But he had to show him who was boss.

"Let's go, Eric," one of the voices pleaded.

"You won't believe what we'll see," another urged.

But Eric continued to wait. The silence lengthened. And then, just when he thought he'd asked for too much and had gone too far, Heylel spoke up. *"All right, my friend. You may return whenever you are ready."*

You promise?

"Of course I promise. You may return whenever you wish."

Something about Heylel's tone made him the slightest bit uneasy. *Whenever I want?* he asked.

"Whenever you want."

Eric still wasn't entirely convinced, but he did have his word. He took a look around the boardroom. *Well, all right then, just as long as—*

But that was as far as he got. As soon as he had given permission there was such a loud, rushing sound that he could no longer hear himself think. For the briefest moment he felt his vocal chords start to vibrate, his mouth start to move ...

"Good afternoon, gentlemen, ladies ..."

And then he was gone, racing into somewhere or something a thousand miles a second. He wanted to scream in fear, in exhilaration, but he moved so fast the cries were swept from his mind before he could think them.

As he pulled their Ford Escort into the Cedar Mall parking lot, Sarah's words kept echoing in his head. *"What kind of God would do this? Is this how he loves his children?"* Brandon turned off the ignition and crawled out of the car. He was stiff and a little achy. The pain wasn't unbearable, just a reminder. But a reminder of what? Of a tyrant God who played hide-and-seek with his will? *"No merciful God would do this!"* He tried ignoring the thoughts, but they kept returning.

He slammed the car door, threw back his hair, and started toward the main entrance. It was 7:45. The bookstore downstairs was Sarah's favorite hangout. It was open until 9:00. He hoped she would be there.

A fog had settled in, absorbing much of the sound of traffic from I–30 while also highlighting the scrape of his shoes against the asphalt. As he walked, his mind continued to spin. What *was* God trying to prove? Yes, he was a God of love and mercy; the Bible made that perfectly clear. And yet, how could a God of love and mercy allow such things to happen? How could he give the two of them such an incredible call on their lives and then go out of his way to keep them in the dark? And what about Salman's sickness? No wonder Sarah was freaked.

But it was more than just Sarah and it was more than just him. What about all the other suffering? Those thousands dying of starvation every day, the Jews and Arabs being wiped out by this malicious virus, the wars raging out of control? It had gotten to the point where he didn't want to turn on the news, afraid of what he'd see.

And yet God, who could see everything, God who was all-loving, who was all-caring, continued to allow these things to happen. Not only allow them, but by the looks of things, endorse them.

The automatic doors hissed open, and Brandon stepped into the mall. He'd barely entered before he heard the first voice . . .

"I'm worth something! I'll make you happy! Please . . ."

It was a girl, so loud, so close that he turned, thinking she was behind him.

But no one was there.

"I'm somebody, look at me . . . please! I've got lots to offer. Please like me. Pay attention to me!"

He glanced about. It was the typical evening crowd—kids, couples, couples with kids, and a few of the elderly. But no one was close enough for him to hear, not like this.

"I'm somebody. Like me. Love me. Please . . ."

And then he saw her, standing by the Coffee Beanery, sipping an espresso. She was fourteen at most. Cutoffs too short, midriff blouse showing plenty of firm belly and a pierced navel. But it was the eyes that broke his heart. Under the thick blue makeup was a look of studied indifference. A rehearsed attempt to disguise her neediness and cover her pleas. Pleas that Brandon heard loud and clear.

"Somebody. Look at me. Like me. Love me."

She didn't say a word. She didn't have to.

"Somebody! Anybody!"

"I'll take 'em out. I'll take 'em all out." It was a different voice. Male. Full of humiliation and anger. "Get the old man's shotgun and blow 'em all away. That would show 'em."

Brandon scanned the crowd.

"Let 'em know you don't mess with me."

It came from the kid ahead of him. He couldn't see the face, only the baggy pants and the swagger.

"Anybody, please." It was the girl again. "Please! I'll make you happy. Love me."

"Better yet, I'll blow away their families. Yeah, that would show 'em."

A third voice joined in. "He'll say we can't support it. Not with Julie and college. He'll say we're too old to start another family . . . *I'm* too old. And what about Down's syndrome? Dear God, I'm too old. He'll make me get rid of it, I know he'll make me get rid of it. Dear God, help me! Show me what to do!"

It came from a middle-aged couple off to his left. She was laughing at something he'd said. But underneath, Brandon sensed her anguish. It's not that he was reading minds; these were louder than specific thoughts. They were overriding fears, never-ending anxieties that constantly plagued and haunted.

"Somebody, anybody—"

"Nobody mess with—"

"Maybe I won't tell him, maybe I'll—"

He'd had similar experiences, sensing people's feelings, but only when he looked into their eyes. Never like this.

"Please."

"I'll show 'em."

"Help me!"

And never this loud. He picked up his pace. If Sarah was there, he'd find her and get out as quickly as possible. The sooner the better.

More voices joined in. Some pleading, others crying—the schoolteacher who'd just lost his retirement in the mutual fund that had crashed, the alcoholic housewife, the young mother convinced of her husband's affair—each crying out in private despair.

The voices grew in number and in volume. They were everywhere now. So much pain. So much sorrow. He broke into a trot. How could a God of love allow this much suffering? There was a nine-year-old Jewish girl, eyes red over the death of her father, terrified for the life of her mother. But she wouldn't be terrified for long. The virus would kill her before summer.

A groan rose in his throat . . . partially from anguish, partially to drown out their cries. But the cries grew worse, turning into screams of overwhelming need, unbearable sorrow.

Up ahead was the escalator leading down to the bookstore. He quickly headed toward it. But a young man approached from the right—crippled arms, dragging foot. He must have recognized Brandon, because he called out to him, his mouth twisting pathetically. Brandon slowed as he approached. He tried to listen, but couldn't hear. The cry of the other voices was too loud. Not that it mattered. He knew what the boy wanted. And he'd be happy to oblige. Anything to relieve at least one person's suffering. Maybe God wouldn't do anything, but he would. He could at least ease one person's agony.

Brandon reached out and took the boy's shoulders. Immediately he felt the heat. And, immediately, the searing pain. It traveled into his hands and up his arms. Brandon stared in horror as his wrists began to twist and his arms turned upon themselves. He looked back to the boy, but the child paid him no attention; he was looking down at his own hands and arms . . . as they straightened.

Brandon tried to speak, to yell, but his mouth was contorting. He felt a drool of saliva spilling from the corner and couldn't stop it. Suddenly his left leg turned in, then crumpled, sending him crashing to the floor. The pain was unbearable. He looked around, eyes wild. People were gathering. With them came even more voices. Desperate voices. Suffering. Screaming. Shrieking.

With the boy's help he struggled to his feet. The kid was talking, but Brandon couldn't hear the words, only stare at the mouth. It was perfectly shaped now, like the rest of his body.

Brandon drew back, horrified, furious at what was happening. No doubt this was more of God's handiwork. Is this what he wanted? For Brandon to take on the suffering of others? Fine. So be it. Let God be the tyrant Sarah had described. Let him be the monster. But not Brandon. Brandon had a gift. He had the ability to end suffering. And he had something God apparently lacked. He had the love.

A mentally retarded woman appeared in the crowd—mid-thirties, holding her mother's hand. Or was it her caretaker's? It didn't matter. She was simply another victim. Someone else in need of healing.

He reached out toward her. The woman cried in fear, but he managed to grab her hand. She tried to pull away, but his twisted grip was like iron. Again there was the heat. But this time no pain. Only a numbness that raced through his mind like a drug. A drug distorting his logic, dissolving his understanding.

He turned to the crowd. Why were all these strangers staring at him? He didn't hurt them. Why did they want to hurt him?

His left foot gave out again. He lunged forward and fell to the floor. Up ahead was the big, shiny exalator. He liked exalators. They were fun to ride. They made him happy. If he could just reach it, maybe he'd be happy, too.

Suddenly a bad man was reaching for his arm. He couldn't hear him over all the crying and screaming. Why were they screaming? Why were they staring? He didn't do nothing to them. Oh look, there's the exalator. He liked exalators. Why was that man grabbing his arm? He was a stranger. He mustn't talk to strangers. He wrenched his arm free and dragged himself to the bright, shiny stairs of the exalators. He liked exalators.

He struggled back to his feet and reached for the moving black belt. There was that arm again. It grabbed him. He tried to break free, but it held so tight that he had to throw himself backwards to break its grip. But the force caused him to lose his balance, sending him backwards, backwards through the air so he thought he was flying, flying until he hit one of those shiny steps with his shoulder and kept rolling onto his head and flipped over and over again, and then again, screaming in fear and pain, knowing Momma would be mad at him for getting his clothes dirty, but he couldn't stop rolling and screaming and falling down and down and down until he reached the place where he was no longer falling or feeling pain or screaming or hearing those awful voices.

Until he reached the place where there was nothing at all . . .

"Eric, sweetheart, wake up." Katherine patted his face gently. "Eric." Then a little harder. "Eric."

He still gave no response.

She was on the polished marble floor with him, his head cradled in her lap. She glared up at members of the Cartel and then at Lucas. "What did you do to him? What happened?"

Lucas kneeled down beside her. Always the voice of reason, he tried to explain, "Katherine, we didn't—"

"What did you do?"

She looked back at her son. By all appearances he was asleep, resting peacefully. "Eric." But he would not wake. "Eric!" She could feel panic trying to take over and used all of her strength to fight it off. "Where is Heylel?" she demanded. "Was Heylel here?"

"Yes," another voice answered.

She looked up to see the fat cigar chewer. "What happened?"

The man shrugged. "He gave us his counsel, and then he left."

"Eric didn't interrupt, he didn't try to take over?"

"That's what's so odd." Lucas continued the explanation. "After Heylel left, Eric simply collapsed, he just went limp." He looked back at her son. Katherine could tell he wanted to reach out and touch the boy, but she also knew he had enough brains not to try.

She turned back to Eric. "Sweetheart . . ."

Nothing.

"Eric . . ."

Now it was Lucas's turn. "Eric . . . Eric, can you hear us? Eric, wake up, son."

Katherine caught some movement under the eyelids. "Eric?"

They shifted several times before they finally fluttered open.

"Eric . . ."

He squinted at the quartz lights over the table, then looked around to get his bearings. When he saw Katherine he relaxed and tried to speak. "Mom." His voice crackled like dry leaves, barely above a whisper.

"I'm right here, baby." She pulled him closer, brushing the hair out of his eyes. "I'm right here."

He slowly closed his lids.

"Eric!"

Then reopened them. As he did, he began to smile.

"What? What is it, sweetheart? Are you okay?"

The smile broadened. "It was beautiful."

"Was it a dream, did you have another dream?"

He shook his head.

"What was it, what did you see?"

"I saw the future."

"The future?"

He nodded. "I was famous, Mom. Everybody loved me."

"Oh, baby." She bent down to kiss his forehead, then stroked his hair again. It was then she caught a glimpse of her hand. It was trembling. Violently. "Everybody loves you, sweetheart. We all love you."

"Katherine." Lucas touched her arm, offering to help.

Instinctively, she pulled Eric away. "Leave us alone."

"Kath—"

"No, no more!"

"I know what you must be—"

"You get that doctor here, and you get her here *now!*"

"We're doing all we—"

"You get her here *now.*" She glared up at Lucas. "You get her here, or we're on the next plane. You hear me? *Do you hear me?*"

She was shouting now. Her whole body trembled, but there was nothing she could do about it. She continued glaring at Lucas, waiting for a response.

Finally, he began to nod.

Sarah's white sneakers squeaked against the worn linoleum as she raced through Bethel Lake Community Hospital. She was on the third floor, the very floor where she'd stayed when recovering from her accident a year ago. She turned left and nearly collided with a gurney as she continued searching for the room number . . . 308, 310, there it was, 312. She burst into the room but was immediately brought to a stop.

There, on the bed, pulled into a twisted fetal position, lay Brandon. His arms were bent and his head cocked sideways. An oxygen line ran to his nose, and a heavy nurse in her late fifties was adjusting some IV lines. But it was the dazed look on his face that took Sarah's breath away. She'd never seen him with such a lifeless expression.

Spotting her, his eyes flickered with recognition. his mouth twitched, slurping back a drool of saliva. It contorted, trying to speak. "Thar . . . wa . . ."

"Brandon!" She started toward him, but the nurse turned and blocked her path. "No, don't touch him."

"What? That's my husband!"

"Are you Mrs. Martus?"

Sarah's head reeled. "Yes, yes, and that's my husband, Brandon Martus."

"The healer guy, right?"

"Yes, right, right."

"Thar ... wa ..." His voice was wracked with pain as he tried to reach out to her.

Again Sarah started toward him and again she was blocked. "What's going on?" she demanded. "What happened?"

"He was at the mall, doing his ..." The nurse searched for the word. "His thing."

Sarah turned to him. "You were healing people? Brandon, you were there trying to heal people?"

He nodded, wincing in pain at the movement.

She turned back to the nurse. "What happened?"

"I can't be sure, I mean I wasn't there, but—"

"Tell me what happened!"

The nurse took a breath and continued. "The people that he touched, the sick ones that he ... healed." She glanced back to the twisted body.

No more had to be said. The realization hit Sarah hard. "He took on their sickness?"

"Tharwa ... et hoorts."

"I'm not saying that. I mean, it may be what others are saying, but ..." The nurse glanced down at her hands and rubbed them self-consciously.

"What?" Sarah demanded. "Tell me!"

"Well, I've had rheumatoid arthritis for years now. Sometimes it gets to hurting real bad."

"And ..."

"When your husband came in, when we were moving him, he grabbed my hands, and I felt this heat, and ..." She held up her hands and slowly wiggled her fingers. "The pain is gone. Completely."

"Tharwaa ..."

"It's okay, Bran." Sarah moved past the nurse and squatted down beside him. "I'm here, I'm here ..." His face was sweaty, and she knew the pain was excruciating.

"Tharwaa ... make it thtop ..."

"Shhh, it's okay. I'm here, I'm here."

"Doon't weave me." The words pierced her heart. She could tell every syllable was difficult for him. "Doon't weave ..."

"I'm right here, hon, I won't leave you, I'm right here." She took his hand and kissed it lightly. It was only then that she saw his knuckles. Each joint was swollen and inflamed. They were turned and gnarled in what could only be the advanced stages of rheumatoid arthritis.

Sarah looked up at the nurse, but the woman had turned away, wiping her own eyes.

"Tharwa . . . et . . . hoorts . . ."

"I know, honey, I know . . ." She could barely get the words out as tears sprang to her eyes. And then, when her throat was too swollen for words, she began to pray.

Dear God . . . Dear Lord, what are you doing to us? What are you doing?

CHAPTER 5

How much longer will you be?" Sarah asked as she flipped through the papers inside another one of the clinic's beat-up filing cabinets.

"Just a couple more minutes. The call's supposed to come in at 11:00. I'll have everything fixed up and running by then, no sweat."

Sarah glanced across her tiny office to the dust-coated clock on the shelf. It was crammed into a bookcase with a thousand other books and periodicals in various stages of spilling onto the floor. It read 10:52. "You've got eight minutes," she said.

"No sweat," the kid repeated.

She watched as he finished attaching a TV camera no bigger than a golf ball to the side of her computer monitor. Although videoconferencing had become more and more common, it was one of the many luxuries she and Brandon had decided to do without. She jimmied the filing cabinet until it shut, then leaned against the wall only to hear the brittle paint crackle and fall to the floor behind her. One of the many luxuries.

It had been two days since she'd first noticed the marks on Brandon's arms. Two days of coffee and bad hospital food. Two days with absolutely no change. He still lay in his bed. He was still twisted. And he still writhed in agony, barely coherent . . . except for the part where he called out her name. That, unfortunately, she understood perfectly.

Of course his mother had arrived and insisted they take shifts, ordering Sarah to go home and get some rest. And, of course, Sarah had tried to refuse. But Mrs. Martus epitomized the term "Steel Magnolia." Despite her Southern charm and hospitality, there was iron inside the lady. An iron that made sure she got her way, whenever she wanted her way. And before Sarah knew it, she was heading home to get some rest.

But after staring at the ceiling fan in the bedroom for the first half of the night and cleaning the apartment throughout the second, she decided to come to the clinic and get some real work done. That's how she handled stress. Some folks had their wine, their TV shows, their aerobics . . . Sarah had her work.

When she arrived, the kid was already there, flirting with Ruth, their receptionist. He was from a local computer store that had been given some very specific instructions. They were to hook up the latest videoconferencing equipment for her without charge.

"And the catch?" Sarah had asked.

"No catch, it's a gift."

"From whom?"

By the look on the kid's face, he must have been waiting all morning to give her the answer. "At eleven o'clock this morning, Lucas Ponte will be giving you a call."

Sarah hadn't been amused. "Right. Tell him I'd love to chat, but I'm having an early lunch with the pope."

"No, I'm not kidding," the boy had said. "They called up the store early this morning and made it real clear what we were to hook up for you."

"They?"

"The guys from the Cartel."

"And you believed they were for real."

The kid had shrugged. "Got me. But the money they wired over was real enough."

That conversation had been thirty minutes ago. After calling his store and being assured that the gift was gratis, that there were "no hidden charges whatsoever either now or anytime in the future," Sarah had finally agreed to the hookup, if only to see who was behind it. Because as practical jokes went, this was about as elaborate as she'd seen.

While the kid puttered with the computer, she returned to her files looking for any material related to what Brandon was suffering. Anything on empathetics (from husbands who actually feel labor pains with their wives to mothers who have to go to the bathroom whenever their children do), to various psychic phenomena, and even to the stigmatics . . . those unfortunate souls, particularly Catholic, who so identified with Christ's suffering that for one reason or another their palms actually begin to bleed.

But she could find nothing resembling Brandon's experience, nothing where a healer so empathized with the sick that he took on their illnesses.

There was, however, material on various individuals who referred to themselves as "intercessors"—men and women who felt they were called to intercede and pray for others. People like Rees Howells, who lived in Wales during the first half of the twentieth century. As a man of great faith whose prayers were responsible for several miracles (including what some believed to be major influences on World War II), Howells had stressed over and over again that the first step in interceding was to lose yourself so deeply in the needs of others that you literally start identifying with their suffering.

Perhaps. But to actually take on the suffering? To identify so strongly with the sick that you actually become sick? No. From what Sarah understood of Scripture, that sort of work bordered on heresy. That was Christ's job, to take on the sins of the world, to suffer in our place. It certainly wasn't man's. But if she was right, then why would God—

"Dr. Martus . . . they're on-line."

Startled from her thoughts, Sarah looked over to the monitor. An image of a handsome woman in a navy blue business suit flickered onto the screen. "Dr. Martus?"

"Yes, uh . . ." Sarah moved somewhat clumsily to her chair and sat. "Right here, this is Dr. Martus." She was unsure whether to look at the camera or at the monitor. She tried a little of both.

"My name is Deena Pappopolis." The woman had a slight accent, probably Greek. "I am executive secretary to Lucas Ponte."

"I see, and that would make me Queen Elizabeth."

"Pardon me . . ."

"I appreciate the toys, Ms. Pappopolis, and junior here and I have been having a real in-depth conversation, but what's going on and who are you really?"

"If you will hold the line for just a moment, Mr. Ponte will be able to explain."

"Uh-huh." For a few chuckles someone was really going out of their way. Then again, maybe it was some sort of commercial, or one of those hidden camera things. Whatever the case, she was already weary of it. She had a lot to do and wanted to get to the punch line as soon as possible.

Suddenly the image cut to a man—young fifties, neatly trimmed beard, distinguished looking, and the same trim figure and riveting black eyes that made the real Lucas Ponte so immediately recognizable.

"Hello, Dr. Martus."

For the briefest second, Sarah thought he might be real. She held her tongue a moment and played along . . . just in case. "Yes?" But even as she answered she remembered hearing of agencies that booked look-alike celebrities for parties and various affairs. Granted, he was a pretty good likeness, but on closer examination even she could tell—

"This is Lucas Ponte."

"So I've been told."

She wasn't certain, but she thought she caught a trace of a smile.

"Actually, I am."

"And I'm the Virgin Mary. Pleased to meet you, Lukey. I can call you Lukey, can't I?"

The smile grew more obvious. "If you wish. And do I call you Mary or Mother, or just plain—"

"You can call me impatient," she interrupted, "and plenty busy. Now who are you, why did you spend money on all this equipment, and what do you want?"

His charm remained though his tone grew a bit more sober. "I appreciate your demanding schedule, Dr. Martus, and please forgive us for the intrusion. But we wanted to make certain you have been receiving our e-mail."

Surprised, Sarah hesitated, then swallowed. Of course she'd read the e-mail, had even given it some consideration. But how did these people know about it? Unless . . . Instinctively her hand shot up to her hair, pulling it over her scar. "I . . . things have been very busy for us lately."

He continued smiling. "I can appreciate that. Especially given your recent marriage. Congratulations."

Sarah felt her face flush. She was beginning to accept it as true—she was actually talking to one of the most influential people in the world. As the fact took hold she felt herself beginning to unravel under his dark penetrating eyes. What had he just said? Congratulating her on the wedding? "Yes, uh . . ." She cleared her throat. "Thank you."

"Your husband is a lucky man."

Sarah's face grew warmer, which made her even more insecure, which began to irritate her. She didn't appreciate being made to feel like some self-conscious schoolgirl. She repositioned herself and swallowed again, only this time there was nothing left to swallow. "Why, uh, why exactly are you calling me?"

"Katherine Lyon, the woman who has been e-mailing you about her son?"

"Yes, now that you mention it, I do recall our staff receiving something." She sounded a little stiff, but definitely more professional.

"She has asked me to personally contact you, to see if there is any way to prevail upon you to spend a few weeks of your valuable time over here. Your training in neuroscience as well as your expertise in the paranormal may prove quite valuable in diagnosing her son's problem."

Sarah cleared her throat. "The mother had said something about seizures and spirit guides?"

"Yes, that is correct."

"Surely there's someone closer to you who can—"

"Dr. Martus, I appreciate your modesty, but her son is very important to all of us at the Cartel. And, consequently, I believe, to the world."

As she listened, Sarah noticed the kid from the computer store edging in closer to get a glimpse of the screen. Again she tugged at her hair. "And you really believe I'm the one to help?"

"From what I have read of your work in neurobiology and psychic research, if you cannot help him, I doubt anyone can."

It was another compliment, and it left Sarah even more unsteady. "Well, I . . . I can't say at the moment. I mean, I'd have to check my schedule and discuss it with the staff." She shifted in the chair. "How long of a stay would you anticipate?"

"That would be entirely up to you. However, once you complete your evaluation, you may wish to stay a few days longer and see the Himalayas. Nepal is beautiful this time of year, and it would be an honor for me to show you some of its sights."

Sarah blinked. Was he flirting with her? She tried swallowing again, but with the same lack of success. "Listen." She cleared her throat. "This is all very flattering, but I need some time to think it over."

"Certainly, and please forgive me for this intrusion."

"That's, uh, that's all right."

"But, as I said, the young man is very important to us."

"I understand."

"All accommodations will be first class, and you and your clinic will be handsomely compensated should you decide to come."

"And if I don't?"

"Then I will take it as a personal loss . . . in more ways than one."

He *was* flirting.

He continued. "Do you mind if someone from my office checks with you in a few days, after you have had time to consult your schedule?"

"Uh, yes, I mean no, I mean that would be fine, certainly." She could feel a cool dampness break out across her forehead.

"Good. Well, thank you for your time, Dr. Martus. And again, please accept my apologies for this intrusion."

"That's all right. No problem. I'll let you know my schedule."

"I shall look forward to that. Good day, Doctor."

"Yes, uh, good day."

She saw him reach for his monitor, and suddenly the picture went blank. Sarah stared at the screen for several seconds, feeling her heart pounding in her chest. She took a deep breath, trying to force herself to relax. And then she took another.

On the morning of the third day Brandon was sweating again. Only this time it had nothing to do with a fever. He wasn't sure if he was awake or asleep, but he knew he wasn't in the hospital. He still lay curled in a twisted knot, and he still writhed with the pain. But he was no longer in his hospital bed. Instead, he lay on a moon-shaped platform above a sea of flames, the same crescent moon he had seen tattooed on Salman's arm and now had on his own, the same crescent moon he had dreamed about.

He didn't know how long he lay there before he saw the light—the blazing brilliance that appeared from somewhere behind him. He tried to turn and face it, but the pain in his body was too great.

A moment later he heard the voice. Its power vibrated the air, the flames, the platform—everything shook with the sound—and yet it resonated gently within his own mind.

"Hello, my child."

Again Brandon struggled to turn his head. The pain was severe, but he fought and strained until he succeeded. He had to.

The light was piercing, blinding like the sun, like a thousand suns. He squinted, trying to protect his eyes until, at last, he saw a form in the light—a form carved from the light. It was the form of a man. In one hand he held what looked like seven glowing stars. From his mouth came a razor-sharp, double-edged sword. And behind him were lampstands . . . seven as well. It was an astonishing sight. But even more astonishing for Brandon was to see this being quietly kneel down at his side.

That's when he noticed the eyes. They were made of fire—pure, leaping flames of fire. But they were not flames of destruction. They were flames of passion. A burning, consuming passion. A passion that Brandon instinctively knew burned for him. It was so intense and overwhelming that he could not move. All he could do was stare at them and drink in the love. There was no doubt who he was looking at. And there was no doubt of the all-inclusive, all-consuming love. That's why, before he could stop himself, Brandon spoke. It came as naturally as a little boy talking to his daddy. "Et hoorts."

Sorrow filled the flaming eyes. The voice responded. This time it contained as much pain as it had tenderness.

"I know."

"Why?"

The voice answered gently. *"You say you love. Yet, my child, you know nothing of love. You know nothing of its depth or of its passion."* The voice was tender, yet the words cut deep into Brandon's soul. *"I have given you the briefest taste of my love. These three days you have felt the merest fraction of what I feel, you have ached the smallest trace of what I ache, you have wept the tiniest portion of what I weep."*

Brandon's head reeled. Were such things possible? Could any one person contain such love?

The voice continued, its passion growing. *"I have purchased my bride with my very life. You know nothing of the depth of my love for her; you know nothing of my passion. You who claim to love more than I."*

Suddenly Brandon felt fear, a tremendous terror rising up inside of him as the voice grew in emotion.

"Do you dare speak to me of love when you know nothing of its meaning? When you cannot comprehend the price I have paid, nor the depths of my devotion?"

Tears sprang to Brandon's eyes. He had to close them. There was no argument to be made. The thoughts running through his mind these past several days, those silent accusations of God, they'd all been heard. They'd all been heard and they'd all been wrong. Brandon knew that was true from the moment he looked into those eyes, from the moment he heard the words. He'd been terribly and ignorantly wrong. A sob of remorse escaped his throat. How could he have been so blind, so presumptuous? Another sob came. And then another. He lowered his head as tears began to fall.

The voice did not respond but waited patiently. Brandon had no idea how long he cried, but finally, when there were no tears left, a hand reached out and touched his cheek. He opened his eyes and recognized it as the hand from his past, the hand from his father's church, the pierced hand that had saved him from the fiery abyss of the serpent's throat.

With excruciating effort, Brandon reached up his own crippled hand to take it. And, as he did, his pain immediately disappeared. But not just the pain in his hand, the pain throughout his entire body ... and his mind. It suddenly ceased.

He looked up, startled. The burning eyes smiled. Reaching out and taking the pierced hand with both of his own, Brandon began to kiss it over and over again as a fresh assault of tears sprang to his eyes and streamed down his cheeks.

"My son ..."

He looked up.

"I have set before you and your bride a great call. I have given you a glorious promise. But you have allowed worldly thinking to turn that promise into worldly glory. You say you are yielded to me, yet yielded is not the same as broken. The promise I have given must die and face darkness. For only in the darkest places dwell my brightest victories. You and the promise must be ground into the powder of contriteness, then mixed with the oil of my Spirit before my glory is manifested."

Brandon nodded, not because he understood, but because he knew truth was being spoken.

"You are able ... but only if you live in my strength. Only if you hold my hand and look into my eyes. You are able. But if you are not willing, I will understand. My love will be no less, but I will understand and I will find another."

Alarm filled Brandon. Was it possible? Would he really pass him over and choose someone else? After all they'd been through?

The eyes waited patiently until Brandon finally realized they were waiting on him. Impulsively he wanted to shout, "Yes, whatever you want and then some! Anything you choose will be fine with me!" But what of the cost? Look what he and Sarah had been through so far, and they'd barely begun. And if the prophecy in Revelation was to be taken literally, the reward for their obedience would be their murder and their bodies left in the streets to rot. Not exactly the happily-ever-after ending one would hope for. Yes, there would be a resurrection, but ...

What was so wrong with having a normal life? What was so wrong with having a wife he could actually make love to, of having children, raising a family, growing old together? What would be so terribly wrong with just being normal?

Brandon looked back into the eyes. He knew there would be no condemnation if he refused. The flames of passion would burn just as intensely for him regardless of his decision. But, as he stared into those eyes, Brandon realized something else. How could anyone say no to such love, to such all-consuming passion?

Slowly, almost imperceptibly, Brandon began to nod.

The eyes sparkled in delight. And it was that expression that burst Brandon's chest with joy. To think that he, a nobody, could actually make the Creator of the universe smile.

The voice spoke again. *"I will give you a gift few have received. I will give you my heart. My words will become a fire in your mouth that you cannot contain. They will burn until you have completed the warning to my bride."*

"What . . ." Brandon's voice was a trembling whisper. "What am I to say?"

"Warn her before it is too late . . .
She who preaches to love herself,
when I have commanded her to hate.
She who prays for her will,
but does not seek mine.
She who claims to be my servant,
yet demands I serve.
She who cries out for answers,
but will not listen.
She who demands healing,
but will not seek me in sickness.
She who indulges her every whim,
yet allows my least to suffer.
She who is quick to raise the sword,
but slow to drop to her knees.
She who chases her dreams
while forgetting my call.
She who raises her skirts to the world
while ignoring my call to holiness."

"But . . . how?" Brandon whispered.

"She no longer has ears to listen, but by seeing, she will understand."

"See what? What are we to do?"

"As my bride's affection has turned from me, so Sarah will turn from you."

Brandon's protest came before he could stop it. "No!"

The eyes looked upon him with overwhelming compassion. Brandon searched them, hoping for a reprieve, for some other solution.

Again the hand reached out, gently touching his cheek. *"It is the only way. But she will return. Just as my bride will return to me, so she will return to you. And her act, the returning to your covenant, will be my testimony to the world."*

The lump in Brandon's throat made it nearly impossible to talk. "But . . . can't there be . . . another way?"

"No."

Brandon looked down, his eyes burning with tears.

The voice continued. *"You and I will share the longing for our bride. And that love, followed by her obedience, is the message the two of you will proclaim to the world."*

Brandon nodded, barely able to breathe for the sorrow.

"Study my letters of love to my bride. Point to their warnings, lest I come and take away her lampstand. Be strong and courageous, my son. Do not tremble or be afraid. For I will be with you. I will be with you always."

Tears spilled down Brandon's cheeks and onto his pillow. The pillow from his hospital bed. The pillow that he was now lying on. He clutched it and continued to weep until it was soaked with his tears.

Sarah was cleaning again. This time she was on her hands and knees in the shower. It was amazing how quickly mineral deposits could build up, especially in the grout, especially in the corners. She'd heard people talk about the city's hard water before; now she understood. For whatever reason, she hadn't seen the accumulation in her first cleaning of the apartment. This time, gratefully, she had. So with spray cleaner in one hand and a brush in the other, she was furiously at work. It was either that or putting down another quart of Swiss Almond Delight which, although kinder to her knees, would be far less considerate of her hips.

She didn't know how long she was down there like that before she heard the front door open. Immediately, she froze. Had she locked it? She wasn't certain.

A moment later, the door shut. Whoever had opened it was now inside the apartment. Sarah held her breath, uncertain what to do. She could call out, demand to know who it was. But that would give away her location. And there, cornered in the shower, on her hands and knees, was not the strongest position in which to ward off an attack. Maybe she should just lay low and stay there in hopes they would take whatever they wanted and get out. It was a difficult decision. Fortunately, she didn't have too long to weigh it. A familiar voice with a terrible Ricky Ricardo accent suddenly echoed down the hall: "Lucy . . . I'm home!"

"Brandon?" She dropped the brush and spray cleaner and jumped to her feet. "Is that you?"

Her husband rounded the corner and her heart leaped. She was so excited that she stumbled over the threshold of the shower.

"Easy!" he warned.

But she didn't care. "Brandon!" Even as she was stumbling and falling, she didn't care. "Brandon!"

He stepped in and managed to catch her just before she slammed into the wall, his arms as strong and healthy as ever. He was laughing now, as he helped her back to her feet, trying to keep his own balance. "Are you okay?" he asked.

She stared at him, not believing her eyes. Then suddenly she threw her arms around him, hugging him, kissing him. "Brandon . . . Brandon, Brandon, Brandon."

He continued to laugh, holding her, until suddenly a dreadful thought filled her mind and she pulled away. "Are you all right, did I hurt you?"

"No." He grinned as he pulled her back into the embrace. "You didn't hurt me at all. I'm fine. I'm absolutely fine."

"And you're positive it was the Lord?" Sarah leaned against their kitchen counter sipping her lukewarm Earl Grey.

Brandon nodded from the table. "Oh, yeah."

"Not some dream, not some hallucination?"

"He was more real than you and I put together."

Sarah paused, carefully thinking it through. Finally she spoke. "Superreality."

"Hmm?"

"That's what Dr. Reichner used to call the supernatural, those dimensions that are higher than our own. Remember? 'Superreality.'"

"He was super something." Brandon looked down at the table, his voice thickening with emotion. "I've never seen such love, I've never felt such intense . . ." But the memory was too much, and he let his words trail off.

Sarah watched silently. It had been nearly three hours since he'd returned to the apartment from the hospital, since he'd strolled in as strong and fit as if nothing had happened. From the looks of things, he'd been made completely well. But, unfortunately for Sarah, she had other types of wounds, ones far less quick to heal.

Of course she was grateful to have him home. Their first hours of reunion had been pure joy. But now they were down to the cold hard facts . . . and some equally hard questions.

As far as Sarah could tell the vision had been legitimate. There had been no drugs administered except for Percodan to help him relax. Nor had he remained in ICU long enough to develop any of the hallucinations common with longer stays. Granted, what he'd been through would be enough to push anyone over the edge, but nearly everything he described corresponded with other documented visions and accounts, both historically and biblically.

Then of course, there was one other fact: her husband, who had been sick and crippled with pain beyond belief, had been instantaneously healed during the encounter. Psychosomatic? Perhaps. Though Sarah had her doubts. This seemed far less psychological than it did paranormal.

She took another sip of her tea. "Do you remember anything else? Anything else he might have mentioned?"

"Sarah, we've been through this a half-dozen times."

"I know, I know . . ." She couldn't put her finger on it, but she sensed he was keeping something from her. "Nothing more about our relationship?"

He shifted slightly. "He still doesn't want us sleeping together, if that's what you mean."

It wasn't what she'd meant. To be honest, she wasn't sure what she meant. Maybe it was just her own insecurity, her lack of self-esteem—it's pretty hard having self-esteem when God says you're not good enough to sleep with your own husband. But there was something else. She couldn't put her finger on it, but there was something else.

She watched as Brandon reached up and pulled a Bible from the shelf behind him. He opened it and flipped through the pages. How odd, a month ago that book had meant everything to her. And now, almost against her will, she found herself growing uncomfortable with it. Uncomfortable with the way it was invading and overturning every aspect of their lives. *Every* aspect. "What are you looking up?" she asked.

"Remember I told you he said something about 'love letters to his bride'?"

She nodded. "I still don't understand that."

Once again Brandon fell silent, and once again she thought he was hiding something. But what?

He continued. "And those seven stars and those seven lampstands?"

"That's from Revelation," she said. "Toward the beginning. The first couple chapters are the ones that talk about lampstands and stars . . ."

"And letters," he said with growing excitement. He riffled through the pages more quickly.

She looked on. Of course she was thrilled to have him back home, and grateful that he seemed completely well. But, then again, she'd never asked for him to be sick. Neither had he, for that matter. So it's not like she should be doing cartwheels in gratitude just because life was almost returning to normal. And what about this business of becoming God's audiovisual aide to the rest of the world? Not exactly the "love, peace, and joy" Brandon had preached to her when she was recovering back in the hospital.

And it's not like they were the first to receive this special attention. After Gerty's e-mail they'd begun studying other Scriptures, discovering how God had used other prophets in the past—men like Isaiah, who was commanded to run around barefoot and naked for three years; or Hosea, the holy man commanded to marry a prostitute; or Jeremiah, who was forbidden to marry at all; or Ezekiel, who wasn't even allowed to cry over the death of his wife.

As far as Sarah could tell, God's track record in dealing with his chosen vessels was anything but pleasant. And if that's how he treated his greatest prophets, she was in no hurry to see what he had in store for them. No, this was not the program she had signed up for. Parting the Red Sea, raising people from the dead, that was more her style. Not this slow, confusing torture. And if that's what he had in mind for them, then maybe it was time to reconsider . . . if, *if* any of it was to be taken literally.

For Sarah that "if" was still the great unanswered question. How much of what was mentioned in Revelation would really happen to them and how much of it was symbolic? How much was literal? How much spiritual? For that matter, the same question could be asked about Brandon's visions, or Gerty's writings, or the hundred and one other signs they'd had. Were they being fools taking everything at face value? Surely if God was Spirit, then he'd talk in spiritual terms, too, wouldn't he? With that in mind, how much of it was up to them to accomplish, and how much of it was up to God? Serious questions. And as the questions churned in her mind, another, more tangible one, surfaced.

"What about Jimmy Tyler's TV show?" she asked.

Brandon looked up.

"Tuesday's the deadline for letting GBN know. During your encounter, did he give you any indication that we shouldn't go through with it?"

Brandon scowled, then slowly shook his head. "No . . ."

"So we can go ahead?"

His frown deepened. "Sarah . . ." She watched as he searched for the words. "Does it feel *right* to you?"

"National exposure, sitting on the platform with one of the most recognizable religious figures of the world? Yes, that feels right to me. That feels real right."

"But this business of, what did he call it, 'pursuing worldly glory.' And remember what Gerty said about the dream and vision having to die first?"

Sarah pulled the chair out and sat across the table from him. "This isn't something we pursued, Brandon. They came to us, remember?"

"I know."

"And to say we're not interested, when we don't have a clear word from the Lord. Isn't it as much a sin to refuse God's blessings as it is to refuse his trials? And couldn't this be just that, one of his blessings, the break we've been waiting for all of this time?"

"I suppose . . ." He was hedging again, obviously struggling with something.

She leaned forward and touched his arm. "What? What is it?"

"It's just . . . well, Tyler wants us to get up there and be a part of this big celebration of unity."

"And . . ."

"And if I'm right about what I heard this morning . . . it doesn't sound like celebration is exactly what God has in mind."

Sarah pushed her hair behind her ear. "No one said you have to get up there and lead cheers. If something needs to be said, we'll have plenty of time to say it later. But later won't come if we don't take these opportunities first."

Brandon continued to think.

She pressed in. "What say we give them a call, give them a tentative yes? And if later God makes it clear we're not to go, then we cancel. That's simple enough, isn't it?"

Brandon gave her a look. One of those that went deep inside of her. The type that, if she let it, would seek out and find her truest, deepest feelings. But not this time. This time she would block it. She'd been doing all she could to ignore the frustration and anger growing inside of her. She didn't need him poking around and discovering what was really going on . . . especially when she wasn't sure herself. Finding an excuse to look away, she rose from the table and crossed to the sink to rinse her mug. "Is that okay, then? I'll call tomorrow and give a tentative yes."

After another long moment he asked, "This is real important to you, isn't it?"

She turned to face him. "Yes, it is. It's very important for *both* of us."

He was still looking at her, but this time she held her ground. She wasn't sure how much he could see, but it didn't matter, at least for now. Now there was the issue of the TV show, whether or not they would take advantage of this obvious, God-given opportunity. Later they would discuss the other issues, like her growing resentment . . . and the invitation to Nepal.

"So?" she asked.

He continued holding her gaze. There was still something else going through his mind, she knew it. But for now, it looked like they'd both be keeping their secrets.

"I'll give them a call then, all right?" She shifted her weight, steeling herself, refusing to look away. "All right?"

Slowly, perhaps a little sadly, Brandon began to nod.

Sarah turned back to the sink and took a silent breath. "Good," she said. "I'll call them in the morning."

CHAPTER 6

"You sure I need all this stuff?" Brandon asked.

The makeup person, a petite Sri Lankan in her late twenties who went by the name of Cassandra, laughed as she continued sponging the number seven pancake onto his face. "First timers always say that. Especially you men." She glanced over her shoulder into the lighted mirror facing them. "Just think of this as an opportunity to see what we ladies put ourselves through every day." She grinned over at Sarah who sat in the other barber chair beside them. "Isn't that right?"

Sarah forced a smile. "I'm afraid she's got a point."

Brandon said nothing and sat sullenly as she continued working on his face.

"The bright lights, they wash everybody out. Even those preachers with the ever-tans from Phoenix and Florida, they wear something." She began applying it under his chin. "So, you guys get out this way much?"

Sarah answered, "I spent most of my time on the West Coast. Grew up in Portland, did my undergraduate and graduate work at Stanford, some research at UCLA. But this is Brandon's first time out of the Midwest."

"No kidding?" Cassandra asked. "Get to see many of the sights?"

"We just got in last night."

"Though we found the gridlock on the 405 particularly interesting," Brandon added.

Cassandra smiled. It was obvious small talk came easy to her. "They put you up in the Beverly Hills Hotel? Pretty fancy digs."

Sarah nodded. "I'll say."

"That's one thing about Jimmy, he only goes for the best. You guys get separate suites or a single?"

"I'm sorry?" Sarah asked.

"Depends who did the booking. If it's Sheryl, she makes sure significant others get to *discreetly* share a suite. If it's one of the, shall we say, less progressive staff members, then you have to stay in separate rooms."

Sarah cleared her throat. "Actually, we're married."

"Oh, no kidding."

"About a month now."

"Well, congratulations. Didn't see a ring, that's why I asked. 'Course a lot of guys are starting to do that, not wear rings, at least for the cameras. Kinda increases their sex appeal, if you know what I mean." She began brushing Brandon's long dark hair. "And nothing increases the donor base like a little old-fashioned sex appeal, ain't that right, guy?" She gave him a wink in the mirror.

Sarah watched as her husband tried to smile, then glanced down.

"Not that you need it, not with this hair." She reached for a bottle of spray and began spritzing it. "I tell you, I know women who would kill for this. Men, too. It's gorgeous."

Brandon coughed. Sarah couldn't tell if it was from embarrassment or from the hair spray. When he'd finished he gave her the definitive, what-have-you-gotten-me-into look. It was all she could do not to break out laughing. Then, coming to his rescue, she changed the subject. "So, have you known Reverend Tyler long?"

"Twenty years ago this July. He found me on the streets of Colombo, begging for food. He and Bridgett, his wife, took me in. They fed and clothed me, gave me an education, and here I am."

"That's great."

"I owe a lot to Jimmy. And not just me. There was a time nearly every member on staff had a similar story. Always something he did to help somebody—lots of times without folks ever knowing about it."

"Really?"

"I know he comes off a little too slick for some, all showbizzy and Mr. Entertainment. But underneath that he's a great man. A really great man."

The description of Tyler's genuineness surprised Sarah, and she glanced over at Brandon. But he was busy hearing something else in the woman's voice and studying her actions. After a moment, he finally spoke.

"You said, 'There was a time.'"

Cassandra looked at him. "I'm sorry, what?"

"You said, there was a time when he used to be there for the staff and help them. Has that changed?"

Sarah watched as her husband continued to search the woman, looking for something deeper.

Cassandra shrugged. "We're a lot bigger now." She glanced away, finding something to busy herself with. But Sarah knew Brandon had found something. The woman continued talking. "In fact, did you know that we now have more stations than any of the secular networks? Isn't that incredible? A Christian network bigger than anything the world has? Praise God."

Brandon nodded as he watched. "And that's a good thing?"

"Of course it's good." Even Sarah could hear the defensive edge coming to Cassandra's voice. "Bigger's always better. At least in ministry. Everyone knows that. The more we grow, the more people we can reach."

Brandon nodded, then answered softly, "And the more of Jimmy everyone loses."

She came to a stop. "What's that supposed to mean?"

Brandon said nothing but held her gaze.

She turned back to her work, a little more briskly. "The man's got pressures you and I can't even begin to imagine. You don't get to be one of the most powerful religious figures in the world without making some concessions along the way."

Brandon slowly nodded. "I understand . . ."

She continued to work, now in silence. Brandon said nothing more. Sarah wasn't sure what all had transpired, but he had found something. Something that had left Cassandra just a little hurt and angry. And something that had left Brandon just a little bit sad.

The silence was interrupted when the door behind them flew open. There, standing in the doorway, was a cameraman with a camera and Tanya Chase with a microphone.

"Hi, guys," she said cheerily. "Glad you could make it."

"Hi," Brandon answered.

"Good to see you," Sarah added.

But Tanya barely heard as she quickly moved into position and motioned for the cameraman to do the same. "We're taping some bumpers to drop in as we go to and from commercial. Little sound bites from our guests explaining why they're so excited to be here. Think you can do that for us, Brandon?"

"Uh . . ." He glanced at Sarah. She knew her husband hated speaking in front of any group, let alone a TV audience, but she gave him an encouraging nod, hoping he'd give it a try. After a moment of reluctance, he agreed.

"Yeah, uh, sure."

"Great. Here we go then."

Cassandra was already removing the plastic sheet from him and turning his chair to face the camera. A bright light glared on above the lens as Tanya shoved the microphone into his face.

"So tell us, Brandon Martus, why are you excited to be here tonight?"

Brandon hesitated, gathering his thoughts.

"Whenever you're ready, Brandon."

He nodded, then finally looked at the camera, wincing slightly at the light. "I . . ." He cleared his throat and started again. "I am grateful to be here so that I can be a part of what Jesus Christ is doing through, uh, *with* Reverend Tyler during—"

"Whoa, hold the phone, tiger." Tanya pulled back the mike and took a step closer. "Can't use the 'J' word on this one."

"I'm sorry?"

"The 'J' word. You know, 'Jesus.' Keep that for the folks back home."

Brandon frowned, not understanding.

Tanya explained. "Lots of secular stations are picking us up. Don't want to antagonize them needlessly. So let's just keep it nice and generic."

"But . . ."

"Just say what you said but don't use the name *Jesus*. Say *God* or *Lord* or something like that instead. That way nobody gets offended."

"Uh . . ." He threw a look at Sarah, who shrugged. It seemed to make sense.

"Just say God instead of Jesus, okay."

"All right . . ."

"Great. Here we go again." She pointed the microphone back at him. "Whenever you're ready."

Again Brandon squinted toward the camera. "I am grateful to be here and to be a part of what God is doing through Reverend Tyler. I think—"

"That's great, Brandon." Tanya gave a thumbs-up. "Just great." She pulled back the mike as the cameraman snapped off the light. "We'll be rolling in about twenty minutes. They'll want you onstage pretty soon. How we doing, Cassandra?"

"Just about there."

"Beautiful. Well, good luck, Brandon." She turned, then suddenly remembered something. "Oh, hang on." She reached into her shoulder bag and pulled out a Bible. "Jimmy wanted all of his guests to have one of these."

"Oh, thanks," Brandon said, "but we've got plenty of Bibles."

"I'm sure you do. But one can never have too many Bibles, can they?" She shoved it into his hands. "Besides, this is the Jimmy Tyler Study Bible." She turned toward the door. "Good seeing you two again and have a great show." Suddenly, she was gone. As quickly as the blonde whirlwind had entered, she had left.

Sarah watched as the door shut. She turned to Brandon with a quizzical look of amusement. But he had already opened the Bible and was scowling down at the title page.

"What's wrong?" she asked.

He didn't hear.

"Bran . . . what's up?"

He glanced at her, then turned the Bible around so she could see the page. "Right here, on the front."

"Yeah."

"It's got Jimmy Tyler's signature."

She still didn't understand. "Meaning . . ."

Brandon's frown deepened as he tried to explain. "Doesn't it seem weird? I mean, the man is autographing God's Holy Word?"

"Aamaa!" The cry was from a young woman, maybe a girl. *"Aamaa!"* With her approaching voice came the slapping of sandals against bare feet and the scraping

of stone. Katherine, who was holding a crusted teakettle at the hearth, turned just in time to see a child of twelve barge in. The red dye where she parted her hair signified she was already married. Although this was frowned upon by the government, child brides were still common in Nepal.

"Aamaa!" she cried breathlessly. It was a term of endearment meaning "mother." Since Eric was a god and since Katherine was Eric's mother, she had become "mother to all"—not exactly a term she relished.

"Ke?" Katherine asked.

"The master . . ." The girl tried to speak English but it wouldn't come. It didn't have to.

"Eric?" Katherine demanded. "Something happened to Eric?"

The girl nodded, motioning frantically. *"Chhito!"*

Katherine dropped the kettle on the hearth, tossed aside the rag that served as a pot holder, and raced for the door.

"Chhito!" the girl cried. *"Chhito!"*

Katherine had barely stepped onto the balcony overlooking the courtyard when she saw them—a half-dozen women just outside the gate. She headed for the stairs, flew down them to the courtyard, then dashed across the cobblestones, past the fountain, and through the arched opening.

Outside, on the dirt road, a large pile of grain glowed from the late afternoon sun. But the women, some still holding their winnowing rakes, were no longer working. They had gathered around a body lying on the ground.

Katherine sucked in her breath, fearing the worst—until she saw it was not her son. It was Deepak, his bodyguard. She started toward him, then spotted Eric off to the side. He looked scared and shaken. "Eric?" His face was wet with tears. She headed toward him. "Eric, what happened?"

"I didn't mean to, honest. I didn't—" He ran the few remaining steps to her. She caught him and he buried his face into her arms, beginning to sob. "It was an accident, I didn't mean to . . ."

"Shh, it's okay. What happened?" She threw a look over her shoulder. The body was not moving.

"We were playing . . . just playing. And Deepak . . ." He was unable to continue.

"And what?" Katherine asked. "What happened to Deepak?"

"He made me really, really mad, and . . ." He gulped in a breath of air and continued. "I tried not to be. Honest. I tried really hard to control it this time, but—"

Katherine felt a chill seize her body. "But what? Eric, what happened to Deepak?"

There was another outburst of tears. She continued, more firmly. "What did you do to Deepak? Eric?"

He looked up at her, eyes red and swollen. "I made his heart stop!"

Katherine could only stare.

"I'm sorry." He buried his face into her shoulder. "I'm so sorry."

Instinctively, she patted his back, "Shh, it's okay . . ." Her head was growing so light that as he pushed against her she nearly lost her balance. But she dug in and held on. For both of them she held on.

"God is love. How many times do we have to hear that before we finally get it through these mule-thick skulls of ours? God is love, God is love, God is love. And anyone who doesn't love, is not of God. It don't get any simpler than that, folks!"

Brandon sat watching as Reverend Jimmy Tyler played the crowd, strutting back and forth across the sixty-foot stage. Late fifties, three-piece suit, flashing silver hair—the man literally looked like a Hollywood actor. In many ways he was. He even used the streams of sweat trickling down his face to their fullest advantage—constantly dabbing at them with his handkerchief. And then there were his dramatic pauses, when he poured water from a nearby pitcher and took gulps from a glass. The man was a pro in every sense of the word.

Brandon turned back to the audience, straining to see past the glare of lights. The L.A. Forum held 18,500 people, and by the looks of things, the place was packed out. Packed out and worked up. Between the forty-piece orchestra, the international choir, and Jimmy Tyler's electrifying delivery, they had no choice but to be. There wasn't an indifferent soul in the house.

"I don't care whether you call him God or Allah or Krishna or Buddha, or some Cosmic Force. The point is, God is love. Everybody say that . . ."

The audience joined him: *"God is love."*

Brandon sat in the third tier of seats on the left of the stage. There were about thirty guests on this side. And thirty more on the other. That made sixty guests representing various races, religions, and creeds. Sixty guests whose presence proved their solidarity behind Jimmy Tyler.

"Now, I don't know 'bout you, but I'm sick and tired, I mean I'm fed up to here, 'bout everybody with their own special brand of religion, their own private interpretation of God." He raised his voice into a pinched, mocking tone. "'Well, Reverend, God never does it their way, he only does it my way. Well, Reverend, God doesn't speak through their holy book, he only speaks through mine. Well, Reverend, God only visits my church or my synagogue or my mosque or my temple.' Well, I got news for you, folks, God can go wherever he wants. He can come in any form he wants to touch and heal and bless whoever he wants. And you want to know why? I'll tell you why. God is . . ."

He stuck the microphone out toward the audience. A portion called back, *"Love."*

"Hey." He tapped the mike. "You folks awake out there? I said, God is . . ."

Again they repeated, only this time louder. *"Love!"*

"I can't hear you. God is . . ."

"LOVE!"

"You think we can remember it these next few minutes?" The audience responded positively, but he shook his head, chuckling. "I have my doubts."

The crowd ate it up. So did Brandon's peers sitting on the stage. But not Brandon. Instead, he felt a growing knot of emotion . . . part embarrassment, part confusion, part frustration.

"This is not a time to dwell upon petty doctrinal differences. I don't care what cemetery, er, I mean, *seminary* you folks are from."

The audience chuckled.

"If you ask me, most of them folks are educated way beyond their intelligence, anyways."

More laughter.

"No, this isn't a time to dwell on our differences, this is a time to dwell upon God's love. Because if there's one thing God is, it's . . ."

Everyone shouted, *"LOVE!"*

Brandon continued to watch. It was the mixture of truth and error that he found so confusing. Yes, God was love and yes, he hated religious pride and spiritual elitism. But wasn't it Jesus himself who said the road to heaven was narrow, that he alone was the door, that he was the *only* way to the Father?

Tyler continued. "So what about all of these plagues, this famine, these financial hard times sweeping the globe? What about all these holier-than-thou, self-righteous Bible thumpers who are jumping up and down screaming, 'It's the judgment of God, it's the judgment of God!' Well, I got news for you, folks. That God sure as . . . heaven . . . ain't my God!"

There was a smattering of applause.

"You've all seen the news. Right now eight people in the world are starving to death every second. Eight people! And most of them are innocent babies and children who can't fend for themselves. Innocent babies and children starving to death? Because of God? No, friends, I don't think so. That may be somebody's God, but it sure ain't mine."

The applause increased.

"'I've come that ye might have life and have it abundantly.' That's what my God says."

More applause.

"And what about this Scorpion virus? In seven months they're claiming that if there's no cure, over half of the Jewish and Arab population will be wiped out. Over half! That's genocide, folks, plain and simple. I don't know about you, but that's not my God. It may be somebody's God . . . but he's sure not mine!"

More applause, louder.

"And these wars? Any minute some third power wanna-be is going to nuke his neighbor, contaminating the rest of the world until we're all giving birth to three-headed babies. I don't know. That may be somebody's God . . . but he's sure not mine!"

Brandon continued to marvel, amazed at how the man could use truth to preach error. How he could quote Scripture to speak falsehood. Yes, God was a God of love, but he'd read in the Bible again and again that God also used suffering to correct and judge. And it clearly taught that that's what would happen in the end times. So how could Tyler preach that these calamities were just an accident? How was it possible for him to use the Bible to disprove the Bible? Then again, wasn't that exactly what Satan had done with Jesus when he tempted him in the wilderness? Used God's truth to tell a lie?

But was Tyler even aware he was doing this? Here was a man who had given his entire life to the gospel, just as Brandon and Sarah had. And what of the hundreds of thousands of lives he'd touched? If the two of them could reach only a fraction of those Tyler had reached, their ministry would be more than a success. And it wasn't just the numbers. According to Cassandra, he'd once spent time doing those invisible acts of love, those self-sacrificing acts that others never even knew about. This had been a man who had loved God and had given everything he had to serve him.

But now . . .

"And what about these out-of-control terrorists with their biological weapons that could wipe out an entire city in seventy-two hours? That may be somebody's God . . ."

By now the audience had picked up his cadence, finishing the line with him. *". . .but he's sure not mine!"*

It was then Brandon felt something stirring and emerging through all the other emotions. He'd felt it once before, when his father's church was under attack. It was welling up inside of him again. Deep, powerful, unwavering. Anger, but not anger. Something stronger.

"And people today, they're so terrified of these financial crashes that their hearts are literally failing from fear. Did you know that right now the suicide rate in every country is higher than it's ever been in the history of the world? I don't know. That may be somebody's God . . ."

". . . but he's sure not mine!"

Part of the stirring Brandon felt came from the lies, but there was more.

"My God of love promised us peace! Peace among men, peace of mind, peace of the pocketbook! That's what my God of love is about. And God is love, God is love, God is . . ." He held out the microphone.

"LOVE!"

"You want a vengeful God? Fine. That may be somebody's God . . ."

". . . but he's sure not mine."

The sensation raced through Brandon's body like fire until it began to condense somewhere in the center of his chest. So powerful that it surprised, even scared him. Of course God was love, but it was a deeper love, one that involved holiness. If he'd learned anything from his brief encounter at the hospital it was that God's love is not a love giving us whatever we want, whenever we want it . . . His is a love that withholds and even disciplines . . . a love that doesn't desire to *give* us the best, but that desires to *make* us the best.

Suddenly Brandon understood the sensation consuming him. This anger taking over his heart and mind was not because of the lies. Misrepresentation didn't threaten God. It was because of what the lies were doing to his people. How they were being ripped off and sold a cheapened bill of goods. How they were being duped into believing in a superficial God of superficial love who had no interest in making them whole.

And the more Tyler preached, the stronger Brandon's rage grew until he could barely stand it. His breathing increased. His heart pounded in his ears.

"Dear God," he whispered. "What's happening to me?"

There was no answer. Only the memory of the promise he'd been given in the hospital. *"My words will become a fire in your mouth that you cannot contain."*

And still Jimmy Tyler continued to preach . . . and still the fire burned and grew and raged.

CHAPTER 7

Sarah sat at the front of the arena in the roped-off section for VIPs and their families. So far she had to admit that it had been quite a show. The orchestra, the choir, and the soloists had all worked hard to bring the audience into a spirit of love and unity. And they had succeeded. Wonderfully. In fact, Sarah couldn't remember a time she'd felt more inspired to reach out and love her fellow human being.

The pretaped endorsements by top world dignitaries had also helped. Respected men and women, both religious and political, everybody from the Dalai Lama to an emissary from the pope, to the UN secretary general, to the vice president. Tyler's folks didn't miss a beat. They even ended the segment with a prerecorded statement by Lucas Ponte—although Sarah had to admit that she really hadn't paid that much attention to what he'd said. She was too busy reflecting on how this was the same man who'd personally phoned her, and musing upon how his looks held up even when projected upon a forty-foot screen. Then, of course, there was the other matter, the one of his invitation for her to come to Nepal. She had discussed it several times with Brandon, and though he seemed strangely uneasy about their being separated, he wasn't entirely closed to the idea.

Finally Jimmy Tyler himself had taken the stage. Everyone was so primed and ready that the man could have hiccuped and gotten a standing ovation. But he did more than that. A lot more. Even though Sarah didn't appreciate his flashy showmanship, she had to admit it was impossible not to get caught up in his message . . . and in the enthusiasm of those surrounding her.

Still, something wasn't right. She couldn't put her finger on it, but there was something. Maybe it was the way he threw Christianity in with all of the other religions, insisting that it was just one of many roads to spirituality. But there was something else. She knew Brandon hated being in front of people—the poor guy's knees nearly buckled when he tried to make a speech at their wedding reception. She also knew he wasn't crazy about appearing to endorse Jimmy Tyler. Still, there he was, doing both, and for that her respect for him only increased. But, as Tyler spoke, she noticed Brandon's growing restlessness. Since she was in the audience sitting low and close to the front of the stage, and since he sat on the third riser behind two rows of guests, it wasn't always possible to see him. But from the glimpses she caught, she could tell he was definitely uncomfortable. A fidget here, a shift of his weight there. Maybe she was just being overly sensitive. Maybe no one else noticed. But the more his anxiety increased, the more her uneasiness rose. She forced herself to look back at the preacher. He'd opened his Bible and was starting to read.

"For I know the thoughts that I think toward you, saith the Lord, thoughts of peace, and not of evil." He looked up. "Do you folks hear that? God wants us to have peace, not evil. And it's not just in this book. I know you'll find the same thing in the Koran, the Bhagavad Gita, any of them other holy books." He turned to the group of guests on either side. "Am I right, folks?"

Several nodded and agreed.

"You bet I'm right. And you want to know why? Because our God is the *same* God."

Once again Sarah caught a glimpse of Brandon. Now she noticed his face. Was it the lights, or was he getting redder? Even under the makeup he almost seemed to glow . . . and then there was the sweat. His entire forehead was covered in beads of perspiration. *Dear Lord,* she prayed, *help him relax.*

Tyler was back in his Bible. "Then shall ye call upon me, and ye shall go and pray unto me, and I will hearken unto you." He looked out to the audience. "You got that people? It's right here in the book of Jeremiah, plain as the nose on your face. If we pray, God has to harken unto us, he *has* to listen. He has no choice in the matter, it's in the contract. He's legally obligated. And you know why? Because he says so! It's right here." He gave the book a rap. "It was true 2500 years ago when he wrote the book of Jeremiah, and it's true today. The Word of God does not change, folks. The grass withereth, the flower fadeth: but the word of our God shall stand forever. Forever! How long will it stand?" He held out the mike.

"Forever!" the audience shouted back.

"Now you're catchin' on." The audience clapped as Tyler wiped down his face and poured another glass of water.

Sarah mechanically joined in the applause as she tried to catch another glimpse of Brandon. A loud *plop* suddenly drew her attention back to Tyler. The man had thrown his Bible down on the stage.

"Ask me what I'm doing." He grinned. "Go ahead, ask me what I'm doing?"

Some of the crowd shouted, *"What are you doing?"*

"What's that?"

More responded. *"What are you doing?"*

He hopped up on the Bible with one foot and grinned. "I'm standing on the Word of God."

The audience laughed.

"Now you little old ladies, don't get your undies in a bunch. I'm trying to make a point here. This holy book is a foundation stone for our society. Fact, some would say for the whole world, am I right?"

More agreement and applause.

"But I've got more than one foot, don't I? Well, don't I?"

The audience shouted back the affirmative.

Continuing to balance, Tyler looked offstage into the wings and shouted, "Boys, can you give me a hand here?" Immediately a half-dozen men ran out onto the stage, each holding a book. "Who's got the Torah?" Tyler asked. A man held out the book. Tyler nodded, "Just set it down there." The man set the book down on the stage near Tyler then stepped back and turned to exit. "What about the Koran?" Tyler asked. Another man raised his book. Tyler nodded, and the man set his book on the other side and exited. "The Bhagavad Gita?" Another man stepped forward and put down his book.

Still on one foot and struggling to keep his balance, Tyler sped up the process. "Go ahead, set them others down, boys—anywhere will do." They obeyed, setting their books on the stage around him, and then turned to leave.

Tyler's balance grew shakier. "We've got more than one foot, so don't we need more than one stone? Isn't that how we stop from falling over?" He grew even more unsteady. "Isn't it?"

Several shouted back. *"Yes!"*

His wobbling grew worse. "Isn't it?"

More shouted, *"Yes!"*

He was beginning to sway, hopping up and down on the one foot. "Isn't it!"

The entire audience yelled, *"YES!"* just as Tyler fell forward, slapping his free foot down on one of the other books. He stood a moment, completely stable, catching his breath. Finally he looked up, grinning. "And that, folks, is called *balance.*"

The crowd broke into applause and cheers.

Jimmy laughed, enjoying it as much as the audience. "Do you understand what I'm sayin'?" He began walking on the other books. "We need these other stones, we need these other beliefs. Otherwise we'd topple over, we'd fall flat on our arrogant, spiritually proud faces. Do you hear me? Differences are good! It's the only way to keep our balance."

The crowd clapped in agreement.

As Tyler continued to walk from book to book, something to his left briefly caught his attention. He ignored it and turned back to the audience. "These are our foundation stones, folks. Not just one rock, not just one belief, but several. They all work together in unison to hold up our society, to give us a better stance and help us keep our balance. And that's why we're here tonight, folks. We're coming together as one balanced people!"

Again, something caught his attention, this time a little longer. And, again, he continued. "We're coming together in unity, putting aside our petty religious differences—" Again, he was distracted. There was a commotion up on one of the risers. Sarah craned her neck and to her surprise saw it was Brandon. He had risen to his feet. Others surrounding him were tugging on his sleeve, urging him to sit back down. But he paid little attention. His face was red and he was trembling.

"Reverend Tyler . . ."

At first Tyler tried to ignore him and continue. "Admitting that on our own none of us has all the answers, but when we're united—"

"Reverend Tyler!"

Soon everyone onstage and in the audience was staring at him. Tyler could no longer ignore him. He looked over and grinned. "What's a matter, son?"

Brandon took a step down from his row toward the stage. His voice was thin and shaky. "Reverend Tyler?"

Tyler continued smiling. "Time for a potty break?"

The audience chuckled. Sarah stiffened as Brandon continued down the steps to the stage.

Tyler gave a nearly imperceptible glance at the security guards who stood down in front of the stage near Sarah. They moved in preparation, but Tyler shook his head, indicating that for now he had it under control. They nodded and he turned back to Brandon. "We'll be over in just a few minutes, son, if you think you can hold it."

More chuckles, but the audience's curiosity was definitely growing.

Gripping the arms of her chair, Sarah noticed how wet her palms had become. *What is he doing? What is he doing!*

"You speak from the Bible . . ." Because Brandon had no microphone, his voice sounded hollow as the other mikes onstage picked him up. "You speak from the prophet Jeremiah. But he has other words as well. Other words for you."

"Well, folks"—Tyler threw a smile to the audience—"looks like I'm in for a little Bible study."

More nervous laughter.

Brandon was nearly center stage now, twenty feet from Tyler.

"What's your name, son?"

"My name is not important. It's what the Lord would say to you that matters."

"I see." He gave a wink to the audience. "And what exactly is that?"

Sarah's hand rose to the scar on her face as she watched Brandon take a deep breath. *Dear God,* she prayed, *what is he doing?*

And then he began: "Woe to the shepherds who are destroying and scattering the sheep of my pasture! declares the Lord. Because you have scattered my flock and driven them away and have not bestowed care on them, I will bestow punishment on you for the evil you have done, declares the Lord."

Tyler was unfazed, remaining cool and calm. "Yes, Jeremiah 23, I believe that is." Then turning back to the audience he quipped. "Looks like the boy's been doing his memory verses."

More chuckles.

But Sarah, whose heart was pounding, knew he was wrong. For the past year the two of them had been poring over Scripture, that was true. But they'd barely cracked Jeremiah, let alone put anything to memory. No, this was something else. Something much different.

Brandon continued, his voice still quivering, but growing stronger. "Do not listen to what the prophets are prophesying to you; they fill you with false hopes. They speak visions from their own minds, not from the mouth of the Lord. They keep saying to those who despise me, The Lord says: You will have peace. And to all who follow the stubbornness of their hearts they say, No harm will come to you."

"Well, thank you for sharing, brother." It was obvious the novelty had worn off, and Tyler had had enough. "Now if you wouldn't mind taking your seat, I'll finish making my point, if I can remember it."

But Brandon was far from through. He turned directly to the audience, trying to see through the glare of the lights. "They dress the wound of my people as though it were not serious. Peace, peace, they say, when there is no peace."

Sarah spotted Tyler signaling the security guards to take over. They moved to action. But seeing them, Brandon held out his hand, motioning for them to stop. And, to Sarah's surprise, they did. They continued to stand and they continued to listen, but for some unknown reason, they did not move toward him.

"Therefore this is what the Lord says about the prophets who are prophesying in my name: I did not send them, yet they are saying, No sword or famine will touch this land."

"Guys." Tyler motioned to the security guards. "Can you help our friend find his seat?"

The guards nodded, but did not move.

"Guys!"

Brandon turned from the audience and back to Tyler, his voice more powerful, almost booming. For an amazing moment Sarah thought she saw a flicker coming from his mouth, almost like a flame. Of course it was an illusion from all the bright lights, and it disappeared as quickly as it had appeared. But the rest was no illusion.

Brandon pointed his finger at Tyler and shouted, "Those same prophets will perish by sword and famine!"

The final phrase echoed through the arena until there was only silence.

Sarah's heart thundered in her ears. *Dear God, let it be over. Please, make it be over!*

In the silence, Tyler calmly reached for his glass of water, trying just a little too hard to appear nonchalant. He obviously didn't understand why the security guards were hesitating, but it was important he appear to be in control. "So tell me, uh, I still didn't catch the name." He waited, but Brandon didn't answer. He reached for the pitcher. "Don't you find that all of this shouting and preaching, ever notice how thirsty it makes a fellow? It sure does me. Not that I've had much opportunity these last few minutes."

The audience chuckled as he poured the water.

Brandon approached, keeping his eyes riveted on Tyler, who tried his best to appear amused. They were ten feet apart when Brandon raised his hand and pointed. "The blood of the sheep will be upon the head of the shepherd."

"I see," Tyler said, raising the glass to his lips and starting to drink. But he barely managed to swallow before he gagged, then leaned over to spit it out. He looked down at the glass in stunned surprise. And for good reason. The water inside had become blood red. His eyes widened. He turned to the pitcher. Its contents had also turned to blood. Astonished, Tyler let the glass slip from his hand. It hit the stage with such a crash that he jumped, causing the pitcher to drop from his other hand. It also shattered onto the stage, sending broken shards and splattered blood in all directions.

The audience gasped and began to murmur. Many rose to their feet. The guests on either side of the stage did the same.

Brandon continued his approach.

Looking up from the blood, Tyler took a half step back. Brandon spoke again, "You have lived as a prostitute with many lovers—would you now return to me? declares the Lord."

That was all the time Tyler needed to recover. Fighting for control, he shot back, "Listen, kid . . . I don't know who you think you are or how you believe these little parlor tricks are going to accomplish anything. But—"

"Repent and return to the Lord!"

Tyler swallowed. "But we've got a lot more important things to cover than to listen to some—"

"Be still!" Again Sarah thought she saw a flicker of flame.

Suddenly, Tyler began coughing, unable to finish his sentence.

And still Brandon continued, breathing hard and speaking intensely. "You son of the devil, you enemy of all righteousness, will you not cease perverting the straight ways of the Lord?"

Tyler tried to respond, but his coughing grew worse.

"The hand of the Lord is upon you, and you shall no longer be able to speak or spread your deceit in my name."

Tyler tried to argue, but the words came out only as coughs and gags.

By now all of the audience had risen to their feet. Some in astonishment, others in anger. Sarah looked around helplessly as they began to shout. "Get him out of here! Get him off the stage!" Others began stomping their feet or booing.

Hearing them for the first time, Brandon turned from Tyler and came down toward the front of the stage to address them. The yelling and catcalls increased. He took a moment and scanned the crowd before breathing deeply and shouting, "Has a nation ever changed its gods? (Yet they are not gods at all.) But my people have changed their Glory for worthless idols. Be appalled at this, O heavens, and shudder with great horror, declares the Lord. My people have committed two sins: They have forsaken me, the spring of living water, and have dug their own cisterns, broken cisterns that cannot hold water."

Booing filled the auditorium.

Brandon continued looking out at them, his face filling with compassion. Sarah could see the moisture in his eyes.

"Stand at the crossroads and look; ask for the ancient paths, ask where the good way is, and walk in it, and you will find rest for your souls."

The audience was shouting so loudly Sarah could barely hear.

"Like a woman unfaithful to her husband, so you have been unfaithful to me, declares the Lord."

Items began flying onto the stage. Wadded-up programs, loose change, pencils and pens, anything the audience could find to throw. Some hit their mark, forcing Brandon to wince. But he continued quoting. "Therefore this is what the Sovereign Lord says: My anger and my wrath will be poured out on this place, on man and beast, on the trees of the field and on the fruit of the ground, and it will burn and not be quenched."

Tyler remained bent over and coughing. By now some of the more courageous guests on the stage had started to approach Brandon.

"Return, declares the Lord, and I will frown on you no longer, for I am merciful. I will not be angry forever. Only acknowledge your guilt . . ."

The group onstage continued to close in.

Sarah started to wave, shouting to get his attention, "Brandon, Brandon, look out!" But he didn't hear.

"You have rebelled against the Lord your God, you have scattered your favors to—"

A young man from the right was the first to charge. He hit Brandon from behind and tackled him hard to the ground. As they hit the stage Sarah screamed. She started pushing her way toward them, but the area in front of the stage was already filled with shouting people. She looked back up to the stage. Other guests had arrived and also began struggling with Brandon, trying to subdue him.

"Brandon . . ."

The audience was in a frenzy—shouting, jeering, many applauding his capture.

The group onstage pulled Brandon to his feet. They began to drag him across the stage, toward the wings. He did not go willingly, twisting and squirming, but there were far too many of them.

Sarah was still trying to push her way through the crowd toward the stage. "Excuse me! Please . . . Excuse me!" But it was jammed, choked with shouting, taunting people. She pushed harder. "Excuse me, please—" until an older teen violently shoved her back, shouting an oath. Sarah blinked and stared. She turned, looking around her, not believing her eyes or her ears. How had it happened? How, in just a matter of minutes, had a loving and caring crowd been turned into a shouting mob? The transformation had been so fast, almost supernatural. Such hatred, such fury. And all directed at one person . . .

Katherine glanced up from filling her second suitcase when Lucas entered the room. There was no one else with him. Not his secretary, none of the peripheral folks that usually surrounded him. Not that it mattered. There could have been a hundred, and she'd still have taken him on.

"I don't want to hear it," she snapped. "Nothing you say will change my mind."

He didn't have to speak. His presence in the doorway spoke volumes.

Katherine crossed to the cedar wardrobe, threw open its doors, and gathered a handful of clothes still on their hangers. "You said you could help. You said you could find a cure. Well, you haven't." She headed back to the bed and dumped the clothes into the suitcase.

He remained silent.

She headed back to the wardrobe for another load. "It's not working, Lucas. He's not getting any better. And Heylel's little visits are only making things worse."

At last he spoke—softly, with understanding. "So where are you going?"

"I don't know. Katmandu, for a while. Till we get enough saved to catch a flight home. Anywhere, just as long as it's not here." The last phrase was a little harsh and she knew it. "I know you've tried. You, the Cartel, you've done all you can. But this place, it's nowhere for a kid to grow up. People treating him like a god, you folks hanging onto his every word, acting like he's some cosmic guru. It's not healthy. You can't blame me for wanting my kid to have some semblance of an ordinary life."

"Eric is no ordinary kid."

She threw him a look as she headed for the dresser. It was then she noticed the envelope he was tapping in his hands.

"What's that?"

He glanced down. "Oh, this. It is two one-way tickets to Seattle along with $5,000 cash to help you get started."

Katherine came to a stop. It took a moment to digest the statement. "Why?"

"Pardon me?"

"Why would you do that?"

"Because you are right, this is no place for a child. Or his mother. Especially ones I have grown so fond of."

Katherine eyed him carefully. She'd seen this maneuver before. Sincere concern, mixed with flattery. It was all part of the Ponte charm. She watched as he quietly set the envelope down on the table. Once again she asked, "Why are you doing this?"

"It is the least we can do, considering all we have put you through." He took a deep breath. "And . . ." He seemed to hesitate, unsure whether he should continue.

Katherine knew it was a ploy, but she took the bait anyway. "And?"

"And, given the fact that from the moment Eric leaves these grounds we will be unable to offer him any type of diplomatic immunity."

"What does that mean?"

"The local officials have called twice and have already paid us one visit. They're charging your son with murder."

Katherine's jaw went slack. "That's . . . absurd. Deepak had a heart attack. Eric didn't even touch him. You can't call that murder."

"In the West, you are correct. But I'm afraid these people here are of a much more superstitious nature."

"They're going to arrest him?"

Lucas shook his head. "If Eric stays on the grounds they will not touch him. The government of Nepal would not risk confrontation with the Cartel."

Katherine's mind raced. "But if he leaves the grounds?"

"If he leaves the grounds . . ." Lucas sighed heavily. "Well, as I have said, it is doubtful they will respect our request for diplomatic immunity."

Once again Katherine felt the noose tightening. As it did, her anger grew. "So that ticket, that money is completely useless."

"Not necessarily. A few of the local officials have been known to look the other way . . . when the right money crosses the right hands."

"A bribe?"

He shrugged. "Call it what you will. The problem, of course, lies in knowing which individuals will accept it."

Katherine stared at the envelope. She was being played in perfect Ponte style. "And you just happen to know who those individuals are, don't you?"

He shook his head. "No, of course not. But in time I am sure we could find out."

"How much . . . time?"

"The neurobiologist from the States will be planning to pay us a visit and to run some tests."

"Dr. Martus? When?"

"Shortly, very shortly."

"And . . ."

"By the time she is finished with her evaluation and recommendation for treatment, I am sure we will have found the proper officials."

Katherine could only stare. The trap had been woven so flawlessly that, even now as she stared at him, hating him, Lucas appeared to have nothing but deepest compassion and consideration. The man was a genius.

"But, of course, it is your decision, Katherine. And whatever you decide, we will do our best to be of assistance. We owe a great deal to the two of you. And, as we have proven, the Cartel does not forget its friends." He gave her a brief smile, then glanced at his watch. "Well, if you will excuse me." He turned and headed for the door. But before exiting he turned back for one final comment. "I know you will make the right decision, Katherine. You always have. That is one of your attributes. One of your many attributes." With that he disappeared out the door.

"It was incredible! It was like this fire burning inside of me, and it kept building and building until I thought I was going to explode."

Sarah and Tanya Chase walked on either side of Brandon as they headed down the hallway of the Hawthorne Police Station. A couple fluorescent tubes overhead were nearly burned out, and they gave the place an eerie blue-green flicker. But Brandon barely noticed. It had been three hours since the event at the Forum, and his adrenaline was still pumping.

"And I knew the words." He turned to Sarah. "It wasn't like the demoniacs we've worked with, where they don't have control of their bodies. I had total control. The words were in my mind before I spoke them. It was just up to me whether I wanted to obey and say them."

"And of course you did." Sarah's voice was flat and noncommittal.

"Well, yes, wouldn't you?"

She gave no answer as they continued down the hall. It was two in the morning and other than a handful of officers, a strung-out gang member, and a couple hookers, the hallway was relatively quiet.

Tanya spoke up. "Seems I remember reading something in the Bible about doing things 'decently and in order.'"

Brandon nodded and looked down at the worn yellowed tile passing under his feet. He knew she was right and the thought had crossed his mind more than once. But still . . .

"The only reason Jimmy's not pressing charges is because of how it will look."

Sarah turned to her. "Is that why he's posting bail?"

"Of course. It's the only way he can put a positive spin on any of this."

Sarah quoted the imaginary headline: "'Merciful Preacher Forgives Nutcase.'"

Tanya threw her a look. "Ever consider journalism?"

Sarah gave no answer as they continued walking.

Brandon glanced over at her with his good eye. The other was swollen by a misdirected elbow . . . or fist. Minutes earlier, when he had first been released from the holding cell, Sarah had greeted him with an embrace and tears of concern. But now, as they headed down the hall toward the front desk, he saw only exhaustion and weariness. The evening had been as rough on her as it had been on him. Maybe worse. He reached out, starting to put his arm around her, but she seemed to anticipate the move and shied away.

The action surprised him, and he looked back at her. She gave no response and continued walking, looking straight ahead. He didn't press the issue, but there was no missing the heavy realization as it settled over him. It was true; it had been harder on her, a lot harder.

Once again Tanya broke the silence. "Any idea when Jimmy's going to speak again?"

He turned to her and asked, "He still can't talk?"

"The doctor says it's psychosomatic . . . something about having a multimillion-dollar TV broadcast destroyed, not to mention an entire ministry. Earliest estimates say we had an audience share of fifty-nine. That's 133.4 million people, more than watched last year's Superbowl."

Brandon said nothing. His sadness grew heavier.

She continued. "I still don't understand that water to blood thing—how you pulled that off."

Brandon shook his head, as baffled as she was. "Me neither. But Revelation 11 says that—"

"Brandon . . ." Sarah interrupted.

He looked at her.

"I think we've had enough Bible quoting for one night." At last she turned to him. "Don't you?"

The fatigue and pain he saw made him wince. She'd been through even more than he had originally thought. But there was something else in her. A hurt. A betrayal.

He desperately wanted to comfort her, to somehow take away the pain, but—

"Oh, great," Tanya sighed.

He turned to her. "What?"

She motioned to the double glass doors just outside the lobby. "It's the press."

Brandon turned to see the sizable crowd that had gathered. "What are they here for?"

She gave him a look. "You've got to be kidding."

"What do we do?" Sarah asked in apprehension.

"There's nothing we can do," Tanya said. "The car and driver are parked in front. When we get out there, don't talk to anyone, don't acknowledge their questions, just head straight for the car's rear door. I'll take the lead and break them up, but you've got to stay right behind me. Just keep pushing and don't lose your momentum, or you'll never get through."

"There has to . . ." Sarah slowed to a stop. They were in the lobby now, near the first set of doors. "There has to be another way out of here."

Tanya shook her head. "Better get used to it, girl." She reached for the first door and called over her shoulder. "This won't be the last."

They stepped through the first set of doors and crossed the five feet of space toward the outer ones. That's when the crowd spotted them and came to life. "They're here!" Lights blazed on as cameramen and reporters jockeyed for position. Tanya reached for the outer door and hesitated. Brandon kept Sarah between them, hoping somehow to protect her. After turning and giving them a nod, Tanya pushed open the door, and the assault began.

"Brandon, is it true that—"

"Do you really think you're some sort of—"

"How long has this rivalry between you and Tyler been—"

Everywhere Brandon looked lights glared, cameras jostled, and eager faces and microphones pressed in.

"Come on, guys!" Tanya was shouting. "Let us through! Come on! Come on, now!"

"How soon before you believe the world will come to an—"

"Is it true that you can call down God's judgment any time you—"

"Do you really believe God hates all—"

As they started down the steps Brandon caught a glimpse of the car below.

"Sarah, how long has he had these powers?"

"Is it true, you've only been married—"

And then he felt it, a shattering egg. It caught his left shoulder and splattered onto his face. He looked up. It came from across the street where at least a dozen other people had gathered. But not reporters. These were hecklers. Some hurled insults, others made obscene gestures. Then, of course, there were the eggs. Another one splattered, this time across Sarah's arm. She gave a startled cry as reporters ducked for cover. Others took advantage and pushed in harder. At last Tanya had the back door to the car open.

"Tell us about the next judgment!"

"Sarah, about that scar? Was that something Brandon did? Another one of God's—"

Sarah ducked in, scooting across the seat. Brandon followed.

Tanya slammed their door and opened the front. Reporters swarmed on all sides, shouting, lights blazing. There were more thumps as eggs hit the windows and roof.

"Let's go!" Tanya shouted to the driver. "Let's go, let's go!"

The car lurched forward, fast enough to make it clear they meant business, slow enough not to run over anyone.

A moment later the chaos was behind them. Brandon looked back as a final egg caught the rear trunk and splattered up to the window.

"Well," Tanya called from the front seat, "that wasn't too bad. 'Course the hotel might be a little worse."

Sarah's eyes shot to her. "Hotel?"

"Oh, yeah. Then of course there's the airport."

Brandon looked at Tanya, dumbfounded. "Why?"

"It was the broadcast event of the year, kids. You claimed on national TV that God was judging the world. And your little special effects with Tyler's voice and that blood trick gave them proof of your credentials. Pretty slick move, buddy boy, pretty slick."

Brandon's head was reeling. "I don't . . . understand."

"In ten minutes you succeeded in achieving everything Jimmy Tyler had spent a lifetime trying to do."

"I'm sorry, I still don't—"

"In ten minutes you became the focal point, the representative of God for the entire nation. Not bad for a night's work."

Brandon frowned.

"Of course, he's not exactly the God most of us want to believe in. But when it comes to representing a judgmental tyrant, someone we can blame all of our troubles on, hey, you two win the prize, hands down."

The first-class flight was as luxurious coming home as it had been when they'd headed out. But Brandon barely noticed. All he heard was the dull roar of the 757 and the deafening silence of Sarah sitting beside him. In the last twenty-four hours neither of them had slept. They couldn't. Sarah was pretending to now, but Brandon knew better. It was simply another excuse not to talk.

His actions had erected an impenetrable wall between them. Something he'd have guessed would have been impossible two days earlier. But now . . . not only had he embarrassed and humiliated his wife, branding them both as lunatics, it was likely that he'd also managed to destroy any reputation the clinic had gained. Why had he been so impulsive? What had he hoped to accomplish? And most importantly, why hadn't he given more thought to what it would do to Sarah?

Pride. That's what it was. Plain and simple. Pride that he was somehow holier than Tyler. Pride that he was the only one with the answers. Pride that his interpretation of Scripture was the only one that counted.

But there was an even greater weight pressing down upon Brandon. The words he'd heard in the hospital. About Sarah. About her leaving. They'd never gone away, they'd always remained nagging in the back of his mind. He'd hoped he could stop them—by being the perfect husband, by doing whatever she wanted, by doing whatever God wanted. But nothing had worked. Everything had been in vain. Like riding a runaway train, there seemed nothing he could do to stop the inevitable.

He looked back over at her. Her eyes were open now as she leaned against the window, staring down at the passing farmland. How he wanted to ease the pain, but it was too late.

He looked down at her hand and saw the wedding band sparkle in the sun. He reached out and took her hand into his. She didn't resist. He raised her fingers to his lips, gave them a kiss, then leaned his cheek against them. She still did not respond. He set her hand down onto his own lap and held it. He saw her chest swell as she took a deep breath. And then, without looking at him, she spoke.

"I think, I think I should go." Her voice was dull and lifeless as she stared out the window.

The back of Brandon's throat ached. "I understand."

"To Nepal, I mean."

"I know."

"It won't be forever. Just a few weeks." She paused a moment, then continued. "It will give me a chance to work with the Cartel. It will be good for the clinic. It will also help us sort things out."

By now the tightness in his throat was so unbearable he could only nod.

They said nothing more. Brandon closed his eyes. He sat for a long time, thinking his heart would burst. But there was still hope. It's not like she would be gone forever. They were still married, they were still a team. And then, remembering he still held her hand, he gave it two little squeezes . . . their private form of communication.

But instead of responding, Sarah shifted in her seat, gently slipped her hand from his, and continued staring out the window.

PART TWO

CHAPTER 8

Look, save me the brain chemistry lectures," Katherine said, "I've heard them all before. Low serotonin, high noradrenaline, whacked-out neurotransmitters. And the drugs they've pumped him full of . . . Prozac, Clozapine, Amperozide, you name it, he's been shot up with it. We even had one quack who wanted to change his diet to chips, cookies, and candy."

Sarah nodded. "High carbohydrates have been known to increase serotonin levels which tends to induce passive behavior."

"And the sugar tends to drive kids through the roof."

Sarah smiled as she strolled with Katherine through the Cartel's long glass and mahogany hallway. To her left was a wall of rich wood with dozens of doors leading to plush offices. To her right was a glass wall and ceiling with the Himalayas looming high above them, their white peaks jutting into a sapphire sky. Below them she could see the ancient three-story compound of stone and stucco where she'd just spent her first night in Nepal.

They walked together in silence for several moments. Sarah liked Katherine and found her candid, no-nonsense approach refreshing, despite the hard shell of defense she'd built around herself and her son. She'd arrived in Katmandu late yesterday afternoon. By the time she'd finished the three-hour, bone-jarring ride up into the mountains, it was too dark to see anything. Thanks to jet lag and all of the excitement, she had not drifted off to sleep until it was nearly dawn. And now, two hours later, Katherine was giving her the grand tour of the Cartel's facility.

"And you believe that stuff?" Katherine asked, finally resuming the conversation. "That we're slaves to whatever chemical happens to be passing through our brains?"

Sarah chose her words carefully. "I believe we are a finely tuned instrument. If just one neurotransmitter alone is off by, say, five percent, it can wreak havoc on the entire nervous system."

"But we're more than just chemistry sets," Katherine argued. "I mean, when Michael Coleman, that fellow who was first infected with the DNA, when he had his problems, he was able to overcome them. It was hard, but he did it."

"How?"

Katherine ran her hand through her short-cropped hair. "You don't think I've asked myself that a million times?"

"And?"

"Michael Coleman was an incredible man."

"That was it?"

Katherine glanced at the floor, frowning.

Sarah knew there was more. "What?"

"Toward the end, when things really got tough, he claimed to have found some sort of faith."

"In?"

"He said it was Christianity. He said his faith in God gave him the power to overcome the evil inside him."

"But you don't buy it."

Katherine's eyes flashed to hers. "My father was a preacher, Dr. Martus. I've seen more than my share of wasted faith and unanswered prayers."

Sarah held her look and then slowly nodded—not because she agreed, but because she understood. It had been two weeks since the Jimmy Tyler broadcast, and things had gotten no better. Well, except for their notoriety. The mail was voluminous, most of it negative. So were the phone calls and visits by reporters. But none of these were as difficult as the attacks on the clinic. Nothing dangerous, just threats, occasional vandalism, and a handful of picketers. Still, that was their life's work, their very service to God. And by the looks of things, God wasn't too awfully interested in accepting that service.

The good-byes had been harder than she'd expected. It was the first time she and Brandon had been apart since they'd fallen in love. And, although he said he agreed that the brief separation would do them and the clinic some good, she knew he didn't believe it for a second.

Unfortunately, she did.

In the forty-eight hours since she'd left O'Hare International Airport she was already feeling a heaviness lifting. Granted, there was still more than enough guilt to go around, but that suffocating frustration, that confusion and resentment which had been building in her for so long, was already loosening its grip. Maybe it was just the exotic location, or the anticipation of working with the Cartel; she wasn't sure. But the sense of freedom both excited her and made her sad.

"So what do *you* think?" Katherine's voice brought her back to the moment.

"I'm sorry?"

"About faith."

Again she was careful with her answer. "I think faith is the catalyst . . . but not the cure."

"Meaning?"

"Meaning I agree with you, that we're more than just chemicals. It's been my experience that there's another level to us, something residing within these . . . 'chemistry sets.'"

"You mean our spirit," Katherine said.

Sarah glanced at her with a smile. "As a Christian I would agree, but the scientist part of me might feel a little better if we were to describe it as 'some form of energy.'"

"Now you sound like a Star Wars movie."

Sarah shook her head. "What I'm talking about is more personal than that. It seems to have a distinct personality. In the labs, to a certain degree, we've been able to catch glimpses of it. No, let me rephrase that. We've been able to catch glimpses of its *effects*. We've been able to see how it can affect the chemistry of our bodies."

Katherine gave her a dubious look.

Sarah continued. "But only if we let it. If not, our bodies can reverse the effect and actually have influence over it instead. It's hard to explain, but when that 'energy' intersects with our chemicals, a hybrid is formed, a unique and very special blend of chemical and spirit, a personality if you will. And that personality can choose to let the 'spirit' override the influence of our chemicals, or it can choose to let the chemicals override the 'spirit.'"

"My dad would have called that personality a soul."

"So would most people of religion. But regardless of the name, it seems to have an ability to make that choice . . . to follow the chemical part of its composition, or to follow the spirit part. And it's that choosing, whether to follow the chemical or the spirit, that I would call 'faith.'"

"So basically you're saying what Coleman said. It was his faith that saved him."

"Yes and no. I'm saying Coleman's faith acted as a catalyst, allowing the spirit to come in and do its work on his chemicals."

Katherine gave a wry smile. "Sounds like you've done a pretty good job of mixing science and faith."

"I don't see any difference between the two. It just takes a little longer for science to get around to proving what we people of faith already accept. I don't believe God performs miracles; I believe God performs 'naturals' that we just haven't understood yet. God performed a 'natural' in Coleman's brain by readjusting the chemicals . . . but only as Coleman gave him permission through faith. God performs 'naturals' when people at our clinic are healed . . . somehow he readjusts their bodies. God performed 'naturals' when he raised Jesus Christ from the dead. What makes it a miracle is that he applied his created laws of chemistry and physics in a manner we simply haven't understood yet."

"But what if we don't have the faith to have faith?" Katherine asked. Sarah couldn't be sure, but it almost seemed like Katherine was enjoying the conversation. "Remember that guy in the Bible asking Jesus to help his unbelief?"

Sarah nodded. "I think that brings us back to that Personality, to that Love. Maybe it's that Love that stacks the deck, that gives us the faith to have faith."

Katherine quoted, "'The Author and Perfecter of our faith.' Another one of God's jobs."

"Exactly. But it doesn't negate the fact that faith is a freewill decision on our part, that we still have to be willing to receive that faith."

Katherine sighed heavily. "So you've taken us right back to having to believe in a loving and compassionate God."

"Why's that so hard for you?" Sarah asked.

Katherine hesitated, then answered quietly, "I've been on the receiving end of that 'love' one too many times, Doctor. The death of my father, the murder of my husband, the killing of Coleman." She turned to look out a passing window, starting to lose herself in thought. "Coleman, though . . . I have to admit, he almost had me convinced." Then she was back, turning to Sarah. "Until I saw what this God of love let them do to my baby, and what he's continuing to do to our lives."

"And that's your proof that a compassionate Deity doesn't exist?"

"Words are cheap, Dr. Martus. Truth lies in what we do, not what we say. *If* there is a God out there, and *if* he really does love us, he's sure not going out of his way to prove it."

Before Sarah could respond, an office door opened a few yards ahead of them. A woman secretary stepped out into the hallway, followed by Lucas Ponte. For the briefest moment Sarah forgot to breathe. He was even more imposing in person than on the videophone. Over six feet tall, broad shoulders, neatly trimmed beard.

"Lucas," Katherine called.

He looked up at Katherine, then over to Sarah. His grin was instant and made her just the slightest bit unsteady. "Dr. Weintraub. It is so good to see you." He handed his papers back to the secretary and strode quickly over to offer his hand.

Barely noticing the use of her maiden name, Sarah took his hand and they shook. His grip was firm, yet gentle. "Good morning, sir," she said. "It's a pleasure to meet you."

His grin broadened. "I assure you, Doctor, the pleasure is mine." And then, just before he could be accused of flirting, he motioned to Katherine. "It is for all of us, am I right, Katherine?"

Katherine smiled, but there was no mistaking the effort it involved. "Whatever you say, Lucas. You're the boss."

"Really." He chuckled. "So why haven't I ever been informed of this fact before?" Smiling at his joke, he turned back to Sarah. "Did you have a pleasant flight?"

"Yes, thank you." She tugged at the hair over her scar.

"Good, good. And our accommodations?"

"No complaints."

"Excellent."

To some this would have been merely small talk. But Sarah felt the man was genuinely concerned as he asked each question and was equally as interested in each answer. That's the type of sincerity she'd read about, and that's the type of sincerity she now saw in person.

"Well," he said, "I will certainly look forward to speaking with you more in depth, but right now—"

"I'm sure you're very busy."

He sighed. "It's this recent outbreak of earthquakes along the Pacific Rim. You've been reading about them?"

Sarah nodded. "We were in Los Angeles just before they started."

"Now there are geological reports of possible volcanic activity. Hawaii, the Pacific Northwest, Japan . . . things may become very serious very quickly."

As he spoke, a young teenager sauntered out of his office and into the hallway. He was thin, almost frail, with sandy blonde hair and glasses. When his eyes connected with Sarah's she caught her breath. For, though they were eight thousand miles apart, Sarah was looking into the very same pair of eyes she'd left back home. Eyes that were already penetrating hers, searching her thoughts, exploring her mind.

Lucas Ponte spotted him and started to make the introduction, but it wasn't necessary. Sarah already knew.

"Dr. Weintraub, this is Eric Lyon."

"Behind me, up on the third story, are the offices to the clinic where Dr. and Mr. Martus had worked for nearly twelve months."

The television picture cut from a close-up of Tanya Chase to a wider angle showing an old four-story brick building in the seedier section of Bethel Lake. Next came a shaky handheld shot moving down the clinic's hallway.

Tanya's voice continued. "It was behind the doors of these rooms that the couple practiced their 'medicine.' And, although many claimed to have been helped by their efforts, there are the others . . ."

The picture cut to a close-up of the mother whose mentally impaired girl Brandon had declined to heal several weeks earlier. "I like Brandon Martus," the woman was saying. "He's a good person. So is Sarah. Debra likes them, too."

The picture switched to the little girl sitting on a tricycle. Her head was tilted and slightly drooped. This was followed by a shot of Mom with her on the floor playing with a preschool toy. As the girl struggled to put the correct block into the correct hole, her retardation became more obvious. The picture returned to the interview as Tanya asked, "How long ago did you visit him?"

"'Bout a month ago."

Back to the two of them on the floor.

"And is she any better?"

"No . . ."

"How does that make you feel?"

"I dunno, kinda disappointed, I guess . . ." The camera remained on the mother. It was obvious she was struggling with her emotions.

Tanya continued. "Just disappointed?"

The woman shook her head, then glanced away. "I mean, we tried everything else. We was just . . ." She swallowed. The camera remained fixed on her and she began again. "We was just hoping that something could be done. I mean with what we heard and everything, we really had our hopes up. We was really, really hoping. But now . . ." She sniffed quietly and looked down. The camera remained on her. Finally, she shook her head, making it clear she was unable to go on.

Tanya's voice continued. "Meanwhile, the plague, the drought, and worldwide famine, which Martus claims to be the judgment of God, continue to increase."

After quick shots of suffering patients, shriveled crops, and starving children, the picture cut to a videotape of Brandon standing on the stage of the L.A. Forum, shouting. "My anger and my wrath will be poured out on this place, on man and beast, on the trees of the field and on the fruit of the ground, and it will burn and not be quenched."

Next came a picture of Brandon being dragged off the stage as Tanya's voice continued. "At best, he is accused by many in the religious community of capitalizing upon current world disasters . . ."

Now some cardinal spoke. He was an older gentleman, with sensitive eyes and a kindly voice. "Such action is nothing but raw exploitation of the world's suffering. It is an unconscionable act, and quite frankly, I believe the lad owes all of us in the religious community an apology."

Back to Tanya. "At worst, he is accused of actually bringing on the suffering."

Now a local businessman appeared—fortyish, sweaty, and with a loosened tie from the heat. "We all know about his power to heal, and what he did to Reverend Tyler on TV . . ." The man shook his head. "You'd have to be crazy not to think he's got some sort of supernatural connection."

Back to Tanya's voice. "Whatever one concludes . . ."

Videotape of the egg-throwing protesters appeared, followed by quick shots of graffiti scrawled across the front of the clinic, and finally ending with a handful of hecklers yelling at Brandon as he tried to enter the clinic.

". . . Brandon Martus has transformed this once mild Midwest hamlet into a conflicting caldron of controversy."

Back to Tanya standing in front of the building. "And now with the recent reports of seismic activity along the Pacific coast, attention is once again turned to this young man."

Back to Brandon onstage shouting in the background as she continued. "Was this also part of his prediction, part of his 'curse'? Is he somehow responsible? Or is he, as many believe, simply a charlatan, an opportunist out to capitalize upon the world's pain and suffering?"

Back to Tanya. "Earlier we'd reported that we'd discovered that the newlyweds had vowed not to physically consummate their relationship, that they felt sex was too demeaning for ones of such a high calling. And now, in an equally bizarre turn of events, it has been confirmed that after less than eight weeks of marriage the couple has separated. Dr. Sarah Martus was reported as being seen—"

Brandon clicked off the remote. He was practically shaking with anger. Like her boss, Tanya Chase had learned the fine art of using truth to tell lies. Other networks had picked up the story, a couple had even asked for interviews for their news magazines. And, although their coverage was equally as uninformed, no one had gone after them like GBN. Little wonder, after what he'd done to Tyler.

At first Brandon had agreed to the interviews, hoping explanations would somehow clarify things. They didn't. In fact they only caused greater confusion, confirming that he was either a huckster, a fruitcake, or some sadistic wizard capable of manipulating the forces of nature for evil. When the interviews didn't work, he tried remaining silent—an even worse mistake that made him all the more mysterious.

And then, just when it looked like things were starting to settle down, all of this seismic activity kicked up along the Pacific Rim. Mount Baker, Mount Hood, Mauna Loa in Hawaii, and a handful of other semidormant volcanoes in Japan, the Philippines, and Indonesia—all suddenly showing signs of potential eruption. And, once again, fingers began to point at him, questioning and asking if he was somehow responsible.

But by far the hardest thing was having to shut down the clinic. That had happened the end of last week. He'd tried to keep it running, but the threats and rising problems had been too much. The place had become a lightning rod, the galvanizing point of attention for everybody from the media, to the picketers with their placards reading: "HE MAY BE SOMEBODY'S GOD ... BUT HE SURE AIN'T MINE," to the opposite extremists who did Brandon little favor with counterdemonstrations involving signs reading: "TURN OR BURN!"

And where was God in all of this?

Silent, as usual.

Shoving aside an undercooked microwave burrito, Brandon rose from the table, shuffled to the computer, and punched it on. He stayed in Sarah's apartment now, and everything he saw reminded him of her. She'd been gone twelve days, and though she was faithful in answering his e-mail, her responses seemed to be growing shorter and less personal. Maybe it was just his imagination. He hoped and prayed that was the case.

The computer came up and the e-mail came on. Nearly a hundred postings this time. It was amazing how quickly they could find his address and flood his mailbox. Early on he'd learned not to open any whose names he didn't know. One virus and crashed hard drive was enough.

Scanning the list, he could find nothing from Sarah, and his heart sank a fraction lower. There was, however, a name he instantly recognized. He popped it up and began reading so fast that he had to stop and start over:

> Dearest Brandon:
>
> I know you are discouraged, but that is a necessary part of the process. The call he has given you is true. You will be doin' great and mighty things for him. But our understanding of great and mighty is different than his. Ours is vain and will burn. His is life-changing and eternal.

Brandon took a breath and slowly let it out.

> Every one of us has a call on our life. I don't care who they are. Like Joseph, God has put a dream in our hearts. But few have the faith to follow that dream through all its steps. You've received the call and that's fine. But that's only the first step. The second came when you messed it up. Like Joseph, you allowed worldly thinking to twist it till it fit into the world's idea of greatness. And if it didn't fit, you gave it a few bends and twists of your own till it did. That's where you've been living this last year as you've tried to accomplish in your flesh what God will do in his Spirit.
>
> But now you've entered the third step, and though it's the most painful, it's also the most necessary. 'Cause it's during this time of discouragement that the Lord untwists the world's twistings, that he removes your handiwork and straightens your dream back into his. Lots of times he lets those closest to us be the most discouraging. For Joseph it was his brothers throwing him into the pit, for Abraham it was his wife laughing at him, for our Lord it was his kinsmen trying to put him away. For you, it is Sarah.

Brandon swallowed hard. The words rang truer than he wanted to believe.

> Embrace this third step. I know the wilderness is hot, I know your wanderings seem aimless. But just like he did with the children of Israel, he will feed you, he will give you water, he will provide shade by day and light by night. Hold the Lord's hand, follow him through the desert, and he will lead you to the land he has promised. But you must do it his way. Because 'Flesh gives birth to flesh, but the Spirit gives birth to spirit.'
>
> Very soon you'll be entering another country. I'm not talking just spiritually, but literally, too. You have seen it lots of times in your dreams, but you haven't sought the Lord about it. When you do, he'll tell you. And when he tells you, obey. For it's the only way your call will bear fruit. Give Sarah my love. Be strong and courageous. Do not tremble or be afraid.
>
> Your servant,
> GM

Brandon sat staring at the words.

That's her, isn't it?

Heylel gave no answer, but Eric knew he was in the room. He'd been in the small conference room ever since Sarah had begun setting up the equipment.

That's her, Eric repeated. *She's the one who isn't the one, isn't she?*

There was still no answer. But Eric didn't need one. He'd known it, he'd sensed it, from the moment he'd first seen her in the hallway.

"Now, Eric . . ."

He turned to her. One of the sensors taped to his forehead pulled against his skin, and he winced.

"Here, let me fix that for you."

"It's all right."

"You sure he needs all of this stuff?" Katherine asked as Sarah readjusted one of the dozen sensor wires attached to his face, fingers, skin, earlobes, chest, and calf. "Makes him look like the back of some VCR."

Sarah smiled. "Some of these, like this GSR, measure the amount of electricity his skin conducts. That tells us how relaxed he is."

She reached across him to adjust another wire. Eric noticed that she smelled nice. In fact, everything about her was nice. Nice body, nice hair, nice smile. If it wasn't for that scar running down her face she might have been a real looker.

"This sensor over here is for the EMG—it records his muscle tension—and these around the scalp are for EEG, to register his brain activity."

"Provided he has any," Katherine quipped.

"Ho-ho," Eric replied, "very funny."

"You comfortable now?" Sarah asked.

He nodded.

"Okay, what I'd like you to do is take this in your right hand." She gave him a computer joystick with a trigger, then pointed to the small monitor on the table directly in front of him. "You see that blue line running across the screen?"

"Yeah."

"And the thinner yellow one on top of it?"

He nodded.

"When we begin, I want you to hold that trigger down and concentrate on pushing that yellow line above the blue one."

"You mean like with my mind?"

"Exactly."

"Cool."

As Sarah busied herself with a digital data recorder to record the results, Katherine asked, "And all of this stuff, it's like serious science?"

Sarah nodded. "What we're employing here is something called an RNG, a random number generator. They've been around about thirty years, and they're still the best way for us to measure a person's PK."

"PK?"

"*Psychokinesis*—the ability to move physical objects through mental concentration."

"You're not serious?" Katherine asked. "You don't actually believe people can do that?"

"There are over a dozen labs around the world studying the phenomena, along with other paranormal activity like PSI, remote viewing, automatic handwriting, and the list goes on. In fact, in the past, the United States Department of Defense has spent over twenty million dollars in paranormal research."

"No kidding."

Sarah nodded. "Many scientists are beginning to believe the human brain has a lot more potential than we originally gave it credit."

"And you buy all that?"

Sarah hesitated, then shook her head. "No. I don't believe the human brain is capable of manipulating anything outside the body."

Katherine looked surprised. "But you just said . . ."

"I know."

"Then why are you doing all of this, if you don't believe it?"

"I believe the human mind is capable of connecting with other forces of energy that are able to penetrate our skulls and communicate with our brains by listening to and firing off specific neurons, particularly in the area of the right temporal lobe."

"You're talking about God again?"

"Not always."

"There's something else?"

Sarah finished her work and slowly rose to face her. "The counterfeits."

"Eric?" It was Heylel.

There you are, Eric answered. *Why have you been so quiet?*

Heylel gave no answer.

Eric pressed in. *It's because she's the one, isn't it? Her husband, he was the one we tried to get that research guy—that Dr. Reicher—to stop, wasn't he?*

"Very good."

And she's the one you tried to kill in the car crash.

"Excellent."

But you failed.

There was no answer.

Eric pursued him more forcefully, almost gleefully. *Both times you blew it. And that's why you're not saying anything now, 'cause you're chicken, aren't you? Cause you're afraid of her, you're afraid that she might be able to—*

"SILENCE!"

The voice roared in his mind. It was terrifying, and his entire body gave a shudder.

"Eric," Sarah said. "Eric, are you okay?"

He wasn't sure he could find his voice.

"Eric?"

He glanced up and was grateful to see her reassuring presence smiling down at him.

"Are you okay?" she repeated. "What happened? You look pale. Are you all right?"

"Yeah," he lied. He pushed up his glasses with his little finger. "I'm, uh, fine."

"You sure? You look a little shaken."

"I'm fine. Are we going to do this thing or not?" He hoped his tone would keep her at bay. She studied him another moment before nodding and turning back to the experiment.

He relaxed, but just slightly.

"You'll be hearing some pinging noises," she said. "When you are succeeding in elevating that yellow line, the tones will increase in pitch. When you are not, they will remain the same. Any questions?"

He shook his head and reached for the joystick. "Let's get this show on the road."

Sarah smiled and reached over to flip a single switch. A low drone came through the speaker beside the monitor. "Go ahead. Hold that trigger down and let's see what happens."

"No sweat," Eric said as he pressed the trigger on the joystick. Instantly the low tone turned into a screaming wail. His eyes shot to the monitor. The yellow line had leaped off the blue line and was pegged against the top of the screen.

Sarah reached for the knobs, checking the calibrations.

"What's wrong?" Katherine shouted over the increasing shrillness. "What's happening?"

Sarah shook her head. "I'm not certain!" she yelled.

The shrillness continued increasing in pitch and in volume.

"Turn it off!" Katherine yelled. "Turn that thing off!"

"I'm trying!" Sarah reached for the computer's electrical plug. She gave it a tug, disconnecting it from the power surge box.

But the screaming whine increased.

Sarah stared dumbfounded.

Now Katherine was on her feet. "What's going on? Turn it off! Turn it off!"

"There's no power!" Sarah shouted. "There's no way it can possibly be—"

And then, it stopped. No screaming whine, no glowing monitor with colored lines. Everything was suddenly silent and still. Sarah stared at the monitor another moment, then to the disconnected power cord. Finally she turned to Eric.

He coughed and fidgeted. It was obviously Heylel's doing. As best as he could tell, his mentor was not in a very good mood.

The scissors were dull and he had to cut smaller portions than he wanted, but slowly, methodically, it was coming off. He'd put a paper towel in the sink to cover the drain, and it was already covered with the long strands of his shiny black hair.

Brandon was not sure why he wanted to cut it. It had been part of his identity since high school. He just thought that maybe . . . maybe it was time for a change. But it was more than a change. As he watched the tufts fall into the sink, he knew it was also a type of death. Everything he'd been, everything he was, and yes, everything he wanted to be, had come to an end. There were no tears, no self-pity. Just numbness. Numbness and bone-weary fatigue.

If Gerty wanted him to stop trying, no problem. When you've got nothing left to try with, quitting is easy. Today, maybe tomorrow he'd go down to Bollenger's Printing and Lithograph. See if he could get his old job back. That at least was something he knew how to do. Maybe, in time, Sarah would come back to him. Maybe people would eventually forget all of the craziness. Maybe, someday, *he* could.

He folded up the paper towel, trying to keep as much hair in it as possible, then pitched it into the garbage. Looking back into the mirror, he checked out the sides and top. It wasn't terrible. True, nothing like he'd get at Supercuts, but going to a Supercuts would mean going out in public. And going out in public would mean having to endure the stares, wisecracks, and occasional confrontation.

It had been a week since Gerty's e-mail. And for a week he'd prayed, he'd fasted, he'd done everything he could think of to find out what God wanted.

And for a week there had been nothing.

She'd mentioned something about searching his dreams. But for the most part they had been equally uneventful. No more special guest appearances by Jesus Christ, no more symbolic imagery. Except for the occasional nightmare of the serpent's head along with the addition of that silly crescent moon and star from Salman Kilyos's tattoo, there wasn't that much to speak of. Mostly just memories of Sarah and the constant reminder of how hollow and empty he was without her.

He stared into the mirror. Not thrilled with his new 'do, he went to plan B. He grabbed a can of shaving cream and a disposable Bic from the cabinet. He wasn't exactly sure how to pull it off, but hopefully shaving his head wouldn't be all that different from shaving his face . . . hopefully.

He turned on the hot water. As he waited for it to heat up he thought through the various fragments of last night's dream. It was no different from the others. He and Sarah at the lake, he and Sarah at work, the two of them shopping. Then came a brief appearance of Salman's tattoo. But instead of being inside the church, Brandon was walking across a giant version of the crescent moon and star. To further confuse the issue there were the seven lampstands he'd seen during his vision at the hospital. The same number of lampstands he'd been reading about in Revelation. And leading him through the maze was none other than Salman Kilyos.

Typically absurd and confusing, it was just like everything else. If there was a code to be cracked here, God would have to do the cracking. Because, as in everything else, Brandon had quit trying.

When the water was good and warm, he stuck his head under the faucet to soften his hair for the shave. He didn't hear the knock on the door until he turned off the tap and reached for the towel. Even then he wasn't sure he wanted to answer it. By now every kook in the county had his address.

But the knocking persisted. Toweling off, Brandon stepped into the hall and headed across the worn carpet toward the door.

"Mr. Brandon, Mr. Brandon, are you there?" More knocking. "Mr. Brandon?" The voice was familiar, but he couldn't place it. "Mr. Brandon?"

He arrived and looked through the peephole. To his surprise it was Salman Kilyos, healthier than he'd ever seen him. Before he could stop it, Brandon's mind sorted through the information, searching for the meaning behind the coincidence. For the millionth time he tried fitting together the puzzle, this time including Salman and the dream tattoo. And for the millionth time he hit a wall.

"Mr. Brandon."

"Hang on." He unlocked the original dead bolt, then the two new ones he'd installed, before sliding back the chain and opening the door.

The man stood, smiling in the bright sunlight. "Good morning." When he registered Brandon's lack of hair, his smile wavered slightly. "It looks . . . good on you."

Brandon eyed him warily. "Good morning, Salman."

The man's grin broadened. "I have them."

"Them?"

He held out a business envelope. "Our tickets. To Istanbul."

Brandon clutched the door just a little bit tighter. "Istanbul?"

"Of course." The man moved past him and entered the apartment. "After all you have done for me, I figure it is the least I may do for you."

CHAPTER 9

Dear Sarah,

A minute doesn't go by that you don't somehow come to my mind . . . wondering what you would say in a situation, what jokes we would make, how we would laugh and talk and argue and pray with each other. I know this time is necessary, but it doesn't make it less painful. Every morning I wake up and feel this huge piece of me missing . . . and every day I'm a little more afraid that we are drifting apart and that that piece of me may never return. Stupid, I know, but the fear is always there in the back of my mind. I'm glad you're finding the boy so challenging . . . you've always liked challenges (as long as you can solve them).

And what you say about Lucas Ponte is interesting. He's on the news every night now, as the debate continues about him taking office and as they prepare to build some sort of temple in Jerusalem. He sounds like a courageous and caring man—just what our world needs to try to bring the peace the Cartel is promising. You're right, working with him is a great opportunity, and it will be interesting to see what purpose his coming into our lives may have.

Sarah blew the hair out of her eyes and reached for her mug of tea. She was annoyed at how, even now while reading a letter from her husband, thoughts of Lucas kept trying to distract her. Of course she found his flirting to be flattering—who wouldn't? A man with all of that power and prestige taking an interest in her? It was enough to make anyone give pause. But that's all she'd done, paused. She'd held off the invitations to dinner, the requests to privately discuss Eric's condition over drinks. She was a married woman. And she was married to an incredible guy. Of course they had their differences; what couples didn't? But they'd work them out. They had to.

She looked back at the screen.

I'm glad this trip to Turkey makes sense to you. When Salman first showed up at my door, telling me that God had told him to buy the tickets, you can bet I had some doubts. Of course I remembered how he'd said the crescent moon and star was the symbol for his beloved homeland, and I knew what Gerty had said about my going on a trip. But it wasn't until you pointed out how all seven churches in Revelation are also in that country that things suddenly made sense.

This is where Christ sent the "love letters" that he commanded us to study. I wouldn't have made the connection if it wasn't for your help. Funny, isn't it? Here we are separated by thousands of miles, and yet we're still working together as a team. Then again, maybe it's not so funny at all.

I'm on the plane now. We'll be in Istanbul in eight more hours, then we'll catch a flight to Izmir, and drive fifty miles to Ephesus, the first of the seven churches. I tell you though, this sitting and doing nothing for hour after hour can sure make a person crazy. Time is dragging in slow motion.

To make it worse, they're showing a little model of our plane up on the TV screens as it creeps across a map of the world. Talk about painful. It's like watching the hour hand of a clock. Some people can sleep. I can't. Too much excitement.

My hope is that I quickly learn what I must learn to "warn the bride." How that's going to happen is beyond me, but then it won't be the first time he's surprised us, will it? All I know is that the sooner I learn the lessons and the sooner you finish your work there, the sooner we will be back together.

Until then, I love and miss you with all of my heart and all of my body and all of my soul.

Yours forever,
Brandon

Sarah looked at the screen a long time before shutting it off. The room was darker now. She rose and crossed to the overstuffed chair near the window. She was already in her nightshirt—actually it was Brandon's shirt, his blue shirt she loved so much. She eased herself down into the chair and pushed back the curtains. The mountains were on fire with another incredible sunset, making everything glow an iridescent pink.

She wasn't sure why she was crying. Some of it had to do with the letter, some of it had to do with missing Brandon. But there was more.

She pulled her legs up under her chin and held them. High up on the slope above her, some of the Cartel office lights were still burning, including Lucas's. She scolded herself for even looking and quickly redirected her gaze.

She rested her forehead on her knees, face in the shirt, and breathed deeply. Even now she could smell Brandon's smell—a little woodsy, a little trace of after-shave. And, as she breathed in, the memories came . . .

It was true, Brandon was the most incredible man she had ever met. And he always would be. Just as importantly, he loved her. He *cherished* her. She snuggled deeper into the chair. She would sleep there, curled up, her face buried in her husband's shirt, smelling his smell. The tears were gone, at least for now, as she continued to sit, breathing in and remembering his love. But they would return. Off and on throughout the night they would return.

It was late and Katherine was bored. Once again she sat in front of Eric's computer and once again she stared at the antisense files, the ones labeled after the first four cities to be infected with Scorpion—Cairo, Mecca, New York, Tel Aviv. Either the Cartel was getting more sophisticated in protecting their information or she was losing her touch. Maybe a little of both. In any case, her earlier attempts at hacking into these files had been unsuccessful. Now it was as much pride as it was curiosity. She *would* get into those files and she *would* find out why they were restricted.

It was the last resort and one she felt a little uneasy using, but hey, they started it . . .

First she brought up the Cartel's system, complete with the graphic field of their logo, the planet Earth with four different races of hands clasped around it in unity.

Next, she tried to log on as Marshal T. Elliott, the system's administrator. She'd never met the man, but as the S.A. he had the highest security access to the Cartel's computers. He could go anywhere he wanted inside the system. Nothing was forbidden to him. The reason? It was his job to oversee and watchdog the computer system, including, among other things, preventing people like Katherine from breaking into it.

A prompt came up asking for Elliott's password, which, of course, Katherine didn't know. But it didn't matter. This was where it got interesting . . .

Instead of trying to guess the correct password and enter it on the Cartel's graphic logo, Katherine simply typed up a program enabling her to make an exact copy of that graphic logo. Once she captured it, she then designed a shadow TSR, or *terminate stay resident,* program to bring her graphic logo up onto Elliott's computer screen instead of the original. It would work like this:

Elliott would boot up his computer. But instead of the Cartel's graphic logo appearing, asking for his password, Katherine's copy of the logo would appear asking for it. He would then enter his password using the standard nonechoing format which replaced his typed letters with asterisks. Next he would hit ENTER. When he did he would see a momentary flicker on the screen, and then the genuine graphic logo would appear, once again asking for his password.

He would hesitate, wondering if there was a glitch in the system. But the only way to find out would be to reenter his password. He would do so, check out the system to make sure everything was running properly, and when he was satisfied he would continue with whatever work he was doing.

In the meantime, Katherine's copy of the graphic logo, complete with the newly typed password, would be recorded into an encrypted file and tagged with a legitimate file name so it wouldn't stand out. Then, at her leisure, Katherine would simply bring up the file, retrieve Elliott's password, and use it anytime she wanted to go into the system.

It was totally dishonest and deceptively simple. But as any hacker or con artist will tell you, the best deceptions are the simplest.

Katherine's fingers flew across the keyboard as she finished the last of the TSR program and entered it into the system. In a day, maybe two, whenever she had some spare time, she would bring up the graphic field, use Elliott's password, and cruise anywhere she wanted . . . particularly into the antisense subfiles listing those four cities.

> To the angel of the church in Ephesus write:
>
> These are the words of him who holds the seven stars in his right hand and walks among the seven golden lampstands: I know your deeds, your hard work and your perseverance. I know that you cannot tolerate wicked men, that you have tested those who claim to be apostles but are not, and have found them false. You have persevered and have endured hardships for my name, and have not grown weary.

Brandon had read the first part of this letter in Revelation a dozen times on the plane and half that many times in the bus on the way to Ephesus. He'd practically memorized it. And now, as he and Salman walked along the uneven marble road amidst the ruins, it was all he could do to imagine that this was the city, the actual location of the first-century church that Christ had addressed in the letter. This was where Timothy had pastored, where Paul had caused a riot, where many believe Mary spent her last years, and where the disciple John came to die.

So much history here—particularly for someone whose idea of the ancient past went only as far back as the Civil War. It was hard to imagine that he was walking on pavement over two thousand years old, that he could actually see the grooves worn into the street from chariot wheels. And Salman was the perfect tour guide. He was only too happy to be back home in his country and to be showing off its rich history. As the son of an archaeologist, he'd been dragged to most of the major ruins a number of times. And Ephesus, nestled in the fog-covered hills near the Aegean Sea, was no different. He made sure Brandon saw everything . . . the temples, the gates, the palaces, the fountains, the baths, and the brothel. For Brandon one crumbling wall, broken set of steps, and marble column looked like the next, and he had to take Salman's word as to what they saw. However, he was certain about the ancient public latrines—there was something about the long row of clearly defined and still functional marble toilet seats that made their authenticity more than obvious.

"And the vestal virgins"—Salman pointed off to the right—"over here is where they lived. They were highly honored in the city. Their job was never to let the sacred flame go out."

"Sacred flame?"

"Yes. The glory of Rome, that is what it represented, and it burned for centuries. These were glorious times, my friend. The times of the Imperial Cult."

"What do you mean, 'Imperial Cult'?"

"That's when the Roman emperors ruled the world, when they were worshiped as gods."

Brandon said nothing as he looked around the ruins. Despite its fallen state, it wasn't hard to imagine the splendor and majesty of the city.

Salman continued. "And the festivals held for the Imperial Cult, they were the most important times of the city, for any of the cities. People, they would come from everywhere to participate in the processions, the ceremonies, the sacrifices, the feasts—they were wonderful times. The government even passed out money to the poor so they could afford an animal sacrifice. For some it was the only meat they would be able to eat for the entire year."

"All of this to celebrate their ruler-gods?"

"Yes, exactly. The Caesars. And that is why Christians, they were not so well liked."

"Because they didn't worship them."

"Exactly. People, they would worship whoever or whatever they wanted, and that was okay. But if they did not also worship Caesar, the leader of the entire civilized world"—Salman ran a finger across his neck with the appropriate sound effect—"things would not go so well for them."

"And this." Salman motioned to an imposing two-story structure complete with towering columns, statues, and intricate carvings. "This is the Celsus Library. It was completed about A.D. 125 and contained twelve thousand scrolls, making it one of the largest libraries in the world. The walls, they were twenty feet thick to protect the scrolls from weather and insects. Magnificent, is it not?"

Brandon had to agree. In fact, the more he took in the sights of this ancient capital, the more magnificent everything became. What a world these first-century Christians had lived in . . . affluent, sophisticated, educated. And what a credit it was for them *not* to have their heads turned by all of this wealth and intellectualism—not to mention the flat-out hostility against them for refusing to worship Caesar. No wonder Christ started his letter to them with such praise.

> I know your deeds, your hard work and your perseverance. I know that you cannot tolerate wicked men. . . . You have persevered and have endured hardships for my name, and have not grown weary.

These were impressive accomplishments. In many ways they made this church the ideal role model for today's churches. Unfortunately, the letter continued . . .

"Mr. Brandon, where are you going?"

"I, uh . . ."

They had traveled about a hundred yards and Salman was turning to a large structure to his right. "The Grand Theater, you will want to see this. This is where the riot occurred."

They had discussed the event during the ride to Ephesus. According to the book of Acts, this was the very amphitheater where an angry crowd had spent two hours shouting down a follower of Paul. Brandon had every intention of seeing it, was looking forward to going inside, but something had suddenly compelled him to head the opposite direction. Something very strong.

"What's this?" he asked, motioning to a long stone road nearly thirty feet wide with broken columns on either side. "Where does this lead?"

"That is the Harbor Street," Salman replied. "It used to lead to the harbor."

"Can we go there first?"

"The sun is nearly down. This is much more important. Did you know that there are over twenty-four thousand seats, and that at one time—"

"That's great, Salman, really impressive—but there's something down here, something I need to see."

"Mr. Brandon, there is nothing at the other end of that road but bushes and blackberry briars."

Brandon nodded. He knew it didn't make sense, but he also knew what he was feeling. It wasn't exactly what he'd felt on the stage in L.A.; it was much more subtle. But it was just as insistent, just as compelling. He knew it didn't make sense, but he also knew he had to obey. "I understand," he called back to Salman. "But . . . there's something down here I need to see."

Salman let out a heavy sigh and started after him. "As you wish, Mr. Brandon, as you wish."

What're all these cloud thingies?

"Clouds?"

Yeah, you know, that misty stuff that's surrounding everybody.

"Ah, you see them as mist. Of course."

What are they?

"They are more of my colleagues. They work with me to protect your people from the harsh and burning light of the enemy."

Eric glanced around the room where he was resting in the recliner . . . well, at least where his body was resting. Because the conscious part of him, the part that was actually Eric Lyon, floated over his body. It hovered eight feet above the room, looking down at the scene with Heylel. The two of them had made up days ago, and now, once again, Heylel was showing him deeper mysteries. They watched as Sarah conducted another experiment while she talked to his mom in hushed tones. Lucas stood nearby.

How come Mom and Lucas got more of the mist stuff around them than Sarah?

"Because they have allowed more of us to surround and protect them."

But Sarah hasn't?

"Precisely."

Why?

"Your mother and Lucas are open to our help. Sarah is not. She still believes in Oppressor's ways."

Eric felt Heylel shudder at the name. He seldom used it, but when he did it was always accompanied by revulsion and fear. The reason was simple. Heylel had never told him the whole story, but from what Eric gathered, a long, long time ago there was a powerful dictator who kept the universe under his ironfisted control. Heylel was one of this dictator's top generals. But he saw the terrible injustices and led a revolt to liberate the universe from this cruel tyrant. He managed to get a third of creation to stand up with him, but two-thirds did not. The rebellion was crushed, and Heylel and his followers were banished here to earth. But even though they were imprisoned here, because of the kindness of their hearts, they had decided to help the planet's inhabitants by protecting anyone who wanted to be protected from Oppressor's ways.

So, Eric thought, *that's why you're so careful around Sarah? She still follows Oppressor.*

"Precisely. In her ignorance, she has potential for doing great harm to us ... and to Lucas."

And Lucas is really important, right?

"Yes. The two of you will be a team. And with my help, there is nothing you will not be able to accomplish."

Eric looked back down at Sarah. *But if she's such a threat, why don't you just take her out?*

"Until her time, Oppressor has forbidden us to touch her . . . unless, of course, she gives us permission."

Permission? Like how?

"You have many questions today, my young friend."

If I'm going to help you run stuff, I better learn as much as I can.

He heard Heylel chuckle. *"Yes, as always you are right. And, as always, I am well pleased. There is no one finer in all the world to help me rule."*

And Lucas, don't forget Lucas.

"Yes, and Lucas. You and Lucas. But it will always be you, first."

Eric felt the pleasure swell inside him. This was another reason he liked Heylel, another reason he put up with the outbursts of anger and the struggles for control. It wasn't just because of the power growing inside of him, or the promises of what he would become; it was also because of the respect and admiration Heylel had for him.

So—Eric looked back down at Sarah—*how are you going to stop her?*

"At the moment there is little we can do. Oppressor's light has blinded her to our truth. However, we are attempting to bring her and Lucas together, so he can help."

Together? What, like boyfriend, girlfriend? I thought she was married.

"Of course, but there is always hope."

Like what? How do you do that?

"So many questions."

Tell me.

"We influence her thoughts. We subtly change the patterns of her thinking."

You can do that?

"Only if she gives us permission."

Cool.

"Yes, it is. But we must be very subtle. If our work is too obvious, she will block it. But if she lets us touch her thoughts, if she allows us to gradually rework her thinking, the two of them may very well become lovers."

Too bad you couldn't do that with Mom.

"We have other plans for your mother."

Really? Like what?

"In good time, my friend, in good time. Would you like to see something else?"

Sure, what else do you—

Suddenly his ears roared with rushing wind. But, instead of falling, as he always did during these times, Eric was shooting up . . . at incredible speed. Before he knew it, he was high above the Earth. Below him were the Himalayas. Further north was what had to be China, and to the south lay India as well as the Indian Ocean. But he wasn't just seeing physical land. He was also seeing larger pockets of the same mist and fog that had surrounded the people in the room. Now, however, the pockets blanketed entire regions. In some places it was very thin, in others very thick.

Wow, Eric thought, *this is incredible!*

"It is quite lovely here."

I'll say. And all those misty and foggy places, those are your buddies, too?

"Yes. Instead of concentrating upon just one person, my more powerful friends concentrate on specific regions and—"

Look out! Eric shouted. He lunged to the side as a pencil-thin shaft of light penetrated a clump of mist below them. It sliced through the air just yards from where they'd been floating, and then it was gone.

What was that?

There was no hiding the irritation in Heylel's voice. *"More of Oppressor's works. Take a careful look and tell me what you see."*

Eric squinted, looking out across the continent. *Nothing. Just land, water, clouds, and your mist buddies.*

"Look closer." The voice was more of a command than a request, and Eric knew better than to disobey.

I am, but I don't see any—oh, wait a minute.

"Do you see them now?"

You mean those light beams?

"Yes."

They're superthin but, yeah, I see them. They're shooting up all over the place.

"Yes. And look what they do to our attempts to protect your people."

Eric squinted harder, focusing upon one particular patch of mist concentrated over what looked like a city. Several narrow shafts of light were cutting through it, and as he watched, he noticed the mist beginning to dissolve and break up.

"Do you see what's happening?" Heylel asked.

It looks like those beams are wiping your guys out.

Heylel said nothing.

Not a lot, though.

"Enough. By itself, no single ray of light can destroy our protection. But, as you see, the more that penetrate us, the weaker our presence becomes and the harder it is for us to protect you."

But what are they? Where do these beams come from?

"They are people like Sarah, the deluded ones who still follow Oppressor's path. This is their communication with him."

That's terrible, Eric thought back.

"Yes."

Isn't there some way to stop them?

"There are many ways. The best is, as you say, 'to take them out.'"

But you said he won't let you.

"No, not on my own. I am only spirit. I need physical tools to manipulate the physical. That is why you and I must work together."

Once again Eric felt his importance rising. *Because,* he asked, *with me, you can do anything?*

"Very good. Together we can do anything."

Eric broke into a grin, then recited what he'd heard a dozen times before. *And the more control I give you, the greater we'll become . . .*

Heylel completed the phrase. *". . . until all is ours."*

But when? Eric demanded. *You keep promising me that, but when?*

"Soon, my young friend. You are nearly ready. Your time of glory will be very, very soon."

The closer Brandon came to the end of the road the harder his heart pounded. He knew he was about to hear something, to learn something. And he knew it had to do with the other half of the Ephesians letter . . . the warning half. Because, as much as Christ had praise for the church at Ephesus, he also had a stern rebuke.

> Yet I hold this against you: You have forsaken your first love. Remember the height from which you have fallen! Repent and do the things you did at first. If you do not repent, I will come to you and remove your lampstand from its place.

But what did that have to do with the end of this particular road?

As they approached, Brandon noticed they were no longer surrounded by tourists. They were entirely by themselves. And why not? The road went nowhere, and it was nearly closing time. They had walked six hundred yards down the uneven stone pavement until it finally came to an end. The stones stopped abruptly and were replaced by a dirt bank three to four feet high, covered in grass and brush.

There was nothing else.

"See," Salman said, squinting at Brandon who stood between him and the setting sun. "It goes nowhere. There is nothing here."

Brandon turned toward the bank, looking out across the flat land. "But it used to go somewhere."

"Of course. It was the great road to the city; it led to the harbor where the ships docked. All of the world's kings and emperors were greeted upon these very stones."

"But there's no water here."

"Not now. The sea is two miles away."

"I don't understand."

"Ephesus, it used to be one of the mightiest seaports in all of the Roman Empire."

"What happened?"

"The Cayster River. Gradually, over time, it filled the harbor with its dirt and silt. Since no one cleaned it out, the harbor eventually filled up. Now there is only dirt and weeds."

Brandon's head began to swim. There was a truth here. Something profound, if he could just grasp it. He looked down at the bank, then kneeled before it. Without looking at Salman he asked, "And since the city no longer had a harbor?"

"It no longer served a purpose."

Brandon slowly turned to him. "And it was deserted."

Salman shrugged. "Of course. What good was it to anyone then?"

Brandon nodded, but barely heard. He looked back at the bank and reached out to finger the dirt. It was good soil, some of the best . . . just like the Ephesians had performed good works, some of the best . . .

> I know your deeds, your hard work and your perseverance. . . . You have persevered and have endured hardships . . . and have not grown weary.

And yet it was that excellent soil that had slowly replaced the most important thing to the city—its harbor . . . just as—now he had it—just as the excellent works of the church had slowly replaced its love.

> Yet I hold this against you: You have forsaken your first love.

Unnoticed, silently, the good quality soil had replaced the city's harbor . . . Unnoticed, silently, the good quality works had replaced the church's love.

Now Brandon understood. That's why he'd been led to the end of this road—to see this truth.

But there was more. The truth didn't end with this city or this church. Wasn't this also what the makeup woman had said about Jimmy Tyler . . . at first he was full of love, but gradually his works consumed him? That somehow they'd "lost" Jimmy Tyler? "You don't become one of the biggest ministries in the world without sacrificing something," wasn't that what she had said?

The thoughts swirled in his mind. How much of it was his own thinking, he didn't know. How much of it was inspiration, he wasn't sure. But understanding raced into his head, almost faster than he could absorb it . . .

Wasn't that the main reason he'd hated church, the reason his friends never darkened its doors, because of the lack of love? Wasn't that what everyone needed more than anything—sincere, genuine love? Sure, there was the teaching, the preaching, the programs—and they were all necessary and they were all good. But, somehow, amidst all of the programs and good . . . love had been forgotten.

But not just their love for others . . . more tragically, he sensed it was the Ephesians' love for God. Their "first love"—that zeal, that joy for being saved, that excitement he'd seen on Sarah's face the first time she understood how loved and forgiven she was. For him, for those who had grown up in the church, it had become old hat, cliché—as lifeless as some other religion's ceremony or prayer beads. Like the silt, good religion had replaced heartfelt love. Godly works had replaced fervent passion.

But what could be done?

"Mr. Brandon, Mr. Brandon, are you all right?" The concern in Salman's voice made it clear he saw the moisture welling up in his eyes.

Brandon nodded and reached into his backpack. He fumbled for his pocket New Testament and Psalms and pulled it out, quickly flipping through the pages to Revelation.

> Remember the height from which you have fallen! Repent and do the things you did at first.

What had he done at first? What had Sarah done?

They'd thanked God, they'd worshiped and adored him. Not from rote, but from their hearts. They didn't recite dusty hymns from dusty hymnals, they didn't recite overhead projection verses. They *truly* worshiped, using their minds *and their hearts*. That's what had started to fade . . . the love from their hearts.

He turned back to the Bible and read.

> If you do not repent, I will come to you and remove your lampstand from its place. . . . He who has an ear, let him hear what the Spirit says to the churches. To him who overcomes, I will give the right to eat from the tree of life, which is in the paradise of God.

But how could the others be warned? How could today's church be reminded of the subtle deception that was slowly creeping in and—

Brandon had the answer before the question had completely formed. Slowly, he rose to his feet and looked back down the road toward the amphitheater. In the distance the multiple rows of stone seats reflected gold in the setting sun. He fought off an involuntary shiver.

But he knew . . .

He would be the one to tell them. Once again, he would be required to stand in front of a crowd. And, just as in L.A., and just as in that amphitheater two thousand years ago, the answer would be booed and shouted down. The thought made him cold inside. But just as surely as he felt the cold gripping his gut, he knew it would be done.

Not here, not now. There were still lessons to be learned. But in time it must be done . . .

CHAPTER 10

"Get out of the street! Hurry!"

Sarah glanced over her shoulder and saw a trickle of people rounding the corner and racing down the street toward her. A trickle which quickly grew into a torrent, and then a mob. And still they poured in. Hundreds, maybe a thousand, all shouting and waving their fists at a frame of burning bamboo held high above their heads.

"In here!" Katherine shouted as she pulled Sarah across the wet cobblestones and into the open doorway of a shop. "We've got to get out of the street *now!*"

They reached the doorway just as the first of the crowd began to pass.

"What's going on?" Sarah shouted. "What are they doing?"

"Watch!"

Sarah pulled further into the safety of the doorway as the throng came by. The trip to Katmandu had been Katherine's idea. "To get you into the city and see some sights," she'd said. And they had seen sights . . . everything from the tea shops to street flower vendors, to the temples complete with spinning prayer wheels, to painted holy men . . . to human bodies being cremated right there on the banks of the Vishnumati River. It took nearly an hour to get the stench out of her nostrils, and she knew she'd never be able to entirely remove the image. Even more unsettling for her was that this same river, where they poured the remaining ash, was where other people ceremonially bathed and cleansed themselves from their sins.

Then there were the children. Everywhere she looked, especially in the temple areas, there were dirty, ragged children. Some begged by playing what looked like cheap, miniature violins, holding them in their laps and lifelessly running a bow back and forth across untuned strings. Others were more direct, dogging them and tugging at their clothes for any money they might have.

"Where do they all come from?" Sarah had asked.

"Lots are orphans."

"They have no home? People don't adopt them?"

"This is a Hindu state, remember."

"What does that mean?"

"It means everyone believes in reincarnation."

"But what's that got to do with these poor—"

"If a child's parents are killed, people figure it's judgment for the evil the child committed in his past life. It's his punishment."

"You're not serious."

"Of course I am. People don't want to interfere with the judgment of the universe, so they leave the kid alone."

"They won't help him?"

"Worse than that. Usually the child is thrown out of the village in hopes that he'll starve to death and die quickly."

"I can't believe that. It's so . . . inhumane."

"That's because you're looking at it through Western eyes. People here feel it's the exact opposite. By helping the child die, they're doing him a favor. They're helping him pay for his past sins, so he can be reincarnated to a better life."

"That's terrible!"

"That's reincarnation." And then Katherine had added, "Guess it doesn't matter what religion people believe in . . . the Supreme Being still winds up embarrassingly short in the love department."

"You really hate him, don't you?"

Katherine had shaken her head. "I don't hate him. I just don't believe him. Truth isn't in words but in action, remember? And I sure don't see any action of a loving God here."

That conversation had been over an hour ago. Sarah had wanted to come to God's defense, but over the weeks, as she had learned all that Katherine had been through, from widowhood, to alcoholism, to fighting for the survival of her only child, she knew there was little the woman would hear. As a preacher's kid who'd seen the worst of life and then some, Katherine seemed to have every reason to doubt God's love. And Sarah, with her own personal doubts and frustrations, knew this was not the time to try and stand up for him. Yes, she still believed there was some sort of call on her life, but every day that believing grew just a little bit fainter, and every day that call became just a bit more dim.

Now the two of them stood in the doorway watching the crowd and the burning frame of bamboo approach. But it was more than just the burning bamboo that the people held above their heads. Lashed to it by his hands and feet was a nearly naked man, his body painted with various symbols and images representing evil. It was he and not the burning bamboo that the crowd was shouting and screaming at.

"Do you know what's happening?" Sarah yelled over the noise.

Katherine nodded. "The man tied up there represents Ghanta Karna, one of the world's most dreaded demons."

"Demons?" Sarah shouted.

"That's right."

By now the man and burning frame were directly in front of them. He writhed and screamed, shouting oaths back at the crowd, which only agitated them more.

"They're not going to burn him to death?" Sarah cried.

Katherine laughed. "No, no. It's all a show, part of the ceremony. By the time they get to the river, he usually frees himself and makes his escape."

"Usually?"

Katherine shrugged and smiled.

Sarah turned back to the crowd. The burning bamboo had passed, and the mob was already beginning to thin.

"So you see, my friend," Katherine said, no longer shouting, "Western religions don't own the market in their belief in demons or, how did you put it the other day, in 'counterfeits.'"

Sarah nodded, watching the last of the crowd head down the street. "I see your point." Then with a grin she added, "But I think our way of handling them is a little easier."

"A good old-fashioned exorcism?"

Sarah looked at her. She was unable to tell if she was mocking her or not. "I've seen it work, Katherine. A half-dozen times at the clinic, I've seen people completely delivered of demonic influence in the name of Jesus Christ."

Katherine glanced away, pretending to watch the remaining stragglers, but it was obvious her mind was someplace else. "Do you think . . ." She cleared her throat. "Do you think that might be what Eric is suffering from?"

Sarah said nothing. The suspicion had been growing in her mind throughout the tests. Eric's psychic abilities, his hosting another "consciousness," his violent behavior—these were all classic patterns of demonic activity. Then there was the increasing difficulty in regaining control from Heylel.

Katherine turned to her, waiting for an answer.

As always, Sarah carefully chose her words. "There's a strong possibility, but his problem could still be physical or psychological. I know others have run tests, but there's still a possibility he may be suffering from schizophrenia or from multiple personality disorder."

"They're not the same as possession?"

"Not always. Possession can display those symptoms, but they can also be created by a chemical imbalance or a psychological disorder. It's not always easy to know the differ—"

"The stuff I've seen my son do, what he's been through—it doesn't sound like any psychological disorder to me. And Heylel . . . there's no way that creep is a part of my son. There's absolutely no way they're connected."

Sarah slowly nodded. "You may be right. But it's important that we finish checking out the natural causes first."

"Aren't you done with that yet?"

"Just about."

"Well, I suggest you hurry and get a move on, Doctor."

Sarah looked at her.

"The sooner you finish up your tests and get down to a major face-to-face with this Heylel thing, the better off we'll all be."

Surprised, Sarah asked, "So you think it's demonic?"

"Come on." Katherine stepped into the street. "Let's head down to the river and see if the poor guy makes it."

> To the angel of the church in Smyrna write:
>
> These are the words of him who is the First and the Last, who died and came to life again. I know your afflictions and your poverty—yet you are rich! I know the slander of those who say they are Jews and are not, but are a synagogue of Satan. Do not be afraid of what you are about to suffer. I tell you, the devil will put some of you in prison to test you, and you will suffer persecution for ten days. Be faithful, even to the point of death, and I will give you the crown of life.
>
> He who has an ear, let him hear what the Spirit says to the churches. He who overcomes will not be hurt at all by the second death.

Brandon stared hard at the page. It was the second letter Christ had sent to the churches in Revelation. But instead of commanding the people to repent and return to their first love, as he had at Ephesus, this letter promised persecution and urged the church to be faithful "even to the point of death."

Persecution? Death? For the church? For his beloved bride? All of his life Brandon had been taught that God protected his own, that Jesus, the loving Shepherd, would not allow anything to happen to his flock. But this . . .

> You will suffer persecution . . . even to the point of death.

It didn't make sense. It wasn't the gospel he'd been taught.

"Mr. Brandon, Mr. Brandon, why the scowl?"

He glanced over to see Salman climbing the steep stone steps of the fortress wall. In his hand he held a sheet of newspaper rolled into a cone. "The children," he called, "they have given us more sunflower seeds."

Brandon smiled. There was no doubt about it, the two of them had become the local children's special project. This was their third day living inside the ruins of Kadifekale, an ancient acropolis of broken walls, crumbling arches, and an underground cavern suitable for sleeping. For three days they had sat atop this nine-hundred-foot hill overlooking the city of Ismir, which in ancient times had been called Smyrna. And for three days the Kurdish children who lived around the ruins had been bringing them sunflower seeds, goat milk, and flat bread baked on the inside roof of stone ovens. These Kurds were the outcasts of Turkish society, yet they were the first to offer hospitality. By day the impoverished children came to them with food. And for the nights, though it was so warm they really didn't need it, an old woman who sold handwoven goods to tourists insisted upon giving them two brightly colored blankets.

Salman remained by Brandon's side the entire time. He didn't have to. He could have easily found a cheap hotel down in the city. But he stayed. Regardless of the discomfort, regardless of the inconvenience, he stayed to explain, to translate, and to tell his stories. Salman Kilyos was a born storyteller, and he loved to practice his gift whenever he could. Their friendship had grown, and a day didn't go by that Brandon didn't thank God for the man's commitment. Their bond was strong . . . and unlikely. But no more unlikely than the journey they were making.

"Hold out your hand."

Brandon obeyed and Salman poured out a large pile of the unshelled seeds.

"Thanks, Salman."

"No problem. But you still do not answer my question. Why the frown?"

"Take a look at this." Brandon handed the Bible to him and pointed to the two small paragraphs in Revelation chapter two. Salman took it and began to read. Although he claimed to be a Christian, Brandon had his doubts. Somehow he suspected it was all part of the Salman Kilyos con. A sincere con, but a con nonetheless. After all, ninety-eight percent of Turkish citizens claimed to be Moslem. For Salman to be part of the two percent and to be a Christian to boot seemed more than a stretch. Then there was his hatred of Ponte and the Cartel. During their frequent conversations with local Muslims, Salman would be the first to side with the most radical fringes, agreeing that Ponte was up to no good, and insisting that he was an "infidel of infidels." An interesting description considering Salman was supposed to be Christian. Still, each time Brandon tried to talk to him about the Lord, Salman insisted that he already knew.

As Salman read, Brandon looked back out over the city from their vantage point high atop the wall. A wall that, according to Salman, had been built by Alexander the Great around 300 B.C. It was a million-dollar view of the city and harbor beyond. A million-dollar view that he and the Kurdish children had for free.

"Of course . . . this is nothing."

Brandon turned to Salman as he handed him back the Bible. "What's nothing?"

Salman shrugged. "Christians, they have been martyred and killed in my country for hundreds of years. Remember what I was telling you about the Imperial Cult?"

"The religion forcing everyone to worship Caesar?"

"It lasted two hundred fifty years."

"That long?"

Salman nodded, pouring a half-dozen sunflower seeds into his mouth. "And the very first martyr to give his life in Asia, he was killed right here on this hill."

"Seriously?"

"Yes, of course, right here. His name, it was Polycarp. Surely you have heard of him?"

Brandon shook his head.

"His death, it is most famous." Brandon didn't answer and Salman continued, a little incredulous. "Your father he was a preacher, and you do not know this story?"

Suddenly, Brandon felt a little stupid. Truth be told, other than the Bible, he knew next to nothing about Christian history. But as Salman repositioned himself, and poured a few more seeds into his mouth, he had a feeling that some of that was about to change . . .

"The year, it was A.D. 156. And the Imperial Cult, they are after Polycarp in a bad way. He is eighty-six years old and as bishop of this church, he was ordained by none other than Saint John himself."

Brandon nodded. Once again he was impressed at the country's rich history.

Salman spit out a couple shells and continued. "His congregation, they insist Polycarp flee the city for his life. Reluctantly, he obeys their wishes, but his location, it is soon found out. And instead of trying to get away, he stays. In fact, he offers the arresting officers food and drink.

"Later, as they drive him back to the city in their carriage, they beg him to change his mind and vow allegiance to the emperor. But he refuses. When they arrive, they take him to the amphitheater to meet the governor just on the side of this hill."

"This hill, here?" Brandon repeated.

"Yes, yes, of course. Anyways, the governor, he orders Polycarp to deny Christ. 'Have respect for your old age,' he says. 'Swear allegiance to Caesar and denounce Christ, then I will release you.'"

Salman paused to drop a few more seeds into his mouth and to no doubt create more suspense.

Brandon fell for it. "Well, what happened? What did Polycarp do?"

"This story, I do not believe you do not know it."

"Will you tell me what happened?"

"I thought everybody—"

"Tell me."

Salman couldn't hide his amusement. He spit out some shells, then continued. "Polycarp, he says, 'For eighty-six years I have been Christ's servant, and he has never done me wrong. How can I blaspheme my king, who has saved me?'

"And the governor, he says, 'I have wild animals I will throw you to.'

"And Polycarp says, 'Bring them on.'

"Now the governor, he sees Polycarp is not afraid so he says, 'If you are not afraid of my animals, then I will burn you by fire.'

"Meanwhile, the Jews inside, they are really getting hot under the collar, so they race to the gates screaming to the crowd outside, 'Polycarp is a Christian, Polycarp is a Christian, Polycarp is a Christian!' And the crowd, they yell back, 'Burn him! Burn him! Burn him!'"

Salman paused to drop a couple more seeds into his mouth.

"And?" Brandon asked.

"The governor, he agrees. But Polycarp, he says he doesn't need to be lashed to a stake. He says all they have to do is tie his hands, and he will remain in the fire. So they do. They tie his hands, put wood all around him, and light the fire. And Polycarp, he doesn't cry, he doesn't scream, all he does is shout to God, 'I thank you that you have thought me worthy to share the cup of Christ among your witnesses!'"

"So he was burned to death?" Brandon asked.

"No . . . not yet. The wind keeps blowing the flames away from him. He feels the heat, but the flames will not kill him. The pain, it must be unbearable, yet eyewitnesses say he had a look of joy on his face until the end."

Brandon ventured, "And the end came—"

"—when a soldier finally runs him through with a sword." Salman said nothing more.

There was no sound, only the hot wind blowing up the hill and through the coastal pines overhead. The story had unnerved Brandon. This was not the "happily ever after" gospel he'd been taught in Sunday school. Why hadn't Polycarp gotten away? Why didn't the governor suddenly have a change of heart or be converted? And why the long, lingering death?

Something was wrong. This was not the good-times, trust-God-to-fulfill-our-American-dream message that Brandon had heard from his father's pulpit all of his life. This was a faith where people gave up their lives. It wasn't a faith where they recited the magic words and cruised to heaven. Yes, there was salvation, yes, it was free . . . but it wasn't cheap. It cost Christ his life, and it cost these people theirs.

Of course there was joy, Polycarp had it even as the fire surrounded him . . . but the fire still surrounded him.

And he was still killed.

Was the church ready to hear of such a thing? If, God forbid, persecution ever returned, was the bride prepared to give up everything for him?

Was *he?*

Was Sarah? In all of his excitement to share the gospel with her, had he forgotten to mention the fine print . . . that to live Christ's life, she may have to die?

Brandon looked back down at the Bible.

> Be faithful, even to the point of death, and I will give you the crown of life. He who has an ear, let him hear what the Spirit says to the churches. He who overcomes will not be hurt at all by the second death.

For Brandon, the first two messages had been revolutionary . . .

If the church in Ephesus wanted to maintain their lampstand they had to return to their first love. If the church of Smyrna wanted the crown of life they would have to be faithful even to the point of death.

But there was more. As radical as these first two messages were for Brandon, he could only guess what the next five would contain . . .

"So you believe that this Heylel, that he's some sort of . . . spirit?"

Sarah toyed with her soda straw as she sat at a wrought iron table next to the Cartel's lap pool. "I'm not certain," she said, "but it's a possibility we have to consider." She looked up, searching Lucas's eyes for any sign of ridicule. There was none. There never was. Just the deep thoughtfulness and consideration she had grown to expect.

And there was something else . . . the connection. She'd felt it the first time they'd spoken in the hallway. And, over the past three and a half weeks, it did nothing but grow each time they met. Which they did, frequently, but only if it applied to business. That was Sarah's unspoken code of ethics, the perimeter of defense she'd built around herself. With what she felt stirring inside of her, she needed a defense. But it didn't stop her from wondering what would have happened if they had met just a year earlier.

He cleared his throat. "And as a scientist, by using the word *spirit* you mean . . . ?"

It was a good question, his questions always were. She took a breath and began to explain. "As you know, there is growing scientific evidence to support what you and I would call the supernatural. You've no doubt seen the results of some of the tests I've run on Eric."

"Yes, I have, and they have been most impressive."

"But it doesn't stop there. Many physicists and mathematicians agree there is evidence that our universe does not end with three dimensions."

He looked on, waiting for more.

"There are several mathematical models that point to at least eleven dimensions, probably more."

"And the reason we do not see these dimensions?"

"Lower dimensions can never see higher dimensions."

"How convenient." It was a good-natured tease and she appreciated the camaraderie. But she also rose to the occasion. She took the straw she'd been holding and laid it on the table.

"If this straw was a two-dimensional creature living on this table, it would understand length"—she indicated the length of the table—"and it would understand width." She motioned to the width. "But it would have no idea of depth, of up and down, since up and down doesn't exist in its world. In fact it would see none of this." She motioned to the rest of the room.

"Nor would it see us," Lucas added.

"Exactly." She took the straw's wrapper and laid it on one side of the straw. "No matter how many walls it built around itself"—she took a napkin and laid it on the other side—"we could still see it."

"Since it doesn't know there is any '*above*' to build a roof over itself."

"Precisely." She lowered her face closer to the straw. "And no matter how close we got, it would never know we were here."

"Unless?" Lucas asked.

"Unless we moved something that it could see in its own dimension." She blew the paper out of the way.

Lucas stared at the paper, slowly formulating his thought. "And you believe that Eric is starting to see into these other dimensions?"

"Yes. I believe that somehow your DNA experiment has made his nervous system more susceptible to their influence."

"*Their* influence."

"The spirits . . . the inhabitants of this other dimension."

"But is that so wrong?"

"Not if they're the good guys."

"Good guys . . . you mean like angels?"

Sarah nodded. "Unfortunately there are other inhabitants of that world . . ."

Lucas listened intently.

"Judaism, Christianity, other religions—many acknowledge their existence and have names for them. Our culture calls them . . . *demons.*"

Lucas frowned. "And you believe that this is what Heylel may be?"

"I'm not sure, but I think in a few days we'll need to find out."

"But he's been so helpful, so generous."

"I understand."

"So much of what we have been able to accomplish has been through his counsel."

Sarah waited as Lucas explored the idea. It was a lot to digest at one time, but if any man was capable of doing so in an intelligent and unbiased manner, he was the one. As she watched, she again found herself wondering what would have happened if she'd have connected earlier with a man of such strength and maturity, a man who knew exactly who he was and where he was going . . . instead of someone so young who, although incredibly kind and compassionate, was still . . . so young.

She pushed the thought out of her mind as she had a hundred other times. But, as always, it came back. Initially, she had tried to replace it with memories of Brandon. She'd even tried to pray them away. It helped some, but when it came to praying to a God that, at times, she barely understood, or daydreaming about one of the most dynamic men in the world, well, there was little contest.

"What do you propose we do?"

She glanced up, momentarily forgetting where they were. "I, uh, we've already completed the psychological aspects of his testing. In just a few days we will be through with the physiological as well."

"And then?"

"Then I'd like to move toward the spiritual. I'd like to speak with Heylel directly. I'd like to convince him to reveal more of his identity."

"Many of us have tried."

"I appreciate that, and I may be equally as unsuccessful. But my experience in these areas might give me a slight advantage."

Lucas nodded quietly.

Sarah took a deep breath and let it out. The meeting had been more taxing than she had anticipated. Then again, she was always nervous with Lucas. She glanced back up and caught him smiling at her.

"What?" she asked self-consciously.

"I appreciate your candidness, Doctor. Many would be reluctant to openly voice such opinions, especially ones of such unconventional nature."

Sarah caught herself tugging at her hair and stopped. "And that's all they are," she emphasized. "Opinions."

"For now."

"Yes, for now."

He remained smiling.

Realizing the meeting had come to an end, Sarah reached down and gathered her papers. "Well, then, that's the direction we'll pursue." She started to rise. "I'll let you get back to work now and—"

"Please." He motioned for her to sit. "I have one other area to discuss with you. If you have the time."

"If *I* have the time? Well, yes, certainly." She sat back down.

"As you know, the Cartel is in the final stages of bringing together the world powers. In a matter of days, and for the first time in history, we may have finally secured world peace."

"A remarkable accomplishment. And as their chairman, you should be quite proud."

Lucas shrugged off the compliment. "A figurehead, that's all I am." Before she could disagree, he continued. "Your work has proven very interesting these past several weeks."

"Thank you."

"And this business of bringing science and the supernatural together is quite intriguing. I'm wondering if it wouldn't be prudent for us to investigate a similar union here at the Cartel. As we enter this new paradigm of history, many things will change. Perhaps it would be well to create our own department bringing these two disciplines together. And what person would be better to head it up than yourself?"

Sarah chuckled. "Is the chairman offering me a job?"

He looked at her, his intense eyes making her feel a little uneasy at the joke. A little uneasy and a lot weak. He spoke quietly. "I know your clinic has closed."

"How did you know that?"

"It is my job to know everything ... especially concerning the people I care about." He hesitated, appearing uncertain if he should go on. "And I care about you, Sarah. By now, you must know I care about you very much."

Sarah's heart stopped. Everything froze as she tried to grasp what she'd just heard. She opened her mouth, but no words would come. She tried moving her lips. Nothing happened. Then, as always, Lucas, the gracious and understanding one, came to the rescue.

"I am sorry. I have embarrassed you."

"No, that's—"

"I was out of line. Thinking only of myself. Please forgive me." For the first time she could remember, he seemed flustered, unsure. "I don't know what I was thinking. It is just . . ." He leaned forward, staring at his palms. "In my position, there are so few people that I trust, that I can confide in." He paused, then continued. "And sometimes, ever since Julia died, sometimes this loneliness—" He glanced up and saw her discomfort. "Ah, but I have done it again. Please, please, I apologize. What you must think of me. And you, a married woman with such deep convictions. Please, accept my apologies. I don't know what I was thinking. When it comes to world powers, I have a good understanding. But these matters of the heart, I guess they'll always be foreign to me."

Sarah looked on, stunned and moved. The more he struggled, the more endearing he became. Here was a major world power, suave, sophisticated, countries bowing at his feet, yet he had suddenly turned to jelly when speaking from his heart. A heart that had apparently placed much of its affections upon her.

He shook his head, unable to look at her. "I am sorry."

"No." She cleared the hoarseness from her throat. "That's okay. Really."

He continued shaking his head.

"Lucas?" He looked up. There were those eyes again. For a moment she forgot to breathe. "Don't worry about it. I'm not offended. Actually, it's quite a compliment." She reached down and regathered her things, preparing to leave. "Most women would consider it an honor." Somehow she was able to rise to her feet and actually stand. "But you're right, I am a married woman and I am committed to my husband."

"Certainly." Lucas also rose to his feet. "I understand completely. Believe me."

She smiled. "I do believe you."

He nodded, but kept his eyes riveted on hers.

"Well." Again she cleared her throat as she checked her papers. "If I have your permission then, when we finish Eric's neurological tests, we'll change gears to see if there's anything spiritual."

"Yes, certainly, whatever you think is best."

"Good." She shifted the papers to her other hand and suddenly reached out to shake his. It was an odd gesture, a little clumsy, but it was the best she could think of considering the circumstances. "Well then, good afternoon, Lucas."

He took her hand and they shook. "Good afternoon."

She moved past him. She heard the click of her pumps against the marble tile, and knew she was making progress toward the glass doors, but she wasn't sure how.

He was still staring, she sensed it. She arrived, pushed open the doors, and stepped into the main building. Somehow she was able to continue forward.

Brandon had been ravenous. And the lunch of cheese, flat bread, cucumbers sprinkled with lemon juice, and a large bowl of yogurt with a glob of unprocessed honey plopped in the middle was a welcomed feast. Once again the food came compliments of Salman's swift tongue. This time he'd convinced the restaurant owner that it would bring him great fortune to feed the "holy man and his disciple." That had been half an hour ago. After that, word quickly spread through the city of Bergama. Now it seemed every time Brandon glanced up from their sidewalk table he caught more faces staring at him. Concerned faces. He'd smiled politely, then did his best to ignore them. And still the crowd continued to grow.

A thousand feet above them on a mountaintop overlooking the city stood another acropolis. It had once been called Pergamum and was the address of the third letter. Of all the locations so far, this one made him the most nervous. He wasn't entirely sure why, though he suspected much of it had to do with Jesus Christ calling it "the throne of Satan."

"Some more drink?" Salman held out a bottle of sweet cherry juice, a favorite of Turks. Brandon shook his head and watched as the young man set it down and refilled his glass from another bottle. Its blue and white label read "Raki." It was also a favorite, but with a bit more kick—a forty-five-proof kick, to be exact.

"I'm still not sure how you pulled this off," Brandon said, marveling at the food before him.

"Take a look around you, my friend. We are in the Bakir Valley—the most fertile in all of Turkey. Nowhere in the world do they grow finer tobacco or cotton."

"But what's that got to do with—"

"Their livelihood, it depends upon farming. And the drought, it is wiping them out."

Brandon looked back up at the faces. "But what's that got to do with me?"

"Mr. Brandon, you're the man who called down this drought."

"What?"

"Please, I saw it on TV—'My anger and fury will be poured out on the trees of the field and the fruit of the ground and it will burn and not be quenched.'"

"But that didn't necessarily mean—"

"So if you can call down a drought from heaven, then you can call it back up and make it rain again." He leaned forward with a smile. "As long as they don't make you too angry."

"Is that what you're telling them?"

Salman shrugged and broke into a grin.

Now the anxiety on their faces made sense. So did the growing crowd. "Salman, I didn't—"

"Well, looky who we have here."

He glanced up and saw Tanya Chase approaching. Looming beside her, his hands stuffed into his pockets and looking miserable in the heat, was her sullen and balding cameraman, the one from L.A.

"We figured you'd show up," Tanya said as she peeled off a 500,000 lira bill, amounting to about two U.S. dollars, and handed it to the boy who had brought her. "It was just a matter of time." She pulled up a chair and joined them. The cameraman followed suit. "You remember Jerry, don't you?"

Brandon and the cameraman exchanged nods.

"Waiter, waiter." She motioned to Salman's glass. "I'll have whatever he's having. Oh, and one of those cheese and honey desert things." She turned to Salman. "What are they called?"

Struck by her beauty and her boldness, Salman was only too happy to be of assistance. "*Hershmalem*. It is called *Hershmalem.*"

"Yeah," Tanya called, "one of those *Hersh*-whatevers."

"Make that two," Jerry muttered.

The waiter nodded and disappeared into the crowd. Brandon watched as Tanya reached for an olive on his plate. "How did you find me?" he asked.

"We knew you'd gone to Turkey. Figured it wasn't exactly a family vacation, with your wife leaving you and all."

Brandon ignored the barb.

"Hometown rumor has it you fancy yourself one of the two witnesses in Revelation. So . . ." She reached for another olive. "Doing our best to think like a delusionist, we figured you'd head for Patmos, the island where the book was written. When you were a no-show there, Jerry here guessed you'd be hitting the seven churches." She glanced at her cameraman. "Nice work."

He shrugged and said nothing.

She glanced around the sidewalk. "You seem to be drawing quite a crowd."

Brandon did his best to keep his voice steady. "What do you want from me?"

"I'm just a reporter after a story."

"Haven't you done enough damage already?"

"*Me?* Haven't *I* done enough damage? Look around you, Brandon. Look at all these people suffering. And not just them. What about the thousands that have been killed in the Pacific Northwest? What do you have to say to—"

"Wait a minute. What thousands?"

"Don't tell me you haven't heard? The volcanoes. Baker and Hood, they've both gone off. Washington and Oregon look like war zones. Twelve thousand dead and counting. And Mount Bandai is getting ready to blow in Japan."

"And you think . . . I'm responsible?"

"You tell me. That's why I'm here. And while you're at it, maybe you can explain again why you believe this God of yours, who's supposed to be an all-merciful, loving Father, has reduced himself to the level of throwing cosmic temper tantrums."

Brandon blinked in surprise. But before he could respond, a little girl's scream suddenly cut through the din of the sidewalk and traffic. Another followed. People turned, looking across the cobblestone road toward the plaza on the other side.

There was another cry, only this one was from a woman.

Other guests at surrounding tables rose, stretching their necks for a look. The screaming continued.

"What is it?" Brandon asked as he stood, trying to see. "What's going on?"

Then he spotted her across the street. A young mother was being held by two other women as she shouted and pointed. Twenty, maybe thirty feet beyond, pressed against the base of an Ataturk statue, was her two-year-old daughter. She was screaming in terror at the fifty-pound mongrel crouched in front of her, snarling. And the more she screamed, the more incensed the dog became.

"He's rabid!" Salman said.

"What?"

"Look at the foam. The dog, he has rabies."

Now Brandon saw it, the white foam frothing and falling from the animal's lips. For the briefest second he wanted to move to action, to try and help. But he felt a check in his spirit. Something told him to be still and to simply watch.

Those closest to the plaza began backing away. Some crowded into the safety of doorways. An older gentleman was doing his best to ease the hysterical mother away.

But the dog saw none of it. His attention was focused only upon the little girl and her awful noise.

A handful of men, four to five, began shouting. They stepped out from the crowd, waving their arms, their hats, doing anything they could to draw the animal's attention. But the girl's cries were too loud, too immediate. The men moved closer, pleading with her to be calm, to be quiet, but she would have none of it. She started toward one of them. The dog immediately crouched, ready to spring. The man shouted for her to stop and she froze, still crying.

Another yelled and started running toward the animal. He came within ten feet before the dog saw him and spun around. The distraction worked, but only for a moment. Because as the man veered off for safety, the little girl's cries drew the dog's attention back to her.

Another one tried. Approaching slower. Shouting louder. Waving his arms until he caught the animal's attention. The dog turned and the man ran. But again the little girl's cries focused the animal's attention back on her. It crouched lower, snarling at the insufferable noise.

Others, near the safety of doorways or behind open windows, shouted and hollered, but they were too far away. The animal was focused only upon the girl, when suddenly—

"Sevim!"

Heads jerked around to see another man running toward the plaza. He was a farmer, dressed in dark clothes, racing directly for the animal.

"Sevim!" It was obviously her name. He shouted other things in Turkish that Brandon did not understand.

"What's he saying?"

"He is the father," Salman explained.

"Sevim!"

The crowd murmured as the man raced across the dead grass and dirt of the plaza. By the look of things he had no intention of stopping.

"What's he going to do?" Tanya yelled. "Is he crazy?"

Salman's response was the same. "He is the father."

The man closed the remaining distance. The dog spun toward him snarling, white froth dripping from its fangs. But, before it could attack, the man leaped at the beast with a ferocious cry.

The dog was strong, fifty pounds of crazed muscle—lunging and biting, clawing and tearing. But the father fought relentlessly, crying out in pain and rage, as he tried to grab the animal's head.

The crowd watched in horror and fascination.

And still the battle continued. Snapping teeth, tearing flesh. The man's face and arms were covered in blood. Some of the others worked in closer, hoping to snatch away the little girl. But it was still too dangerous.

The snarling changed to gasps and grunts as the father wrapped his bleeding arms around the animal's chest and began to squeeze. If he couldn't break its neck, then he would crush it to death.

The dog yelped and writhed, twisting its head, lunging for the father's face, but the man continued to squeeze. With superhuman strength he began breaking ribs, crying in rage until he let the animal slip a foot between his arms, then grabbed its head and lathering muzzle and jerked it hard to the right.

The dog went limp and dropped to the ground.

The little girl shouted and started toward him, but she was immediately swept up by the surrounding men.

Chest heaving, dripping in sweat and blood, the father looked down at his arms, at his torn and bloody clothing, and finally at the dog that lay at his feet. He was as dazed and as astonished as anyone.

Others approached, motioning him to follow, careful not to get too close, lest they, too, become infected by the saliva.

"Did you see it?" Tanya turned in amazement to Brandon and Salman. "Did you see what he did? How he risked his life?"

Salman nodded. "He is the father."

"Such love, such anger. I've never seen anything like it. No one else would get in there. But he did. And did you see what he did to that animal?"

"It was about to destroy his child."

"Yes, but such passion . . . and rage."

"He is the father."

As Brandon watched the scene, his understanding grew. God's anger, his wrath had nothing to do with the throwing of what Tanya had called temper tantrums. Instead, it had everything to do with his love, with his overwhelming passion for his children. Instead of petty rage, it had everything to do with awesome love . . . and with destroying the very thing that was destroying those he loved. Because, as Salman had so clearly put it:

"He is the Father."

CHAPTER 11

Dearest Sarah,

I'm constantly amazed at how great God's love is. It seems every time I turn around I see it appearing in deeper ways. Of course I'm clueless about how to use all this information to "warn the bride." Then again it's better I don't know or I'd probably freak. I guess not knowing is just another part of that love.

What you said about Eric's EEG doesn't sound good. If strong delta waves are what demoniacs and psychics experience during their trances . . . and if that's what Eric's brain is doing when Heylel is around, then I think it's pretty clear we're talking possession. As a Christian it shouldn't be a problem for you to send him running . . . if that's what Eric wants. But if he doesn't, that's a whole 'nother ball game. Let me know what happens.

Is the heat as unbearable where you are as it is here? And the pollution from those volcanoes—the sky here is getting so thick with haze that it's almost impossible to see the mountains just across the valley.

I miss you, Sarah. Not a moment goes by that I don't think of you. Sometimes it's in the way I hear a person laugh, or see them tilt their head, or when I watch other couples together. It's like you're everywhere. Everything speaks of you and reminds me how much I want for us to be together. Of course I wish you would write more, but I understand when you say you're so busy. But not forever. Soon we'll be back in each other's arms, and we'll never let each other go again. I look forward to that moment with all of my heart and with all of my soul.

Yours forever,
Brandon

Sarah closed the lid to her laptop computer. Of course he was right about Eric. The kid was displaying typical signs of demon possession. Well, not quite so typical. Because this Heylel, or whoever he was, was not displaying typical signs of being a demon. The profound insights he was sharing with the Cartel, the intense visions he was giving the child ... these were not normal for what she'd confronted in the past. Still, everything else pointed in that direction ... and she knew what course must now be taken.

Then there were Brandon's comments about the drought and the volcanoes. Who knew what effect the millions of tons of contaminants in the atmosphere would have? At one point a third of the world had reported "darkness at noon." And it was anyone's guess how those pollutants would affect the rest of the ecosystem. People were already complaining about water so bitter that it was unfit to drink. And it would only get worse.

But neither of these issues weighed as heavily upon Sarah as the other. She sighed wearily as she snapped off the computer and walked barefoot across the worn pine floor to her dresser. She slid open the top drawer and looked at Brandon's neatly folded shirt. She reached down and unfolded it. As always, the women of the compound had done an excellent job washing the clothes. Every morning they left for the river with baskets full of dirty laundry. And every afternoon they returned with wonderfully clean and fresh-smelling clothes.

She pressed the shirt to her face and drew in a deep breath. There was only the smell of soap and fresh water now. No trace of Brandon remained. She felt the burning in her eyes. The tears happened almost nightly now. She peeled off her clothes, letting them drop to the floor, and slipped into his shirt. She crossed toward the bed, holding one of the sleeves to her face. There was nothing at all.

She curled up under the blankets. It was late, but sleep would not come. The knot in her stomach and the heaviness in her chest made that impossible. The last thing in the world she wanted to do was hurt him. He was such a good kid, so committed, so loyal. But that was the problem, he was a kid.

And Lucas Ponte was a man.

She rolled onto her side, pulling the spare pillow into her and clutching it tightly.

> To the angel of the church in Pergamum write:
>
> These are the words of him who has the sharp, double-edged sword. I know where you live—where Satan has his throne. Yet you remain true to my name. You did not renounce your faith in me, even in the days of Antipas, my faithful witness, who was put to death in your city—where Satan lives.
>
> Nevertheless, I have a few things against you: You have people there who hold to the teaching of Balaam, who taught Balak to entice the Israelites to sin by eating food sacrificed to idols and by committing sexual immorality. Likewise you also have those who hold to the teaching of the Nicolaitans. Repent therefore! Otherwise, I will soon come to you and will fight against them with the sword of my mouth.

He who has an ear, let him hear what the Spirit says to the churches. To him who overcomes, I will give some of the hidden manna. I will also give him a white stone with a new name written on it, known only to him who receives it.

Brandon woke within the ruins of a large round room. There was no sound, just crickets and a soft wind blowing across the dry grass of the Bakir Valley. The moon was nearly full, but because of the smoke high in the atmosphere, it produced a red hue that gave an eerie glow to the crumbling walls above him. He rose up on one elbow and spotted Salman sleeping a few yards away. At first he didn't understand why the man slept curled on the dirt with no blanket to soften the hard ground . . . until he looked down and saw that he was sleeping on two.

Earlier, Brandon had complained about the rocky ground, and Salman had offered him his blanket. Of course Brandon had refused. But after he had fallen asleep, it appeared that Salman had stolen over and somehow slipped it under him. Brandon smiled. The greatness of the man's heart continually surprised him.

It had been Salman's idea for the two of them to sleep here at the Sanctuary of Asclepion, just a couple miles below the main acropolis. "It was one of the main healing centers of the world," he had said. "Named after the 'healing god.'" He'd given Brandon a wink. "Something you can relate to, I am sure."

It was also upon Salman's insistence that Brandon had agreed to sleep inside the remains of this treatment center, or dream house. "It is where the patients used to sleep," he'd said. "It is where they waited for Asclepion to give them dreams for the priests to analyze."

Although Brandon wasn't superstitious, he wasn't crazy about sleeping in the remains of some building once used for occult practices. But, between arguing with Tanya—who kept wanting to chronicle his pilgrimage "for the folks back home"—and visiting the mind-boggling sights up on the acropolis earlier that afternoon, Brandon had little energy to argue.

Yet now he was wide awake.

When sleep showed no promise of returning, he rose and stepped out of the ruins. High above he could see the acropolis hovering in the distance, its white marble pillars glowing crimson in the moonlight.

"Where Satan has his throne," that's what Christ had said of the area. But what did that mean? And where was this throne? Brandon had been up on that hill all afternoon but hadn't found an answer. Nor did he receive any further insights into the letter. Maybe that's why he was unable to sleep. And maybe that's why he had this sudden compulsion to return. Without the noise of tourists, the incessant chattering of Salman, or the scrutiny of Tanya and her cameraman, maybe now he could learn something.

It would take less than an hour to climb back up to the top. The night, although bathed in the moon's unearthly red glow, was peaceful, and the solitude would be a good time for waiting upon the Lord. Although, even as he started forward, Brandon nervously wondered what time would ever be good for visiting Satan's throne.

"Dr. Martus . . . Dr. Martus, over here!"

Sarah looked up from her papers to see one of Lucas's aides motioning to her. The pressroom bustled with noise and confusion as members of the Cartel and other significant figures took their position onstage. Last-minute adjustments were being made to lights, makeup, and the pleats on the navy blue backdrop curtain. The reason? Less than an hour ago the Cartel's scientific team in Brussels had found the cure to Scorpion.

Now they were about to make it public.

"Dr. Martus . . ." The aide continued motioning for her to join them.

Sarah glanced to the other distinguished members taking the stage, then turned back to him and shook her head. He'd obviously made a mistake; she had no business being in their company.

She returned to the report that had been thrust into her hands, a copy of the preliminary findings. Although viral diseases were definitely out of her field, from what she understood, the results looked very promising. No wonder everyone was so excited.

"Dr. Martus . . ." It was Ponte's voice. Her head jerked up, and she saw him standing on the back riser, motioning for her to join them.

She pointed to herself. "Me?"

"Come, come," he called, "you're part of this, too."

She hesitated, not understanding.

"Carlos, Deena," he called to his aides, "please help Dr. Martus up here."

A moment later Sarah was being guided through the crowd and up onto the platform.

"Over here." It was Lucas again. "Please, bring her here, beside me."

The crowd parted, not without a few raised eyebrows. Sarah felt her ears growing warm as she moved up the risers, until she was standing beside the grinning Lucas.

"What do you think?" he asked, referring to the report in her hands.

"From what I can tell it looks great."

His grin broadened. "Good, good . . ."

"All right, everybody, if I may have your attention, please?" It was the press secretary, a short man with a nasal voice. He was clapping his hands and calling from below. "May I have your attention. If everyone would look this way, please?"

Sarah and the group turned toward him. He was surrounded by a small battalion of video and still photographers. Lights blazed as cameras whirred and clicked. Instinctively, Sarah's hand rose to tug on her hair, but just as quickly Lucas reached out, took it, and gently brought it down to her side. She shot him a quick look of gratitude, but he did not respond. Instead, he continued posing and smiling for the cameras. He was, however, doing something else. Hidden by the others in front of them, he continued to hold Sarah's hand.

And she did not withdraw it.

The climb was steep, but Brandon made good time. In fact, he was surprised at how quickly he'd arrived. Unfortunately, that wasn't his only surprise. He'd not quite crested to the top of the hill when he heard rustling in the grass behind him. But it was more than rustling. It sounded like rushing water. Lots of it. He threw a look over his shoulder and saw that the entire hillside below him was now alive with snakes. Millions of them . . . slithering through the grass, crawling over rocks, and swarming across the broken ruins. He knew they weren't real. They couldn't be. At least not real in the physical sense. It was a vision, like so many he used to have—back when heaven had first called him, back when hell had used every power at its disposal to stop him. But, vision or not, it was just as frightening. And, on another level, just as real.

They came from the Asclepion healing center he'd just left. He suspected they represented the snakes the people there had worshiped as part of their healing. He didn't know if they were poisonous. He wasn't sticking around to find out. Although tired and winded from his climb, he picked up his pace.

As he stumbled up to the top of the hill, the first ruins to come into view was the Altar of Zeus. Only now it was no longer ruins. Instead of five rows of broken steps leading to rocks and grass, it was now a magnificent altar with dozens of polished marble stairs along with intricately carved reliefs, columns, and statues. And there, standing at the top, directly behind the altar, was a dazzling bright form of a man at least ten feet tall.

He radiated such power that, at first, Brandon thought it might be another vision of Christ. Or at least an angel. He glanced over his shoulder. The snakes continued their approach up the hill. Maybe the creature would stop them, maybe it would protect him. But as Brandon turned back to him, he noticed the eyes. They burned like Christ's, but instead of burning with love, the flames flickered and leaped with hate.

Brandon continued to run, veering to the right to give the thing a wide berth. That's when it roared, shaking the very ground under his feet. He stole a quick look over his shoulder and to his horror saw that the creature had started down the altar steps. And there was only one place it was going . . . after him!

Already exhausted from the climb, he forced himself to keep running. He staggered up a slight knoll and entered the large flat area that Salman had described earlier that afternoon as the Sanctuary of Athena, the goddess of wisdom and war. But instead of the broken pillars overrun with grass and shrubs that he'd previously seen, there was now a giant two-story marble building and gate. And exiting that gate, heading straight toward him, was another figure of light, almost as tall, but female. In her arms she carried several books. Her mouth did not move, but he could sense her calling out to him. There were no words, but he felt an incredible attraction to her. A powerful impulse to sit down and discuss what was happening, to search the books she was holding for some clue, to put their heads together and try to reason out what was going on.

But this was not the time for sitting and reasoning. The snakes were gaining on him; so was the creature from Zeus's altar. He darted around her to the left . . . and a moment later she, too, had joined in the pursuit.

Up ahead was where the library had once been. Salman had said it had contained two hundred thousand scrolls. When it was standing it was the second largest library in the world. Well, it was standing now. And as far as Brandon could see, there were no glowing giants or slithering snakes anywhere around it. That was good enough for him. Near exhaustion and gasping for breath, he staggered toward it hoping to find someplace inside to hide and rest.

He arrived and entered the first room of the massive building. That's when he heard the voices. At first only two. They came from the shelves. No, they came from the scrolls on the shelves. He didn't understand the language, but they were murmuring, as if alive. Others joined in. He sensed they were giving opinions, advice. Soon there was a dozen—each trying to be heard above the other.

With legs turning to rubber, he stumbled through the dimly lit room. The voices grew in number, hundreds of them now, coming to life as he passed the shelves, shouting at him, yelling at him, desperate to be heard.

He entered a second room. More voices. Growing to a roar. Deafening. He covered his ears. He had to get out. He couldn't think. He forced his legs to keep moving, but they no longer had feeling. His lungs burned for air. Off to the side, he spotted the red glow of moonlight. It was coming through a distant doorway. He headed for it, staggering, stumbling, fighting to keep his balance until, finally, he burst outside into the night air.

He could go no further. He had to stop and lean over, to fill his lungs, to regain his strength. The voices faded only slightly, but even that was a relief. So many attacks on so many fronts. *Why, God?* he prayed. *What's going on?* Glancing up he saw he was standing on the top row of a huge amphitheater. Just beyond, off to the right, was the temple of Bacchus, the wine god. *Tell me, what are you trying to say?*

Suddenly he felt his spirit quicken, his understanding expand . . .

This is exactly what the people of Pergamum had faced every day of their lives. The occult practices of Asclepion, the hostile Greek and Roman religions, the spiritual warfare, the intellectual reasonings, the overwhelming information—all constantly attacking their minds and their spirits. And when the assault was too much—Brandon looked down to the theater and over to the temple of Bacchus—they had plenty of diversions to distract and numb the pain.

> I know where you live—where Satan has his throne. Yet you remain true to my name. You did not renounce your faith in me . . .

What faith these Christians must have had. To withstand so many attacks on so many levels. And yet—his mind focused more sharply—wasn't that exactly what the church of today faced? Today, in this age of information with all of its truths and science and spirituality? So much information attacking from every side. And so many opportunities to throw up our hands, to give up, to quit the fight and zone out with the world's diversions. Although separated by nearly two millenniums, the cultures suddenly appeared identical.

Amidst such assault, how could either culture distinguish the difference between truth and error? Amidst such cacophony, how could anyone hear, let alone discern, that still, small voice of God?

And yet, didn't our culture have at least one advantage? Brandon turned his head toward the Temple of Trajan that loomed above and to his right. As the center of the Imperial Cult, it was the crowning masterpiece of the acropolis and towered over the entire valley, making it clear where the ultimate power and authority lay. At least Christians today didn't have to worry about the totalitarian government that Salman had described. At least they didn't have to worry about worshiping a one-world dictator.

The thought had barely registered before he heard the snakes. They'd rounded the library and were rushing toward him in a giant wave. From the other side came Athena with her pleas for reason, and behind her, Zeus with his thundering demands.

There was no place to go. It was either down into the theater or up to the Temple of Trajan. He'd known since Ephesus that his future involved a large arena, but he also knew that it wasn't now. He turned to his right and scrambled up the rocky remains toward the temple.

And that's when the rules changed . . .

He'd barely reached the temple with its moonlit, blood-red pillars, when an unearthly cry spun him around. To his astonishment, he saw the snakes engulfing Zeus. But it was more than that. Zeus was also engulfing the snakes and Athena . . . as she was engulfing them. All of the creatures were coming together, joining forces, turning into one large entity—a darkness that resembled none of them separately, but all of them corporately.

Brandon watched, paralyzed with fear.

I know where you live—where Satan has his throne.

Suddenly, he understood. Satan's throne wasn't just the altar of Zeus, or Athena, or the medicine of Asclepion, or the library with its thousands of "truths." It was all of these combined. And now they had all come together, combining forces here at the center of Imperial Cult worship. As he watched, the black shadow collapsed upon itself, condensing into a denser, more tangible form . . . one he recognized immediately. It was the giant serpent head from his dreams.

It started toward him.

Brandon stepped back. "Stay away!" he cried hoarsely. "Stay back!"

It said nothing, but continued its approach. Brandon could see its tongue flickering in and out and back and forth. His thoughts raced. There had been no way to battle this thing in his dreams nor when it had appeared in his father's church. If he couldn't stop the thing then, how could he stop it now?

He struggled to remember Christ's words, his letter to the Christians here. Surely God had not left them defenseless. If this was Satan's throne, God must have given them something to fight with. But what? What could defeat all the noise, the deceptions, the falsehood? What had the letter said?

I will fight against them with the sword of my mouth.

But what did that mean?

The serpent's head closed in. It slowly opened its jaw, revealing the swirling, fiery abyss inside. An abyss that had nearly consumed him before. The wind increased. It began pulling at him, tugging at his clothes, his body, exactly as it had in the church. Desperately, he looked for an escape, but it was already cornering him against the back wall of the temple.

His mind churned, running the phrase: *Sword of my mouth, sword of my mouth, sword of my mouth.* He recalled the small, double-edged sword he'd seen inside Christ's mouth at the hospital. The one that had replaced his tongue. It was a scary image, almost obscene, but now . . .

The sword, the sword . . . Wait. A verse was coming to mind. One of those he hated memorizing back in Sunday school. *"The Word is sharper than any double-edged sword . . . able to divide, to divide—"* He couldn't remember the rest, but that was enough.

The mouth was a dozen feet away now. Its jaw unhinged, opening even wider. Now there was nothing but fire. Fire and wind screaming in Brandon's ears, trying to pull him in. Other memories of other confrontations raced through his mind. What had other people done? What had Jesus—

He remembered the battle between Jesus and Satan. In the wilderness. It had been one of his dad's favorite stories. How the most evil force of the universe fought the Creator of the universe. Not with guns or bombs—they hadn't even tried to nuke each other. Instead, these two powerful forces of the universe battled with the most powerful weapon of the universe: They quoted God's Word. Wielding it back and forth, like swords, like—

That was it! That was the sword of Christ's mouth, his Word!

Even in L.A., wasn't that how he'd silenced Jimmy Tyler? Not with *his* words, but with *God's.* And maybe that's what was bringing God's judgments down on the world now. Not what Brandon had said up there on that stage, but what God had said through him. That's where the power was. That's the weapon that had been given them!

Brandon reached into his back pocket for the New Testament. He'd barely touched it before he heard the scream.

"Nooooo!"

He looked up. The head had stopped its approach. He finished pulling out the Bible and with trembling hands opened it—somewhere, anywhere, it didn't matter. But, even as he did, he noticed the wind beginning to subside.

Again he looked up. The serpent head was already beginning to lose its form, turning back into a nebulous shadow. Brandon watched, transfixed, as the shadow started to dissipate, allowing the red moonlight to penetrate it. A moment later it had turned into a fine mist, then wafted and blew until nothing more of it remained. Nothing but two words, or at least Brandon's impression of those words.

Soon . . . The voice echoed inside his head. *Very soon . . .*

And then it was gone. There was no sound, except Brandon's heavy breathing. No shadows, except those cast by the crumbled ruins. And no more majestic temples. Everything was exactly as he had seen it that afternoon with Salman.

A thousand feet below, down in the city, the first Moslem call to prayer began. Dawn was about to break. Other mosques around the city joined in until the entire valley echoed in competing calls to worship.

So many voices.

Brandon would head back down to join Salman soon enough. But for now he needed to rest. To rest and to contemplate what he'd seen. It was true. The struggles of Pergamum were no different than those of today's church. So much information, so many versions of *truth*. Both cultures had their roaring distractions. But both had an identical weapon available, not only to battle those errors, but to uncover the truth.

Because, just as surely as love was required for Ephesus, and faithfulness to death for Smyrna, so truth was required for the survival of Pergamum.

Katherine stared at the computer screen, unable to believe what she saw.

Earlier she'd pulled the system administrator's password, *Mongoose Warrior*, from her encrypted file. Then, using his name and password, she'd logged onto the system and was given free access to all files. Everything went exactly as planned. No problem . . .

Until she started reading the classified information on Scorpion. She'd already checked the Cairo and Mecca files. Now she was scrolling through the New York one. Like the others, it contained a brief log of time and events. And, although the locations and times were different, the sequence was nearly identical—particularly in regard to the "dehydration of product," "transportation of product to specified site," and "dispersal of product over site."

It was this last phrase that sent a shudder through her. With trembling fingers, Katherine brought up the fourth and final file. "Tel Aviv."

Again there were minor alterations, but the basic sequence of events was the same . . . dehydration, transportation, and finally, the dispersal of product over site.

She closed her eyes and took a deep breath. Was it possible? Here were the first four cities that Scorpion had struck. And here, before her, was a record of the Cartel producing and releasing something over those very same cities.

No. The thought was too outrageous. It had to be a coincidence. A bizarre coincidence. Her thoughts raced, exploring a thousand other options. There had to be something else, some other tie-in that could either prove or disprove the possibility. Something more that could—

Wait a minute. Dates and times. Yes, of course. The incubation period of Scorpion was between twenty-eight and thirty-one days. If she could find the date that its outbreak was first reported in each of the four cities, and compare that to the date of the product's dispersal, that would be more than enough proof.

For the briefest moment Katherine hesitated, afraid of what she would find. Then the anger kicked in. Anger over the wasted months and years. And anger over all the deceptions that she'd suspected but could never prove. Fueled by this anger and with growing resolution, she jotted down the release dates and exited the system.

A moment later, she logged onto the Internet and began her search of dates and locations.

Sarah leaned over Lucas Ponte's bathroom counter and stared into the mirror. Her face was flush from the wine and her eyes watery. "Get a hold of yourself," she whispered crossly. "Stop it. Stop it right now." She grabbed a tissue and dabbed at her eyes, careful not to smear the mascara.

The dinner had been Lucas's idea . . . part celebration, part sitting down with Katherine and Eric to lay out her beliefs about Heylel and to explain what must be done. That was the only reason she'd agreed to come to Lucas's living quarters, because Katherine and Eric would be there. But, for whatever the reason, mother and son had not shown. And, after waiting nearly an hour (and consuming two, or was it three, glasses of Chianti), they agreed to start eating dinner without them.

The dinner was excellent. Greek salad, sautéed mushrooms, veal scallopini, and more vino, lots and lots of vino. They talked about everything. And they laughed. Lucas did not bring up his feelings about her again, at least not in words, though she could see it in the hundred and one ways he was attentive to her. In fact, as best she could tell, those feelings had grown.

So had hers.

An hour didn't go by that she didn't catch herself thinking about him, about them. His sensitivity, his maturity, his power . . . who he was, and what she could have been with him.

"Stop it," she repeated. "You're a married woman. You have a husband."

She took a deep breath to clear her head, then adjusted the spaghetti straps to her dress and tugged at its hem. Why she had worn such a skimpy thing was beyond her. She turned from the mirror and with determined resolve strode across the white marble floor toward the door.

When she reentered the room she saw that Lucas was no longer sitting at the table. He had dimmed the lights and had stepped over to look out the large picture window with its moonlit view. His silhouette was impressive. That tall frame, those broad shoulders, a physique that he obviously took great care—

Stop it!

Sensing her presence, he turned. "There you are," he said. "Are you all right? I was beginning to worry."

His concern was touching. "Yes." She cleared the raspiness from her throat. "I'm fine." As she passed the table she had to briefly reach out to steady herself. There was no doubt about it; it was definitely time to be going.

Lucas turned to look back out the window. "Beautiful, isn't it?" She arrived at his side, so close they were practically touching. The mountains glowed brilliantly. The shadowed terraces spilled to the valley floor where lights from the tiny village twinkled. He continued, softer. "How could anything be more perfect?"

She quietly agreed.

"That's one of the many reasons they selected this location. Certainly not because of its easy access." He chuckled, and she felt his arm brush hers. Suddenly she was very aware of their closeness. "Though, I must say, sometimes this isolation, this loneliness . . ." He took a deep breath. She felt his arm swell against hers, then deflate as he quietly sighed.

How hard it must be on him. So powerful, yet so lonely. Here was one of the mightiest men in the world, beside her, alone with her, yet having no one with whom to share his intimate thoughts. What she could do for him, how she could help—

No! You're a married woman. There's Brandon! Your vows!

She continued to stand beside him, absorbing the scenery, feeling the warmth of his presence, wondering if he felt hers. Her head was growing light as feelings of well-being and euphoria washed over her.

Your vows! That piece of paper!

But that's all it was, a piece of paper. There was no moral contract, nothing physical had taken place. Their marriage had never been consummated. In some cultures that meant it wasn't even legal. Could she really be considered unfaithful? Unfaithful to what? A written document, a piece of paper? What about faithfulness to her own heart?

"Sarah . . ."

She looked up at him, wondering if he knew her thoughts, seeing and feeling the room move slightly.

What about Brandon? What about God?

She waited for him to say more, but he did not. Instead, he looked down and shook his head, unable to continue. But she knew. She always knew. She could see the glint of moisture in his eyes. She touched his arm, offering support, assuring him she understood, that she felt it, too. The impossibility of their situation.

And then he looked at her. Those soulful, penetrating eyes that reached in and held her heart, that dissolved her very insides. The room started to move again, and she tightened her grip on his arm for support.

What about Brandon? What about—

He slipped his arm around her waist, helping her to stand. He understood everything. They were close, their bodies touching. Closer than they'd ever been. She could feel his breathing, the pounding of his heart.

She was no longer certain if she was standing or being held. It didn't matter. The room was moving again, and they were so close, and so much alike, and so perfect for one another.

His mouth moved toward hers.

What about—

She tried to think of Brandon, of God, of some reason to resist. But they no longer mattered. There was only Lucas, their embrace, his pounding heart, the spinning room . . .

She closed her eyes, felt his warm breath on her face. She tilted back her head until, finally, their lips found one another's.

CHAPTER 12

To the angel of the church in Thyatira write:

These are the words of the Son of God, whose eyes are like blazing fire and whose feet are like burnished bronze. I know your deeds, your love and faith, your service and perseverance, and that you are now doing more than you did at first.

Nevertheless, I have this against you: You tolerate that woman Jezebel, who calls herself a prophetess. By her teaching she misleads my servants into sexual immorality and the eating of food sacrificed to idols. I have given her time to repent of her immorality, but she is unwilling. So I will cast her on a bed of suffering, and I will make those who commit adultery with her suffer intensely, unless they repent of her ways. I will strike her children dead. Then all the churches will know that I am he who searches hearts and minds, and I will repay each of you according to your deeds. Now I say to the rest of you in Thyatira, to you who do not hold to her teaching and have not learned Satan's so-called deep secrets (I will not impose any other burden on you): Only hold on to what you have until I come.

To him who overcomes and does my will to the end, I will give authority over the nations—

"He will rule them with an iron scepter;
    he will dash them to pieces like pottery"—

just as I have received authority from my Father. I will also give him the morning star. He who has an ear, let him hear what the Spirit says to the churches.

The sun had set an hour ago, but the darkness offered little relief from the heat. Brandon had spent all afternoon inside the coffee shop reading his Bible. A television set droned quietly in the background as a large electric fan swept back and forth across the sweating men who sat around Formica tables drinking tea, discussing politics, or playing a tile game called Okay. They were a hundred yards down the street from the ruins of Thyatira, now called Akhisar. There was little to see. Just more dried grass and scrub pines in ruins that were no bigger than a city block . . . a city block located directly in the center of the existing town.

Salman was up in the hotel room resting. Despite Brandon's protests, Tanya Chase had insisted upon paying for their room. "Don't be ridiculous," she'd scolded him when he'd tried to refuse. "It's good for all of us. They'll kick you out the second you try to sleep in those ruins, and Jerry and I have no intention of traipsing all around the countryside tracking you down wherever you decide to camp out."

It seemed a fair trade-off: a real bed to rest his travel-weary bones, for life under some minor media scrutiny that would be inevitable anyway. But there was another reason he had agreed. Although Tanya insisted she was only going after a story, pushing him to make his "great declaration to the world" so she could wrap it up and put it to bed, Brandon saw something else. A softening. Maybe not on the outside, but something was happening to her heart. As she and Jerry continued to hang around, watching him day in and day out, occasionally discussing the Scriptures, something was happening to her. Slowly, but surely, something was happening. He turned back to the New Testament and smiled quietly. There seemed to be no end to God's miracles.

As he continued reading and waiting on the Lord, an unusual truth had started to emerge. But this one wasn't about the church of Thyatira . . . it wasn't even about the church of today. It was about Brandon Martus. A truth exposed and revealed by "he who searches the hearts and minds." A truth about the Jezebels in his own soul. The sins he was tolerating and allowing to dwell within his own heart.

All of his life he'd been taught that holiness was a good thing to pursue, a worthwhile . . . pastime. But it was nothing as important as life and death. After all, if we sinned, there was always Christ's sacrifice on the cross to pay for it. And if we wanted to indulge a little longer or deeper in those sins it may not be for the best, but it was okay. Christ's grace was endless; there was no ceiling to the debt we could run up on his credit card of forgiveness.

But now . . . as Brandon studied the Scriptures, he was beginning to see a much different God, with a much higher purpose. He turned back and reread 1 Peter:

> But just as he who called you is holy, so be holy in all you do; for it is written: "Be holy, because I am holy."

Brandon was beginning to understand that holiness wasn't a suggestion. It wasn't even a goal. It was a command. A command just as important as not killing, not stealing, not committing adultery.

He flipped over to Galatians 5:19–21. He'd read it several days earlier—a virtual shopping list of immoralities.

> The acts of the sinful nature are obvious: sexual immorality, impurity and debauchery; idolatry and witchcraft; hatred, discord, jealousy, fits of rage, selfish ambition, dissensions, factions and envy; drunkenness, orgies, and the like.

Of course he wasn't guilty of all of these, at least not on the outside. But, like the church of Thyatira, how many of these immoralities did he secretly tolerate on the inside? And if that wasn't bad enough, there was the final verse. The kicker:

> I warn you, as I did before, that those who live like this will not inherit the kingdom of God.

"Will not inherit the kingdom of God." Did God honestly expect him to live a life that pure and holy? Yes, he knew holiness was something God *preferred*, and he always figured if he succeeded, great, but if not, no sweat. After all, he no longer lived under the law, but grace.

Yet these verses seemed to take the matter far more seriously. He felt compelled to flip over to the book of Romans.

> Don't you know that when you offer yourselves to someone to obey him as slaves, you are slaves to the one whom you obey—whether you are slaves to sin, which leads to death, or to obedience, which leads to righteousness? But thanks be to God that, though you used to be slaves to sin, you wholeheartedly obeyed the form of teaching to which you were entrusted. You have been set free from sin and have become slaves to righteousness.

Was it possible? All of his life Brandon had been taught that he had been set free from the *penalty* of sin. But now he was seeing something deeper. According to these verses and others like them he was not only free from sin's punishment . . . he was free from its *power*.

He turned to 1 John.

> No one who is born of God will continue to sin, because God's seed remains in him; he cannot go on sinning, because he has been born of God. This is how we know who the children of God are and who the children of the devil are: Anyone who does not do what is right is not a child of God.

It had always been there, in the Scriptures and somewhere in the back of his head, but it had never taken hold. He had never known the importance, no, the *requirement* God made regarding holiness. Did others? Did the church? Had she preached it here in Thyatira? Did she preach it today? Or, in her zeal to save people, had she forgotten the second half of the gospel—the fact that God not only freed us from the *penalty* of sin . . . but that he freed us from the *power* of sin. A power we could choose to embrace—or ignore. But one that if ignored would bring a devastating penalty.

> I warn you, as I did before, that those who live like this will not inherit the kingdom of God.

The concept was astonishing.

"Brandon?"

He looked up. It was Tanya.

"I think you need to see this." She tried to avoid his eyes, but it was too late. He already knew something was wrong.

"What's the matter?"

The men in the coffee shop had started to murmur. This was a place for them to gather; no women were allowed.

"What is it?" Brandon repeated.

Tanya turned and left the shop without a word. Brandon quickly gathered his papers, stuffed the New Testament into his back pocket, and followed. His heart was already beginning to pound as he stepped outside and into the night.

"You scum . . ." Katherine searched for a more degrading term, but she was shaking so badly she could barely speak. "You despicable monster."

"Good evening, Katherine." Lucas turned to squint at the clock across his living room. "Or should I say good morning." Even as he stood in his disheveled state of mussed hair and swollen eyes he looked gorgeous. "To what do I owe this honor—and how, might I ask, did you get past the electronic security?"

"I know a little about computers, remember."

"Ah, of course." He finished tying the belt to his robe while heading past the leather sofa to the bar at the end of the room. "May I get you something to drink?"

It was then she noticed Sarah's open satchel and scattered briefs on the coffee table . . . and her shoes beside the sofa. "Dr. Martus is here?"

Lucas glanced up. "Hmm? Oh, yes. I am afraid your friend had a bit too much to drink at dinner, and she is now sleeping it off."

Katherine threw an involuntary glance to the bedroom with its door half ajar. "She had dinner here? With you?"

He was searching through the bottles in the cabinet. "Does that surprise you?"

"I just thought she was smarter than that."

"Yes, well, when you and Eric failed to show, our evening became a bit more—how shall I say—intimate."

"When Eric and I failed to show?"

"Yes, we waited, had a few drinks, but you never—"

"We were never invited."

"Ah, an unfortunate oversight by my staff. I shall have to speak to Deena. Here we go." He pulled out a bottle from the back. "Scotch is still your preferred drink, is it not?"

It was now or never. Katherine played her card. "I know about Scorpion, Lucas."

He glanced up. "I'm sorry?"

"I know the Cartel . . . I know that you created the virus."

He paused just a fraction of a second, then reached for two glasses. "Created . . . the virus?"

She remained silent. She'd thrown him off balance, and now he was stalling to recover.

He opened the bottle and began to pour. "I have been accused of many things, Katherine, but I must admit this one really surprises—"

"I saw the files, Lucas." She stepped further into the room. "Cairo, Mecca, New York, Tel Aviv—the first four cities to break out with the plague. I don't know how you created it, but I know you transported and air-dropped the Scorpion virus over each of those four cities. I know that you purposely started the epidemic."

He hesitated. By now her heart was pounding like a jackhammer. She watched his every move, waiting to see what he would do, what he would say. After an eternity, he turned and crossed toward her, drinks in hand.

"You're right, of course." He arrived and held out a glass. She only stared at him, her rage building. When it was obvious she wouldn't take it, he carefully set the glass on the coffee table, beside Sarah's papers, and eased himself into the leather sofa. "Please." He motioned for her to sit opposite him.

She remained standing.

He became very quiet, staring down at his glass a long moment. Katherine shifted and waited. Finally, he spoke, but he did not look up. "It was a very difficult step to take." His voice was soft and thick with emotion. "And, although the Cartel fully endorsed the action, I am the one who must take the ultimate responsibility."

Katherine watched, refusing to be taken in. Still, she had to ask, "Why?"

He looked up. "The Arabs, the Jews, you know they will never get along. We all know this. The rest of the world, we may agree to live in peace, but not these two cousins. And that is what they are . . . cousins. Did you know that both come from the line of Abraham? The Jews from Isaac, Sarah's son—the Arabs from Ishmael, her handmaiden's child?"

She said nothing.

He continued. "That is why it wasn't hard to design a virus to attack only their gene pool."

She repeated the question. "Why?"

"It seemed so unfair, for the entire world's peace to be held hostage by nothing more than a . . . family squabble."

"So you decided to wipe them both out."

"No, no. Is that what you think?" He looked up at her, his eyes full of hurt, even betrayal. But it didn't work. Not this time. Katherine would not be drawn in. "No, that's not it at all," he said. "You must understand, the only way to bring these two parties together, to force them to cooperate, was to somehow provide them with—how shall I put it—an incentive."

Katherine frowned, not understanding.

He continued. "The Jews, the Arabs, they are dying off by the thousands."

"Try millions."

Lucas shrugged. "Yes, you are right. And here we are, an organization dedicated to world peace that is suddenly holding the only cure."

Katherine's jaw went slack. "You're . . . blackmailing them? If they don't cooperate, you're going to withhold the vaccine?"

"Blackmail is a very ugly word. As I said, our purpose is only to provide an incentive."

"They'll never go for it. The people will never—"

"The people will never know. But their leaders already do. And by all appearances they are already coming around."

"That's not possible."

"We are talking life and death here."

"You're talking genocide."

"That would be their decision, not mine."

Katherine reached out to the sofa to steady herself as Lucas continued.

"In less than a week, every major country will have given the Cartel the authority we need to enforce world peace. That's when I will officially be taking office and when we'll have the groundbreaking for the new temple. Think of it. For the first time in five thousand years, the Jew and Arab will exist side by side in peace. Not that there won't be tensions. But, as I have said, we do hold the incentive."

Katherine's voice was dry and raspy. "That's . . . monstrous."

"It is the only way."

"The only way? Innocent Jews and Arabs are being destroyed all around the world, and you say it's the only way?"

Lucas leaned back and sighed wearily. "It is an unfortunate by-product, yes."

"By-product?" She was practically shouting. *"By-product?"*

He said nothing.

Unable to contain her anger, Katherine was ready to explode. She had to do something. Anything. She spun around and started toward the door.

"Where are you going?"

"I don't know, but we're going. We have to get out of here."

"Katherine, if you're thinking about disclosing this information to the general public, I assure you, it will not be—"

She spun back at him. "I'm not disclosing anything. I'm getting out of here. You're sick, Lucas. Deranged! All of you! And we're not going to be a part of your sickness any longer!"

"So you're taking Eric and leaving?"

"That's right."

"Despite the authorities."

"We'll take our chances."

"And if Eric chooses to stay?"

"I'm his mother; he'll leave if I tell him to leave."

"I'm afraid that may be wishful thinking."

She looked at him, incredulous. "What?"

"Eric is more connected to us than you would like to believe. He is more connected to me. I've made sure of it."

When her voice finally came it was husky and full of venom. "You scheming, manipulative—"

"Katherine, please, let us forego name-calling, shall we?"

She turned on her heels and stormed back to the door. There was nothing left to be said. Now there was only action. She'd get them out of there. She had to. And if Eric put up a fuss . . . well, she was still his mother, wasn't she? She could still make him obey, couldn't she?

"Katherine . . ."

But even as she flew out the door, slamming it behind her, doubts began to rise. Lucas had sounded so confident, and he was always so thorough. What other tricks did he have?

Brandon raced outside, past the children kicking the deflated soccer ball, barely noticing the old men sitting at the tables, puffing on their giant hookahs.

Something inside of him was beginning to *know*. Once again his spirit was quickening. Once again the world surrounding him grew less and less real as the understanding became more and more vivid. The truths of the letter to Thyatira hadn't been completely revealed, not yet. There was something else.

He pulled up alongside Tanya. Her heels clicked against the tile sidewalk, drawing the attention of every male whose vision was not completely impaired. "Is it Salman?" he asked.

She looked straight ahead. "I told Jerry not to tape it, as a courtesy to you. But sometimes his ambition gets out of hand." She said nothing more, her face flashing from light to shadow as they walked under the bare bulbs strung from the fronts of shops to the mulberry trees lining the street.

The hotel was a dive at best. A handful of apartments in one of the five-story buildings that surrounded the square. They'd barely arrived outside the structure when Brandon heard the music and looked up. Three stories above, on his balcony, a young couple was locked in a passionate embrace. And by the noise coming from inside he suspected they weren't his only company.

He entered the lobby with Tanya and started up the concrete steps. Brandon didn't need the Spirit of God to fill in the details. Salman was on the road, Salman finally had a place to stay, Salman was unwinding and letting off a little steam with some newfound friends. No big deal. But other impressions rushed in. Salman drunk, Salman carousing, Salman having sex. The thoughts were unsettling, and he knew he'd have to speak to him. Still, it certainly wasn't his style to judge or condemn—

"Nevertheless, I have this against you: You tolerate that woman Jezebel, who calls herself a prophetess. By her teaching she misleads my servants into sexual immorality . . ."

The words surprised him. Surely God wasn't talking about Salman. The guy was a baby Christian, nominal at best. Brandon's job wasn't to judge. He was to be loving and kind. Salman would eventually come into deeper maturity and—

"I have given her time to repent of her immorality, but she is unwilling."

He grabbed the iron railing as they moved up the stairs. *Lord, that's too harsh.*

There was no response.

He's a good friend. It's not my job to judge.

"You tolerate . . ."

He's a good man. Look at all he's done.

"He is unwilling."

Only for now. He will be later. We just have to give him more—

"I have given him time to repent, but he is unwilling."

It's just . . . sex. It's part of today's culture. Everybody is—

"You tolerate . . ."

That's so . . . judgmental. It's so . . .

"You tolerate . . ."

Brandon was growing more desperate. *Please . . . I wouldn't even be here if it wasn't for him. Look at all he's done for me, all he's given up.*

"You tolerate . . ."

But you say we're supposed to love, we're supposed to be merciful and forgiving.

"I have given him time to repent, but he is unwilling."

They were on the second story now. He gripped the railing tighter, fighting back the anguish. *I can't. I can't do that.*

"I have this against you."

Please . . . what about your love? But even as the words came, Brandon knew their answer. He'd already seen God's love back in the hospital, back in the square with the rabid dog. The love that surpassed human sentimentality, a love that destroyed anything that threatened his beloved. In desperation, Brandon turned back to the other argument, the one minimizing Salman's sin. *It's just . . . sex.*

"And eating the fruit of the tree was merely eating the fruit of the tree."

The insight was so powerful that it nearly slowed him to a stop. It was true. Rebellion was rebellion. It made no difference what shape, what form. It made no difference how large or small, how injurious or benign. Rebellion was rebellion.

They arrived at the third-story landing and crossed to the apartment. The music throbbed as Tanya stepped aside to let him open the door. He leaned against the handle, steeling himself. This was hard. Next to saying good-bye to Sarah and losing the clinic, this was the toughest.

Taking one last breath, he turned the knob, pushed open the door, and stepped into the party. There weren't a lot of people. About a dozen. Some talked, others danced to the clanging rhythms and mournful wails of contemporary Turkish music.

He called out to the nearest couple. "Where's Salman?"

"Ne?" the young man shouted.

"Salman, where is Salman?"

His partner, a bottle blonde, motioned toward the bedroom.

Brandon looked over at the closed door. Heaviness grew in his chest as if a huge stone had been placed on it. He started through the crowd and had barely crossed halfway when the door opened and Salman appeared, tucking in his shirt. The girl with him was sixteen, seventeen at most. She reminded Brandon of the girl at the mall. The one so hungry for love and attention.

Salman looked up and for a moment appeared startled to see him. "Mr. Brandon!" He recovered and sauntered toward him. Disguising his uneasiness with a grin, he arrived and slapped Brandon on the back. "Welcome!"

Brandon swallowed hard, took another breath, and then quietly gave the order. "Leave."

"I am sorry. What?"

Although he tried to sound angry, the ache in his heart gave him away. "Leave."

"But the party, it has just begun." He glanced about. "Banu, Banu!" He motioned for one of the nearby girls—easily as young as his. She wobbled toward Brandon in high heels, obviously drunk, the interest in her dark eyes emboldened by the alcohol.

Salman laughed. "You're in luck, I think she likes you."

Brandon repeated himself. "I want you to leave, and I want you to leave now."

Banu wrapped her arms around one of his. He barely noticed as he remained focused on Salman. "What you are doing is wrong." The words came harder. He had to breathe between each sentence. "It is wrong and you know it."

Salman chuckled. "Wrong? It is a little indulgence. A little reward after our hard labors."

"It's wrong." From the corner of his eye he noticed Jerry across the room, hoisting the camera on his shoulder, beginning to tape.

"Maybe it is a little wrong," Salman admitted with a twinkle, "but a little wrong is sometimes good. Banu, show Mr. Brandon how good a little wrong can be."

Before he could stop her, the girl had reached her arms around his neck and pulled herself up to him, kissing him fully on the lips. He tried to push her away, but she clung with tenacity. He tried again, harder, until he finally broke her grip. But the force sent her staggering backwards. She hit a table filled with glasses. It collapsed and crashed with her to the floor. Booze splashed, glass shattered, and people gasped. Suddenly, Salman and Brandon were center stage.

Trying to ignore the stares, Brandon repeated himself as evenly as he could. "What you are doing is wrong."

"Wrong? Celebrating with a few friends, it is wrong?"

Brandon spoke more softly. "You know what I mean."

"No, I do not. You tell me which is wrong." He raised his voice so everyone in the room could hear. "Is it wrong for someone to buy an airline ticket for a friend in trouble? Is it wrong to be his companion and guide in a country he would be lost in? Is it wrong to live outdoors with him, to starve with him, to suffer with him? Is that wrong? Or is it wrong for that friend to suddenly throw him onto the streets as thanks for his hard work and dedication?"

Salman's logic was irrefutable. Brandon had no argument, only what he knew to be true. "You must go, Salman. If you repent, if you sincerely ask God's forgiveness, then maybe—"

"Repent? Repent of what?" There was no missing the contempt filling his voice. "Of being a man? Of having manly desires?" He reached for the girl he'd slept with, pulling her mouth toward his, kissing her passionately, long and hard. The crowd voiced approval.

"There," he said, finally releasing her and catching his breath. "That's what I think of your repentance. Or would you prefer me to treat her as you do your own wife . . . never fulfilling your duties to her as a man!"

Brandon wasn't angry. He knew it was the alcohol talking. He also knew it was Salman feeling the betrayal of their friendship. And who could blame him? Certainly not Brandon. Instead, Brandon slowly nodded and looked at him with deep sincerity. "I am sorry, my friend."

The word triggered something in Salman. Suddenly his voice grew husky with emotion. "Friend? This is not how you treat a friend." His jaw stiffened, making it clear he was trying to maintain his anger. "This is how you treat an enemy. And you"—he pointed an accusing finger—"you do not even know the difference."

He turned to one of the group. "Orhan! The newspaper, bring it here." A young man in his twenties produced a newspaper. Salman grabbed it and threw it down on the table. "That!" He slammed his hand down on the front-page photo. The one of Lucas Ponte standing with a handful of dignitaries. "That is your enemy! He is all of our enemy!"

Brandon glanced at it, then back at Salman. He'd heard the speech about the evils of Ponte and the Cartel a dozen times—if not from Salman, then from his militant friends. This was an obvious attempt to change the subject. But Brandon would not be sidetracked. "I'm sorry, Salman." There was a large lump in his throat. "We can no longer work together."

"Look!" Salman roared. "Look at the picture!"

Brandon glanced back down. Salman's finger was not on Lucas Ponte; instead, it was pointing to a woman. A woman standing beside him, looking on with deep gratitude. But it was far more than gratitude . . . she was looking at him with heartfelt admiration.

Suddenly Brandon could no longer breathe. He gripped the table, having to lean against it just to stand. Salman continued to talk to him, to berate him, but he no longer heard. People from the party moved in for a better look, but he barely noticed.

All he could do was stare at the photograph of his wife gazing at Lucas Ponte with adoration . . . and burning love.

CHAPTER 13

Sarah dragged herself up the courtyard stairs. Her head throbbed, her mouth felt like cotton, and she still didn't completely trust the ground under her feet. She'd barely made it to the second flight when her stomach heaved and she bent over vomiting. But it was more than just wine that had made her sick. Sarah Martus was sick with guilt.

Lucas had been kind and understanding as always. Once she woke, he had done everything to convince her to stay. He'd even offered to sleep on the sofa. But she had to get away, she had to sort things out. It was Katherine's shouts and slamming of the door that had awakened her. She didn't hear all the words, couldn't understand the argument, but she knew Katherine was awake and that she was at least one person who would listen.

She pulled herself back to her feet, wiped her mouth, and somehow started across the landing. Fortunately, Katherine's door was open and her light on. Pausing to gather herself, Sarah pushed her hair behind her ears, straightened her clothes, and approached.

Inside, Katherine flew around the room, packing furiously. She glanced up, was briefly startled at Sarah's presence, then continued. "What do you want?"

"I . . ." Sarah squinted at the glaring light. "Where are you going?"

"We're leaving. Eric and me, we're out of here."

"But . . . the treatments . . ."

"They're over. You did what you could."

"What about the deliverance session? I haven't gotten together with Eric to—"

Katherine stopped. "To what? To cast out his demon?" She motioned cynically to Sarah's appearance. "You, the mighty woman of God?"

Sarah's face grew hot as she adjusted her dress.

Katherine continued. "You can't even control your own libido, and you think you can get some demon to obey you?"

"I . . ." Sarah stammered, "We didn't . . ."

Katherine turned back to her packing, her voice dripping with disdain. "Please . . ."

The conversation was racing faster than Sarah could keep up. Suddenly she heard herself blurt out, "I love my husband!"

Katherine looked back at her. "You really believe that, don't you?"

Sarah nodded, already feeling tears in her eyes.

Katherine shook her head, then resumed packing. "That just makes you more pitiful than I thought."

"Katherine . . ." It was more plea than argument.

But Katherine continued packing, not looking up. "As I've said before, Doctor, truth is in what we do, not what we say. You say you love your husband, yet you sleep with Lucas Ponte. You tell me which is the truth."

Her stomach was churning again. Brine filled her mouth as she leaned against the frame of the door, swallowing it back.

"Not that I blame you. What woman in her right mind would pass up the opportunity—especially a woman with so much . . . ambition."

Ambition . . . there was that word again. The one that had haunted her all of her life. The reason behind her abortion, her sordid past. The reason she'd become a Christian and tried to start over with a clean slate. Yet, here it was again, raising its head, just as Gerty had warned, just as Brandon had sensed. Nothing she did could free her of it. Katherine was right. How much of her attraction to Lucas was love and how much of it was simply his power? Surely, it was more than coincidence that she happened to have fallen for one of the most influential men in the world.

But Katherine wasn't finished. "You two are cut from the same cloth; you always have been." She reached for the door, making it clear she wanted her privacy. Sarah took a step back. "But be careful, my friend. Lucas Ponte is not as he appears. But then again, I guess, neither are you."

She shut the door, leaving the indictment ringing in Sarah's ears.

To the angel of the church in Sardis write:

These are the words of him who holds the seven spirits of God and the seven stars. I know your deeds; you have a reputation of being alive, but you are dead. Wake up! Strengthen what remains and is about to die, for I have not found your deeds complete in the sight of my God. Remember, therefore, what you have received and heard; obey it, and repent. But if you do not wake up, I will come like a thief, and you will not know at what time I will come to you.

> Yet you have a few people in Sardis who have not soiled their clothes. They will walk with me, dressed in white, for they are worthy. He who overcomes will, like them, be dressed in white. I will never blot out his name from the book of life, but will acknowledge his name before my Father and his angels. He who has an ear, let him hear what the Spirit says to the churches.

Just outside the small village of Sart, the Hall of the Imperial Cult towered fifty, nearly sixty feet above Brandon's head. Of everything he'd seen in Turkey, this reconstructed portion of building with its multiple columns, balconies, and towering brick walls was the most foreboding and intimidating. Part of it was its architecture, part of it was its history. Built during the peak of the Roman Empire, it symbolized the power of the ancient one-world government, and just as importantly, the worship of its leader.

But there was something else that frightened him. He couldn't put his finger on it, but he knew it involved Sarah, it involved himself, and somehow it involved the future. But what did this ancient past have to do with their future?

"I just spoke with Salman."

He turned to see Tanya approach through the grassy field that had once been the Sardis gymnasium.

"How is he?"

"He's in the village. Wants to team up with you again. If you'll have him."

Brandon felt a surge of joy. "Of course I'll have him. I'd love for him to join us."

"So would he. Except . . ."

"Except?"

"His girlfriend from the party is with him. He says she's part of the deal."

Brandon's heart sank just as quickly as it had leaped. He glanced away, then answered softly, "I'm sorry to hear that."

"That's your answer, then?"

"My answer is the same as it was back in Thyatira."

"I told him it would be."

The two grew quiet. Only the wind and the rustling of dry grass broke the silence.

Changing the subject, Tanya finally asked, "Have you been up to the Citadel yet?" She motioned toward the craggy hill across the road and above them.

He shook his head.

"Not much up there, though the history's kind of interesting."

"How's that?"

"About twenty-five hundred years ago the Pactolus River was *the* source of gold in the world. That made the ruler, here, a fellow by the name of Croesus, the richest man on earth. And that's where he stored his riches, right up there in the Citadel."

Brandon looked at the hilltop. As Tanya spoke, he listened carefully. So far every church letter from Revelation had also been related to that city's history or geography. He suspected this would be no different.

"The place was absolutely impregnable," she explained, "except for one small opening in the wall. So Croesus stationed two watchmen there to guard it. Everything was fine, until Cyrus, King of Persia, decided he wanted the ruler's gold. But there was no way to get in and get it. So he brought his army into this valley, and he waited and waited and waited."

"Until?" Brandon asked.

"Until one night both watchmen fell asleep. That's when Cyrus made his move. He broke through the wall, stormed the Citadel, and defeated Croesus, taking all of the man's gold and riches."

"All because the watchmen fell asleep?"

"Exactly."

> But if you do not wake up, I will come like a thief, and you will not know at what time I will come to you.

Immediately Brandon recognized the symbolism. Five hundred years after Croesus, a church at this same location had existed which seemed to have had a rich history of good works. There was no false teaching, no lack of love, and no immorality. Christ had nothing against them . . . except that they had fallen asleep. They had rested on their past accomplishments. Like the two watchmen they had slept when they should have been on duty. And eventually . . . Brandon looked around the ruins . . . *the thief had come to steal.* And now there was nothing.

Again he wondered how similar that was to today's church. He wondered how often good people pointed to past accomplishments as an excuse not to act, as a reason to retire from the battle. But the battle always continues. And, like Cyrus, the enemy is always waiting . . . waiting for us to quit, waiting for us to retire, waiting for us to fall asleep . . . so he can storm the gates.

> Wake up! Strengthen what remains and is about to die, for I have not found your deeds complete in the sight of my God. Remember, therefore, what you have received and heard; obey it, and repent.

The more Brandon thought on this truth, the more he understood. Christian service is not historical fact, it's contemporary action. It is not past glory, it is current doing. Retirement would have to wait until heaven. Because right now the battle continued to rage for the hearts and minds and souls of people God loved more than his own life.

"Brandon . . . Brandon?"

He looked up, returning from his thoughts.

"There's another bit of information you need to know . . . considering Sarah and the Cartel and all."

He couldn't hide the anxiety in his voice. "What's that?"

"The last of the holdout countries has agreed to endorse the Cartel. Seventy-two hours from now, in Jerusalem, the Cartel will be given full authority over matters of world peace. That's when Lucas Ponte will officially be installed as their chairman."

Brandon looked back up at the Hall of the Imperial Cult. Once again, he felt the stirring of the Spirit, the movement of pieces falling into place. He gave an involuntary shudder. Something had been happening. Something under his very nose. And now it was stirring from its slumber.

"Wake up!"

"Brandon, are you all right?"

"It's happening." His voice was barely above a whisper.

"What?"

"The Imperial Cult."

"What are you talking about?"

He swallowed hard and continued. "One world government, one world leader... Ponte and the Cartel, they're coming into power. They're bringing everything to an end, exactly as it began."

"Whoa, wait a minute, now you're sounding like Salman."

He turned to her. "Salman was right."

"What? You're not serious?"

He was as surprised as she was. "It's been staring me in the face all this time, and I just hadn't seen it. About the Cartel, about Ponte . . . Salman was right." Brandon slowly shook his head, amazed at his own thickheadedness.

Tanya continued searching his face. "You really believe that?"

He turned back to her. "I *know* that."

An eerie silence crept over them.

Tanya cleared her throat. "So what are you talking about here? Some sort of Antichrist thing?" She tried to show her scorn, but it came out more as a nervous chuckle.

Brandon answered quietly, "Whoever he is, he will rise up to become the next ruler of the Imperial Cult—he will become the next world . . . god."

"Come on," Tanya scoffed.

Brandon said nothing.

She continued. "Who are we kidding? The people would never allow something like that. They'd never stand for it."

He agreed. "Not if they knew."

More silence, more thinking.

Finally Tanya spoke again. "If you really think it's true, then the people have to be warned. Somebody has to tell them."

Brandon nodded. He knew she was trying to capitalize on the situation, but that didn't stop the pieces from moving about in his mind, from him seeking some way to try and make them fit. She saved him the trouble. "Brandon . . ."

He glanced at her.

"It's you."

The words caught his breath.

"It's you, isn't it?"

He shook his head. "No."

"But—"

"There's nothing I can do."

"But you agree, the people have to be warned. And if you're supposed to be some sort of end-time prophet guy, shouldn't that be your—"

"No . . . I'm not the one." He turned away.

"But if it's true, if you *really* believe it's happening, then somebody has to warn them, somebody has to wake them up."

The phrase spun him back to her, but she had no idea what she'd said. Without a word he turned and began walking away.

"Brandon?"

"No . . ."

She scrambled to his side, doing her best to keep up with his long strides in the grass. "If you seriously believe that, then you need to say it. You need to go public and say it."

He remained silent. He'd "gone public" once before, in Los Angeles. And one disaster like that per lifetime was enough.

But Tanya didn't let up. "Isn't that your job?" He knew full well she was more interested in a story than the truth, but that didn't make her any less right. "Who's going to tell them if you don't?" Nor did it prevent her from going for the jugular. "And what about Sarah, who's going to warn Sarah?"

The question nearly stopped him, but he pushed ahead. "I'm not ready."

"The installation is in three days. When *will* you be ready?"

He gave no answer.

"We could fly to Jerusalem. I could pull a few strings, maybe arrange a public face-to-face. Shoot, we might even be able to stage a debate if—"

"No!"

And still she dogged him. "Okay, then we could make that tape I've been asking for, broadcast it over GBN, and—"

"No!"

"Why not?"

"I'm not the one . . . I can't do stuff like that."

"Brandon?"

"It's not me."

Growing out of breath, she slowed to a stop. "Brandon?"

"Leave me alone!"

"Brandon!"

But he kept walking, practically running, doing anything he could to get away from her. But the truth remained. And it would remain, gnawing away at him the rest of the day . . . and on into the night.

CHAPTER 14

Sometimes death rushes in like a flood, sometimes it trickles in unnoticed. For Brandon both cases were true. The first death, the flood, had hit him with the TV broadcast back in L.A. The trickle death had slowly seeped in as he traveled the villages of Turkey until, suddenly, he was over his head and drowning at Sart. Yes, he had received insight. Yes, he had learned truths to warn the bride. But, at last, he understood who he would have to oppose in order to proclaim those truths. That's when he realized how absolutely unqualified he was.

And that's when he had given up.

It's not that he was rebelling against God. It was just a cold hard fact. There was no way he could step up and take on the world's most powerful organization. Would the Lord be disappointed? He didn't know. But he did know it was not his fault that God had picked the wrong person for the job.

His tears, his protests, and yes, his shouting at the Lord, had continued throughout yesterday afternoon and on through the night. Pacing, yelling, crying, raging . . . until he was entirely spent. Now there was only fatigue . . . and a sad, melancholy peace. There was something peaceful about being dead.

He was sitting on one of a half-dozen stone sarcophagi strewn about the tiny ruins of Philadelphia. Except for an occasional puttering moped on the street behind him and the distant shouts of children playing, the morning was still. The mulberry trees offered shade from the relentless sun as well as a haven for a family of doves cooing in its branches.

Funny, a month ago he'd dreamed about taking on the world for God. Now he realized he was unqualified to do anything except give up. But that was okay. He'd tried, he'd put up the good fight. He simply didn't have what it took. In time, maybe Sarah would return to him, though he wondered what he could possibly offer in comparison to the great Lucas Ponte. In time, someone else would warn the church about her need to prepare for Christ's return. In time, someone else would stand up against this new Imperial Cult.

But it wouldn't be him. That much was certain. For him, it was over. It was painful, yes. It left him numb, of course.

But it was over.

The sun continued to rise and the day grew hotter. More out of habit as well as some curiosity, Brandon eventually pulled out his pocket New Testament and flipped it open to the sixth letter, the one addressed to the church that had inhabited these ruins.

And, after a long pause, he began to read:

> To the angel of the church in Philadelphia write:
>
> These are the words of him who is holy and true, who holds the key of David. What he opens no one can shut, and what he shuts no one can open. I know your deeds. See, I have placed before you an open door that no one can shut. I know that you have little strength, yet you have kept my word and have not denied my name. I will make those who are of the synagogue of Satan, who claim to be Jews though they are not, but are liars—I will make them come and fall down at your feet and acknowledge that I have loved you. Since you have kept my command to endure patiently, I will also keep you from the hour of trial that is going to come upon the whole world to test those who live on the earth.
>
> I am coming soon. Hold on to what you have, so that no one will take your crown. Him who overcomes I will make a pillar in the temple of my God. Never again will he leave it. I will write on him the name of my God and the name of the city of my God, the new Jerusalem, which is coming down out of heaven from my God; and I will also write on him my new name. He who as an ear, let him hear what the Spirit says to the churches.

The words were comforting. There were no rebukes, no commands, nothing that needed to be repented of. Just encouragement and the promise that if he held on to what he had, God would reward him. No problem there—when you've got nothing left, hanging on isn't hard.

There was, however, one phrase that stuck in his mind. He tried to dismiss it, but it kept returning. *"I have placed before you an open door that no one can shut."* Of course the promise could have merely been for the church here, or for today's church in general. But, somehow, he suspected there was more. Then again, what purpose did an open door serve for a dead man with dead dreams and dead hopes?

The answer came back just as clearly, just as sadly . . .

None.

"Brandon . . ."

He glanced up to see Tanya wind her way through the ruins toward him. They'd dropped him off earlier that morning and had left to check into a hotel. He was grateful for the ride from Sart to Philadelphia, but could have done without her continual persistence for him to go to Jerusalem and confront the Cartel . . . or to at least make a video that she could broadcast. On the other hand, Tanya could persist all she wanted. Another nice thing about being dead is, persistence doesn't matter.

"I've got something for you." She approached, waving a piece of paper. "I printed it up from the Internet. I don't recognize the name, but she sent it to you in care of my e-mail."

"She?"

"Yeah." Tanya handed him the paper. "Somebody by the name of Morris—Gerty Morris."

The name startled him, and she saw it. "You know her?"

He nodded, then looked down at the paper she had given him. How could she have known? How, over a year ago, did Gerty know who to send this through to get it to him? Both a chill and a sense of anticipation started to rise in him. It was happening again. He could feel it. The fear. The excitement. Already he was starting to breathe harder. His spirit was quickening. Once again, God was making his presence known. There was no mistaking it. More importantly, He was about to make his will known.

> My dearest Brandon:
>
> This is gonna be my last letter to you. My prayer is that you've made your journey safely and that now you're preparing to be doing battle.

Brandon almost laughed. Prepared to do battle? If there was one time in his life he was unready to fight anybody for anything, it was now. He continued reading:

> 'Cause it's only when you're the weakest and the most defeated, that you're the most pliable in his hands. It's only when your vision is dead, that God's vision comes alive.

Brandon gripped the letter more tightly.

> I have told you of the four steps to fulfilling your dream. First you received it, then you twisted it into your version of greatness, and now, at long last, it's dead. But it is only dead as Abraham's dream of Isaac was dead on the altar, as Joseph's dream of ruling his brothers was dead in prison, as our Lord's dream to save the world was dead on the cross, as Moses' dream of freeing his people was dead when he fled to the wilderness.

The words began to blur from the moisture welling up in his eyes. Were such things possible? Had this been planned all along?

> Unlike Moses, your time in the wilderness was short. But your death is just as thorough. God commanded Moses to throw down his staff so he could transform it. But, just as importantly, he ordered Moses to pick it back up. You are

God's now. Brandon Martus is dead. His dream is dead. His call is dead. No one can be harming or hurting you 'cause no one can harm or hurt a dead man. No one can be killing you 'cause no one can kill a dead man. All that you are is Christ's . . . and all that is Christ's is yours.

Now it is time for the fourth and final step. Now you must be picking up your staff. You have received the call. You have distorted it. You have watched it die. Now, you must let him resurrect it.

He has set an open door before you, Brandon Martus, that no one can close. All you got to do is walk through it. The seed has fallen to the ground and died. Now it is time for it to sprout and bear fruit. Your work is complete. Now, pick up your staff and watch as God completes his.

Good-bye, my brother. I look forward to meeting you again.

GM

A full minute passed before Brandon looked up. He did not bother hiding the tears streaming down his face.

"Hey." Tanya reached out and touched his knee. "Are you okay?"

He nodded and quietly whispered, "Yeah."

"You sure?"

"Yeah." He forced a grin. "For a dead man, I couldn't be better."

Sarah raced across the courtyard. Even from this distance she could hear the screaming. She ran up the outside steps and sprinted toward the men's quarters, not slowing until Eric's room came into view. Outside, a handful of disciples had gathered. Others remained below in the courtyard. Both groups stood in silent concern as, inside, the mother and son were embroiled in a terrible fight.

That's why Katherine had called her. Eric was out of control. He had to be stopped. Given his history of violence, Sarah had grabbed her medical kit, including some Versed, a powerful sedative, and come as fast as she could. The guard stationed outside the door recognized her and stepped aside. Sarah nodded, took a moment to catch her breath, then pushed open the door.

The room was a war zone. Torn posters, broken chairs, even the computer screen was smashed. She spotted Katherine first and then Eric. He was holding two men against a wall by their necks. Their feet dangled just off of the ground.

"Eric!" Katherine was screaming. "Eric, let them go! Eric!" She turned to Sarah, her face wet with perspiration. "I told him we were leaving! I told him, but he refused. He said we're going to Jerusalem!"

Sarah looked at the two men pinned against the wall. Their eyes bulged; their faces glowed a bright red. And Eric, far too scrawny to be exerting this type of strength, was a study of deep concentration.

"You're killing them!" Katherine screamed. "Eric, let go! Eric!"

Sarah took a couple steps closer.

"I brought them in to help us pack," Katherine cried. "That's when he went crazy. Eric!" she shouted. "Eric!" She turned back to Sarah. "It's like he doesn't hear me, like he's not even there!"

Sarah nodded. She'd reached the same conclusion. Eric's rage, his superhuman strength, the look in his eyes. There was no question in her mind that it was time to make her move. She'd seen Brandon do this a half-dozen times at the clinic. Sometimes she'd helped. But this time she was all on her own. She took another breath, then shouted, "Heylel!"

Eric showed no signs of hearing. For the briefest moment Sarah thought she was mistaken. She cleared her throat and tried again, this time with greater authority. "Whoever you are . . . I order you to stop this!" Still no response. "In the name of Jesus Christ, I order you to stop it, now!"

In an incredible display of strength, Eric slowly brought the men down until their feet touched the floor. But he did not let go of their throats. And he still did not acknowledge Sarah's presence.

"Release them completely!" Sarah shouted. "I order you to release them, now!"

The hands withdrew from the throats, and the men slipped to the ground, coughing and gasping for air.

Then, ever so slowly, Eric turned to face her. She braced herself, expecting the worst. She was not disappointed. His eyes locked onto hers with such hatred that she gave an involuntary gasp. His lips curled back into a maniacal grin.

Katherine started toward him. "Eric—"

"No." Sarah held out her hand to stop her. "Don't. That's not Eric." She turned back to the boy. "Are you?"

The grin broadened.

"You're the one they call Heylel, aren't you?"

At last the mouth moved. "Very good." It was still Eric's voice but much deeper and more guttural. "But tell me, Dr. Martus, who exactly are you?"

Sarah swallowed, unsure of the question.

Katherine took a step closer. "What have you done with Eric? Where's my boy?"

The head swiveled in her direction. "At the moment he is preoccupied with more private instruction."

Katherine bristled and took another step toward him. "What are you doing to my son?"

Sarah touched her arm. "Easy . . ."

But Katherine didn't notice. Her voice trembled as she spoke. "What do you want from him?"

"Why, the same as you do, Katherine. I simply want his happiness."

The answer appeared to set her back. "How?" She pointed toward the men rubbing their throats, struggling to their feet. "By using him to destroy people? By turning him into some kind of monster?"

"Oh, but Katherine, he has already become that."

The statement made her shudder. The voice continued. "But you mustn't blame me, my dear. Turning your son into a monster was not my doing. That was the hand of your scientists. I am merely completing spiritually what they had begun physically."

Katherine's trembling grew worse. The voice continued. "It is the perfect marriage, don't you think? Man's desire to become God . . . joining forces with mine?"

Katherine bit her lip.

He continued. "And the two shall become one."

"No . . ." She gasped. "That's . . . my son."

And still the voice continued, relishing the torture. "Not anymore, Katherine Lyon. He is mine."

"No . . ."

"Oh, yes. Your little boy barely exists. He's given me nearly everything. After all, he understands the importance of our goal and—"

"Goal?" Sarah had seen enough. She quickly stepped between the two. "What is your goal? What are you going to do with him?"

The eyes shot to hers. "Why, rule the world, of course."

The candidness surprised her. But he wasn't finished.

"Just as the Christ was the incarnation of your Oppressor, so Eric has become the incarnation of me."

Sarah went cold. "Who . . . who are you?"

"I am the voice of reason, the Illuminated One. I am he who is committed to enlightening your planet and setting it free."

"Free? Of what?"

"Of he who claims love, yet demands holiness. Of he who offers freedom, while demanding servitude."

"You're . . . talking about God?"

"I am speaking of Oppressor. He who cast me from heaven, who imprisoned my host upon your planet."

Sarah caught her breath. She'd encountered several demons but never one who made such boasts. When she finally found her voice, she repeated her question. "Who . . . are you?"

"Oh, but Sarah, you know me." The casual use of her name made her stiffen. "You've always known me." Eric took a half step closer—his eyes focused so entirely upon her, their hatred so cold that she felt an icy embrace wrap around her chest, making it nearly impossible to breathe. "I was there when you put Suzie Burton into the hospital."

"What?"

"You remember . . . that little bicycle incident?"

The comment stunned her. "It . . . it was an accident."

"Yes, that is what you told your parents. That is what you told everybody. But you and I know better, don't we?"

Sarah's face reddened as thoughts of her most embarrassing childhood moment filled her mind. "I was eight years old."

"You were not eight when you cheated your way through calculus to get that scholarship for Stanford."

Shame poured in on top of her embarrassment. "How did—"

"I was there with you and your best friend's boyfriend, in the backseat of his parent's Nova. Remember?"

More memories rushed in . . . along with other emotions—remorse, humiliation. The accusations came faster.

"When you 'borrowed' that money from your mother's purse, when you stole from your employer's till. When you were so drunk at that frat party you didn't even know who or how many young men—"

"Stop it!"

But Heylel didn't stop. The blows came harder and more rapid. "I was there when Harrison was conceived—"

"Harris—?"

"Your baby boy. That's what you were going to name him, remember?"

Sarah was reeling. "I—"

"I was there when you sacrificed him for grad school. I was in the abortion clinic when they reached inside of you—"

"Please . . ." She gasped. "Stop . . ."

"When they grabbed your baby's skull with the forceps—"

"Stop it!"

"When you let them crush—"

"Stop it!" She covered her ears. "I will not listen!"

But the voice was also screaming inside her head. "I was there when you let them kill your baby boy, Sarah! When you sacrificed your only child for your selfish *ambition!*"

There was that word again, like a blow to her chest. And still he spoke, driving each phrase home with a vengeance. "Ambition! That's all you are, Sarah Weintraub. That's all you'll ever be!"

She tried to answer, but she could barely breathe.

"I was there when your ambition nearly killed Brandon, your own husband!"

Mustering all of her strength, Sarah cried, "That's history! I'm a Christian now! I'm forgiven!"

"Are you?"

"Yes . . ." She gasped. The words tumbled out by rote, using the last of her energy. "Christ died on the cross for my sins. I'm forgiven, I'm a new creature in Christ."

"Is that why you drove your husband to humiliate himself on national television? Is that why you destroyed the clinic? Is that why you destroyed your own marriage? Because you are a new creature?"

Sarah had no defense. And still the blows came, so relentless she grew weak at the knees. "Is that why you're here, because you've changed? Is that why you're Lucas Ponte's concubine?"

"Please . . ." She could barely hear herself speak. She could barely think. There was only the voice and its awful truth.

"Is that why you're an adulteress? Tell me, Dr. Martus, is there anybody you won't sleep with to further your goals? Is there anyone you will not prostitute yourself to?"

She shook her head. "I am not—"

"Of course you are. You always have been—you always will be. The whore of Babylon."

Her body convulsed in a stifled sob.

"You have not changed. You never will change. That is why Oppressor selected you. The whore of Babylon. That is what you are. The harlot full of ambition . . . adultery and ambition, that is all you ever will be. Admit it! Who better to symbolize the prostitute! ADMIT IT!"

Another sob escaped.

"Who better to be the whore! ADMIT IT!" The entire room vibrated with his roar. "ADMIT IT! THAT IS ALL YOU ARE. THAT IS ALL YOU WILL EVER BE!

"ADMIT IT!

"ADMIT IT!"

Almost imperceptibly, Sarah began to nod. She could no longer deny the truth. A truth she'd been running from for months, for her entire life. There was no change. She'd tried, but it had done no good. There'd never be change. Not for her.

"Sarah Weintraub. . . ," the voice sneered, spitting out the words. "Liar, cheater, thief, adulterer . . . killer of her marriage, killer of her children, killer of all she touches . . . You're pathetic. Disgusting. You're worse than Eric ever could be. At least Eric is honest enough to admit what he wants. But you . . . the whore of Babylon. THE WHORE OF BABYLON!"

Sarah continued to sob, uncontrollably now. She felt Katherine at her side, heard her speaking words of comfort. But it didn't matter. Words no longer mattered. Truth was truth. There was no hope. Not for her. Not even God could help her. Not now, not ever . . .

The remains of Laodicea were so isolated and so desolate that the mere act of walking through them made Brandon's heart heavy. There were no glimmering marble ruins here, no towering columns or arches. There were only broken-down walls and scattered piles of brick and rubble. There were no trees, not even brush—just one barren hill after another covered in dry, dead grass. For one of the richest cities in the Roman empire, it was now one of the most forsaken. For one of the wealthiest of the seven churches, its physical remains were the least.

The sun had just dropped behind the hills as Brandon stretched out his blanket beside the ruins of what a faded metal sign claimed to have been the actual church building. Earlier he had given in. He had finally agreed that tomorrow he would make the videotape for Tanya. Granted, a tape wasn't exactly the same as standing up to the Cartel in a dramatic confrontation, but it was better than nothing.

That was scheduled for the morning. But tonight, he had just wanted to be alone, to spend time out in these deserted hills, meditating on the last of the seven letters. He had no idea what the future held. Perhaps he'd take Tanya up on her offer to go to Jerusalem. He didn't know.

But that was okay, dead men don't need to know anything. They don't have to do anything. They don't have to be anything.

As the wisdom continued to take root, the peace continued to grow. If there was a battle, it would not be his. If there was a confrontation, it would only be as the Lord directed. He was merely along for the ride.

He reached for his pocket Bible. Although he planned to turn to Revelation, Psalm 37 caught his attention. He glanced down at the first few verses and began to read.

Do not fret because of evil men
  or be envious of those who do wrong;
for like the grass they will soon wither,
  like green plants they will soon die away.

Brandon paused to look out over the hills of dead brown grass. Hills that had once been so full of commerce and life were now withered and dead.

Trust in the LORD and do good;
  dwell in the land and enjoy safe pasture.
Delight yourself in the LORD
  and he will give you the desires of your heart.
Commit your way to the LORD;
  trust in him and he will do this:
He will make your righteousness shine like the dawn,
  the justice of your cause like the noonday sun.
Be still before the LORD and wait patiently for him;
  do not fret when men succeed in their ways,
  when they carry out their wicked schemes.
Refrain from anger and turn from wrath;
  do not fret—it leads only to evil.
For evil men will be cut off,
  but those who hope in the LORD will inherit the land.
A little while, and the wicked will be no more;
  though you look for them, they will not be found.
But the meek will inherit the land
  and enjoy great peace.

"Peace, *great* peace." That was his inheritance. It was not up to him to fret or worry about evil. God would take care of it in his time. He had promised to use Brandon and that was fine, but only as he chose, not as Brandon schemed or planned or worried.

Dead men don't worry.

He rested against one of the ancient stone blocks of the church. Behind him, in the distance, he heard a pack of wild dogs. They sounded like they were near the remains of the Laodicean stadium. He had visited that area a little earlier and had sensed, just as he had in Ephesus and in Pergamum, that such a place would be part of his future, maybe part of his physical death. But that was okay.

Dead men don't die.

Ahead of him stretched one rolling hill after another. He could hear the distant tinkling of sheep bells as a shepherd guided his flock to safety for the night. The symbolism was not lost on him: the barking dogs versus the gentle shepherd protecting his flock from approaching night. And night was approaching . . . faster than he'd imagined. In the dimming light he quickly turned to Revelation, to the final letter to the final church:

> To the angel of the church in Laodicea write:
>
> These are the words of the Amen, the faithful and true witness, the ruler of God's creation. I know your deeds, that you are neither cold nor hot. I wish you were either one or the other! So, because you are lukewarm—neither hot nor cold—I am about to spit you out of my mouth. You say, "I am rich; I have acquired wealth and do not need a thing." But you do not realize that you are wretched, pitiful, poor, blind and naked. I counsel you to buy from me gold refined in the fire, so you can become rich; and white clothes to wear, so you can cover your shameful nakedness; and salve to put on your eyes, so you can see.
>
> Those whom I love I rebuke and discipline. So be earnest, and repent. Here I am! I stand at the door and knock. If anyone hears my voice and opens the door, I will come in and eat with him, and he with me.
>
> To him who overcomes, I will give the right to sit with me on my throne, just as I overcame and sat down with my Father on his throne. He who has an ear, let him hear what the Spirit says to the churches.

It was darker now. And Brandon's heart was heavier. He looked out over the bleak, forsaken hills. It was obvious the church had not paid attention to the warning. According to the guidebooks, there had been a major textile center here—so successful that apparently they had no need for Christ's garments. A medical center so famous for its eye balm that they didn't need Christ to help them see. A church so wealthy that they didn't realize they were "wretched, pitiful, poor, blind and naked." And, because they felt no need to repent, Christ had apparently spit them out of his mouth. As Brandon scanned the stark desolation before him, he wondered how different today's church, in all of its affluence, was. He also wondered how different, if any, its fate would be.

As he thought of today's church his mind drifted to Sarah. Their fates were so intertwined, he saw that now. As always, Gerty had been right. Sarah's actions symbolized a portion of the church—her ambition, her wanderings, her . . . He swallowed back the thought, but knew it was true . . . her adultery. Yet, even this knowledge hadn't stopped his love and longing for her. Nor did he suspect it stopped the Lord's love for his bride. If anything, her unfaithfulness only increased his desire to hold and console her.

With a quiet sigh, Brandon closed the book and stuffed it into his back pocket. He lay down and watched the stars begin to appear. But sleep would not come. Eventually he threw off the blanket and rose to his feet. He started to pace. He started to pray. Before long, he was wandering the deserted hills, praying and pacing.

He prayed as the last light of evening faded . . . and he would still be praying at the first light of dawn.

Sarah sat alone in the dark.

It was her last evening in Nepal. She'd agreed to accompany Lucas and his entourage to Jerusalem. What other choice did she have? Heylel had been right. She couldn't return to Brandon. She was not worthy of him. And this business of being an end-time prophet? Who was she kidding? She wasn't qualified to serve God, she wasn't even qualified to be a Christian. What had Katherine said about actions speaking louder than words? She could claim to be whatever she wanted. But the truth was in what she did. And what she did proved her to be nothing but an ambitious, manipulating . . . adulterer.

"The whore of Babylon"? Not a bad description. But instead of selling her favors for money, she'd held out for a higher currency: power.

She'd not slept with Lucas again; in fact she'd barely seen him. But she knew it was just a matter of time. Word had already spread that the two of them were "an item." Not that it mattered. Not now. Now that she'd finally seen the truth.

Sarah looked around the room. All her bags were packed except for the notebook computer which she'd left charging on the table for tomorrow's trip. But its tiny light was already glowing green indicating its battery was charged. She rose and crossed to it. For the briefest moment she thought of turning it on, of seeing if there was any e-mail from Brandon. But she fought off the temptation. It didn't matter. Not anymore.

She unplugged the power cord and packed it away.

"Okay. Stop tape, please."

For what must have been the hundredth time, the red light went off from Jerry's camera, and for the hundredth time he lowered it from his shoulder.

"I'm sorry, guys," Brandon apologized.

"No, that's okay," Tanya said, though there was no missing the weariness in her voice. "Just take a couple minutes to gather your thoughts and we'll start again. Do you want some water or anything?"

Brandon shook his head.

"Okay, let's just relax a couple minutes then."

Brandon sat on a nearby pile of stones and rolled his head, trying to stretch the stiffening muscles in his neck. They'd been at it all morning, and as far as he could tell they were no closer to getting it right than when they had started. But it was understandable. How do you condense a month's worth of learning into a single speech . . . especially when the person giving the speech doesn't know the first thing about speaking?

Brandon had so much to say, messages from each of the seven letters, and it all wanted to come out at once. From Ephesus, the warning for Christians to return to their first love. From Smyrna, to prepare them for possible persecution. From Pergamum, that they could cut through the distracting voices with the sword of Christ's mouth. From Thyatira, the insistence upon holiness. From Sartis, to wake up and quit resting on past accomplishments. From Philadelphia, the opportunities opening up to proclaim the gospel. And finally, from Laodecia, that wealth and strength will be the church's downfall if she doesn't humble herself and receive Christ's real riches.

And, if that wasn't enough, there was his knowledge of the Cartel—how the organization of peace would eventually turn into another Imperial Cult whose ruler would set himself up to be worshiped as God.

How could someone like Brandon say all of this? Sure, he'd jotted down notes and had practiced, but everything he said still came out jumbled and confused.

"Don't worry," Tanya had assured him earlier, "we can save it in the editing."

Maybe she was telling the truth, maybe she wasn't. Still, it would be nice to get it right at least once.

"Brandon?" He looked up as she knelt next to him. "Can I make a suggestion?"

"Sure, anything."

"I've got bits and pieces of what you're trying to say—"

"I know and I'm sorry. I've got an outline, but—"

"Why don't we try another approach?"

"Another approach? Like what?"

"Do you remember back in L.A. how easy the words came for you, how you said they were like fire?"

He nodded. "They burned so hot I couldn't hold them back."

"So let's do that. Instead of trying to remember everything, just relax and let the fire come."

"I'm sorry, I don't know what—"

"I mean get out of the way. Stop trying to do it on your own."

Brandon frowned.

"You've been talking about being this dead man, right?"

"Right."

"So be dead. Stop trying. I'll tell Jerry to stand by while you pray or do whatever you do. And if you feel this fire stuff starting to come, just let us know and we'll turn on the camera."

"And if it doesn't come?"

"Well, no offense, my friend, but we couldn't be any worse off than we are now." She flashed him a grin, which he couldn't help but return. She patted his shoulder, then rose to go speak with Jerry.

Waves of heat shimmered off the tarmac at Tribhuvan International Airport. The temperature outside was insufferable, but it dropped a good twenty degrees as soon as Sarah stepped into the Cartel's Gulfstream Five corporate jet. Toward the front of the cabin was a plush sofa, a handful of overstuffed swivel chairs, a wet bar, and a large mahogany table. Beyond that was an office meeting area, and past that what looked like quarters for sleeping.

"Sarah." Lucas glanced up from his paperwork and motioned for her to sit in one of the chairs beside him. As usual he was all charm and attention. Gesturing around the plane, he asked, "What do you think? It's on loan to us for a trial run."

She continued looking around the cabin, taking in the rich wood paneling, the communication center behind them with its phones, faxes, and computers, and the royal blue curtains tied back from the windows with gold rope. "It's . . ." She couldn't quite find the words. "Nice. Very nice."

"You don't think it's too much?"

She joined him and took a seat. The upholstery was leather, probably calfskin. "A person could get used to it."

"Good." He grinned. "How was your ride to the airport?"

"A little bumpy. But I'm sure we managed to miss a few potholes along the way."

He chuckled while reaching out and patting her hand. "Well, that shall all be changing. Very shortly we will leave behind the potholes and all the other joys of life in the wilderness."

"You're not going to return?"

He shook his head and sighed. "I don't think so. The work before me is too great. I am afraid the days of semiseclusion have finally come to an end."

Unable to miss the sadness in his voice, Sarah was about to comment when something outside the window caught her eye. A police jeep had pulled up just past the jet's white wing. Two officers had emerged and were now intercepting Katherine and Eric on their walk from the car to the plane.

Eric had won the argument with his mother about remaining with Lucas and the Cartel . . . at least for now. Not that Katherine had much say in the matter. Just the same, she took great pains to stay glued to her son's side every available second. Sarah had barely spoken to her since the encounter in his room. Except for the not-so-subtle warning about getting too close to Lucas, Katherine had returned to her usual distant and aloof self.

Outside, the argument grew more animated. It appeared the police were trying to escort Eric away.

Sarah turned to Lucas. "Do you see this?"

He had returned to his work. "Hmm?"

"The police, it looks like they're trying to arrest Eric."

He glanced over at the window. "You're not serious?"

"Take a look." They watched as the altercation grew more physical, until the officers were actually pulling Eric toward their jeep. "Shouldn't you do something?"

"Mr. Chairman?" An aide knelt at Lucas's side. "The American secretary of state is on the phone."

"Now?"

"Yes, sir."

He rose from his seat and turned to Sarah. "I am afraid I must handle this."

"What about Eric?"

"I think . . ." He gave a slight smile. "I think Eric can take care of himself."

"But—" Sarah motioned toward the window, confused.

"Trust me, he will be fine." And after another smile, Lucas was gone.

Sarah turned back to the window. Now the larger of the two officers was stumbling backwards. He was grabbing his collar, ripping at it, trying to loosen it. Others looked on, not understanding. He motioned wildly, clawing his neck. He stumbled against the jeep, then dropped to his knees, tearing at his throat. His partner raced to his side, shouting, trying to understand what was happening. Other members of the party moved in to try and help.

But not Eric. He had simply turned and started toward the plane again. For the briefest second he glanced up, and his eyes locked onto Sarah's. They were filled with smirking amusement. She looked away and over to Katherine. The woman was ashen white, watching with a hand over her mouth. Sarah turned back to the officer. He was sprawled out on the concrete, his body heaving, gasping for air.

She spun around to Lucas, who was in the communication center, chatting away. He nodded to her with a reassuring smile and continued to speak. She turned back to the window. The officer on the ground had stopped moving. As far as Sarah could tell, he was no longer breathing.

A chill crept through her body. "Eric can take care of himself," he'd said. "Trust me . . . he will be fine."

It had started. Not because Brandon had forced it, or even sought it. It began simply as he thanked the Lord. He started thanking him for the small immediate things—the stark beauty of the rolling hills in front of him, their various shades of brown and gold and beige. The rocks at his feet—their shapes, their colors, their texture. He glanced over at Tanya and Jerry. What wondrous creations they were, each with their unique looks and gifts and personalities—Tanya with her honey blonde hair and perpetual drive, Jerry with his sweating bald top and sullen weariness. What marvelous diversity.

These first few thoughts of thanks were purposely willed by Brandon. But once the pump had been primed, the praise came easier. Soon it was taking on a life of its own. The worship began to blossom, growing until he was caught up in it wholeheartedly. But not just worship over what God had created . . . worship over who God was. His goodness. His faithfulness. His majesty. With the worship came a reverent sense of awe . . . and with that awe came the love.

As he basked in his love for the Lord, he began to feel the Lord's love for him. It became a cycle. A cycle of adoration and love, one for the other, spiraling, drawing them closer and closer into each other, until Brandon was totally and completely immersed. And with the immersion came the spilling over. Unable to contain the love, it overflowed, pouring out from him toward all of creation. Once again Brandon was experiencing the Creator's heart. And with that heart came the fire. It was the same fire he'd seen in the Lord's eyes. The same all-consuming passion.

Tears filled his eyes. But they were not his tears. The love, the gut-wrenching ache was God's—his longing to embrace his children.

And still the fire grew, radiating through his body until it centered in his chest. So much needless pain, so much self-inflicted suffering . . . when all they had to do was listen. The rules were not for him, they were for his children, for their wellbeing. Why wouldn't they see? Why wouldn't they obey?

Tears spilled onto his cheeks. He couldn't stop them. So much love. So much pain. He felt Tanya touch his knee. "Tell us," she said softly, "tell us what you're feeling."

He tried to speak, but the ache was unbearable.

"Tell us . . ."

He looked up. There was Jerry with his camera lens four feet away. But it was no longer just a lens. It was God's children, millions of suffering children who needed their Father, who needed to be held. It was his bride, longing for her bridegroom, aching for his embrace, hungry for the only one who could satisfy her.

A Scripture leaped into his mind, another memory verse. But it was more than a verse. It was alive—filled with the very presence of God, filled with his fire. At last Brandon opened his mouth, and at last he began to speak.

"When I shut up the heavens so that there is no rain, or command locusts to devour the land or send a plague among my people . . ."

He took a ragged breath and continued: "If my people, who are called by my name, will humble themselves . . ."

Other words rushed in. They were not Scripture, but he knew they could be trusted, he knew they came from the fire. "My children! My bride! I have chosen you from before the beginning of the world. You carry my name, yet you do not live my life. Though I have given you power, you have not used it to pursue my holiness. Hear my plea. Heed my warning. Quit seeking your desires, quit seeking your kingdom. Humble yourselves and receive mine. Receive all that I am."

More words poured in and Brandon obeyed, speaking them as they came to his consciousness.

"I am eternal. All else you pursue will burn. You fast in vain. You pray and plead and beg, but your efforts are futile. Look into my eyes and know what is eternal. Only when you behold my glory will your desires conform to mine. Only when you know me can you pray in my name.

"Repent! Turn! I have given you the power to overcome. All you need to do is choose: your wickedness or my holiness, your death or my life. For without repentance there is no forgiveness. And without forgiveness we have no fellowship."

For the briefest second, Brandon caught a glimpse of life without God, and it nearly devastated him. A heaving sob escaped, and it was all he could do to hold back others.

"Humble yourselves!" he shouted. "Seek my face! Turn! Then will I hear from heaven and will forgive your sin and will heal your land. My bride . . . my precious bride." The words choked in Brandon's throat as he realized he was also speaking to Sarah, *his* Sarah. "How my heart yearns for you. How I love and adore you . . . more than I did my very life. How I long for this time of suffering to end, and for the cup of my wrath to be emptied. But you will not have it.

"You try to stop evil by changing others. Yet you do not cease from your own evil. Repent. Repent and turn your heart toward me. Repent and see if there is anything I would withhold from you. My arms are opened wide."

He continued to shout, pleading to the camera, pleading to Sarah, to whomever would listen. He could no longer tell if they were his words or the Lord's. He suspected they were one and the same.

"Turn from your adultery. Let my love break your grip on iniquity. Let my love strip you of your sin. Turn and run into my arms that I may hold you as I once did. Come to me that we may again share the intimacies of husband and wife. That we may again be one."

The final words came heavy and uneven. "For when we are one . . . when you are lost in my arms and when our hearts are intertwined, all of creation watches in awe. When we are one, delighting in each other's pleasure, there is nothing, absolutely nothing you can withhold from me, and nothing I will withhold from you."

Brandon was hit by another set of wracking sobs. And then another. But there were no more words. Just the tears. He lowered his head. He had felt God's presence; he had been consumed by his love and had spoken his words.

Now there was only silence.

PART
THREE

CHAPTER 15

For Sarah Martus the ride from Ben Gurion International Airport to Jerusalem was an eye-opener. In some ways she'd forgotten the worldwide fame of Lucas Ponte, let alone the international importance of the upcoming event. But now, everywhere she looked, there were reminders. There were the crowds standing outside the airport with banners to greet them. There was the fifty-two-kilometer drive to the city with every other streetlight along the highway supporting a different country's flag. And as the motorcade wound its way through the limestone cliffs, there were the honking cars and waving drivers. They had no idea which of the three limos Lucas was in (one of the many Israeli security precautions), so they waved at all of them.

When Sarah had pointed out the fervent devotion, Lucas had shaken his head and smiled. "It's not for me; it's only what I stand for."

"You mean the upcoming peace?" she asked.

"Yes." He sighed with weary satisfaction. "Finally our planet can have some rest."

Sarah nodded. Amidst her own life's turmoil, it was easy to forget the significance of the last few days . . . and the upcoming ones. Still, there was the matter of Eric and her knowledge of who or what he was hosting. And, since there was no place for Lucas to hide or duck the issue inside the limo, she decided to bring it up again.

As always, he listened with great attention. When she had finally finished voicing her concerns he spoke. "And yet, as far as you can tell, Heylel offers no physical danger to the boy."

"That's true. But the psychological trauma for anyone, particularly in these early stages of adolescence, can be devastating. Surely, Katherine has told you what she's seen."

Lucas shook his head. "A few brief remarks, but nothing of substance. Katherine can be quite elusive when she wants to be."

Sarah frowned. "But you knew about the death of his bodyguard? His outbursts of violence?"

"Oh, that. Yes, yes of course. That I knew. That's why we initially invited you to join us."

"And now this incident at the airport."

He shook his head. "Terrible, terrible." He leaned over to his secretary who was brooding over an itinerary in the seat facing them. "Deena, when we get to the hotel be sure to send our condolences to the family."

"Certainly." She jotted down the note.

"Also flowers."

Deena nodded and continued to write.

Sarah watched. What had Katherine said? "He's not as he appears." She was beginning to understand. She saw it on the airport tarmac, and she saw it now. Lucas Ponte, the ultimate statesman—not only had he a gift for saying the right thing at the right time, but he was a pro at keeping his hands clean and avoiding any unpleasant confrontation.

This time, however, she would not give up. "My point is—"

"Oh." He turned back to Deena. "And something for his partner, perhaps a gift reminding him that the Cartel would greatly appreciate his discretion in this matter."

"I understand."

"Lucas?"

He turned back to her. "Yes, Sarah." The sincerity in his eyes was so earnest that she almost believed him. Almost.

"If Heylel is so dangerous," she asked, "to both Eric and to others, why do you keep going to him for counsel?"

"Because he has always proved accurate."

"That's it?"

"Should there be more?"

"He's a killer."

"Lucas?" Deena interrupted. "Excuse me, Sarah." Without waiting for permission, she continued. "You have a meeting scheduled with the vice-chair at 1:15, but if you meet with Premier Orowitz at 2:00 I'm afraid we could create some diplomatic upsmanship. Perhaps it would be better to . . ."

She continued speaking, but Sarah barely heard. It had happened again. The interruption. The sidestep. As they spoke, she turned and looked back out the tinted window. They were in the city now, heading down Jaffa Road. She craned her neck, hoping to catch a glimpse of the Old City, but the buildings blocked her view.

When Deena finally finished, Sarah turned back to him. She would not be put off again. "Lucas?"

He was studying his papers. There was the slightest trace of impatience in his voice. "Yes, Sarah."

"If Heylel is a killer, if he's so dangerous, it seems incongruous that you would work with him toward world peace."

Lucas looked over to her, then broke into a smile. "You know so little of politics."

"I know Heylel is incredibly evil."

"We provide Heylel a service. In return he rewards us with his counsel."

"And that service . . . is Eric?"

"Eric has voiced little opposition, and for his participation Heylel has promised him great things."

"You mean to let him rule the world." Lucas hesitated, and she took advantage of the opportunity. "He's just a boy, Lucas. You're letting a boy prostitute himself for some sort of demonic power. Don't you see it? The Cartel, all of you, you're all prostituting yourselves for whatever information this Heylel has to offer."

"Sarah . . ."

"What about your ethics? What about your ideals, what about—"

"Ideals?"

"Yes, what about—"

"Ideals?"

Sarah came to a stop.

There was the smile again. This time he gently shook his head. "Sarah, Sarah, Sarah. The world is a very hostile place. Ideals are interesting in theory, good for classroom discussion. But I am afraid they don't fare so well in world politics. Take a look out there."

Sarah turned to the window. They were approaching the King David Hotel, and people were lining the street to catch a glimpse of them. Some waved, others clapped.

"These people, they are not interested in ideals. They are interested in survival. They want to live. They want their children to live. And in the end they will do whatever is necessary to make it so. In the real world everyone must pay a price. Everyone must prostitute themselves some way. It's how we survive." He patted her hand. "Prostitution does not have to be an evil thing, Sarah. Surely you understand that by now. You, better than most."

She wasn't sure she'd heard correctly. "Pardon me?"

The car, which had pulled into the driveway of the hotel, came to a stop. "Ah, here we are."

Sarah glanced outside. People were gathered along the driveway. They crowded onto the sidewalk and spilled over to the front yard of the large YMCA building across the street.

The car door opened and a young man in a dark blazer appeared. "Welcome to Jerusalem, Mr. Chairman."

Lucas smiled and turned on the charm. "Thank you . . . Mr. . . ." He paused, waiting for a name.

"Zimmerman, sir. William Zimmerman. I'm head of security."

"Thank you, William." Lucas stepped out of the car, and the crowd broke into cheers. He waved as bodyguards appeared from nowhere and quickly escorted him toward the entrance of the large six-story stone structure.

Inside the car, Deena had gathered her things and stepped outside to follow. But as Sarah scooted across the seat to join her, she turned back and motioned for her to stay put. "You don't get out here."

"I'm sorry?"

"For appearances. It is best you wait until the limo pulls to the service entrance on the side."

"Service entrance?"

She nodded. "We don't want the conservative factions to get the wrong impression, do we?"

Sarah sat stunned.

Deena smiled. "Don't worry, we've secured a suite for you beside Lucas's. I've been told it has a discreet connecting door." Before Sarah could react, Deena smiled and shut the car door. The limo gave a slight jolt and pulled away.

"But you can fight it, I know you can."

"Mom . . ."

"Just like Coleman, remember? You still have free will."

"Mom . . ." Eric watched his mother rise to her feet. She began pacing around the large fifth-story suite that overlooked the Old City.

"Maybe if we were to pray," she offered. "Maybe if we were to ask God—"

"Mom!" The sharpness of his voice turned her back to him. "I don't want him to leave."

She crossed back to him. "Sweetheart . . . it may be exciting now, he may be making all sorts of promises. But eventually, eventually you'll have to pay the price."

"I don't care."

"You don't . . . care?"

He nodded and pushed up his glasses with his little finger. She took a deep breath and eased herself beside him on the sofa. He could tell she wanted to brush the hair out of his eyes the way she used to. He was grateful she didn't try.

"Don't you see?" she asked. "You've become a different person. The sweet, loving Eric I used to know is—"

"That Eric was a wimp!"

"No." The kindness in her voice made him uneasy. "That Eric was sensitive and kind. And he always used his gifts for good. Remember?"

He felt his old weaknesses trying to creep in, and he glanced away.

"Remember how he used to help people? Remember how you healed my face? How you helped that little blind girl at the compound?"

"Tell her." He wasn't sure if it was his thoughts or Heylel's. *"Tell her the truth."*

He rose and moved away from her toward the window. The Old City and its wall rested on the hill just a few blocks away. It had a green hue from the bulletproof glass in front of him. "You don't know what you're talking about."

"I know what I see." Her voice remained gentle.

"We *are* using my gifts for good!"

"Killing that policeman at the airport yesterday?"

"He was in our way."

"And Deepak? He was a good friend, Eric. One of your favorites."

He felt himself faltering. "He . . . he made me mad."

"Eric, sweetheart . . ." She was up again, crossing toward him. "You have to make this thing stop."

"No!"

"Do you want me to take over?" That was definitely Heylel speaking, though the two were becoming so close, it wasn't always easy to tell. And that was the idea—to become so much at one with each other that when he thought, it was Heylel thinking, that when Heylel spoke, it was him speaking.

His mother continued, softer. "I know you love Lucas, but—"

He turned on her. "Love has nothing to do with it! He's been valuable to us in the past, and he'll be even more valuable in the future. Just you wait."

His mother hesitated, then continued. "I know you like the idea of the Cartel listening to you, that it makes you feel important—"

"I am important!"

"—but these people are not good, Eric. They're evil."

"They're going to help us rule the world!"

His mother hesitated. "Maybe. But that doesn't make them good. They've done things, sweetheart. Awful things. And they'll continue to do them. They'll continue to do them until—"

"If you're talking about Scorpion, I already know."

That stopped her. But only for a moment. "You . . . know about it?" Her voice was a little unsteady.

Eric had the upper hand now. It was important to keep it. "Of course."

"You knew that all those people—that the Jews and Arabs—were being murdered?"

"Knew about it?" He let out a short laugh. This would get her. "We told them how they could do it!"

"Eric . . ."

"Sure. Me and Heylel, we drew them the diagrams, we showed their genetic guys how to make it."

She could only stare.

"And that won't be the end of it," he said. "Others are going to try to stop us, and we're going to kill them, too. We'll kill them all. We'll kill anybody who gets in the way. Anybody."

He wanted to keep going, but his mother was already fighting back tears. It was enough for the time being. After all, she was still his mother. At least for now.

If Brandon had been impressed by Turkey's history and culture, he was overwhelmed by Jerusalem's. With a past history thirty times longer than the United

States, the Old City was home to four hundred holy sites, thirty denominations, three Sabbath days, seven alphabets, and fifteen languages. It was a jarring cacophony of life-threatening politics, swarming humanity, fierce prejudice, devout holiness, deep-rooted hatred, and beckoning merchants . . . all crammed within a half square mile of narrow streets and stone buildings. But there was something else here—beyond the history and humanity.

There was the desire to touch holiness.

Brandon felt it no stronger than in the Church of the Holy Sepulcher, the large structure built over what many believe to be the hill where Jesus was crucified as well as the tomb from which he rose. Tanya had dropped Brandon off here while she went to persuade a news producer friend into editing and beaming his taped message back to the States. That had been nearly two hours ago, and Brandon was no more tired of the place now than when he had arrived.

For the first hour he'd been lost, wandering the grottos and carved-out niches staked out by somber-looking clergy of various sects. He choked on the incense and smoking candles, was jostled by the waves of pushing pilgrims, and was amused at the chants and songs of competing clergy all pretending to be oblivious to each other. It wasn't until he'd completely circled the inside of the church and started up the steep nineteen stone steps to Calvary that Brandon started to feel a connection. Even then, it wasn't immediate.

At first, like so many others, he was put off by the gaudy lampstands, the hanging candleholders (attached to nearly every square foot of ceiling), the pretentious amount of gold and silver (including the loincloth of the life-size crucifix looming above and behind the altar), the inlaid pearl, the religious icons, and the intricate mosaics covering the entire ceiling of vaulted arches. In fact, for Brandon, the whole place gave new meaning to the word *kitsch*. If Christ really had been crucified here, why did they have to turn it into such an overindulged spectacle of bad taste?

But as he sat on a worn marble bench against the sidewall, he began to see something deeper. He began to sense the awe and the love here. He saw it in the hundreds of faces parading past the crucifix stuck into the rock. He saw it in the line of those patiently waiting to stoop under the altar and reach into a small hole to touch part of that rock. He saw it in the nuns kneeling, the Greek Orthodox priest meditating, the Armenians moving their lips in whispered unison, the Protestants standing to the side softly singing, a lone Coptic priest silently weeping. He saw it as each attempted, in their own way, to touch the infinite, to express their inexpressible appreciation for what had been accomplished on that hill so many centuries before.

And the longer Brandon sat, the more he understood. He tilted back his head to look up at the mosaic ceiling above him—dozens of stars and angels in a midnight blue sky. Each stone was laid with such care and precision that it actually looked like an intricate painting. The work must have been excruciatingly difficult. Wasn't this all the same? Wasn't this the same as the old black woman who was now being helped down to her knees so she could touch the rock? Wasn't this simply another attempt at trying to embrace God, some way of expressing the inexpressible? And although the pictures, candles, and gaudiness were not his style, just as many of the theologies parading before him were not, Brandon felt their reverence, awe, and love.

And, as he felt their love, he sensed a deeper Love returning.

Feeling God's love and sensing his presence were happening more and more for Brandon. Now that he'd given up his own life, he was more open to experiencing God's ... no matter what form it came in. He found it interesting that he was no longer concerned about affirming his own views of Christ. In fact, the more he lost himself in Christ's love, the more he realized his views didn't matter. All that mattered was Jesus Christ. Not Brandon's theology, not Brandon's ministry. God would advance these as he saw fit. All that mattered was Jesus Christ and him crucified. Everything else was vain ... as vain as the debate over which brand of worship here was better ... or which type of art was the most tasteful.

As he felt God's love, he felt the fire—the burning desire to draw each of these children into his arms. To encourage them to bask and soak and drink in as much love as they could. Because there was no end to it. The love for each was infinite. And there was no spot on earth where that love was more apparent than here.

Here, where the God of the universe unleashed his wrath upon his Son. Here, where at any moment, the Son could have cried, "Enough, let them suffer their own punishment!" Here, where, sin by sin, anguished torture upon anguished torture, the Son received full punishment for each of our failures ... where, for six excruciating hours, all of creation watched in stunned silence as the human race, who had once sold itself into slavery, was being repurchased.

Such love. Such infinite, unfathomable, indiscernible love. That was the love that saturated Brandon and fed the fire. And that was why here, on this tiny hill, in this noisy, eclectic sanctuary, Brandon closed his eyes and began to pray for the bride. For God's bride ... and his own.

Sarah sat naked on the edge of the white Jacuzzi, staring at the water as it filled the tub. She was drunk. She'd been drunk for hours. A fully stocked bar was one of the perks in the VIP suites. She had taken a fancy to the Coke and Puerto Rican rum. She'd hoped it would silence the voice, the one she'd been hearing to some degree or another ever since the encounter in Eric's room at Nepal. The one she'd first heard on her wedding day ... *the whore of Babylon!* But it did not. Instead, the more she drank the louder it grew ... and the more relentless it became. *Adultery and ambition, that is all you are!*

In Nepal she'd been able to drown it out with the preparations for Jerusalem, with the excitement of the installation, and with the love and respect she had felt from Lucas. But now ... *Prostitution ... surely, you understand better than most.* That was yesterday afternoon, the last time she'd seen him in person. He'd been in meetings ever since.

For whatever reason, security thought it was best she not leave the hotel, at least until after the installation. So with Lucas gone and Katherine making a point to stay cloistered in her room with Eric, Sarah was left pretty much on her own.

Except for the voice. *You have never changed, you never will.*

She'd tried the TV, but all she seemed to see was Chairman Ponte speaking with some president, Chairman Ponte talking with this group, Chairman Ponte offering assurance to that group. Anticipation for tomorrow's installation was high, and rightfully so. With the Cartel pulling strings behind the scenes and pressing for last-minute favors, it looked like it would be the international event of the decade. And her boyfriend was right in the center. But for now he was the last thing in the world she wanted to see. Not since the little incident out on the terrace.

She'd been sunning herself at the hotel's pool, one of the few distractions she'd found since she'd arrived. She'd already lost track of the number of glasses of Chardonnay she'd put down when she spotted Lucas dining up on the terrace. He was chatting with a handful of Hollywood celebs. Big names. So big that she thought strolling up to the table and meeting them would be interesting—especially since their talk didn't appear to be too official—especially since one of the actresses seemed to be becoming a bit too affectionate.

Sarah pulled herself from the lawn chair, waited for the ground to stop moving, then placed one foot in front of the other and headed toward the terrace. She'd barely made it halfway when Lucas spotted her. She smiled. But, without even acknowledging her, he glanced to one of the security men and discreetly nodded in her direction. Taking his cue, security quietly crossed the lawn and cut her off.

"May I help you, Doctor?"

"I'm going up to say hi."

"I don't think that's such a good idea. Chairman Ponte is preoccupied at the moment."

"No, he's not. He's right there." She tried to pass him, but the man blocked her.

"I'm sorry, ma'am, he's asked not to be disturbed."

"What?" The ground had started to move again. "Do you know who I am?"

"Yes, I know exactly who you are."

"Then you'll let me by."

Again she tried to move around him, and again he blocked her. "I am sorry, Doctor."

She raised her voice louder. "I want to see Lucas. Let me by."

"Doctor, maybe you should go back to your room."

"Lucas!" she waved her hand. "Lucas!"

Other tables glanced in her direction, but not Lucas. He became more engrossed in his discussion.

"Lucas!"

"That's enough, Doctor." The security man motioned to one of the dining guests, who immediately rose to his feet and joined them. "Show Dr. Martus to her room, will you please?" The "guest" nodded and took her arm.

"But that's . . ." Sarah tried to twist free. "Lucas and I, we're, we're . . ."

"I know what you are," the security man answered. "Good day, Doctor."

The guest began leading her around the terrace and up toward the hotel. She tried to break free, but his grip was like iron. "Lucas! Lucas!" Other tables turned and stared. By now she'd drawn nearly everyone's attention. Everyone but Lucas's. He continued talking and laughing in perfect oblivion.

That had been forty minutes ago.

Sarah turned to the bathroom counter behind her and poured the last of the rum into her glass. When she set the bottle down, she missed the counter and it crashed onto the marble floor, sending shards of splintered glass in all directions. She looked down, startled at her own clumsiness, then felt the tears coming to her eyes.

Can't you do anything right?

She closed her eyes, but the voice continued. *You can lie. You can cheat. You can kill.*

"I know exactly who you are, Doctor." That's what the security guard had said. And maybe he did. But did she?

Adulterer.

I know exactly what you are, Doctor . . .

Behold, the Whore of Babylon!

And she was learning more and more who the great Lucas Ponte was as well . . .

Be careful, he's not all that he appears.

She'd seen it before, but had done her best to deny it. Lucas Ponte . . . master of charm, perfecter of politics. Wasn't it interesting how once they'd slept together he had never again mentioned his offer for her to join the team? Wasn't it interesting that he was always insulated from the dirty work of power? Wasn't it interesting how he always pretended to listen, but how he always got his way . . . even when it came to Eric . . . even when it involved the young man's destruction?

No, Lucas Ponte was not as he appeared.

But, then again, neither are you.

Liar . . . Baby killer . . . Adulterer . . . Whore . . .

She looked back to the water in the tub. Is that really what she'd become? The great Sarah Weintraub, doctor, cutting-edge neurobiologist, end-time prophet . . . now reduced to nothing but an elaborate call girl?

"Brandon!" The name surprised her. It came deep from her gut before she could stop it. "Bran . . . don . . ." But even Brandon couldn't help now. No one could. Naked and all alone, Sarah lowered her head and tried to cry tears of self-pity. But they would not come. There was no pity. Not anymore. It was hard to pity someone you hated so deeply.

CHAPTER 16

I tell you, kiddo, it's the biggest broadcast I've ever been a part of. We've got downlinks in nearly every country. In theory we could be reaching every household with a television in the entire world."

"If those households are interested in tuning in," Tanya corrected.

"Oh, they'll be interested. With the promos and all the past coverage on Ponte, they'll think it's the media event of the century."

Tanya looked at Ryan Holton skeptically.

"See for yourself." He motioned to the row of monitors along the top of the wall of the Channel Two newsroom. They monitored the competing channels beamed in from other countries. Except for one screen showing the latest volcano disaster in the Philippines, and another playing a fabric softener commercial, all others were broadcasting various aspects of Lucas Ponte's visit to Jerusalem or commenting upon the upcoming installation.

Tanya whistled softly. "The Cartel's doing all this?"

Ryan nodded. "They're twisting some pretty heavy arms. Every major network in the world is being 'encouraged' to support this 'pivotal moment of world history.'"

"That's how it's being promoted? A little rich, isn't it?"

He shrugged. "The people are eating it up."

Tanya looked out across the newsroom. A dozen reporters, all under thirty and most chain-smoking, were typing at computer terminals or working the phones. Israel had basically two major networks. Channel One, run by the government, and Channel Two, which was owned and operated independently. The latter's facilities filled the entire ninth floor of the impressive Egged Building on Jaffa Road. On the outside the building looked modern and impressive. On the inside it was purely functional. Worn carpeting, low ceiling, fluorescent lights, and grimy white walls. But Channel Two was the best. And that's why Ryan Holton had chosen to use their services. Because he was the best.

Tanya had fallen in love with Ryan's good looks and sharp intelligence right out of college. And, despite their breakup two years later, she knew a part of her would always love him. But he wanted a family and she wanted a career. Then there was her faith. Not that it prevented them from living together for nearly ten months. Still, she claimed to be a devout Christian. And Ryan—well, Ryan's only devotion was to being a great TV producer/director and a faithful friend. He had succeeded in both.

Tanya stared up at the various screens showing Ponte meeting this dignitary, Ponte visiting this site, Ponte chatting with this common person. According to Ryan, the images were being broadcast all around the world. "These guys are good," she conceded. "Very, very good."

Ryan nodded. "They've got the power, kiddo, and they know how to use it. You should see what they're letting me do for the broadcast. I've got twelve cameras with live feeds from around the world. Endorsements from Moscow, the Vatican, Washington, that sort of thing. Another half dozen for immediate man-on-the-street responses, and fourteen stationed around the Temple Mount where I'll call the show."

"They let you bring remote trucks onto the Mount?"

"No, the trailers are parked just outside the Wall. We had to string cable over it *and* the cemetery beside it. But they're letting me bring in a couple Jumbotron screens so the crowd at the back of the Mount can see what's happening up onstage."

"Sounds like you've got your plate full."

He flashed her a smile. "Just the way I like it."

Another pause settled over the conversation. Nearly eighteen months had passed since they'd last touched base. She hadn't even known about his divorce, though she suspected it coming. And as far as his looks went? The more worn and weathered he became, the more handsome it made him.

He tapped the tapes she'd handed him. "You say this kid is the one who ruined your show in L.A.?"

"Yeah. Any chance of scoring some time in one of these edit suites?" She motioned to the cramped rooms behind them. "Turn Jerry loose on an Avid so we can put together something for broadcast?"

Ryan broke into a mischievous grin. "Payback time, huh?" Before she could respond, he asked, "Did you know your boss is in town?"

"Jimmy Tyler?"

"Yeah, he's staying over at the Hyatt. During the ceremony he'll be one of the dignitaries on the platform. Not that he'll be doing much talking." Ryan glanced back to the tapes in his hand. "So what you're looking for with these is a little eye for an eye, am I right?"

Tanya shook her head. "Not really. Actually, I believe there's something legit about him."

"You're not serious?"

She nodded. "He's young, and he's made his share of mistakes, but what I saw in Turkey and what I have on tape proves he's not some religious con artist. And he's definitely not a fruitcake. I think he just might be the genuine article."

"A prophet crying in the wilderness?" Ryan teased.

Tanya shrugged, doing her best to maintain her skepticism. After all, that was a reporter's stock-in-trade. "The kid's got a lot to say . . . I just think somebody should give him the opportunity to say it."

Ryan held her look a moment, then glanced down at the tapes. "We've booked time on all their Avids until after the installation."

"Prerecorded segments during the broadcast?"

He nodded, then referred back to the tapes. "What do you have, about three hours here?"

She nodded. "I'm looking for an eight-, maybe ten-minute piece when it's completed."

"Do you mind working at night?"

"Hey, we'll take what we can get."

"Send Jerry up. Have him start digitizing them. Once they're loaded I can give up one of the machines."

Tanya broke into a smile. "Thanks, Ryan."

"No problem, kiddo."

"What do I owe you?"

"This one's on the Cartel."

"You're serious?"

"Sure." He grinned, then added good-naturedly, "'Course it might cost you some drinks with me when you're done. Maybe stop by the hotel . . . we've got plenty of catching up to do."

Tanya knew what he meant, and she was not offended. After all, they were both single again, and he *was* looking pretty good. But she'd already planned her answer. "I don't think so, Ryan." There was a flicker of surprise in his eyes, and she explained, "Don't get me wrong, there's nothing in the world I'd rather do than spend the night catching up on old times."

"But?"

"You know my faith, my religion."

He looked perplexed. "It never stopped you before."

"You're right." She inhaled, then let it out. "But, this kid. I don't know. After listening to him . . ." She dropped off, trying to find the right words.

"He really got to you, huh?"

She looked up at him, then slowly nodded. "Yeah . . . he really got to me."

As Brandon remained in the church praying, a deeper urgency began to rise up within him. At first he thought it was coming from the old Brandon Martus, the dead one, the one trying to make him worry and draw him away from the presence of God. This sort of thing happened frequently, but he was getting used to its tricks. In fact, he'd learned a few of his own. He'd discovered the best way to keep the old man dead was by focusing upon Christ. He discovered if he filled his mind so full of worshiping and dwelling upon him, he could literally force the old thoughts to flee. Sometimes this would take ten seconds, sometimes ten minutes, but if he persisted, it always worked. He could enter the presence of God and remain until the Father's thoughts became his thoughts.

Except for now.

Now, the more he dwelled upon Christ, the more his thoughts filled with Sarah. He bore down harder, closing his eyes, concentrating upon Jesus' grace, his tenderness, his glory. And yet the thoughts of Sarah continued to grow and expand. An idea began to take shape. Was it possible that the reason he couldn't remove the thoughts of Sarah was because they were the thoughts of the Father?

Eyes still closed, he sensed a difference in the light striking his face. Somebody had approached and was standing in front of him. He heard faint, labored breathing, but kept his eyes shut and continued to pray. Then he heard the brush of clothing and felt something touch his arm. He opened his eyes and saw a frail old woman leaning toward him. She was hunched over and wore a loose dark brown dress and a cream-colored Palestinian head scarf. Her face was leathered and grooved from decades of sun, and her once-blue eyes were watery gray from cataracts.

She patted his arm again, this time motioning for him to rise and follow her.

He smiled, but indicated that he was praying.

She took his arm. He looked down at her hand. It was mostly bone and blue veins. She pulled, motioning that he must come with her. Her grip was weak but persistent, and when he looked back into her eyes, he sensed how important it was for her that he obey. Finally, reluctantly, he rose from the marble bench.

She did not release her grip, but continued to pull. She hobbled toward the steep steps and started down them, relying on him for balance, until they reached the main floor of the church. Once there, she turned and started toward the exit.

"Whoa, wait a minute." Brandon brought them to a stop. "I have friends. They are coming to pick me up."

She paid no attention and continued to pull, motioning for him to follow.

He spoke again, louder and slower. "I must stay." He indicated the church. "Here. I must stay here."

She shook her head and continued to pull. It was obvious the woman would not let up until she got her way. Brandon scanned the crowded church, making sure Tanya had not already arrived. When he didn't see her, he looked back at the woman's anxious eyes. Finally he agreed to follow.

They stepped through the wooden door and into the blazing bright courtyard. He winced at the sunlight reflecting off the limestone pavement and buildings. She led him to the right, up the steps, and out onto St. Helena, a narrow street. Fifty yards later they turned left onto Christian Quarter Road. Like all the other streets and roads in the Old City, it was a crowded walkway jammed with small shops hawking everything from onions to leather coats, Turkish delight, batteries, dried dates, blue jeans, pistachios, and a thousand and one tourist trinkets—from cheap olive wood chessboards to holographic pictures that changed from Jesus to Mary and back to Jesus again as you walked past.

And still the woman pulled, tirelessly, treading up the worn stones until they turned right again, past more shops, and eventually arrived at a square just inside Jaffa Gate. A square big enough for a few cars.

"Taxi?" A driver called out. "Taxi?"

Brandon shook his head.

They continued through the square toward the towering wall of giant stone blocks. The woman was puffing now, struggling to breathe. Brandon tried to slow her down, indicating that she should sit on one of the benches and catch her breath. But she would not stop. They stepped through Jaffa Gate and out into the new city.

And still the voices accused.

Failure! Destroyer! Whore!

As Sarah's hopelessness grew, her need to be near the one person who had ever given her hope increased. She struggled to rise from the edge of the tub. Her first unsteady step ended with a sharp burn. She looked down to see a jagged piece of the broken glass cutting into her right heel. She watched the dark blood spread out onto the white marble. But it didn't matter. She continued walking, stepping on other pieces of glass, hearing them pop and snap under her bare feet, feeling the sharp pain as they tore into her toes, her arches, her heels. But it didn't matter. In fact, it almost felt good, proof that the universe was still a sane place that demanded justice.

She staggered into the bedroom, leaving bloody footprints on the beige carpet. Some of the glass remained stuck in her feet, but it didn't matter. She arrived at the dresser and pulled open the bottom drawer. She dug through the cloths until she found it. Brandon's shirt. She pulled it out, sending the other clothes tumbling to the floor. She slipped it on. Of course the smell was gone, but there were still the memories.

She hugged herself, holding it close, shutting her eyes and imagining it to be Brandon's embrace. She wasn't sure how long she stood, lost in his goodness, his kindness, his love. It had been the happiest time in her life, in both of their lives. Until she had ruined it . . .

Adultery and ambition, that is all you are!

"No!" she whispered harshly.

Liar!

"No!"

Cheater!

"Stop it!"

Thief! Murderer!

She wrapped her arms tighter, holding Brandon's shirt closer. But the comfort had already faded. There was nothing he could do. Nothing anyone could do. For the briefest second she thought of praying. But she'd failed at that, too.

You have never changed, you never will.

It wasn't God's fault. It was nobody's fault . . . but hers. Like everything else, she was the one to blame.

Killer! Adulterer!

She lowered her head, but the tears still did not come. Now there was only the self-hatred, the accusing voice, and the unbearable pain. These were things no one could stop.

Or could they?

She turned. With unsteady steps, she shuffled back toward the bathroom. A plan was beginning to form.

Baby killer!

There was a way to silence the voice. There was a way to stop the pain.

By now the water was pouring over the top of the tub, mixing with the blood on the marble and darkening the carpet where it soaked. Another mess of her making.

She sloshed across the floor, her feet finding another piece of broken glass before she arrived and turned off the water. Now everything was quiet. Strangely still, except for the echoing drip of the faucet. And the voice.

Stooping down, she rummaged through the pieces of glass until she found just the right one—blunt at one end, razor sharp at the other. There was a way to stop the pain and the voice. And, as a doctor, she knew the least painful and most effective way to do it. Holding onto the tub for balance, she rose back up and then stepped into the water. For the briefest moment she started to remove Brandon's shirt, then thought better of it. It was all she had left. And she needed him now more than ever.

She lowered herself into the water, sending more of it spilling over the side and onto the floor. But it didn't matter. No one would know. The Cartel would see to that. It would be too much of an embarrassment. But, then again, she was always an embarrassment.

She looked at the water. It was turning pink from her bleeding feet. She looked down at her wrists. This much she could do right. After all, she was a doctor. Taking the piece of glass in her right hand, she lowered her left arm into the warm water. There was barely any pain as she expertly opened the vein. She switched the glass shard to the other hand and slit open the other vein. Darkness spread into the water.

Sarah set the glass on the side of the tub. As she scooted down into the water, more sloshed onto the floor. But that was okay, everything would be okay. All she had to do was wait. She pulled Brandon's shirt tighter around her body and drew his collar up around her face. This is how she would go to sleep. This is how she would die. Dreaming of Brandon, of all that they had, of all that they could have been.

"Mom," Eric whined from inside the limo. "Lucas is already there. Come on."

"Right, honey, just a second." Katherine stood in the open car door. Lucas had sent word for Eric to join him as he reviewed the preparations at the Temple Mount before tomorrow's installation. They were just leaving when a slight commotion in front of the hotel caught her attention. A young man and an old Palestinian woman were being blocked from entering by two plainclothes security. Normally such a scene wouldn't concern her, but there was something vaguely familiar about the man, and she felt drawn to check it out.

"Mom!"

"I'll be right back." She turned from the limo and walked briskly toward the entrance. "Excuse me," she called. "Excuse me, is there a problem?"

The young man looked at her. He was in his mid-twenties. And, although the face was unshaven and his hair closely cropped, she recognized the steel gray eyes instantly. They were the same eyes from the photos Sarah had shown her. "You're Dr. Martus's husband?"

He was surprised at the recognition and nodded. "Yes, I'm Brandon Martus. And you're—"

"You know these people, Ms. Lyon?" the older of the two security guards asked.

"Yes, I . . ." Katherine glanced back at Brandon. "This is Brandon Martus, Dr. Martus's husband." There was no missing the glance between the two guards. They'd all been briefed on Sarah's relationship to Lucas.

She turned back to Brandon. "You're here to see Sarah."

"Is she here?" He sounded surprised.

"Of course."

"Mom!"

Katherine glanced back at the limo. Eric was growing agitated. If she didn't hurry, he could have another outburst. She turned to the older guard and asked, "You'll see to it Mr. Martus gets to her room?"

The guard fidgeted. "Ms. Lyon, I'm not sure if he's cleared security for—"

"He's the woman's husband."

"Yes, I can appreciate that, but—"

"Mom!"

"Certainly a man's entitled to see his own wife."

"I agree, but—"

She heard a car door slam and turned to see the limo begin pulling away. "Eric!" She started after him. "Eric, wait a minute! Eric!" The car picked up speed. "Eric!" She ran a half-dozen steps before slowing to a stop. The limo pulled out of the driveway and onto King David Road, where it took a right and disappeared down the street. Frustrated and angry, Katherine turned and stormed back to the group.

"He'll be okay," the guard said as she arrived. "We've got two of our best people with him."

She gave him a look, then called out to the doorman, "Order me a taxi."

The older guard shook his head. "Can't do that."

"What?"

"Not until we get you some security."

"Then get me some!"

"It will take at least thirty minutes."

"Then do it," she snapped. Spotting Brandon and the old lady still waiting, she asked, "So are you going to get them up to see Dr. Martus or not?"

The older guard hesitated, not wanting to upset Katherine any more than she already was.

"Well?" she demanded.

More hesitation.

"Ponte's not even here! What's the risk in taking this man up to see his own wife?" she demanded.

Finally, reluctantly, the guard turned to his partner and motioned toward the entrance. The partner nodded and escorted them to the door, but not before the older guard called, "He can go, but not the old woman."

"What?" Katherine turned to him.

"Not the old lady."

"She's obviously a friend."

"Not the old lady," the man repeated.

Katherine realized it was a power play, the only way for the guard to save face. But before she could continue, the old woman produced a business card on paper-thin stock. She handed it to Brandon, pointing to the card, then to herself.

"What's this?" Brandon asked.

Again, she pointed.

"It's her home," the guard answered in mild irritation.

Brandon frowned. "I don't understand."

"It's an invitation. If you don't have a place to stay she's offering her home." The guard motioned her toward the street and ordered something in Arabic. She nodded, but before she turned to leave, Brandon reached out and took her hand.

He spoke loud and slow. "Thank you."

She patted his arm, gave a semitoothless smile, and pointed toward the heavens. Brandon understood and nodded.

Once again the guard ordered her to leave. This time she obeyed, turning and starting to shuffle down the driveway toward the road. Katherine watched as the younger guard ushered Brandon through the large revolving door and into the hotel. She hesitated a moment, glanced at her watch, then turned to the first guard.

"Thirty minutes?"

He nodded.

She sighed in frustration. "Call me," she said, then turned and followed the other two inside. The lobby was two stories of yellow marble, dark wood, brass, and freshly cut flowers. The floor was made of long, alternating slabs of green and yellow marble. Along the walls were portraits so dark and indiscernible that Katherine figured they must have cost a fortune. Not that she cared. All she cared about was getting back to her son.

She caught Brandon's elevator just before the door closed and rode up with him and the security guard. It was there in the privacy of the small elevator that the guard motioned to Brandon with upturned palms. "May I?"

It took a moment until Brandon suddenly understood. Without a word he raised his arms and the guard quickly, but expertly, ran his hands over his back, chest, and sides, then down each of his legs.

"Thank you."

Brandon nodded as Katherine continued to watch. He was a good-looking kid, intriguing. Then there were those eyes. Sarah was right when she'd said there was nothing they didn't see. And when they caught her evaluating him, even she felt the slightest bit uneasy, as if he was somehow able to see into her.

She cleared her throat. "I take it Sarah isn't expecting you."

"No, I uh . . . no." He was nervous, and for good reason. She wondered if he had any idea what he was walking into.

"My name is Katherine. Katherine Lyon."

"Eric's mom?" The eyes were kind, but still probing.

"Yes."

"How is he?"

"He's okay. He's fine."

She tried to hold his look, but couldn't. He obviously knew she was lying. It was time to change the subject. "Sarah's . . . she's been going through some tough times."

His answer was quiet and full of understanding. "I know."

She looked at him, wondering how much he did know. The elevator came to a stop and the doors opened onto the hallway of the sixth floor. This was the location of the Royal Suite, the suite in which nearly every visiting head of state had stayed in the past fifty years. Deciding to tag along, Katherine stepped out of the elevator and followed the guard as he escorted them down the hallway of plush blue carpet and dramatically lit limestone arches. In the center of the hallway to the right was a white tiled door with a guard posted on either side. Each was armed with an Uzi. They passed the two guards, who gave stoic nods, and then approached a door another twenty feet further down the hall.

When they arrived their escort knocked loudly. There was no answer. He tried again. The result was the same. He turned to Brandon and gave a shrug.

But Katherine would not be put off. "I guess he'll have to wait inside until she returns."

The guard gave her an uneasy look.

"You do know the security code, don't you?" Katherine asked.

He nodded.

Katherine sighed heavily, trying her best to intimidate him—no easy job since he was Israeli. "Then will you please open the door so this man can go in and wait for his wife?"

The guard hesitated.

"You see how dirty he is."

More hesitation.

"Look, I take full responsibility. Just let him in there and get cleaned up before she arrives." Unable to clearly read him, she set her jaw more firmly. "Either that . . . or we go down, drag up your boss, and waste even more time that you fellows obviously don't have."

She held his gaze, unblinking. Finally, more in irritation than compliance, he reached for the keypad and pressed four buttons. The door clicked and he pushed it open. Brandon entered, followed by Katherine. The guard said, "We'll call you when a car is available," then turned and headed back down the hall.

Almost amused, Katherine shut the door and turned to Brandon. "Well, that went rather—"

But he'd noticed something off to his right. She followed his gaze to the carpet leading to the bedroom. It looked like footprints. "What on—"

"Sarah?" He sprinted into the room. "Sarah!" He turned right, following the stains into the bathroom.

Katherine was right behind him. The best she could tell, the footprints looked like blood. Then she saw the soaked carpet near the bathroom entrance and the rose-colored water on the bathroom floor. She heard splashing as Brandon reached into the tub and then she saw him rise up, holding Sarah's limp body in his arms. The young woman's face was the color of snow. She wore a blue work shirt stained crimson, the same color as the water streaming down her pale white legs and arms. And then she saw the wrists.

Brandon carried the dripping body past her. "Sarah . . ." he cried softly. "Oh, Sarah." He brought her to the bed and laid her down. "Sarah . . . Sarah, can you hear me? Sarah!"

Finally Katherine could move. She crossed to the bed stand and picked up the phone.

He looked up. "What are you doing?"

"I'm calling the front desk for a doctor."

"No."

The response surprised her. "What?"

"Not yet."

"She needs help."

"Not yet."

Katherine hesitated, not understanding—then she started to dial.

Brandon's hand shot to her arm and gently held it. "Please . . ."

"If we don't call now, she'll—" That's when she felt the heat from his hand. She looked down. It was wet with water and blood. But the palm felt like fire. She looked back up at him.

"Please," he asked, "just give me a few seconds . . ."

She knew she should refuse. But there were those eyes. They were full of absolute knowing, of intense passion. Against her better judgment, she slowly lowered the phone.

Brandon turned back to Sarah. He'd already pulled one of her arms from the wet shirt. Now he removed the other, bringing the sliced, bleeding veins into full view. Katherine winced at the sight, but Brandon barely seemed to notice. Instead, he began applying pressure to the wounds. But on closer look Katherine saw he wasn't applying pressure. He was merely holding them.

She looked back up at him. His eyes were closed and his lips silently moved. She looked down at the arms. Was it her imagination, or had the flow of blood stopped? She tilted her head for a better look. As best she could tell the wounds under his hands were no longer bleeding. It was amazing. But that wasn't all. Because as she watched, Katherine saw something even more astonishing.

At first she thought it was an illusion, the play of light and shadow on Sarah's arms. But it wasn't. Instead, the collapsed veins, the very ones Brandon was holding, actually began to swell. Not a lot, just enough as if they were filling back with blood. The swelling continued to move up her arm, until it began branching out into other vessels. And, as Katherine watched, she could actually see color returning to the arms, then the shoulders and chest.

"That's incredible," she whispered. "What are you doing?"

Brandon didn't answer. His eyes remained closed and he continued praying.

She looked back down. The color was moving into Sarah's abdomen now, then her thighs, and up into her face. She could actually see the arteries in the woman's neck plumping up. The process continued, lasting well over a minute, until Brandon was finally done. At last he opened his eyes. And when he removed his hands, wiping the sweat from his forehead, Katherine saw another amazing fact. The cuts in both of Sarah's arms were gone. Completely.

"Let's get her under the blankets," Brandon said.

Katherine nodded. She pulled back the sheet and blankets while Brandon slipped her under the covers. But Sarah's head had barely touched the pillow before her eyes began to flutter . . . then slowly open.

Katherine touched his arm. "Look . . ."

He already saw.

It took several seconds for Sarah's eyes to focus. When they did, she recognized Brandon smiling down at her and closed them again, obviously thinking it was a dream. But this was no dream. When she reopened them, he was still there, still smiling.

Her lips quivered, trying to smile back.

Katherine glanced up at Brandon. He was practically beaming.

Sarah tried to speak.

"Shhh," he whispered. He brushed the matted hair from her forehead. "Just rest."

"I thought . . ." Her voice was a breathy crackle. "I thought I'd never see you again."

He grinned. "You were wrong."

Tears filled her eyes. "Bran . . ."

"Shhh . . . I'm right here."

They streamed down her cheeks and onto the pillow. "Don't leave me . . ."

"Shhh . . ."

"Please . . ."

He bent down and kissed her forehead. Then he rested his face on the pillow beside her. He was crying, too. "I won't leave you," he whispered, his own voice breaking. "I won't ever leave you."

Sarah gave a faint smile. Then she closed her eyes and slept.

CHAPTER 17

In some ways Sarah felt like they had never been apart—as if her loathsome behavior were from some other life, from some other Sarah. It was almost like she was once again the clean Sarah, the Christian Sarah, the Sarah her husband had cherished and adored. For Sarah his presence was like a cool wind blowing through a hot, stench-filled room. A breeze that filled her sails, lifting her, reminding her how she could soar with his love as her only support. But those feelings soon gave way to heavier reality. A reality that tasted like tarnished metal in her mouth, that felt like an overcoat soaked in her own sweat, reeking with her own filth and odor, so heavy with failure that she could barely move, much less fly.

And she knew Brandon knew. Those eyes knew everything. That's why she avoided them, why she found excuses to look around the room, out the window, anywhere but at him. She knew he knew. And, regardless of what happened, things would never again be the same between them.

She'd barely slept an hour. When she awoke, other than being ravenously hungry, there seemed to be no other side effect. Even the hangover was missing. Brandon figured it came with the fresh blood supply, though he joked that it shouldn't be a recommended cure for too much partying. Sarah returned the humor by mentioning the scar still remaining on her face. "What's the matter?" she'd teased. "You couldn't make it a package deal?"

At Katherine's insistence a doctor had come up and given her a quick look over. As far as he could tell everything was fine. And, once she'd been assured that Sarah was okay, Katherine headed for the Temple Mount to find her son.

Now, Sarah sat on the edge of the bed finishing off a lunch, courtesy of room service, as Brandon filled her in on his travels through Turkey. He described what he'd seen and learned, and explained how an unquenchable fire to warn and prepare the church had returned and continued to burn in his soul.

"It's like the fire I felt in L.A., but different." He paused, then shook his head. "No, no . . . I'm what's different."

"How so?"

"I've given up."

Sarah frowned.

"I'm not running my life anymore, Sarah. I've given up and died. No more agendas, no more trying to make God's will happen, no more anything."

"And this is good?"

"Yes. Because when I'm dead, that only leaves Christ. Remember that verse Gerty gave us. Unless a kernel of wheat falls to the ground and dies, it remains a single seed. But if it dies, it produces many seeds? Well, that's what's happened. I've died. I've traded my life in for his. And, if you ask me"—he flashed a grin—"I think I got the better end of the deal."

Sarah returned the smile, a little less sure. "How does that tie in with the fire?"

"Now I'm letting it burn however it wants." He rose to his feet. "I've stepped out of the way, Sarah. I'm letting God do it. It doesn't matter how stupid or ignorant it feels, I'm letting God call the shots. To be honest, I've never been so free, I've never felt such peace . . . and power."

"It sounds a little frightening."

"Of course it's frightening, but if you're dead, what difference does it make? And I've noticed something else."

"What's that?"

"When I get out of the way and let that fire do its thing . . . there's a lot less chance of me getting burned." He gave her another grin and she responded in kind. But it lasted only a moment, before the guilt rose up again and began pulling her down.

It was true, during their time apart Brandon had gone through some obvious changes. He'd left a boy and returned a man. But it was more than that. He was freer. He was more at peace than she'd ever seen him.

And what changes had she undergone?

Whore of Babylon!

The voice was still there. Even Brandon's presence could not remove it. *Oh God!* she cried out in silent prayer. *Can you forgive me? Can you ever forgive me? Can Brandon?*

He reached out and took her hands. "Hey," he whispered. "I missed you."

She glanced away, fighting back the tears. He knew. And yet he still loved her, he still treated her with adoring respect. Was it possible . . . was it possible that God . . . did he feel the same way toward her? Even now?

"You up for more food?" Brandon asked, reaching for the phone.

"Yeah. . . ," she answered hoarsely.

"What'll it be this time?"

After placing the order, Brandon urged her to tell him what she'd been through since they'd been apart. It was hard, but through the tears, the anger, and the self-hatred, she told him . . . everything.

She could see by the workout he was giving his jaw that it wasn't easy for him. She could also see the hurt in his eyes. But she saw no anger, nor any condemnation. When she finished she was exhausted, feeling much like a limp and very dirty dishrag.

Nearly a minute passed before Brandon finally spoke. "So . . . where do you want to go from here?"

"Where do *I* want to go? Where do *you* want to go? You're the one I've wronged. You and God. I'm the one that's ruined everything."

"You've ruined nothing." Brandon's voice was soft but firm. "There's nothing you've ruined that God can't restore. If you let him."

"Brandon, it's not that simple."

"Sure it is."

"What about *your* emotions, your feelings of betrayal? You have the right to be furious with me."

"If I had any rights, I might be."

"Brandon . . ."

"But dead men don't have rights." He knelt down at her side. "Sarah, you're God's gift to me. Whatever he gives of you to me, I rejoice in; whatever he withholds, I accept. When you're dead everything is a gift."

"But what about your feelings? Your emotions?"

He paused a moment, thinking it through. "They're like children," he said. "When they're good, I enjoy them. When they misbehave, I don't let them rule my home. Like every other part of me, they are subject to Christ."

"Brandon . . ." She closed her eyes in frustration.

"What?"

"Feelings are important . . . you just can't repress them."

Brandon smiled warmly. "I'm not repressing anything." He reached out to her face and gently brushed back her hair. "Christ is in charge, Sarah. Not my feelings. Christ has already paid the price for your sin. He's already forgiven you . . . how can I do anything less?"

And then it happened. Almost before she knew it. A deep, heaving sob. And then another. And another. Suddenly the floodgates were opened. It was as if all the bile that had been building up over the weeks, over the months, was suddenly coming up—doubts, ambitions, adultery, attempted suicide—all of it—and with an intensity that completely overwhelmed her. "I'm sorry!" she gasped between sobs. "I'm so sorry."

She felt him sit beside her, his arms gently wrapping around her. He pulled her closer. "I know," he whispered softly into her ear, his own voice filled with emotion. "I know . . . and I forgive you."

At that exact moment she knew the Lord had forgiven her as well. For as her husband continued to hold her, she could feel the arms of Christ gently wrapping around her, tenderly embracing the depths of her soul. The experience was so intense, so powerful, that she could not speak. She didn't have to. All she could do was cry—each silent sob bringing another failure to the surface, another failure that the Lord instantly removed and discarded. It was as if she was taking a long, refreshing shower, but from the inside . . . as if the water was loosening and washing away the filth of every failure, cleansing and forever rinsing away the foul stench that had been clinging to her for so many months.

How long they held one another like that she did not know. But when they were finally finished, she was exhausted. As she pulled back, wiping her cheeks, she saw her husband's own red eyes and wet face. "Sorry about that." She sniffed as she reached out to wipe his cheeks with her hands. He grinned and did the same for her. Now it truly was as if they had never been apart.

Eventually, the conversation resumed. Soon they began talking about Eric. Sarah recapped all that she had discovered, speaking of the tests she'd run, what they'd revealed, and about the long delta brain waves that were recorded whenever Heylel was present.

Brandon slowly nodded. "So we're talking about basic demon activity?"

Sarah shook her head. "Not so basic. Don't forget, the genetic structure of his blood has been altered. According to the lab reports, his DNA is like no other in the world. There's no telling what combination of hormones and neurotransmitters his blood is triggering his brain to release."

"Meaning?"

"Meaning, it could just be creating some sort of unknown connection between the physiological and the spiritual."

Brandon whistled softly. "Poor kid, he got it from both ends, didn't he?"

Sarah nodded. "The worst science has to offer and the worst of the spiritual world."

"We're agreed then," Brandon asked, "that Heylel is demonic?"

Sarah paused. "I think . . . Brandon, he might be more than that. I think the evil is more powerful than just a demon's."

"More powerful than a demon? The only evil more powerful than a demon is . . ." Brandon slowed to a stop. "Are you saying what I think you're saying?"

She nodded and watched as he fought off a shiver. The same shiver she'd experienced the first time she'd worked through the possibilities. But something else was running through Brandon's head as well. She could see the wheels turning. Once again he rose to his feet.

"What is it?" she asked.

He started to pace, trying to piece it together. "You're saying we have a person like no other in the world."

"Correct."

"A human who has been biologically manipulated and now may be hosting Satan himself."

"That's only speculation."

He nodded. "But he is a multiple murderer, and he does offer supernatural counsel to the Cartel."

"Yes."

"The very organization that's ushering in this one-world peace thing, that's setting Lucas Ponte up as its figurehead."

"I don't see the connection. What's that got to do with—"

"I'm not sure, but somehow it's connected to the Imperial Cult."

"Imperial what?"

"The one-world government that was killing off Christians for not worshiping their Caesars. That's what they thought the Antichrist was back then, back when Revelation was first written, back when they believed 666 was the code for Nero's name."

"What are you saying?"

"I'm not certain. But here we are, the two witnesses in Revelation—"

"At least one of us."

He ignored her and continued. "We're in Jerusalem where we're supposed to have some kind of showdown with the forces of hell . . . and there's supposed to be an Antichrist and a false prophet and—"

"That's only if you're taking everything literally."

Brandon turned to her.

She continued. "We've always agreed that some of Revelation was to be interpreted historically, like your Antichrist Caesar stuff, and that some of it was to be interpreted spiritually, and that only some of it was to be taken—"

"—literally. Yes, the three views of Revelation, that's how it's always been interpreted."

"So . . . what are you saying now? I mean which is it, historical, spiritual, or literal?"

"Yes."

"What?"

"It's all three!"

"At the same time?"

"Yes." Brandon grew more excited. "Don't you see, you're the one who's always talked about a multidimensional God. One that's everywhere at the same time."

"Omnipresence is one of his characteristics; the Scriptures make that clear."

"So if he's omnipresent, if he's multidimensional, why can't his writings be, too? Why can't he be talking about a historical event as well as a spiritual event as well as a literal future event . . . all at the same time?"

Sarah's head began to spin.

Brandon crossed the room back to her. "That's what I learned in Turkey. Even though those seven letters were written to seven specific churches in history, they also have deep spiritual and symbolic significance, while at the same time applying to issues facing today's church."

"Yes, but—"

"That's what Scripture always does with prophecy, even the ones about Christ! That's why nobody figured them out until after he came. Yes, they pointed to events in Old Testament history; yes, they pointed to spiritual events; and yes, they pointed to very real and tangible future happenings . . . all at the same time! Don't you see? A multidimensional God writing on multidimensional levels!"

Sarah forced herself to speak calmly. "So you still believe there's a literal quality to all of these events in Revelation?"

"There's something. We'd be fools if we thought we could figure it out before it happens. I mean, that's what they did with Christ's first coming. Nobody got it right. Three hundred prophecies and not a single Bible scholar got it right. Nobody can figure out prophecy until after it happens. But there's too much here just to be coincidence. Eric . . . the Imperial Cult . . . Ponte . . ."

An eerie silence stole over the room. Was it possible? Were they smack-dab in the middle of Revelation without even knowing it?

The knock on the door caused them both to jump. "Room service."

Brandon crossed over to the door and opened it. A young bellhop rattled in with a cart. "Sorry I'm late. Everyone's watching the shooting on TV."

"Shooting?" Sarah asked.

"Didn't you hear?"

"Hear what?"

"Some majnoon just shot Chairman Ponte. Over at Temple Mount. Gunned him down in cold blood."

"What's the kid doing!"

"Somebody stop him!"

"Eric!" Katherine cried. She struggled to move, but she was pinned to the pavement by a security guard. "Eric?" He had tackled her to the ground when the shooting had started. Now she was fighting to catch a glimpse of her son through the running feet and fallen bodies. "Eric!"

"Somebody grab the kid!"

They'd been a hundred yards north of the Dome of the Rock when the shot rang out. A single bullet fired by a sniper across the courtyard. Katherine had been standing so close to Lucas that she'd actually seen blood and bone explode from his chest. Now he lay eight feet away—the front of his body soaked in blood, his eyes fixed open in a death stare.

But she could not find her son. "Eric!"

They'd just left the stage, fifty yards from the newly opened East Gate, and were strolling toward the site of the temple groundbreaking. That's when the shot had been fired.

"Let me go!" It was Eric. She recognized his voice immediately. "Let me go, I can help!"

There was a scuffle. She caught a glimpse of Eric's trousers and shoes.

"Eric!"

"I can help him. Let me—"

"Let him go." It was a member of the Cartel. The secretary general.

"But, sir—," a guard protested.

"Let the kid go." The command was firm and unwavering. "Now!" And then a little more reflective. "Let's see what he can do."

"Okay, everybody," another guard spoke up. "Step back now, let's clear the area."

Instantly, the weight came off Katherine. Another guard was helping her to her feet. Now at last she could see the whole picture. There was Lucas lying on the ground in a widening pool of blood, and standing directly above him was her son ... *safe.* The relief was immeasurable.

"Eric!" she called. "Eric!"

But he didn't hear. Instead, he stared down at the lifeless body.

"Everyone stand back." Security continued moving the crowd. "Give us some room here ..." She felt hands around her arms, pulling her back with the rest of the crowd.

"But I'm the boy's mother. I'm—Eric!"

It did no good. She was pulled back fifteen feet until she became part of the perimeter surrounding Eric, the secretary, and the body. She watched breathlessly as Eric slowly lowered to his knees. She knew how much he loved the man, and she'd give anything to be by his side to comfort him. But when she looked at her son's face, she saw no tears. She saw no emotion at all.

Eric gently took Lucas's right arm, which had fallen across his abdomen, and stretched it out onto the stone pavement. He did the same with the other arm. The crowd grew still. In the distance an approaching EMS vehicle could be heard. Eric reached down and straightened one leg and then the other. Then he rolled the head forward until it faced up. Finally he reached down to the staring eyes and closed them.

A gentle breeze stirred through the courtyard. News cameras adjusted for better positions. Everything became absolutely silent.

Still on his knees, Eric lifted one leg over the body until he was straddling it. A faint murmur rippled through the crowd. Then, ever so carefully, he stretched out and lowered himself directly on top of the body—chest to chest, arms to arms, legs to legs.

The murmuring increased. Security started to move in, but the secretary repeated his order. "Leave him."

"But, sir—"

"Watch."

Eric took a deep breath and lowered his head. He put his mouth directly over the man's mouth, face to face, lips to lips ... and then he blew. It was a type of mouth-to-mouth resuscitation, but one like nobody had ever seen. Eric exhaled completely, then turned his face to let the air escape from the corpse's lungs. He took another breath and repeated the process. The crowd began to fidget, a couple voiced concern, but Eric paid no attention.

Katherine watched. She wanted to cry out his name, but she knew he would not respond. He took a third breath and blew it into the mouth of the body. The crowd grew more restless.

Then, ever so faintly, the fingers of Lucas's left hand began to twitch—once, twice. A moment later, those of his right hand started to move.

Katherine looked on in astonishment.

Suddenly the right foot jerked. Then Lucas's entire body convulsed. Then, at last, he began to cough.

The crowd whispered and buzzed in amazement.

A moment later Eric crawled off of the body, and a moment after that, Chairman Lucas Ponte opened his eyes.

Sarah stared at the medical chart, not believing what she saw. Blood pressure, ECG, respiration rate, everything about Lucas was normal. He wasn't even running a temperature.

She turned to the physician who'd let her take a look at the chart. "What about the chest wound?"

"What chest wound?" he asked.

"It's all over the news. Eyewitness reports. A bullet tearing through the chest. Lots of blood."

"The reports are wrong."

"I'm sorry, what?"

"There is no chest wound. There is no wound of any kind."

She searched his face.

He shifted uncomfortably and repeated himself, "There is no wound. Now, if you'll excuse me."

She nodded, then motioned to the chart in her hand. "May I look at this another moment?"

"As you wish." He turned and exited past one of the two sets of security guards stationed at either end of the long ICU bay. The room was designed for nine separate beds and ICU stations, which was still only a fraction of those available in the new emergency wing at Mount Scopus Hospital. But today it was cordoned off with only two occupants . . . Chairman Lucas Ponte a few beds over, and directly at her side, young Eric Lyon.

Both were sleeping. And why not? Raising someone from the dead is probably just as exhausting as being raised from the dead. The thought gave Sarah little comfort as she turned back to Lucas's chart. Against Brandon's advice she'd insisted upon rushing to the hospital. He'd accompanied her as far as the waiting room. But having no security clearance, he was now sitting out there with Katherine sipping lukewarm Nescafe.

Sarah flipped through Lucas's chart until she reached his EEG, the measurement of the brain's electrical activity. This was her specialty. If there was any abnormality she could probably spot it. But she was not prepared for what greeted her. According to the chart, Lucas Ponte was registering the exact same delta waves that Eric displayed whenever Heylel had entered him. In fact, their patterns appeared absolutely identical. A fist-sized knot formed in her stomach.

"Quite a coincidence, isn't it, Doctor?"

She looked up to see Ponte, across the room, wide awake. "Lucas . . ." She took a step toward him, then caught herself. She wasn't entirely sure why. "You gave us quite a scare."

"I gave myself quite a scare, Dr. Martus."

It was the way he spoke. Something about how he used her name. She did her best to cover the uneasiness. "You're not feeling any pain? No side effects?"

"Not a thing. Well, except my vision seems to have been slightly affected. Still, at my age, spectacles become a reality sooner or later. They want us here for overnight observation, but I guarantee you we'll be out of here by nightfall."

"It's . . . amazing."

"Yes, it is. So you see, Doctor, your husband is not the only one who can perform miracles."

The knot tightened. She unconsciously reached for the newly healed skin on her wrists. "You know . . . what happened?"

Lucas smiled. "Yes, Doctor, I know everything about you."

There was that phrase again, that tone. She glanced down at his chart.

"It really is quite remarkable, isn't it?" he said. "For two entirely different people to have identical brain waves?"

"You've seen this?"

"No, as I have said, my vision seems to be suffering slightly. I asked them to test it. What do they have it down as?"

She looked back at the chart. It read 20–400. "They have you down as—"

"20–400, yes."

She looked up, startled. "How did you . . ." She slowed to a stop. He was grinning, but not at her. He was looking just beyond her. She quickly turned and was startled to see Eric now sitting up in the bed beside her. He was busy reading the chart in her hands.

"Eric," she said, "how are you feeling?"

"Just fine, Dr. Martus."

She felt a slight chill. Something wasn't right, something about the voice. She continued. "That was quite a feat you pulled on the Temple Mount."

"Yes." Eric smiled and pushed up his glasses with his little finger. "But it wasn't me, Doctor. You of all people should know that by now."

The chill grew deeper. She forced herself to continue. "I was just telling Lucas how remarkable all of this is. I mean, to go through that kind of trauma with virtually no side effects."

"Except for my vision and those brain waves," Lucas corrected.

She turned back to him. "I still don't understand. If you can't read the chart how did—"

"A hundred and sixty over a hundred!" Lucas interrupted. "That's ridiculous, I've never had blood pressure that high!"

Sarah glanced down at the chart. Sure enough, that's what they'd written down, 160/100. She looked back up. "How did you know, if—" She came to a stop.

The grin increased. She slowly turned back to Eric. Once again, he'd been reading the chart in her hands. She spun back to Lucas, whose grin broadened, almost menacingly.

"That's . . . that's not possible," she stuttered. She turned back to Eric, who wore the identical grin.

"What's that, Doctor?" Lucas asked.

Her breathing came harder. She started backing away.

"What's that, Doctor?" Eric asked. It was a different voice but the same.

She turned back to the boy. He was gloating in delight. So was Lucas. It was a game. It had to be. The two of them were playing some sort of game.

"What's that, Doctor?" Now it was Lucas.

She bumped into a bed table on wheels, nearly knocking its contents to the floor, then she turned and started for the door.

"What's that, Doctor?" She didn't know who it was that time. She didn't care. All she knew was she had to get out of there. She had to breathe. She broke past the guards, through the doorway, and out into the hall.

"Brandon . . . Brandon Martus!"

Brandon turned from his conversation with Katherine and looked across the milling crowd of press and security that filled the waiting room. Tanya Chase's honey blonde hair emerged through the faces. She was pushing the wheelchair of an old man.

"Look who I found!" she called.

At first Brandon didn't recognize him.

"It's Reverend Tyler," she exclaimed as they pulled up to his side. "You remember Jimmy Tyler."

Brandon stared at the man. He'd put on a good fifteen years . . . and had lost twice that many pounds. He was hunched over and drawn, and when he looked up at Brandon his eyes were full of pain and helplessness.

Brandon dropped down to his side. "How are you, sir?"

The old man gave a hacking cough, then motioned to the back of his hands and the back of his arms, indicating their sensitivity to touch.

"It's Scorpion," Tanya explained. "He's come down with the virus."

Brandon nodded. He knew the symptoms. First came the nausea and fevers, then the sensitivity to touch. Next the lining of his blood vessels would start to leak, followed by his organs bleeding, filling his stomach and intestines. Eventually blood would begin seeping out of his nose, mouth, eyes—every orifice in his body. Slower than Ebola, it was just as deadly, and because of its more leisurely pace, it was even more torturous.

Tanya continued. "I told him what you've been up to, about the video we made. And he's agreed to broadcast it, in its entirety, on his network."

"That's great," Brandon said.

"In fact," Tanya said, "Jerry's over at the station right now, editing the piece."

Brandon looked from her back to Tyler. "Thank you," he said gently.

The old man shut his eyes and nodded, accepting Brandon's gratitude. It was clear he wanted to bury the hatchet. But as Brandon started to rise, he grunted and motioned for him to remain a moment. Brandon stooped back down. With more grunting and pantomime, Tyler pointed to Brandon, then to himself, and then up to heaven. It was clear he wanted Brandon to pray for him. He motioned to the back of his hands and his arms. He wanted him to pray for his healing.

Brandon nodded, only too happy to oblige. He reached toward the old man, who greedily took his hands into his. That's when Brandon felt the check. Something wasn't right. He wanted to pray over Tyler, but somehow he shouldn't. He looked at the old man. It made no sense. Tyler's eyes were full of pain and sorrow—and there was no mistaking his contriteness. So why couldn't Brandon pray?

"No, not yet." The command resonated in his head.

Why? Brandon asked.

"His repentance is not real."

I don't understand.

He waited for further clarification. But none came. The command had been given. Brandon looked back into the old man's eyes. They were brimming with tears of thankfulness. But slowly, sadly, Brandon had to withdraw his hands. "I'm sorry," he whispered. "I'm . . . sorry."

The withered hands reached out to his, trying to pull them back, his eyes filling with growing fear and confusion. The expression broke Brandon's heart. He could clearly see the man was repentant. But he had his orders and regardless of how unreasonable they seemed, he would not disobey. "I'm sorry," he whispered softly.

Suddenly the man's countenance shifted. His eyes flashed with anger. He coughed, clearing his throat, and before Brandon could rise, Jimmy Tyler spit a mouthful of phlegm into his face. Brandon winced but did not move. Instead, he looked at Tyler. The man seethed with rage.

Now Brandon understood. There was no repentance here. No contriteness. There was only the desire to stop the pain, to end the Lord's discipline. And wanting to stop God's discipline is a far cry from wanting to repent.

But even now, Brandon was filled with compassion. A Bible verse came to mind. He didn't know where it was in Scripture, but he knew it was from the Lord. And, despite its apparent harshness, he knew it must be said. Because, past the harshness was God's love, his infinite yearning to touch and save his child.

As gently as possible, Brandon spoke, "Not everyone who says to me, 'Lord, Lord,' will enter the kingdom of heaven, but only he who does the will of my Father who is in heaven."

Tyler stared at him, his anger hardening to hate.

But there was more and Brandon continued. "Many will say to me on that day, 'Lord, Lord, did we not prophesy in your name, and in your name drive out demons and perform many miracles?' Then I will tell them plainly, 'I never knew you. Away from me, you evildoers!'"

Brandon searched the man's face, looking for any trace of humility. There was none. Then, quietly, tenderly, he added his own postscript. "I'm sorry," he whispered, "I'm so very sorry." Slowly he rose to his feet, wiping off the spittle with his sleeve.

"Are you okay?" Katherine asked.

He nodded. "Yeah . . ." He turned back to Tyler, but the man had already grabbed the wheels of his chair and started rolling himself through the crowd.

Brandon, Tanya, and Katherine watched silently as he disappeared into the mob.

"I don't understand," Tanya said. "It would have been the perfect solution. Jimmy would have gotten his healing, you would have gotten your broadcast, and God would have reached the world with his message. Everybody would have won."

Brandon shook his head. "Everybody, but Jimmy . . ."

"What?"

"God is as concerned about the one lost sheep as he is the ninety-nine."

"Brandon . . . Katherine?"

He turned to see Sarah working her way through the crowd. Even then he noticed how drawn she looked.

"What's the matter?" he asked as she arrived. "Are you all right?"

"Yes." She nodded, a little out of breath.

"Are they still sleeping?" Katherine asked.

Sarah shook her head.

Brandon repeated, "What's wrong?"

She turned to Katherine. "Eric, your son's eyesight . . . do you know what it is?"

"His eyesight?"

"Yes, the prescription for his glasses. What's his eyesight?"

"Not great, but—"

"What is it?"

"Uh, 20–400, I think. Why?"

If Sarah was pale before, she turned absolutely white now.

"What's wrong?" Brandon repeated. "Sarah, what is it?"

She glanced around.

"Sarah?"

"We've got to talk," she answered quietly. "In private."

"Back at the hotel?" Katherine asked.

Sarah shook her head. "No." She glanced at the security and the press milling about. "We've got to talk someplace where we won't be recognized and where we won't be heard."

CHAPTER 18

It had been Brandon's idea to meet at the home of the old Palestinian woman. Actually, he hadn't even thought about her until he'd stuffed his hands into his pockets and pulled out the card she'd given him with her address. But as soon as he saw it, he knew that was the place.

She lived in the Palestinian village of Silwan, just south of the Mount of Olives. The flat-roofed buildings made of ancient stone and rubble stood two, sometimes three, stories high. They were packed tightly beside each other and clung to the steep hillside. Directly to the west lay the Hinnom Valley, once called Gehenna. According to Tanya this was where, in the Old Testament, the Israelites had sacrificed their babies to Baal and later, where Judas had hung himself. For Sarah, it seemed everywhere she looked there was history. In fact the taxi ride from the hospital to Silwan had taken them through the Kidron Valley, the very valley Jesus had crossed during his triumphal entrance into the city on Palm Sunday and prior to his arrest five nights later.

"That's the Garden of Gethsemane," Tanya said as they passed a church and small olive grove to their left.

The group turned to look and Brandon half-whispered in awe, "That's where it all began . . ."

"What do you mean?" Sarah asked.

"That's where the war was fought . . . where the fate of the entire world hung in the balance."

"What about Calvary?"

Brandon shook his head. "The decision to go there, to die to his own will, that war was waged right here."

"Dying to self," Sarah said as she looked back out the window, recalling their earlier conversation. "Even Jesus Christ had to do it."

Brandon nodded. "That's the only battle that counts."

Sarah glanced at her husband. There was so much wisdom there now. So much maturity.

The taxi pulled up to the address, and everyone was certain the driver had made a mistake. It was nothing but a garage carved out of a hillside with an impoverished two-story house beside it. But the driver insisted this was the place, and reluctantly the four of them piled out. The sun had already dropped behind the hill as they approached the entrance, a large corrugated door with the address spray painted across the top left corner. Off to one side a patch of wild roses withered from the heat. On the other, a grape arbor was propped up by a barrel used for burning trash.

Katherine banged on the steel door. The reverberating echo set off one or two neighborhood dogs. Sarah looked around. An old bedspring set atop cinder blocks served as a fence separating them from the neighbors. After a louder set of knocks and more barking dogs, the door finally slid open. The hunched woman with the nearly toothless grin greeted them. She'd already met Brandon and Katherine, but not Tanya or Sarah. After carefully shaking each of their hands, she ushered them inside.

It wasn't much. A tattered throw rug lay across cracked concrete. Two lamps (one without a shade) lit the bright yellow walls. A worn wooden table and three chairs sat in one corner, while the bench seat of an old car served as a sofa against the far wall. But the poverty had little effect upon the woman's hospitality. They'd barely taken their seats before she disappeared into what must have been the kitchen/bedroom and returned with a large serving tray. On it were four small glasses of coffee with the consistency of grainy syrup, along with four glasses of water to help wash it down.

"Okay." Tanya turned to Sarah. "You definitely have our attention. Now, what's going on?"

Sarah finished her sip of coffee, set the glass down, and began. "I don't think Lucas Ponte . . . I don't think he's with us any longer."

"What's that supposed to mean?" Katherine demanded.

"It means that what made up Lucas, his personality, his soul, whatever you want to call it . . . I believe it's no longer controlling his body."

"But he's alive," Katherine said, "you just saw him. You said you talked to him."

"I talked to somebody, but I don't believe it was him." She took a breath and continued. "I believe it's the same personality, the same entity that inhabits and controls Eric."

"You mean . . . Heylel?" Katherine asked.

"Lucas Ponte's brain waves are identical to your son's when Heylel inhabits him."

"Long deltas?" Brandon said.

"Exactly."

"Who is Heylel?" Tanya asked.

"That's the million-dollar question," Katherine muttered.

"But he inhabits your son?"

Katherine held her look a moment, then glanced away. Silence stole over the group until Tanya turned back to Sarah. "So you're saying the Lucas Ponte we know is dead."

Sarah nodded. "I believe so."

"And inhabited by this Heylel?"

"That's only one of his names. I believe he has others."

"Such as?"

"This is only speculative, there's no way to prove it, but I believe . . ." It was harder for Sarah to say than she thought. She backed up and tried again. "I believe what was once Lucas Ponte is now being—"

Katherine finished her sentence. "—controlled by Satan."

The group turned to her in surprise.

"I was with you in Eric's room," she said to Sarah. "I heard his claims. To be honest, I've suspected something like that for a while."

More silence. Finally Brandon spoke, staring at the floor. "The Antichrist." Uneasy glances were traded across the room. He looked up. "He is the Antichrist that was prophesied to rise up and rule the world." Turning to Katherine, he continued. "He and the false prophet."

"Which would be my son," Katherine flatly concluded. Without waiting for his response she turned to the group. "That's what Heylel has been promising him from the beginning, to rule the world."

"And . . ." Tanya was thinking out loud. "Tomorrow's installation is . . ."

Brandon answered. "Tomorrow's installation is the beginning of their reign."

Another pause. "Is there any way we can stop it?" Tanya asked. "If this is true, shouldn't somebody try to stop it?"

"Enter Revelation's two witnesses," Katherine said as she turned to Sarah and Brandon.

Sarah said nothing, waiting for Brandon to respond. He began shaking his head. "No . . ."

Tanya scowled. "But if that's who you're supposed to be, isn't that what you're supposed to do? If you really are the two witnesses, then you have to stand up to him and—"

"No," Brandon interrupted. "My job"—he threw a glance to Sarah—"*our* job has been the same as it's always been. We're to proclaim truth—through the Word of God and through our lives. Nothing more."

"But we're talking the Antichrist here," Tanya argued. "The great deceiver and destroyer. If you don't get in there and physically stop him, who will?"

Sarah ventured, "I think what Brandon's saying is that our weapons are not physical . . . they never have been."

Brandon nodded as Katherine quoted, "He who lives by the sword, dies by the sword."

"So what's left?" Tanya demanded.

"What always has been," Brandon replied. "To warn the world, to prepare the saints of God."

"Prepare?" Tanya asked. "For what?"

Brandon answered, "For the return of Jesus Christ." The group exchanged looks. He continued. "Christ is on the brink of returning. But his bride isn't ready. She needs to repent, to prepare herself."

"And," Sarah interjected, "she needs to be warned that Lucas is the counterfeit messiah and not to be followed."

Brandon nodded. "That's our job—to proclaim the truth. Nothing more."

"But how?" Tanya repeated, then suddenly she had an answer. "The videotape! Of course. You can tell them through the tape we made of your message from Turkey!"

Katherine shook her head. "You need more than some tape. I've seen these guys operate; they can spin and distort truth any way they want."

Sarah nodded. "I'm afraid she's right."

Katherine continued. "What you need is to present something live and in person, something they can't come back and twist all up."

Brandon agreed. "And it has to be done before the installation. Before anyone bows their knee."

"Or," Sarah said thoughtfully, "during it."

"You mean get him up there on the stage, like in L.A.?" Tanya asked. "Get Brandon to prophesy and call down some sort of curse on Ponte?"

Sarah threw another glance at Brandon. The idea literally made him stiffen with fear. Still, it had some merit.

Katherine shook her head. "There's no way Heylel will let you get close to the stage, much less get on it."

"Maybe ..." Sarah turned back to the group. "But I've seen how he operates. And if there's any residue of Lucas left, I have a pretty good handle on him, as well."

"Meaning?" Tanya asked.

"Meaning, I might be able to convince him."

"That's absurd," Katherine scoffed. "He's worked years for this moment. He's got far too much pride and ambition wrapped up in this to share it with anybody."

Sarah began to nod. "And that's the key."

"What is?"

"His pride and ambition."

"What are you talking about?"

"If this Heylel really is who he claims to be, who we think he is, what's his one weakness, what's his Achilles' heel?"

The group stared at her blankly.

"His ambition," Brandon ventured. His voice sounded weaker. Obviously the thought of going back onstage had taken its toll.

"Exactly," Sarah agreed. "Everything we read about Satan in Scripture ... his temptation of Adam and Eve, his promises to Christ, his being kicked out of heaven ... everything points to him trying to usurp God's authority, to a pride and ambition that wants to rule." She turned back to Katherine. "Look at his promises to your son."

Katherine agreed. "Pride and ambition . . . that pretty well covers it."

Sarah nodded. "Unfortunately, I've had a little experience in that area myself." She continued. "If there was some way we could play off of that pride . . ."

"You actually think he'd give Brandon permission to speak?" Tanya asked.

"Only if he thinks he can make a fool out of him," Katherine answered.

"And out of God," Sarah added.

Brandon coughed nervously. "Given my past record in front of crowds, I'd say that's a strong possibility."

"But it doesn't matter." Sarah turned back to him. "All you have to do is deliver the truth. It doesn't matter how stupid he makes you look or how foolish you feel. It doesn't matter if he cuts you down or verbally destroys you."

Brandon held her look, still obviously nervous, but at least understanding. "Because dead people don't die," he said.

"Precisely. All that matters is that you speak the truth. That's all God ever commanded us."

Brandon swallowed. "And . . . the rest is up to him."

"Yes!" Sarah was excited. "Don't you see? Our strength is that we don't have to be victorious, we don't have to win!"

"And Satan's weakness is . . ."

"That he has to!"

A moment passed as the group slowly digested the paradox. Sarah caught Brandon's eye and gave him a small smile of encouragement. He tried to return it, but the fear was obviously too great.

"And what about my tape?" Tanya asked. "Any chance of convincing Lucas or Heylel or whoever to let us play the tape during the broadcast, too?"

"Don't be ridiculous," Katherine scoffed.

Tanya countered, "It's no more ridiculous than winning a war by losing it."

"You want me to ask Ponte if he'll also play the tape?" Sarah asked.

"Doesn't hurt to ask."

"And if he says no?"

Tanya grinned. "Ponte's not the only game in town. I've got a few other strings I can pull."

Another moment passed before Katherine asked, "What about Eric?"

Sarah scowled, thinking it through. "I'm not sure of the logistics . . . but I doubt even Satan can inhabit two places at once."

"Only God is omnipresent," Tanya offered.

"I may be splitting hairs, and maybe it's only a matter of microseconds, but I believe Heylel probably moves back and forth between your son and Lucas."

"Then who's inhabiting Lucas when Heylel is in Eric?"

"Maybe some weaker power, maybe nobody. But you bring up an interesting point . . . if we can keep them separated, there may be less consolidation of power."

Katherine nodded. "Lucas thrived off of him in life; now he's doing it in death."

Sarah agreed.

"I should keep Eric away from tomorrow's ceremony, then?"

"Can you do that?"

"I'm still his mother, aren't I?"

"I don't know, guys . . ." Brandon's voice was thin, the way it always sounded when he was nervous. "To expect Sarah to talk Ponte into letting some hick like me up onstage." He turned to Tanya. "I mean, you saw me in L.A. And in Turkey I could barely put two sentences together for that tape. And now you want me to get up in front of the whole world?"

"Not you, Brandon," Sarah answered softly.

He turned to her.

"You're dead, remember?"

He tried to hold her look, but his eyes faltered. He turned to the rest of the group. "And Tanya, you're going to try and drop in some tape during an international broadcast?" He rose to his feet and began to pace. "Listen to you people. I mean, who are we kidding? There's no way we can pull this off."

Sarah knew he was speaking out of fear. Getting back onstage in front of all those people was his worst nightmare. She glanced around the room. Everyone sat silently, weighing his words, maybe even coming to his same conclusion. It might even be the right one. It certainly made more sense. But still . . .

Finally, Tanya looked up at him and asked, "So you don't think we should even try it?"

All eyes turned to Brandon. He had crossed to a small barred window, keeping his back to them. Sarah knew the pressure he felt was enormous, the thought of going back onstage, terrifying. A half minute passed before he finally answered, his back still toward them. "I don't know if it's possible or not." He paused, then continued. "But I know what I've always known." He slowly turned to face the group. "The bride has to be prepared . . . and she has to be warned of Ponte's seduction."

"And all of these 'impossible odds'?" Sarah asked.

His voice was softer now as he answered. "You said it yourself. If we fail, all we do is wind up looking foolish. Our job is to proclaim the truth . . . the rest is up to the Lord."

"The whole thing is ludicrous," Katherine muttered.

Brandon turned to her. "Probably . . . but what other course do we have?"

She started to respond, then glanced away. It was obvious she had nothing further to say.

Once again silence stole over the group. Finally, Brandon repeated himself quietly, but with more determination. "Our job is to proclaim the truth. The rest is up to the Lord."

For Sarah, one of Jerusalem's many surprises was the close proximity of everything. According to Tanya even the walk from Silwan to the King David Hotel was less than thirty minutes. That's why she'd decided to take it. It would give her a chance to clear her head, to sort through the day's events . . . and to prepare for the upcoming talk with Lucas or Heylel or whoever he was. If his prediction was correct he was probably already out of the hospital and back at the hotel, where she should speak to him as soon as possible.

Katherine had asked if she could accompany her. Of course Sarah had agreed. From what she'd seen of Eric's iron will and explosive temper, she figured Katherine's task would be as difficult as hers, and she'd probably need just as much time to think things through. Tanya had taken a taxi downtown to Channel Two to check on the progress of the editing. And Brandon, at everyone's insistence, had agreed to stay behind at the old woman's home. Everyone had their assignments, and his was to prepare for the unlikely possibility of speaking tomorrow.

The moon was full, and because of the growing impurities in the atmosphere, it cast a dull red glow over their shoulders as the two of them made their way along the single-lane road that passed through the Hinnom Valley. To their right towered the south wall of the Old City, and to their left was a steep ridge with occasional cliffs.

"So this is where the Israelites sacrificed their kids," Katherine mused. "What did Tanya call it, 'The Valley of Sorrows'?"

Sarah looked around them. The narrow ravine was silent and tranquil, the air still warm and smelling of dust and sage. There was no trace of the suffering that had filled this valley so many thousands of years ago.

"I wonder what that must have felt like," Katherine said, "sacrificing your own kid." Sarah turned to her as the woman continued thinking. "Giving up your child's life in the belief that you're securing the safety of millions."

Sarah wasn't sure what she was saying, but she didn't like the sound of it. "Katherine . . ."

Katherine turned away, looking up at the cliffs. "He's a monster, Sarah. My son is a killer. He's killed before and he'll kill again and he'll keep on killing. Only it won't be by ones or twos. Soon it will be by the thousands, maybe millions."

"You don't know that for certain."

"Of course I do. And so do you. But if somebody could stop him—"

"Katherine . . ."

"Were the mothers' actions here really so despicable . . . sacrificing one life in the belief that they could save millions?"

"Katherine, what are you saying?"

At last she turned to face her, and for the first time Sarah could remember, there were tears in the woman's eyes. "He's my baby . . . He's all I've got."

Sarah took her arm. "I know. I know . . . But there's got to be some other way."

"What?"

"I don't know. But sacrificing your only son . . ."

Katherine said nothing.

Sarah continued. "Eric still has a free will. Somewhere deep inside of him he must still be able to make decisions. If you could just reach him, talk to him. If you could get him to see that Heylel is wrong and that God's ways are better. If you could convince him that God's love is greater than all the—"

"Don't you dare talk to me about God's love!" The outburst surprised her. "Not after what I've been through."

"But—"

"No God of love would allow this type of torture. And if he did I certainly wouldn't want anything to do with him."

"Katherine . . ."

"I'm serious. No more!"

Sarah nodded and answered softly, "I'm sorry."

They walked in silence for several minutes before conversation finally resumed. They talked about how Katherine might convince Eric to go with her tomorrow. Perhaps a tranquilizing drug to sedate him would be helpful. Sarah had some Versed back at the hotel with her medical supplies. She could give her a small vial and show her how to use the syringe if she was interested.

Katherine had agreed.

Eventually the conversation turned back to Heylel—what Sarah should say, how she would have to again stand before his accusations, how she would have to use all of her strength and intelligence to persuade him to let her husband speak. Then again, maybe she wouldn't have to use her strength and intelligence at all. Maybe she would simply follow her husband's example and die. Die and let God do it. But how? They were fancy words, but how could she actually put them into practice?

Sarah shook her head. She couldn't. Not yet. But she could pray. And, as silence again stole over the conversation, that's what she did.

The elevator doors opened and Tanya stepped into the run-down foyer just outside Channel Two. She nodded to the guard who had been dozing at a small metal desk. She pushed open the double glass doors and entered the newsroom. Compared to this morning's crowd, there were only two kids working the computers and puffing cigarettes, which almost made the air breathable. No one acknowledged her presence as she headed back to the edit suite where she and Jerry had begun their work.

But Jerry wasn't there.

The overhead fluorescents were on, but the monitors and computer editing system had been shut down. Tanya scowled. Maybe he was on break. But that wouldn't explain why he'd turned everything off.

Beside the keyboard, she spotted a stack of three tapes. She crossed to them and read the backs. One was labeled "Brandon Martus, Turkey montage." It was marked with a red "edited master" sticker. The other two were the original tapes they'd made of Brandon's speech back in Laodecia.

Tanya was puzzled and angry. She had left clear instructions that Brandon's speech was the first thing to be cut together. And later, only if he had the time, was he to put together something on his travels through Turkey. But, by the looks of things, Jerry had done just the opposite. He'd wasted valuable hours editing Brandon's travels and hadn't even touched his speech.

Something was wrong. This type of incompetence wasn't like Jerry.

Tanya stepped out into the hallway and poked her head into the next edit suite. A stringy-haired brunette was hunched over the keyboard, mumbling and smoking.

"Excuse me?" Tanya asked. "Excuse me?"

"What?" the girl demanded without looking up.

"The gentleman that was in here with me this afternoon. You don't happen to know where he went, do you?"

There was no response.

"Excuse me."

The girl swore at the picture playing on her monitor. She hit a few keys, and tried again.

"Excuse me."

"Here," the girl called over her shoulder, "take a look at this." On the monitor a shaky handheld shot zoomed into a crowd on Temple Mount, then it cut to a closeup of Eric placing his mouth over Ponte's, lip to lip, and slowly exhaling. Tanya watched with morbid fascination until the picture abruptly ended and the girl turned to her. "So what do you think?"

"It's fine . . ."

"Not too weird."

"You're using it for tomorrow's broadcast?"

"Maybe. The director wants tons of prerecorded drop-ins. Probably won't use half of 'em, but he wants them just in case."

Tanya nodded. "That's his style. So tell me, did you happen to know where the guy in the next suite went?"

"How should I know?"

"I just, uh—"

Without a word the girl turned back to the keyboard and resumed working. It was clear the conversation was over. Frustrated, Tanya stepped back to her room and mulled over the situation. The good news was the last take of Brandon's speech in Laodecia was great. It would only take an hour or so to tighten it up. The bad news was it had been a long time since Tanya had operated the Avid editing system on her own. Still, valuable time was ticking away. So, with a heavy sigh, she eased herself into the sticky vinyl chair, booted up the system, and went to work.

"So tell me, Dr. Martus, how was your meeting?"

Sarah stiffened. "What meeting is that?"

"Come now," Ponte chided. "As I have told you, there is little I do not know. Your husband, he has gone through many impressive changes, am I correct? Making someone of your filth and immorality even less worthy to remain in his company."

"I'm not here to talk about my past behavior."

"Past, future, it is all the same with you, Doctor. You will never change."

Sarah recognized the ploy. It was the same one Heylel had used in Eric's room in Nepal, and more recently when she had tried to kill herself. But she would not fall for it. Regardless of her past, regardless of her future, she was forgiven. Maybe she didn't fully understand it as Brandon did, but she knew it in her head. Just as her husband had forgiven her, so had her God.

She remained standing at the end of the conference table in the north section of the Royal Suite. Lucas Ponte, or what was left of him, sat at the other. He looked as he always had, except for the pair of glasses he now wore. A stack of papers lay on the table before him. It was 10:00 P.M. and they were alone.

Sarah cleared her throat. "If you know about our meeting, then you know what we would like from you."

"I only know when and where you had the meeting. My associates were forbidden from entering."

The fact gave Sarah some comfort. It was good to know there were still limits put on his powers. Bracing herself, she went straight to the heart of the matter. "We know who you are and what you plan to—"

"You know nothing of me!"

The shouting surprised her, but she held her ground. "I know what I've read."

"You know only what Oppressor has written. You know only his version of truth. You know nothing of the glory that was mine—of my vast power and majesty. I was his greatest accomplishment, his shining act of creation. I led the stars in their songs, I was the bright and exalted one, directing all of heaven's host in his worship."

"Until you got greedy."

The eyes locked onto hers in icy rage—the hate so intense that she physically felt air pulled from her lungs. "They *wanted* me to rule! A third chose me as king! A third! And now"—a seething chuckle escaped from his throat—"his beloved children are about to do the same."

The emotion was so dark and cold that instinctively, Sarah started to pray. *Dear Lord—*

"Stop it!" He ordered. "Stop it!" The voice echoed through the suite. He took a moment to regain control. "I cannot hurt you. Even now there are forces surrounding you that prevent my approach. But not forever, Sarah Martus. Rest assured, your time is nearly at hand." Leaning back with the faintest trace of a smile, he began to quote. "When they have finished their testimony, the beast that comes up from the Abyss will attack them, and overpower and kill them. Their bodies will lie in the street of the great city . . . where also their Lord was crucified."

Sarah steadied herself. She was all too familiar with the prophecy, but that didn't stop him from continuing. "For three and a half days men from every people, tribe, language and nation will gaze on their bodies and refuse them burial. The inhabitants of the earth will gloat over them and will celebrate by sending each other gifts because these two prophets had tormented those who live on the earth."

Ponte paused, then shrugged. "An unfortunate ending given your loyal and unswerving commitment. Then again, that's how Oppressor always operates, making impossible demands upon those he claims to 'love,' while offering little in return. But if you were to serve me"—he tilted his head—"well, now, that would be a different story. For I know how to reward my servants."

Suddenly Sarah's mind swam with immeasurable pleasures. Feelings, emotions, impressions—gorgeous men desperate to please her every whim, access to the highest powers, unlimited glory, worldwide adoration—pleasures so overwhelming that Sarah had to lean against the table to stand.

And then, just as quickly as they came, they were gone—leaving her gasping in the sudden silence.

"You see." Lucas chuckled quietly. "I do know how to reward."

"I thought . . ." She took a gulp of air and finally managed to look up. "I thought you couldn't touch me."

"I can't, not without your permission."

"Then what was—"

"Just a few of the doors you've left open to me."

Sarah looked back down at the table, her mind and body still reeling from the assault.

"Those are *my* promises, Dr. Martus. Those are *my* truths."

She knew she couldn't withstand another attack, not like that. She had to play her card and get out of there. "But . . . your truths," she said, "they're only half-truths. What of the pain they bring, the suffering that follows?" She looked up at him. "What of the whole, the eternal truth?"

Lucas laughed. It wasn't malicious, just amused. "Eternal truth? Nobody is interested in eternal truth." He pushed up his glasses with his little finger, just as Eric always had. "The only truth they are concerned with is mine."

"Is it?"

"Open your eyes, Doctor. Take a look at the world. Nobody cares for the eternal. My truth is all that counts. My pleasures are all they pursue. They have made their decision, Doctor. Through their own free will they have chosen me to rule. By their own volition they have rejected Oppressor and have selected me."

"You're wrong."

Lucas looked at her, waiting for more.

Sarah made her play. "They have chosen you out of ignorance. They have chosen your truth because they know no better."

"They have always had Oppressor's Word."

"Distorted by you."

"No, my pleasures have distorted many of its teachers. Their teachings have, in turn, distorted the Word."

Sarah could feel the ground slipping away. His logic was too strong. *Dear Jesus,* she silently prayed, *help me, please help*—Instantly, she understood that Heylel was again trying to distract her. She shook her head. "No, that doesn't matter," she said. "What matters is that tomorrow the world will be making their choice out of distorted facts and ignorance. And making a choice out of ignorance is not making a choice at all."

"My dear Doctor, even with all the facts, they would choose me. Even if every man, woman, and child knew every detail, they would still choose my truths over Oppressor."

"Possibly."

"Definitely."

"But you'll never know, will you? Not for sure. You'll always wonder if they chose you because you really are the greatest, or simply because they didn't know better."

Another smile crossed Lucas's face. "You are very clever, Doctor."

She said nothing.

"And your solution to my dilemma is . . ."

"Let the people make an intelligent choice. Give them all the facts. Then, if they want to follow you, so much the better."

His smile broadened. "But you've forgotten one important fact, Doctor. They *will* follow me, regardless. Oppressor's prophecies must be fulfilled."

"Then you'll have nothing to lose. They'll follow you regardless, even when they know the facts. And you can rule with the satisfaction that they truly have rejected God and that they really have chosen you to be their ruler."

There was a moment's pause. "You make an intriguing argument, Doctor." He pushed up his glasses. "So tell me, how would they hear these facts?"

"Let my husband speak from your stage tomorrow."

Lucas burst out laughing. "You would have Brandon Martus debate me?"

"No, not a debate. Just let him speak from his heart for a few minutes."

"The boy is terrified to stand in front of the smallest group. He will make an utter fool out of himself. He will completely discredit your cause."

"Then you'll have nothing to lose, will you?"

"Except, as you have said, if he embarrasses himself and your position, the people will still be unable to make an intelligent decision."

Sarah's mind raced. Had she just defeated her own argument? Suddenly another thought came, another opening. "That's why we'd also like to play a video. In case Brandon gets tongue-tied."

"The video he and Tanya Chase made in Turkey."

Again Sarah was unnerved at how much he knew. "Yes."

Silence settled over the room. She waited patiently.

Finally Lucas spoke. "You have presented your case well, Doctor. Allow me to think upon it. The prophecies must be fulfilled. The people will choose me and reject Oppressor, this we know. But to have them make this choice with the full knowledge of who they are rejecting and who they are choosing . . . this would be an even greater triumph."

Sarah nodded. "Exactly."

He turned his gaze fully upon her. "I know what you are planning, Doctor. Do not think your cleverness has deceived me. But your proposal has every possibility of making tomorrow's victory all the sweeter. Through your own wiliness you may have actually made my victory greater. You will have my answer in the morning. Good night, Doctor." He looked back down to his papers and resumed his work. The meeting was over.

Sarah turned and saw herself to the door. She felt a sense of triumph, but even now, wrapping around it, there was a deeper sense of dread. She'd sensed the Lord sharpening her mind so she could effectively state her case. But had she out-thought herself? Had she inadvertently played into Heylel's hand, giving him, as he had said, an even greater victory? Only time would tell. And, glancing at her watch, she realized that time was fast approaching.

CHAPTER 19

Brandon sat in the deep silence of the Garden of Gethsemane. He watched the dappled patterns of moonlight that had filtered through the olive trees as they inched their way across the ground. The stillness was absolute. He wasn't sure why the Franciscan caretaker had left the gate unlocked, but he knew this is where he wanted to be. This is where his Savior had been.

Earlier he had prayed and paced and cried and prayed some more. *Are we doing the right thing . . . what am I to say . . . are we stepping out where we shouldn't . . . is this really your will?* Around and around the questions went. But there had been no answer.

Only silence.

And with the silence came the doubts. What was he thinking? He'd already proven his inability to stand in front of people. He ruined one man's ministry, destroyed his own. He'd subjected Sarah and himself to unbelievable ridicule and scorn. And now he was expected to do it all over again? This time in front of billions of people? What *was* he thinking?

And with the doubts came the fear. Memories of glaring television lights, unblinking cameras, a hostile audience yelling and booing him, hating him. And it would be worse tomorrow. Much worse. This was no national broadcast he was appearing on, this was *international;* it was going to be shown around the world. And this was no televangelist he was going against. This had every appearance of a standoff with Satan himself!

What was he thinking!

Please, Jesus . . . I'm not ready for this . . . there has to be some other way . . . tell me some other way . . . whatever you want, just tell me . . .

The silence continued.

He wasn't sure what he had expected. A word would be nice, another guest appearance by the Lord would be even better. He'd even settle for one of those supernatural impressions he sometimes felt in his spirit.

But there was nothing.

He didn't know how long he had sat there waiting, listening to the silence—maybe an hour, maybe two. But eventually he heard the faint squeak of the iron gate. He'd finally been discovered. He was about to be thrown out. Not exactly the answer he'd hoped for. The sound of feet crunching gravel approached. He pulled into the shadows with the futile hope that he wouldn't be noticed. But, of course, he was.

"Brandon . . . is that you?"

"Sarah?" He rose to see her coming up the path, then quickly moved to her for an embrace. "What are you doing out here? How did you find me?"

"I went to the house. The old lady said you were coming here. And the caretaker, he said he was expecting me."

Brandon looked at her in surprise. "The caretaker . . . he knows?"

Sarah shrugged. "He pointed out where you were sitting. Said he was concerned about all your pacing wearing out his grass."

Astonished, Brandon looked over his shoulder toward the garden gate. There was nothing there but shadows. That's all he'd ever seen. Pushing aside the thought, he turned back to Sarah. "You shouldn't be out here, not alone."

"I talked to Lucas."

"What did he say?"

"I think he'll go for it."

"That's . . . good."

"You don't sound too excited."

"No, I think that's great. It's . . . great."

"And . . ."

He looked at her. She was staring up at him, searching his face. He'd never been good at hiding things from her. This was no different. Finally, he confessed, "I'm scared, Sarah."

"I know."

"I mean, it's one thing to dream up all these clever plans, but to actually go through with them . . ."

She nodded.

"In just a few hours I'm supposed to go up onstage, in front of the whole world, and have some sort of showdown with the Antichrist? Who are we kidding? I still don't have the faintest clue about what I'm going to say or do. At best I'm just going to wind up looking like the world's biggest jerk."

She took his hands and answered quietly, "What does it matter? As long as you're dead in Christ, what does it matter what you look like?"

He looked at her, appreciating what she was trying to do, but it didn't work. He broke from her and turned to resume his pacing. "Those are just words. They sound real good in theory, but this isn't theory. This is reality. And tomorrow's reality is that I'm going up there battling the most evil force in the world, and I'm not the slightest bit qualified."

"You're right, you're not. You never have been."

He looked back at her.

"But isn't that your strength, Brandon? Hasn't the key to everything you've done so far been your weakness? Think about it. Hasn't your success been knowing you're unqualified, knowing that the only way you can possibly succeed is by relying on God?"

"This is different."

"How?"

"It . . . just is."

"Why . . . because it's bigger?"

He tried to answer, but could not.

She stepped closer. "You keep talking about dying—about letting the old man die and letting Jesus rule. That's all well and good. I mean, that's really important, but I think you've missed something even more important."

He waited.

"You've missed faith, Brandon. Without faith you've got nothing, without faith you are nothing. Yes, be dead, yes, let Christ rule . . . but then have the faith that he *will* rule."

"You don't think I want that? You don't think I've been trying to believe?"

Her answer was soft. "Then maybe . . . you should stop trying."

"What's that supposed to mean?"

"It means dead people don't try."

She was beginning to make sense, in an odd sort of way. And she was starting to break through. "What am I supposed to do about all of these fears, about all these emotions?"

She approached him, looking up into his face. "Let me tell you what a good friend once told me about emotions. He said they're like children. We can enjoy them when they're good, but we don't have to let them rule our house."

Brandon gave her a look.

She reached out her hands and rested them on his waist. "It's not a matter of emotion, my love. It's a matter of choice. Just as you chose to die in Christ . . . you have to choose whether or not to believe."

"You make it sound so simple."

"It is simple . . . it's not easy, but it is simple."

He closed his eyes for a moment and then sighed. "For a scientist, you're a pretty good theologian."

She smiled. "I have a pretty good teacher." She snuggled into him and he wrapped his arms around her. She was right, of course. But how had she done it? How, in just a few seconds, had she managed to calm the storm? The woman was amazing. He'd almost forgotten how amazing.

She said nothing more but simply rested her head on his shoulder and waited. It felt good holding her like that. Natural. Like she always belonged. Pressed against him, he could feel her warmth, and with that warmth came the assurance. He could do anything with her there. Anything at all. He took a deep breath of the night air and slowly let it out. She snuggled in closer.

"It's getting late," he said.

"Yes."

"We should be heading back."

"I know." Then, looking up at him, she held his gaze for a long moment. He felt a strong impulse to kiss her. He reached down and brushed the hair from her face.

"What about you?" he whispered.

"What about me?" she said, tilting back her head, lifting her face closer.

"We keep talking about my death in Christ . . . what about yours?"

She gave no answer but closed her eyes and raised her mouth to his. He lowered his head and their lips found one another.

When they parted he looked back down at her. "Well?"

"I'm working on it," she said as she pulled his mouth back to hers. "I'm working on it." They kissed again longer, slower.

When they had finished, Brandon looked down at her. She smiled, and it made him warm all over. Without a word they turned. Still holding one another, they headed back down the path toward the gate. And there, walking in the moonlight, through the garden, for the first time that Brandon could remember, he felt like they were truly one.

Tanya had spent much of her professional life around remote television setups, and she wasn't the least bit surprised to see that everything for tomorrow's shoot was state of the art. After all, Ryan Holton was in charge. The equipment and trucks were parked along a narrow road that ran parallel to and a mere twenty feet from the Eastern Wall. It was a typical arrangement: a boxy-looking generator truck to supply the electricity, a semitruck whose long trailer served as the production center, and the miles and miles of black cable. What was not typical was the scaffolding that carefully suspended the cable, preventing it from touching the thousands of graves packed tightly along the outside of the wall.

It had always amazed Tanya that such a location had been chosen for a cemetery . . . until she learned the method behind the madness. Tradition claimed that Jesus Christ, upon his return, would enter through the large Golden Gate in the center of the wall. This explained why in the seventh century the Moslems had sealed it up with stone. Then, as an added precaution, they had buried their dead directly in front of it. After all, the Law said a priest could not walk over the grave of a human, and since Jesus was a priest, and since there was nothing but wall-to-wall graves in front of the gate, it was obvious in their minds that they had efficiently blocked the second coming of Jesus Christ.

The blue and white production trailer was lit by two self-contained quartz lights on either end. Besides various storage bays underneath, the trailer had three separate doors leading to three separate rooms. The front room was where the director, technical director, and production assistant sat. Before them would be rows and rows of monitors along with a switcher to change cameras and an effects board. This is where Ryan would call the angles and direct the show. Behind him and just slightly higher was the sound engineering room. Here the sound technicians would sit, checking levels and watching the broadcast over the director's shoulder through a pane of glass. And finally, at the back, was the VTR, or videotape replay, room. This was where the show would be recorded and where the prerecorded tapes would be dropped in and played on Ryan's cue.

It was this last room that Tanya needed to enter and discreetly place her two edited tapes. She'd not heard from Sarah and had no idea what if any progress she'd made with Ponte. She'd put a call in to Ryan, but he was not available. She'd left a fairly detailed message on his service but knew that it would be unlikely she could see him before the show. So, as far as she could tell, prepositioning the tapes for the VTR operator was her next best option.

A single guard with an M-16 was posted outside the trailer. He didn't look Israeli but appeared to be part of the international coalition . . . which meant he might be easier to con. Gripping the plastic shopping bag that held the tapes, Tanya took a brief breath and stepped out of the shadows toward the trailer. She walked with what she figured to be the right sense of purpose and professional boredom.

The guard heard her and turned.

"Good evening," she said, nodding.

"I.D. please." He sounded American, from the south. He tapped his chest indicating where her crew I.D. should be hanging from her neck.

"It's right . . ." She looked down, then feigned surprise at its absence. "That's funny, it should be . . ." She pulled aside her jacket to look. "Oh great . . ." She glanced back up, pretending to be flustered. "I left it back in his van."

"Van?"

"Yeah, Ryan Holton's."

"The director?"

"Yeah, it got in our way when we were . . . I mean to say, he took it off when, we, uh . . ." She ran her hands through her hair, pretending to be even more embarrassed. She caught a flicker of amusement crossing his face. Good, it was working. "Look," she said, "if anybody found out about us, I'd probably lose my job. But he's kind of nervous, you know preshow jitters and everything, and, well hey, a girl's got to do what she can to get ahead . . . if you know what I mean." She dropped off, pretending to fidget some more. "Look, if you'll just let me deliver these two tapes for him, I'll be on my way."

He shook his head in amusement.

"What?"

"You showbiz people, you're all alike, ain't you."

She looked up through her bangs and smiled. "Yeah, I guess we are."

"Let me see in the bag."

She crossed to him and opened it. For the briefest moment she thought of leaning forward and distracting him a bit further—after all, she was wearing her favorite V-neck pullover—but something inside said no. Something about Brandon and what he'd been saying.

After checking the tapes, he motioned her toward the trailer. "Go ahead."

She gave him another smile. "Thanks." She crossed to the aluminum steps leading to the VTR room, climbed up them, and entered. It was small, almost claustrophobic. Two chairs faced a narrow desk which faced various rows of monitors. On the side wall hung cables and patch cords. The rear wall consisted of a dozen tape machines with two metal racks holding videotapes. These were the tapes to be dropped in during tomorrow's broadcast.

For some unknown reason, a wave of uneasiness crept over her. She wasn't sure why. Maybe it was because in just a few hours this tiny space would be responsible for influencing the entire future of the world. A sobering thought. But it wasn't her first. She would always remember the confrontation she'd had with a congressman in Washington when she'd first started out. He'd openly ridiculed her choice of profession, and when they were alone in the elevator she got in his face with one of the best sound bites of her life. "Listen, congressman," she'd said, jabbing a finger at him, "you folks may legislate what the people want, but we *tell* them what they want."

It was true back then, and it was just as true today . . . and tomorrow.

Pushing aside her uneasiness, Tanya unfolded the plastic bag and reached for the first tape. It was the one she'd just finished editing over at Channel Two, the speech Brandon had delivered with such conviction at Laodecia. As she pulled it out of the bag, she noticed her hand shaking.

"What's the matter with you, girl," she scolded herself. "It's just a segment." But she knew it was more than that. She knew that if played, this single tape could change the entire outcome of the broadcast.

She turned toward the metal tape rack and riffled through the tapes, looking for the ideal place to put it. They would be positioned in the rough order Ryan would call them. She hesitated, then decided to put the speech in the fifth or sixth position, well after the logos and intros, but not too far into the show.

That's when she heard the voices. Men talking, outside.

She froze, listening carefully, but she couldn't make out the words. She knew it wasn't the crew. They wouldn't be called for three or four more hours.

Her heart began to pound.

Quickly, she pulled the other tape from the bag, the montage of Brandon's travels through Turkey. She hadn't had time to view it, but she trusted Jerry. Despite their differences, despite his annoying habits and ever-present ambition, he was good.

Suddenly the trailer vibrated as heavy feet moved up the steps. Tanya reached for the rack, trying to drop the tape in somewhere, anywhere . . . when the door quickly opened.

"Hold it right there, please."

She stopped, hand in midair.

"Turn around slowly, if you do not mind."

Tanya obeyed. As she turned toward the door she squinted, trying to make out details of the silhouette standing there.

"Ms. Chase? Tanya Chase?"

She continued to squint. "Who's asking?"

"What is that you have in your hand?"

"Oh, this?" She referred to the tape. "I was just putting this back where I—"

"May I see it, please?"

"Sure." She handed him the tape. That's when she saw the dull glint of light reflect off what looked like a silencer. Her mind raced as she did her best to sound calm. "What's all this about?"

The figure turned and handed the tape outside, to someone just out of sight. "Is this the one you edited?"

Another voice read the label. "'Brandon Martus, Turkey montage,' that's the one."

Tanya immediately recognized him. "Jerry . . . is that you?"

"Good." The first figure nodded and retrieved the tape.

"Jerry!"

"You gave us a scare, Ms. Chase," the silhouette said. "Mr. Jerry has worked very hard on that for us. We were afraid you might have misappropriated it."

"Worked . . . for you?" She tried to see past him. "Jerry, what is this about?"

"Please, go ahead and put this back where you had it."

Tanya took the tape. "What do you mean, 'worked for you'?"

"Please . . ." The gun motioned toward the rack.

Tanya turned and dropped the tape into the second shelf, wherever there was room. Knowing the best defense was an offense, or at least a belligerent attitude, she tried to turn the tables. "Now, tell me, exactly who are you and what is Jerry Perkins doing—"

There was the faintest flash from the muzzle of the silencer, a muted *zip-thud*, and a roaring explosion inside her chest. The force was so powerful that it threw her back into the wall. She tried to gasp, but for some reason she could not breathe. Her chest raged with fire and she clutched a handful of patch cords before she slid to the floor. There was another flash. But this one brought no pain as it slammed her body hard into the floor. If she could have breathed, she would have cried out. The room was already growing bright white. She was losing consciousness.

"What did you do?" It was Jerry's voice, screaming in protest, but sounding very, very far away. "What did you . . . No, don't. What are you doing? No, please. We had a deal! Please, for the love of—"

She heard two more *zip-thuds* . . . and then there was nothing. By now the whiteness was everywhere and her eyes were unbelievably heavy. She had to close them, just for a moment. No, she was a reporter, she had to see what was happening. She could no longer hear Jerry, she could no longer hear anything. And her eyes, they were so heavy. She would close them, just for the briefest moment. Slowly . . . she lowered her lids . . . just for a second . . . only for a second.

Rose-colored moonlight spilled through the window and onto Eric's face as his mother watched him sleep. He was always so peaceful when he slept. There was no sign of the explosive anger or the violence. There was no sign of Heylel. Just the sweet, tenderhearted child she had once known.

She remembered one day when he was six and she had dropped him off at day care—how, after she'd kissed him good-bye, she had watched him from the car. She remembered how his little body stood at the foot of the stairs, lunch box in hand, staring up at the huge house before him. How badly she wanted to jump back out and race to him, scooping him into her arms, explaining that she had made a mistake, that he was too young, that she'd never let him go. And she remembered how he had turned, giving her a brave little smile, more for her sake than his, and started up the porch steps, never looking back again.

The thought brought tears to her eyes. It always did. Over the years she'd gradually given up hope that she could ever find peace and happiness. Those days had come and gone. But not for Eric. His whole future lay ahead of him. That's why she'd invested so much into him, providing every opportunity she could afford for him. She thought if she could draw the line and stop the suffering with herself, letting him enjoy peace and goodness, then her life would have had some purpose.

That had always been her hope. And looking down at the sweet, innocent face before her, that hope was almost revived. Almost.

In the next room sat the vial of Versed and the syringe Sarah had given her before leaving—plus another full vial Katherine had stolen after Sarah had left. Two ccs would be all that was needed to sedate Eric to the point of cooperation. It would still allow him to walk, if she helped support him. Any more than that could be dangerous. By Katherine's estimate, she now had twenty ccs.

There were many important decisions she'd have to make in the next few hours. But right now she was too exhausted. Not that she'd be able to go to sleep. But, at least for now, she could curl up in the armchair across the room and watch her child in the moonlight. Here, she would muse and smile over memories of what he had been . . . and here, she would silently weep over what he would never be.

The walk from the Garden of Gethsemane to the old woman's house was only twenty minutes, and no matter how slowly they took it, it was coming to an end far too soon. There were so many issues Sarah wanted to discuss and catch up on, but they'd all have to wait. All but one.

"Brandon . . . I want to go up on that stage with you tomorrow."

He slowed to a stop. They were less than fifty yards from the door. "Are you crazy?"

"I think it's important."

"Why?"

"I've always let you stand up and take the heat. I've always hid in the background and let you be the one to get the beating."

"I don't have a problem with that."

"I do. We're a team, Brandon. That's what the Lord has always told us—in the Scriptures, in the prophecies. We've gone our different directions, but we're together now, just like he said. We're a team."

Brandon nodded.

"If you go up there, I want to go up there."

"But . . . what are you going to do, what are you going to say?"

"I don't know. Do you?"

"That's not the point." He shook his head and resumed walking. "No, I don't think it's a good idea."

"Brandon . . ." She caught up to him. "If you and I are supposed to represent Christ and his bride, isn't there a time when the bride has to stand up with her husband and share in his suffering? Isn't that one of the things you learned in Turkey, that the bride should expect persecution?"

"Yes, but—"

"So what type of symbol am I if I sit back and let you take all the heat?"

He picked up his pace, obviously agitated. "I don't think it's a good idea," he repeated.

She stayed glued to his side. "Why not?"

"It's . . . it's not right."

"Of course it is."

"It's too dangerous."

"Brandon . . ."

He said nothing.

"Brandon, talk to me. Brandon."

He didn't slow until they reached the front of the old woman's home.

Finally he turned to her. "Look, you know the prophecies. If they're to be taken literally, you know there's a chance that tomorrow could be our last day alive."

"Exactly. *Our* last day."

"It's not right."

"You keep saying that. What's not right?"

"Jesus Christ laid down his life for his bride."

"Yes . . . and he requires the bride to do the same for him. That's what you've been learning, Brandon. That's what those letters say." He tried to look away, but she wouldn't let him. As she searched his face she saw the fear and concern. "It's all right," she whispered. "I want to do this."

"But . . . I'm afraid. I mean it's one thing for me . . . but for you . . ."

"It's okay."

"Sarah . . ."

She put her fingers over his lips, silencing him. "You've given up your life," she whispered, "now let me give up mine."

He looked into her eyes a long moment. But this time she felt no uneasiness. This time she had nothing to hide. At last, he began to nod, almost imperceptibly.

She rose up and kissed him on the cheek. "Thank you," she whispered.

They turned back to the house. He reached for the steel garage door and pulled it open. Both were surprised at what greeted them. The lights were off and the old lady was nowhere to be found.

"Hello?" Brandon called. "Hello."

Everything was dark except for faint flickering coming from the next room.

"Hello . . ."

They exchanged looks, then moved in to investigate. They passed the table and chairs, the car seat sofa, until the other room came into view. But the woman wasn't there, either. Instead, a queen-sized mattress with clean pillows and a pulled-back sheet lay in the center of the floor. Beside the head of the mattress sat an ornate wooden tray with two recently filled champagne glasses and an opened bottle of sparkling grape juice. From the ceiling hung several white crepe paper streamers. They came together in the center above the bed, where two cardboard wedding bells hung. Everything was bathed in the soft romantic glow of a dozen flickering candles.

Brandon and Sarah stood speechless.

When Sarah found her voice it was barely above a whisper. "How did . . . how did she know?"

Brandon shook his head and nervously cleared his throat. "Do you think maybe the Lord's trying to tell us something?"

Sarah said nothing.

"Well." Brandon cleared his throat again. "It's not exactly Chicago's Hyatt Regency . . ."

By now Sarah was so overwhelmed she could barely speak. "No," she whispered as she wrapped both arms around Brandon. "It's a thousand times better."

CHAPTER 20

Brandon held Sarah in his arms throughout the night. He found everything about her intoxicating . . . the slow breathing of her sleeping body against his, the softness of her breath upon his chest, her warmth, her smoothness, the smell of her hair. Everything filled him with both peace and exhilaration. And, as the hours passed, he tried his best not to fall asleep so that he might savor the time for as long as possible.

But her presence was more than physical or even emotional. Yes, he was whole now, complete. But there was something else here. Something deeper, something . . . spiritual—a truth he could almost grasp, but not quite. If Sarah's presence could bring him such joy and if Sarah represented the bride of Christ . . . was it possible that he, as a part of that bride, could bring equal joy to his Lord? Was it possible that as a mere human he could bring such pleasure to the Creator of the universe . . . simply through his presence and fellowship? Could this be part of the "profound mystery" Paul spoke of in Ephesians?

Brandon tried to explore the idea, but it was deeper than he could think—at least for now, at least for tonight. Instead, he was content to simply lie beside his sleeping wife, enjoying her presence. Eventually he rose up on one elbow and looked down upon her lovely face, quietly thanking God for his goodness. But soon his eyes grew tired and he had to lay his head back down on the pillow. Still, even as he drifted off to sleep, he was rejoicing over his bride and silently worshiping his Lord.

"Brandon . . . Bran . . ."

He woke to see Sarah smiling down at him. It was morning and she was already dressed. Even more surprising, she had cut her hair. So short, that it no longer hid the scar.

She bent over and kissed him lightly. "Good morning."

"Hi." He grinned, then reached out and pulled her to him.

They kissed again, and when they parted she whispered, "It's getting late."

"You cut your hair."

"Yes."

"It's like the picture," he said. "The one Gerty sketched of us confronting the serpent head. Remember?"

"Yes, I know."

Suddenly he understood. Sarah had finally accepted all of Gerty's words. And all of Revelation's.

"Today's the day, isn't it?" he asked.

"I think so."

He sat up. "Are you frightened?"

"No." She shook her head and sat beside him. "Not when I'm with you. When I'm with you, I can face anything."

Her long jagged scar was in plain view now, its shiny pinkness accentuated by the harsh morning sun. As he looked at it, he felt his hands beginning to grow warm. The palms first and then radiating out into his fingers. He glanced down and saw their growing redness.

So did Sarah.

He looked back up into her face. Then, slowly, tenderly, he raised his hand toward the scar. But before his fingers touched her cheek, she took them and gently moved them away. "No, Brandon."

He looked at her, puzzled.

"This is who I am. Today of all days, I want to be exactly as he's made me."

A smile spread across his face. He didn't fully understand, but he realized this was her way of accepting all that God had called her to be. Like the cutting of her hair, this was a confirmation, a marker proving she had totally and unequivocally given Jesus Christ complete control of her life.

He leaned over and kissed her again. She sighed in quiet contentment, then whispered, "We better get going."

He nodded and rose to dress.

Moments later she called from the other room. "Brandon. Come look at this."

He slipped on his shoes and entered the room. On the table sat two sesame bread rings, several slices of goat cheese, some grapes, and two oranges.

"This wasn't here last night, was it?" she asked.

Brandon slowly shook his head. "I guess there's no end to her surprises."

"I guess not."

Although there wasn't a lot of food, it was enough and it was refreshing. After they'd finished eating, Sarah suggested they spend some time in prayer. Kneeling had never been their habit, but they both felt it was appropriate for today. Lowering to their knees, they held one another's hands and began to pour out their hearts to the Lord. They thanked him for his goodness and his faithfulness. They blessed him for his protection these many months and for accomplishing his will regardless of their doubts and failures. Finally, they asked for the courage and faith to finish the task he'd set before them.

"And, above everything," Brandon concluded, "we ask for your perfect will to be done. Regardless of our success or our failure, we ask that you accomplish your purposes fully and completely . . ."

"Yes," Sarah agreed. "Your will and only yours."

"Because it is in your name that we pray . . . and that we live or die . . ."

They both said amen together but remained kneeling in silence for several more moments. When they finally looked up, Brandon saw Sarah's eyes were brimming with moisture. So were his. But they were not tears of sadness or fear. They were tears of appreciation.

As they rose and prepared to leave, they outlined the plan one more time. The installation and groundbreaking were scheduled to begin at 11:00. Lucas and his entourage would have already left the hotel. Sarah would speak with him at the Temple Mount, confirm his decision, and get word to Brandon, who should be standing nearby.

"Do you know what you're going to say yet?" she asked.

He shook his head. "It's like I have two different topics. One is a judgment against evil, and the other is a warning and encouragement for the bride. I'm not sure which he wants."

"It will come," Sarah assured him. "Whatever is to be said, it will be said."

"I wish I had your confidence."

"We just prayed for his will to be done, didn't we?"

"Yeah."

She broke into a grin. "Then even you can't mess that up. Whatever is to be said, will be said."

He chuckled softly and they started for the door. "What about Tanya?" he asked. "If Lucas says yes to showing the tape, how will you get word to her?"

"She said she had other avenues. I don't think we have to worry about Tanya Chase."

Something about the phrase rang truer than Sarah had intended, but Brandon couldn't tell what. All he knew was that she was safe now—very, very safe.

"What about Katherine?" he asked.

Sarah turned to him. "As you're praying about what you're going to say, send up a prayer or two for her—she needs it."

Brandon caught something terribly troubled in her eyes, but she said no more. He made a point to pursue it later, as they headed toward the city. They stepped outside. The haze of ash was much thicker and the heat was already unbearable. He reached for the steel door and slid it shut.

"Do you think we should lock it?" Sarah asked.

"Probably wouldn't hurt." He reached for the padlock and snapped it into place. Finally, they turned and started up the steep road leading toward the Old City.

"She was so sweet," Sarah mused. "I wish we could have left her a gift or note or something to show our appreciation."

Brandon nodded in agreement, though he suspected she already knew. She seemed to have known nearly everything. They'd barely taken a half-dozen steps before they spotted a middle-aged Palestinian at the next house, locking his own door.

"Excuse me," Brandon called. "Excuse me. Do you speak English?"

The man turned. "Of course."

"I was wondering. The old woman that lives there?" He pointed toward the garage.

"What?"

"The old lady that lives there . . . in that garage? If you happen to see her, would you mind—"

"There is no old lady living there."

Brandon pointed, "No, I mean in that garage, right there."

"That's what I said, nobody lives there."

"Well, actually," Sarah explained, "there is. We had—"

"The owners, they have been away for nearly a month."

Brandon frowned. "But the woman who lives in the garage—"

"I told you, no woman lives there."

"Well . . . maybe she's like homeless or—"

"I watch their property. I feed their canary. There are only two keys, one for the garage, one for the house. I have them both. Nobody lives there." He finished locking his door, then turned and headed past them up the road.

Brandon and Sarah looked at each other, then back at the garage. Neither could say a word.

"Momm . . . whas woong? Mommm . . ."

Katherine put her hand to Eric's forehead. "Oh, sweetheart, you're burning up."

He frowned, obviously trying to clear his mind. "Whas . . . gooing on . . ."

"You're delirious, dear. We've got to get you back to the hospital. Here, let me help you get dressed."

It pained Katherine to lie to her son, but she could think of no other way. This would at least ensure his cooperation. And if Heylel should drop in and experience Eric's drugged state, he might buy it as well. She had her doubts, but it was worth a try.

He'd winced slightly and stirred from his sleep when she'd injected the Versed a few minutes earlier, and now it was performing exactly as Sarah had promised. She'd already called a taxi, leaving clear instructions for the driver to meet them down in the lower service entrance. She wanted to avoid the lobby and the security personnel she knew would be present.

After dressing Eric and grabbing her handbag with the other vial of the drug, Katherine led him out the door and down the hall toward the elevator. Unlike Ponte's Royal Suite, upstairs, there were no guards on this floor. The two of them arrived at the elevator and waited as Eric drifted in and out of coherency . . . sometimes appearing nearly wide awake, other times dozing off into dreamy sleep.

The elevator arrived. Katherine walked them both inside and pressed the button to the basement. With any luck they'd be able to go straight to the service entrance without stopping on any floors.

Unfortunately, Katherine's luck had never been good. They stopped at the fourth floor to let on an old Jewish couple and at the second to let on a child. Neither party asked questions, and she didn't offer any explanations. It took forever, but they finally arrived at the lobby. The doors opened and it was just as she had feared—the place was crawling with security.

The child exited first, followed by the couple. As they left, Katherine did her best to block Eric from any curious onlookers. When the doors were clear she reached out and pressed the *close* button. Once again time seemed to crawl until the doors started to shut.

"Ms. Lyon . . . Ms. Lyon." A hand suddenly appeared between the doors, slamming one side and causing them to reopen. It was the security guard from yesterday. The one who had led her and Brandon up to Sarah's room. "Is everything all right?" he asked.

She nodded. "For the most part."

He'd already spotted Eric. "Is he okay?"

Eric opened an eye, gave a smile, then drifted back to sleep. As he did he shifted his weight against Katherine, nearly throwing her off balance.

"Whoa." The guard moved to the other side to assist.

"I'm not sure what's wrong," Katherine said. "It's probably a complication from yesterday. I told them they should have spent the night at the hospital for observation, but with today's installation and everything . . ."

"Here, let's get him out and—"

"No, that's okay. I have a taxi downstairs. He's waiting to take us back to the hospital."

"Without security?"

"No, I called you guys. There's probably somebody waiting there now."

"Just the same." He pushed the *close* button. "I better go down with you and make sure."

"No, really, you don't have—"

But the doors were already closing. Fortunately, Eric remained sleeping as the elevator crept to the basement. Doing her best to make small talk, Katherine asked, "Is everybody else over at the Mount?"

"Just about. Couple more groups to transport, including yourselves. I'll let them know the situation and see what arrangements we can make for you."

"Thank you."

At last the doors opened.

"Here . . ." The guard began to help Eric out of the elevator.

"That's okay, I can handle it from here."

"Don't be ridiculous."

They stepped out of the elevator and headed down a dimly lit hall with Eric between them. The boy did little to help.

"That's funny," the guard said. "I don't see anyone here. You sure you called us?"

"Absolutely." Katherine breathed harder as Eric grew heavier. "He's probably just outside."

But when they stepped through the doors and into the bright sunlight there was no one there. Just an idling taxi with its Palestinian driver standing outside, grabbing a quick smoke. When he spotted them he quickly crossed to the passenger door and opened it.

"You seen anybody else here?" the guard asked as they arrived. "Any security people?"

The driver ground out his cigarette and shook his head.

The guard surveyed the area. "This is not right."

"Maybe he's up on the street," Katherine offered. She pulled Eric toward the door. "Here, help me get him inside."

The guard obliged, easing Eric into the car. But when he rose again, he still saw no sign of help. "Listen," he said, raising his sleeve toward his mouth. "Just stay put a moment and we'll find out what's going on."

"We don't have time to wait," Katherine insisted. "He's getting sicker by the minute."

The guard motioned for her to hang on and then turned to speak into the mike hidden in the cuff of his blazer sleeve. As he did, Katherine quickly crossed to the other side of the car and climbed in. "Mount Scopus Hospital, hurry."

The driver, who was still standing outside, motioned to the guard.

"Hurry!"

He did not move.

"Now. Let's go. *Let's go!*"

He hesitated.

"Now!"

Finally, reluctantly, he crossed back to the driver side, trying unsuccessfully to catch the guard's eye. But the man still had his back to them. At last the driver climbed behind the wheel and shut his door.

"The hospital," Katherine ordered. "It's an emergency!"

"But"—the driver motioned toward the guard—"the man . . ."

"Hurry! Hurry!"

Muttering something in Arabic, he put the car into gear.

"Now, let's go!"

They started forward.

Hearing the movement, the guard finally turned. "Hey, wait a minute. Wait a minute!"

"Go!" Katherine shouted. "Go!"

"But—"

"I'm paying the fare, not him. Let's go!"

More than a little frustrated, the driver accelerated. He looked nervously through the rearview mirror as the guard started after them.

"Keep going!" Katherine cried. "Keep going!"

The driver cursed in Arabic but continued driving. They headed up and around the building. Katherine stole a look over her shoulder. The guard was squinting to read their cab I.D. number and shouting back into his sleeve.

The cab pulled up to King David Road and the driver started to turn right. This would take them past the hotel's entrance and ensure certain capture.

"No!" Katherine shouted. "Turn left! Turn left!"

"But the hospital, it is—"

"Left!"

Throwing up his hands in frustration, the driver uttered another oath and turned left, causing more than one driver in the opposing lane to slam on his brakes, giving opportunity for the driver to curse even more.

Katherine looked over her shoulder.

"Where to now, lady?"

She gave no answer, continuing to look out the back window as they headed down the hill until the hotel disappeared from sight. When she turned back she recognized they were heading toward the same area she and Sarah had walked the night before.

"Lady . . . you still want hospital?"

"No, uh . . ." She looked around. "No, drop us off here."

"What?"

"Here, right here!"

"But we have not—"

"I'll pay you full fare, just drop us off here. Now! Stop the car and drop us off!"

As she hoped, her anger got her way. He swerved toward the right curb near the bottom of the hill. The cab barely stopped before she jumped out, grabbed Eric, and threw a handful of bills at the driver. Then, with minimal help from Eric, they crossed the busy street against the light and headed east, toward the Valley of Hinnom.

The Temple Mount was packed. The area of paved limestone north and east of the Dome of the Rock, the expansive park of cypress and olive trees north of that, even the rooftops that surrounded this twenty-five-plus acres of the most hotly contested real estate in the world were crammed with people trying to see the ceremonies on the stage which was located less than a hundred yards from the Golden

Gate. And if they couldn't see the stage, there were always the two Jumbotron video screens rising high into the air on either side.

Brandon stood and watched the opening ceremonies upon the stairs called the Scales of Souls. These were a series of steps directly under the stone arches where Muslims believed men's souls would be weighed on Judgment Day. To his immediate right, on the stone pavement, was an area many believed to have been the site of the original temple, and just past that was the famous gold-roofed Dome of the Rock, one of the most holy sites in all of Islam. Inside was the rock upon which Jews, Christians, and Muslims believed Abraham had offered Isaac up to the Lord. The Mount was a somber, reverent place, and it seemed that everywhere Brandon looked some major religious event had occurred.

He had a strong sense that those events weren't entirely over.

He directed his attention back to the stage where an orchestra was playing various national anthems as country after country marched forward presenting their flags. Lucas Ponte sat onstage surrounded by nearly a hundred dignitaries. He watched the ceremony with the perfect mixture of strength and humility, nodding graciously to each flag bearer who placed their flags into one of the hundreds of holders surrounding the stage.

Brandon turned to look out over the crowd, searching the sea of faces for Sarah. She should have been there by now, but he saw no sign of her.

A cheer rose up and he turned back to the stage. The last of the flags had been presented and the music had changed to something noble and stirring as a video clip on the life of Lucas Ponte appeared up on the Jumbotrons. It covered everything from his humble beginnings as a grandson of Italian immigrants in Chicago, to photos of his valedictorian speech, to his emerging social consciousness at Notre Dame, to his stint in the Peace Corps, to his political career which started locally, then rose to Illinois governor, culminating in his illustrious career as president of the United States. It included the tragedy of losing his wife to cancer and yet his determination to fill out his second term for the good of the country, followed by his decision to continue serving the world through his work with the Cartel. It spoke of the organization's struggles to usher in world peace and their recent cure for the Scorpion virus. The piece was stirring and worked the crowd into such excited anticipation that the entire Mount roared in appreciation as Lucas Ponte was finally introduced and approached the lectern.

Brandon turned back to the crowd. They shouted, they cheered, they clapped, many wiped tears from their eyes. He'd never seen anything like it. And still the roar continued. A full minute passed, and then another as, up on the screen, Ponte smiled in both appreciation and humility, while wiping away a tear or two of his own. It was quite a performance.

"Brandon . . . Brandon . . ."

He turned to see Sarah working her way through the crowd toward him. When she arrived he shouted over the noise, "Are you okay?"

She nodded.

"Did you talk to him?"

She leaned forward. "What?"

"Did you talk to him? What did he say?"

"He said yes."

Brandon's heart sank and soared.

"It won't be for long," she shouted. "Just enough to call you up onstage—to use you as an example of his 'accessibility' and 'open-mindedness.'"

"He hasn't missed a trick, has he?"

"He doesn't think so."

The cheers started to subside. They turned back toward the stage. Several more seconds passed before the applause quieted down enough for Ponte to begin.

"Friends . . ."

But that was all it took before the crowd started up again. Brandon turned back to scan the cheering, shouting, tearstained faces. And he was expected to go up against this? Was he crazy? They'd rip him apart!

That's when he felt Sarah take his hand. He looked at her. She smiled, doing her best to appear encouraging.

When the crowd finally settled, Ponte resumed. "Standing before you this day, upon this sacred and holy site, I can only say that I am overwhelmed. Humbled and overwhelmed."

More applause. When it ceased he continued. "Jerusalem . . . the city of peace. Yet, for how many centuries, no, for how many millennia has that name been scorned and mocked. Jerusalem . . . she who has been destroyed and rebuilt eighteen times. Jerusalem . . . she who has changed religions eleven times. Jerusalem . . . she who has never been a city of peace . . . but the symbol of seething hatred and unspeakable violence."

A hush fell over the Mount. A quarter million people grew very, very still. Ponte said nothing, holding the pause for as long as possible before he continued. "But all that is about to change. Starting today, Jerusalem will finally become all that she was destined to be. Starting today, Jerusalem will be a city of hope, of understanding, and most importantly, a city of peace!"

The crowd clapped and cheered.

"But not just a city of peace. Starting from this moment forward she will become the symbol of humankind's ability to overcome our barbaric past, the symbol of our entrance into a new age, the center of a new world order whose one and only theme is . . . peace!"

More cheers.

"Peace!"

Still more.

"Peace!"

Once again the roar was deafening. Brandon looked down and shook his head, marveling. But when he glanced back up, something above the stage caught his attention. A cloud of mist had begun to form. And as the crowd cheered and Ponte resumed, it continued to grow.

"And why are we entering that peace? It is not because of anything I have accomplished." He motioned to the dignitaries behind him. "It is not because of anything my friends, your leaders, have accomplished. No." He pushed up his glasses and continued. "It is simply because our time has arrived. Just as seasons come and go, so do the seasons of human history."

The cloud began to condense, slowing taking the shape Brandon had seen far too often.

"And now we are entering into a brand-new season. The season of humankind. A season where we will no longer focus upon our differences in race, in nationality, and perhaps even more importantly, our differences in religion—for, as this city can attest, it is differences in religion which have proven the most dangerous of all."

"Brandon ..."

He threw Sarah a glance. She was staring straight ahead. "You see it, too?" he asked.

"I see something."

"This is the day, perhaps the first since the glory of Rome, that we will be able to throw off the yoke of religious division, that we will no longer allow it to manipulate and control our destiny ..."

A tightness began to grip Brandon's gut. He suddenly felt very, very cold—not only about what he was hearing, but about what he was seeing. For there, hovering over the stage, with Lucas Ponte directly below it, was the head of the serpent.

At the mouth of the Hinnom Valley lay a grassy park. Despite the ceremony on the Mount two miles away, a Palestinian family sat under one of the many pine trees enjoying a picnic lunch. They seemed the quintessential family—a husband, wife, two beautiful children. They ate and teased, shouted and laughed, obviously enjoying each other's company. Katherine couldn't help but stare as she and Eric made their way across the narrow ravine to the dirt road leading up the other side. That's all she had ever wanted, a family like that.

And she'd nearly had it, too ... until her husband's murder, until her father's death, until her bout with alcohol. And then, just when everything looked hopeless, Michael Coleman came upon the scene. Like her father and Sarah and a dozen others, Michael had also spoken of faith and of God's love. And then, just when she was starting to believe that there might really be some goodness in life, that there might really be a God of love, Michael was also taken. End of topic. End of discussion. End of hope.

Now there was only Eric.

The drug had barely started to wear off. She thought of giving him another injection, but Sarah's earlier words about free will and that he could still denounce Heylel rang in her ears. As far as she could tell, that was his last remaining chance. And, since it's hard to make a freewill decision doped up out of your mind, she decided to let more of it wear off.

They continued climbing the ridge.

"Whar we goin'?" His speech was still slurred, but he was definitely more coherent. "Whar you takin' us?"

"Just a little farther, sweetheart. See those nice cliffs over there?" She pointed to where the Hinnom and Kidron Valleys met. "I thought maybe we could sit there and talk."

"Talk?"

"Yeah, you know, like we used to. Just the two of us."

"Wha abou Lucas . . . an Heylel. Whar's Heylel?"

"They're busy, sweetheart. Right now it's just you and me. Just you and me . . ."

"But those of you who know me, who know what I have been striving to accomplish these many years, know of my insistence upon tolerance and mutual respect."

The crowd applauded in agreement.

Brandon looked on, his mouth bone dry, as he watched the serpent's head condense over the stage.

Sarah turned to him. "That's what killed your father—what attacked you?"

He nodded.

"Just because we do not agree with any one person does not give us the right to deprive that person of their voice. Just because their views are extreme, or even hurtful, does not give us the right to silence them. That is not the mutual respect and love for which I have worked so long and hard. Despite our disagreements, they are still our brothers and sisters, they are still part of our unique oneness. Because we are all one, my friends. We are one people . . . we are one community . . . we are one planet!"

The applause grew more enthusiastic.

Brandon threw another look at Sarah. Her eyes were riveted to the serpent's head. She appeared even more frightened than he was. He reached out and put an arm around her. She barely noticed.

"That is why I have personally invited a dissenting voice to come and briefly share our platform. You may disagree with what he has to say, perhaps even find it repulsive. Some would insist that his narrow religious thinking is a throwback to the very hatred and intolerance we are eliminating here today. Others may see him as a symbol of what has crippled and shackled our human spirit for so many centuries. So why do I invite him? Because he still deserves the right to be heard, because he is still my brother, he is still part of our human family."

By now the image of the head was so clear Brandon could see the tongue flicking in and out ... just as it had in his visions, just as it had in his father's church ... moments before it had opened its mouth and consumed him.

"Many of you from the West may remember the televised event featuring our good friend, Reverend Jimmy Tyler." Ponte turned to those onstage behind him and acknowledged the man in the wheelchair. With great effort, Jimmy Tyler raised his hand in a wave. "That was when this young man I am about to introduce first came to the world's attention. But for those of you unfamiliar with him, a news crew has assembled a brief video that should serve as an adequate introduction before he comes forward."

"All right, Tanya," Sarah whispered.

Brandon nodded.

"In it you will hear statements that may strike you as outrageous, even offensive. You will see things that may defy science and the laws of physics. Do I believe such things are possible? What I believe is of no consequence. All I ask is for you to listen to his claims, look at the world around us, and draw your own conclusions. Ask yourself if his views are not the embodiment of the chains that have enslaved our planet since the beginning of time. Ask yourself if the writhing our planet is currently undergoing is nothing but a final effort to, once and for all, throw off those shackles."

Brandon lowered his head. He was being set up. Even now, even with world opinion on Heylel's side, even with the prophecies clearly stating the people would follow him, he was still stacking the deck.

"And let me apologize in advance for any bias you may note in this videotaped introduction. Although the news team tried to be objective, it was obvious they found the material deeply disturbing, and like the rest of us, they are only human ..."

Ponte stepped back, motioned to the screens, and Brandon and Sarah joined the rest of the world in watching.

The narrator's voice was unfamiliar to him, but the images were crystal clear.

"Born of religious parents, Brandon Martus was raised in a strict fundamentalist Christian household ..."

A series of photos flashed upon the screen. Seeing his parents displayed before the world filled Brandon with both anger and sorrow. Was there nothing this man would not stoop to?

"But it wasn't until the death of his sister in an auto accident for which he was responsible that Martus began to experience the deeper aspects of guilt and condemnation for which his faith is known."

The screen showed photos of him with his little sister—images that brought instant tears to his eyes. He had to look down. A moment later he felt Sarah moving closer to him for support.

But it was only the beginning. Soon the video was discussing his "so-called psychic powers," replaying portions of the older report Tanya had broadcast that included interviews of angry and disappointed patients. Next came the photos of Sarah and mention of their "sexual repressions" and "failed marriage."

He glanced at Sarah. She was taking it no better than he.

After that came clips from Jimmy Tyler's TV rally. Images of Brandon shouting, Brandon screaming, Brandon approaching Tyler and yelling, "The blood of the sheep will be upon the head of the shepherd!" This was followed by the pitcher of blood, the shattering glass, Tyler choking and coughing helplessly as Brandon, appearing out of control, shrieked, "The hand of the Lord is upon you, and you shall no longer be able to speak or spread your deceit in my name!" All of this was intercut with shots of the Los Angeles audience booing and throwing things onstage . . . as the live audience on the Mount also grew more and more agitated over what they saw.

New images began. A video of a party with plenty of drinking, dancing, carousing. At first Brandon didn't recognize it, until he caught a glimpse of Salman. This was the party he had thrown at Thyatira. There were other shots, angles of half-naked men and women which may or may not have been part of the party, but which definitely gave it every appearance of an orgy.

Now they were back in L.A. with Brandon onstage shouting: "Surely as a wife treacherously departs from her husband so have you dealt treacherously with me!"

Now, back to the party—shots of young Banu snuggling into Brandon's arms with the narrator explaining, "But such hypocrisy cannot be hidden for long . . ." A close-up of the intoxicated girl. " . . . especially when it comes to underaged children, no more than fourteen or fifteen years old."

The anger and disapproval of the Temple Mount grew louder.

More angles of Brandon screaming onstage, "You have played the harlot with many lovers!"

Back to Brandon at the orgy where he was seen abusing the child by throwing her across the room into the table, sending glass and booze crashing all around her.

By now the Mount's anger had turned to audible boos and hissing. And still the video continued . . .

"But I don't wan' things diff'ren'!"

"Eric, sweetheart—"

"Heylel promised . . . and nothin's gonna stop us! Nothin'!"

For the briefest moment Eric's anger had pushed through the effects of the drug. Katherine hesitated, wondering if she should inject more or wait and see if he settled back under its influence. They'd found a seat on a boulder atop one of the cliffs. Forty feet below was rocky rubble, dead grass, and parched olive trees that stretched across the ravine and up the other side toward the Old City. Occasionally they could hear the cheers and roar of the crowd from the Temple Mount that was about a mile and a half away.

She glanced at her son. His eyes were already growing heavy and starting to close. "Eric?"

They opened.

"If you continue with Heylel, you'll be responsible for more people dying, maybe even more than Scorpion."

"Tha's their problem," he mumbled.

"Eric?"

He woke more. "If they get in the way, tha's their problem."

The coldness of the statement hit Katherine hard. Even in his half-asleep stupor, he knew what he wanted . . . and the consequences. And at that moment Katherine knew he would not change, he would never change. He would hold to the decision he'd made so many months before. He would follow Heylel, he would always follow him, and there was nothing she could say or do to change his mind. Regardless of the millions that had died in the recent past or that may soon die in the future, her son had made his decision.

Numbly, Katherine Lyon reached into her purse.

Memories of Eric flooded in—his sweetness, his kindness, his tearstained face when he'd caught his first fish and saw it struggling for breath on the riverbank. But other images came as well . . . the bloody carnage of the birds atop that rock in Nepal. The death of his friend, Deepak. *Momma, I made his heart stop!* The murder of the officer on the airport tarmac.

An unbearable ache spread through her chest, making it impossible to breathe as she pulled the first vial from her purse, followed by the syringe. She looked at her son. He was dozing peacefully. How was it possible? How could this child, this flesh of her flesh, this soul of her soul, be the murderer of millions?

She took a ragged breath, then pulled out the syringe. She removed the protective tip she had placed back over the needle. With trembling hands she inserted it into the first vial and drew out the remaining eight ccs of the clear liquid. She hesitated a moment, unsure, then reached back into her purse to pull out the new vial. She inserted the needle, and though it was difficult to see through the tears, she drew out the full ten ccs.

Another wave of cheers wafted across the valley.

Eric stirred and she watched him. So tender, so innocent . . . and yet a murderer, a mass murderer. Her heart screamed in agony, and she bit her lip so the words would not escape. *Dear God, dear God, please don't make me do this!*

But of course there was no God. At least for her. And, even if there was, he would not answer.

She reached back into her purse and pulled out a narrow cloth belt, the one that went with her green floral dress. Everything was blurring. She could see only the syringe, the belt, her shaking hands.

For God so loved the world that he gave his only begotten Son . . .

The phrase surprised her. It was a Bible verse, the one printed over the door of her father's church. She hadn't thought of it in years. Once again it echoed in her head.

For God so loved the world . . .

"God's love," the same words her father had preached, that Michael had preached, that Sarah had preached. Words. That's all they had to offer. That's all anyone had to offer except . . . except, perhaps . . . God.

. . . that he gave his only begotten Son . . .

Giving up his only Son . . . Well, at least maybe he knew a little of what she was going through.

She reached down to Eric's arm. It was tan and the hair was just starting to thicken from manhood. She looked down at his hand, the one that had clutched hers at the state fair during his first ride on the Octopus.

Momma, I'm scared!

Just hang on to me, baby. It'll be okay, just hang on . . .

She reached down and lifted the hand to her lips, then tenderly kissed its open palm.

For God so loved the world that he gave his only begotten Son . . .

Was this what God had felt? This impossible grief, when he'd given up *his* Son?

She pushed up Eric's sleeve, then wrapped the belt around his arm, pulling it tight until the veins began to bulge.

He stirred, opening his eyes. "Whar you doin'?"

"It's okay, baby . . ." It was all she could do to force out the words. "This will make you better . . . This will make everything better."

She searched her lap for the syringe. It was difficult to see it through the tears.

For God so loved the world . . .

If this was the type of pain he'd gone through . . . for the world . . . then maybe she'd been wrong, maybe he did have some love in him . . .

She found the syringe and lifted it up. Sarah had explained the need to tap up the bubbles and squirt them out, but her vision wasn't clear enough to see them. Not that it mattered, not with eighteen ccs. She lay his arm in her lap. For the briefest moment she lowered her head and rested it against his shoulder, unable to continue. She turned and kissed his neck. A sob escaped. This was her child, her cooing, gurgling, laughing baby.

He would also be the murderer of millions.

She raised her head from his shoulder. She tightened her legs around his arm to hold it in place, wiped the tears from her eyes, and searched for the largest vein.

That's when she heard Heylel's voice. *"What do you think you're doing?"*

Her words came out choking but determined. "I'm stopping you. You'll not use my son to kill anymore."

Suddenly Eric's body came alive. He tried to twist, to pull away his arm. *"Stop it!"* Heylel bellowed. *"Stop it!"*

But he didn't have a chance. Despite the movement, Katherine held his arm firmly between her legs. She brought the needle toward a puffy blue vein. It pressed into the skin, starting to pierce the flesh, when she heard—

"Momma . . ." It was the voice of her baby boy, of little Eric. "Momma, I'm scared."

And it burst her heart. She was overcome. She could not do it. She could not kill her only son.

That's when Heylel made his move. He jerked Eric's arm out of her lap. The movement startled her and before she could react, he grabbed the hand with the syringe and tore it from her grip. Then, with one swift move, he raised it into the air and plunged it deep into her chest.

"Eric . . ."

She caught a glimpse of his eyes but Eric wasn't there. Only Heylel.

She raised her hands to her chest, trying to pull out the syringe, which gave Heylel opportunity to scoot away from her, letting her tumble off the rock. As she fell, he slid down to join her, using her momentum to kick her the rest of the way . . . until she rolled over the edge of the cliff.

"Eric . . . !"

She hit one rock and sailed through the air. Then she hit another and another—falling, flying, flailing. Time slowed. She could hear Heylel's laughter high above, but she felt no betrayal or anger. Instead, her mind focused, growing amazingly sharp. She couldn't do it. She loved her son too much to kill him. And yet God's love was greater than that—because he *had* gone through with it. He *had* killed his Son . . . for the world . . . *for her!* Was such a thing possible? As much as she loved Eric, was it possible that God loved her even more?

The answer was vividly clear . . . not in words, but in action. He *had* killed his Son for her, he *had* gone through the agony that she could not endure . . . for *her*, to save *her*, because he loved *her!*

. . . that whosoever believes in him shall not perish but have everlasting life.

Suddenly it made sense. Suddenly she understood. Katherine had no idea how long she fell. The concept of time was gone. All she knew was that now, at last, she finally understood the fullness of God's love. And for the first time since her childhood, she asked that he would once again hold her in his arms.

Katherine Lyon's prayer was answered before she hit the ground.

As Sarah watched the video, she noticed the theme had begun to change. Instead of dealing with Brandon's "anger" and "hypocrisy" it began drawing connections between his statements and the world catastrophes. Using portions of Tanya's old broadcast, it discussed the worldwide drought, the consequent famine, the earthquakes, the volcanoes, even the outbreak of Scorpion, while cutting back and forth to Brandon on the L.A. stage, shouting the passages from Jeremiah.

"My anger and my fury will be poured out on this place . . ." The scene was followed by various shots of eruptions, blasting plumes of smoke and ash. "On man . . ." Next came portraits of suffering humanity, dying men and women, living skeletons, a starving child trying to nurse from his dead mother. "And beast . . ." Malnourished cattle, a thousand chickens dead from heat prostration. "On the trees of the field ..." Pacific Northwest forests igniting in flames from fiery lava. "And on the fruit of the ground ..." Shriveled crops, desert farmlands. "And it will burn and not be quenched!"

The narrator resumed: "Perhaps this is all just coincidence ..."

Back to the video of Brandon onstage, shouting: "Be astonished oh heavens at this and be horribly afraid." Next a shot of him and Sarah pelted by rotten eggs. Back to Brandon. "Be very desolate, says the Lord ..."

The narrator continued. "Then again, perhaps it is not."

Sarah watched the screen in amazement. Heylel's fear and hatred was even greater than she had imagined. He was working the crowd into a frenzy. Many were shouting, swearing, shaking their fists as if they had finally found the source of their torment.

And still the images continued, recapping the most horrific moments as the narrator concluded: "Could one man really be responsible for all of this turmoil? It is doubtful. And yet we must ask ourselves, could these natural disasters be a death knell? Could they be, as he insists, the final act of a jealous God—a divine temper tantrum thrown by a desperate deity who knows he has lost control, who knows that we as a people will no longer endure his tyranny? Interesting questions and ones that may never be answered. And yet as we join together to face this new era, these are questions that we must all begin to ask."

Sarah couldn't believe her ears. In less than two minutes, he had started making the transition from blaming Brandon to blaming God. She suspected it would only be the beginning. Over the next few months, perhaps years, it would continue. The pride and hatred she had experienced last night up in Heylel's room would grow and spread until he persuaded the whole earth to attempt what a third of heaven had failed to do ... to rebel and overthrow God.

Now she understood more than ever why Brandon had to speak today, why it was important the people be warned and the facts presented. Each and every individual would have to make a choice. If not now, then soon—very, very soon.

The music swelled to an ominous ending as the video freeze-framed on Brandon shouting. The image remained on screen several seconds before it slowly faded. But the crowd's anger did not. It continued to grow, feeding upon itself. And, the louder it grew, the more solid the serpent's head above the stage became. To Sarah it no longer appeared as a thick mist. It had become a tangible flesh-and-blood entity.

Lucas Ponte began to speak. "Please...," he shouted, "please ..." He motioned for the crowd to quiet. "Please ... I told you the video could be provocative, and I must apologize for its bias. Surely, not all of these facts could be true. Some must be exaggerated."

The crowd disagreed.

"Please ... regardless of what we think of him, or his religion, he is allowed his opinion. Please." Again Lucas held out his hands. "Please, we must show restraint. Allow him to explain. We must allow him to justify his actions and his God. Please . . ."

Gradually the crowd began to quiet.

"Good . . . good." Then, scanning the Mount, he called out, "Brandon . . . Brandon Martus, are you out there? Mr. Martus, please come forward and share with us your views. Mr. Martus . . ."

Sarah turned to her husband. He was as white as a sheet . . . and trembling.

"Mr. Martus, I know you are out there."

She wrapped an arm around him. Now was the time. All that they'd been through, all that they'd learned, it was for this one single moment. He took a shaky breath and looked at her. For the briefest second she thought he was too frightened to continue. "Be strong and courageous," she shouted over the crowd.

He swallowed hard and nodded. Then he shouted back, "What can they do to a dead man?" He tried giving his killer grin, but it would not come. She smiled anyway, hoping he didn't see the concern on her own face.

Wiping the sweat from his forehead with his sleeve, he took her hand and they started forward. The crowd in front of them began to part . . . not without grumbling, shouting occasional oaths, and spitting on the ground before them.

But they continued.

Sarah looked up ahead to the stage. The serpent's head began opening its mouth, as if preparing to devour them. Maybe it would. She knew Brandon saw it, probably more clearly than she. But she also knew he had faced its gaping mouth before and had survived.

She prayed he could do it again.

CHAPTER 21

I *HAVE WAITED A LONG TIME FOR THIS."*

Brandon recognized the voice instantly. He looked up at the serpent's head, which hovered twenty yards before them over the stage. Its jaw had opened wide enough for Brandon to see into the throat. But it was not the throat of a snake. Instead it was the swirling vortex of screaming, fiery faces, the anguished specters whose mouths twisted and shrieked in unearthly wails.

He glanced at Sarah. She saw them, too.

"YOU ARE MINE."

Although the voice came from the head, the mouth did not move. Just below the apparition stood Ponte, looking kindly down upon them as they approached the stage. They were fifteen yards away when a young man lunged toward them, screaming a curse in French. He was intercepted by security and immediately swept away.

For Brandon everything was turning ethereal, as in a dream, as in the dozen nightmares he'd had since his encounter in the church. They were ten yards from the stage now. He was so frightened he barely had feeling in his legs. In fact he was surprised he could even walk. But he continued forward, one foot after another.

The jaw unhinged, opening even wider. It was no longer possible to see the eyes or snout—only the fangs, the flicking tongue, and the twisting, screaming faces of fire. More memories rushed in. How he'd been sucked into that very throat—how he'd felt the fire searing his waist, his chest, his neck, and finally his face until . . . until . . .

"Don't look," Sarah shouted. "Think about the Lord."

Yes. That's what he'd done before. At the church. He'd kept his attention fixed on the Lord. Back then it had been on the vision of a nail-pierced hand. But this was not the church; there was no hand. And he could not look away. As he stared, the swirling faces began taking on forms of those he knew—first his little sister, then his father, then others who had passed away. Each cried out to him, beckoning for him to join them. He knew it was a trick, another deception.

But they looked so real.

"The Lord!" Sarah shouted. "Think of the Lord!"

Brandon barely heard. This was the mouth that had devoured him, that had nearly destroyed him. And now he was walking directly into it. Of his own free will! He wanted to bolt, to run away. But where do you run when you're surrounded by a quarter million people? You don't. The machine had been set in motion, and there was nothing he could do to escape it.

They arrived at the stairs leading up to the stage. He hesitated, unable to continue.

"Please . . ." He looked up to see Ponte spreading open his arms. "There is nothing to fear. We are all friends."

He glanced at Sarah. She was pale and almost as frightened as he. Still, somehow, she managed to give him the slightest of nods. And that was all he needed. He gripped her hand tighter, and the two of them started up the steps. As they did, the crowd's displeasure grew even louder.

"Please . . ." Ponte addressed the audience again. "Please . . . this will only take a few moments. Please . . ." But the crowd was far less gracious. "Please, if you do not give him an opportunity to speak, then that makes us no better than he. Please, now . . ."

The crowd settled slightly as Brandon and Sarah arrived at the top of the steps and started the long trek toward Ponte . . . and the open throat of fiery faces just above him. But as they forced themselves to continue walking in obedience and in faith, a most unusual thing happened . . . the apparition began to retreat.

"Brandon. . . ," Sarah whispered.

"I see it."

It continued pulling back, maintaining the exact same distance from them until it was hovering over the dignitaries at the rear of the stage.

"It's afraid of us," Brandon said.

"Not just us." Sarah nodded toward the audience.

Brandon turned and caught his breath. Interspersed throughout the crowd, every twenty yards or so, were what appeared to be giant towering men. They were a good three to four feet taller than any men around them, and they were wrapped in robes of dazzling brightness.

He turned to Sarah in astonishment.

"That's not all." She motioned toward the hills surrounding them.

He turned to look. On every hill, as far as the eye could see, stood thousands of the same creatures . . . all glowing, all watching.

He knew who they were. And with that realization came the understanding that he and Sarah were not alone. Regardless of what would happen, they were not alone. As he stood there, before the host of heaven, he felt a confidence and a faith begin to swell inside of him. And with that faith came the warmth of the fire. It started in his belly, then slowly rose into his chest.

Ponte greeted them as they arrived. "Thank you both for joining us. I can imagine it is not easy to appear before such a large audience—not only in front of the hundreds of thousands of people here in Jerusalem, but before the billions of people watching on television around the world. To appear in front of so many people must be very intimidating, very intimidating, indeed."

Brandon knew what Ponte was doing. He could feel the terror at the edge of his mind eager to rush in. And it would take so little effort to allow it. A tiny choice of his will. But he also knew that was where the battle was being fought. Regardless of the odds, regardless of the outcome, the real battle was being waged within his will.

Keeping that in mind, Brandon chose not to look out at the audience, nor back at the serpent head. Instead of caving in and obeying his fears, he did as Sarah had suggested and looked upon the Lord. Quietly, in his heart, he began to worship him. And, as he worshiped, the fire grew hotter.

"Dr. Weintraub." Ponte smiled warmly. "It's so good to see you again."

Brandon watched as the man focused his gaze upon her. He could only guess what doubts and feelings of unworthiness he was stirring inside her mind. She took an unsteady breath, and for a moment Brandon thought she might crumble. But as she exhaled he saw her lips begin to move, almost imperceptibly. She was also praying.

"So tell us, Mr. Martus . . ." Ponte continued to speak as he gave Brandon a microphone which a stagehand had passed up to him. "As briefly as possible, have we in any way misrepresented your beliefs? Is there anything you'd like to clarify for us?"

There was another surge of panic. Brandon still had no idea what he was to say. Judgment of the world or warning to the bride? Which? But before he allowed the fear to take hold, he forced himself to blurt out an answer. "Yes!"

Instantly, the clouds of confusion parted, as if this act of faith alone had cleared his mind.

"Well," Ponte said, "we're waiting."

Realizations poured in. Now, Brandon understood why he'd been unable to decide which of the two topics he was to speak on. He was to talk about them both. He wasn't sure how, but that wasn't his concern. He turned to Ponte. And, in another act of faith, he opened his mouth. The words began to come. "The Lord would say two things to you."

"Two things?" Ponte asked.

Brandon nodded. "The Word of his mouth is a double-edged sword." The fire had risen to his throat now, emboldening him until he could look out into the audience. "One edge will protect and instruct the righteous . . . the other will cut down and destroy the evil."

"I see." Ponte pretended to chuckle. "Sort of good news, bad news."

Amusement rippled through the audience.

"Please"—Ponte motioned to him—"share with us. Tell us what more we can expect from this God of yours."

The fire burst from Brandon's mouth. Words barely came to mind before he spoke them. And the more he spoke, the hotter they grew. "Who will have pity on you, O Jerusalem? Who will mourn for you? Who will stop to ask how you are?"

Ponte turned his back and walked a few steps away, obviously distancing himself from what was being said.

"You have rejected me, declares the Lord. You keep on backsliding. So I will lay hands on you and destroy you; I can no longer show compassion. I will winnow them with a winnowing fork at the city gates of the land. I will bring bereavement and destruction on my people, for they have not changed their ways."

Once again the audience began to voice their displeasure. But the broiling intensity inside Brandon could not be contained.

"I will make their widows more numerous than the sand of the sea. At midday I will bring a destroyer against the mothers of their young men; suddenly I will bring down on them anguish and terror."

Boos and catcalls began, but Brandon would not be stopped. He started focusing upon specific faces in the crowd, pleading with them, begging them to see.

"The mother of seven will grow faint and breathe her last. Her sun will set while it is still day; she will be disgraced and humiliated. I will put the survivors to the sword before their enemies, declares the—"

"Yes, well, I think you've made your point, Mr. Martus."

"But—"

Ponte approached. "Once again you've proven to us that your God knows nothing of love. He cares only for his own interests and nothing for ours. And, as far as I can tell, that's anything but love."

"But it is." Sarah leaned over and spoke into Brandon's microphone. There was a brief squeal of feedback. Brandon handed it over to her and she continued. "It's a deeper love. It's a greater love."

A flicker of concern crossed Ponte's face. He was not expecting this.

Sarah continued. "It's a love that tells us what we need to hear, not what we want to hear. It's a love that cares more for our lives than our feelings."

Brandon looked at her, marveling. She glanced at him, as pleased with her performance as he was. Obviously, the same fire had ignited her soul. She turned back to the audience. "Don't you see? God loves us so much that he'll sacrifice anything to save us . . . even our love toward him. If it means disciplining us, he'll discipline us . . . even if it means our hating him."

"Please, Dr. Weintraub," Ponte interrupted, "it makes no difference how you try to spin it, the truth of the matter is—"

"He loves us so much that he destroyed his own Son . . . for us."

"Dr.—"

"And"—she turned directly on him—"he will destroy anyone who tries to cut off that love."

"Love?" Ponte was no longer able to hide his scorn. "How can anyone describe what we saw up on the screen as love? Human suffering, indescribable agony, unspeakable sorrow? That's not love. The writhings, screamings, the ignored cries for mercy? How can you call that love?"

The audience applauded in agreement, and Ponte turned to them. "The intolerable bondage we, the human family, have been under all of these centuries ... that is not love!"

Cheers of agreement followed.

Ponte grew more agitated ... which had the desired effect upon the audience, giving them permission to vent even more anger. Brandon looked back out at the shouting faces ... and that's when he spotted him. Just a few rows back, moving toward the stage. Salman Kilyos.

As Ponte worked up the crowd, Salman took advantage of the distraction, moving closer and closer. He was holding a sweater. Brandon's mind raced. Why was anyone carrying a sweater on such a hot day? Unless they were hiding something underneath. Unless they were—

Instantly, Brandon understood.

Ponte continued to rail. "You talk about a self-sacrificing love. An interesting theory ... but where is the proof? I ask you, where is the truth to validate such claims?"

Brandon watched Salman, praying that someone would stop him before he got himself hurt or killed. He was in the second row now, working his way through the agitated crowd. Surely the dozens of security personnel around the stage would spot him. But they didn't. They saw nothing, almost as if they were blinded.

"Real love is based upon action. Like stopping the deadly Scorpion virus."

The audience broke into cheers.

"Like uniting every person, tribe, and nation."

The cheering grew louder.

"Like ushering in an age of peace and prosperity such as the world has never known!"

The Mount roared in approval. They were ecstatic—shouting, stomping their feet, waving their arms.

Salman made his move. He pulled the large black revolver from his sweater and lunged toward the stage.

"No!" Brandon shouted. But he couldn't be heard over the crowd.

Ponte stood less than six feet from the edge of the stage when he glanced down and saw Salman taking aim. Everything turned to slow motion as he began to turn, as he began to shout.

Brandon started toward him. He could not stop Salman, but he could knock Ponte out of the way.

Salman prepared to fire.

Brandon leaped toward Ponte, once again shouting. "Nooo . . ."

Salman pulled the trigger.

Brandon slammed into Ponte, wrapping his arms around him and pulling him to the ground . . . just as Salman fired once, twice, three times.

The first bullet went wide, the second shattered Brandon's clavicle, and the third pierced his lung and pulmonary artery. The impacts were so powerful that he didn't feel himself hitting the stage . . . though he did hear a multitude of shots fired and knew security had finally discovered Salman.

"Brandon!"

Lying on the stage, he saw Sarah's approach. He wanted to yell at her to stay back, that they'd misunderstand. But he could not move. Instead, he watched in numb horror as a half-dozen red laser dots found her body and a half-dozen hollow-point bullets tore into her flesh.

She landed inches from his face.

Security swarmed the stage. All Brandon saw were rushing feet and legs. What had gone wrong? Why had he only been allowed to deliver one-half of the message, the judgment? What about the other, the message to the bride?

Reality began disintegrating, strobing bits and pieces flashed at unexpected moments. He saw Ponte rising. Heard him shouting. He knew the man wasn't happy. He knew Ponte was all too aware of how Brandon's self-sacrifice would be construed. He'd been double-crossed. He'd been out-loved. "No," Ponte was shouting. "This isn't right! This isn't how it's supposed to be!"

"What's he doing?" the technical director cried.

Ryan Holton shook his head as he watched Ponte rant and rave over the monitors. "It's not right!" the chairman was shouting. "It isn't fair. You tricked me, you tricked me!"

"He's lost it," Ryan answered.

"We got to get off him. Cut to something else!"

Ryan nodded and quickly spoke into his headset. "VTR . . . give me a segment."

"What do you—"

"Anything. I don't care what you have, just give me something, now!"

"Stand by."

Ryan watched the monitors in amazement as Ponte's anger continued. The man was definitely out of control. He was standing on the stage, seeming to shout at no one in particular. "It's not fair, you promised, it's not fair—"

"Tape ready," came the response through the headset.

"Roll tape," Ryan ordered.

"Tape rolling."

The VTR monitor before him came up. It was another segment on Brandon Martus. Only now he was standing in what looked like ancient ruins. Behind him were broken arches and stone rubble and beyond that was what looked like the remains of an ancient stadium. The kid turned to face the camera. Tears were streaming down his face as he began to speak.

"Where'd that come from?" the technical director demanded.

Ryan shook his head and leaned forward to listen.

"When I shut up the heavens so that there is no rain, or command locusts to devour the land or send a plague among my people . . ."

"Punch it up," Ryan ordered.

"But we don't know what it—"

"Punch it up. We've got to dump Ponte, punch it up!"

The technical director reached down to the board in front of him and hit one of the dozens of illuminated buttons. Suddenly Brandon Martus was on the main monitor. Suddenly he was up on the two Jumbotron screens. And suddenly he was being broadcast around the world.

"If my people, who are called by my name, will humble themselves . . ."

The technical director turned to Ryan. "Do we really need more of this guy?"

Ryan watched the screen. "Let's see where it goes . . ."

"My children!" Brandon cried, "my bride! I have chosen you from before the beginning of the world. You carry my name, yet you do not live my life. Though I have given you power, you have not used it to pursue my holiness. Hear my plea. Heed my warning. Quit seeking your desires, quit seeking your kingdom. Humble yourselves and receive mine. Receive all that I am."

Brandon heard his voice echoing through the Mount. Consciousness came in fits and starts. For a moment he thought he might be hallucinating . . . until he heard the familiar verse . . . until he realized the other edge of the sword was now being wielded.

"If my people will pray and seek my face . . ."

He looked over at Sarah. She lay in an expanding pool of blood staring at him. She was struggling to breathe, every gasp a torturous ordeal. But she heard his voice, too. And, for the briefest instant, a smile broke through the pain and flickered across her face.

He returned it.

His voice continued. "I am eternal. All else you pursue will burn."

Then he saw her hand. It was outstretched, just inches from his. To touch it, to hold it these last remaining moments suddenly became the most important thing in Brandon's world. He struggled to move his hand toward hers. The effort was excruciating, but it was something he had to do.

Ryan continued to watch the monitor.

"You fast in vain. You pray and plead and beg, but your efforts are futile. Look into my eyes and know what is eternal. Only when you behold my glory will your desires conform to mine. Only when you know me can you pray in my name."

The technical director cleared his throat. "I don't like this. I'm not sure what he's doing."

Ryan said nothing. He was looking at the love and compassion in the boy's eyes, and he was thinking about his last conversation with Tanya . . .

He really got to you, didn't he?

Yeah, he really got to me.

"Let's cut to something. Ryan?"

He thought of the message she'd left on his service, the report he'd been given of her trying to break in, and of the "accidental shooting" by the guard . . .

"Ryan? Ryan, do you hear me?"

. . . and he thought of his own ever-present emptiness.

"VTR," the technical director spoke into the intercom. "Give us something else. Maybe a—"

"No." Ryan cut in firmly. "Keep it."

"But—"

"Keep the tape rolling."

The technical director gave him a look, but Ryan had made up his mind. And, as he settled back into his seat, crossing his arms to watch, he half-whispered, half-prayed, "This one's for you, kiddo. This one's for you . . ."

Brandon's voice continued to reverberate across the Temple Mount.

"Repent! Turn! I have given you the power to overcome. All you need to do is choose: your wickedness or my holiness . . . your death or my life. For without repentance there is no forgiveness. And without forgiveness we have no fellowship."

But, lying on the stage, Brandon barely heard. He was using all of his concentration and strength to reach for Sarah's hand. He no longer felt pain. And he knew by the blurring and spinning that he'd be losing consciousness any second. If he could just get to her hand, if he could just move his hand those last fractions of an inch—there! He had it! His heart swelled with gratitude as he glanced back to her face. But her eyes were already closed.

No! his mind cried. *Please, God, not yet!*

But he was also going. He could feel it. He'd fought the fight and he'd won. He'd delivered the message. How it would be received was not his responsibility. His task was over. He gave Sarah's hand a tender squeeze, a gentle good-bye. Sights and sounds slipped away. He could no longer see, he could barely hear. And then, to his surprise, he felt Sarah's hand respond. It was weak, no doubt using the very last of her strength. But there it was, two distinct squeezes answering his one.

Then she was gone.

And, smiling faintly, Brandon followed.

"Humble yourselves! Seek my face! Turn! Then will I hear from heaven and will forgive your sin and will heal your land. My bride . . . my precious bride. How my heart yearns for you. How I love and adore you . . . more than I did my very life. How I long for this time of suffering to end, and for the cup of my wrath to be emptied. But you will not have it."

In Washington State, Beth O'Brien woke her husband, Dr. Philip O'Brien, and their two girls to watch the great Chairman Ponte speak. It was an important moment in history and one she felt they shouldn't miss. She'd even fixed coffee and hot chocolate to coax them out of bed. But as the family sat on the sofa watching TV, Beth began to think. It had been several years since she'd given God any serious thought, and longer than that since she'd attended church. And yet, watching and listening to this young man, she wondered if maybe, just maybe, it wouldn't hurt to expose the children to what she once believed in so strongly. Maybe it wouldn't hurt at all.

"You try to stop evil by changing others. Yet you do not cease from your own evil. Repent. Repent and turn your heart toward me. Repent and see if there is anything I would withhold from you. My arms are opened wide. Turn from your adultery."

Frank shook his head sadly. He'd just returned from a late-night, full-on party, and despite the booze and beer, he stood before his TV set stone sober. That had once been his friend on the screen there, a fellow "townie"—before he'd gotten religion, before he'd turned fanatic. Of course Frank had tried to get him to see reason, and they'd had more than their fair share of shouting matches. After all, it was one thing to believe in something, but to let it take over your life like that? No way. Yet Brandon refused to see reason. Even when the people had shut down the clinic. Even when he made a total fool of himself in L.A.

And now this . . .

Again Frank shook his head. This was a perfect example of the old order that Chairman Ponte was talking about—a perfect example of what happens when someone lets himself get too carried away with all that God stuff. Frank crossed over to the sofa and rummaged through the dirty clothes and magazines until he found the remote. He pointed it toward the TV and shut it off. He could not, he would not watch anymore.

Tisha Youngman could not stop the tears as she watched the broadcast from the Motel 6 room. Her friend for the night, some guy whose name she'd already forgotten, but who had more than enough access to the smack she'd fallen in love with so many months before, lay beside her, snoring, sweating, naked—sprawled out like some giant beached whale. But she didn't notice. Her mind was a thousand miles away. Back home, back when she was a little girl, back when she was sitting with her momma and daddy in church . . .

"Let my love break your grip on inequity. Let my love strip you of your sin. Turn and run into my arms that I may hold you as I once did. Come to me that we may again share the intimacies of husband and wife. That we may again be one."

Brandon's picture and voice continued to be broadcast in homes and countries all around the world. As the speech drew to its conclusion, those who felt drawn to him listened thoughtfully while those who disagreed counted him even more of a lunatic.

"For when we are one . . . when you are lost in my arms and when our hearts are intertwined, all of creation watches in awe. When we are one, delighting in each other's pleasure, there is nothing, absolutely nothing you can withhold from me, and nothing I will withhold from you."

On the TV screen, the taped Brandon Martus finally lowered his head. His message had concluded. And viewers all around the globe were forming opinions. There was no longer room for feigned impartialities, there was no longer an excuse for wavering indecision. The time had come. Now, everyone would have to make a choice. One way or the other, they would all have to decide.

EPILOGUE

William Zimmerman hated the assignment. Standing in the oppressive heat at four hours a shift, eyes burning from the smoke. He knew it was strictly disciplinary and he certainly had no one to blame but himself. Truth be told, it was a small price to pay for the astonishing lapse of judgment his security team had displayed over at the King David as well as here on the Mount. How they had let someone like Salman Kilyos slip past them was beyond him. But that was three days ago. And, as always, the brilliant Lucas Ponte had managed to take an ugly chain of events and turn it into something positive. Hence the two glass caskets to Zimmerman's immediate right . . . and their unspoken warning to any who had similar ideas of opposing the new regime.

Carefully, Zimmerman scrutinized each member in the passing line. From dawn to dusk they came, enduring the sweltering heat, sometimes breathing through handkerchiefs because of the smoke . . . every age, every race, every nationality. They'd already passed through security and the metal detectors—a requirement for anyone now visiting the Temple Mount—but emotions still ran high. Any one of them could break past the ropes, race across the fifteen feet of stone pavement, and attack the two coffins. In fact, this morning alone there had been two such attempts. Not that he could blame them. In record time these two corpses, resting under the white nylon canopy, had become the symbol for all that was wrong and oppressive with the old world order.

That's why Ponte, at the Cartel's insistence, had agreed to put their bullet-riddled bodies on display—here, less than a hundred yards away from the construction of the new temple. It was a riveting symbol of new versus old. The giant beams of steel, the powerful cranes, the raw vitality, the hustle, bustle, and camaraderie of building the new . . . versus the silence, the decaying remains, and the inevitable destruction of the old.

In line, one or two people had started to look up. At first Zimmerman paid little attention, until more and more began tilting back their heads and shading their eyes. Finally he stepped out from under the canopy to see for himself. It was only a cloud. White and puffy, no different from any other cloud. Except it was the only one in the sky . . . and it was growing. At least that's what he first thought. But the longer he watched, the more he realized that the cloud wasn't growing . . . it was approaching.

By now all of the crowd was murmuring and staring. And for good reason. Not only was the cloud approaching, but as it drew closer it was possible to see some sort of glow radiating from inside. Even in the bright midmorning sun, light was clearly visible. It was a remarkable phenomenon. Unfortunately, Zimmerman had become so engrossed in it that he did not see who had sneaked up to the coffins and suddenly struck both of their glass tops.

But somebody had. That was the only explanation for their simultaneous shattering as they broke into a thousand spiderwebs that crumpled and rained down on top of the bodies inside. The crowd gasped. Some cried out in surprise.

Zimmerman raced the five or six paces back to the coffins, preparing to apprehend the culprit. But he could find no one. He glanced over at his partner, who was searching the other side with the same lack of success. And then he saw it . . . the shifting of broken glass inside the casket. A little at first and then more and more. Something was moving. The corpse's arm. Both of the arms. No, it was the entire body. It was sitting up!

Zimmerman held his fear in check. He'd heard stories of corpses doing similar things. Sometimes when the tendons dry, they contract the larger muscles, literally moving the body or, in extreme cases, causing it to sit up. That's all this was. He glanced over to the other casket, the woman's. Her body was doing the same thing. A remarkable coincidence. Still, that's all this was, a coincidence.

At least that's what he thought until the corpse raised its arms and began brushing the broken glass off of its face . . . then finally opened its eyes. Now, Zimmerman could only stare in astonishment as the body put both of its hands on the edge of the casket and eased itself up and out of the container.

Beyond the ropes, the crowd panicked—shouting, running for protection. Zimmerman was unsure what to do. Yell out orders for them to stop? Demand that they stay calm? And what about the corpse? Should he order it to get back into its casket?

By now the body was standing. It was still in its bloodstained clothes, the bullet holes clearly visible. Then to Zimmerman's greater astonishment, the head slowly turned toward him. It was all the guard could do to hold his ground. But the gaze was not zombielike or unseeing. This person was now alive. Fully. In fact, he was looking deeper into Zimmerman than he had ever been looked into before—searching him, probing his mind, his heart. An expression of pity slowly filled the face . . . as if what he'd seen greatly saddened him. Then, just as slowly, he turned and started toward the other coffin.

Zimmerman could not move. He stood frozen, dumbfounded, as Brandon Martus arrived at his wife's casket. Zimmerman threw a look at his partner who was undergoing equal shock and paralysis of action. Now Martus was reaching out to his wife, smiling warmly at her, helping her up and out of the coffin until she was standing at his side. Despite the matted hair and blood-smeared faces there was no missing the look of love between the two as they gazed into each other's eyes. Then Martus reached out to his wife's hand. She took it. And they turned and strolled out from under the canopy.

By now, the crowd had scattered . . . at least those who could move had scattered. A handful had fainted. A few lay prostrate on the ground. It was definitely time to act. Time to override his fear and move into action. But to do what? As Zimmerman frantically weighed the possibilities, a voice boomed from overhead, clapping like thunder.

"COME UP HERE!"

He stepped out from under the canopy and looked back up to the cloud. It loomed fifty feet above them. And, although Zimmerman's logic dictated the sound came from the cloud, most likely thunder, it also came from everything surrounding him—from the stone pavement at his feet, the fabric of the canopy, its poles, even the remains of the caskets. It was as if every molecule vibrated with the terrifying voice.

He looked back at the couple. A wind had started to surround them. It came from nowhere, whipping and whirling about them. But neither appeared concerned. Instead, they moved closer to each other, facing one another, he wrapping his arms around her waist, she resting her hands upon his neck. Then the most remarkable thing happened. Ever so gently, the two began to rise up off the ground. Slowly, but steadily, they rose, higher and higher. But they barely noticed. As the wind continued to surround them and as they continued to rise, they directed their attention from each other and up to the cloud. The same love and adoration filled their faces, only now it was directed toward the cloud. The expressions were that of total awe and abandonment. The look of two people completely immersed in love.

As they continued rising, their features became more difficult to distinguish against the cloud's blinding brilliance. Eventually, the bottom wisps of the cloud began to wrap around the couple, enveloping them . . . until, finally, they disappeared altogether.

Then Zimmerman heard it. A deep, throaty rumble that grew until it was a deafening roar, until the ground beneath his feet suddenly turned liquid. Shifting, pitching, writhing. Wave after wave of earth and pavement rolling like the ocean. He opened his mouth but could not hear himself scream as he was thrown to the ground. And still the earth heaved and buckled.

From the pavement he caught glimpses of the buildings surrounding the Mount. They were falling, crumbling like toys. He turned to the Dome of the Rock. It, too, was disintegrating . . . as if it were made of sand, as if it were nothing but dust. It was as if the entire area, the entire city—all of man's finest and grandest creations—as if it was all being reduced to nothing but dust.

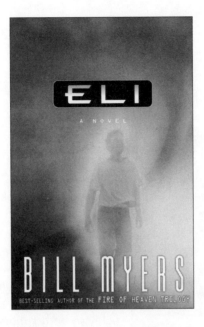

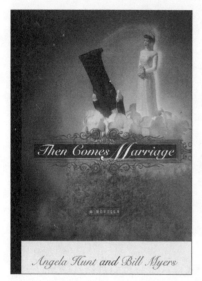

and Bill Myers!

WHEN THE LAST LEAF FALLS

BILL MYERS

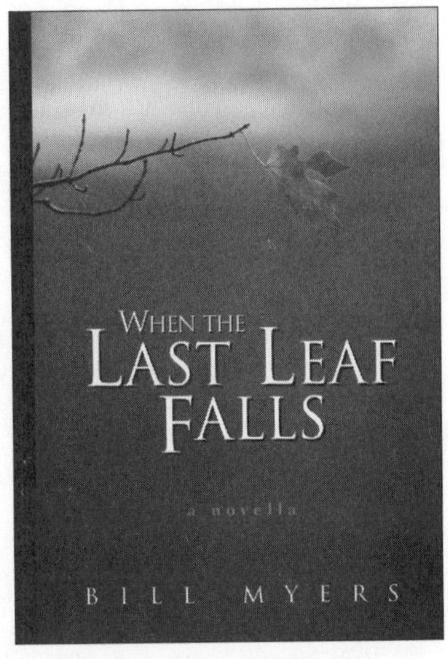

When everything seems lost, God's love has a way of turning life around.

This retelling of O. Henry's classic short story *The Last Leaf* begins with an adolescent girl, Ally, who is deathly ill and angry at God. Her grief-stricken father, a pastor on the verge of losing his faith, narrates the story as it unfolds.

Ally's grandpa lives with the family and has become Ally's best friend. He is an artist who has attempted—but never been able—to capture in a painting the essence of God's love. One day, in stubborn despair, Ally declares that she will die when the last leaf falls from the tree outside her bedroom window. Her doctor fears that her negative attitude will hinder her recovery and her words will become a self-fulfilling prophecy.

This stirring story of anger and love, of doubt and hope, speaks about the pain of living in this world, and the reality of the Other world that is not easily seen, but can be deeply felt. Talented storyteller Bill Myers enhances and updates a storyline from one of the masters and brings to light the awesome power of love and sacrifice.

Hardcover 0-310-23091-8
Audio Pages, When the Last Leaf Falls/The Faded Flower
0-310-24046-8

Pick up a copy today at your favorite bookstore!

We want to hear from you. Please send your comments about this book to us in care of the address below. Thank you.

GRAND RAPIDS, MICHIGAN 49530

www.zondervan.com